Penguin Books
The Second Michael Innes Omnibus

Michael Innes is the pseudonym of J.I.M. Stewart who was a
Student of Christ Church, Oxford, from 1949 until his retirement in
1973. He was born in 1906 and was educated at Edinburgh
Academy and Oriel College, Oxford. He was lecturer in English at
the University of Leeds from 1930 to 1935, Jury Professor of
English at the University of Adelaide, South Australia, from 1935 to
1945, and lecturer in Queen's University, Belfast, between 1946 and
1948.

He has published many novels – including the quintet *A Staircase in
Surrey* (*The Gaudy, Young Pattullo, A Memorial Service, The
Madonna of the Astrolabe* and *Full Term*) – several volumes of short
stories, as well as books of criticism and essays, under his own
name. His *Eight Modern Writers* appeared in 1963 as the final
volume of *The Oxford History of English Literature*, and he is also the
author of *Rudyard Kipling* (1966) and *Joseph Conrad* (1968). His
most recent books are *Andrew and Tobias* (1981) and *The Bridge at
Arta and other stories* (1981).

Under the pseudonym of Michael Innes, he has written broadcast
scripts and many crime novels including *Appleby's End* (1945),
The Bloody Wood (1966), *An Awkward Lie* (1971), *Appleby's Answer*
(1973), *Appleby's Other Story* (1974), *The Appleby File* (1975),
The Gay Phoenix (1976), *Honeybath's Haven* (1977), *The Ampersand
Papers* (1978), *Going It Alone* (1980) and *Lord Mullion's Secret*
(1981). Several of these are published in Penguin together with *The
Michael Innes Omnibus* containing *Death at the President's Lodging,
Hamlet, Revenge!* and *The Daffodil Affair*.

The Second
Michael Innes Omnibus

The Journeying Boy
Operation Pax
The Man from the Sea

Penguin Books

Penguin Books Ltd, Harmondsworth, Middlesex, England
Penguin Books, 625 Madison Avenue, New York, New York 10022, U.S.A.
Penguin Books Australia Ltd, Ringwood, Victoria, Australia
Penguin Books Canada Ltd, 2801 John Street, Markham, Ontario, Canada L3R 1B4
Penguin Books (N.Z.) Ltd, 182–190 Wairau Road, Auckland 10, New Zealand

The Journeying Boy first published by Victor Gollancz 1949
Published in Penguin Books 1961
Copyright © J.I.M. Stewart, 1949

Operation Pax first published by Victor Gollancz 1951
Published in Penguin Books 1964
Copyright © J.I.M. Stewart, 1951

The Man from the Sea first published by Victor Gollancz 1955
Published in Penguin Books 1961
Copyright © J.I.M. Stewart, 1955

This collection published in Penguin Books 1983
Copyright © J.I.M. Stewart, 1983
All rights reserved

Made and printed in Great Britain by
Hazell Watson & Viney Ltd, Aylesbury, Bucks

Set in Plantin 9/10.5 (Linotron 202)
by Syarikat Seng Teik Sdn. Bhd., K.L.

Contents

The Journeying Boy   7

Operation Pax   235

The Man from the Sea   463

The Journeying Boy

Chapter 1

On the morning of Monday, the 4th of August 1947, Mr Richard Thewless walked in pleasant sunshine through the West End of London. His object was commonplace enough, being simply that of obtaining temporary employment as a private tutor. Nevertheless, he had the sense of an occasion, and of an interest much transcending that which commonly accompanied his finding a new pupil. For *this* pupil – if indeed he landed the job – was somebody. Or rather – since small boys are necessarily nobodies – he was the son of one very decidedly somebody. Sir Bernard Paxton's reputation was world-wide. He was beyond question the greatest of living physicists.

From his proposed connexion with this eminent person, Mr Thewless already extracted considerable satisfaction – to the point, indeed, of being quite unwontedly disposed to a somewhat premature counting of his chickens. It was, to begin with, with the learned and professional classes that, in general, he got on best. He liked people substantially of his own sort, and often continued to like them when they turned out not very readily able to meet his bills. Impecunious barristers, bankrupt country gentlemen, or harassed provincial professors with sons who must either win an Eton scholarship or be swept into the hideous maw of national education: these were persons whom Mr Thewless took pleasure in succouring. True, it was his duty sometimes to represent to them that Magdalen or Christ Church, King's or Trinity – those farther goals – might be as readily attained through new and virtually costless establishments as through others still addressing themselves to the world of Alfred the Great or William of Wykeham or the Prince Consort. Nevertheless, Mr Thewless profoundly sympathized with the conservative disposition evinced by this category of his employers. For by instinct he was, as he sometimes told himself, a sober and self-respecting snob, just as by vocation he was a hanger-on of people themselves now no more than desperately hanging-on. And precisely here lay the particular attraction of Sir Bernard Paxton. Already – Mr Thewless reluctantly admitted it – the lower stratum of the intellectual class was being proletarianized, and there was always a limit to what the most conscientious tutor could achieve in households in which there appeared unnaturally and perpetually to preponderate distracting vistas of unwashed dishes and unsegregated babies. In that particular world nowadays only the high-ups had their heads substantially above the soapsuds. Yet here, surely, Sir Bernard Paxton must belong . . . Mr Thewless, hoping that his services might be retained by this eminent scientist, looked forward to a congenial environment still materially cushioned by a substantial prosperity.

But Mr Thewless was a man of measure. Mounting as he presently did the broad flight of steps to Sir Bernard's front door, and responding with practised certainty to sundry preliminary indications of what lay within, he was visited by sharp misgiving. Often enough before he had been in this sort of house, but never with satisfaction for very long. Positive opulence was something which he found uncomfortably to jar with the spirit of the time; the poet whose social occasions obliged him to spend a day at Timon's villa was not rendered more uneasy by its splendours than was Mr Thewless by anything resembling their latterday counterpart. And why – the question suggested itself even as he raised his hand to the door-bell – yes, why in the world should a really great man take the trouble to surround himself with so emphatic a material magnificence?

A large element of taking trouble there must certainly be. Not even wealth (and what he was confronted with, he saw, was inherited wealth rather than the mere fruits of a substantial earned income) – not even wealth made this sort of thing trouble-free nowadays. Anxiety about where the housemaids were to come from and how the place was to be heated must, under present conditions, tiresomely creep out of housekeeper's room and butler's pantry and assault the owner. Nor – Mr Thewless understood – was there a Lady Paxton. Sir Bernard was a widower, so that female vanity could not be responsible for the maintaining of these splendours. Doubtless there were noblemen and others in high place for whom the utility of such a way of life still outweighed its inconvenience; people, Mr Thewless vaguely thought, who give political parties. But for a man whose labours were on that frontier where the higher physics passes into the inapprehensible it was distinctly odd.

And Mr Thewless shook his head. Whereupon Sir Bernard's butler, taking this as indicating a disinclination on the part of the visitor to remove his overcoat, made a noise at once respectful and peremptory. Mr Thewless took off the overcoat. He handed the man his hat, and suffered the discomfiture of seeing an expert scrutiny passed upon the unimpressive label inside the crown. He had already relinquished his umbrella, which happened to be a good one; he had the impression that he was suspected of having purloined it during some momentary failure of surveillance in just such another resplendent place as this.

Then he was ushered into a library, where he waited for some time.

This interval, had he known it, was heavy with destiny. But Mr Thewless was aware of no more than a growing sense of oppression which he put down partly to the sultry quality of this London morning and partly to the sombre richness of the apartment. The furniture was ancient, carven, and massive, upholstered in dark velvets upon which glinted dull silver studs. Horripilant velvet, thought Mr Thewless – and being unable without discomfort even to think of sitting down he discreetly prowled about. It must all be Spanish, he decided, even to the heavy presses sheltering the books. And, of course, both pictures in the room were Spanish; indeed they were almost certainly the original work of Velazquez. Mr Thewless was somewhat humiliated to find that his first impulse before these masterpieces was in the direction of financial calculation. Persons who moved more familiarly among private collections of Old Masters were presumably superior to this vulgarity. Conscientiously then Mr Thewless elevated his mind to aesthetic contemplation. The first painting represented a peculiarly repulsive court dwarf; the second was of a radiant little prince, dark-haired and dark-eyed, who clasped a formidable musket in his right hand and glanced slantwise out from a scene of improbable carnage among wolves and boars. It was a vision of the felicity of childhood, and the whole room – it suddenly occurred to Mr Thewless – was contrived to contrast with it and set it off. And this made Mr Thewless uneasy. His uneasiness in turn made him feel bourgeois and provincial. And by this his uneasiness was increased yet further.

Caught in this unfortunate circle, Mr Thewless found himself distrusting everything around him. He distrusted an eminent physicist who lived like a grandee; he even distrusted his butler. But this was absurd. Why should he nurse dark suspicions of a man simply because he had been impertinently curious about a visitor's hatter? Mr Thewless realized what was happening. He was simply more and more distrusting *himself* – and of the burden of this abasement he was endeavouring to lighten his ego by projecting the occasions of his distrust upon the world around him.

If Mr Thewless was not altogether confident about himself, this was certainly not because he had disappointed any very general expectations. Little had been prophesied of him, either by himself or others, which he had not fulfilled. First as a schoolmaster and later as a private coach he had given satisfaction to his employers, and these in return fed, clothed, and housed him, as well as providing small but fairly regular sums of money for recreation and to set against old age. This was the whole history of Mr Thewless as he sat in Sir Bernard Paxton's library waiting to be interviewed. It is true that he sometimes found himself believing that other situations, had they come his way, would have aroused in him responses not altogether inadequate. But such secret persuasions were no doubt commonly harboured by the unsuccessful, and Mr Thewless attached small significance to them. On the other hand the self-distrust that intermittently assailed him worried him a good deal. Was it not baseless, after all, since what he was called upon to do he did reasonably well?

However all this might be, Mr Thewless upon the present occasion found himself growing irrationally cross – cross with himself and cross with the environment and presumed personality of Sir Bernard Paxton. This feeling might well have led him to a resolve to proceed no further, to decline the proposed engagement if it were offered to him. But actually it had a contrary effect. Mr Thewless resolved to get the job, and to get it as the result of displaying an uncompromising professional severity. He had just come to this decision when he was ushered in upon Sir Bernard.

It was rather like a trick played by a fashionable physician. From surroundings of elaborately contrived oppression and gloom he was abruptly transferred amid tones, proportions, and objects evocative of confidence, repose, and a buoyant, nervous tone. The room had all this even while being markedly exotic, for there was almost nothing in it which was not of the authentic arts and crafts of ancient China. Those strangely logical landscapes and those birds perched amid blossoms miraculously disposed were, Mr Thewless conjectured, about a thousand years old. In the British Museum he would have appreciated them very much; now, unfortunately, his first thought was again that a lot of money must have been spent on them. And, more than ever, he instinctively disapproved. A man who kept Spain and China cheek by jowl in this way almost certainly ordered his rooms wholesale. Yes, that would be it. Sir Bernard Paxton would simply decree a room and some professional person would forthwith purvey it. And not a merely commercial person by whom Sir Bernard might be roundly and wholesomely cheated. Rather some great connoisseur would be employed, some unfortunate pitchforked out of a ruined continent . . . At this rambling and undisciplined moment Mr Thewless saw Paxton.

At once everything faded out except the man himself. He was not even 'Sir Bernard'; he was a single great name, belonging with Galileo, Bacon, Newton. He might live amid a menagerie; he might indulge not in mere ostentation and acquisitiveness, but in eccentricities, lunacies, deplorable vices – and there would remain the single overwhelming fact of his being Paxton still.

He stood in a window embrasure, bathed in sunshine. He turned as Mr Thewless advanced and the light caught that prodigious brow, that whole skull so tremendous that it would have been freakish and horrible had the man's whole frame not been cast in a gigantic mould. The capacity for profound speculation was evident at once, and a moment later the habit of it was revealed in the settled lines of the forehead and mouth. Mr Thewless was impressed. But when he saw Paxton's eyes he was overcome. Deeply and darkly blue, they were the eyes of a child who sees his first illuminated Christmas tree, or his first fall of snow. Only whereas the child's emotion is transient Paxton's was enduring. Whatever was the universe that Paxton contemplated it was one evoking the response of perpetual wonder and awe. All other men – Mr Thewless suddenly felt – lived with their noses hard up against a wall and their eyes painfully focused upon some few inches of brick and mortar. But Paxton's stature carried him clear of the barrier and he looked out upon an illimitable prospect which he recognized as his heritage and his home.

The impression of all this was for some moments so overwhelming that Mr Thewless went almost automatically through the preliminary exchanges that followed. When the voice of genius did eventually reach him with any clarity it seemed to come, at first, from a long way off.

'One way and another, my son has been unlucky for a number of years. I am afraid that his teaching has been something worse than indifferent. Wartime conditions, no doubt.'

Mr Thewless blinked. These were words extremely familiar to him. They might almost be described as standard at this stage of such an interview. Quite automatically, Mr Thewless looked judicial and nodded as does one man of superior understanding to another. But within him he was immediately aware of the impertinence of this when such a one as Paxton was in question.

'A sensitive and slightly nervous boy. He has been judged unruly at times – and it is certainly true that he is not very amenable to discipline of the ordinary sort.'

'Quite so.' Mr Thewless's tone conveyed complete understanding of the situation and complete confidence in his own power to deal with it. Mr Thewless was in fact (as an inward voice told him) going through his tricks. 'Special arrangements may well be necessary in such a case, Sir Bernard. But they should be made with as little fuss as possible. The danger of too much indulgence should be frankly faced. It is no kindness to cocker and coddle a lad who will be obliged to face the world on his own one day. The advantage of a public school lies in its being, roughly speaking, a microcosm of that world. It reproduces that world's rough-and-tumble, among other things. If a boy can stick it, he should. We must not be too quick to think in terms of guarding the young nerves from shock. On the other hand, when a sensitive child . . .'

Mr Thewless was eyeing Sir Bernard Paxton firmly and his voice did not falter. Nevertheless, he was keenly aware of the fatuity of presenting this shallow and platitudinous chatter to a man whose views must necessarily be both extensive and profound. Nor was his uneasiness diminished by the observation that Sir Bernard was responding much as commonplace parents did; that is to say, he was slightly disconcerted, slightly hostile, and more than a little impressed. And by the time Mr Thewless had reached the conclusion of his remarks (this conclusion being to the effect that, all things considered, young Paxton might well be delivered over to him for just so much modified cockering as a ripe experience should endorse) – by the time Mr Thewless got so far, Sir Bernard showed every sign of eating out of his hand.

For some moments Mr Thewless was triumphant. He had successfully presented just that air of professional severity upon which he had resolved while in the library, and the consequence was that the job appeared as good as his. With Sir Bernard Paxton he had kept his end up; he had been abased by neither his intellectual eminence nor the splendours of his way of living. And this was very satisfying to the ego.

These feelings on the part of Mr Thewless are so natural as scarcely to be worthy of record. More important is the fact that he had other feelings as well. In all this he saw himself as about one millimetre high. Of course Sir Bernard Paxton could be scored off; genius always can. And perhaps *this* genius was more vulnerable than many – for Mr Thewless had come to discern the weakness in the man before him. His will by no means matched his intellect. The creaking magnificence of this great London house attested it, for here was simply the issue of an irrelevant part of himself – his wealth – which he had been unable to resist. But more striking than this was what was already discernible of the relationship between Sir Bernard and his son. The father doted on the son, the son pushed the father around, and now the father was seeking extraneous aid. To Mr Thewless, who contrived to manage boys simply by taking his ability to do so for granted, this was a familiar situation in which there was always something slightly ridiculous. And the absurdity grew when the father was a towering person like Paxton. What was diminutive in Mr Thewless drew him for a moment into an attitude of pleased superiority.

But this was to take the matter basely. One has the duty of reverencing genius in its frailties as well as in its strength. And certainly it was not for Mr Thewless, confronting the intellectual beacon that was Paxton, to pride himself on the continued independence of his own flickering farthing candle. In any perplexity into which this great man had fallen it was his duty to assist to the maximum of his power . . . This resolution on the part of Mr Thewless, which was sincere and generous, added considerably to the jolt he was presently to experience. But, as it happened, it was to have consequences far wider than that. Upon it, and in the near future, imponderable things were to hang.

Meanwhile, Mr Thewless discoursed on School Certificate. 'Still', he said, 'substantially below the standard? I am afraid there must be something very far wrong. Is he a capable boy?'

With parents, this was one of Mr Thewless's strongest words. A small boy who was likely enough to become a Senior Wrangler or a Fellow of Balliol he would by no means describe in terms more extravagant. And this he had found was a capital technique.

'Capable?' Sir Bernard sounded dubious. 'Humphrey's intelligence quotient is fair. In fact it is very high so far as the common run of able people go. But he does seem to be retarded in certain respects.'

Mr Thewless wondered whether he himself might be ranked among the common run of able people. He doubted it.

'On the other hand' – Sir Bernard spoke with an effort – 'there are matters in which he is uncommonly precocious. That is particularly so in – um – the sphere of the emotional life.'

This sounded far from promising. Mr Thewless considered. 'But he has at least held his place at school?'

Sir Bernard looked extremely gloomy. 'They wouldn't be in a hurry to turn out my son, you know. I doubt whether latterly the position has been other than that. Humphrey is somewhat ungovernable, as I said.'

'But the holidays have begun, and he is at home? I think I had better see the boy, Sir Bernard, before even the most tentative arrangement is made.'

'That is very reasonable. And I believe Humphrey is actually in the house at this moment. Only – it is really rather an awkward thing – he is at present quite resolved not to show himself.'

Mr Thewless, receiving this information, was expressively silent.

'But he is quite keen on a certain holiday that has been proposed. Cousins on my late wife's side – folk, actually, whom I seldom meet – have asked him to join them in Ireland for a month. It is there that I would wish you to accompany him, and keep him to his reading as well as you can. If Humphrey is given to understand that he may only go on condition that he has a tutor –'

'I quite understand.' And Mr Thewless was indeed perfectly familiar with bargaining and compromising parents. 'Do these cousins live permanently in Ireland?'

'I know almost nothing about them. But I imagine they merely have a place there to which they go at this time of year for shooting and diversions of that sort.'

'In fact, the proposal would be that I should take Humphrey for purposes of study to what will probably prove to be a large house-party in a hunting-lodge or shooting-box? I hardly think that such conditions would be likely to favour application in a wayward lad.'

Sir Bernard looked harassed and depressed. 'I quite see the force of what you say. And you do very well to insist on it. Only –'

At this moment there came a low buzzing sound from somewhere on the exquisitely lacquered table behind which Sir Bernard sat. With a word of apology, he picked up a telephone receiver. It was merely an instrument, Mr Thewless conjectured, by which he maintained communication with other parts of this ramifying establishment – and indeed what appeared to issue faintly from the ear-piece was the voice of the objectionable butler. Mr Thewless disapproved of a gentleman thus ordering matters as if his home were a laboratory or an office. But genius, he reflected, makes its own rules. And again he surveyed the noble brow and perpetually wondering eyes of the great scientist. It was really satisfactory – it was really very satisfactory, after all – to find oneself drawn into the affairs of one so eminent.

'At once,' said Sir Bernard. There was something like surprise and relief in his tone. He replaced the receiver, and in the same moment his hand went down in what might have been the action of pressing an electric bell. He looked at Mr Thewless in an abstraction so extreme as to suggest that some profound speculation on the structure of the physical universe had suddenly come to him from the void. And then he spoke. 'I shall give myself the pleasure', he said, 'of writing to you by this evening's post. Should it be possible . . .'

And thus in a matter of seconds – although not before achieving a full realization of what had happened – Mr Thewless found himself being shown out. Some more acceptable candidate for the distinction of tutoring young Humphrey Paxton had turned up. What manner of man was his successful rival? Mr Thewless had his answer as he stood in the hall waiting to be handed his suspect umbrella and his insufficient hat. For through the open door of the library he glimpsed a young man of athletic figure and confident bearing who was beguiling his brief period of waiting by turning over the pages of *The Times*. Mr Thewless knew the type.

He walked down the broad steps of the Paxton mansion into London sunlight. The letter which Sir Bernard would write that evening already lay open in his mind. He had received it before. That it was a disconcerting letter to receive was a fact lying not at all in the economic sphere. Mr Thewless was never unable to obtain employment, and that on terms as good as it ever occurred to him to bargain for. No, the jolt lay elsewhere . . . Mr Thewless reached the pavement and took a deep breath of air – an air equally redolent of lime trees and petrol engines. He was, he tried to persuade himself, well out of it. The Paxton establishment had irritated him; Humphrey Paxton sounded a most unpromising boy; the proposed arrangement would have been altogether unsatisfactory from a working point of view.

Nevertheless, Mr Thewless was disappointed. And this, since he was an honest man, he presently admitted to himself. Galileo, Bacon, Newton . . . that morning he had been with the gods. Genius had half turned to him in its frailty and he had been prepared to shoulder whatever responsibility followed. In his heart Mr Thewless believed that he would have done not badly. As he turned away from the Paxton portico and walked through the quiet, almost empty square, he felt the universe contracting about him and building up, not many inches from his nose, its old and familiar horizons. It was as if, while in the great man's presence, he too had for a moment contrived to peer over that brick wall. But now – to put it less graphically – the humdrum was establishing itself once more as his natural environment. For some little time his life would feel the narrower as a result of this episode. And then he would forget all about it.

But in this prognostication Mr Thewless was wrong. As a consequence of his visit to Sir Bernard Paxton, an altogether fuller life was presently to be his. And in this his fate was to contrast markedly with that of the young man whom he had glimpsed in the library.

Chapter 2

The Spanish library had a good deal impressed Captain Cox, and now the Chinese study impressed him too. Nevertheless, the marked deference with which he shook hands with Sir Bernard Paxton was only partly a tribute to wealth. Captain Cox, quite as much as Mr Thewless, respected genius. And Sir Bernard certainly had abundance of it. He could, likely enough, show you how to press a button and blow up any gang of rascals who were making a nuisance of themselves on the other side of Europe – and was it not something of a red-letter day to be in the presence of *that*?

The mind of Captain Cox as he made this reflection quite kindled to the idea of science; there floated before him such vague images of its unfolding wonders as the genius of the American people has given to the world through the medium of strip fiction. Sir Bernard had a head like an egg, which was entirely as it should be; and he was probably mad. 'Honoured to meet you, sir,' said Captain Cox, quite carried away. Then, feeling the shockingly foreign lack of restraint in this, he blushed deeply. 'Warm day,' he added hastily. 'Wonderful season, I'm told, up in the north. Birds strong on the wing.'

Sir Bernard Paxton bowed. Having among his other endowments a substantial insight into human nature, he saw at once that the muscular young barbarian before him was not a bad fellow. It was for this fundamental fact of character, no doubt, that he had been so highly recommended by persons enjoying Sir Bernard's confidence. For an intellect, clearly, he represented something like absolute zero. But, of course – thought Sir Bernard confusedly – that might be all to the good.

For in undoubted fact Sir Bernard *was* confused. In that part of his life which concerned itself with family responsibilities his son Humphrey had reduced him to sheer muddle-headedness. He was devoted to the boy, and this although he seldom had more than ten minutes of the day in which to think of him. Yet in Sir Bernard obscure forces had come to ensure that when a decision about Humphrey had to be made that decision would generally be wrong. This was hard on Sir Bernard, and of course a little hard on Humphrey too; certainly it did not contribute to the building up in him of the purposive young scientist whom Sir Bernard desired to achieve. And now Sir Bernard, preparing to swallow Captain Cox whole, was no doubt making an error which could have been pointed out to him by his gardener or his cook.

'There are directions,' said Sir Bernard, 'in which my son has been over-stimulated for his years. I fear that the society which I tend to draw around myself might be charged with being excessively intellectual, and this has reacted unfavourably on the boy.'

Captain Cox nodded. 'A bit too much of a book-worm, I suppose? Still, we've caught him young, and it ought to be possible to get back to a healthier state of affairs. I generally recommend horses.'

'Horses?' Sir Bernard appeared slightly at sea. 'No; it is not that Humphrey has become over-studious. It is rather that he has reacted against the intellectual – or at least the scientific – bias of his home. The stimulus has led him – um – to overcompensate in other directions. I do not know even that his morals are good.'

'Ah! Well, I should be inclined to say that the answer was cold baths. And perhaps I would cut out the horses at first. Fishing would be better.' And Captain Cox, who, like Mr Thewless, was not without his repertory of tricks, appeared to consult some fount of inner experience. 'Yes; the thing to do will be to get him out with a rod and line.'

'As a matter of fact, I am thinking of sending him to Ireland now. And there will be plenty of fishing with the relations to whom he is to go. As to horses, I cannot say. My recollection is that people keep donkeys in such places.' Sir Bernard paused, aware that this was not a very well directed line of thought – aware too that he was somewhat disingenuously concealing the fact that the Irish visit represented Humphrey's own determination. 'I have no doubt that an outdoor life would be most desirable. But, as a matter of fact, there is School Certificate to consider. Humphrey should have got that this summer.'

'Don't worry, sir – don't worry over that at all.' And Captain Cox shook his head dismissively. 'I've found it to be just a matter of mugging up the old papers and seeing how the examining blighters' minds work. We'll wangle him through that in no time. It's not as if it were Higher Certificate. There it does seem as if you have to know the stuff.'

Sir Bernard frowned – this being not at all his conception of the right way to pass an examination. But the spell of Captain Cox – of Captain Cox's remoteness, even weirdness – was upon him. Humphrey plainly needed an altogether new type of approach. And no doubt this was it. Cold baths, fly-fishing, possibly equitation whether on horses or donkeys – assuredly this was what a demoralized – or at least problematical – boy required.

And Captain Cox was consulting a diary. 'Well,' he said, 'the sooner we are off the better. Those relations got a shoot? We must decide about a gun. Nothing more important for the lad than that. And I think I know how just the right thing can be picked up. What's his height, sir? Perhaps we'd better have him in.'

'Perhaps that would be best.' And Sir Bernard hesitated. It was more difficult, he found, with this young man than it had been with Mr Thewless to confess to the distressing fact that Humphrey was not choosing to show himself.

And the simple Captain Cox, misinterpreting this hesitation, again blushed beneath his healthy tan. 'That is to say, sir, if you do by any chance think of taking me on. I'd do my best to pull the little blighter together for you, and all that. But perhaps some other fellow –'

Sir Bernard was in a quandary. He recalled Mr Thewless, an experienced person in whom some traces of what might be called mental life had been discernible, and he felt a lingering doubt. And now the healthy automaton before him had brought the matter to an issue. Being not quite able to decide, Sir Bernard adopted the resource of being carefully explanatory. 'Captain Cox,' he said, 'you misinterpret my hesitation. I was merely reflecting' – and here Sir Bernard's courage fairly failed him – 'that Humphrey may not at the moment be available.'

The effect of this speech was startling – being nothing less than a whoop of satirical laughter from behind a door on the far side of the room. There was a moment's silence, and now it was Sir Bernard's turn to blush. He rose, strode to the door, and threw it open. Only an empty ante-room was visible.

Captain Cox took this shocking interruption very well. 'Not quite the thing, eh?' he said. 'But boys do get out of hand from time to time. I don't know that I'd be severe. Just try to explain, you know, that there are things one doesn't do. Start by insisting quietly on good manners and other matters will probably dry straight.'

'It is possible that you are right.' Sir Bernard doubted whether this simple code, admirable in a general way, would, with Humphrey, quite see Captain Cox through. But his opinion of the young man rose; he would at least not be brutally heavy-handed, which was clearly the danger with his type. Yes, those who recommended Captain Cox had no doubt substantial reason for doing so.

'Perhaps', suggested Captain Cox helpfully, 'I might chase him up now and explain that it is only in comics that people listen at keyholes? It's not quite a thing one should let pass.'

'On the whole, I judge that it would be better not.' Sir Bernard disliked having his beautiful rooms turned to the uses of a bear-garden. And Humphrey, he knew, whose mental age was bewilderingly variable, would be quite capable of answering the proposed admonitions by seizing a priceless Han vase and pitching it at Captain Cox's head. 'The truth is that I have been obliged to enter into a sort of compact with the boy.' Before Captain Cox's respectful but uncomprehending gaze he again hesitated. 'If he is to have a tutor for the holidays, it is to be not before he sets out for Ireland – where, I ought to have explained, he much wishes to go.'

Captain Cox, being out of his depth in such a family situation, wisely held his tongue. And Sir Bernard led the conversation back to School Certificate and then to the cousins with whom the holiday was proposed. One of them – actually a sort of nephew – had recently called and shown a disposition to improve what had hitherto been only a slender acquaintance, inviting both Sir Bernard and Humphrey to Ireland. That, of course, was impossible, for Sir Bernard had a great deal of work on hand. For years, indeed, holidays had been things unknown to him. But the invitation had suggested a possible solution of the problem of Humphrey's vacation . . . Sir Bernard talked on, aware that he was not really getting anywhere. And as he talked the clock moved on too. At length he tried to settle the matter. 'Captain Cox,' he said abruptly, 'I would like you to –' And then a last twinge of doubt assailed him. 'I would like you to stop to luncheon, if you are not engaged.'

And the luncheon – at which Humphrey did not appear – was quite a success. Sir Bernard, who rarely sat down at table in company other than that of fellow members of the Royal Society, did his best to accommodate his conversation to the interests of his guest. He ought, after all, to know more about this prospective tutor than he did. He proceeded therefore to draw him out. This proved not at all easy – and that for reasons which were entirely to the credit of Captain Cox's good sense and modesty. Already Sir Bernard knew that the young man was something of a fire-eater; now he gathered that he had been a good deal abóut the world upon missions in which courage and steadiness were required. And in the war he had certainly seen his share of fighting. Pursuing this theme first with pertinacity and then with downright authoritativeness, Sir Bernard eventually extracted from Captain Cox the admission that he had been awarded the Victoria Cross. And Sir Bernard, who was as impressed by this circumstance as any normal schoolboy would be, wondered how it would strike Humphrey. It might be a strong card – on the other hand, to this too that unaccountable child's response might be a hoot of satirical mirth . . . Sir Bernard, still doubtful as to a decision in this matter of tutors, found that the mere progress of the meal had made that decision for him. Over the soup it was an open question, but the serving of the sole virtually committed him – and to this commitment Sir Bernard's butler, moving softly about the room, was a sort of gloomy witness. By the time that Captain Cox plunged his fork into a second pancake it had become apparent that there was no drawing back. Sir Bernard, therefore, went forward.

'It will be best', he said, 'that you should leave on Thursday, should that be convenient to you.'

'That's A1 by me, sir.'

'I am glad to hear it. The Heysham boat-train leaves Euston at four fifty-five, and I will arrange that the necessary bookings shall be made.'

Captain Cox produced a pocket diary. 'In that case, I had better be along here about half past three.'

Sir Bernard hesitated. 'I am afraid', he said, 'that it is a matter in which Humphrey must be a little humoured. I shall bring him to Euston myself and introduce you there.'

'I see.' Captain Cox sounded slightly dubious. 'In fact, Humphrey and I will be pretty well pigs in a poke to each other until we are on our way together?'

Sir Bernard nodded a little stiffly. 'I trust that you will not find him objectionable. Although difficult, he is really a very attractive lad. Nor do I think that you will find the relations in Ireland altogether uncongenial. They are near a place called Killyboffin. The name is Bolderwood and the family is most respectable.'

'Ah,' said Captain Cox. 'They wouldn't be the Bolderwoods I know.'

Sir Bernard, who took this for a pleasantry and found it not quite to his liking, signed to the butler for a final glass of claret. 'I was remarking that the Bolderwoods are of considerable antiquity – I believe in the county of Kent. Latterly, however, the main branch of the family has lived much in South America, where I understand them to have considerable interests.

We must not disparage commerce, Captain Cox – provided, of course, that it is on the large scale.' And Sir Bernard (in whose eyes, as we have seen, shone the awe of one whose universe is on a very large scale indeed) sipped his claret with some complacency.

Captain Cox, who appeared not given to undercurrents of satirical feeling, concentrated upon writing 'Bolderwood' in his diary – a quite new diary, unseasonable to the time of year, which he might have bought for the express purpose of recording the requirements and occasions of his prospective employer. 'And the address?' he asked.

But Sir Bernard's mind had strayed elsewhere. 'Humphrey –' he began – and paused as he observed Captain Cox's pencil once more travel over the paper. It was perhaps a sleepiness following upon the excellent Paxton claret that this momentarily reduced the young man to an automatism so accurately recalling the jurors in *Alice in Wonderland*. Becoming conscious of what he was doing, he blushed and hastily thrust the diary into his hippocket – this apparently as the most inaccessible place he could at the moment command.

'Humphrey –?' said Captain Cox.

'I was about to remark that Humphrey, not unnaturally, has a good deal interested such schoolmasters as he has had. It is a pity they have not managed to make a little more of him. Understanding, I am sure, is what he needs. But these people have at times written quite voluminous reports, and it occurs to me that you might usefully run through them. If we take our coffee in the study, it will be possible for you to do so.'

If Captain Cox reflected that Humphrey himself might be a good deal more illuminating than his reports he had the tact not to say so, and Sir Bernard's plan was accordingly adopted. Many of Humphrey's previous preceptors, it turned out, had expatiated at some length on his abilities and shortcomings in Latin, Maths, Geography, Scripture, and similar intellectual pursuits, while others had made remarks on his industry, degree of personal cleanliness, attitude to manly sports, table manners, veracity, loquacity, and sundry other character traits commonly coming beneath a schoolmaster's eye. Captain Cox conscientiously perused these memorials for about an hour, and at the end of this period informed Sir Bernard that no very clear picture of the boy emerged. Sir Bernard, approving of this honesty, gloomily concurred. He then wrote out a cheque, requested the new tutor to buy a shot-gun and any other necessary gear, led him out into the hall, and bade him farewell.

As Captain Cox walked away from the Paxton mansion and its magnificence, and as the Paxton coffee continued to settle down upon the Paxton claret, he reflected upon a certain unacknowledged mistrust which had lurked in his consciousness for some time. Was young Humphrey Paxton such that any prospective tutor might be expected to retreat in dismay upon a first ripening of acquaintance? Certainly there was ground for suspecting something of the sort. For, as matters at present stood, they were to meet only in the uncompromising atmosphere of Euston railway station, and some ten minutes thereafter they would be travelling together in an express which made its first stop at Crewe. Was this the cunning of Sir Bernard, who was so plainly a terribly brainy old bird? Captain Cox feared that it was. He had, in fact, let himself in for what might prove an uncommonly tiresome job. But this did not, perhaps, greatly disturb him. He would do his conscientious best with Humphrey. And as they were going to stay with people apparently adequately provided with lakes and streams, there ought to be enough salmon, snipe, and waterfowl to compensate for his tutorial labours.

No; it was by something else that Captain Cox was obscurely troubled. It had been the occasion of that odd abstraction which had led him into the little misadventure with his diary . . . Captain Cox, who was now walking through the square next adjoining to Sir Bernard Paxton's, had advanced so far in his meditations when they were interrupted by the sound of rapidly running feet behind him. He glanced back in time to see a slender youth come dashing round the corner he had himself turned a minute before. 'Hi!' shouted the youth. 'Hold on!'

Captain Cox halted. That this untidy, fair-haired boy was Humphrey Paxton appeared certain, and he found it necessary positively to brace himself for the unexpected encounter. But his first impression was favourable. The lad possessed a turn of speed and ease of breathing that suggested a very fair athletic trim. Moreover, he looked Captain Cox straight in the eye. 'Are you my new tutor?' he asked.

'I am. And I think you were at that keyhole quite long enough to know it.'

'Keyhole?' The boy appeared momentarily disconcerted. 'Oh well, why not?'

'It isn't done. Not by our sort. A housemaid might do it because she isn't a lady.' Captain Cox frowned. 'I mean, might do it if she hadn't the *feelings* of a lady. You mustn't do everything that you see young louts doing in comics.'

'All right. I'll drop it.' Humphrey, Captain Cox reflected, appeared suitably abashed. 'Are we going to Ireland together?'

'Certainly we are. We leave at four fifty-five on Thursday. And I've suggested to your father that before that I'd better buy you a gun.'

'A gun? I say, that was jolly decent of you.' The boy, however dark a view he and the public-school system took of each other, appeared to possess the right articulations – which were made the more attractive in his case by a very slight lisp. Not that Captain Cox was wholly reassured as to his charge, for in the lad's eye as it confidently met his there was an impression of remote and rapid calculation which, in one so young, was not altogether inspiring of confidence. But his total bearing was frank enough. 'Couldn't we', he asked, 'buy it together?'

'Well, perhaps we could. In fact, it mightn't be at all a bad idea.'

'What about Thursday afternoon? That's the first time I'm free. Only I want to go to the Metrodrome at two-fifteen and see *Plutonium Blonde*.'

'Whatever is that?'

'It's a film with an atom bomb in it. They say it's absolutely smashing.'

'It might well be that.' And Captain Cox chuckled, pleased with this unwonted flight of wit in himself. 'Well, I'm afraid you will have to choose.'

The boy considered. 'I say, couldn't you come to *Plutonium Blonde*, too? It really is sticking out. We could buy the gun first, and then go to the flicks, and then straight across to the railway station. I'd have sent my things ahead.'

'I think your father was intending to bring you to Euston.'

'Dad can meet us at the station for the proper sort of farewells. Do come.'

Captain Cox considered. This eagerness for his earlier society on the part of the kittle young Humphrey was distinctly gratifying, and his forebodings were beginning to dissipate themselves. 'We could have the gun sent straight to Euston and put in the Left Luggage,' he said. 'And if we met at half past one –' He made rapid calculations. 'We could just do it. But I shall consult your father first.'

'Ring him up this evening. Where do we meet?'

'At Bone's in Piccadilly for a quick snack first. And now you'd better cut along.' Captain Cox was a great believer in the moral effect of abrupt dismissals of the young. 'You won't see many films in Ireland. We shall have other things to do. Goodbye.'

And Humphrey Paxton's new tutor strode on his way. The holiday job, he felt, was going to be satisfactory, after all. Snipe drummed and salmon leapt before him as he marched.

Chapter 3

Monday afternoon

Sir Bernard Paxton to Mr Thewless

Dear Mr Thewless, – Since our meeting this morning it has unfortunately proved necessary to make arrangements other than those of the kind then contemplated. I am greatly obliged to you for your kindness in calling.

Yours v. truly,
Bernard Paxton.

Humphrey Paxton to Universal Stores

Dear Sirs, – Please deliver at once by special mesanger one pair of strong binoculars for bird-watching and a good camera (not box). Please send also these books: *Biggles Flies East, Biggles Flies West, Biggles Flies North, Big-*

gles Fails to Return, Bertrand Russell's *History of Western Phisolophy*, George Moore's *Daphnis and Chloe, Biggles and the Camel Squadron*, Bleinstein's *More and More Practical Sex*, Blunden's *Life of Shelley*, also *Atalanta in Calydon, Biggles in Borneo, Women in Love*, and any *close* translations of *Caesar's Civil Wars*, Book III and *Phaedrus' Fables*. I repeat special mesanger and charge to my account.

> *Yours truly,*
> *Bernard Paxton (p.p. H. P.).*

Humphrey Paxton to Miss Mary Carruthers

My dear Miss Carruthers, – I am leaving on Thursday for Ireland. As you know about my wanting to go I hope you won't mind my writing to tell you. I shall miss not being able to come and see you while I am away but I hope you will let me come when I get back. It has been so very wonderful really meeting you and then hearing you read your wonderful poems. As you know I have not been happy among the oppressive and deadening influences of this place where there is nothing but

> a world of woes
> The harsh and grating strife of tyrants and of foes

but I hope that in Ireland amid the influances of Nature (about which you write so beautifully in your Ode) I shall

> burst
> My spirit's sleep.

I have also to read a lot of Latin they say but when I return it will be

> So now my summer task is ended, Mary,
> And I return to thee, mine own heart's home.

I think Latin silly particularly since you said you do not read it very much. But fortunitly I shall be able to take some other books won from Opression by Guile!

> nothing that my tyrants knew or taught
> I cared to learn, but from that secret store
> Wrought linked armours for my soul, before
> It might walk forth to war among mankind.

> *Your sincere and admiring friend,*
> *Humphrey Paxton.*

Humphrey Paxton to Master John Potter

Dear Potts, – I can't come to look at your stamps on Thursday afternoon because I'm going to Ireland – as I jolly well said I would. Actually I'm not going till late in the afternoon but I have to be at the dentists's all the time before that.

> *Humphrey Paxton.*

Humphrey Paxton to Miss Beverley Anne Crupp

Buxom Beverley, – I am going away on Thursday afternoon but first I will take you out. Be at the usual place at half past twelve. I will give you a meal and take you to the pictures. I will book two seats in the back row. Do not muffle yourself up as for Siberian snows. Among those wanting to sit beside a cloakroom or clothes-horse

Is not Numbered

H. P.

    P.S. – Alas, that love should be a blight and snare
        To those who seek all sympathies in one!
You need not trouble with this.

Tuesday morning

Universal Stores to Sir Bernard Paxton

Dear Sir, – We enclose a letter received from your address this morning and await the favour of your further instructions.
    Assuring you of our best attention at all times,

We remain,

Yours faithfully,

J. Muirhead

(Universal Stores Ltd).

Telegram to Sir Bernard Paxton

MUCH REGRET SUDDEN DEATH RENDERS IT IMPOSSIBLE ACCEPT POST AS ARRANGED COX.

Sir Bernard Paxton to Universal Stores

Dear Sirs, – Please deliver the goods ordered on my behalf by my son. You may however omit the treatise *More and More Practical Sex*, and add a reliable pocket compass.

Yours faithfully,

B. Paxton.

Sir Bernard Paxton to Mr Thewless

My dear Mr Thewless, – Since writing to you yesterday afternoon I find the situation again changed. It will be best to say frankly that I had engaged as tutor to Humphrey a young man highly recommended to me, whose chief virtues appeared to me athletic interest and simplicity of mind: these I thought might commend themselves to the boy in the particular circumstances of the holiday proposed. But this gentleman has been called away – seemingly by a family bereavement – and I am hoping that you may still be free, and inclined, to assist us. If so, would you have the great kindness to ring up, or send a telegram, upon the receipt of this, in order that we may arrange to meet at Euston on Thursday?

It is not within my recollection that we discussed terms. If you are now so good as to undertake the work, would you please let me know whether, for the month or so that it will last, the sum of fifteen guineas weekly would appear to you to be reasonable? I am uninformed in these matters and you must forgive me if this should be to propose an inadequate remuneration.

With kind regards,
Yours sincerely,
Bernard Paxton.

P.S. – May I say how much I enjoyed, in the *Journal of Roman Archaeology*, your lucid and informative account of the villa which you assisted in excavating at Little Slumber some years ago?

B.P.

Tuesday evening

Mr Thewless to Sir Bernard Paxton

THANK YOU FOR YOUR LETTER STOP WILL TAKE HUMPHREY TO IRELAND SUBJECT RETURN AT DISCRETION SHOULD ENVIRONMENT IN MY OPINION BE PREJUDICIAL MORAL AND OR NERVOUS AND OR INTELLECTUAL PROGRESS OF PUPIL STOP TERMS SATISFACTORY BUT PLEASE REPLY ON ABOVE THEWLESS.

Sir Bernard Paxton to Mr Thewless

My dear Mr Thewless, – Very many thanks for your telegram to which I reply at once by special messenger. I am glad that you find it possible to take Humphrey on his holiday and need hardly say that I highly approve the reservation you make. However, although I know little of the Bolderwoods I have a substantial hope that they will provide the quiet and stability which are so desirable. They have been apprised of Humphrey's present somewhat unsettled state.

I enclose a cheque for £65, being three weeks' salary as agreed between us and a further sum upon which to draw for such expenses as you may incur. Humphrey will be provided with pocket-money, but you will of course make any further disbursements of this kind that you think judicious.

It was my intention on Thursday afternoon to take Humphrey to visit an aunt and then come straight to Euston. He now tells me, however, that he has made an appointment with his dentist, so I suggest that we all meet at the station at half past four. Near the main hall you may recall a plan showing the location of the various buildings and platforms, and this would seem to be a convenient place for our rendezvous. Unfortunately there is a possibility that within the next couple of days I may be called urgently away.

In this event Humphrey will have the necessary tickets, and a note with anything further that it may occur to me as being convenient for you to know. I need only add now that he is looking forward to the change and already appears to be drawing benefit from its prospect. He has taken occasion to acquire various books and objects – some of them very sensible – which he proposes to take with him. What alone causes me some anxiety is a growing tendency to imagine various conspiracies and enmities as hovering around him. I will later consult Lord Polder (a very old friend) about this, and he may recommend some form of psychiatric treatment. Meanwhile, Humphrey will be in excellent hands.

> *Yours very sincerely,*
> *Bernard Paxton.*

Humphrey Paxton to Mr A. B., c/o Bunce, Newsagent, Bolt Road

Sir, – You make a misstake. I am ashamed of nothing I say or do. So you may see me with whom you like, when you like. Wretched man! if I did not think that all law was Tyrany I would have you put in goal. If you approach me personally I will punch you on the nose.

> *Farewell and beware*
> *Humphrey Edwyn Honyel Paxton.*

Miss Margaret Liberty to Miss Agnes Hopper

My dear Agnes, – I am writing to excuse myself, with many apologies, from what I am sure will be a most delightful Mah Jong party on Friday. The fact is – I am going for a holiday – and to the West of Ireland! I leave on Thursday! And this means such a terrible *rush!*

You will wonder how this has come about. Well, when my brother, Sir Charles, came to see me a short time ago it appeared to him that I was (only, I am sure, ever so slightly) *run down*, and he recommended the change and was so very generous as to provide for the financial side. You will appreciate the thoughtfulness of this the more when I tell you that my brother's work is now *extremely important and most confidential* – and so absorbing that it is really charming of him to give such thought to the happiness and health of an elderly spinster sister. Were my dear father, Sir Herbert, alive he would, I am sure, be proud of his *equally distinguished son*. Woollens are the problem, even at this time of year, and particularly when one is going abroad. I am sure to be particularly interested in everything I find in Eire, as my father, a truly liberal man, was a great supporter of the late Mr Gladstone. And on the literary side there will be, I believe, views of Slieve League, Ben Bulben, and other places most romantically associated with Allingham, Mr Yeats, and other wonderful Irish writers.

In great haste from one who is about to go out and hunt for *woollen stockings* (!!) and who remains

> *Your affectionate friend,*
> *Margaret Liberty.*

Captain Cox to Miss Joyce Vane

Dear Joyce, – I'm terribly sorry I shan't be seeing you for some time, as on Thursday I'm off to Ireland with a kid who sounds a bit of a handful all round. This is a terrible bore! I've been making inquiries since I got the job and it appears that the lad's father is a terrible scientific swell. He has a laboratory in which he cracks atoms much as you and I might crack nuts when lucky enough to be having one of our jolly dinners together. Perhaps this is why the lad is insisting on taking me to see a film with atom bombs in it just before we leave. It's called *Plutonium Blonde*. But there is only one blonde for me and I will see her again as soon as I can.

Love,

Peter.

Ivor Bolderwood to Cyril Bolderwood, Killyboffin Hall, Co. Donegal

My dear Dad, – I shall be returning by Stranraer tomorrow night, nearly everything here being satisfactorily cleared up, I am glad to say. Meanwhile this ought to catch this evening's plane and let you have one piece of news. I called on cousin Paxton and expressed the hope that, being now more settled on this side of the world, we might a little better our acquaintance with him. Bernard is very much the great man (as is right and proper) but perhaps a little lacking in the simplicity of life and manner which one likes to think of as attaching to genius. He is – as we rather expected – unable to visit us this summer, having very important researches in hand. I was of course sorry about this but at the same time a shade relieved – suspecting that when he does go into the wilds it is to do all the orthodox things during the day, and to express complete rustication of an evening by donning nothing more elaborate than a boiled shirt and a black tie. But he did accept your invitation for his only boy, Humphrey, who will be crossing with a tutor on Thursday. Humphrey is of public-school age and will presumably want to fish and perhaps shoot. Billy will no doubt be able to do something about that. Bernard hinted darkly that Humphrey is something of a handful, and indeed that he has sometimes been afraid of his running away! What do you think of that? But soon he soft-pedalled on this theme, no doubt as not wanting to scale off relations like ourselves benevolently prepared to 'solve the problems of the holidays'. As for the tutor, I gathered in a telephone conversation that he was to have been a Captain Peter Cox, V.C., a worthy much too straight out of the romances of 'Sapper' to be quite our cup of tea. Do not, however, be alarmed! Now, it seems, the charge has been transferred to a Mr Thewless, whom Bernard described as 'a very genteel man and something of a scholar'. Bernard had looked him up in some work of reference and found that he is given to writing little articles on Roman remains. So he may be quite a congenial man, and it occurs to me that he might be interested in the conical mound near Ballybags, which appears to me to be almost certainly defensive in type. Humphrey and this excellent bear-leader will be taking the light railway from Dundrane on Friday and you will no doubt send Billy to meet them.

Your affectionate son,

Ivor.

Chapter 4

As he drove to Euston, Mr Thewless, having a tidy mind, endeavoured to sort out his misgivings. He did not believe that Sir Bernard Paxton had read his article on the Roman villa excavated at Little Slumber. Being anxious to secure his services after all, Sir Bernard had simply looked him up in the likelier bibliographies and added a postscript designed to please. Every summer, as Mr Thewless very well knew, scores of Thewlesses attach themselves to little archaeological enterprises and happily potter away their holidays in insignificant siftings of the rubbish-dumps of the legionaries . . . But in Ireland – thought Mr Thewless irrelevantly – the armies of Rome had never set foot. There the Imperial Eagles had never been borne along the unending arrow-like roads that were the arteries of Latin culture. And the island was the worse of it to this day. Because the praetors of Augustus had left it to the generals of Elizabeth, to the Earl of Essex and Lord Grey de Wilton . . .

But these scholastic reveries – thought Mr Thewless, bumped awake as his taxi jerked to a stop in a traffic-block – were off the present point. Sir Bernard was paying too much, too. For a residential holiday post five guineas would have been adequate and eight handsome. Fifteen was merely ominous. And along with the offer of it there had come fresh and disconcerting information. Humphrey Paxton was not merely difficult. There was now the suggestion that the unfortunate lad was a little off his head, and disposed to imagine conspiracies and dangers around him. It was with this that Mr Thewless was to be landed in the depths of Ireland and in a household of which he knew nothing.

Mr Thewless frowned at the humped back of the taxi-driver. These were merely the reactions of a new housemaid who learns that it is two miles to the nearest bus-stop. Rightly regarded, if the job was difficult it thereby carried only the more dignity. This was Paxton's boy – say Newton's, Galileo's boy. The child of genius . . . And it was up to the new tutor to see him through.

But there was the additional annoyance that Sir Bernard himself might not appear again. There had been the suggestion that the great man might be 'urgently called away'. The quite childish suspicion came to Mr Thewless that he was really, in the vulgar phrase, being led up the garden path – or left holding the baby. Perhaps Sir Bernard had reason to avoid or dread a parting at a railway station. Perhaps in all innocence, but at the beckoning of the unconscious mind, he had contrived that the urgent calling away should happen. Perhaps here at Euston there would be immediate and embarrassing difficulty. Mr Thewless had a horrid vision of a lusty fifteen-year-old boy indulging in a hysterical fit on the platform . . . Various ineffective schemes occurred to him. They would see if any of the automatic machines were working. They would walk up and look at the engine. They would buy large numbers of banal illustrated journals. They would look for chocolate-coated ice-creams. Distraction was the proper technique.

The taxi-door was flung open and Mr Thewless, emerging, gave directions for the disposal of his luggage. Unlike many of those who excavate Roman villas, he never found small matters of this sort harassing and he seldom muddled them. It was already a couple of minutes after half past four as he made his way to the appointed rendezvous. There was nobody there.

Misgiving returned. If Sir Bernard was indeed not bringing the boy to the station, what reason was there to suppose that the boy would actually come? It was true that his father believed him anxious to go to Ireland – but what more likely than that when it came to the point panic might seize a nervous child? Mr Thewless paced up and down. He bought some tobacco and paced up and down once more. It was after twenty-five to five. Suddenly a fantastic thought – or rather a fantastic mental experience – came to him. Sir Bernard Paxton was one of the most important men in England – and not important in any insulated world of science merely. There no longer existed such an insulated world. He must be important – vastly important – to those who played for power. For *ultimate* power. For the very dominion of the earth. Was it not conceivable that his own child . . .?

Mr Thewless halted, amazed at himself. He never read gangster stories. He never even read that milder sensational fiction, nicely top-dressed with a compost of literature and the arts, which is produced by idle persons living in colleges and rectories. Whence, then, did this sudden vivid fantasy come? He found himself staring unseeingly at some unintelligible piece of machinery displayed in a glass case. He turned and hurried out into the main courtyard of the station.

A taxi was just drawing up. The door burst open and he saw untidy black hair and black eyes glancing slantwise from a pale face – with crowning these the sort of flattened bowler hat which some public schools still consider essential for young travellers. The boy jumped from the taxi, and as he did so hauled from an inner pocket a large watch on a leather strap. Mr Thewless went up to him. 'Are you Humphrey Paxton?'

Startled eyes regarded him. 'Yes.'

'I thought' – and Mr Thewless nodded at the watch – 'that I recognized Master Humphrey's Clock.'

The boy gave a yelp of laughter, instantly taking and joyously appreciating the unremarkable joke. Then his eyes narrowed and Mr Thewless saw them suddenly flood with anxiety, suspicion, distrust. 'Are you Mr Thewless, my tutor?' he asked abruptly.

'I am. And you have arrived just in comfortable time.'

'Let me see your passport, please.'

Mr Thewless opened his mouth – and checked himself. From an inner pocket he produced the document and handed it over.

And the boy scanned it with extraordinary intensity. Then he handed it back. 'Excuse me.' He turned away and tumbled some coins into the hands of the taxi-driver – and his own hands, Mr Thewless noticed, were trembling. Another taxi had drawn up behind. The boy spun round upon it. An elderly lady got out. The boy gave an odd gasp; it might have been of either relief or dismay. 'Well,' he said, 'here I am. And I'm most terribly sorry to be late. I've got the tickets and my gear is in the Left Luggage. Daddy couldn't come. It's not *too* late?'

'Not a bit. Did the dentist keep you?'

'The dentist?' The boy looked blank. 'Oh, well – it was all horrid. And then I had to go home for something. I just *had* to go. I'm frightfully sorry. It was terrible cheek, keeping you waiting.' He paused, and his eyes flashed again at Mr Thewless. 'What's the first line of the *Aeneid*?'

'*Arma virumque cano, Troiae qui primus ab oris.*' And Mr Thewless smiled. 'Perhaps you can tell me the second?'

'The second?'

'Certainly. If you want to be sure it's me, I want to be sure it's you.'

'I see.' And Humphrey Paxton gave a quick and decisive nod. '*Italiam fato profugus Laviniaque venit.*' He frowned. 'Would we have time to make a short telephone call?'

'Only just.'

'Is there anyone in London that you know very well?'

'I have a sister who lives in London.'

They had been walking through the station, and now Humphrey halted by a telephone box. 'Will you ring her up and say just the words I tell you?'

Mr Thewless nodded gravely. 'Unless they are quite unsuitable words, I have no objection at all. Come along.' They entered the telephone box together and he produced twopence. 'What is it that I am to say?'

Humphrey considered. 'What is your sister's name, please?'

'Harriet.'

'Then say "Hullo, Harriet, I hoped I'd find you in" – and hand the receiver to me.'

Mr Thewless did as he was bid. The lad, he thought, *was* quite unbalanced. Nevertheless, he was capable; he ought certainly to have got School Certificate long ago . . . He heard his sister's voice. 'Hullo, Harriet,' he said, 'I hoped I'd find you in.' And he handed the receiver to Humphrey.

'I'm so sorry.' Humphrey's voice was apologetic, but not exaggeratedly so. 'Would you mind telling me who has just spoken to you?' He listened. 'Thank you,' he said. 'Would you please hold on?' He handed the receiver back to Mr Thewless. 'You may care to explain,' he said seriously. And he slipped from the telephone box.

Mr Thewless explained – briefly, for his eye was on his watch. He set down the receiver and emerged briskly. 'And now we run for it, Humphrey. We have ten minutes, but there's often a queue at the Left Luggage. Porter!' And he hurried forward. Humphrey Paxton, it was clear, fought with phantoms, and a sympathetic understanding was necessary. After all, it was only in point of their intensity that such dire imaginings as apparently beset the boy were abnormal. Only a few minutes before his own well-ordered mind had been invaded by some sensational and alarming notion – fleetingly indeed, so that he no longer remembered what it had been about . . . At the moment he must simply show Humphrey that the phantoms had no power over the actual world; that the holiday upon which they were embarked went smoothly forward on its predetermined way. 'What about the tickets?' he asked briskly.

And Humphrey produced an envelope. 'Everything is there, sir.' His voice was meek and suddenly that of a much younger boy. Mr Thewless glanced at him. He was moving dreamily forward, sucking his thumb.

They still had seven minutes when Humphrey's suitcases had been added to those of Mr Thewless on a barrow. Their porter was moving off when he was recalled by the man at the counter. 'Paxton, was that? There's something else came in later.' And he pushed forward a heavy and slender object in a canvas case.

Humphrey's thumb came out of his mouth; he turned and himself seized this new piece of luggage with quick curiosity. 'It's a *gun*!' he cried – and so loudly that people turned to stare. His eyes blazed. To be young! thought Mr Thewless. To have so swift and passionate a capacity for pleasure, for exultation! A clatter disturbed this reflection. Humphrey had flung the swathed shotgun back on the counter. 'I don't want the horrible thing,' he said. 'Take it away. It's not mine.'

Mr Thewless looked at the label. 'It's addressed to you, Humphrey, and has been delivered here by special messenger. Your father must have meant it for a surprise.'

'He wouldn't do such a thing – unless prompted. Did *you* prompt him?' And Humphrey looked at his tutor accusingly. 'Do *you* think I want a horrible gun to go shooting living things with?'

'I can see you don't. And I certainly didn't suggest a gun to your father. But there it is.'

Humphrey shot out a finger and pointed at the clerk behind the counter. The whole scene was uncomfortably dramatic, and there was now a little crowd to watch it. 'Do you think *he* would like it? He could sell it and buy toys for his children.'

Mr Thewless smiled. 'I don't think he would be allowed to take it, just like that. But if you don't want it we can leave it here and make some arrangement when we get back.'

'I don't know that we *shall* get back.' Humphrey's glance as he uttered this dark absurdity was travelling rapidly over the people round about. 'We'll take it,' he said abruptly. 'Come on.' And he tucked the shot-gun under his arm and strode forward.

Mr Thewless, had there been leisure for the action, might have paused to mop his brow. As it was, he hurried after the porter, who was trotting in sinister haste far in front of them. Their coach was A3, which meant right at the front of the interminable train. They gained it, however, with a good half-minute to spare. The man piled their luggage on the racks. Mr Thewless handed him a shilling and then, after rapid calculation, a further sixpence. The train was moving.

'We've done it!'

Humphrey's voice had rung out surprisingly. So might the earth's first space-traveller exclaim as his rocket took off for the moon. The two other occupants of the compartment looked up, smiling. One was a bearded man with pebbly glasses. The other was the elderly lady who had been in the taxi behind Humphrey's. On one side a towering brick wall was gliding past them; on the other were lines of sleeping-cars, themselves apparently fast asleep in the afternoon sunshine. Presently the whole sprawl of North London would be hurtling southwards. Then the Midlands. There would be no pause till Crewe.

Mr Thewless, tucking his gloves into a crevice on the rack above his head, heard a sigh behind him, and when he turned to his pupil it was to observe that some quick reaction had seized the boy. Humphrey was curled up in the corner seat opposite, his head just above the level of the window-frame, staring out with unseeing eyes. He had grown to a casual seeming smaller and younger, and yet at the same time he appeared to be supporting some unnatural burden of years. His brow was slightly puckered and for the first time Mr Thewless noticed that there were dark lines under his black eyes.

In fact, Humphrey Paxton had retired into a sort of infantile privacy, like some unhappy small boy being taken to his first private school. And into that privacy it was necessary to intrude. That, Mr Thewless saw with some misgiving, was a condition of getting anywhere. Somehow – and the sooner the better – he had to rap firmly on the door and walk in.

But it would assuredly be useless to force the lock. For the moment at least it might be best to leave Humphrey alone. Mr Thewless, therefore, got out his book – it was a volume of verse – and opened it. He read a page with reasonable concentration – it would never do to let his professional problem of the moment obsess him – and turned over to the next. And here his mind must a little have wandered, for it was some moments before the oddity of what had occurred came home to him. What he had stumbled on was in the form of a rhetorical question; and it was substantially the question that he now realized to be forming itself with some urgency in his own mind about his new pupil. Acting on impulse, he leant forward and handed Humphrey the book. 'Do you know this?' he asked. 'The one called "Midnight on the Great Western".' And he pointed to the place on the page.

> What past can be yours, O journeying boy,
>   Towards a world unknown,
> Who calmly, as if incurious quite
> On all at stake, can undertake
>   This plunge alone?

Humphrey read the lines, frowning. He read them again and abruptly sat up. 'Is that by Shelley?' he demanded.

'No; it's by Thomas Hardy.'

'Was he as good a poet as Shelley?'

'I happen to like some of his poetry better. But he was not nearly so good a poet. He kept on being depressed. And although you can write poetry out of despair, just as you can write it out of joy, it's very hard to write it out of depression.'

'I see.' Humphrey sounded as if, in fact, he did see, and he was looking at his tutor wide-eyed. 'I wasn't told you knew about those things.' His voice was, if anything, rather hostile, and he handed Mr Thewless back his book at once. 'Have you been told to find out about *my* past?' he demanded abruptly.

Mr Thewless smiled. 'I've been told to give you a hand with your future. But if you care to tell me about your past I shall be quite interested.'

Humphrey ignored this. 'Did you show me that poem because I look as if I'm taking a plunge into a world unknown?'

'You do a little look as if you think you are.'

'The poem says "calmly". Do I look as if I'm doing it that way?'

Mr Thewless hesitated. 'No, you don't. You look as if you found it rather more exciting than is comfortable. But I think you could manage quite a lot of calmness at a pinch.'

Faintly but perceptibly, Humphrey Paxton blushed. 'About poetry,' he said abruptly. 'Do you know the verse Mary Carruthers writes?'

'Yes.'

'Do you think it good?'

'No.'

Humphrey's eyes widened further. He looked almost guiltily round him. 'Not good! I – I know her quite well. She has me to tea. She's awfully decent.'

'As a person? Perhaps she is. But not her poetry. It's awfully indecent, as a matter of fact.'

Humphrey gave a sudden whoop of wild laughter. 'Do you mean because it makes you blush inside?'

'Just that. You see, you know it's no good, really.'

Humphrey gasped. It was an unambiguous gasp this time – like that of a person who has been lightened of at least one of many confusions. 'I say,' he said, 'do we get tea?'

'Yes. I think I hear the fellow coming now. Let's go along. And we get dinner on the train, too.'

'Wizard!' And Humphrey Paxton tumbled himself into the corridor. He looked like any one of the innumerable small fry whom summer releases from English schools. Without any illusions, Mr Thewless followed him.

The first-class restaurant car was empty when they entered it; a minute later the elderly lady from their own compartment came in and sat down in a far corner. Humphrey picked up a printed card from the table and handed it politely to his tutor. Mr Thewless glanced at it. 'I don't think it tells one much.'

'And not about the dinner either.' Humphrey shook his head so that his gleaming black hair tossed on his forehead. 'Some man in Whitehall sits and tells the railway just how many slices of bread and scrape it may give us, and just how thick to cut the railway slab. It's tyranny.'

'Is it? Suppose that we –' Mr Thewless looked across at Humphrey. 'Are you a Cavalier or a Roundhead?'

'I'm a Roundhead.' Humphrey spoke decidedly.

'Very well. Suppose we were a group of Roundheads besieged in a castle and that there were only so many tins of biscuits –'

'They didn't have tins. And I don't know that they had biscuits.'

'Then say so many kegs of salted beef. Would it be tyranny in the man in charge to insist on a proper shareout?'

'It would depend on how he was elected.'

Mr Thewless shook his head. 'I don't think it would. As long as he made a good job of it, the particular manner of his election would be irrelevant. Irrelevant, that is to say, to the particular point at issue. And if he worked very hard at his job –'

Humphrey gave his sudden peal of laughter. 'You work terribly hard at *yours*,' he said.

This was a disconcerting thrust. Mr Thewless was somewhat inclined to the doctrine that education should go on all the time. But now he abandoned the Roundheads and poured himself out a cup of tea. 'Can you eat all right?' he asked.

'Eat all right? Why ever not?'

'Because of the dentist. He sometimes leaves one a bit sore.'

'Oh, that! Old Partridge is never too bad.'

Mr Thewless put down his cup. 'Is that Mr Partridge in Devonshire Crescent?'

'Yes. I always go to him.' And Humphrey looked his tutor straight in the eye.

Mr Thewless felt a sudden sinking of the heart. For Mr Partridge happened to be his sister's dentist and that very morning Mr Partridge's nurse had rung up to cancel an appointment. When Humphrey claimed to have visited his dentist that dentist had been in bed with influenza.

35

Prevarication in a pupil is always tiresome. But in this instance, Mr Thewless found, it was also strangely disturbing. Why? He could discover no sufficient answer, and was aware only of the elements of some fantastic suspicion stirring anew in the depth of his mind. He decided on an obstinate return to education. 'My point', he said, 'was that England is rather like a besieged castle today. And that's why we none of us get more than our share.'

'I did. I just asked.' And Humphrey pointed to his plate.

The boy had certainly managed to get two pieces of cake. 'I imagine', said Mr Thewless austerely, 'that you were given mine as well.'

'No, sir. As a matter of fact you've eaten yours. Only you were thinking so much about the Roundheads – or Mr Partridge – that you didn't notice.'

Looking down at his own plate, Mr Thewless saw sufficient crumby evidence to substantiate this. Humphrey Paxton, he realized, could be extremely annoying – and only the more so because he was not in the least impertinent. He had good manners. Or perhaps he had merely a natural and undisciplined charm which passed as these. Whatever he had – Mr Thewless reflected with sudden irritation – he abundantly needed. The world is never for long very patient with its Humphrey Paxtons. To get along at all, they must necessarily exploit whatever powers of pleasing they may possess. For a moment – and all inconsequently – Mr Thewless felt himself invaded by an unwholesome sense of pathos. Just so must Thomas Hardy have felt as he contemplated that journeying boy – docketing him both for a doleful poem and for the most shattering of his novels. But it was not Mr Thewless's business to develop cosmic feelings about young Humphrey. What was required was some provisional analysis of the lad's strength and weakness – and not merely in mathematics and Latin. How serious was this queer sense of surrounding conspiracy and danger amid which he moved?

Mr Thewless glanced across the table. Humphrey, having eaten all there was to eat, was showing a disposition to curl up once more and suck his thumb. This clearly was a species of retreating to the nursery and locking the door. But against what? Mr Thewless looked out at the window. Perched on a fence, two little girls were waving at the train and behind them on a long, dull canal a gaily painted barge was moving southwards; sitting on the deck in the level evening sunshine was a woman peeling potatoes. There could have been no more peaceful scene; all the security of England lay in it. But Humphrey, it was to be presumed, moved during much of his waking life in an invisible world, stubbornly sustaining nerve-racking roles. Humphrey Paxton, Special Agent . . . Humphrey Paxton, the Secret Service Boy. And all this had begun to usurp upon reality, as had been instanced by the absurdities at Euston. Yes – thought Mr Thewless, laboriously reassuring himself against unformulated alarms – that was how the matter stood. It was a state of affairs common enough, and nothing was more foolish than to make a profound psychological pother over it, as the boy's father was perhaps unhappily prone to do. Yet –

And Mr Thewless frowned absently at the bill which had been laid in front of him. For something, he found, prompted him to distrust this simple diagnosis. About Humphrey when he was alert and aware there was a sense of covert calculation which was disturbingly of the waking world. He had been sizing Mr Thewless up. And he had been sizing up too a novel but perfectly actual situation – one which his day-dreams had perhaps helped in building, but which was itself by no means a day-dream. Or so some instinct in Mr Thewless declared. And instinct declared further – obscurely and most disturbingly – that more than one sort of danger would attend any disposition to deny that Humphrey Paxton knew a hawk from a handsaw. He did not simply spar with shadows in quite the way that Sir Bernard supposed. He was imaginative, unruly, ill-adjusted – an uncompromising problem at a dozen points. But to explain his conduct, his bearing, the essential impression he gave, by declaring that he was an incipient little lunatic suffering from delusions of persecution: this was to run counter to some powerful inner persuasion.

It would perhaps have been well had Mr Thewless, getting thus considerably far in his speculations in a novel field, as it were paused to take breath. As it was, his mind took a further leap, and found itself thereby on a perch so hazardous that mere vertigo was for a time the result. The impulse to scramble down again – only made the more overwhelming by a certain nightmarish power of reproduction with variation which the horrid eminence was henceforward to display: this must be held accountable for the deplorable muddle with which he was ever afterwards to associate the successive stages of his journey to the west of Ireland. It was as if the celebrated twilight with which that region is romantically associated were already a little clouding his intellectual processes.

What now at once came to him was a suspicion, a sudden and topsy-turvy suspicion having for the time much more of power than of precision. Something of the sort had come fleetingly into his mind earlier, when he had been perturbed by the tardy appearance of his charge at Euston. But his new speculation elaborated upon that. If the atmosphere of lurking melodrama which this totally unknown boy carried with him belonged somehow not to a fantastic but to an actual world, then what significance must attach to that extraordinary performance at the station whereby Mr Thewless's first encounter with him had been entirely a matter of his, Mr Thewless's, having elaborately to establish *his* identity? And why had the boy told a lie about Mr Partridge the dentist? Why had he not known that Mr Partridge was ill? Why had the shot-gun taken him wholly by surprise? Why, above all, did he involuntarily give the impression of one embarking with full awareness upon a novel and hazardous adventure requiring constant wary calculation?

It is very possible that had Mr Thewless continued this surprising train of thought undisturbed he would have been able to lay out a number of alternative hypotheses in an orderly manner, and so have begun to see some way round the problem by which he was confronted. Unfortunately at this moment he looked up and caught the boy's eye. It was this that gave him his sudden and disabling impression of being perched or poised as it were above some horrid precipice. For the boy's gaze was no longer abstracted. It was directed upon Mr Thewless in naked distrust and fear. But just so – Mr Thewless realized with horror – was he looking at the boy. It was as if a nameless and corrosive suspicion had instantaneously propagated itself between them.

Hence Mr Thewless's hasty hunt, one may say, for a downward path. This would never do. In a moment of indiscipline (he told himself) he had allowed a bizarre and sinisterly-beckoning mistrust to seize him. And Humphrey Paxton, this nervous and unfortunate boy, was instantly aware of it. Almost irreparable damage to their tentative and insecure relationship might be the result. Mr Thewless, partly because he remembered that this was Paxton's boy, and partly for reasons more immediately human, cursed himself heartily. It was essential that he should try to retrieve the situation as quickly as might be. And he must begin by sweeping his own mind clear of the penny-dreadful rubbish which – perhaps through the operation of some suggestive force from the teeming brain of Humphrey – had so unwontedly invaded it. Here – Mr Thewless in headlong downward scramble reluctantly asserted to himself – was a nervous boy who fancied things; who went in fear of all sorts of non-existent threats to his security. His confidence must be restored. These threats must be treated as the shadows they were.

Thus did Mr Thewless march his thoughts to the top of the hill and march them down again – or rather (to put it frankly) did he give them licence, which they were abundantly to take advantage of quite soon, to scurry up and down as they pleased. At the moment, however, he had them more or less quietly stowed – permitting them, indeed, but one more mild foray. In other words, one final flicker of queer distrust he did at this moment allow himself. 'Humphrey,' he asked, 'have you ever met any of these cousins we are going to stay with?'

The boy shook his head. His gaze had gone blank and uncommunicative. 'No,' he said; 'they've never set eyes on me.' There was a long silence. Humphrey's thumb stole towards his mouth. Then he checked himself and looked at his tutor steadily. With a movement as of abrupt decision he leant across the table. 'Sir,' he asked seriously, 'have you ever been blackmailed?'

Mr Thewless, because now determined at all costs to be sedative, smiled indulgently and leisurely filled his pipe. 'No,' he said; 'nothing of that sort has ever happened to me.'

'It has to me.'

'Has it, Humphrey? You must tell me about it.' Mr Thewless paused.

'But when I was a boy I used to get a good deal of fun out of telling myself stories in which things like that happened. Only sometimes the stories got a bit out of hand and worried me.'

'I see.'

And Humphrey Paxton gave an odd sigh. Mr Thewless rose to return to their compartment. Once more something illusive and disturbing had invaded his consciousness. As he swayed down the corridor – following Humphrey and with the elderly lady behind him – he realized that it was the profound isolation of Hardy's journeying boy.

Chapter 5

While Mr Thewless and his charge were moving unsteadily down the corridor of the 4.55 from Euston Detective-Inspector Thomas Cadover was crossing a broad London thoroughfare with the unconcern of a man once accustomed to controlling the traffic in such places with a pair of large white gloves. Nowadays his attire was pervasively sombre and his hair the only thing that was white about him: it had gone that way as the result of thirty years of fighting Metropolitan crime. During this long period he had seen many men come to the same job and not a few of these leave again – promoted, demoted, retired, or resigned. The fanatical Hudspith was gone and so was the wayward Appleby. But Cadover himself hung on, his hair a little thinner each year as well as whiter, his expression a little grimmer, his eyes sadder, his mouth compressed in an ever firmer line. He had seen tide upon tide of vice and lawlessness rise and lap round the city. Of low life and criminal practice he had seen whole new kinds sprout and flourish; he had seen criminology, answering these, transform itself and transform itself again. Sometimes he thought it about time he was giving over. Still, he was not giving over yet.

He paused on the kerb and bought an evening paper. He turned to the stop press. *West End Cinema Tragedy*, he read. *Scotland Yard Suspects Foul Play*.

Well, *he* was Scotland Yard – and the cinema was still a hundred yards off. Newspapers were wonderfully ahead with the news these days. He walked on and the Metrodrome rose before him. Across its monstrous façade sprawled a vast plywood lady. If erect, she would be perhaps fifty feet high; she was reclining, however, in an attitude of sultry abandon amid equatorial vegetation and in a garment the only prominent feature of which was a disordered shoulder-strap. As a background to the broadly accentuated charms of her person – pleasantly framed, indeed, between her six-foot, skyward-pointing breasts – was what appeared to be a two-ocean navy in process of sinking through tropical waters like a stone. One limp hand held a smoking revolver seemingly responsible for this extensive catastrophe. The other, supporting her head, was concealed in a spouting ectoplasm of flaxen hair. Her expression was languorous, provocative, and irradiated by a sort of sanctified lecherousness highly creditable to both the craft and the ardent soul of the unknown painter who had created her. Poised in air, and in curves boldly made to follow the line of her swelling hips, were the words AMOROUS, ARROGANT, ARMED! Above this, in letters ten feet high, was the title PLUTONIUM BLONDE. And higher still, and in rubric scarcely less gigantic, was the simple announcement: ART'S SUPREME ACHIEVEMENT TO DATE.

There were queues all round the cinema. The crowd could afford to be patient. Here, as at Eve's first party in the Garden, there was no fear lest supper cool; within this monstrous temple of unreason the celluloid feast perpetually renewed itself. And aloft in her other Paradise that second Eve, a prodigal confusion of tropical flesh and nordic tresses, spread wide the snare of her loosened zone and grotesquely elongated limbs. She was like a vast mechanized idol sucking in to her own uses these slowly moving conveyor-belts of humanity . . . And the crowds were growing as Cadover watched. People were buying the evening paper, reading the stop press and lining up. For here was sensation within sensation. *Art's supreme achievement to date. Scotland Yard Suspects Foul Play.*

Another squalid crime . . . Circumstances had made Inspector Cadover a philosopher, and because he was a philosopher he was now depressed. This was the celebrated atom film. This was the manner in which his species chose to take its new command of natural law. Fifty thousand people had died at Hiroshima, and at Bikini ironclads had been tossed in challenge to those other disintegrating nuclei of the sun. The blood-red tide was loosed. And here it was turned to hog's wash at five shillings the trough, and entertainment tax extra. That some wretched Londoner had met a violent death while taking his fill seemed a very unimportant circumstance. To track down the murderer – if murderer there was – appeared a revoltingly useless task. Mere anarchy was loosed upon the world – so what the hell did it matter? Better step into a telephone-box and call the Yard. Then he could send in his resignation in the morning and join some crank movement demanding international sovereignty . . .

Inspector Cadover's feet carried him automatically forward – as automatically as if he had been on his beat nearly forty years before. He was skirting the long queue for the cheaper seats. There was a woman clutching the hand of a fretful five-year-old boy with a chocolate-smeared mouth and sleep-heavy eyes. There were two lovers already beginning to cuddle in the crush. There was an apostate intellectual, furtive and embarrassed, caught by that scanty cincture overhead like a fly on a fly-paper. Cadover went firmly forward and the vast building received him. Underfoot the padded carpet was heavy as desert sand.

Three constables stood in the foyer. They could be no manner of use there; the management had doubtless wangled their presence as a little extra advertisement for its latest, and unforeseen, sensation. Cadover was about to scowl when he remembered that this would dismay them, and that they were only doing what they were told. So he nodded briskly and passed on. A slinky young man had appeared and was proposing to conduct him to the manager. The slinky young man contrived to insinuate that this was a privilege. Cadover, smouldering, marched forward still. Banks of flowers floated past him, gilt and scarlet chairs on which no one had ever sat, little fountains playing beneath changing coloured lights. Hectically tinted photographs as big as tablecloths, each with a disconcerting tilt to its picture-plane, presented curly-headed young men with butterfly ties, sleek-haired not-so-young men with smeared moustaches, a Negro in a straw hat, a nude girl knock-kneed and simpering behind a muff, the members of an entire symphony orchestra dressed like circus clowns . . . A door was opened and Cadover was aware of bare boards and a good rug, of bare walls and Dürer's *Apollo and Diana*. This was the manager's room. Its conscious superiority to the wares peddled outside was very nasty. Cadover's gloom increased.

The manager was sitting at a Chippendale table lightly scattered with objects suggesting administrative cares. On a couch at the far end of the room lay what was evidently a human body, covered with a sheet. By the window stood a glum, uniformed sergeant of police, staring out over London.

The manager rose. His manner appeared to aim at that of somebody very high up in a bank, and he received Cadover as if he came from among the middle reaches of his more substantial clients. 'An unpleasant thing, this,' he said. 'But if we must show a film of which the highlight is a holocaust what can we honestly say of a mere solitary killing in the Grand Circle? "Irony," I said to myself at once when they told me about it. "It's like cheap irony." And then I had them bring the body straight in here. Now we shall have nothing but standing room for a fortnight. The cinema industry, my dear Inspector, is nothing but a great whore. And you might call this the tart's supreme achievement to date.'

The slinky young man giggled deferentially. Cadover, who did not care for this cynical travesty of his own responses, looked round the room. 'The tart', he said, 'would appear to treat her doorkeepers handsomely enough.' There was a brief silence. The slinky young man giggled on another and an abruptly checked note. Cadover walked over to the body and twitched away the sheet. 'Unknown?' he asked.

The sergeant had come up beside him. 'No identification yet, sir. It's been made deliberately difficult.'

'This happened in the auditorium?' Cadover turned to the manager. 'And you had the body hauled out on your own responsibility?'

'Certainly. There was nothing else to do. And it wasn't known that the fellow was dead until they had him out in the upper foyer.' The manager returned to his desk and consulted a note. 'Lights went up at the end of

Plutonium Blonde, the time being three minutes past four. One of the girls we call usherettes' – and the manager made a fastidious face over this barbarism – 'saw the fellow slumped in his seat and went up to have a look at him. He didn't look right, so she called the floor manager. That was the regular procedure. The floor manager gave him a shake, and then saw the blood. By that time there was a bit of a fuss round about, so he sent one of the girls for a couple of commissionaires and to call up a doctor. He supposed, you know, that the fellow had suffered a haemorrhage, or something like that. By this time the lights were due to go down, and he didn't stop them, since he didn't want more disturbance than need be. But as the body was lifted out he saw that it *was* a body – that the fellow was dead – and he tells me that the notion of foul play did enter his mind. He called two firemen to stand by where the thing had happened – fortunately it was right in the back row – and then he came straight up to me. I gave instructions for the body to be brought in here and for the police to be called up at once. Then I went in to see how it was with the seats where the thing had happened. The row immediately in front was full. But the dead man's seat was, of course, still empty, and so was one seat on his right and three on his left. So I ordered the whole five to be roped off and guarded. Then your men arrived and my responsibility ended. Lights go up again in five minutes. Of course, if you want the theatre cleared and closed, I will have it done. Only you might put me through to your Assistant Commissioner first. I have to consider my directors, you know.'

Cadover made no reply. He turned to the sergeant. 'Well?'

'We arrived while they were still showing the short that follows *Plutonium Blonde*. There seemed no point in sealing the place. People had been pouring out and in during the previous interval – the one during which the discovery of the body was made. But, of course, there was the question of people nearby when the thing occurred who might still be in the theatre. There was that, and there was what the usherettes might know, and there was clearing a space round the spot where the thing had happened, and searching it in the interval after the short. Inspector Morton is on that now, sir, with half a dozen men from the district. But I understand they've come on nothing yet. The crime appears to have passed unnoticed.'

'Unnoticed? But this man was shot. You can't shoot a man in a public place without –'

The remainder of Cadover's sentence was drowned in a sudden crashing explosion which made Dürer's engraving rattle on the wall. The manager sighed resignedly. 'Disgraceful,' he murmured. 'Do you know that between the auditorium and this room there are two supposedly sound-proof walls? We shall have people calling quacks from Harley Street to swear that they've been deafened, and we shall have to pay thousands of pounds. And, of course, it's indecent too. Much more indecent than rows of ghastly little trollops waggling their photogenic haunches. The Lord Chamberlain should intervene. When I was a young man I had idealism, Inspector, I assure you.

I saw Film as a great new aesthetic form. Those were the days of the early Clairs, and of *Potemkin* and *Storm over Asia*. And to think that it should all come to this . . .! Would you care for a cigar?'

The slinky young man, looking awed, produced a box of Coronas from a drawer. Cadover petrified him with a scowl. 'Was that meant to be an exploding bomb?' he asked.

The manager nodded. 'An atomic one. The biggest noise in the entire noisesome history of the screen. Sound's greatest triumph. The explosion kills seventy-five thousand supers hired at five dollars a head. It also blows the clothes off a gaggle of girls in a cabaret. It's all very disheartening to people like ourselves. To say nothing of being an invitation to murder. For plainly the shot was fired just as the sound-track triumphantly broke the record. Ingenious, come to think of it. The poor fellow must have been lured in expressly to be shot under cover of that hideous row. And then he was robbed.'

'Robbed?' Cadover turned sharply on the sergeant.

'I don't think it should be called that, sir. Everything – or nearly everything – was certainly lifted from the body. But there was more to it than that. Bits of the clothing were cut away.'

'Bits of the clothing.'

'Yes, sir. You know there are three places where a good tailor usually sews in a tab with a name – an inner jacket pocket, a waistcoat pocket, and the inside of the trouser-tops at the back. Well, all these places have been cut out.'

There was a silence while Cadover verified this. 'I can understand the shooting,' he said. 'With a smokeless powder, and when the audience was stunned and distracted by that uproar, the thing would be possible enough. But that anyone should then be able to tumble the body about –'

The slinky young man giggled. 'It was in the back row, Inspector, and you must remember how people do behave in a cinema – and particularly there. Lovers embrace and fondle each other in the darkness –'

'That's deplorably true.' The manager had assumed an expression of refined repugnance. 'With a little care, this bold rifling of the body could be made to bear the appearance of mere amorous dalliance. What a splendid point for the Sunday papers that will be.'

Cadover frowned. 'Initials? Laundry marks?'

'Yes, sir.' The sergeant nodded. 'Several of the under-garments have the initials P.C.'

Once more the slinky young man giggled. 'I don't suppose that they could stand for Police Constable, could they?'

The manager looked offended. 'Really, Louis, this is no occasion for unfeeling jokes. A hard-boiled attitude is quite out of place.' The manager lit a cigarette, strolled across the room, and glanced indifferently down at the body. 'About thirty, would you say? And a military type. Nothing like the Army for wiping off any individuality a face may once have been blessed with. You could pick half a dozen almost identical young officers out of any line regiment.'

This was true. For that sort of identification which is sometimes achieved with the aid of smudgy photographs exhibited outside police-stations or in the Press there could scarcely, Cadover reflected, be a less promising subject. Not that it ought to come to that. Perhaps, within a few hours, and almost certainly within a few days, there would be a link-up with one of the endless inquiries after missing persons that flow in upon the Metropolitan Police. A body not ultimately thus identified would be a rarity indeed . . . He turned to the sergeant. 'Everything been done here?'

'Yes, sir. And Inspector Morton is in a room just opposite.'

'I'll see him now. Have the body removed.' Cadover nodded curtly to the manager and walked out. The foyer was crowded. *Plutonium Blonde* was over. The evening's final showing of the programme was about to begin.

Inspector Morton was interviewing a succession of girls dressed in bell-bottomed white trousers and enormous scarlet bows. Two constables were making shorthand notes and another was recording the proceedings on a dictaphone. The room was a humbler version of that occupied by the manager, and there was another Dürer engraving on the wall. Perhaps it belonged to the slinky young man called Louis.

'All we found.' Inspector Morton had interrupted himself to jerk a thumb at a table behind him. Cadover crossed to it and saw a bunch of keys, a pile of loose change, and a pocket diary.

'Finger-prints?'

'Been attended to. The diary was in the hip-pocket and must have been missed when the body was rifled. It has a few interesting scribbles.' Morton turned back to the girl before him.

Cadover picked up the diary. It was new and at a first glance appeared entirely unused. He turned to the page for that day. Scrawled in pencil he read:

gun for boy 1.15.

He turned to the preceding page and found:

N.I. police re guns etc.
Light railway from Dundrane

Two days earlier he found:

Bolderwood
Hump

He continued to search. Throughout the diary there was only one other entry. It occurred six days before and read:

Smith's 7.30

Cadover put down the diary, picked up the bunch of keys, and examined them carefully one by one. Then he did the same with the little pile of silver and copper coins. One florin he inspected for some time. Then he turned round. A pair of sailor's trousers – very tight above and baggy below – was swaying from the room, and Inspector Morton was staring at this departure in unflattering absence of mind. 'Cadover,' he said, 'do you think it might be terrorists?'

'No.'

Morton sighed. 'It was easy to do, and the setting will give it sensational value. But no doubt you're right. Some of these girls are far from being fools. A lot behind, but something on top as well.' Morton paused and, getting no response to this, sighed again. 'To begin with, something emerges from the box-office. They have been showing to full houses, but when the lights went up and the body was noticed there was one empty seat on its left and three on its right. Four people had left before the end of *Plutonium Blonde* – before the end, that is to say, of its first showing of the day. So there was no question of those people leaving when the film reached the point at which they had come in. Moreover, for that showing those seats could be booked – and they *had* been booked. So I thought at once of quite a little gang on the job. They had their victim nicely isolated, and after killing him they all cleared out. But there is a point that is pretty conclusively against that.'

'The booking?'

'Exactly. When you book, the girl in the box-office hands you the numbered tickets and makes a blue cross on the correspondingly numbered seats on a plan. And here we come upon the blessings of industrial psychology. How to make the blue-pencil crosses on a plan with most speed and least fatigue. Pushing up production per man-hour – or girl-hour, in this case.'

'Ah.' Cadover's expression indicated no appreciation of this embroidery.

'Two seats is *zig-zag, zig-zag*. Three seats is *zig-zag-zig, zig-zag-zig*. In other words, you can study the line of crosses and distinguish the number of seats booked at a time. Of the five seats in question, three were booked at one go, and two at another. There can have been no concerted booking of all five.'

'Does that follow? The bookings may have been successive. One fellow comes immediately behind the other and simply says he'll have the next three.'

Morton shook his head. 'In this case, I think not. The block of three has been crossed off with a much more recently sharpened pencil than the block of two. And if one wanted to make sure of all five seats one would scarcely –'

'Quite. But does the girl in the box-office remember anything about the people concerned?'

'Definitely not. It couldn't be expected. The job is purely mechanical and she must have lost all interest in the faces peering in on her long ago. But it's a different matter when we come upstairs to the usherettes. We get far more than we might hope for from them . . . Look here, I'll draw a plan. It will explain the situation until you can see for yourself.' And Morton reached for a pencil. 'The seats in question we'll call $A B C D E$, and you can see that A comes next to a gangway. It's the back row, remember, so there's nobody behind. From the people in front and to the right we may get something, though I doubt it now. The body was in B. And it was A $B C$ that were booked together in a block of three, and $D E$ that were booked together in a block of two . . . I think we may say that something of a picture begins to emerge.' And Morton tapped his pencil with some complacency on the table before him.

Cadover grunted. 'What about those usherettes?'

'Ah! Well, there's a girl who remembers showing the dead man to his seat. But he didn't bring three tickets; he brought two. And there was already someone – a woman – in A. Nobody remembers the woman arriving. She may just have had her counterfoil taken at the entrance and found her way to her seat herself. You can see it was an easy one to find. But her ticket, mind you, had been bought along with B and C.'

Cadover committed himself to his first judgement. 'Good,' he said.

'And this girl remembers who came with the dead man. It was a boy. He might have been about fifteen. Now, of course, that's pretty queer. It suggests that the crime was perpetrated by a woman and a lad. Not but what the woman's function isn't clear.'

'It is at least conjecturable.'

Morton nodded. 'Put it that way, if you like. The dead man believed that on his left there was a stranger having no interest in him. Actually, the woman may have been his murderer. And certainly she had her part to play as soon as he was dead. Everything that might serve to identify the body –'

'Quite so. The manager here has tumbled to that. The job was done under the appearance of hugging and being hugged.' Cadover stared sombrely at Morton's plan. 'And then this woman, and the boy who had lured the victim to his fate, slipped out. Did anyone remark that?'

'No. We have nothing but the arrival of the man and boy. By the way, though, it was something about the boy that had struck the usherette's attention. He wore a bowler hat.'

'Is there anything so remarkable in that? You and I both wear bowler hats.'

Morton chuckled. 'That's because we are both a particular sort of policeman. Mere lads don't often wear them nowadays. Possibly some conservatively inclined office-boys in the city still do, but on the whole it's a habit confined to a few public schools which like their boys to dress like that when in Town. That's what attracted the notice of this usherette – the glamour attaching to our fading institutions of privilege.' Morton lingered over this phrase with evident pride. 'And she says that he didn't look quite right. She *says* that *that's* why she noticed him. Bowler hat and all, he didn't look quite right . . . But one would expect her to say that now.'

'Of course one would – but then might she not be correct?' Cadover smiled a rare smile. 'Public schoolboys with lethal intentions are quite wrong.' His expression grew dark again. 'Commonly they have to wait till they grow up and we turn them into airmen and soldiers.'

'No doubt.' Morton was slightly shocked. 'Anyway, that's all we have about *A B C*. But we also have something about *D E*. Another usherette is sure she noticed two people who must have come from *D E*. She noticed them because they came out in a bit of a hurry and almost caused a disturbance. They came out *to the right* – that is to say, not past *A B C*, but past a much longer line of seats, all occupied, on the other side. People sometimes come blundering out because they are feeling ill, and this usherette came forward in case it was anything like that. She shone a torch for them and then caught a glimpse of them in the light of an opening door. It was a boy and a girl.'

'Children, does she mean?'

'Not exactly. As a matter of fact, there's something odd there. She is quite clear that the girl was about seventeen. But when I asked the age of the boy, she first said that he looked no more than twelve, but later corrected that and declared he might have been sixteen.'

Cadover considered. 'Well, it was only a momentary glimpse, and a conflicting impression of the sort might be quite possible. Did she notice anything about them in particular?'

'It was the lad who was really in a hurry, she says. He was bustling out the girl, who was just bewildered and a little cross. Well, of course there was one attractive explanation of that. This lad, sitting perhaps in *D*, became aware that something horrid had happened on his left, and he decided to get his girl and himself clear of it. An adult, as we very well know, is apt to behave in just that way, and it would be very understandable in a boy. But, as it happens, there's a big difficulty in taking that view. For the usherette is quite confident that those two young people pushed out *before* the big bang. They were clear of the auditorium *before* the girl in the picture is represented as letting off the bomb.'

'The girl lets it off?' Cadover frowned at his own irrelevance. 'Of course, the lad may simply have tumbled to the fact that, although nothing nasty had actually happened on his left, something of the kind was working up. Not that that's a likely explanation. The essence of the killing must have lain in sudden and unsuspected assault. Perhaps the film makes another big noise a bit earlier?'

'Apparently it doesn't. Even for a revolver with a silencer – which is a clumsy thing – there would be just the one chance. We must take it that the couple in *D E* left before either murder or hint of murder. In fact, it looks as if they are out of the picture. Whatever their reason for leaving early, it just doesn't concern our affair.' Morton hesitated. 'Only the usherette noticed one other odd thing. I wonder if you could guess what it was?'

Cadover shook his head, his expression indicating the conviction that the case stood in no need of conundrums arbitrarily added.

'The lad she saw leaving had a bowler hat.'

'Um.' Cadover's was a quintessentially noncommittal grunt.

'So it almost looks as if the lad who appeared to leave *D E* was the same who arrived in company of the dead man to occupy *B C*.'

'It is far from a safe assumption. And if the booking of *A B C* and *D E* respectively were indeed entirely independent it is also a difficult one.'

Morton nodded glumly. 'I suppose that's so. But this usherette's response – the one who showed the boy and girl out – corresponds oddly to that of the other – the one who showed a man and boy to *B C*.'

'You mean that she felt there was something wrong about the boy?'

'No, not that – although there is the odd fact of her being in doubt about his age. I mean that a bit of class-consciousness again came in. She was aware of the bowler hat as a manifesto – as saying, "My education costs papa at least two hundred a year".'

'Your manner of questioning usherettes must be extraordinarily skilful.' Cadover spoke quite without irony. 'But does this lead out anywhere?'

'Only to this – that the usherette then went on to distinguish the girl as not coming out of at all the same drawer. Whatever the feminine equivalent of the bowler hat may be, the girl didn't possess it. "A cheap little thing" – that's what the usherette called her.' And Morton shook his head. 'It's extraordinary how snobbish people are. But it's a little stroke added to the picture – though whether to *our* picture one can't say. We do know one thing we have to look for. If the two lads were *not* the same, and if the usherette's nice social sense was not astray, we have to find and question a prosperous youth of problematical age who was giving some little shop-girl an afternoon at the pictures.'

Cadover nodded. 'I'm afraid', he said seriously, 'that it opens what might be called a wide field of reference. One of the uses of prosperity is to entertain little shop-girls in that way . . . There is nothing else on the cinema side of the affair?'

'Nothing at all, so far. And I doubt whether more will emerge. It's already more than we might hope for.'

'I agree with you. Now, what about this diary which was in a hip pocket and therefore missed? Can we make much of it?'

'It's most tiresomely new.' Morton stood up and walked to a window. 'One might guess that the dead man lost his diary something like a fortnight ago, that he then bought this new one, and that, anyway, he didn't use such a thing very much. The first entry occurs a week last Tuesday and says, "*Smith's 7.30.*" Is that right?'

'Just that. It sounds like a dinner engagement.'

'And with a pal who couldn't have a less helpful name.' Morton was drumming moodily on a window-pane. ' "Robinson" wouldn't be so hopeless by half.'

'I don't at all know about it's being hopeless.' Cadover had looked up sharply. 'It might be the restaurant, might it not?'

'Good lord – you've got something there! It's the first real light we've struck, likely enough. Can you work the same trick with the other entries? The next is on Monday, isn't it? Just the name *"Bolderwood"* followed by something odd that I've forgotten.'

'It's followed by *"Hump"* – just that. The way it's arranged looks rather like the beginning of an address. We might do worse than look for somebody of the name of Bolderwood living at –' Cadover shook his head. 'Some English villages have precious queer names, but I doubt whether we'd find one called Hump.'

'What about a house?' Morton's face brightened. 'People give the most idiotic names to houses. Dash Bolderwood, Esqre, The Hump . . . What do you think of that?'

'At the moment I think we'll pass on. The next entry occurs yesterday. *"N.I. police re guns etc."* – and immediately below *Light railway from "Dundrane"*.'

'Well, *Dundrane* explains *N.I.*, because it's a town in Northern Ireland. And seeing police about guns may not be as sinister as it sounds. If you travel to Eire by way of Northern Ireland and want to take dutiable objects in with you and out again you have to collect some sort of certificate from the Northern Ireland Police on the way.' Morton sat down, well pleased with his own grasp here. 'Again, it is the remoter parts of Ireland which are served by light railways, and it's a reasonable inference that the dead man was proposing a trip there and had been making some inquiries about how to proceed. And, of course, there seems to be a tie-up with the final entry – that under today's date. *"Gun for boy 1.15"* it reads, doesn't it? The figures can scarcely represent a bore, or anything technical like that. They must be a time of day – and presumably not in the middle of the night. At a quarter past one this afternoon something was to be done about a gun for a boy. And if guns and the dead man were going to Ireland so presumably was the boy. And a boy was with the dead man in this cinema within an hour of that time. Now, you don't *hunt out* a gun for a boy at one fifteen, or *forward* one, or *pack* one. That note of a precise time means an appointment – and, ten to one, an appointment to *buy* a gun. They bought a gun together – a shot-gun of some sort, one must presume – and then they came on here, and then the boy was a party to the man's murder and to the concealment of his identity. It's a most extraordinary picture.'

Cadover as he listened to this efficient analysis was gloomily pacing the room. He paused before the Dürer. This one was a fantastic representation of the Assumption of the Magdalen. She was poised nude in air and appeared to be sprouting cherubs all over her like a Surinam toad. Down below a clerkly person raised a hand as if to study this phenomenon against the glare of the sun. Probably the clerkly person was blankly incredulous. But the world really is full of tall stories . . . 'Yes,' said Cadover; 'it's a most extraordinary picture.'

'But gives us several lines.'

'Quite so. They will have photographs of the dead man by now. I can try Smith's. In the morning I can try the likely gunsmiths. Then there are possible bookings to Ireland by anyone with the initials P.C. Then what about it being by a light railway from Dundrane that one reaches Mr Bolderwood of the Hump? As you say, there are several lines.'

'To be sure there are.' And Morton looked at his watch and stood up – a man not dissatisfied. 'The problem's a tough one, but it can be worn down in time.'

Cadover had risen too, and now he reached for his hat – his bowler hat. 'Has it occurred to you', he asked abruptly, 'that this crime may have no meaning in itself?'

'In itself?'

'Just that. It may be a mere clearing the ground for some other devilish thing – perhaps in a few hours' time, perhaps tomorrow or the next day. I'll make what speed I can. Good night.'

Chapter 6

Dinner was over and the train still ran through sunshine. Double Summer Time – England's last and most detestable contribution to civilization, Mr Thewless irritably thought – made the evening uneasy and unreal. The engine, a creature whose ancient pride had been to enter stations unblown and on the dot, now pursued with depressed but dogged wheezings a time-table hopelessly beyond its senescent powers. On either side the forlorn and dismal backs of terrace houses stretched like a tedious and inescapable discouraging argument; through their windows peered hideous vases, iron bedsteads, the plywood backs of showy dressing-tables being bought at eighteen-pence a week. As a refined person, Mr Thewless felt guilty and glum as he ran this gauntlet. Those miles of brick concealed squalors at which he could only guess; they also concealed heroisms which he was unlikely to touch. Mr Thewless sat back and meditated the building of a better England. For the achieving of that, after all, how many people more talented and powerful than he must passionately care! And yet how slow, how painful every step that was being won! For his own part, he felt very helpless, very irrelevant. An usher, a comparatively expensive leader of privileged little bears . . . He looked at Humphrey Paxton, curled up on the seat opposite. And a new thought came to him. Perhaps that sense of his own irrelevance was no more than a discouragement whispered by the Devil – say, by way of protecting those dark satanic mills of his which here smoked on the horizon. Perhaps to set Humphrey straight was to set England straighter forty years on. For how much might a single able and imaginative man achieve!

Mr Thewless frowned at himself, distrusting inflated notions, distrusting these wafts of emotion. He picked up *The Times*. It was true that he had read most of it already. But he would convince himself that he was mildly diverted by the fourth leader . . .

At this moment the elderly lady put down her book and glanced rather nervously about her. Hitherto she had not spoken. But now she looked at Humphrey. 'Have *you* got an exciting story?' she asked.

'Thank you; it is quite exciting here and there.'

Mr Thewless stirred uneasily. Humphrey, he had noticed, was provided with a number of books of a suitable if slightly juvenile sort; these dealt with the heroic and surprising exploits of aeronauts in various quarters of the globe. But in addition to these the boy had others, and of these the only one that Mr Thewless had been able to survey was the book he was reading now. It was the late George Moore's version of the erotic romance of *Daphnis and Chloe*. That Humphrey should inform himself from this volume – and even find it quite exciting here and there – Mr Thewless as an enlightened pedagogue judged not reprehensible. Nevertheless, he was not quite pleased. And now this amiable lady would perhaps peer at the book and be a little shocked.

Sure enough, the lady peered. '*The Pastoral Loves of Daphnis and Chloe*,' she read aloud. 'Ah, yes – I remember quite liking that. There are pirates, are there not? But I don't remember if they are important in the story.'

Humphrey, startled, mumbled some inaudible reply. The bearded man with pebble glasses appeared to consider joining in the conversation and to think better of it. The elderly lady tapped the volume on her lap. 'Now, this really makes me quite nervous. In your book there is nothing that could actually happen to one. Is there?'

At this Humphrey blushed a bright scarlet beneath his dark hair and mumbled more hopelessly than before.

'For example, pirates are quite out of date. But this' – and again the elderly lady tapped her book – 'is a Secret Service novel. And quite a lot of it takes place in a *train*.'

'I should have thought the Secret Service a bit out of date too.' The bearded man spoke in an appropriately rumbling voice. 'The sort of thing that is exciting in time of war.'

'But I assure you that it is always going on!' And the elderly lady nodded with surprising emphasis. 'I have been told so by persons who are *most* well-informed. Only this April I met an extremely interesting woman at Bournemouth who had good reason to believe that an intimate friend of her brother's was nothing less than a special agent of the Government! I confess that it is since that meeting that I have been inclined to read novels of this sort.'

Humphrey had tucked *Daphnis and Chloe* unobtrusively away and was looking at the elderly lady intently. 'My name is Humphrey Paxton,' he said abruptly.

'And mine is Margaret Liberty.' The elderly lady gave a brisk nod by way of completing the introduction. There was a smile of pleasure on her face.

Mr Thewless's uneasy feeling grew. He was aware of a mounting tension in his pupil. He was aware too of the stirring, once more, of just those alarming doubts and fantasies which he had promised himself to banish from his own mind.

'Do you think', asked Humphrey, 'that in things of that sort – spies and so on – truth is really stranger than fiction?'

Miss Liberty shook her head. 'I wouldn't say that. I only say that things of that sort do happen, and that sometimes quite ordinary people – people like ourselves in this compartment – become mixed up in them. And that, of course, is why this book makes me a little nervous; one can never be quite sure – and particularly in *trains*.'

From behind the shelter of *The Times* Mr Thewless cursed the woman heartily. For if Humphrey irrationally believed himself to be surrounded by blackmail and conspiracy what sort of talk could be more injurious than this? And Mr Thewless put down his newspaper. 'I myself', he said firmly, 'am quite sure – even during a railway journey. I have no inclination to believe that melodrama will leap out at me from between the pages of a novel. And, even if I were myself nervous, I would hesitate before doing anything to propagate the feeling.'

Some little time before he got to the end of this speech, Mr Thewless became aware that it was not a success. For one thing – and even if the elderly lady called Miss Liberty had prattled foolishly – it was definitely uncivil. But also – and this was more important – it was untrue. Mr Thewless was himself substantially jittery. By what stages the feeling had grown again he could now scarcely say. But it was as if a sinister and improbable world really *had* escaped from Miss Liberty's book. If the man with the beard and the pebble glasses had whipped off both these appearances and incontinently revealed himself as a beautiful adventuress toying with an automatic pistol, Mr Thewless would have been alarmed, certainly, but scarcely surprised.

Miss Liberty smiled brightly. She had every appearance of one who is not easily snubbed. 'What the writers of these books know so well how to contrive', she said, 'is *distrust*. Who knows anything, really, about anybody else? How often in our casual relationships with others we take their very identity for granted! I am taking it for granted now that this young man's name is truly Humphrey Paxton – just as he is perhaps taking it for granted that mine is Margaret Liberty.'

From across the compartment Mr Thewless heard Humphrey give his characteristic gasp. There was now a glitter – a positively frightening glitter – in the concentrated glance he was directing upon this cursed busybody. And suddenly he burst into speech. 'That's true,' he said. 'I mayn't be

Humphrey Paxton at all.' He laughed queerly. 'I may just be having some-body on.'

The bearded man rumbled. 'You're not having me on, my boy. Do you know you have your pullover on inside-out? And there's a tab that shows when you bend forward. It says "Humphrey Paxton" in neat red letters.' And the bearded man chuckled, his eyes twinkling behind their massive lenses. '*I'm* quite satisfied as to who you are.'

'But that is altogether primitive!' With a kindled eye, Miss Liberty was protesting warmly. 'If he is pretending to be Humphrey Paxton – other, I mean, than as a mere passing joke – *of course* his things will be appropriately labelled. And he will know a great deal about the real Humphrey Paxton, too. It would probably be quite difficult for anyone not knowing the Paxtons well to catch him out.'

'That's right – I'm thoroughly well up in my part.' Humphrey was now leaning forward in mounting excitement. He swung round upon Mr Thewless. 'Can you catch me out?'

For a moment Mr Thewless was bereft of speech. For it was not the boy whom this detestable woman had unnerved; it was himself. This grotesque conversation, starting up out of nothing, had brought him face to face with that fantastic suspicion which – he realized it now – had been haunting the fringes of his mind for hours. *Was this Humphrey Paxton?*

What had the jabbering woman said? How often in our casual relation-ships with others we take their very identity for granted! That had been it . . . Well, the boy had certainly not so taken *his* identity for granted; he had authenticated it by scrutinizing a passport, by reference to the *Aeneid*, and by an ingenious use of the telephone. But why? Was it really because the boy, being the veritable Humphrey Paxton, had doubted the *bona fides* of his new tutor? Might it not rather have been a sort of bluff, an adroitly distracting turning of the tables designed to drive any answering doubts from Mr Thewless's own mind? What of the boy's scarcely controlled agitation and his recurrent air of rapid and furtive calculation? These might well be the signs of a clever youth playing a dangerous and difficult game. And the dentist! Had the youth an uneasy sense that over the dentist he had somehow given himself away, and was he now attempting to discover how the land lay when he jestingly challenged his tutor to catch him out? Was his queer and spasmodic behaviour an overplaying of the part of a nervous boy which he had been instructed to take up?

Mr Thewless, even as he sat silent and amazed at himself, let this jumble of speculations pour into consciousness. His suspicions were better out in the light of day, he realized, than lurking disturbingly in the depths of his mind. But what had planted them there in the first case? Not the foolish talk of Miss Liberty; that had merely precipitated a crisis. He had, he now saw, been worried from the first. The prospect of taking charge of the dif-ficult son of the great Bernard Paxton had been more formidable than he had allowed himself to think. And the actual circumstances in which the responsibility was transferred to him had been disturbing too. Sir Bernard's failure to appear; the boy's belated arrival and odd behaviour; the queer business of the gun: all these things had contributed to the downright uneasiness he now felt.

And then in a flash Mr Thewless saw the full possibilities of the situation in which he had involved himself. He was conducting a boy who called himself Humphrey Paxton to a remote part of Ireland and upon a visit to relations *who would not know whether he was Humphrey Paxton or not.* If the boy was a fraud and played his part well, and if the ticklish matter of letters home were successfully coped with, there was not the least reason why the deception might not continue successfully for several weeks. And – supposing all this to be true – what end would it serve? The answer was starkly obvious. Humphrey Paxton – the real Humphrey Paxton – was the son of a very rich man from whom large sums of money might be extorted under threats. But he was also – and this leapt to Mr Thewless's mind again at once – the son of one of the world's most eminent scientists, so that it was conceivably something quite other than money that the criminals required. Yes! Criminals had kidnapped the real Humphrey Paxton and now had weeks in hand to get him safely away – out of the country, doubtless – while Mr Thewless with this abominable young villain went goose-chasing off to the wilds of western Ireland!

Quite suddenly Mr Thewless felt himself to be trembling in every limb. He had an irrational impulse to spring up and pull the communication cord, or to thrust out an arm and take the boy sitting opposite him by the collar. Had the bearded man and the fatal Miss Liberty not been in the compartment, he might actually have adopted this latter course out-of-hand. But for some seconds a mere sense of social decorum kept him immobile in his seat. And in those seconds his mind again began to work – began to work in the deplorable seesaw fashion to which it now seemed committed.

Certainly the boy had joined him in circumstances which would have made a kidnapping and substitution perfectly feasible. Humphrey, since he was under sixteen and travelling with an adult, required no passport to visit Ireland; there was therefore no photograph with which to check his identity. And the matter of the dentist was very striking indeed. But was it conclusive? This wayward boy might have given out that he was going to the dentist when he had some quite different plan for spending his last afternoon in Town. What, then, if Mr Thewless was wrong? What if here were the real Humphrey after all?

Two things seemed to follow. First, it must be admitted that he, Mr Thewless, was of a mind considerably more impressionable and erratic than it had ever occurred to him to own to before. For to have arrived so fast and so far in the spreading of a net of baseless suspicion was an achievement altogether surprising in him; indeed, he found himself obstinately reluctant to believe that nothing but fancy was responsible. Secondly, he had been on the verge of some act of almost criminal irresponsibility. For, supposing that this was in fact the genuine Humphrey, consider the lad's case. He was a highly excitable creature who had surrounded himself with alarming, perhaps with terrifying, figments of conspiracy and persecution. These figments had by some obscure telepathic process communicated themselves to his new tutor; had perhaps served, too, to activate a similarly melodramatic strain in the mind of the fortuitously encountered Miss Liberty. Now these two grown-ups were playing up to Humphrey and building an atmosphere which was bound to intensify his fears. And Mr Thewless himself, although he had attempted a few minutes before to indicate this to the lady firmly enough, was now on the verge of seizing the unlucky lad by the collar and doing, maybe, irreparable nervous harm.

'The technique of such yarns', Miss Liberty was saying brightly, 'differs both from the detective story on the one hand and the simple thriller on the other. As I said, it is not primarily a matter of mystery, and not primarily a matter of violent action. What is aimed at is distrust . . . sometimes sudden and apparently fantastic distrust.'

The boy leant forward further still. 'What about the other thing?' he demanded. 'Sudden confidence? Taking a chance?'

'That is very true. It is also an excellent thing to bring in. We have always supposed X to be X – a thoroughly reliable man. But all at once there springs up the spine-chilling question: what if X is really Y . . . Y whom we know only to be our deadliest enemy? That is one of the possibilities. But the other is as you say. Z is wholly problematical. We have every reason to suspect him. But something obscurely prompts us and we take a chance.' Miss Liberty laughed. 'And, of course, it turns out well. He is revealed in the end as nothing less than the ace operator in our own Secret Service.'

Humphrey laughed too – his wild and sudden laugh. His eyes were still shining. It was hard to believe that he was the same boy who curled up brooding in a corner and sucked his thumb like a three-year-old. He turned to Mr Thewless. 'You look glum,' he said. 'But I expect we'll have a perfectly calm crossing.'

The harmless impudence of this juvenile sally ought to have cheered Mr Thewless up. But he was, he found, too extensively disturbed to be much encouraged by a momentary mood of confidence in his mercurial charge. He heartily wished the two strangers away. If they had the compartment to themselves he could surely have it out with the lad and come to a definite conclusion one way or another – and this without doing any great damage supposing him to be indeed the true Humphrey Paxton. But now there was no chance of that. Preston was behind them. Their two fellow passengers were seemingly bound for Ireland. Not till they were on the steamer would he have a chance of getting the boy to himself. And by the time he could come to any determination on his problem they would be at sea. Mr Thewless frowned. Then, recollecting himself, he smiled benevolently both on his pupil and on the calamitous Miss Liberty. For good measure, he even smiled on the bearded man, who was fiddling with a fishing-rod, and who received this gratuitous emotional display with some signs of confusion. Whereupon Mr Thewless looked out through the window, surveyed a landscape which was now just beginning to admit the shades of evening, and fell to a more mature consideration of his predicament.

Suppose, once more, that this was indeed Humphrey Paxton. The boy had been living in a world of oppressive fantasies, until he had reached a state of hallucinating himself with terrifying day-dreams. But now he was making a break; a change of environment lay before him; in his new tutor he had one who would at least handle the situation as intelligently and conscientiously as he could. Moreover, Miss Liberty had not, perhaps, been an unmitigated pest. Her cheerful talk about thrillers and spy stories had produced in Humphrey – if Humphrey it was! – what seemed a healthy response; it was as if he had succeeded for the time in reducing his fantasies to their original status of exciting make-believe. Perhaps, indeed, the lady had unconsciously provided something like a key for dealing with him. But now suppose that Mr Thewless broke through this make-believe with an actual and sober challenge to the lad's identity – such a challenge as the lad on his part had uttered when at his most disturbed at Euston. Could he really do this without the risk of inflicting serious nervous shock? On second thoughts, and without the advantage of professional knowledge on such matters, Mr Thewless doubted it. It would be a step of the utmost gravity. And prompting it there might be nothing more solid than a vagary of his own mind – one induced by those very vagaries in his pupil which in accepting his present employment he had given an implied assurance of his ability to cope with!

But now consider again the other side of the picture. What if, in London, the first stages of an audacious and atrocious crime had indeed accomplished themselves? Humphrey Paxton was to be taken by a tutor who had never set eyes on him to visit relations who were in precisely the same case. His father had been prevented from accompanying him to the railway station; presumably, therefore, Humphrey had set out for it alone. *Had he ever got there?* Could more favourable circumstances for a ruthless kidnapping be conceived? For the criminals had only to be provided with a colourable pseudo-Humphrey and they had a chance of achieving something altogether out of the way – nothing less than a kidnapping unsuspected until they chose to reveal it at their own convenience; an abduction unsucceeded by the slightest hue-and-cry! And in this scheme Mr Thewless, the unsuspecting tutor pottering through Caesar or Virgil with the pseudo-Humphrey in the depths of Ireland, would be the prime if unconscious instrument.

It was an intolerable thought. Moreover, if he really believed his suspicions to have any substance he had a clear duty to act. Not to do so would be to concur weakly in a train of events leading to none could tell what degree of horror. But what could he do? Insist upon returning to London at once? Communicate his fantastic suspicion to Sir Bernard Paxton and request that somebody be sent to identify the boy? But Sir Bernard had been called away, and it might not be easy to get at once into touch with him. Should he hurry on to the Bolderwood cousins and explain the situation to them? Should he call in the police? Harassed thus by one disagreeable project and another, Mr Thewless heartily wished his problematical pupil to Jericho.

As he did so, he turned from the window to view the compartment, and found that the boy had disappeared.

Chapter 7

Very little reflection would have suggested to Mr Thewless that here was a circumstance in no way remarkable. On long-distance trains people do leave their compartments and potter down corridors. And as yet the boy who might, or might not, be Humphrey Paxton could not have been more than a couple of minutes gone – for certainly Mr Thewless's troubled abstraction had lasted no longer. Moreover, on neither supposition was there strictly anything to be alarmed about. If this was the real Humphrey Paxton, then the whole fevered supposition which his tutor had been building up was a figment and there was no reason to suppose any sort of plot whatever. And correspondingly if this was a bogus Humphrey, then anything untoward – such as the lad's losing his nerve for the imposture and bolting – could represent no more than a welcome clearing of the air.

But at this juncture Mr Thewless was in the grip not of rational calculation, but of instinct. The boy – very possibly the young criminal – was only two minutes gone, and on the mere score of this even the slightest uneasiness was absurd. Yet Mr Thewless was swept not so much by misgiving as by panic.

The man with the beard and the pebble glasses was gone too. On his seat, like the cast skin of some dingy reptile, lay the canvas case of his fishing-rod. Sections of the rod itself were propped in the corner, and beside them lay a gleaming brass-and-ivory reel. On the rack above was that sort of basket with an oblong hole through which one is supposed to drop fish like letters into a pillar-box. At all these things Mr Thewless absently stared – and as he did so his irrational alarm grew. Quite suddenly the bearded man had become in his heated imagination a figure wholly sinister. *For he had never fished in his life.* All these properties were entirely new – and what genuine fisherman ever renewed his entire outfit simultaneously? Moreover, there had been something in the way in which the fellow had fiddled with his rod –

Having got so far in fantastic speculation, Mr Thewless felt his head begin to swim. It was just as the woman in the corner had said; distrust was spreading itself like a miasma around him; he had a nightmarish feeling that he could be certain of nobody; were he to summon the guard, even that official would presently suggest himself as an emissary of darkness. But Miss Liberty herself, although annoying, was at least genuine; there could be no doubt about *her*. And Mr Thewless glanced across at the elderly lady's corner. As he did so he felt a queer stirring in his scalp, and this was immediately succeeded by an even more unpleasant pricking in the spine. The woman in the corner was *not* Miss Liberty . . .

Long ago Mr Thewless had been deeply impressed by a certain scientific romance. It told how (just as in H. G. Wells's novel) the Martians wished to possess the earth. But they could do so only by projecting their own intelligences into human bodies – and this they had begun to do. No earthly being was safe. A man might turn to his wife – and in that instant the being who looked out through his eyes might be that of a malign invader from a distant planet . . . And now, as he looked at Miss Liberty, it was something of the same sort that Mr Thewless experienced. For a second – a mere fraction of time – the person answering his gaze *was someone else*. But this was madness! And even as he held the woman's gaze the hallucination passed. More, it even explained itself. Miss Liberty had been at her exciting book again; its illusion had her in its grip; that absurd impression he had received of a cold mind grappling with a crisis was no more than a reflection of whatever absurdities were transacting themselves within its pages.

Nevertheless, Mr Thewless's perturbation grew. He got to his feet, shoved at the sliding-door giving on the corridor, and scrambled out of the compartment. Doing this somewhat blindly, he collided with the bearded man, who was now returning to his seat. The impact would in any event have been not inconsiderable. But at this moment it happened that the train, now spurting like a seasoned runner down the final stretch of track to Morecambe and Heysham, swayed over some system of points – with the result that Mr Thewless found himself precipitated upon the bearded man with all the violence of a deliberate assault. And as a result, the bearded man's glasses were knocked off. For a moment the two men looked at each other – and Mr Thewless realized with a fresh stab of apprehension that the eyes fixed upon his own were perfectly focused. Assuredly they were *not* the eyes of a man who has just been deprived of unusually strong lenses of a genuine sort. Moreover – and this completed Mr Thewless's dismay – the glance which they fleetingly held had a fresh familiarity which it took only a fraction of time to place. It was that same glance of cold appraisal of some invisible situation that Mr Thewless had fantastically imagined himself to discern in the innocent Miss Liberty . . .

The bearded man picked up his glasses and rumbled an apology. Mr Thewless, who had been much more in fault, found himself without the power of reply; he edged past the bearded man in a mere impulse to get away, and found himself stumbling up the corridor. Outside, dusk had now fallen and was deepening rapidly. It was like an impalpable tunnel closing in upon the hurtling train, and already the flying wheels and pounding pistons were taking on the deeper note they seem to sound at night.

The boy was missing . . . Mr Thewless made his way up the corridor, peering into the succession of first-class compartments on his right. Business men, Army officers, dogs, expensive children: each held its appropriate quota of these. But of the boy there was, of course, no sign. Why should there be? Mr Thewless got to the end of the corridor and tried the lavatory. It was empty. He passed into the next coach. Here there were two lavatories and one was occupied. But even as Mr Thewless paused doubtfully the door opened and something cannoned unaccountably against his knees. Looking down, he had the shock of feeling that open madness had seized him at last. For what he saw was an elderly and rather intelligent-looking man – but put together on a scale of something like four inches to the foot. With a word of apology, this apparition scurried down the corridor, occasionally pausing to stand on tip-toe and peer into a compartment. And at almost the same moment a door opened halfway down the coach and there advanced upon Mr Thewless what appeared to be a schoolboy of about Humphrey Paxton's age. Only this schoolboy was some eight feet high and correspondingly broad, and he came down the corridor only by a series of muscular exertions which made him pant as he moved . . . Mr Thewless glanced in a kind of despair into the first compartment upon which he came – and met the impassive gaze of a Chinese lady who was holding a white monkey on a chain. At the farther end of the compartment two Indians were playing cards, and in the middle an enormous Negro smoked a cigar. And the compartment held a fifth occupant – an inert figure entirely swathed in bandages . . .

The train swayed. The engine could not be far away, for its roar was very loud. Nevertheless, other sounds predominated. There was a buzz of excited chatter in half a dozen outlandish tongues; there was a further baffling babel of growls and hisses, snarls and chirps; there was an intermittent and wholly mysterious deep reverberation, as if some valve were being periodically opened in a vast and grating machine.

Upon all these appearances and sensations Mr Thewless did not pause to reflect. He was surrounded by a congeries of foreigners and prodigies; he saw in them only the massive menace which anything of the sort may occasion in a mind swayed by primitive impulse; here was the enemy, and that was that! Nor was Mr Thewless any longer very clear on the first promptings of his confusion. The boy was gone. He had vanished in a sinister way. And his genuineness or otherwise – which was really the crux of the matter – had for the moment passed out of focus.

Mr Thewless glanced again at the Negro, who was dressed with great ostentation as an Edwardian dandy. Had he been in possession of his customary lucidity of mind, it is doubtful whether this circumstance would have appeared to him as particularly suggestive of covert conspiracy. But now he had no hesitation. He pushed back the door and entered the compartment.

In the reading of Mr Thewless the romance about the Martians had been an early vagary representing something altogether out of the way. Moreover, with the possible exception of the episcopate and of His Majesty's judges, he frequented the cinema as sparingly as any man in England. What now came to him, therefore, must be regarded as no matter of easy reminiscence, but rather as an exhibition of native intellectual vigour. Mr Thewless pointed sternly at the almost obliterated figure hunched opposite the Negro and pronounced the words, 'Remove those bandages!'

For there could surely be no doubt of it. This swathed and limp figure was something below adult size. The boy had been drugged, and was now being thus ingeniously smuggled away. 'Remove those bandages!' repeated Mr Thewless, and glanced commandingly round the compartment.

The Indians desisted from their card-playing. 'Please?' they said simultaneously. Their eyes were moist; their linen was finical; they had shoes with very pointed toes.

The Chinese lady leant sideways and dived swiftly into a silk bag. Mr Thewless nerved himself for the emergence of a fire-arm. But what actually appeared was a nut, and this the Chinese lady handed to the white monkey. Then she looked at Mr Thewless. 'Iss,' she said – not very intelligibly but with perfect agreeableness. 'Iss.'

The Negro, who had been more particularly addressed, took the cigar from his mouth, balanced it carefully on a newspaper beside him, and with the hand thus disengaged gravely took his hat off to Mr Thewless. It was a grey bowler and must, Mr Thewless thought, have been specially manufactured to encompass that enormous skull. And now, having completed this salute, the Negro spoke in a voice the depth of which would have made the bearded man's rumblings sound like a thin falsetto. 'Sir,' he said, 'I am this gentleman's medical adviser. And I cannot agree to your proposal.'

Anger welled in Mr Thewless. 'Remove those bandages!' he thundered.

The Chinese lady reached for another nut. The Indians looked at each other wonderingly, and then at Mr Thewless. 'Please?' they said.

And the Negro considered. He appeared altogether unperturbed. 'The fee', he said, 'will be half a guinea.'

'I beg your pardon?'

'In the common way of business, and at regular hours, the sum required is sixpence, payable at the door. But here I cannot sanction anything of the sort under half a guinea – or, if it is more convenient to you, say a ten-shilling note.'

'Release the boy!' said Mr Thewless.

This time the Negro looked genuinely surprised. 'My patient', he said, 'is Mr Wambus. Professionally, he is known as the Great Elasto, the India-rubber Man. I insist upon his travelling in this way because of the constant danger of lesion and infection. Technically, of course, his is a morbid condition of the skin. Allow me.' Rapidly the Negro untied a bandage on the arm of the listless creature opposite. 'Be so good as to pinch,' he said; 'pinch and pull.'

Mr Thewless pinched and pulled. The skin responded with a horrid spongy resilience. As a nasty sensation it would be uncommonly cheap at sixpence; Mr Thewless produced ten shillings, thrust them hastily upon the Edwardian Negro, and stumbled from the compartment feeling sick. The white monkey gibbered at him as he passed. 'Iss,' said the Chinese lady. He was again in the corridor.

Humphrey, the pseudo-Humphrey, the Great Elasto . . . in considerable confusion of mind Mr Thewless continued to plod towards the engine. This whole coach must have been reserved for the circus troupe – or whatever the abominable creatures might be – and in the remaining compartments there was nobody upon whom he was prompted to pause. It was now dark outside and he moved down his narrow shaft of swaying space – on one side of him a night grown indefinably ominous; on the other this nightmarish collection of freaks, the unaccomplished works of Nature's hand, abortive, monstrous, or unkindly mixed . . . To the human and sub-human gibbering there was now increasingly added a mere brute bellowing, with above this that deep periodic reverberation which one could almost feel it was beyond the power of the labouring engine itself to produce.

At the end of the coach was a single lavatory. Mr Thewless peered in and found it empty; he passed on and discovered himself to be in a guard's van, dimly lit and full of tumultuous sound. For here in baskets and hutches and cages, or slumbering or straining at the ends of chains, were lemurs and Alsatians, goats and cockatoos, cobras and Shetland ponies, racoons and rabbits. Of the animal part of the circus there was missing only the horses, the elephants, and the larger carnivora. But even without the roar of lions the place was a pandemonium. For the rest, it was filled with the usual assortment of luggage: trunks, suitcases, baskets, a pair of drums, a cased and swathed double-bass looking unnaturally large in the dim light, a weigh-ing-machine with some heavy weights, a couple of motor-mowers tied up in canvas. But it was neither the animals nor any of these objects that immediately caught and held Mr Thewless's attention; it was the single human occupant of the van. Sitting plumb in the middle on a large steel and leather chair was a woman of gargantuan proportions, fast asleep and snoring. It was this snoring, indeed, that had been so mysteriously echoing down the train.

Here, in fact, was the Fat Lady. And there could be no doubt as to *why* she was here. Into no ordinary railway compartment could her bulk possibly be introduced; only the double doors of a luggage van would admit this mountain of humanity . . . Mr Thewless stared, fascinated. Despite him-self, he had a sudden and acute vision of this creature stripped of the gaudy clothes in which she was swaddled – a vision of flesh piled upon flesh in continental vistas.

> 'License my roving hands, and let them go,
> Before, behind, between, above, below . . .'

Mr Thewless felt his brain reel. Not often did his well-ordered mind behave in this way. *O my America! my new-found-land!* . . . At this moment the engine hooted and the Fat Lady woke up.

She opened one eye – an operation involving the systematic redisposition of fold upon fold of puffy and proliferating tissue. She gave a single vast respiration under the influence of which her bosom heaved like a monstrous and straining dirigible (*the Sestos and Abydos of her breasts*, thought Mr Thewless wildly) and then she opened her other eye with the same laboriousness as the first. ''Ullo,' she said suspiciously. 'Wot are you after?' And, much as if she divined the extreme impropriety of Mr Thewless's disordered imaginings, she drew several yards of outer garment with a careful modesty more closely around herself. 'If you come to water them dorgs,' she said, 'stop making passes and get on with it. 'Ere, where's my tablets?'

'I am looking for a schoolboy.' Mr Thewless raised his voice to a shout in order to be heard above the animal noises around him. 'A *schoolboy*, ma'am! You haven't seen him pass through here?'

'I ain't seen no schoolboy. 'Aving my forty winks, I been. But likely enough 'e taken my tablets.' The Fat Lady began systematically to shake and wobble the several parts of her person, apparently with the idea of dislodging and so discovering the missing articles. Mr Thewless followed the resulting undulations with horrid and unabated fascination; they were seismic or oceanic in character, or they suggested the sort of deep rubbery shudder which a passing bus may communicate to an adjacent building. Strangely, before this spectacle, the erotic imaginings of the poet Donne continued to possess him:

> 'Succeeds a boundless sea, but yet thine eye
> Some Island moles may scattered there descry;
> And sailing towards her India, in that way
> Shall at her fair Atlantick . . .'

''Ere they are!' cried the Fat Lady, and held up a bottle triumphantly. 'I don't care to be without them – not between one forty winks and the next, I don't. You 'ave to remember the night starvation orl right when you 'ave a domestic economy like mine.' The Fat Lady tapped herself on what the poet would have described as the Hellespont of her bosom. 'And 'ave you reckoned the turning over? The doctors calculate as 'ow we turn over thirty-five times in the night. Now, just consider what that means with me!' And the Fat Lady shook her head darkly, so that her cheeks quivered like pallid jellies. 'Burning up sugar all the time – that's me!'

'You cannot tell whether a boy has passed through here?'

'Of course I can. You can't get no further than this van. Try and see.'

Mr Thewless did so and found that the Fat Lady was right. Perhaps the engine was immediately ahead. Certainly the door at the end of the van was locked. 'But you have been asleep?'

'Of course I been asleep. It's lonesome sitting in here among all them brutes. Makes you feel 'ardly 'uman.' The Fat Lady was suddenly tearful. 'I can tell you, I sometimes feel I'd rather be a dwarf or a monster. Yes, a monster' – reiterated the Fat Lady emphatically – 'or a freak. I'd as soon be a freak, I often say, if in all this dratted travelling I could enjoy the society of my own kind. Two 'eads, I wouldn't mind 'aving – or no arms and able to play the piano with my toes. Do you know what they 'ave to do with me tonight on the steamer? Do you know 'ow they 'as to stow my sort? Why –' At this moment one of the Fat Lady's eyes closed. 'Why –' she repeated – and her other eye closed too. 'As if I were one of them Indian's heffalumps,' she murmured . . . The Fat Lady vastly respired, and was asleep.

For a moment Mr Thewless paused, irresolute. A cream-coloured donkey, diminutive as if in a toyshop, began to bray in a corner. The sound, mingled with the Fat Lady's snoring, the pounding of the engine, and the miscellaneous animal hullabaloo all around seemed for the moment to represent to him a final overthrow of all sanity; he hastily quitted the guard's van and made his way down the train. The Chinese lady, he noticed, was still giving nuts to the white monkey, the Indians were still at their cards, the Great Elasto – Mr Wambus, in private life – lay back inert as before, the Edwardian Negro was puffing at his cigar again and perusing a copy of the *British Medical Journal*. Mr Thewless moved on, somewhat somnambulistically continuing to try the lavatories as he went. Near his own compartment he met Miss Liberty, who squeezed past him with every appearance of faint maidenly embarrassment. Perhaps he would find the boy back in his place, and this whole episode to have been mere eggs in moonshine.

Eggs in moonshine, Mr Thewless repeated to himself – and dimly wondered from what odd corner of his reading the phrase had started up. Eggs – but the boy was not in the compartment. Nor was the bearded man. The compartment showed nothing but luggage and a litter of books and papers. In Mr Thewless's excited imagination this void and upholstered space was hurtling through the night in an uncommonly sinister way.

Moreover, it was no time since the bearded man had returned from a prowl in one direction; why should he now be off in another? And at once Mr Thewless felt that he knew the answer. He and the pseudo-Humphrey were accomplices; they had planned to confer in privacy; but by some misunderstanding the boy had gone the wrong way. At the moment of that odd collision in the doorway the bearded man had been returning from a false cast. He was off again now in the other direction – and it was in that direction too that the boy must have vanished.

Once more Mr Thewless set out on his wanderings. But this time, he knew, a virtually endless succession of coaches lay before him, and most of them would be very crowded. In order to confer together, moreover, the pseudo-Humphrey and the bearded man could easily lock themselves in a lavatory – and unless he told his sensational story to a guard and invoked assistance it would be impossible to check up on this possibility.

Nevertheless, Mr Thewless plunged down the train, for a sort of automatism now possessed him. Firsts and thirds were alike for the most part overflowing, and he marvelled at the number of people who had the ambition to sail for Belfast that night. Many were soldiers, sailors, and girls in uniform; it was deplorable, thought Mr Thewless vaguely, to see how England had become like any Continental country before the war, its railway stations and public places a perpetual filter of drifting and shabby conscripts. A small professional Army, decently clad in scarlet and black –

The reflection, for what it was worth, remained unfinished. For at this moment, and at the farther end of the coach down which he was plunging, Mr Thewless descried the bearded man hurrying before him. But although evidently in haste, he was making an exact scrutiny of each compartment as he passed it – and even in the moment in which he was thus descried he turned round and his pebble glasses glinted as he cast a wary look behind him. Mr Thewless, with remarkable quickness for one not accustomed to this sort of thing, doubled up as if to tie a shoe-lace. The number of people lounging or squatting in the corridor was such that he had a confident belief that this manoeuvre had saved him from detection. But now he proceeded more cautiously. That the bearded man was making his way to an assignation he took to be established. If it was indeed with the boy, and if the two could be glimpsed together, the main point of doubt in this dreadful adventure would be resolved.

The train was here increasingly crowded, each coach seemingly more crammed with travel-weary humanity than the last. It was that stage of a long journey that is consecrated to a haze of tobacco-smoke, the smell of orange-peel, and a litter and silt of abandoned periodicals and newspapers. Astonishing, thought Mr Thewless, how many people contrive to sleep amid these mild miseries; everywhere around him was the sprawl, the pathos, and the strange vulnerability of human bodies sagged and slumped into slumber. Did a large part of the adult population spend too little time in bed? Mr Thewless stepped carefully over a straying infant, negotiated a woman who was rummaging in a suitcase, and became aware that the bearded man had disappeared. Perhaps he had simply put on an extra turn of speed and gained the next coach. But Mr Thewless believed that he had at last dived into a lavatory. He therefore hurried forward to reconnoitre. Fortunately, the corridor was so crowded that one could squeeze oneself into virtually any position without exciting remark. He succeeded in getting himself close up to the suspected lavatory door – so close indeed that he could unobtrusively put his ear to it.

That such a drab proceeding caused Mr Thewless some discomfort is a point requiring no emphasis. It was to this that the somewhat ineffective termination of the incident was due. That voices were to be heard behind the door was unquestionable, and that the second voice had a boy's higher pitch Mr Thewless almost persuaded himself to believe, and his plain policy appeared to be to stand his ground and achieve a decisive *exposé* there and then. But, even as he decided upon this, there was a general stir and bustle in the corridor. Mr Thewless conjectured – inaccurately, as it happened – that the train was about to reach its destination. And he was alarmed.

It may be that in this whole succession of episodes there was more of alarm than was altogether creditable to Mr Thewless's nervous tone. It must be recalled, however, that he had most abruptly become involved in events – or in the suspicion of events – altogether remote from his common way of life, and that he was enduring a period of intensive acclimatization. Be this as it may, his alarm now was not discreditable, for it proceeded from a renewal of his power of judgement. Coolly regarded, it was surely over-whelmingly probable that he had merely in all this involved himself in fantasy after all, and that in twelve hours' time he would be looking back on it with mingled amusement and embarrassment. But if this was so he was at present being most remiss in relation to his charge. Wherever Humphrey had strayed to on the train, he would presumably return to his own compartment – and his tutor should certainly not be absent from it as they ran into Heysham. If he were not at hand during what would probably be something of a rush for the steamer, the boy might be considerably upset.

These were rational reflections – but the answering behaviour of Mr Thewless was not wholly so. There is something in a whole train load of people beginning to stir that can communicate a mysterious inner sense of insecurity and the need for hurried action. It was this that had gripped him. And he turned now and began to hurry back towards his base. But as he reached the farther end of the corridor he turned, as it were, one longing, lingering look behind upon his late suspicions – and with a mildly catastrophic result. The bearded man had reappeared and was following him down the train. In this there was nothing sensational. The privy conference which had been held in the lavatory was over, and the bearded man was returning to his compartment. What was startling was the appearance of somebody whom Mr Thewless just glimpsed disappearing in the other direction. This was the back of just such a schoolboy as the lad calling himself Humphrey Paxton, and clad precisely as he.

Once more, perhaps, cool reason would have been able to render Mr Thewless a somewhat different estimate of this incident to that which his agitated imagination formed. A psychologist would have spoken to him on the theme of eidetic imagery, and of the power of the mind to see the image of what painfully absorbs it, not within the brain but projected upon the world without. A critic not thus learnedly equipped but endowed with moderate common sense would have represented that schoolboys are frequent enough, that their formal attire varies little between individual and individual, and that the particular specimen thus glimpsed (not even as having been in any certain communication with the bearded man, but merely in a rela-. tion of simple contiguity) might well have been any one under the sun. But whatever promptings of this sort his own mind was capable of Mr Thewless was at the present moment deaf to. And to the marked facility of his suspicion now must be ascribed the fatal absoluteness of his revulsion later. In this mechanism of emotional recoil (the final lurch, as it were, of that seesaw upon which we have already seen him rather helplessly ride) lay the occasion of much disaster to follow.

Clambering over kit-bags and babies, Mr Thewless hurried back to his compartment – physically as mentally a shuttlecock in the swaying corridors of this interminable train. That the bearded man did stand to him in some profoundly malign relationship he was convinced; there was nothing shadowy or intermittent about this; he could feel as he stumbled and squeezed his way forward that the fellow's eyes behind their bogus lenses were boring uncomfortably into his back. But around this there was only wild surmise. The boy was a fraud; with rather shaky logic, Mr Thewless felt him to be a traitor; the real Humphrey Paxton was in the hands of these same people who were plotting thus mysteriously around him and leading him this harassing and humiliating dance; action must be taken at once if he was not to be a mere cat's-paw in the commission of an atrocious crime . . .

The compartment was still empty. Mr Thewless entered it and sat down heavily in his seat. He had now been in a state of more or less continuous agitation for more than five hours – and to this the last half hour had stood as a sort of mounting climax. Such excitement told upon an elderly man. Not that Mr Thewless felt himself beaten. Nothing indeed was to be more remarkable about the whole history of these days than that he never felt himself to be precisely that. He was slow; he was bewildered; he was even irresolute at times. But Nature did appear to have given him the obstinate feeling that it was always possible to fight back.

He took breath. And as he did so the bearded man entered the compartment. His expression was not easy to discern, but his manner had become amicable. 'That's done with, praise heaven!' he rumbled, and fell to packing up his suspect fishing-rod.

What was done with, presumably, was the journey, and Mr Thewless felt called upon to make some reply. 'We are coming into Heysham?' he asked. It went against the grain thus casually to converse with the enemy, but it might be as well to give no appearance of suspicion.

'No, sir – that's some way off yet.' The bearded man dumped his pillarbox basket on the seat beside him. 'The train stops at Morecambe first, and I myself go no further.' The bearded man paused. 'Having no occasion to,' he added. Mr Thewless seemed definitely to discern an inflexion of sinister triumph in this. 'Capital place for fishing, Morecambe. You can make an uncommonly big catch there.'

Mr Thewless had no means of telling whether these words were literally true, but as pronounced by the bearded man he felt that they bore some sardonic secondary sense. And for a moment he found himself surprisingly near to random violence. Already, and by mere accident, he had knocked the bearded man's glasses off. In this perhaps he had tasted blood. For he certainly felt now that it would be pleasing to set about this questionable fisherman and give him a bashing. It was a long time since he had cherished such an impulse towards a fellow man. Mr Thewless grabbed *The Times* and took shelter behind it once more. And in a matter of seconds the train had stopped and the bearded man had left the compartment.

Mr Thewless dropped his paper, lowered the window, and looked anxiously out. If his charge had been the real Humphrey Paxton, and he had gone into hiding on the train, what more likely than that he should now be proposing to make a bolt for it? And, correspondingly, if his charge had been an impostor, was it not possible that the same thing was taking place? There might have been no plan to maintain a long-continued deception in Ireland; the criminals might feel that they had already been given sufficient grace. And Mr Thewless peered up and down the platform for signs of an absconding boy. But all he saw was the bearded man once more. The fellow had been joined by what appeared to be a private chauffeur, and this retainer was assisting a porter to unload something from the van. The light was poor at just that point, and Mr Thewless had for a moment the absurd impression that what the two men were grappling with was a coffin . . . But the reality, when he succeeded in distinguishing it, surprised him scarcely less. The bearded man, it appeared, was the owner of that swathed double bass which had kept the Fat Lady and the various circus creatures company in the guard's van. The instrument was being extricated with considerable difficulty – almost as if it were heavy as well as bulky – and the bearded man (whose piscatorial paraphernalia looked doubly absurd in one now revealed as a devotee not of the naiads, but the muses) was superintending the operation with some anxiety. Even as Mr Thewless watched, however, the thing was accomplished, and the bearded man and his retinue made their way to a waiting car. To do so they had to pass close by once more, and upon seeing his late travelling companion the bearded man gave a cordial wave. 'I hope you'll have a good crossing!' he called cheerfully, and was about to pass on. But an afterthought appeared to strike him, and he turned. 'You and the boy, that is to say. Good night!' He was gone. And at the same moment Miss Liberty re-entered the compartment.

Mr Thewless had forgotten about her. But now he turned his eyes on her suspiciously – and noticed that hers were upon the retreating form of the bearded man. At once his suspicions grew. Between these people – and between these people and the boy – he felt some occult connexion. Perhaps this harmless-seeming female was being left as a sort of rearguard to keep an eye on him . . .

But this was insanity. A more harmless type than Miss Liberty, with her trepidations over an exciting novel, it would be impossible to conceive. And to break the ridiculous spell which he felt growing upon him Mr Thewless spoke out. 'May I ask,' he said, 'if you have seen my young companion? He has been missing for some time, and I am getting quite worried about him.'

Miss Liberty withdrew her gaze into the compartment and directed it upon her interrogator. Since she wore no pebble glasses, it was possible to assess something of its quality. What Mr Thewless read in it was distrust. But it was not, he felt, a muzzy and generalized distrust, such as a mind seeped in sensational fiction might evince. It was rather the suspended judgement of one before whom he had by no means as yet passed some crucial examination. 'Humphrey?' said Miss Liberty. 'I am sure he must be quite all right. Ah, we are moving again! A delightful boy, if I may say so, only perhaps a little highly-strung. He will be back any minute, I expect.' She glanced towards the corridor. 'Indeed, here he is.'

It was certainly Humphrey – whether the true or the feigned. Without a glance at either of his companions, he pushed the door to and tumbled into his seat. He was deathly pale, breathing hard, and – it seemed to Mr Thewless – oddly crumpled. His eyes between their dark eyebrows and dark shadows held a brighter glitter than they had yet shown – a piercing gleam which might have been of fear or excitement or even anger. He curled himself up and his thumb stole towards his mouth; suddenly he straightened himself with a jerk, sat up, and thrust his hands into his trouser pockets. 'Is the next stop Heysham?' he asked.

Mr Thewless, who had been about to make some reference to his unaccountable disappearance during the past half hour, was startled by the voice, which was at once unnecessarily loud and trembling beneath some uncontrollable agitation. 'Yes,' he said. 'We shall be there in a few minutes now.'

'And go straight on board the steamer?' The boy laughed – and his laugh was more disturbing still. 'Do you believe in tests?'

'Tests?' Mr Thewless looked at him blankly.

'*I* believe in tests.' It was Miss Liberty who spoke.

And the boy turned to her eagerly. 'You don't turn back?'

'Not so long as something inside says to go forward.'

'Not even if it's all plainly going to be more than you bargained for?'

'Not even then. To go on, you see, may make you. And to turn back may – well, may mar you quite.'

'Is that from a poem?'

Miss Liberty smiled. 'I believe it is.'

'From Shelley?'

'No. But it is something that Shelley thoroughly believed in, I should say.'

The boy peered out into the dark. As he did so the engine whistled, and the sound was eerie. He spoke without looking round, and in a strangely adult voice. 'One may not be what one dreams,' he said. 'I think I *shall* turn back.' He wheeled upon Mr Thewless. 'You may as well know –' He hesitated and his glance wandered to Miss Liberty. 'Is that right?' he asked her.

'It entirely depends on your inner mind.'

'I see.' The boy was silent. The engine hooted again and the train began to slow down. 'One should have a sword upstairs,' he said.

Miss Liberty looked puzzled. 'A sword upstairs?'

'Yes. Even if one was going to be a poet one should have that.' He sprang to his feet. 'But at least I've got a gun!' He climbed on the seat and brought down from the rack the mysterious parcel that had caused such perturbation at Euston. 'The bump at the end must be some cartridges to be going on with. I say! We've stopped.'

'This is Heysham.'

'Then here goes.' The boy's face was lit up strangely. 'Do you remember Protesilaus? He was first ashore at Troy, even though he'd had a warning. I think I'll be first ashore at Heysham.'

And the boy thrust open the carriage door and leapt out. Mr Thewless, who had sat through this odd talk in a sort of misdoubting daze, reached for luggage. Had his mind been more actively working, the queer experience of the next few seconds might not have come to him – or if it had come at all must have done so with modified effect. But the fact is that by this time Mr Thewless's thinking had set into a groove of deepening suspicion. And in this mood the boy's dark conversation with this foolish old woman appeared to him as no more than the impudent mystery-mongering of a young rascal conscious of playing the central part in a successful conspiracy – one which had led him, only a little time before, into horrid confabulation with the sinister bearded man in a lavatory.

And so Mr Thewless's mind was made up – so definitely so that he now opened his mouth and stretched out his arm with intent to denounce and apprehend the impostor. As he did so the boy, already on the platform, turned his head –

Sound died upon Mr Thewless's lips; his gesture froze. For *this* – just this – he had seen before. The bare-headed boy set in a sort of deep chiaroscuro by the harsh station light; the bare-headed boy glancing slantwise at him from beneath raven hair; the boy, thus lit and thus standing, grasping a gun . . . all this he had seen, fixed for ever by Velazquez, in Sir Bernard Paxton's Spanish library. And that was why Sir Bernard *had* such a library – as a setting for a picture acquired because of its overpowering likeness to his cherished son. Humphrey had produced a passport after all, and one authenticated far more certainly than by any photograph.

A sadder and a wiser man, Mr Thewless descended quietly to the platform. During these nightmarish five hours he had allowed the strange power of suggestion to carry him into a land of shadows, of figments as insubstantial as those in Miss Liberty's romance. He had believed wonders. And now – and after a fashion strange enough – the simple truth had been restored to him. This was Sir Bernard Paxton's son – a boy hopelessly submerged in highly-coloured fantasies, indeed, but in point of identity none other than he claimed to be. That the future held substantial difficulties was likely enough – but they were only those with which a competent leader of young bears might confidently look to cope.

Mr Thewless took his hat off to Miss Liberty, made an authoritative gesture which secured him one of the few porters in evidence, and with Humphrey Paxton proceeded to board the night steamer for Belfast.

Chapter 8

The queues had grown longer outside the Metrodrome. Emerging from the cinema, Inspector Cadover scowled at them as he strode away. Here were people unaware that at their back hurried Time's wingéd chariot . . . people giving half an evening to nuzzling nearer to the armed, the arrogant, the amorous lady. And beyond that less than paper-thin illusion what awaited them? Deserts of vast eternity, Cadover told himself. Assuredly they would miss the Blonde. But they would get the Plutonium, likely enough, in its nastiest fissile form . . .

At this point Inspector Cadover, an experienced Londoner, was nearly killed by a bus. In which case the laugh would have been distinctly with the folk in the queues, he thought. And it would have been awkward. For nobody else seemed to feel that in the death of this unknown man in a cinema there lay a challenge that was urgent.

> But at my back I always hear
> Time's wingéd chariot hurrying near.

The rhythm of the lines distorted itself as Cadover walked. *I* always hear, *I* always hear, *I* always hear . . . the words thumped themselves out in his brain like a phrase which one has fitted to the inescapable jolt of rails or pounding of pistons as one hurtles through the night in a train. But why think of a train . . .? Cadover's eye fell upon that rare and blessed visitant of London streets, a cruising taxi. He hailed it. 'Smith's,' he said.

With the stump of the cigarette between his lips the driver gave a signal of comprehension. Cadover was pleased. He had been by no means certain that Smith's possessed the sort of status that made possible the directing oneself to it in this monosyllabic way; that it was so appeared to lend slightly more colour to the possibility that this small restaurant was indeed what was pointed to in the dead man's diary. How wretchedly meagre the entries that little book had contained! Cadover ran over them once more in his mind.

Smith's 7.30

That had been a week last Tuesday. All the other entries belonged to the present week. On Monday there had been

> *Bolderwood*
> *Hump*

and on Wednesday

> *N.I. police re guns etc*
> *Light railway from Dundrane*

while the final entry was on Thursday – this very day, that was to say, on which the fellow had met his death. And it read:

> *gun for boy 1.15*

For boy . . . It was conceivable that in a brief jotting a man might so indicate his son. 'I must get the boy a gun.' Yes, one could hear a father saying that. But the phrase as written down had another flavour. Was it a flavour suggesting a professional relationship? 'That lad So-and-So had better have a gun.' Was that it? A man whose initials were *P. C.* proposing to take a pupil or ward to Ireland, and as a first step proposing to get the boy a gun . . . A good deal in the way of inference might proceed from this. For example, a boy is not commonly given a shot-gun, surely, until he is about fifteen. And again, if he is so provided before a trip from London to Ireland there are economic, social, and even geographical implications; he is not going to take the thing to Dublin, for instance, for use on Stephen's Green. But likely enough he will be taking a light railway from Dundrane – and travelling first-class should such distinctions carry so far into the wilds of Ireland.

Again, there was a point there. The west of Ireland was not like the highlands of Scotland, a rich man's playground into which there poured at this time of year the residue of England's plutocracy. It was country really remote still; and of such large houses as it had once possessed many were now ruins or burnt-out shells. One might, of course, go off with guns to stay at an hotel, but if P. C. had been taking the boy to stay with landed folk approached by a light railway from Dundrane the hunt from that direction might not be altogether hopeless. But assuredly it would take time . . . And here was Smith's. Cadover jumped from the taxi.

It was a small restaurant which he had not entered for years. From the outside it looked shabby enough and he eyed it gloomily. The probability was that like many of its kind it had tumbled hopelessly downhill and that its only pronounced feature would be in a tacit, dogged denial – hanging heavy in the air as the smell of synthetic gravy – that the human palate exists. But this – Cadover told himself conscientiously – was neither here nor there, except as it might affect the probability of the dead man's frequenting the place. He pushed open the door and entered.

Smith's, he saw, had gone in for being discreet. Partitions, alcoves, and the sort of lighting that is described as subdued appeared to be its chief selling-point. Behind decaying palms elderly and besotted men argued with elderly and anxious women; younger women were paired tensely in corners;

here and there youths given over to ignoble calculation pressed chianti or what was doubtless execrable brandy upon predatory girls. Over these futilities presided a frock-coated proprietor and half a dozen waiters so softly and sinisterly confidential as to suggest that they kept unnamable horrors conveniently disposed in an annex at the back. Actually, thought Cadover, all one would find there would be black-market butter and a quantity of illicit horseflesh in process of being transmogrified into venison. He sat down and ordered something out of a tin. Nobody was near him except two undergraduates in *démodé* polo-jumpers, endeavouring before two revolting-looking troughs of *minestrone* to preserve that sacramental attitude to exotic foods publicized in the writings of Mr Evelyn Waugh. Cadover beckoned the proprietor.

'I am from Scotland Yard and engaged upon an inquiry in which it is possible that you can help me. Have you a regular customer – a young man with the appearance of an Army officer – whose initials are P. C.?'

The proprietor looked blank. 'We don't often know their names,' he said.

'Oh, come. In a restaurant like this you must have a great many habitués – people who dine here quite regularly.'

The proprietor looked as if he would like to have the hardihood to declare that this was indeed so. But he was a man whom discouragement was beginning to render indifferent and therefore almost honest. 'Well, we don't have so many of that sort as we once had. People have become very floating – very floating, indeed. Of course there are people who ring up and book tables fairly often.' The proprietor paused, as if he suddenly saw that there was something rather odd in this. 'Yes, people do book tables and give names. Browns, mostly. You'd be surprised at the number of Browns who dine at Smith's. But I can't place your P. C. Sounds like a postcard, don't it?'

Cadover received this inane pleasantry coldly. 'There are about twenty people in here now,' he said. 'Just look round, will you, and tell me how many you recognize.'

The proprietor made a slow survey of the room. Then he shook his head. 'Really, it's difficult to say. Quite a lot of them do *seem* familiar.' His gaze was upon the two undergraduates. These, having some dim knowledge of the ways of their kind before the deluge, had ordered a carafe of red wine and were now contemplating it in a gloom which might be either gustatory or financial. 'But, do you know, I think it's just their *expressions*?' The proprietor looked puzzled. 'Yes – I think it is only that.'

'Here is the man I am talking about.' And Cadover produced a photograph which had arrived just as he left the Metrodrome. 'Do you recognize him?'

'I think I do.' The proprietor hesitated. 'Or is it just the expression again? I'm afraid it's only that. People who have been dining here . . . there's some odd likeness . . .'

'This man is *dead*. It's the photograph of a corpse.'

The proprietor nodded – as if the matter now explained itself. 'Ah,' he said. 'Well, life is a banquet, after all. And here we have the expression of one who is finished with it . . . Will you have some venison? It is the *spécialité de la maison*.'

'I'll have tinned pears, please – without custard. And I congratulate you on your baked beans.'

The proprietor received this compliment with a deep bow, dredged up from the nineteen-twenties. 'To receive the praise of our patrons', he said, 'is our only happiness. Our *chef* –' He was interrupted by one of the undergraduates, who had risen from table with a complexion gone suddenly pea-green and was now making his way to some inner chamber with both hands clutched to his stomach. 'But about this *P. C.* it is to be feared that I cannot help you. The features are not distinguished and he would not dwell in the memory.'

This, Cadover had already realized, was deplorably true. He put the photograph down on the worn tablecloth before him and produced a bunch of keys. 'You don't happen to have noticed anybody with these?'

'I am afraid not.'

'Nor with this?' And Cadover produced the dead man's pocket diary.

'No. These are really very insignificant objects. Even if a customer were to produce them over and over again –'

'Quite so. And here is my last exhibit.' Cadover brought out a little pile of silver and copper and spread it on the table. 'What about that?'

The proprietor looked bewildered. 'But of course not! How can one hope to identify a man from a heap of coins?'

'I'm afraid that's very true. How could one identify your restaurant from a plate of tinned pears? Now, if it were the *spécialité de la maison . . .*' Cadover was spreading out the coins on the table. 'But have a look at them, all the same. You see, we've nothing else to go on.'

Markedly without enthusiasm, the proprietor poked among the coins. Suddenly he picked up a florin. 'But this is most remarkable,' he said.

'Ah.' Cadover's comment had the carefully restrained quality of a man who plays out of a deep bunker and incredibly sees his ball make the green and trickle straight towards the hole.

'It is a counterfeit, and rather an odd one. The waiter brought it to me and I explained to the gentleman.'

'And how did the gentleman respond?'

'He was most correct and took it back with an apology. There were reciprocal expressions of esteem and he remarked on the excellent quality of the venison. Just as you have done on the – um – baked beans. Just occasionally it is quite like old times . . . Good heavens, what is that – an ambulance?'

The pea-green undergraduate was indeed being carried out on a stretcher; his agonized voice could be heard incoherently repeating from *Brideshead Revisited* the majestic passage on *caviar aux blinis* and the hot, thin, bitter, frothy *oseille* . . . But Cadover paid no attention to this unsurprising incident. He had produced his photograph again. 'And was this', he asked, 'the man?'

The proprietor studied it anew and then shook his head. 'I really cannot say. It is so much less characteristic than the florin, is it not? And the gentleman himself was assuredly of the kind who is like so many gentlemen. *That* I do remember. It is unfortunate that I am so little able to assist you.'

'But at least you can remember approximately when this took place?'

'It would be about ten days ago.'

'And did the fellow have a companion or companions?'

'There was a lady. But I cannot say that I recall her to mind. She was of the kind who is like so many ladies.' The proprietor shook his head mournfully. 'You have noticed how it is nowadays? Nothing of individuality any longer attached to the idea of style. And it is to be feared that the same influence attaches to modern cuisine. Times are hard and distinction difficult to attain. Even when one is so fortunate as to receive ample supplies of venison from Sutherland – or is it Ross and Cromarty? – one is sometimes at a loss –'

'You do not recollect that you had ever seen either the man or the woman before? Neither came here regularly?'

'I begin to recollect. Yes, I believe they have come together from time to time.' The proprietor brightened. 'Perhaps they may come again.'

'The man is dead, remember. As a matter of fact, he has been murdered. So *he* won't come again – unless he decides to haunt your kitchens. But the woman is another matter. If she –'

'But she is here now!' Even as he spoke the proprietor visibly blenched. 'They are *both* here now – over at the table in the corner.' He looked wistfully at Cadover. 'Do you think a ghost might be good for trade?'

'I think he might – if he were of the affable and familiar sort. Of course, if he went from table to table clutching his bowels and crying "*Revenge!*" it might be another matter.' Having delivered himself of this unkind nonsense, Cadover felt that he might allow himself to glance cautiously over his shoulder. The man whom the proprietor had discerned was certainly not unlike the man who had died in the Metrodrome that afternoon. Nevertheless, nothing supernatural was involved; this was no more than another person of markedly similar type. 'And the woman?' he asked the proprietor. 'You are sure of her?'

'Quite sure. I clearly recall that emerald ring. Yes, the lady is assuredly the same. But the gentleman' – and the proprietor gave a sigh of relief – 'is not.'

'He is similar – that is all? In fact you might say he is the sort of man the lady dines with?'

The proprietor nodded. 'You may put it that way. And she, of course, is the sort of lady who dines with that sort of man. In such moments as I can snatch from supervising the service and the cuisine the study of human

74

nature is my main preoccupation. And here we have an interesting type.'

Cadover stirred his coffee and pushed his chair sideways so that he could command the couple in the corner by a sideways glance. 'Would you say', he asked heavily, 'that she is an improper woman?'

The proprietor sighed nostalgically. 'My dear sir, you recall, if I may say so, memories of happier days. An improper woman – how many years is it since I have heard that exquisitely *fin-de-siècle* expression! I should judge that the lady is employed in some secretarial capacity in the City, and that she has a small circle of male friends.'

'Also from the City?'

'Possibly so. They will certainly not belong to the intellectual or artistic classes. The lady, although no doubt in one sense as improper as you aver, is extremely respectable. My experience, my dear sir, assures me of that at once. She is attractive to young men who, certain sharply defined necessities apart, require a healthy moral tone, such as every headmaster of a public school would approve.'

'I see.' Cadover felt old, and that the world and its types were passing beyond him. 'Are the relationships to which you refer of a mercenary nature?'

'The lady will undoubtedly receive presents – quite substantial ones. But she will herself give presents of lesser value. It is all quite simple. And I judge that she will have no special lover or protector behind the scenes. It is life, is it not?' And the proprietor, although his eye was uneasily on a customer who looked as if he might be about to give trouble over the fricassee of chicken, contrived to look nebulously philosophic.

Cadover, having clearly formed notions of the nature of vice, scowled unappreciatively. But he was studying the young man in the corner. 'Would you say that the young man has been in the Army?'

The proprietor considered. 'The Air Force, I should venture to judge.'

'And that he is sociable, with an extensive but vague acquaintance, and that he hasn't much in the way of brains?'

'That would be very much my impression.' The proprietor was gratified by these reiterated appeals to his judgement. 'Distinctly what they used to call an operational type.'

Cadover rose. 'I am going out to ring you up from the nearest call-box. You will then fetch that young man to the telephone.'

'But we do not even know his name! Such a summons would be quite without plausibility.'

'Possibly so. But when called to the telephone many people don't pause to think.'

'Very well. I shall endeavour to summon him *avec instance*, and we must hope for the best. I take it that your object is to get rid of him?'

'Precisely. And – unlike that unfortunate youth – without the aid of an ambulance. But it would be as well if you had a taxi at the door, so that he

75

can be whirled away without stopping to think. *A bientôt!*' And with this tactful concession to the cosmopolitan character of Smith's, Cadover slipped from the restaurant.

He found an empty call-box almost immediately, and the proprietor's voice answered his call. He pressed Button A. 'Go ahead,' he said.

There was silence for something over a minute. Then a slightly surprised but cheerful voice spoke. 'Hullo,' it said.

'Hullo?' Cadover spoke as one of massively sunny disposition who is momentarily vexed. 'Hullo . . . hullo? I can't hear you.'

'Hullo,' said the voice.

'Hullo . . . am I through? Who's that speaking?'

'Jake Syme speaking,' said the voice innocently.

'Good old Jake! Larry here.'

'Larry!' The voice was blank.

'Not Larry – Harry.'

'Good old Harry!' The voice was instantly expansive. 'How goes, Harry, you old whorehound?'

Cadover was disconcerted by this. Appropriate speech failed him. 'Very well,' he said.

'Like hell? Well, that's grand. Good old Larry.'

'Harry,' said Cadover.

'Good old Harry. And how's Larry?'

'Like hell,' said Cadover.

'Well, that's grand. Come round and have a drink.'

'*You* come round and have a drink,' said Cadover. 'Know the Square Peg? Top-hole little party here. Hop into a taxi and come round now.'

'Got a girl here.' Jake Syme's voice was suddenly confidential. 'Bring her along too?'

'What sort of girl?'

'Girl.'

'Better not.' Cadover strained his invention. 'The mater's here,' he said. 'Top-hole party, but we've got the mater.'

'I see.' Jake's voice was properly respectful. 'Wouldn't do, of course. I'll leave her here for a bit.'

'That's right. Fill the old nose-bag and let her browse.'

'What's that?'

'Nothing, old boy.' Cadover realized that he had over-reached himself with this outmoded trope. 'Come right round now. So long.'

'So long.'

Cadover left the call-box and walked with modest satisfaction back to Smith's. He grew old, but his dexterity did not altogether fail him. A taxi was drawing out from the kerb as he approached, and he had the satisfaction of catching a glimpse of Jake Syme, his expression alive with innocent anticipations of pleasure. No vice in him, Cadover reflected – and then shook his head, remembering the lady within. A small circle of male friends

. . . Well, there was a vacancy. And he had better announce the fact straight away.

The girl was eating an ice. Her expression of displeasure might have proceeded either from this or from the fact of Jake Syme's having left her so cavalierly. Cadover sat down opposite her without ceremony. 'Good evening,' he said. 'I want to speak to you.'

'I don't intend to.' Cadover looked at her austerely and saw with discomfort friend. He has had to go out to meet somebody's mother, but he will be back in a few minutes. I advise you to go away.'

'I am Detective-Inspector Cadover of the Metropolitan Police. What I have to say will not take long, but it may distress you. Would you like to withdraw to the manager's room?'

With a hand that trembled suddenly, the girl pushed away her ice and dived into a bag for her cigarette-case. 'I don't think you can have any business with me,' she said. 'You have no right to interfere with my private affairs.'

'I don't intend to.' Cadover looked at her austerely and saw with discomfort that she was debating whether to try a little allure. But even as he looked she decided against this. Perhaps, he thought fleetingly, he had not the appearance of one who requires a healthy moral tone, such as every headmaster would approve, from the shady ladies of his acquaintance . . . 'I merely want information about a man whom I have reason to believe to be known to you.'

The lady raised her eyebrows, and contrived to look at once spontaneously relieved and elaborately puzzled. 'A man?' she said – much as if Cadover had mentioned an iguanodon or a tapir. 'I don't think I know many men.'

'I believe you know a sufficient number for my purpose.' Cadover was suddenly grim. 'And this is a photograph of the body.'

'The *body* . . .?' The girl stared at the square of pasteboard. 'Is Peter dead?'

'I am sorry to have to tell you that he died of a bullet-wound in a West End cinema this afternoon. He appears to have been accompanied by a woman and a boy.'

With a nervous and automatic movement the girl smoothed her hair. 'I'm terribly sorry,' she said. 'He was awfully nice . . . a really good sort.' Her voice broke. 'He was the soul of honour and fair play. I liked him more . . . more than anybody I know. We both liked music.' She looked at Cadover with eyes suddenly perfectly ingenuous and swimming in tears. 'We usually went to a concert first.'

'I am sorry to have such bad news.' Cadover's discomfort in this strange world was not abated. 'At least I have little more with which to trouble you. What was your friend's name?'

'His name?' The girl was puzzled. 'His name was Peter.'

'But his surname – and his address?'

'I – I'm afraid I don't know. He – he was rather a casual acquaintance, in a way. We met at a party about a year ago. He used just to drop me a line – not one with any address on it – and we would meet for a show or something.'

'I see.' Cadover had not reckoned upon this extreme discretion in young men disposed to combine dalliance and moral tone. 'But he must have spoken about himself and his circumstances?'

'Hardly at all. I think he had done pretty well at dangerous jobs in the war. I know he had been about the world a bit. And I rather think he was looking for something to settle down to. But he never spoke of his people, or anything like that. He was rather shy.'

'That is no doubt one way of expressing it. But about those notes that he sent you – when did you receive the last?'

'Only a few days ago. And it was jolly decent of him to write.' The young woman looked at Cadover with suddenly startled eyes. 'But there was something in it about a cinema! And about a boy, too. He was going away with a boy. It was nice of him to let me know . . .' She was now fumbling in a bag. 'Yes, I thought so. Here it is.' And she handed Cadover a letter.

He looked at the envelope and saw that it was directed to Miss Joyce Vane at an address in Maida Vale; he opened it and read.

Dear Joyce, – I'm terribly sorry I shan't be seeing you for some time, as on Thursday I'm off to Ireland with a kid who sounds a bit of a handful all round. This is a terrible bore! I've been making inquiries since I got the job and it appears that the lad's father is a terrible scientific swell. He has a laboratory in which he cracks atoms much as you and I might crack nuts when lucky enough to be having one of our jolly dinners together. Perhaps this is why the lad is insisting on taking me to see a film with atom bombs in it just before we leave. It's called *Plutonium Blonde*. But there is only one blonde for me and I will see her again as soon as I can.

Love,
Peter.

The letter bore no address and it had been posted in the West End; nevertheless, Cadover scanned it with something like exultation. Smith's and the counterfeit florin had been mere wisps of hope – but they had led to what, compared with the situation an hour before, were inestimable riches. He took a slip of paper from his pocket and scribbled. 'Miss Vane,' he said, handing it to her, 'here is your receipt for this document. This is your address in Maida Vale? And you have no other information that you can give?' Cadover's eye as he spoke was on the door; it would be as well to beat a retreat before the return of the indignant Jake Syme. He rose. 'By the way,' he added, 'I think I'd have a drink ready for your friend when he gets back. He may be a little cross. And I'm sorry if my news has been a shock to you. Good evening.'

And Cadover hurried into the street, glancing at his watch as he did so. It was eight o'clock. Still compelled by an obscure sense of urgency, he set himself a time-limit. By midnight he would have found a terrible scientific swell who possessed, first, a laboratory in which atoms were cracked like nuts, and, second, a son who was a bit of a handful all round.

But more haste, less speed. He stood on the kerb, waiting patiently. And presently an obvious calculation fulfilled itself. A taxi drew up and there emerged from it an angry and bewildered young man. Cadover took his place and was driven to Scotland Yard.

Chapter 9

The clock stood at eight-twenty when Cadover's call came through. 'Information about physicists in London?' said the voice at the other end. 'Oh, certainly – no objection at all.'

'Nuclear physics,' said Cadover. 'At least, I think that's the term. Atoms, and so on. The matter is highly confidential.'

'It always is.' The voice was politely exasperated. 'Let people of your sort begin talking about atoms and we are sure to be told how confidential it is. That's all nonsense, you know. Only you can't see it.'

'Ah,' said Cadover. For to this voice it would be discreet to listen with deference.

'Science has grown up talkative and is bound to remain so. Stop the talkativeness and you stop the science. Whether that would be good or bad is quite speculative. But the fact is undoubted. You see?' The voice rose with the hopeful inflexion of one discoursing to a small group of advanced students. 'Or don't you see?'

'I see.'

'But, of course, if it pleases the police to hold what they consider confidential conversations over a telephone line I am quite willing to join in. Please go ahead.'

Cadover scowled at his scribbling-pad. 'Time is an important factor, sir, or I would have called. And the inquiry is this. I am looking for a physicist, probably resident in London, who has at least one son somewhere round about the age of fifteen.'

'I see. Well, sixteen years ago numerous scientists were continuing to beget children. In fact, they do it still. So it would appear that they are no wiser than other folk. And indeed there are other grounds for supposing the same thing.'

'Quite so, sir.' This time Cadover spoke with conviction.

'So unless you can tell me something more about this physicist –'

'I have a letter in which he is described as a terrible scientific swell.' And Cadover glanced at the note he had obtained from Miss Joyce Vane. 'He has a laboratory in which he cracks atoms much as you and I might crack nuts when lucky enough to be having one of our jolly dinners together.'

'My dear sir, I don't recall that I ever had the pleasure –'

'I'm only quoting the letter.' Cadover made vicious jabs at the scribbling-pad with his pencil. 'And it says no more than that. My problem is to identify the scientist quickly.'

'Very well.' The voice became brisk. 'You know, of course, that the writer of your letter is either remarkably ignorant or speaking with conscious extravagance. Scientific swells, however terrible, do not own laboratories in which atoms are cracked like nuts. Unfortunately, the laboratories own *them*. You see?' The voice was not very hopeful this time. 'Or don't you see?'

'I see.'

'Well, now, your problem is really this. First, how many scientists live in London who are what would popularly be termed "high up" in atomic research. Second, how many of these have a son or sons round about fifteen years old. I can give you a list of the likeliest men. And for their progeny you can turn to *Who's Who*. It generally tells about people's children – though I can't think why.'

'Thank you very much.'

'First, of course, comes Sir Bernard Paxton. *You* will have heard of him.' The emphasis in this last sentence was not very flattering. But Cadover scribbled impassively. 'Sir Bernard Paxton,' he repeated. 'Yes.'

'And as a matter of fact, I happen to know that he *has* a son. I recall going to luncheon with Paxton, and this boy being present. A very well-mannered boy. I never quite understood why he threw the cream-jug.'

'Why he *what*?'

'Threw the cream-jug at Lord Buffery. An unusual experience for a President of the Royal Society. Buffery had been talking about poetry – surely not a subject to rouse strong emotions in anyone.'

Cadover glanced again at his letter. 'Do you know', he said, 'that that sounds very hopeful? The boy I'm looking for is described as a bit of a handful all round. But, of course, I'd better have your other names as well.'

'Lord Buffery himself,' said the voice. 'Sir Adrian Ramm, Professor Musket, Dr Marriage, Sir Ferdinand Gotlop . . .'

Cadover sighed as he noted down the long list of names. It looked like being a full night's work. And how would these eminent persons react when hauled out of bed to testify to their having, or not having, a son who was a bit of a handful all round? But at least *Who's Who* might eliminate some. He put down the receiver and reached for the volume. Fifteen minutes later he returned it to the shelf and gloomily picked up his bowler hat. Between atomic physics and schoolboy sons there appeared to exist what his recent informant might have called a high positive correlation. Still, he must tackle it – and tackle it himself. To set a little squad of men seeking information from these eminent persons might have the appearance of saving time. But in general Cadover believed that the solution of a crime ought to be a one-man job. One man trudging from point to point was slow and laborious, but he carried round with him a single probing, pouncing, arguing brain. Set A, B, and C to work and, as likely as not, some vital fact would slip through the mesh of the resulting reports. A, the man in charge, would fail amid all the material unloaded on him to relate B's x to C's y. But if both x and y formed part of A's direct and unmediated experience, then his chance of hitting upon their significant relationship was considerably higher . . .

In arguing with himself thus, Cadover was no doubt only rationalizing an instinct to go about things in an old-fashioned way. Being not without a sort of dogged ingenuity, he could probably have found colourable reasons for continuing to wear the 1912 species of bowler which he was now lodging firmly on the tips of his ears. Thus habited, he strode from the building, climbed into a waiting car, and gave the driver Sir Bernard Paxton's address.

It was a quarter to nine and London was still incongruously bathed in the neutral light of early evening. The armed, arrogant, and amorous lady of *Plutonium Blonde* was everywhere in evidence upon the hoardings. It struck Cadover that her expression had subtly changed; in addition to animal provocation, it now held a hint of mockery. He felt the stirrings of a sort of personal relationship to this sprawling figure – a sort of confused antagonism which was doubtless, he gloomily reflected, disreputably erotic in origin. Was it desirable, he wondered, that he should see the film? Apart from the fact that the loud noise of the exploding bomb had made the murder in the cinema easy, could there be any relationship between the film and what had actually occurred? The speculation, he saw, was singularly barren; he had no conceivable means of proceeding with it.

The car came smoothly to a halt and Cadover peered out. 'Are you sure this is right?' he asked. For the mansion before him was exceedingly imposing and did not at at all answer to his notion of a scientist's abode.

'This is it, all right.' The plain-clothes constable at the wheel peered out in his turn. 'Crime's becoming quite the thing among the upper classes, isn't it? Currency case, I suppose – nobs making the dibs fly on the dear old Riviera?'

Cadover made no reply to these over-familiar observations, but jumped from the car and made his way up a broad flight of steps to Sir Bernard Paxton's front door. He rang the bell and then glanced back over his shoulder at the august square in which the house stood. It was all extremely solid; unlike most of post-war London it was all very adequately painted, glazed, and polished. Money still commanded services and materials here. But whereas the folk who had built this square lived comfortably on their income, those who now inhabited it were living – almost equally comfortably – on their capital. Towards the end of the century it would give out, and the reality of social revolution would then become apparent . . .

Cadover became aware that the door had opened and that he was being studied by an unprepossessing but wholly correct manservant. 'Is Sir Bernard Paxton at home?' he inquired.

The man was eyeing his bowler hat – and even noting, it might be felt, its propinquity to Cadover's ears. Then his glance travelled down to Cadover's boots, and from thence to the car waiting in the square below. 'Sir Bernard', he said impassively, 'is not at home.'

'Can you tell me when he will be in?'

'Sir Bernard will not be at home tonight.'

'You mean he's not sleeping here?'

The man slightly raised his eyebrows, as if to indicate his surprise that even one so uncouth as this caller should be ignorant of the conventions of admittance and exclusion. 'Sir Bernard', he said, 'is not at present in the house. And he will be unable to receive callers later tonight.'

Cadover produced a card. 'I am a detective-inspector from Scotland Yard,' he said.

'Indeed, sir.' Ever so faintly, the tone contrived to imply that some such melancholy fact had already been only too apparent. 'I shall not fail to inform Sir Bernard of your call.'

'I am afraid the matter is more urgent than that. Is he dining out – or at his club?'

'I'm afraid I don't know, sir.'

'Well, what are his clubs? I think I'll try them.'

'Yes, sir.' For the first time the man hesitated. 'As a matter of fact, I am fairly confident that Sir Bernard will be home in about an hour's time. Perhaps you would care to wait?'

'I'll come back.'

'Thank you, sir. I would not leave it much later than the hour. It is conceivable that Sir Bernard may be going out again.'

'Very well.' Cadover nodded and returned to his car – an inexplicable shadow of misgiving at the back of his mind. 'Next address,' he snapped.

'That's Lord Buffery's.' The car slid from the kerb and the driver spoke over his shoulder. 'Blackmail, is it? I rather thought as much.'

Cadover frowned. 'You appear', he said acidly, 'to be a young man remarkably well furnished with hypotheses. But the fact that this is a wealthy part of London is scarcely a sufficient ground upon which to base such an inference. So far as I know, it is *not* blackmail.'

'You've got me wrong, sir.' The driver was aggrieved. 'I wasn't just judging by the fact that we're among the nobs. I was judging by Soapy Clodd. He was lounging at the corner there as we drove up.'

'The devil he was!'

'Nasty bit of work, isn't he? Now, if we were getting him a stretch we could go to bed feeling we had done something useful. Think of all them kids he makes miserable! And naturally I thought it was something to do with him.'

Cadover shook his head. 'Nothing of the sort. And I only know him by name. Never been my line.'

'Specializes in blackmailing adolescents, Clodd does. Wealthy people's kids who can raise five pounds now and then to keep his mouth shut. Plays on the queer sense of sin kids have. Have you been petting a girl in the park? Were you coaxed into paying five bob to see something you've always been a bit curious about? I'll tell your mother and she'll be heartbroken for life. That sort of thing. If Soapy had been a bit nearer the kerb I'd have felt like a little hit and run.'

'That is a most improper thing to say, even as a joke.' Cadover relented. 'I rather agree with you, all the same. But Clodd's affairs have nothing to do with us at the moment.'

Cadover sank into a reverie which lasted until he was shown into the presence of Lord Buffery. The eminent scientist was playing with an electric train arranged round the circumference of a billiard-room, and he showed no disposition to abrupt this activity when Cadover was announced. 'Police?' he said, raising his voice above the rattle of a goods train which was clattering across a viaduct. 'Well, what d'you want? . . . Son? Of course I've got a son.' He flicked a lever and an express emerged precipitately from a tunnel. 'Going away with a tutor? Naturally he is. What else should I do with him in these absurd summer holidays? . . . Peter? Certainly not. Going with a Frenchman to somewhere near Grenoble . . . Interested in model railways?'

A second goods train had now come into operation and was avoiding the first at sundry crossings in a hair's-breadth way reminiscent of an antique comic film. The refrigerated vans appeared to be particularly noisy. Lord Buffery pressed a button on a switchboard beside him and the express engine instantly emitted a series of realistic and penetrating whistles. And now a great deal of shunting appeared to be taking place in the obscure and extensive area beneath the billiard-table. The uproar grew. Cadover took a pace forward by way of indicating polite attention to these phenomena, and was at once made aware that the floor was an ordered litter of porters, passengers, cars, taxis, Bren-gun carriers, ambulances, motor-cyclists, hay-wagons, and other miscellaneous paraphernalia of locomotion all of an appropriate scale. Lord Buffery looked with some apprehensiveness at the size of Cadover's boots, and then at a collection of navvies complete with tools, brazier, and nightwatchman's hut which was dangerously in their proximity. 'Deuced hard to replace, these,' he said apprehensively. 'Just mind the steam-roller.'

Cadover, minding the steam-roller, resolutely returned to business. 'Your son', he asked, 'doesn't happen to be a bit of a handful all round?'

Lord Buffery deftly brought another express into action and simultaneously indicated that he had not quite caught the question. Cadover bellowed it anew. Lord Buffery's features assumed an expression of sudden exasperation; he stretched out his hand and the whole various uproar died away on the tracks; he stood up and moved gingerly towards the door. 'This way,' he said. His voice had sunk into a sudden gloom.

Cadover followed him through a long corridor and saw a door thrown open before him. Inside was a great stillness and clear white light – this and the faint smell which electricity seems to generate when being used in oblique and ingenious ways. The place was some sort of advanced laboratory. And its sole occupant was a small, weedy boy with a bumpy forehead, large glasses, and prominent teeth. For a moment he looked up from the complicated system of retorts and test-tubes over which he was bending, contemplating Cadover without curiosity and Lord Buffery with disapproval tempered with tolerance. And then he returned to his affairs.

Lord Buffery murmured an apology and closed the door. 'Harold', he said resignedly, 'is entirely given over to study. I call it a damned dull life. Now, if you want to see a boy who *is* a bit of a handful, I advise you to go round to Paxton. Not long ago his lad threw a cream-jug at me.' Lord Buffery paused admiringly. 'Deuced expensive one too, I should think. Great connoisseur is Paxton – ceramics, pictures – all that sort of thing . . . But it would be a long time before Harold would throw so much as a calorimeter at you. Would you care to come upstairs and see my workshop? I'm just finishing rather a good model of the Forth Bridge . . . No? Well, good evening to you.'

At least, Cadover thought as he made his way to the car, Lord Buffery appeared untroubled by the larger issues involved in the exploitation of atomic power. 'Sir Adrian Ramm,' he said to the driver, and once more sank back into reverie.

But Sir Adrian Ramm's only son was in a nursing home with appendicitis; he was a reasonably well-conducted child; and there was no proposal that he should go anywhere with a tutor. Sir Adrian could not afford a tutor and would not employ one if he could. As a class of men, he regarded their morals as bad.

But now it was time to return to the Paxton mansion. Cadover realized that his hopes were substantially set in this quarter. For this he had perhaps small logical justification. Indeed, he found that he was attaching obscure significance to the lurking presence of Soapy Clodd, although this petty scoundrel was almost certainly no more than an accidental intrusion upon the picture. All he really had to go upon was this: that the dead man's pupil had been unruly, and that young Paxton had thrown a cream-jug at the President of the Royal Society. Nevertheless, he knew that he would be disconcerted were the Paxton trail to prove a dead end.

The same manservant admitted him – and in what he felt was a sinister quiet. Had some horrid revelation burst upon the household and prostrated it with gloom? Cadover hoped so – and followed the soft-footed butler into a sombre library. A tall, pale man with a high forehead sat writing at a dark, heavily-carved table which served as a desk. He rose as Cadover was announced and advanced across the dimly-lit room. 'I understand that you are a police officer?' The voice was low and precisely cultivated. 'What is your business with me?'

'I apologize for intruding upon you, Sir Bernard. But the matter is of some urgency.' Paxton, Cadover knew, was a person of much consequence in the world – of much more consequence than Lord Buffery. And he found himself treating the great man with a more than usually wary respect – and explaining the reason of his call without at all resenting the fact that he was not invited to sit down.

The tall figure listened in silence. Then he shook his head. 'I can be of no help to you. There is no proposal that my son should go away with a tutor.'

'The boy is at home now?'

'He is on a short visit to an aunt in another part of London. As it happens, I called upon her and saw them both less than an hour ago.'

'Has your son been in any way out of hand recently?'

The tall man could just be discerned in the subdued light as raising his eyebrows. 'As my son can demonstrably have no connexion with the person who has died in the cinema,' he said stiffly, 'the question does not arise.' Then he suddenly smiled faintly, as if charitably willing to relieve his obscure caller's embarrassment under this rebuke. 'As a matter of fact, the boy is sometimes the very devil. Not very long ago he threw a cream-jug at Lord Buffery.'

At this Cadover, doing what was plainly expected of him, gave evidence of mild mirth. Then, moved by a sudden impulse, he spoke again. 'I have another question, which I hope you will not find vexatious, sir. Have you any suspicion that there may recently have been an attempt to blackmail your son?'

'To blackmail him!' The words came with a curious quality – almost as if from one suspecting a trap and momentarily out of his depth. 'Certainly not. It is a most improbable circumstance.' The tone was confident again now. 'Had I reason to suppose anything of the sort I would at once call in the police.'

'It is merely that a criminal who specializes in that sort of thing – in preying upon the common misdemeanours and concealments of adolescents – has been observed lurking near your house. It is more than probable that your son is not involved. But I should advise you, Sir Bernard, to bear the circumstance in mind. A sensitive boy so preyed upon may be enduring a very dangerous strain. On our side, we shall see that the man's present activities are investigated. And now I must not take up more of your time.'

The tall figure had already touched a bell and was steering Cadover dismissively towards the door. As he did so he appeared to notice Cadover's eyes upon a painting at the end of the room. 'Ah, yes,' he said, 'I have that hanging there because it is so uncommonly like my son.'

Cadover, thus prompted, looked at the painting more carefully; it was of an aristocratic little boy, dark-haired and dark-eyed, dressed in hunting

costume. Cadover wished that the light was better; he was fond of painting –
and here surely was an original Velazquez! He remembered Lord Buffery's
remarking that Sir Bernard Paxton was a connoisseur. 'Surely –' he said.

'Yes – to be sure.' The tall figure was now waiting impatiently for the
door to open. 'It's an old picture – very old indeed . . . If I can be of further
help to you, please let me know. But, as you see, you are on a false scent
here. Good evening.'

The silent manservant conducted Cadover across the hall and handed him
his bowler hat, not without taking a glance inside it first. Cadover set it
firmly on his head, and fleetingly inspected himself as he did so in a large
mirror before him. This mirror revealed the door through which he had just
come; it opened as he looked and the figure of the eminent scientist whom
he had disturbed came rapidly out and disappeared into the gloom of a
corridor.

The manservant had opened the front door and Cadover saw his car wait-
ing at the bottom of the flight of steps and beyond the broad pavement.
And at the same time he heard a voice speaking sharply and authoritatively
from what might have been the direction of the main staircase of the house.
'Jollard . . .' said the voice. The manservant closed the door softly upon
Cadover and he heard no more.

So that was that. The boy who had thrown the cream-jug was out of it.
Cadover, with an irrational feeling that he had just failed to make a lively
acquaintance, climbed wearily but doggedly into the car. 'Professor Musket
at Dulwich,' he said. 'Then round to Sir Ferdinand Gotlop at Bromley and
on to Dr Marriage at Greenwich. After that we go right across to Highgate
and Wood Green and New Barnet . . .'

How very queer the association of these familiar and unassuming names
with the recesses of atomic physics! How infinitely alarming, when one came
to think of it, the spectacle of Lord Buffery and his electric trains! Cadover
sat back in the gathering London night and enfolded himself in gloom like
a blanket. The car ran over Waterloo Bridge; he peered westward and shook
his head at the blank and innocent face of Big Ben, as if doubtful whether
those within the shadow of St Stephen's Tower had quite as sharp an eye
as was desirable upon that sinister billiard-room . . . The car, sequacious
of Professor Musket, purred through the emptying streets.

Cadover got to bed in the small hours – irritated by defeat; more obscurely
irritated by he knew not what. Of those few of London's millions who were
on familiar terms with proton and electron the male progeny were all
comfortably – or in some cases uncomfortably – accounted for. Eminent
scientists, it appeared, had no special skill in maintaining amicable
relationships with their young. Sir Ferdinand Gotlop's son had run away
to sea, another boy made mysterious disappearances for a week at a time,
but was at present safely at home studying existentialism; a third was
believed to be living in a cellar with a group of juvenile anarchists learned

in the manufacture of explosives. But of any youth about to set out for Ireland with a tutor there was no sign whatever.

Restlessly Cadover searched for an explanation. And the likeliest surely was this: that the dead man's letter to Miss Joyce Vane was wholly misleading. The father of the lad referred to might indeed be a terrible scientific swell, while his connexion with atomic physics was illusory. The young man might have thrown in this touch just to be impressive – or perhaps he had a vague notion that smashing atoms was the invariable business of all scientists sufficiently eminent. And if something of this sort was the case, the clue provided by this letter was altogether slighter than it had seemed. It was a pointer still, but a pointer into the haystack of London's scientific folk in general. Long before one could get at the matter this way the identity of the dead man would have emerged by some other route. What Cadover had looked for was a short cut. After numerous exhausting windings it had turned out to be only a dead end. And he still had the uneasy persuasion that time was all important in the case.

Dawn was breaking before Cadover fell asleep. He dreamed of interminable journeys through the night, of the deep vibration of steamers and the rattle and sway of trains. Sometimes Lord Buffery would appear gigantic in a fitful moonlight, a portentous presence brooding over interminable sidings, here stooping to pick up a steamroller and there straddling across a valley like the cantilevers of a bridge. And up and down the corridors of the labouring trains, round the decks and hatches of the plunging steamers strode a great blonde woman in a wisp of shift – amorous, arrogant, and armed. Now she was stalking Cadover himself – and now a dark-haired, dark-eyed boy dressed in the rich and sombre garments of imperial Spain. The rhythm of the train, of the steamer, formed itself into a single word, pounded out a single insistent trisyllabic word . . .

Cadover woke up, aware of a mind at once dream-sodden and on the verge of discovery. In all that maze of talk which he had threaded through London and its environs the night before – in all that maze of talk there had been a single significant word. Or had there been the *lack* of that word; instead of it had there been an awkward, an unexpected periphrasis? Cadover sat up and shook his head, aware now that he was pursuing only some phantom of thought. He planned the day's work, the new attack that he would make upon the problem of the unknown body in the cinema.

Chapter 10

The sea was perfectly smooth; the deep vibration of the steamer was scarcely perceptible; of the myriad stars overhead each was precisely in its appropriate place for that particular hour, century, aeon. All these facts were reassuring to Mr Thewless. He stood on deck watching the diminishing lights of Heysham Harbour. Beside him stood a perfectly ordinary boy called – undoubtedly called – Humphrey Paxton. In front of him stretched six weeks or so of considerable but by no means overwhelming difficulty. For these weeks Mr Thewless was already making various competent plans. They would read the fourth book of the *Aeneid* and thereby bring sex and the emotional difficulties of adolescence a little into the open. They would give a good deal of time – much more time than would normally be justifiable – to English poetry, and they would incidentally consider fancy, imagination, day-dreaming, and the possible confusions of fiction and fact into which certain types of minds – particularly growing minds – may fall. English composition might take the form of writing, on the one hand, an adventure story in which the narrator was the hero, and, on the other hand, a sober but not uninteresting diary of actual observations made upon people and things. Such common-sense measures might clear matters up quite as effectively as the probings of child psychologists.

For, of course, that there *were* matters to be cleared up was undeniable. Humphrey, although a perfectly ordinary boy when broadly regarded, had admittedly his uncomfortable side. He imagined things. More than that, he imagined things with such intensity that he set other people imagining too. During the fatigues of the recent railway journey had not Mr Thewless himself been persuaded into imagining quite a lot? He was resolved that with this sort of thing he would have no more to do. Let it be admitted that the boy had an almost hypnotic power of edging one into a world of fantasy. Let this be recognized and firmly guarded against . . .

'I'm terribly afraid there's something I ought to have told you earlier.'

Pitched conspiratorially low, Humphrey's voice came out of the semi-darkness beside him. Mr Thewless smiled as one who now possesses an assured wisdom. For here was the boy off again; his tone betrayed it; he must be briefly humoured and then packed off to bed. It was already unconscionably late and they would be berthed in Belfast long before any normal breakfast-time.

'Something you ought to have told me, Humphrey? Well, out with it. But – by Jove! – what about getting a final ginger-beer? I noticed that the bar is still open.' Mr Thewless was uneasily aware that the epithet 'sporty' might be applied to his manner of making this proposition. With a movement towards gravity, he therefore continued, 'And then we must certainly turn in.'

'I suppose so.' Humphrey had immediately begun to move towards the bar and the proposed refreshment, but his tone sounded slightly dejected. 'Yes, I suppose we must try to sleep.'

'Try to sleep!' What Mr Thewless now heard in himself was an unnecessary jollity. 'I'm certain you will sleep without rocking tonight. And tomorrow should be a good day. The light railway sounds most amusing.'

'Yes.' Humphrey sat down and placed his shot-gun (which he now rather absurdly persisted in carrying round) carefully beside him. 'Do you know why I brought this? It wasn't to go out shooting helpless birds.'

'Perhaps it was in case the sheep look unhappy.'

'The sheep?' Humphrey was startled.

'Didn't Shelley somewhere go round with a gun benevolently putting sheep out of what he conceived to be their misery? It made the farmers very cross.' Mr Thewless paused and sipped with a dishonest appearance of relish at his ginger-beer. 'The story may not be true. But it does represent fairly enough Shelley on his freakish side. It was his marked weakness.'

'I see.' Humphrey stirred uneasily in his chair. 'But what I wanted to –'

'The powerful imagination of a poet', pursued Mr Thewless, 'requires ceaseless discipline. Only by being confined within its own proper bounds does it maintain sufficient force and impetus for creative work. For a young artist any involving of his own day-to-day affairs in mere fanciful reverie is bad. It is likely to cripple his final achievement. By a strong effort of the will, therefore, he should abstain.' Mr Thewless frowned, momentarily aware of the echo of some magistral voice long ago lecturing his own perplexed innocence on a somewhat different theme. 'And this was what was meant by a poet in some ways superior even to Shelley – I refer, Humphrey, to John Keats, whom I am sure you have eagerly read – when he declared that the poet and the mere day-dreamer are sheer opposites. And what is the practical lesson of this? We should not allow ourselves to confuse –'

'I didn't bring the gun to shoot sheep. I brought it to shoot plotters and blackmailers and spies.' Humphrey Paxton banged down his glass on the table before him and raised his voice to something like a shout. Fortunately, there was still a good deal of noise in the smoke-room and only one or two people looked round. 'And I ought never to have left that compartment without it this evening.'

'It sounds', said Mr Thewless, 'as if what you really need is a revolver.'

'Exactly.' And Humphrey nodded soberly. 'Have *you* got a revolver?'

'Dear me, no. You see, plotters and spies don't much come my way.'

'I'm terribly afraid they are bound to . . . now.' Into Humphrey's voice had come something like compunction and apology. 'Perhaps I should have considered that. It wasn't really quite fair to drag you in. I hope Daddy pays you a decent screw?'

Mr Thewless smiled. 'As a matter of fact, Humphrey, he is proposing to pay me a good deal more than is customary.'

'That's odd.' And Humphrey Paxton looked sharply thoughtful. 'Would it be dirt money, do you think?'

'That sounds like something rather disagreeable.'

'So it is. It's the extra pay dockers and people get when doing something thoroughly nasty. Perhaps Daddy thinks that being my tutor is that.' An expression of rather complacent pathos spread itself for a moment over Humphrey's features. 'Do you think I might have another ginger-beer?'

Mr Thewless fetched the ginger-beer. 'No,' he said; 'definitely not dirt money. I believe your father finds you a little trying in spots. But he was confident that we should find considerable pleasure in working together. Which reminds me that we can make out a scheme of things when on the train tomorrow.'

'Of course *dangerous* work gets extra pay too. Perhaps it was that. Perhaps he really did have an inkling.'

'Perhaps he had an inkling that you would pitch me some pretty tall stories.' Mr Thewless determined to be good-humoured. 'I wonder if I could do it too? Tomorrow we might have a competition and see which of us can imagine the biggest adventure.'

Humphrey took a gulp at his ginger-beer. 'This is going to be difficult,' he said. 'Of course I didn't mean to tell you at all. I meant you just to find out – as you're pretty sure to do. I meant it to be pretty well my own adventure right through. But now I don't think I can do that. Not after what happened on the train.'

Mr Thewless looked at his watch. By one means or another this disjointed nonsense of Humphrey's must be stopped. 'I think –' he began.

'I suppose I'm frightened . . . rather.' Humphrey looked gloomily at his gun. 'Have you noticed how sometimes I get just like a kid?'

'Yes, I have.' Mr Thewless responded soberly to this odd appeal. 'Our age is not always just what our birthday says. It's the same with grown people sometimes. They can't decide what age it's sensible for them to be. Often people manage to be suddenly much older. Sometimes they manage to stay the same age for years and years. Sometimes they become younger and stay younger for quite a bit. It depends on the sort of things that happen to them. And sometimes people decide that it's time to be no age at all – and then they die. So there's nothing very odd or special in occasionally feeling rather a kid. I've known big chaps do it quite regularly at bed-time. Had to hug a teddy-bear – that sort of thing.'

Humphrey, who had listened carefully to this, slightly blushed. Perhaps he had some private reason for finding the reference to teddy-bears embarrassing. 'You are a very sensible person,' he said seriously. 'It's a pity you're going to be such an ass over this.' His blush deepened. 'Sorry. I oughtn't to have said "ass". Not when I wasn't in a temper.'

'I certainly don't want to be an ass. But had we not better have this talk in the morning?'

'Very well.' And Humphrey got to his feet, submissive but plainly discouraged. 'You see,' he said, 'it was the blackmailing that misled me. I – I handled that. And so I thought – But this turns out to be different.'

Mr Thewless allowed himself an inward sigh. Whatever fantasy was urgently waiting to tumble from Humphrey Paxton's mind had better tumble now. For assuredly he would not sleep if sent to his cabin in his present nervous state. And Mr Thewless produced from his pocket a bar of milk chocolate which he proceeded to divide. 'Well, now,' he said, 'we're pretty private in this corner. So let me hear the trouble, Humphrey. And I'll try not to be an ass.'

But Humphrey now seemed to find some difficulty in communication. He munched his chocolate, put up a thumb to lick – and was plainly disposed to let it remain performing the function of an infant's comforter. Mr Thewless tried prompting. 'You said something about blackmail before. What was it about?'

'It was about a girl.'

'A girl?' Humphrey at this moment seemed so absurdly young that the words now jerked from him came to Mr Thewless without implication. 'What do you mean, my dear boy?'

'I know several girls.' Humphrey was momentarily circuitous. 'There's Mary Carruthers, the poetess – although, of course, she's really a grown woman. But this was Beverley Crupp. She works in a shop. Not that that's any disgrace.'

'Certainly not,' said Mr Thewless, automatically but forebodingly.

'You *have* to learn about things and do them for the first time.'

Mr Thewless judged that a general acquiescence in this sentiment might be inexpedient. So he ate his last piece of chocolate and said nothing.

'I used to fool around with Beverley in parks, and that sort of thing. The way you see people doing all over the place. It used to puzzle me a lot, even although I'd read books about it. But I wasn't puzzled after knowing Beverley. It's quite extraordinary, isn't it? So unlike anything else. So frightfully *exciting*.'

By the perfect innocence of this last word Mr Thewless felt considerably relieved. 'Well,' he said briskly, 'what about this Beverley?'

'One day there was a man taking photographs – the sort of man who snaps passers-by with a little camera and then hands them a card. I didn't think anything of it. But it turned out to be blackmail.'

'I see.' Humphrey's tutor looked at him thoughtfully. 'Were you very much worried?'

'At first I was – quite frightfully. It made me feel an absolute kid. But then I managed to use my brains. I could see that the thing was something that this photographer-man did regularly. It was more or less his trade. Well, if I refused to give him money and he sent the photograph to Daddy, or anything like that, it would probably be even more awkward for him than for me. For Daddy, of course, would tell the police, and the fellow would be hunted down and sent to prison. And, anyway, the risk wasn't great. It wasn't as if I had a mother to be upset. Daddy would be cross, but that isn't so – so formidable. And he would quickly come to take a man's view. He would even tell his more particular friends out of a sort of obscure vanity. For a man likes it to be – be borne in upon him that he has a son capable of having sons. A very queer and deep approval of just keeping the human race going is a factor in such cases.'

Mr Thewless felt within himself a moment's mild panic. That Humphrey had managed to use his brains was undeniable. Attaining to the mere practical common sense of the matter had been in itself a considerable achievement of intelligence. But his appreciation of what might be called the underlying psychology of the situation was positively intimidating. 'I take it, then, Humphrey, that you ignored this criminal's demands?'

'I handled the situation.' Humphrey seemed to take particular satisfaction in this phrase. 'Actually I don't know that the fellow is quite choked off yet. But he has just ceased to worry me. And that has made me rather uppish. And that's why I'm landed in *this*.' Humphrey's glance went warily round the now almost empty smoke-room. 'It's a pretty tight place. But I've asked for it.'

'There is no doubt that you have had an unpleasant experience.' Mr Thewless was genuinely sympathetic – and the more so because he now comfortably felt that full light on Humphrey had come to him. The narrative to which he had listened was sober truth, and at the same time it explained the genesis of a great deal of fiction. Early sexual experience, even of the comparatively innocent kind in which the boy had involved himself with his friend Beverley, may entail considerable nervous strain. Massive feelings of guilt (reflected Mr Thewless, who was a conscientiously well-read man) have to be contended with in the unconscious mind. And upon Humphrey, a sensitive boy so circumstanced, there had broken this horrid business of a petty blackmailer who preyed systematically upon adolescents. Humphrey's brain, it was true – as also, what was not quite the same thing, an ability to use it in an awkward situation – had proved too much for the fellow. But the shock must have been there, all the same. And it had precipitated the deplorable world of fantasy into which the boy now so readily sank.

Mr Thewless felt relieved. There is always great satisfaction in the complete intellectual clarification of a problem. And now surely he had the key – the weapon, indeed, with which he could combat the lad's insubstantial fears. He looked at Humphrey, still clutching his gun, with an increase of benevolence. 'I am extremely glad', he said, 'that you have told me all this. You don't think, do you, that there was anything deeply shameful in your – your acquaintance with the girl Beverley?'

Humphrey frowned, as if he now had to recover this topic from a considerable distance. 'Of course not,' he said.

'But the trouble is that there is a part of the mind – particularly of the *young* mind – which does think that. It is very deeply disturbed, and imagines all sorts of punishments which are bound to follow. The person finds himself imagining that he is ill –'

Humphrey looked startled. 'I know about that,' he said. 'Just after I found out about babies I began to think I was going to die of appendicitis. It cleared up when I worked it out that somehow the two things were connected.'

'Or the person imagines that he is being plotted against and has all sorts of cunning enemies. In the case of a boy, his father often figures in such fantasies. But we needn't go into the reasons for that.'

Mr Thewless had abstracted his gaze in the endeavour to deal discreetly and lucidly with this unwanted territory. Otherwise Humphrey's expression might have given him pause, for it was certainly not that of one who begins to feel lightened of a load of imaginary fears.

'Again, he may feel that he is being dogged or shadowed by spies or avengers, that he will be imprisoned – or even that he has been imprisoned – in dark confined spaces. He may even see his imaginings just as if they were actually happening in the outside world. Shelley did that. He may see himself, or one like himself, apparently involved in similar obscure adventures. And all this just because he believes himself to have come into possession of some dangerous secret.'

The hour was late; the ship, although sailing in calm waters, had a gentle motion which Mr Thewless was too poor a sailor to like; the day had produced a succession of obscure and exhausting alarms for which this boy's fevered mind had been assuredly responsible. Moreover, the boy himself, although sometimes extremely young, had a certain intellectual precocity, receptive to mature ideas. Had it not been for all these facts Mr Thewless would scarcely have plunged in this reckless way into what he now supposed to be the well-head of Humphrey's troubles. Naturally, he expected his pupil to be startled; and he was not without an uneasy suspicion that there is much hazard in abruptly exposing or controverting delusions that have painfully built themselves up in a distressed mind. What he hoped was that by this outspokenness there might rather be achieved some salutary shock. He looked at Humphrey warily and was far from reassured. The boy was now sitting very still. His breathing was short and the pupils of his eyes appeared dilated. But at least he was thinking. Indeed it was evident that some battle was going on between an emotional and an intellectual response to what his tutor had been saying.

And at length he spoke. 'You don't think that I could *really* be in possession of some dangerous secret?'

'I think it quite likely that you believe yourself to have gained some guilty knowledge that you ought not to have. You see, Humphrey, having – um – made friends rather early with this girl –'

'Oh, *that*!' There was a disconcerting shade of intellectual impatience in Humphrey's voice. 'I'm not talking about that at all.'

'It's what sets you imagining things, nevertheless.' Mr Thewless was tired, dogmatic. 'And you must face the fact.'

'I'm facing quite a lot of facts. For instance, the fact that you are right in quite a lot of the things you say. I *do* think that I am being plotted against by cunning enemies. And I *do* think that I am being shadowed by spies. And I *do* think that my father is mixed up in it. But that's not the end, by any means.' Humphrey was now looking at his tutor with an expression oddly compounded of desperation and malice. 'What you called meeting oneself apparently involved in some obscure adventure. I've done that too. In fact, I saw myself this afternoon. It was terribly queer.'

Mr Thewless felt rather queer himself. He recalled with a twinge of particular uneasiness his own momentary impression of a second Humphrey on board the train. He recalled too that in folklore there is no more certain presage of disaster than to meet oneself face to face – to meet what the Germans call one's *Doppelgänger*. And no doubt the superstition reflected some actual fact of mind. If Humphrey really believed that he had thus encountered himself his nervous condition must indeed be deplorable. 'Nonsense!' Mr Thewless said loudly to the empty smoke-room.

'Actually, I ought to say that I *heard* myself – but I suppose it's much the same thing. It was in a cinema. And you were there too – more or less.'

'*I* was there!' Mr Thewless's dismay was now tempered with indignation.

'You see, I didn't really go to the dentist's this afternoon. I took Beverley to see a rotten film called *Plutonium Blonde*. I dare say some people were quite amused. But with Daddy being the sort of person he is, I get quite enough about smashing the atom at home. And this one was just silly. There was a sort of tropical heroine, all bottom and breastworks –'

'Um,' said Mr Thewless.

'And she had a revolver with a special bullet, so that in the end –' Here Humphrey suddenly paused. 'Only we didn't wait for the end. Because when I found that I was sitting next to myself I got into a panic and bolted, dragging Beverley with me. She was terribly puzzled. And naturally I couldn't explain to her. She's quite, quite dumb.'

'Of course, Humphrey, I am very glad that you are telling me all this. But are you quite sure that you were not acting rather extravagantly? You say you only *heard* this boy. And just because his voice sounded rather like your own –'

'It didn't. As it happened, I could be quite sure of that. Because, you see, this other boy had a lisp.'

'Then if it was *not* –'

'But it *was*. You see, they whispered a bit – and chiefly about a gun. And the boy was Humphrey Paxton. And the man was his new tutor. And they were going to Ireland.'

Humphrey paused again. The throb of the ship's engines vibrated in the stale air of the empty smoking-room and very faintly they could hear the slap of water against the hull. Mr Thewless found it necessary to speak. 'I am afraid –' he began.

'I know.' Humphrey appeared to be quite calm now, and he was momentarily at his most mature. 'It must be a great worry having been landed with so imaginative a child. What do you think of the story so far?'

'I am more convinced than ever that we ought to be in bed.' And Mr Thewless got to his feet with a firmness that somewhat belied his inner mind.

'But the really odd part is still to come.' Humphrey remained obstinately curled up in his chair. 'I mean about your being so right on all the things I fancy to myself. Didn't you say something about being imprisoned in dark, confined spaces?'

'Possibly I did. But I realize now that these things are not to be discussed with any advantage at present.'

'Well, that was what happened in the train.' As Humphrey made this announcement, he looked straight at his tutor, and Mr Thewless was aware of what was surely an almost hypnotic power in the dark glance thus directed upon him. Before it, indeed, he felt the need of bracing himself to firm incredulity – for had not some emanation or aura from the boy already wrought havoc in his own plain common sense that day? Almost Mr Thewless would have stopped his ears. But this was something that dignity made impossible, and Humphrey talked on.

'I imagined that I was imprisoned in a dark, confined space. *Very* confined. Would you expect it to be that?'

Mr Thewless, although he had for some time been moving in an intellectual fog, was nevertheless not without certain instinctive perceptions still. He recognized the irony; recognized that his pupil was making fun of him; and recognized too that in doing so Humphrey had found a sort of safety-valve for great emotional pressure. So he made no reply to the gibe, but simply knocked out his pipe and sat down again on the arm of a chair. The ship was now rolling slightly and the silence was punctuated by the inter-mittent creak of timber.

'It was when I left the compartment and went along to the lavatory.' Humphrey's voice was suddenly casual. But as the same time it rose a note – and with an effect that Mr Thewless by no means cared for, since it sug-gested something like hysteria beneath the boy's malicious calm. 'I can't tell you precisely what happened. I only know that I opened the lavatory door, and that it suddenly went dark, and that I was dizzy and quite powerless and being heaved or bundled somewhere – quite a short distance, I think. And then I found that I had been tied up – my hands, I mean – and packed into a box. It was a very frightening thing – well, to imagine.'

Once more Mr Thewless was silent, but his heart was sinking. With a young mind so disordered as this what could possibly be done? At the end of this exhausting and tragic journey to Ireland doctors must be called and Humphrey be taken home. There was nothing for it but that.

'But then almost at once, and again without my really knowing how it happened, I was pulled out and set free, and a voice said: "There's the lavatory. Stay in it till the train stops and starts again." And I did. And there my – my imaginings ended. For the time, that is to say. Besides, of course, one can't tell what tomorrow may bring.' Humphrey reached for his gun. 'And now that you know how right you were, I think we really had better go to bed.'

Mr Thewless, although he had now for some hours been devoutly desiring just this acquiescence on his charge's part, nodded almost absently. Perhaps –

he was doggedly thinking – perhaps it was not so *very* bad after all. The boy had undeniably a nervous intensity that made the communication of these fevered day-dreams an alarming experience. But, for all Mr Thewless knew, the actual confusion of fact and fantasy might be neither very uncommon nor very ominous in one of Humphrey's years. Was it not, indeed, rather more disconcerting that he himself, a mature man, should quickly have been drawn into an identical insubstantial world on board the Heysham train? And yet one point in Humphrey's rigmarole particularly worried him. The boy imagined not only that he had been *shut* up, but also that he had been *tied* up as well. And for some reason – the reading, perhaps, of one or another newspaper horror long ago – Mr Thewless regarded this as peculiarly unfortunate. Upon those who indulged in fantasies of fetters and bonds it was likely that the most dismal forms of madness would eventually pounce. If only, thought Mr Thewless, the boy had not persuaded himself of just *that* . . .

Humphrey's hand had closed on the canvas-swathed gun. As it did so he winced slightly. 'It still hurts, rather,' he said.

'Hurts?'

'These.' And Humphrey stretched out his arms so that the cuffs of his jacket shot backwards. And Mr Thewless's head swam as he looked. Round each wrist was the red weal left by a cord drawn tight.

'Tomorrow,' said Humphrey, 'it may be dragons or giants. Or pirates or smugglers or torture by Red Indian braves. Or, of course, it may just be spy stuff all over again.'

Chapter 11

It is probable that, had Mr Thewless's education been less extensive than it was, he could not have continued blind to the actual posture of his and Humphrey Paxton's affairs for so long as he did. To be well informed is not in itself any more certain a blessing than to be rich in material endowment; similar risks in the misapplication of one's resources have to be accepted in either case. And knowledge is really more dangerous than a bank balance. It will not stay put until we sign a cheque, but must ever, like an importunate child, be nudging us into an awareness of its existence, and encumbering us in whatever we may be about by tumbling at the wrong moment into the wrong place. Had a man of simple mind and circumscribed information rolled wearily into a bunk hard upon being afforded the spectacle of Humphrey's chafed wrists it is unlikely that he would have got out again next morning without a tolerably firm conviction that the boy had been manhandled. But it was not so with Humphrey's new tutor.

On the subject of Roman Britain Mr Thewless knew pretty well all that was to be known. In the field of School Certificate, Higher Certificate, Responsions, and Little-go he was almost equally omniscient. And on an enormous number of other matters he had a smattering of information that was both reasonably accurate and reasonably up to date. One of these was morbid psychology. And of this species of learning it is particularly true that slender draughts intoxicate the brain – though whether we are sobered again by large drinking is a matter still perhaps a little in doubt. However this may be, Mr Thewless had undoubtedly read quite a lot about the freakish powers and vagaries of the human mind. It thus came about that early next morning, and as he peered out of his porthole at the mouldering pile of Carrickfergus Castle, there rose fatally into his field of consciousness the beguiling topic of Hysterical Stigmatization.

In particular, Mr Thewless recalled, it is adolescents who are prone to putting up these strange performances. A young girl may be lying quite alone in bed; she will give a sharp cry of pain; and there will straightway be found upon her cheek or back the physical evidences of a bite or scratch or blow. But the mischievous spirits or goblins who are sometimes credited with inflicting these injuries have assuredly no objective existence, and the process illustrates nothing more than the mysterious power that a mind can exercise over the body it inhabits. And so it must be with poor Humphrey. If he was able to persuade himself that he had been pinioned he might well be perfectly able spontaneously to produce the stigmata that would support the fantasy.

As a logical approach to the facts involved there is little doubt that this could have been improved upon. But if the merit of a hypothesis is to be judged merely by the confidence it gives us in jogging through life's diurnal bewilderments it must be admitted that Mr Thewless's intelligence had functioned admirably. Walking down the gangway at Belfast, he felt in every sense that he was no longer at sea; and from this feeling of an adequate grasp of the situation he drew resolution to proceed with Sir Bernard Paxton's holiday plans undisturbed. That his young charge would eventually require the help of medical science was a fact upon which, unhappily, he could now feel little doubt. But to abrupt his journey in a strange town and to announce himself in some bleak consulting room as the itinerant and helpless warden of a demented schoolboy was a procedure at once uncomfortable to contemplate and unnecessarily drastic in face of the immediate situation. It would be altogether wiser to travel straight on to the Paxtons' relatives – persons of position and substance with whom the responsibility for any further decision might very properly be shared.

Meantime, he might, of course, send an immediate report to Humphrey's father. But Mr Thewless rather shrank from announcing to Sir Bernard – and that with the baldness required by telegraphic communication – that his cherished son had announced encountering himself in a cinema and later being dramatically, if briefly, bound and shut up in a box. Mr Thewless decided therefore to go straight ahead, and to support the harassments of the coming day upon a resolutely buoyant, nervous tone. In all this he must by no means forfeit his claim to the reader's sympathy. Nature had made Humphrey Paxton a decidedly odd child; circumstances had dictated that his revelations should be odder still; certain obscure purposes of his own had necessitated these revelations being partial and therefore singularly unconvincing. Moreover, Mr Thewless steadily remembered that this was Paxton's boy; that genius in its weakness had turned to him for help; and that his obligations in this sad and exhausting affair were by no means to be measured in terms of fifteen guineas a week. An inspector of the C.I.D. (Cadover, for example – who was at this moment still being pursued by uneasy dreams in his semi-detached villa at Pinner) or a physician professionally versed in those psychological labyrinths into which Mr Thewless had with an unwary amateurism been dangerously drawn: either of these might have been more immediately useful to Humphrey. But neither could have been any more conscientious according to his lights.

An air of cheerful confidence, however, proved at first not easy to sustain. Belfast, grimly utilitarian and shrouded in rain, was very little evocative of any gateway to the holiday spirit; it suggested rather a various detritus from the less appealing parts of Glasgow washed across the Irish Sea during the darker years of the nineteenth century. But this may have been an unfairly coloured view, since no city looks at its best when observed on a wet morning from a four-wheeler cab the progress of which irresistibly hints at a destination not in a railway station but in a municipal cemetery. Nor did Humphrey help in any ready uplifting of the heart, since he was silent, withdrawn, and apparently indisposed to favour his sceptical guardian with further fantasies. This, although in a sense reassuring, was depressing as well. Mr Thewless could not quite forget that Humphrey was, among other things, a *capable* boy. It seemed deplorable that his temperamental troubles (to put the matter mildly) should stand in the way of those activities to which capable boys are rightly dedicated. The mental dexterity that he had put into the business of identifying his new tutor at Euston, the precocious subtlety with which he had analysed a father's inner responses to adolescent behaviour in his son, the complex manner in which he had for a time checked his own irrational fears by an intellectually conceived mockery of his tutor: how fast and far these abilities would take a properly conducted boy into the recesses of the Greek and Latin languages! Peering out through the rain at the Great Northern railway terminus, and feeling in his pocket for half a crown, Mr Thewless fell for a moment into a weak nostalgia. The images of former pupils rose up before him – chubby-faced fourteen-year-olds solemnly construing from the immensely remote world of Juvenal, of the *Alcestis*; children learned in particles, lisping faultlessly in Sapphics and Alcaics . . . Mr Thewless glanced at Humphrey beside him . . . pale, mum, and refusing to be separated for a second from that shot-gun which he had been so anxious to repudiate less than twelve hours before. And momentarily he caught the dark glance of the boy – caught that slightly hypnotic gaze once more. It showed no response or recognition. In fact, it was fixed, Mr Thewless saw, upon some unseen goal or conception with quite as much concentration as any of those earlier pupils had ever brought to the ultimate mysteries of the Glyconic and Pherecratean metres . . . Mr Thewless, feeling the first stirrings of obscure doubt rising in him once more, jumped hastily from the cab and contrived his customary efficient capture of a porter. Humphrey followed. The railway station spread before them a classical portico nicely painted to look like milk chocolate. On one side stood an immobile policeman of gigantic size proportionately armed with truncheon and revolver. On the other a placard, equally generously conceived, announced

> LIFE IS SHORT
> DEATH IS COMING
> ETERNITY – WHERE?

And upon this brief glimpse of the cultural life of Belfast their train received them and they were presently hurtling west.

There was one other passenger in their compartment, and presently Mr Thewless was eyeing her with considerable gloom. For she was none other than that tiresome Miss Liberty to whose futile chatter over her spy story he attributed a good deal of his own and Humphrey's nervous follies on the previous afternoon.

They breakfasted together. This was by Humphrey's initiative and somewhat to the annoyance of Mr Thewless, who had planned to begin with his pupil a discussion – thoroughgoing but not unnecessarily solemn – on the nature and functions of deponent verbs. What – he heard himself asking Humphrey with a spice of harmless fun – was the difference between a deponent verb and the Prime Minister? Mr Thewless had achieved a good deal of success in his time along such lines as these. A deponent verb . . .

'Not the kipper,' Miss Liberty was saying. 'They say kipper or sausage; but if one waits, the sausage turns out to be egg and tomato as well. Not that I am an experienced traveller' – and Miss Liberty turned from Humphrey to Mr Thewless as if anxious that there should be no false pretences in the matter. 'It is simply part of the advice that I was given before setting out by my brother, Sir Charles.'

Mr Thewless bowed. Remembering that he had not been very polite to Miss Liberty on the previous day, he felt obliged to accept her advice himself – and this although kipper was a breakfast of which he was particularly fond. With suitable resignation, he watched the dish being borne away. A deponent verb *looks* harmless and passive –

'When travelling on the Highland railway with my dear father, Sir Herbert,' Miss Liberty was saying, 'we commonly obtained a luncheon basket at Kingussie. The cold chicken was sometimes a little tough, but the moment was a romantic one, all the same.'

Mr Thewless made an insincere noise, indicative of imaginative understanding of this remote thrill in Miss Liberty's past. He had an uncomfortable feeling that the sausage, to the confusion of Miss Liberty and the discrediting of her brother Sir Charles, would prove to be only sausage, after all. This, of course, made it particularly necessary to continue being polite. 'A journey into the Highlands, ma'am,' he said, 'must always be a romantic experience for an – um – capable child.'

'Precisely so. And the west of Ireland, I am told, is almost equally beautiful. So I am so grateful for the kindness of my brother –'

'Sir Charles?' Humphrey asked.

Mr Thewless was appalled. That his pupil should be on the verge of lunacy was one thing. But that he should suddenly become ill-bred was quite another. And there had undoubtedly been mockery in the boy's tone. And yet there was something else as well. Into this dining-car there had crept a faint atmosphere which Mr Thewless found it impossible to define. It *felt* like conspiracy. But how could it possibly be that? Could Miss Liberty, like a deponent verb, be a wolf in sheep's clothing? The idea was patently absurd.

'*Precisely* so.' Miss Liberty was helping herself with surprising lavishness to what had veritably proved to be sausage, egg, and tomato. 'It was my brother who was so kind as to suggest this holiday at Killyboffin. The inn had been recommended to him as satisfactory. So often in hotels nowadays one cannot be sure of well-aired beds.'

Mr Thewless was peering through a window. The train had slowed down and on the parapet of a stone bridge he could read the inscription

PREPARE TO MEET THY GOD.

Now he turned back and regarded Miss Liberty with a heroic effort at pleased surprise. 'Killyboffin? That happens to be where Humphrey and I are going too.'

'How very odd.'

'Very odd, indeed,' echoed Humphrey, and gulped coffee. Perhaps because the train was gaining speed and rocking slightly, he gave a sudden squirm and splutter. 'But then a lot of odd things do happen.'

A sort of baffled uneasiness – now only too familiar to him – assailed Mr Thewless. He had the illusion of a momentary vivid penetration into the mind of this tiresome old chatterbox – and what he found there was a fixed determination to carry out some formidable task. But this was nonsense. It was a fancy hitching on to nothing whatever in the actual world; it belonged to last night's nightmare on the express. What was desirable was to finish breakfast quickly and announce a frontal assault upon the Latin language. A deponent verb comes up to you looking quite harmless; then it throws off its fleece . . . Gazing through the window again in the direction of Lough Neigh, Mr Thewless frowned absently. What troubled him this time was a suspicion that Humphrey had in some way changed. He had planned a day in which his own cheerful common sense would do something to hearten this sadly possessed child; but now it was Humphrey's spirits which were in some odd way rising, while Mr Thewless himself was becoming a prey to irrational foreboding and gloom. Was it possible that the presence of Miss Liberty had some subtle effect on the boy? Or was there a relationship more definite than that? Was it possible, for example, that they had held some conference on board ship in the small hours of the morning; that Humphrey had poured out the pernicious fantasies by which he was beset; and that Miss Liberty, instead of insisting upon their true character as mere figments, had irresponsibly accepted them as gospel, thereby gaining the lad's confidence upon thoroughly reprehensible terms? If this were so, nothing, surely, could be more dangerous. For a time the boy's confidence might rise at finding himself seriously taken as the hero of an adventure story. But Mr Thewless knew only too well the sort of nervous reaction that was likely to follow. All this was conceivable, and it would explain that sense of conspiracy which he felt was rising about him.

Mr Thewless stared glumly at the remains of his sausage and then once more out across the landscape. The green and yellow fields were now flecked with sunshine, and a blue line of mountains lay far to the south. It was a deeply peaceful scene. The train rounded a bend and across a lush meadow a long whitewashed barn swung into view. Along its whole length it bore the words:

BOAST NOT THYSELF OF TOMORROW.

The habits of the Northern Irish, although godly, appeared scarcely gay. In Mr Thewless the sense of foreboding and bafflement irrationally grew; he had a feeling that he was being hurtled at sixty miles an hour into the threatening sickle of a vast question-mark formed by the bogs and mountains that he knew lay ahead of him. Humphrey and Miss Liberty were exchanging critical opinions on the works of 'Sapper' – and were apparently proposing to treat these one by one, in chronological order. In desperation, Mr Thewless opened the local paper he had bought at the railway station. It contained circumstantial accounts of several funerals, each ending with the information that the highly successful catering had been carried out by Messrs Tiffin and Tiffin. He turned to the back page and sought a meagre refuge in much incomprehensible information on horses and association footballers. Near the bottom somebody had bought quite a lot of space and caused to be printed:

THOU FOOL THIS NIGHT
THY SOUL SHALL BE
REQUIRED OF THEE.

Mr Thewless put down the paper, and as he did so Miss Liberty paused in her anatomy of one of the earlier exploits of Captain Hugh Drummond and smiled at him with maidenly cheer. 'And soon,' she said, 'we shall be on this most entertaining little train.'

But Mr Thewless's reply was a mere mumble. For with his intermittent and always disturbing intuition he had, as it were, looked clean through that smile. He had looked into the grey eyes of the lady. And what he there encountered he recognized instantly, although to the best of his knowledge he had never seen it before. It was the clear light of battle.

Those intuitions by which Humphrey's tutor was occasionally troubled by no means extended to any form of prescience, and it is not possible that he can have foreseen the accident. Nevertheless, his heart undoubtedly sank a little further when he saw the entertaining little train to which Miss Liberty had referred. They encountered it after an indefinite wait at a junction during which they were subjected to a somewhat perfunctory Customs examination, and when it finally appeared it looked less like a train of any description than a stunted single-decker bus – or it would have so appeared had it not much more powerfully suggested one of the lower forms of organic life monstrously enlarged to some problematical but assuredly sinister end. Into the belly of this bug-like creature they were presently bundled, but not before Mr Thewless had cast a final lingering look behind. He possessed, it is necessary to admit, something of an urban mind; and all too plainly the entertaining little train spoke of a destination at the back of beyond. Moreover, at this point of the journey there ceased to be anything of that segregation of classes which the philosopher in him was accustomed to deplore but which the social man was apt to take as part of the order of nature. Three or four impoverished persons with bundles were already on board, and immediately behind him an embarrassingly undernourished old woman was singing in a dismal, surprising, and Celtic manner – although whether for monetary reward or the pleasures of self-expression was obscure. Presently the driver appeared. He was a melancholy man lost in reverie – and almost equally lost in an immensely old suit of Connemara cloth, evidently tailored for one of the giants before the Flood. He sat down before the controls, eyed them with that flicker of interest which a person of abstract mind may evince before some unfamiliar material thing, and presently pulled a lever with every appearance of random experiment. The bug instantly coughed violently, shuddered as if unkindly roused from sleep, gave a loud angry roar, and then abruptly fell silent and motionless once more. The driver again pulled the lever, but this time nothing happened at all. He tried several other controls with an equally negative result. Whereupon – but with the reluctance of one who is innately kindly – he reached for a large hammer, climbed down from his seat, and proceeded to beat the bug violently about the snout. At this the bug, as if far advanced in some horrid masochistic perversion, contentedly purred. The driver climbed back into his seat and settled himself with an air of deep metaphysical abstraction. The bug continued to purr. After this nothing happened for quite a long time.

The bug purred and the August sun warmed both its entrails and that temporary ingestion represented by Mr Thewless and his fellow travellers. Further impoverished persons crowded on board, the majority carrying ill-wrapped brown-paper parcels or uncertainly clothed children. Somebody brought up a number of cardboard boxes and proceeded to hoist them on the roof; these apparently contained young pigs and were rather smelly. Humphrey and Miss Liberty were discussing some nice point in the character portrayal of their author's middle period. The undernourished woman had stopped singing and was talking unintelligibly and uncomfortably down Mr Thewless's neck. Probably she was soliciting alms. But as it was just possible that she was obligingly explaining some point of Hibernian scholarship germane to her minstrelsy he felt unable to take any action. Suddenly the purring deepened and the bug, without warning, shot off with a swaying and bouncing motion down the narrow-gauge line before it. At this the conductor, a fat boy with a squint who had been eating sandwiches at the back, showed much presence of mind by violently ringing a bell. Whereupon the driver, emerging in some degree from his abstract speculations, as also from his enveloping suit, looked about him in some perplexity and experimentally pressed a button. Immediately a siren whooped demoniacally in the bowels of the bug and amid a series of bumps and bucketings the creature made for the open country. Overhead the piglets in their cardboard boxes squealed in justifiable alarm. The undernourished woman continued to talk down Mr Thewless's neck, but her tone had changed and was now quite evidently one of imprecation against a monster of parsimony. A number of people ate oranges and close to Mr Thewless a small boy announced what was evidently a most implacable intention to be sick. Everywhere the greatest good-humour prevailed. From a wayside hoarding Northern Ireland took a Parthian shot at the unregenerate:

THEIR WORM DIETH NOT
AND THE FIRE IS NOT QUENCHED.

Through the early afternoon sunshine the bug trundled westwards and the landscape began to take upon itself with surprising fidelity the characteristics of those railway posters that celebrate the beauties of Erin. In the distance the mountains showed bluer and more blue; blue peat smoke rose from the whitewashed cottages; stacks of peat lay about the bogs or moved mysteriously down the lanes, superincumbent upon invisible donkeys. It was a natural scene in which poetry was steadily gaining upon prose, and Mr Thewless endeavoured, amid the perturbations still active within him, to assume that aesthetic mode of contemplation proper in the circumstances to a cultivated English traveller. The boy who had said he was going to be sick was sick.

The bug stopped at a little whitewashed hut and there was another customs examination. A pillar-box bearing the monogram of Queen Victoria had been painted a nice green. On the platform stood a policeman of normal proportions, and instead of a revolver and a truncheon he carried a copy of

Ben Hur translated into Irish, which he was evidently studying for an examination important to his professional advancement. Mr Thewless realized that the imperial might of Great Britain lay behind him and that in front was the philosophic republic of Mr de Valera. He several times endeavoured to show his passport and was somewhat hurt to find that the authorities took no interest in it. The attention of the policeman and the Customs officer was entirely given to the piglets, which they examined with many expressions of admiration and surprise. Contrary to popular supposition, it appeared that a pig was almost as much of a curiosity in Ireland as an armadillo would have been in Elizabethan London.

The bug moved on – inexplicably on any merely mechanistic hypothesis regarding its constitution, since both the driver and conductor became aware of the fact only in time to race down the platform and leap on board as it rounded a bend and headed towards the Atlantic Ocean. For a couple of hours it purred and clanked from station to station, but these halts grew gradually more indeterminate in character as the afternoon advanced, and eventually it simply stopped whenever summoned to do so by agitated persons hurrying across an adjoining field. Once when the single track upon which it ran breasted a rise Mr Thewless was startled to see an identical bug rapidly advancing upon them in the middle distance. The driver, also by chance observing this appearance, called to the conductor, and the two engaged for some minutes in dispassionate conversation, bending curiously over the controls of the vehicle and pointing now to one lever and now to another. Meanwhile, the advancing bug hurtled towards them. The conductor made some suggestion which the driver upon consideration rejected; the conductor reflected and then urged some further argument; the driver, being plainly a man of open mind, agreed to give the suggestion a trial and depressed some object with his foot; with an agonizing jolt the bug came to a dead halt. Some ten yards away the second bug had done the same, and the two appeared to eye each other balefully, much like two fleas that have been taught to simulate pugilistic encounter. The drivers and conductors, however, climbing out to meet upon neutral ground, debated the situation in the friendliest spirit over cans of tea and a cigarette; eventually the oncoming bug was coaxed by its crew to back for half a mile into a siding which had been discovered by the enterprise of a reconnoitring conductor – whereon the journey was resumed. One other hitch occurred about an hour later, when the bug came to a halt, baffled by a bifurcation of the line before it. And this occasioned the only flaw in the complete harmony of the afternoon's proceedings, for whereas the driver was in favour of taking the line to the left the conductor was obstinately wedded to the notion of taking the one to the right. Various passengers took part in the discussion, which presently re-echoed to a spirited bandying of the musical place-names of the district. Miss Liberty, hearing the driver several times enunciate in tones of disgust and repudiation the name of Killyboffin, joined in vigorously on the conductor's side; and it was this opinion that eventually carried the day.

The journey went interminably on. Apart from two or three silent men who sat at the back, conversation was general on various points of crop and animal husbandry. A friendly farmer observing that Mr Thewless had nothing more entertaining to read than a novel by Mr Charles Morgan, insisted on lending him the current issue of the *Tullycleave, Derryness, and Kinnoghly Recorder*, and from this he learnt that at Crockacooan on the following Thursday it would be possible to bid for three store heifers in forward condition, four dairy cows springing and in full milk, a slipe, three rundlets, and a number of double and single trees. He was just speculating on the nature of a double tree when the train ran into the tunnel.

One short tunnel there had already been; traversing it had made Mr Thewless notice the absence of any form of artificial light in this primitive vehicle. One simply sat in the dark and waited. And this time the period of darkness was longer. It must be fully –

At this moment the thing happened: first a shattering jar; then a splintering crash and a tinkle of breaking glass as the bug lurched over on its side; then shouts, cries and – from somewhere at the back – a succession of spine-chilling screams.

It was a situation made all the more unnerving by the complete darkness which enveloped it. Mr Thewless, clinging with one arm to a seat which had reared itself up at an angle of some thirty degrees, stretched out the other in the direction in which he judged the shoulder of his pupil ought to be. 'Humphrey,' he called, 'are you all right?' But there was too much noise for him to be sure if there was any reply. The driver and conductor were endeavouring to restore calm by each shouting at the top of his voice; children were dismally howling; overhead the piglets sustainedly squealed. In the restricted space of the tunnel the resulting reverberations were altogether bewildering, and it was not easy to decide whether what was involved was a major disaster or a largely baseless panic. Somebody struck a match and there was a momentary vision of sprawled bodies and scared faces. From the rear a man's voice called: 'I'll get back along the tunnel and bring help' – and this was followed by a further shivering of glass, as of somebody breaking resolutely out of the coach. From the rear too the most agonized groans continued to come, and when another match was struck Mr Thewless saw that one man there was writhing as if in agony and another slumped in his seat, apparently streaming with blood. This last glimpse presented so clamant a call for aid that Mr Thewless began to scramble over the seats, the lessons of long-past first-aid classes reassembling themselves surprisingly in his mind. But he got no distance in this charitable endeavour. For in the darkness and continued confusion something struck him with unaccountable violence on the head and all consciousness left him.

He came to his senses knowing somehow that no great interval of time had elapsed. Nor had the situation greatly changed, except that he himself was now outside the coach and propped against the curved side of the tunnel. Here and there a torch flickered, but there was still more of impenetrable blackness than of light – as also more of turmoil than of order. It was clear, however, that some outside help had arrived. It must, indeed, have arrived with surprising speed, since almost the first object of which he was aware in a passing flicker of light was an efficient-looking stretcher upon which, momentarily unattended, a shrouded form reposed. And Mr Thewless felt a sudden cold fear. Could it be Humphrey who lay in sinister stillness there? The mere thought brought him staggering to his feet and he reached out towards the stretcher. As he did so another uncertain beam of light showed him Miss Liberty close by – Miss Liberty with her features set in swift calculation and with her arm oddly raised . . . Unaccountably, once more Mr Thewless was struck on the head and was just aware of being gripped in strong arms as he fell.

When he recovered consciousness for the second time it was to discover that a throbbing which he had supposed to be the subjective consequence of his own battered cranium was in fact the steady pulse of a powerful engine, and for a moment he had the confused impression that the bug, with that resistance to even extensive injury characteristic of lowly organisms, had again got under way. But this was an altogether smoother mode of progression, and some subtle report of the senses assured him that it was much more rapid as well. There was still complete darkness around him, but presently he discovered with great surprise that this was merely because he had his eyes shut. Opening them, he found himself to be lying on a stretcher in an admirably appointed ambulance, all chromium, white enamel, and antiseptic smell. Despite the warmth of the afternoon, a little electric radiator was thoughtfully burning, and above it was a tastefully arranged vase of flowers. There was a gay frieze of delightful nursery scenes, and perched at Mr Thewless's feet was an uncompromisingly hygienic but nevertheless cuddlesome teddy-bear. On the other side of the vehicle was a second, and empty, stretcher.

From all this there was only one reasonable inference. He had been badly injured in the accident and was now being borne away in an ambulance hastily requisitioned from some children's hospital. But it was odd that there was nobody else in need of similar conveyance; for example, there had been the two badly hurt men at the back. And what had happened to Humphrey? Even if he had escaped injury, what would be the consequence of these untoward events upon a boy so easily thrown off his balance?

Confronted by this thought, Mr Thewless realized that it was his first duty to ascertain the extent of his injuries and thereupon come to a determination as to what was best to be done. There being no nurse or attendant in the ambulance of whom to inquire, he decided upon a cautious exploration. Apart from a moderate headache and a decided tenderness on the top of the skull, he was aware in himself of no unusual sensation. He knew, however, that sometimes for a considerable interval after the sustaining even of grave injuries very little pain may be felt. But if sensation were delusive, movement could scarcely be so. Now, what was the worst that could have befallen him? The answer, he decided, was a broken back. And, with a broken back, there was one thing assuredly that one could not possibly do: sit up. Bracing himself against some sharp agony, Mr Thewless made the effort to achieve this position. And immediately he found that he was sitting up with as little inconvenience as he experienced every morning in bed.

Mr Thewless moved a limb. He moved all his limbs. He twiddled his toes and twisted his neck. Then, as an afterthought, he vigorously champed his jaws, blinked his eyelids, and retracted the muscles of his abdomen. The issue of all these experiments was incontrovertible. Whatever minor sprains or abrasions he might have received, he was by no means in the sort of condition that justified his thus being treated as a cot case and hurtled away from his young charge hard upon an alarming and dangerous experience. And as soon as he realized this Mr Thewless acted with vigour. 'Stop!' he shouted loudly. 'Please stop at once. There has been some ridiculous mistake.'

Nothing happened. He called more loudly still, but again in vain. The hum of the engine must be rendering his cries inaudible through the partition separating him from the driver and anyone else in front. He therefore explored the back, and found only double doors which appeared to be locked on the outside. At the other end, however, and quite close to where the driver's ear must presumably be, there was what proved to be a sliding shutter – and this Mr Thewless opened with considerable relief. 'Excuse me,' he said politely through it; 'would you mind stopping, and opening the door? I find that I have sustained no serious injury.'

These remarks being, even if faintly surprising, eminently rational, Mr Thewless was a good deal startled to hear them received with a loud laugh. 'Shut your trap, son,' said a rough voice. 'Hollering won't do no good. Sit down and play with yer bloody bear.'

Mr Thewless was not unnaturally much shocked. It was evident that the driver, being accustomed to conveying children, had forgotten that upon this occasion he was dealing with an adult. But that sick children should ever be spoken to in such a way aroused his extreme indignation at once. 'Stop the ambulance instantly,' he said. 'Your language is disgraceful, and you may be sure that I shall report upon it with the utmost severity to the proper authorities.'

Again the driver laughed loudly. 'Gawd,' he said, 'what a rum kid.'

''Ere' – it was a second voice that spoke this time – '*is* it a kid? It don't sound much like a kid to me.'

'Wot's that?' The driver was startled and jammed on his brakes. 'Didn't yer have a look at 'im under that ruddy sheet?' The ambulance jolted to a stop. 'Let's 'ave a look.'

And a moment later the doors were flung open. Mr Thewless, boiling with indignation, jumped to the ground and confronted two surly and oddly uncertain men, who had not at all the appearance of hospital attendants. 'Strewth!' said one. ''Ere's a go.'

But the second appeared more self-possessed, and now presented Mr Thewless with an ingratiating smile. 'You mustn't mind his language, sir,' he said. 'He don't belong at all regular with the ambulance; it's just that the regular driver's away like.'

At this the first man growled what might have been an apology. When he spoke, however, it was in tones of indignation almost matching Mr Thewless's own. 'Look 'ere,' he said, 'ain't yer tripes 'arf torn out? Ain't yer at death's door? Ain't yer a bleeding mess?'

Mr Thewless uttered a comprehensive denial of these charges. 'I am perfectly well,' he said sternly. 'And I demand to know –'

'Then we ain't got no time to waste on yer. What d'jer mean coming joy-riding with them as is employed strikly on errands of mercy? Serious calls is wot we attend to. Come along, mate. And jigger off, yer silly old goat.'

At this the two men leapt with surprising speed into their ambulance and drove away. Mr Thewless was left standing by the roadside, speechless with bewilderment and rage. All around him stretched an empty moor, now growing bleak and inhospitable in the late afternoon sunlight. Miles away, a single white spot on the horizon suggested some humble species of human dwelling. Further sign of life or habitation there was none. He examined the dusty surface of the road. No tracks were visible except those of the ambulance which was now growing small in the distance. It was only too evident that the back of beyond had veritably received him.

Doggedly he began to trudge towards the distant white speck.

Chapter 12

'No eggs! No eggs!! Good heavens, man, what do you mean by no eggs?' And, as one thunderstruck, Mr Cyril Bolderwood of Killyboffin Hall stared at Denis, the general factotum whom, in expansive moments, he was pleased to describe as his steward. Then less vehemently he added: 'You did say *no* eggs?'

'It's a shameful fact, sir, that I'm just after discovering.' Denis paused to remove a straw from his hair and drop it in his master's waste-paper basket. 'But Mr Ivor had the last of our own for his breakfast surely, and now there's never an egg to be bought in all Killyboffin on account of the fish having come.'

'God bless my soul!' Mr Bolderwood raised both hands in the air with an expressiveness possibly indicating his long sojourn in Latin-American countries. 'Do you realize, Denis, that here is Mr Ivor's cousin coming from London, where not the King himself has an egg to his breakfast except once in a way – and coming, mark you, with a tutor, Denis, a great doctor from the universities, no doubt – and you stand there and tell me the eggs are all gone from Killyboffin because the fish have come? Is it the tinned salmon in old Mrs Fallon's little window that have risen up in the night and sucked them dry, Denis? Now tell me that.' And Mr Bolderwood, who prided himself on a manner of speech both feudal and familiar, sat down with regained composure and began to stuff an ancient pipe.

'Indeed and your honour knows it is no such thing, but rather the live fish coming up the loughs in their millions like the stars of heaven and all the world's ships labouring after them from Hull and Narvik and Nineveh. And it's myself have seen boatloads of them coming ashore all morning, and taking Tannian's car and Donohoe's, yes and Michael Orr's old Ford too, and scouring the land to eat it up like the locusts, and ourselves in want of a simple dish to set before a fine lad from London itself, broad and fair and blue-eyed as he is, that none of us has ever had the joy of setting eyes on, and him Mr Ivor's own cousin.' Denis paused on this. He found a rhetoric based upon uncertain memories of his grandmother distinctly exhausting to keep up. But since his cosmopolitan employer liked to play at being surrounded by old Ireland, and was prepared to pay for the illusion, Denis did his best to get the atmosphere right. 'Isn't it a hard case, your honour, myself and yourself to be treated –'

'So that's it!' Cyril Bolderwood had risen again and walked to the window of the long shabby room he called his sudy. 'Steam trawlers, eh? And rascals off them wandering the countryside buying by day what they haven't already stolen by night? Why don't the police see to them? Why doesn't the *garda* act?'

'Indeed, sir, he well might.' Denis shook his head. 'And yet it would maybe be beyond reason to expect a poor lad like Shaun Cushin, with a great examination in the Irish before him that would tax the bottomless learning of the Taoiseach himself, to concern himself with chasing after a rabble of foreigners and gaoling them for stealing a goose or a hen or a handful of eggs. Unless' – Denis added as an afterthought – 'they should be your honour's own, indeed.'

Mr Bolderwood was now staring thoughtfully at a curl of smoke which rose presumably from one of the offending trawlers in the little harbour beyond the village. 'If we can't have eggs –' he began, and abruptly broke off. 'What the devil is all that noise about?'

Killyboffin Hall was a large, bare, rambling building, Georgian in a bleak way and falling down at the corners. The lightest breeze, on gaining entry through its many cracks, crevices, and broken panes, became mysteriously transformed into a gale that sobbed and moaned through its lofty rooms, stirring the dust from shadowy cornices and immemorial hangings, and making the worn carpets rise and fall in the long corridors. It was the sort of house in which, in the small hours, boards start from worm-eaten joists, and ancient wicker furniture creaks in shrouded rooms, and invisible fingers are at play upon doors and windows. That the Bolderwoods were positively obliged to live amid such a *décor* nobody very seriously believed, for clearly it was old Mr Bolderwood's whim thus to assimilate himself with impoverished landowners upon whom such conditions were obligatory, and the fancy was licensed by sundry tortuous but indubitable blood-ties with the nobility and gentry of the region. Life at Killyboffin, then, had superficially every appearance of all the discomforts associated with genteel penury, and had Sir Bernard Paxton gained any inkling of this eccentric humour on the part of his kinsman he would certainly not – prizing life's material surfaces as he was inclined to do – have sanctioned the expedition upon which his only son had recently embarked.

One consequence of the somewhat bare condition of the mansion was the tendency of noise in any volume to gain resonance as it travelled from room to room, and to propagate itself through a complex system of echoes. It was a phenomenon of this sort that was disturbing Mr Bolderwood now. 'Denis,' he repeated, 'what the devil is that?'

Denis considered. 'It might be the half-Ayrshire, your honour, got unbeknownst among the turnips, and Gracie and Billy and the lad Pat and the dogs –'

'Stuff and nonsense, man! It's coming up the kitchen stairs – and whoever heard of a half-Ayrshire doing that? But here's Mr Ivor. Ivor, in heaven's name –'

Ivor Bolderwood, a mild young man behind large round glasses, had entered his father's study by a door at its far end; and at the same moment a confused rout of persons had burst in opposite. One of these latter, a stout woman in an apron, appeared to possess some power of articulate speech, and her voice presently rose clear of the babel around her. 'The terrible disaster that it is!' she cried. 'And the poor lad nigh at the end of his long journey and all – alas! that Killyboffin should see such a day.'

To these words a general consenting murmur arose from Mr Bolderwood's other retainers. And Denis, although without any notion of what all this betokened, judged that some more specifically Celtic reaction would be appropriate. 'Ochone,' he cried with great satisfaction, and began swaying his body in a rhythmical manner from the hips. 'Ochone, ochone!'

'Hold your tongue, man!' Ivor Bolderwood spoke with a decision unexpected in one whose eyes gleamed so vaguely from behind their expanses of glass. 'Now, Gracie, why –' But here the young man stopped, his glance having fallen for the first time upon another of the intruders. 'Billy, weren't you told to be off to the station long ago?'

'And indeed I was, Mr Ivor.' The man addressed took a step forward, acknowledging the presence of his employer as he did so by pulling at a forelock. 'And I'm after driving back this moment with the terrible news of the great disaster to the train. And sorry I am that it's without the poor young gentleman that I've returned here.'

'A disaster to the train!' The elder Mr Bolderwood paled. 'You don't mean the train on which my nephew and his tutor were –'

'Indeed he does, sir.' The woman called Gracie spoke again. 'A great and terrible accident in the tunnel it has been, and the mangled bodies and severed limbs strewn far under the wide heaven, and the cries of those in their agony like to be heard from here to Sligo.'

'But this is too ghastly to believe.' Mr Bolderwood looked in consternation at his son, whose perturbation was equal to his own. 'And is the poor boy –'

'The poor boy, indeed!' Denis was no longer to be restrained. 'The fine lad that was to be coming amongst us, triumphant and brave, to be no more than one of a dark line of corpses crying shame upon the railways of Ireland!'

'And the learned man that was with him to be less even than that, by far and far.' Gracie had risen and raised imprecating hands against the heavens. 'For no morsel of him have they pieced to morsel in all that dolorous field.'

'Not with all the labour of all the doctors that be there now with all their fair and shining instruments,' said Denis with conviction. 'But thanks be to God we can do better for the boy. For with a stitch here, and maybe some hay or tow thrust in there, he can be laid neat and decent in his coffin and it shipped at no great expense to his sorrowing dad in London. And no trouble on the way except it may be a bit rummaged, reverently undertaken, in the Customs sheds of Dublin.'

At this Mr Bolderwood produced a large coloured handkerchief and mopped his brow. 'Am I to understand,' he cried, 'that my nephew is *dead*?'

Billy, who was chiefly addressed, made a motion with his head which contrived to be at once vigorous and completely ambiguous. 'As soon', he began, 'as ever the train got into the station –'

'Got into the station?' It was Ivor Bolderwood who exclaimed this time. 'And how the deuce could the train get into the station when it had had a terrible accident in the tunnel?'

'Indeed and why should it not?' Billy was innocently surprised. 'The great disaster was safely over, praise God, and what should the train do but arrive where it was intended?'

'It's enough to drive a man out of his senses!' Mr Bolderwood's voice rose in despair. 'Haven't you been telling us, you abominable rascal, of mangled bodies and severed limbs and dark lines of corpses and – and doctors and surgeons by the bevy. And now you –'

'But indeed, your honour, there was an ambulance.' Billy produced this with a good deal of triumph. 'There's five or six of them that was on the train to swear to it – although others will yet be denying of it, to be sure, since it was gone it seems almost as soon as come.'

'There was an accident – but not so bad that the train couldn't continue on its way.' Mr Bolderwood had advanced and was grasping Billy sternly by the lapel of his coat. 'And there was an ambulance – but it saw no reason to stay long. Now, what of all the rest of this outrageous nonsense? Was *anyone* killed? Was *anyone* injured?'

'Or' – and Ivor Bolderwood intervened sharply – 'is anyone missing?'

Billy threw up admiring hands – thereby dexterously freeing himself from his employer's grasp. 'There, now!' he said. 'It's a great intelligence that your honour's son has, and a great pride that he must be to his father. For there were three strangers at the back of the train, it seems, and they the most sorely wounded of all. Screaming in their agony, they were, and the blood all about them as deep as fish-pools, while the others, as it appeared in the end, were no more than shaken and bruised. And when all that great fear and panic was over it was seen that these three had vanished entirely, and with them the learned man that was your honour's nephew's tutor. And this same that I'm after telling you is but another proof that there was an ambulance there surely, for how else could the wounded men have vanished? And the tutor, Christ help him, must have been taken as at death's door too.'

'Then it comes to this.' Ivor Bolderwood turned to address his father, who, wrathful and bewildered, still confronted Billy. 'The accident resulted in three strangers and Mr Thewless being injured and taken away in an ambulance. That is bad enough, although not nearly so bad as all this excited chatter suggested. But where is the boy?'

'Exactly so.' The elder Mr Bolderwood was now trembling with mingled anxiety and irritation. 'Where is Mr Humphrey, you blackguard? Why haven't you brought him home? Do you realize how – how *important* this is?'

'And that we are responsible', Ivor added, 'to his father?'

'There, now!' said Denis indignantly. 'And can't you answer his honour with some mite or drop of reason, Billy Bone, instead of blathering, God help you, over every irrelevant thing?'

'And causing the limbs to drop and the blood to flow', cried Gracie, 'from untold Irish souls, when there was no mischief but to three poor creatures from the North, and maybe to the young lad's tutor, which is a person of great learning, God be praised, but of small consideration either among Christian folk or gentry?'

Under this general reprobation, Billy Bone shifted uneasily from one foot to the other. 'Should I not be sparing his honour's feelings', he demanded of the company at large, 'and waiting some more seemly time for telling him that his nephew has gone off with a woman in Tannian's car?'

'Gone off with a woman? Stuff and nonsense!' The elder Mr Bolderwood threw up his arms in despair. 'Why should Mr Humphrey do a fantastic thing like that?'

'And why should he do anything else?' Billy was bewildered. 'With the tutor that was set at guard over him laid low in an ambulance, and a fine woman in her perfumes and her pearls and her rich and rustling garments waiting for him in Tannian's great car, and himself a young heretic without fear of priest or purgatory or the blessed St Patrick –'

'Lunacy – utter lunacy!' Mr Bolderwood's manner wavered between incredulity and apprehensiveness. 'Do you ask me to believe that a – a woman of this character should be waiting in the wilds of Killyboffin on the chance that a railway accident might incapacitate my nephew's tutor?'

Ivor Bolderwood had strolled to the window and was staring out at the wisp of smoke rising from the hidden trawler. Now he turned back and looked at his father soberly. 'To me', he said, 'the unlikely touch is Tannian's car. One would expect the equipage of such an adventuress to match the perfumes and the pearls and the alluring limbs.'

Mr Bolderwood looked at his son in some surprise. 'But surely you can't think –'

'Well, the boy *has* vanished. And something odd *does* seem to have happened on the train. I begin to wonder if we quite reckoned with what we might be taking on.' He glanced round the circle of his father's retainers. '*Paxton père*,' he said, '*n'est-il pas très riche et très célèbre? Peut-être on trame l'enlèvement de l'enfant.*'

The element of play-acting commonly discernible in the elder Mr Bolderwood quite evaporated under this dire hint. He sat down heavily and without the intention of creating an effect. 'You disturb me,' he said. 'You disturb me very much.'

Ivor's eyebrows had dipped beneath his glasses in a thoughtful scowl. 'The tutor – this Mr Thewless – sounded extremely respectable. But, of course, there might have been a second adventuress waiting to nail *him*. She might have lurked in the tunnel. She might have been disguised as a beautiful nurse and laid on with the ambulance.'

The elder Mr Bolderwood looked momentarily relieved. 'You ought not to make these jokes,' he said. 'I am naturally worried; naturally very worried indeed.'

'If, of course, this Mr Thewless who has travelled with the boy is the genuine Mr Thewless. We can't really be sure . . . Ah – that may tell us something!'

This exclamation was occasioned by the shrill ringing of a telephone bell in a far corner of the room. Ivor Bolderwood made for it, but not before he had ejected his father's retainers with the gesture of one who drives sheep expertly through a gate. He picked up the receiver. 'Yes,' he said, '. . . yes. This is Ivor Bolderwood speaking . . . No, he hasn't turned up yet. As a matter of fact, we have become a little anxious. One of the servants says he has gone off with a lady . . . No, I didn't say there had been something shady. I said that we are told he has gone off with a lady . . . Yes, we are certainly going to inquire at once. I hope that you yourself . . . Dear me . . . *dear* me! Yes, indeed. A most alarming experience . . . Good lord! Extremely careless . . . Certainly a stiff letter will be the thing. Can we send the car? . . . I see. Yes, we look forward to it . . . Yes, we will start a search now . . . You think it will be all right? I am so glad. It will allay my father's anxieties . . . A prank? Quite possibly . . . Goodbye.'

Ivor Bolderwood put back the receiver and turned to his father. His eyebrows had risen expressively over the rims of his glasses. 'Thewless,' he said. 'Thewless, as you may have guessed. There really was some sort of accident in the tunnel. He was hit on the head.'

'In the accident?'

'It sounded to me more like *after* the accident. And then he was put into an ambulance – so there really was an ambulance – and driven away. Apparently it was a *children's* ambulance. And when the people in charge of it discovered that *he* was not a child they more or less dropped him like a hot potato and disappeared.'

'Well I'm damned!' The elder Mr Bolderwood looked doubtfully at his son. 'And was he terribly upset when he heard that Humphrey hasn't turned up?'

'Not a bit of it. He says it must be some boyish prank.'

'Bless me! And does he think being carried off in an ambulance was a boyish prank too?'

'He considers that it was careless – really unpardonably careless. He is going to write a letter about it to the local authorities.'

'It is certainly a sort of thing that must be stopped.' Cyril Bolderwood frowned. 'But, my dear Ivor, this is most disturbing – positively sinister, indeed – whatever this fool of a tutor thinks of it. The lad may be in the hands of Lord knows what set of gangsters or professional kidnappers at this very moment. This Thewless must be a confoundedly casual chap.'

'He didn't give me quite that impression.' And Ivor Bolderwood stared at the telephone as if that instrument might be capable of throwing light on the matter. 'He struck me as a man who was almost irrationally determined to deny that the universe holds anything dangerous or surprising.'

'An admirable temperament! I wish I could feel the same.'

Ivor Bolderwood shook his head. 'I didn't feel it was a matter of his temperament. The learned tutor is in some rather abnormal state of mind. His ordinary way of taking things may be quite different.'

'Well, it's our way of taking things that is the question. What the devil are we to do?'

'Make sure that the excellent Thewless isn't right, and that the boy's disappearance isn't, in one way or another, a mare's nest. After that – well, we must send a wire to Bernard Paxton and call in the police.'

'Oh dear, oh dear!'

'But do Irish rural policemen believe stories of kidnappers and beautiful decoys? I doubt it.' And Ivor Bolderwood, disregarding his father's evident perturbation, placidly chuckled. 'It would be better – yes, decidedly better – to rescue the boy ourselves. Don't you think?'

'I think I'll get the police station now.' Cyril Bolderwood rose with sudden resolution and approached the telephone. 'They may at least tell us something like the truth about the train . . . Whatever is that?'

From somewhere beyond the precincts of Killyboffin Hall there had come a sound as of the ragged firing of small-arms. It drew nearer and presently disclosed itself as being in the nature of a death-rattle from some internal combustion engine.

'Tannian's car!' exclaimed Ivor. 'Perhaps it's the adventuress come to do a deal with us.' He strode to the window, threw it open, and leant out. There was a moment's pause and then his laughter floated back into the room. 'It's the lady, sure enough. But she's fifty, if she's a day. And she's brought the boy with her.'

Cyril Bolderwood produced his handkerchief and once more mopped his brow. 'Bewildering,' he said, 'really bewildering. One doesn't at all know what to make of it. And – do you know? – there isn't a single egg in the place.'

Chapter 13

The various anxieties to which Mr Thewless had been subject since accepting the guardianship of Humphrey Paxton had indeed produced very much the effect divined by Ivor Bolderwood over the telephone. He was, he assured himself, a commonplace person who had undertaken commonplace employment. Law, order, and security surrounded him as they had always done, and the only disturbing factor in the situation was the lurid and infectious imagination of his pupil. The affair of the ambulance had certainly been a little out of the way; but this was all the more reason for his being on his guard against treating it as Humphrey would do – as a springboard to some alarming fantasy. Even to write that stiff letter of complaint might be to make too much of the incident. The Irish, after all, were known to be a somewhat erratic people, and the mistake that had been made, although perplexing and vexatious, was not serious. Much more disturbing was the fact that Humphrey, although uninjured in the affair in the tunnel, had made another of his foolish disappearances.

And Mr Thewless (who had found little difficulty in hiring a car which was now carrying him comfortably towards Killyboffin Hall) remembered with mortification the absurd suspicions he had harboured upon the occasion of Humphrey's vanishing on the Heysham train. Those suspicions had not even held any coherency among themselves. For instance, there had been that muddled idea that the boy travelling with him was an impostor – an idea upon which he might positively have acted (to the vast detriment of poor Humphrey's nervous balance) but for that fortunate flash-back to the Velazquez in Sir Bernard Paxton's library. But now the whole of that bad twenty-four hours was behind him; the life of a country-house in this remote region could scarcely be other than tranquil; and once Humphrey had turned up again a quiet and wholesome routine could be established. Unless, indeed, the house-party assembled by Sir Bernard's cousins was of an order so large, brilliant or – abominable thought! – rackety as to make quiet and study difficult.

But for the moment, at least, complete tranquillity was possible. Mr Thewless's pipe and tobacco had come safely through his adventures; he employed himself with them comfortably now, while he surveyed a countryside which was quite unfamiliar to him. Ahead were occasional glimpses of an ocean the deep blue of which was beginning to take the glitter of the declining sun; and here and there, too, he had seen cliffs and headlands which hinted at a rugged and deeply indented coast. Behind and on either hand stretched gently undulating country, intensely green, divided by stone dykes into fields and paddocks that grew larger and more ill-defined as they climbed from the valleys towards the higher ground. Sparsely threaded on invisible tracks that ran diagonally up and down the hills were the low white cottages which were almost the sole sign of human occupation. Their doors, windows, and chimneys were so disposed as to make them strongly suggestive of sentient beings, crouched with wide eyes and pricked ears to mark the intruder. Twice the car had passed the burnt-out shell of a large mansion amid abandoned gardens, and Mr Thewless's driver took it upon himself to explain that this state of affairs dated from the Troubles, and was the work of persons whom he, the driver, held in the strongest reprobation; whom he regarded, indeed, as possessing a reach of wickedness quite beyond even the common large tether of humanity. Mr Thewless, having a strong persuasion that his informant had himself been a handy man with a firebrand, supposed that this political attitude was not unconnected with the amount of the fare he should presently be expected to pay. Perhaps (speculated Mr Thewless, thoughtful for his employer's pocket) the Bolderwoods would have some idea of what was reasonable. Two shillings would certainly be an adequate tip.

At this moment the car swung sharply and the driver announced that they were on the drive to the big house. Mr Thewless would not have guessed it, but looking back at what appeared to be a cart-track he discerned that they had passed the ruins of a small lodge. These were unblackened by flame, and the mere product, it was to be conjectured, of the effluction of time. The car took another bend and the house was before them. Mr Thewless looked at it with some surprise. For here too time seemed to have been let play almost unimpeded. The mansion, although it was not actually ruinous – having recently received, indeed, a sort of token restoration in the form of much amateurishly applied white paint – was not such as Sir Bernard Paxton's manner would have prepared one to expect. It contrived to suggest the idea of an immemorial and settled possession, of the confident tenure that comes only with generations; but at the same time there appeared to be whole wings and floors that were deserted, so that the life of the whole place conveyed the notion of a gentle peripheral decay. This effect was enhanced by a long balustraded terrace along the line of which were disposed sundry groups of statuary so drastically decayed as to display little more than a tangle of lower limbs, human and brute, from which an anatomist might possibly have reconstructed the various super-incumbent dramas now missing. Behind this somewhat mournful detritus of classical culture a woman was moving about in what appeared to be the motion of feeding hens.

When he had recovered from his first mild surprise at these unexpected appearances, Mr Thewless was distinctly pleased. There was unlikely to be anything rackety or pretentious here. It seemed to be a very good setting, indeed, for that labour of rehabilitation, both nervous and scholastic, to which he and his charge were dedicated. And, even as he made this reflection, Mr Thewless found further reassurance in an eminently quiet domestic scene. Below the terrace, and upon a large space of ground mid-way in character between a lawn and a hayfield, an elderly lady and gentleman sat beneath an ancient coloured umbrella the shade of which had crept away from them with the sinking sun. Beside them on a wicker table a silver tea equipage of considerable complication suggested an ordering of things at once sober and substantial. Some fifty yards beyond, and on the farther side of a low hedge, were two other figures whom Mr Thewless could at first distinguish merely as those of a younger man and a boy. These were bent over some object presently invisible; they straightened up and Mr Thewless heard a dull report; their conference was renewed and in a flash its nature became clear. The boy was being instructed in the use of a shot-gun – that same shot-gun which he had been disposed violently to repudiate at Euston. Humphrey had turned up.

Perhaps because he was more relieved than he was prepared to acknowledge, Mr Thewless paid his fare without inquiry. He was then led, by a female servant markedly more disposed to hospitality than deference, across the decaying terrace and into the presence of the persons beneath the umbrella. He had only time to remark, with a twinge of obscure misgiving, that the lady was none other than his old acquaintance, Miss Liberty, when his attention was commanded by the volubility of his host.

'My dear sir, I'm delighted to see you safe – most delighted. Gracie! bring another pot of tea . . . Yes, very pleased indeed and I hope you're not unduly fatigued. Dinner, woman – dinner? Hold your tongue and do as you're told – am I to be dinnered in my own house when I choose that it shall be tea-time still? . . . I think you know Miss Liberty. She took charge of Humphrey, you know – a nice lad, Bernard's boy, and intelligent, I'd be inclined to say – took charge of him, you know, and they went off to search for you in Tannian's car. But here you are, after the rascals have done their damnedest, eh?'

'Done their damnedest?' Mr Thewless was disturbed.

But Mr Bolderwood largely laughed. 'No animus, of course; nothing directed against you in particular, my dear sir. But first they let fly at you with a railway accident and then with this odd ambulance affair, eh? It's their stupidity, you know. All the Irish are intensely stupid. Charming, of course; full of poetry and often extremely industrious; religious too – positively religious to a fault.' Mr Bolderwood paused for a moment, and Mr Thewless conjectured that he was proposing to supply this last statement with some larger theological context. But all he did was to take breath the more effectively to shout across the length of the terrace: 'Gracie, send out another fruit cake! And tell that woman to stop feeding the fowls.' Mr Bolderwood turned this time to Miss Liberty. 'Positively,' he said, 'I won't feed the fowls if the fowls refuse to feed me. Would you believe, now, that there's not an egg in the place, and that they won't even send up a dozen – not a dozen, mark you! – from the village? And on a day, as Ivor there would tell you, that I distinctly had it in mind to order an omelette for dinner. By the way, I hope you'll stop for a meal?'

During these wandering remarks, Miss Liberty had been studying Humphrey's tutor with a good deal of attention – and this with a frankness making the latter feel faintly like an object exposed behind plate-glass. But now the lady rose and drew on her gloves. 'Thank you,' she said, 'but I am afraid I cannot accept your most *kind* invitation. Not, Mr Bolderwood, that I will claim to feel a stranger, or in any way unintroduced, after the *curious* circumstances in which we have met and the most friendly reception you gave me. When Humphrey was parted from Mr Thewless as a result of the mishap in the tunnel I felt it right to make what inquiries I could, and then to bring the boy on to his destination. But now I must find my inn. It is said to be most *comfortable*. Indeed, it was strongly recommended to my brother, Sir Charles. Personal recommendation is most important, do you not think? And now I propose to walk to the village, and nobody is to accompany me a single step.'

Delivering herself of this command, Miss Liberty paused as if for a final survey of the scene. Ivor Bolderwood, unaware of the arrival of Mr Thewless, had wandered the length of some fields away, but the occasional pop of the shot-gun told that the boy's education was proceeding. Further off in the same direction could be seen an arm of the sea, and beyond it a promontory running out and up to a commanding eminence from which cliffs dropped sheer to the water below. At this Miss Liberty pointed suddenly and with a decisive finger. 'There must be a very fine view from there,' she said to Mr Bolderwood.

'View?' Her host's gaze went somewhat vaguely after her finger. 'Oh, yes, capital – really capital.'

'Particularly in the morning.' Miss Liberty was now critically taking her bearings by the sun. She turned to Mr Thewless. 'Say at ten o'clock.'

'I beg your pardon?' Fleetingly – he was by now decidedly fatigued – Mr Thewless was aware of something dropping softly into the depths of his mind.

'The shadows,' said Miss Liberty. 'The shadows over the bay must be just right then. Mr Bolderwood, I quite envy you living amid such beauties of Nature. *Good*-bye.'

And Miss Liberty, having shaken hands with some ceremony, walked composedly away.

This departure was the signal for Mr Thewless to be shown to his room – an operation which Mr Bolderwood directed in person, and which involved the services of a surprising number of assistants. The factotum Denis was present in something of the position of an interpreter, reiterating and augmenting the sufficiently considerable volubility of his employer. The lad called Billy Bone bumped about with suitcases. Gracie, having thumped the bed upon which the guest was to repose himself, with results very little to her satisfaction, fell to re-making it amid loud exclamations of indignation and shame. Two further maids appeared with large jugs of hot and cold water, and proceeded with such concentration to the mixing together of these in a basin that Mr Thewless had an alarmed feeling that these maidens, with a positively Homeric simplicity, intended themselves to wash him down there and then. This sense of mild personal insecurity was further increased when an enthusiastic youth, in feature disconcertingly like the traditional Irishman celebrated on comic postcards, slipped deftly behind him and neatly stripped him of his jacket – while at the same moment another lad, possibly a twin to the first, threw himself on the floor and seized Mr Thewless by a leg, although with no more hurtful intention, as it presently appeared, than of depriving him of his shoes and socks. Mr Bolderwood, meanwhile, stamped about the apartment, tugging at curtains which came off their rings, and knobs which came off their drawers, and cupboard doors which came off their hinges. The whole effect was like a page by Smollett or a print after Rowlandson; and Mr Thewless was rather sleepily aware of it as being – although by no means displeasingly – somewhat factitious in character. It was evidently a turn which this retired South American commercial magnate (for Mr Bolderwood, he recalled, was really that) pleased himself with putting up. And although Mr Thewless would certainly have preferred running water, decent seclusion, and drawers from which there was some prospect of extracting shirts and ties without exhausting operations with pocket-knives and shoe-horns, he was nevertheless quite prepared to take this harmless feudal fantasy in good part. Besides, he reflected, it might amuse Humphrey.

Presently, however, Mr Bolderwood brought down the curtain abruptly on the scene by driving his retainers with something approximating to sudden physical violence from the room. Mr Thewless rather expected that he would follow, leaving his guest to pursue his own occasions until summoned to dinner. But Mr Bolderwood simply seated himself comfortably on the faded cretonne of a window-seat – gaining himself thereby a pleasant bath of evening sunshine – and prepared to keep his guest company during his ablutions. 'Soap?' he said. 'Yes, I see the rascals have remembered soap. Our ways are very informal at Killyboffin, very informal indeed. But I assure you, my dear sir, that we are very glad to see you. And I like cousin Bernard's boy. Ivor and he are going to get on admirably. Ivor has a good touch with lads. For my part, I look forward to a very pleasant time while you are with us.' Mr Bolderwood paused, and it appeared to his companion, peering at him from amid an abundant soapy lather, that some shade of doubt momentarily clouded his ingenuous brow. But this instantly explained itself. 'If it wasn't for the eggs,' said Mr Bolderwood. 'Did you ever hear of so outrageous a thing? And when we had positively planned an enormous omelette. I greatly fear that for dinner now we shall have to fall back upon stelk. Do you awfully mind?'

Mr Thewless, reaching for a towel, murmured some inarticulate civility. Conceivably stelk was some very considerable delicacy which his host was heralding with modest disclaimers. But somehow it did not sound altogether promising.

'But, of course, we might have boxty.' Mr Bolderwood brightened. 'Gracie's boxty is very eatable, very eatable indeed. And you'll agree that that's more than can be said for boxty as a general rule.'

Mr Thewless was again inarticulate. He did not think he would care for boxty – whether Gracie's or another's – and moreover he felt a scarcely rational apprehension lest Humphrey, also disliking it, might be prompted to some demonstration as with Lord Buffery and the cream-jug. He was casting round for some means of changing the subject when his host himself did this with some abruptness. 'I say,' he said, 'that old girl – do you think she's all right?'

'All right?' It took Mr Thewless some seconds to realize that this question, which had broken from Mr Bolderwood in a manner betraying considerable inner anxiety, referred to his late travelling-companion. And even when assured of this he was quite at sea as to its bearing. It was his first thought that the lady's morals were being brought to the question; then it occurred to him that it was perhaps her social acceptability, and that Mr Bolderwood was fearful that accident had brought him into too familiar contact with a person of insufficient consideration. But these were both suppositions so absurd as to be untenable. 'I really don't know much about her,' he said. 'But, one way and another, she had a good deal of conversation with Humphrey.'

'That is what I gathered. Did she talk –?' And from his patch of sunshine, Mr Bolderwood looked in sharp interrogation at Humphrey's tutor.

'I thought she talked a lot of dangerous nonsense.'

There was the effect of a good deal of stored-up irritation in Mr Thewless's tone. For a moment Mr Bolderwood appeared to consider it on that basis. 'Ah,' he said.

'Spy stories', said Mr Thewless, 'and stuff of that sort. In ordinary circumstances it would, of course, be harmless enough. But in this particular case –'

Here Mr Thewless hesitated. He was a man who, even when tired, continued to act from delicate feelings; and it went a little against the grain to announce so soon, even to one in whom confidence might quite properly be reposed, his discovery of his pupil's infirmities. In this situation Mr Bolderwood, with a nice tact of which one would not have suspected him in his feudal moments, took the initiative. 'Yes,' he said, 'I gather that Humphrey is a little difficult. A pity in so capable a boy.'

'Exactly!' Mr Thewless was much pleased by this perception. 'The lad is thoroughly capable – which is no more than one would expect of his father's son. Moreover, he is very attractive. Oddly young for his years at times, and yet at other times with a streak of disconcerting precociousness. But thoroughly nice.' Mr Thewless paused, it may be, fleetingly surprised by the decided character of his own sentiments. 'There is no doubt, however, that Humphrey can day-dream himself into some rather alarming world of romantic adventure, with nervous consequences that are by no means desirable. And I was a little annoyed with Miss Liberty – although I don't doubt she is a well-meaning woman enough – for encouraging him. When there was this little hitch in the tunnel, and I was taken off under some absurd misapprehension in that ambulance, it appears that she got hold of a car and drove about the country with the boy looking for me. Heaven knows what melodramatic nonsense they stuffed into each other's heads. And fancies of that sort propagate themselves rather easily.' Mr Thewless paused. 'As a matter of fact, I must confess to have got a little fanciful myself.'

If Mr Bolderwood was at all interested in this tentative confession, his sense of civility prevented him from betraying the fact. 'I quite follow you', he said, 'about what is desirable for the boy. We have, of course, heard about him from Bernard. A little apt to do undisciplined and alarming things.'

'He threw a cream-jug at Lord Buffery.'

Mr Bolderwood received this information for what his guest designed it – a humorous touch on the situation which at the same time staked out a claim for forbearance should any such small untoward incidents occur at Killyboffin. 'I'm afraid', he said, 'that we shall have no distinguished targets of that sort. But I can find Humphrey plenty of common-or-garden ones. I have a dozen rascals about the place for whom the experience would be thoroughly wholesome. Don't, by the way, think of taking that dinner-jacket off its hanger. Our habits are of the simplest here from month's end to month's end.'

By this time Mr Thewless had got used to the engaging familiarity of his host, who sat by him while he changed for all the world as if they had been at school together. So he now responded with unwonted warmth. 'I look forward to my stay with you all the more. Going round doing private tutoring as I do, I get a little tired of formal households.' He smiled. 'Nor would they suit Humphrey. I have an idea that Sir Bernard's rather magnificent manner of living may have rather an oppressive effect where his son is concerned.'

'Quite so.' Mr Bolderwood was now looking in some absence of mind out of the window, rather as if he had detected in the grounds below an illicit attempt to feed the disgraced Killyboffin poultry. 'Hence, no doubt, the running away.'

'The running away?' Mr Thewless was startled.

Mr Bolderwood chuckled. 'Just something that Ivor tells me cousin Bernard mentioned about our young handful – that it wouldn't be surprising if he cut off to sea or joined up with a circus. I suppose boys still do these things from time to time.'

'I see.' Mr Thewless, finding himself a pair of house-slippers in a suitcase, was dimly aware that, in fact, he didn't quite see. 'Well, we must make sure that we are not landed with anything like that.'

'Most certainly we must.' Mr Bolderwood was at once properly emphatic and charmingly amused. 'Although, with exploits of that sort, one never knows, does one?'

'Never knows?' Despite his tardy tea, Mr Thewless was feeling hungry as well as tired, and the combination made him stupid.

'Something was put in my head. *Captains Courageous*, and that sort of thing. I imagine that Humphrey has been a little fussed by his father – I don't intend any serious criticism of Bernard, I need hardly say – and been brought up in an atmosphere of wealth, and formality, and at the same time of abstract and intellectual preoccupations rather depressing to a young mind. A bit of an escapade, and a bit of roughing it, might actually do him a world of good. Of course I may be quite wrong – and you, my dear fellow, have infinitely more experience with lads than I. It need hardly be said that we shall entirely rely upon you for the regulating of Humphrey's ways during your stay.'

This last was altogether a proper declaration. On the strength of it, Mr Thewless was quite prepared to accept in a cordial spirit his becoming his host's dear fellow a little early in the day. And now Mr Bolderwood got to his feet. 'If Humphrey did cast loose,' he said idly, 'it would be a considerable comfort that he has a brain to deal with things.'

Mr Thewless, had he not been engaged in brushing his hair, would certainly have accorded this proposition an emphatic nod. He recalled his pupil's story of the blackmailer – a story which he was still disposed to regard as a little island of true report in the ocean of the unfortunate lad's imaginings. And he decidedly agreed that if a child must be rum he had better be brainy as well.

'You must tell us about your routine; when you want to work with the boy and when you want him taken off your hands. Ivor will be able, and most willing, to give him quite a lot of time. They seem to be getting on very well already. Steady work, plenty of absorbing occupation out of doors – shooting, swimming, and that sort of thing – and, above all, the sense of a quiet, ordered life.' And Mr Bolderwood smiled benevolently on his guest, altogether the understanding and sympathetic host. 'Yes,' he repeated, 'a quiet, ordered life.' He glanced at his watch. 'Damnation!' he shouted –

and charging at Mr Thewless's door, flung it open with the utmost violence, and proceeded bellowing angrily to the staircase across the corridor. Here, hanging hazardously over the battered elegance of a Georgian balustrade which looked as if it had suffered a good deal of Bolderwood impetuosity in its time, he fell to upbraiding the negligence and unpunctuality of his retainers after a fashion which the notable resonance of Killyboffin Hall rendered startlingly effective. Moreover, the cry was presently taken up by Denis somewhere below, and this impudent proposal to transmit rather than receive his master's displeasure so irritated Mr Bolderwood that his own vociferations were redoubled. Mr Thewless was aware of a rather startled Humphrey peering out of the room adjoining his own, and then of the quiet voice of Ivor Bolderwood apparently composing and expediting matters below. Ivor seemed to be without his father's disposition to put on squire-archal turns. Mr Thewless, as he made his way through the din in order to have a little conversation with his pupil, felt that the son of the house might turn out to be someone to rely upon.

Chapter 14

There seemed to be no reason why Humphrey should have been taken by surprise, since Mr Thewless had most meticulously knocked on his door and waited to be called upon to enter. But Humphrey, who, since making his own reconnaissance, had sat down at a small desk by his window, had it seemed responded automatically, with the result that his tutor came upon him making a flurried attempt to thrust an exercise book into a drawer. The drawer, since it was a true Killyboffin drawer, resisted the attempt. Where-upon Humphrey, with considerable presence of mind, dropped the exercise book on the floor, edged it with a deft toe beneath the carpet, and turned to Mr Thewless with a charming smile. 'Hullo,' he said. 'I'm so glad to see they didn't handle you too roughly. Although they *must* have hit you on the head.'

'I was certainly knocked unconscious for a time, my dear Humphrey, when things began falling about us in the tunnel. If it suits you to think that some villain was involved – why, I see no substantial reason why you should not do so.'

As Mr Thewless delivered himself of this indulgent speech it struck him that here was precisely what *did* suit Humphrey. The boy was clearly sur-rounded still by his delusions; his eye and cheek spoke of considerable excitement; and at the same time he looked in much better trim than his tutor had yet known him. Moreover, Mr Thewless could feel a new element – it was a sort of easy benevolence rather reminiscent of Mr Bolderwood – in Humphrey's attitude to him. The boy was no longer disturbed by the fact that his tutor was sceptical; he gave the impression of rather liking him that way. At the moment Mr Thewless was given no leisure to be more than briefly puzzled by this, since Humphrey was very wholesomely intent upon proceeding to dinner. He had changed circumspectly into a dark suit; an insufficiency of soap and water was seemingly not among his numerous personal indisciplines; at the moment he nicely displayed the extravagantly scrubbed and mildly cheerful features which are the orthodox insignia of the well-conducted public schoolboy. Mr Thewless, heartened by this sight and auguring well from it for much dutifully conned French and Latin in the coming quiet and ordered life that his host had promised, fell to teasing Humphrey about his immoderate expectations from the meal they were awaiting. It was Friday, he pointed out, and what had been projected was an omelette. But owing to the ill-regulated conduct of the Killyboffin hens nothing except boxty was likely to meet them below. Humphrey must by no means expect a whopping steak, misled by his insufficient erudition into supposing the word in any way connected with *bulls*; rather that peculiar species of sea-fish sacred to Hermes, the *box* or, βοαξ, so named because of its unfishlike ability to emit a short, plopping noise, gave the true derivation of the word. They would undoubtedly find that boxty was in every sense a wholly fishy dish.

With such gamesome talk as this, immemorial to his kind, did Mr Thewless presently conduct his charge downstairs. An evening breeze had risen, blowing in from the ocean; its effect upon the respectable antiquity of Killyboffin was to set a hundred soft tongues whispering, a thousand tiny creatures moving, all around one in the bare, pervasively dilapidated house. Mr Thewless again remarked that it was a place of considerable size. Everywhere corridors ran off in a dimness of white walls and faded cream paint, with here and there the dark rectangle of an oil painting in which troops of hunters moved obscurely through Italian landscapes which time or the varnish bottle had umbered to a cavernous gloom. The house, moreover, had this peculiarity: that its contents, so soon as one should stray in person or in glance from, as it were, certain narrow channels leading from various inhabited corners to the living-rooms of the family, were for the most part swathed and sheeted after the fashion of large establishments from which the owner has taken his departure for the time. Mr Bolderwood had among his fancies, it appeared, that of living like a caretaker in his own rambling halls, and this although the confused multitude of his retainers would surely have been adequate to the dusting and polishing of the mansion several times over. Moreover, some past Bolderwood had owned a taste in statuary; another had collected armour; a third had been interested in grandfather clocks. All these objects, in common with the chairs, benches, tables, and the like which lined, after the common fashion of ornament rather than utility, the broad corridors of the house, were swathed in a white sheeting from which one could have puffed the dust in passing. The effect could not well be other than spectral. It was as if, in addition to the vociferous Denis and his rout, the place owned another body of inhabitants, who waited, shrouded and silent in the gathering dusk, the stroke of some hour that should release them to their own nocturnal offices. Nor indeed did their silence appear entire, since the wind as it sighed through Killyboffin had the effect of prompting them to sinister confabulation, the result of which was already an uneasy twitch and stir in their enveloping garments.

Mr Thewless, when he remarked this rather uncanny effect, glanced in some anxiety at Humphrey. But at the moment, at least, the boy made nothing of it. He had paused, driven by hunger though he professed to be, by a window on a broad landing, attracted by an equal prospect of sea and mountain there revealed. The gentle declivities by which Killyboffin Hall was surrounded already lay for the most part in shadow, but, on higher ground beyond, the level light of late evening was still brilliant upon emerald fields, white or pink cottages, and, in the farther distance, dun bogs scarred by the darker brown of peat cuttings. Here and there along the dykes and hedges that demarcated the tiny fields lay inexplicable streaks and splashes of colour – orange and crimson and ultramarine – much as if, casually but to a happy effect, an artist had scattered his brightest pigments over the picture.

'Wool,' said Humphrey. 'Isn't that it? They dye it themselves and put it out like that to dry. And look! There's an old woman boiling something up in a cauldron. That must be wool too. And those girls are taking it from her and carrying it on their heads in baskets. I've seen that in Italy. They're taking it to those others to wash in the stream. And – I say! – just look at the hillsides. You'd think they were so empty, and yet there are people all over them. And in those same gorgeous colours too.'

Mr Thewless looked, and saw that all these appearances were as Humphrey had remarked. Everywhere on the hillsides, and to distances that were almost remote, one could pick out slowly moving specks of brilliant colour.

'There's always something happening in an Irish countryside.'

It was Ivor Bolderwood who spoke; he had come up behind them and was looking mildly out through his large glasses. Humphrey turned to him with an alacrity from which Mr Thewless gathered that the young man had substantially gained his pupil's confidence. 'Are these people very poor?' Humphrey asked.

Ivor nodded soberly. 'Very poor indeed, most of them. They have to go miles and miles to the bogs where they can cut peat, and not all of them have even a donkey to bring it home on. And you will see them gathering seaweed as the only manure they can afford for their patches of potatoes. Still, they dye the cloth they make for themselves in those brave colours, and they know a lot of stories and poetry and songs. Some of those bright, moving specks are thinking of no more than their suppers, I expect – as you and I are doing.' Ivor paused and chuckled as Humphrey faintly blushed. 'But the minds of others are moving through old, old poems that nobody, perhaps, has ever written down – poems about kings and heroes and all the sad and splendid things that beautiful women have brought into the world.'

'Is that really true?' Humphrey was round-eyed. 'Could I go among them, and would they tell me, and could I put it in a book?'

Ivor Bolderwood laughed. 'A good many people have tried to do that. And there is a difficult language you would have to learn before you could hope to understand a great deal. But I think some of them might tell you something.'

Humphrey glanced from Ivor to his tutor, and Mr Thewless thought proper to offer an interested and approving murmur. Here, he judged, was a vein of interest altogether more wholesome than anything represented by the boy's current reading, or by the matters on which he conversed with Miss Liberty. 'We shall certainly', he said, 'try to get into conversation with some of them.'

'So long as they don't suppose you to be folk off the trawlers.' And Ivor pointed in the other direction, where from their present height they could just see the masts and funnel of a vessel anchored some way out from a little pier. 'They dislike the way the foreigners, who don't speak even English, often enough, come and eat out the country. But some of these sailors are interesting folk too. There's Viking blood in some of them, and presently they will be off in their dirty little ships to the places from which their ancestors sailed to harry Ireland. In quite a short time that tub out there may have rounded the North Cape, and instead of these tiny Irish fields and cottages the sailors may be seeing the sort of things the Ancient Mariner saw: icebergs and the aurora borealis – or, at this time of year, the midnight sun.'

> 'And ice mast-high came flowing by
> As green as emerald.'

Humphrey, now staring out to sea, quoted the lines shyly but in a glow of pleasure. 'But don't you think the bit about the moon is the best? *The moving moon went up the sky* –' He broke off suddenly. 'Hullo, here's something else. And – I say! – isn't she wizard?'

Round a precipitous headland which bounded the scene – the same from which Miss Liberty had conjectured that there must be a superlative view – there had appeared a vessel which Mr Thewless, unversed in maritime matters, could have defined only as an outsize motorboat. An affair of gleaming white paint and flashing brass, its thrusting bows, flowing lines, and flattened stern suggested formidable speed and power, while the scale upon which it was built seemed indicative of a craft built for blue water. Mr Thewless looked at it with mild but genuine interest, Humphrey with an enthusiasm which this time was a little conventional, Ivor Bolderwood in swift and knowledgeable appraisal. 'She's certainly rather grand,' the last-named said. 'We usually get only the most modest pleasure-craft bothering about Killyboffin.' His fingers drummed for a moment on the window-pane.

'Well, we had better go down, or Denis will have the triumph of announcing dinner before we're all there, after all.' He turned pleasantly to Mr Thewless. 'I do hope that you will get more amusement than annoyance out of our way of things here. We can at least make some interesting expeditions. The pre-Celtic antiquities are numerous, and I have always wanted to go over them with an authority.'

Mr Thewless was pleased. That an amateur in Roman archaeology was competent to pronounce upon the monuments of prehistoric Ireland was assuredly something that young Ivor Bolderwood was much too well informed to suppose. But the success of this sort of compliment lies all in its manner, and at the end of his exhausting day (or what he supposed to himself to be its end) Mr Thewless found himself sitting down to dinner with feelings of considerable pleasure in the society of his hosts.

Nor, he presently discovered, was the dinner itself such as to depress the spirits. Although the boxty was certainly in evidence, it was given more prominence by the elder Mr Bolderwood in his conversation than by Denis as he handed the dishes; and Mr Thewless was more aware of the excellence of the salmon and the perfection of the hock. His host, it is true, was still much troubled about the eggs, and supposed that for breakfast it was impossible that they should have anything but siot or skirlie-mirlie. Ivor, while he refrained from disputing this, pointed to the sustaining fact that in four days they would undoubtedly be eating grouse – and grouse, moreover, which they should owe to Humphrey's rapidly increasing skill with a shot-gun. And at this Humphrey, who not much more than twenty-four hours before had been repudiating with vast humanitarian indignation the suggestion that he should slaughter living things, and who after that again had been clutching the same weapon as a resource against imaginary spies and assassins, produced in high pleasure the modest disclaimers proper in well-mannered persons of his age. Mr Thewless felt eminently satisfied, and his various meaningless alarms, together with the absurd but harmless conduct of the men with the ambulance, altogether assumed their proper proportions in his mind. He had discovered that Killyboffin was on the telephone, and he had thus been able to send a telegram to Sir Bernard Paxton, informing him of the safe arrival of his son. And when he considered Humphrey's present equable state, and remembered the sort of dire intelligence which at one time he had been persuaded it might be necessary to despatch to his father, he saw how much he himself must at one point have been thrown off his balance. Humphrey, it was true, was still going to be nervously disturbed and thoroughly difficult from time to time; Mr Thewless stood in no doubt as to that. But Ivor Bolderwood was going to be an excellent person to take part of the strain; already he was absorbing the boy's interest with well-informed talk about remote places and peoples; he was much what Mr Thewless himself aspired to be: simultaneously instructive and entertaining.

Nevertheless, Mr Thewless, despite his own sense of nervous relaxation, presently found himself wondering whether Humphrey was not up to his tricks again. There are children in whose presence small objects are liable to drop inexplicably off the mantelpiece, or to levitate in air and glide quaintly to another corner of the room. But in the presence of his pupil, Mr Thewless had come to believe, it was rather the furniture of the mind that was apt to suffer disconcerting small displacements; and he was by no means certain that something of the sort was not now beginning to tinge the consciousness of his elder companions. It was possible, again, that the boy had produced this effect not merely telepathically but by some direct communication to Ivor Bolderwood during their first ramble with the shot-gun. Perhaps he had assured his newly-found cousin that during his journey from London he had been the interesting centre of sundry alarming melodramatic adventures. And perhaps Ivor, abundantly sensible as he appeared to be, had been a little shaken by the odd conviction which Humphrey had the trick of importing into his fantasies.

It was certainly true that Ivor, in spite of his competence as an entertainer, was unable to keep some part of his thoughts from straying elsewhere. It was as if he felt intermittently impelled to fine calculation on some state of affairs altogether unforeseen. Perhaps Humphrey had indeed told him a vast deal of nonsense and he was debating with himself whether the boy's tutor was likely to have received the same absurd confidences; and, if not, whether he was the sort of man with whom a difficult situation might usefully be discussed. And this reading of the matter Mr Thewless was for a time the more inclined to in that he had very markedly the sense of being appraised. Miss Liberty herself in fact, fixing upon him her wholly enigmatical eye, had scarcely given him this uncomfortable feeling more strongly. He was reminded that he was, after all, a mere substitute for Captain Cox, that favoured young man whom some intimate bereavement had removed at the last moment from the scene. It was natural that his hosts should be disposed to wonder whether Sir Bernard Paxton's second choice was a reliable man for his job.

But this chastening reflection was presently replaced by another. It became evident as Mr Thewless's perceptions sharpened themselves under the material recruitment afforded by Mr Bolderwood's table that if considerations of this sort were active in Ivor's mind so too were others of a different order. To what might be termed the atmospheric effects of Killyboffin – the genius of the place for disconcerting suggestions of murmured colloquy, stealthy movement, and all the imponderables commonly associated with edifices of much greater antiquity – the young man must be abundantly inured. It was natural, when the night wind, flapping the worn carpets in remote corridors or tinkling somewhere in abandoned candelabra, suggested the rapid tread and clinking accoutrements of some army of invading dwarves, or the rattle of some mouldering upper casement sounded like a discharge of small arms, that Mr Thewless himself should feel a certain irrational disposition to glance over his shoulder. But it was surprising that Ivor Bolderwood should indefinably betray a similar tendency, or convey, by a certain wariness of regard upon door and window, an obscure apprehension of physical insecurity. A poet, Humphrey had declared, should keep a sword upstairs; Ivor's manner, even as he conversed absorbingly about the Sahara and the Caribbean, betrayed some sense that it might be useful to have one under the table. And at this a horrid doubt came to Mr Thewless. He feared that Ivor – whose talk, after all, hinted at an imagination romantic in cast – might, despite his appearance of eminent good sense, prove to be such another as Miss Liberty – one with whom he would have to wrestle in the task of keeping cobweb and chimera out of Humphrey's head.

But at least it was different with the elder Mr Bolderwood. Despite the strain of fancy revealed in his manner of life at Killyboffin, his mind appeared to be of a reassuringly solid cast, and the only disturbance to which it was at present subject was one still connected with his recalcitrant poultry. A fourth glass of hock had produced in this matter something like the dawn of illumination, and it was becoming clear to him that he was confronted, not with an unnatural and unseasonable continence on the part of the creatures concerned, but simply with a new and monstrous instance of the worthlessness and dishonesty of his retainers. It was his misfortune to be subjected by these to every species of robbery and extortion, and now they were taking the very eggs out of his guests' mouths – doubtless to sell them at unreasonable prices to the black marketeers, smugglers, and bandits by whom the whole countryside was now overrun. Not since the heyday of the Troubles, indeed, had a wellnigh universal lawlessness so prevailed; housebreaking had become common and arson might be expected to spring up again at any time. For two pins he would return to South America or settle in some atrocious part of Surrey.

This comparatively harmless talk was for the most part directed to Mr Thewless. Humphrey, engaged with Ivor, clearly gave no heed to it. And thus dinner passed comfortably enough. It was followed, as a preliminary to packing Humphrey off to bed, by a stroll upon the terrace. Mr Thewless found the ritual a trifle chilly, and he judged that the tumbledown statuary, dimly revealed by a moon now in its last quarter, was depressing rather than picturesque. Behind the house the sough of the ocean could be faintly heard; sparsely on the hillsides, and to an effect of great loneliness, there gleamed a yellow light from cottage windows; periodically the beam from a lighthouse on some adjacent headland swept over the uppermost story of the house and passed on like a hunter's noose that has failed to snare its prey. Humphrey was delighted with the effect, and at this Mr Thewless found himself being foolishly relieved. The truth was, he realized, that he had fallen into the way of being unnecessarily apprehensive as to what might alarm his pupil's sensibilities and precipitate undesirable imaginative repercussions. He was the more startled, therefore, at the sudden starting up of what might well have proved disastrous in this regard.

The Bolderwoods, father and son, had fallen behind together for domestic discussion, and Mr Thewless was about to make some remark to Humphrey about the possibility of one day visiting the lighthouse that was at play above them, when the voice of the elder Mr Bolderwood was heard clearly behind them in tones of characteristic incautious exasperation.

'Bless my soul, Ivor! You don't mean to tell me that the imbeciles have put the boy in the haunted room?'

Mr Thewless, appalled by this luckless stroke of fate, glanced swiftly at Humphrey and saw that mischief had indeed been done. The boy looked thoroughly alarmed. But in a second Ivor had overtaken them, and laid his hand on Humphrey's shoulder with a cheerful laugh. 'Humphrey', he said, 'would give quite a lot for the chance of sleeping in a haunted room! But, as a matter of fact, I rather want to move him to the one next my own. Shall you mind, Humphrey? It means that we can slip out quite early with the guns, and nobody need be disturbed.'

'Excellent!' Mr Thewless had the wit instantly to back up this deft sparing of his pupil's *amour propre*. 'I should hate to be wakened up by Humphrey and his gun bumping about together next door to *me*. And perhaps you will be able to bring something back for breakfast.'

Ivor laughed again. 'To eke out the skirlie-mirlie? Perhaps we shall. Well, come along, and we'll make the move now.'

And at this the party returned to the house and, without calling upon menial assistance, transferred an evidently relieved Humphrey to his new quarters. There he was bidden good night, and Mr Thewless was carried off by his hosts to desultory conversation and a generous provision of Irish whiskey in Mr Bolderwood's study. At eleven o'clock Mr Bolderwood announced that he proposed to lock up the house.

This proved to be an occupation of some labour, and began with the securing of a door which shut off the servants' quarters – an out-of-the-way proceeding sufficiently explained by Mr Bolderwood's whimsical conviction of the unreliability and dishonesty of those who attended him. There was then much bolting of other doors and securing of windows – and this again was unremarkable in one who believed the countryside to be alive with robbers. Mr Thewless, however – although by this time thoroughly sleepy, slightly fuddled and only intermittently attentive – was mildly surprised when his host proceeded to make a thorough search of the house. In this operation, which was rendered considerably more troublesome by the fact that the only artificial light at Killyboffin was supplied by oil-lamps and candles, Mr Bolderwood was assisted by his son with rather more vigour than was necessary simply for the purpose of humouring an eccentric parent. Whether the proceeding was customary, and with a rational basis in the apprehension of robbery, or whether it was a matter of the tiresome imaginative aura of Humphrey Paxton at work once more, was a question that Mr Thewless was now much too tired to entertain. When the Bolderwoods had satisfied themselves that reasonable security reigned at Killyboffin he took up his candle, bade his hosts good night, and took himself thankfully to bed.

Chapter 15

It was the healthful custom of Mr Thewless to sleep with his window open to its fullest extent. When he had undressed, therefore, he extinguished the lamp which had been burning in his room, drew back his curtains, and threw open the casement. The waning moon was hidden in cloud and the night was almost completely dark; he had the sense, rather than the perception, of standing at a considerable elevation, and he remembered that what was commanded from this aspect of the house must be a view of the sea. A single light was visible at a distance not easy to determine; presently he distinguished that this was faintly reflected in water; and it occurred to him that it might well represent a riding-light on the motor cruiser noticed by Humphrey before dinner. There was still a chilly breeze, and Mr Thewless climbed without more ado into bed. He had been not without fears, reasonably bred by the marked unreliability of the furniture around him, that the night might bring discomforts of its own. He found, however, that the bed was in excellent order and soothingly sheeted in the finest linen. As he tumbled in, he became aware of a dim radiance gliding smoothly across the ceiling of his room. It must be the faint reflection of the beam from the lighthouse that he had previously remarked as touching the upper part of the house. The effect was too slight to be disturbing. Within a minute Mr Thewless was asleep.

It would have been no more than fair had his late vicissitudes earned him a full night's oblivion. But his undisturbed sleep was of short duration, and was succeeded by uneasy and perplexing dreams. In these he was himself at first the only living participant and he moved amid a décor which his waking consciousness – as we have seen, nicely informed in such matters – would have assured him reflected the alarms and dismays which had attended a singularly frightening episode of his career undertaken jointly with his mother some fifty years before. Painful progressions through narrow tunnels, terrifying drops through space, sudden assaults upon eye and ear by unanalysable lights and sounds, the dread presage of unknown modes of being: all these things, in a confusion somewhat suggestive of the best modern music, formed as it were the overture to his nocturnal drama. And then it was as if the curtain rose and slowly, with a careful regard for the sluggish understanding of the audience, the actors appeared one by one. The first of these was Mr Thewless himself, aware – and surprised, but only mildly so, at his awareness – that he was no longer very substantially Mr Thewless, since he had assumed the vastly more distinguished role or identity of Sir Bernard Paxton. Mr Thewless having become Sir Bernard, and having gained thereby an insight into Sir Bernard, remarked that Sir Bernard (who was himself) was by no means so impressive a spectacle when viewed from within as he (Mr Thewless, that was to say) had found him when viewed from without. In particular he was prone to behave in an indecisive and timorous fashion when confronted by heights. And this was the position now. In a vast, void darkness Thewless-Paxton trod falteringly the brink of some unimaginable precipice. Far below shone a single light dimly reflected in dreadful waters; to a sickening plunge towards this he felt himself irresistibly impelled; his head swam, his knees gave way beneath him and he fell. But from the darkness a strong arm stretched out and held him and, turning in air, he recognized that his preserver was Humphrey Paxton, who was his son. Again he trod the precipice, the boy holding his hand and guiding him as he went, and presently their path through darkness began to rock and pulse beneath them. It was a path no longer, but the corridor of an express train, its outer side cut away to expose them to the hurtling night, its inner giving upon a series of compartments through the glass of which there gibbered and mowed monsters and prodigies in endless sinister diversity. But in every compartment too sat Ivor Bolderwood – always in the same corner an Ivor Bolderwood, his glance composed and direct through his large round glasses, in his lap a bowl of boxty from which he ceaselessly fed the horrors around him with a long-handled wooden spoon. But whether Ivor was master of the rout or whether he was in their thrall Mr Thewless could by no means determine as the boy hurried him onwards down the interminable train, his lips parted and his eyes, bright with challenge, fixed upon some distant and shrouded goal.

The dream seemed interminable: always the monsters, always an Ivor, always the swaying corridor beneath the feet. Once Mr Thewless turned his head and behind him saw the bearded man with pebble glasses, in his hand a bludgeon raised and prepared to strike. But even as Mr Thewless shrank in anticipation of the blow the bearded man was transformed into Mr Wambus, swathed and powerless in his bandages, like a corpse in some old picture. Once – and once only – the dread monotony of the teeming compartments was varied, and Mr Thewless glimpsed the solitary figure of Miss Liberty, a volume by Sapper in her lap. But her face was blank and sightless; or rather – he realized with a chill of sudden horror – it was no face at all, but simply the dial of a clock from which the hands had been wrenched so as to render it useless.

And now the unending train was devouring not only space but time as well; it was hurtling at such speed through aeons of time that Mr Thewless recognized in a rhythmic sweep of light and darkness about him an actual procession of nights and days. And suddenly he knew the destination of the train. It was hurtling towards the sun. This was the goal upon which the eyes of the boy who still guided and supported him were set; ahead was nothing but empty space, with that vast conflagration at the end. And then it was before him – burning, incandescent light. Mr Thewless felt the leap and lick of its vast tongues of flame upon his brow. He woke up.

Mr Thewless woke up and on his retina there glowed and swam a single orb of orange fire. He stared at it and instantly, from its voyaging place a thousand million miles away, his mind made a wonderful leap at objective fact. Somebody had shone an electric torch in his face. Hence the sun as terminus to that unending journey; hence now this fading spot of colour on his brain. And this realization was followed by another almost as immediate. The swift procession of nights and days through which his dream had moved as over a chequer-board of darkness and light had also been physically determined. It was dark now; presently there would pass over his ceiling the faint illumination from the lighthouse. In this illumination it would be possible to *see*.

Yet long before that tiny wash of light swept into the room he knew by some sufficient instinct what would be revealed by it. Watchers stood beside his bed, waiting in absolute stillness to know whether their inspection had aroused him. Mr Thewless kept his eyes shut and opened all his ears. A soft breathing was unquestionably distinguishable on either side of him.

The humble creatures that turn immobile at danger, and whom not even a thrusting stick or nudging toe can stir to any sign of life, have no monopoly of this primitive notion of self-protection. Mr Thewless had a very strong impulse simply to lie still, keep his eyes shut, and trust that the mysterious presences would depart. Indeed, this was less a proposal of his mind, a plan or craft to act on, than simply something that was happening to his body as it lay. Cautiously he endeavoured to flex a knee and was by no means convinced that he had the power to do so. He wondered if he could even open his mouth, and he remembered those worst nocturnal terrors of childhood in which there is reft from one the power of calling out.

And Mr Thewless endeavoured to seek security by returning into his dream. In his dream there had been safety amid innumerable hazards because . . . yes, because he had been in the charge of Humphrey Paxton. And suddenly, with an agility altogether surprising, Mr Thewless leapt out of bed. For Humphrey Paxton was *his* charge; he was responsible for the safety of the boy; and to hesitate in the face of undefined danger was to cling ignobly to the topsy-turvy realm of sleep. It might be by his own bedside that threatening figures hovered. Nevertheless, he knew himself to be a person of no consequence, and if they did so hover there this was merely incidental in some way to a design against the boy. Therefore it was the boy's safety that was to be seen to.

Thus did Mr Thewless for the moment bring wisdom from his dream. He leapt from his bed, aware of startled movement on either side of him, and by some paranormal sense of direction also dredged up from sleep, precipitated himself across and out of the room. In an instant he was at the next door, and as he opened it and entered the dim illumination from the lighthouse swept across it. It was, of course, empty and the bed undisturbed; his mind in prompting him to sudden action had missed a step, and he had forgotten about Humphrey's having been moved to another part of the house. He paused irresolutely, and as action failed him fear returned. There *were* people in his own room. It was a testing moment – and the more so because he saw before him a rational yet surely craven plan. The door on which his hand now rested had a key on its inner side. In an instant he could lock himself in, and from the refuge thus obtained raise a loud alarm. In a sense this was even his wisest, his most responsible, course. For if he returned to encounter the intruders alone it was very possible that he might be instantly and silently overpowered, and the villains might then achieve with impunity whatever further mischief they proposed.

But as these sensible considerations presented themselves to Mr Thewless's mind something altogether more potent and primitive stirred in his blood. Sapper, it might be said, and not simple sapience took control; a glorious anger sang suddenly in his ears; he took a deep breath and marched back to his own room. The corridor which he had briefly to traverse was for the moment sufficiently lit through some skylight to make observation possible to his sharpened sense. Nothing stirred in the long vista it presented. The intruders must be awaiting him in his own room still.

Mr Thewless belonged to a clerkly caste whose immemorial weapon has been words. As he took the half-dozen further steps that would confront him with the enemy he absurdly tested out on his inner ear some form of words that would confound them. He would point out that they had been detected, that the household contained a considerable number of able-bodied men, that firearms were available to these and – since prevarication was surely permissible in a situation like the present – that the police had already been summoned by telephone. But at the same time as he prepared this mere logomachy he had the good sense to wish himself possessed of a poker or even an empty bottle. And in default of anything of the sort, he clenched his fists in a manner suggesting itself to him as the right posture for pugilistic encounter and walked into his room.

He was standing in the middle of it and nothing had happened. The glint of light came and went, revealing seeming emptiness. He walked boldly to his bedside and lit his candle. Still nothing revealed itself. He searched, and satisfied himself that he was alone. And at that, feeling slightly giddy, he sat down on the bed.

Deep in the mind there is a clock that never goes wrong. Hypnotists can exploit it as an alarm, enjoining one to blow one's nose at four twenty-five next Thursday. Of this instrument, which is said to work with particular nicety during sleep, Mr Thewless was still sufficiently possessed to have an instinctive assurance that the interval during which he had been in Humphrey's late room was insufficient to have permitted anyone to escape down the corridor. He stood up and had a second look under his bed. He crossed to the window and satisfied himself that no creature not possessed of wings could have departed that way with any hope of an unbroken neck. And at this he sat down again upon his bed, possessed by a new alarm. The nature of this may be guessed. He feared that his imagination had been playing tricks with him – and doing so with more resounding success than any substantial sanity would have allowed. He was now resigned to believing himself highly susceptible to melodrama viewed as a sort of infection or plague, and even to the hypothesis – nebulous but nevertheless haunting – that he and his pupil were in some degree of *rapport* in matters of the sort. Yes, that would be it. Humphrey had been having a nightmare on the lines upon which his fantasy commonly ran, and the shadow of it had fallen upon himself at the other end of the house. But at least Humphrey, whether or not he too had actually awakened to the conviction of lurking presences, had not made night hideous with his alarms; and Mr Thewless was thankful that he had himself at the critical moment at least managed to refrain from doing this. Assuredly it had all been a figment. The only thing to do was to go to sleep again.

His candle afforded only the most feeble illumination, but when he turned to light the oil lamp which had stood at the bottom of his bed he found that in his hasty rising he had overturned it and knocked it to the floor. This was both tiresome and embarrassing, as was also the evidence of an extreme of terrified violence with which he must have acted. For his bed was in quite surprising confusion, its various furnishings tumbled around it and a heavy mattress, of the kind comfortably constructed with an interior springing, dragged cornerwise to the floor. This he now set about remedying, an apparently simple if vexatious task which presently revealed itself as an unexpected difficulty. At first he made considerable progress, only to find upon scrutiny that he had employed as an under sheet what was demonstrably some species of linen coverlet. To leave matters so disposed might be to excite surprise and even ridicule in Mr Bolderwood's domestics in the morning. He therefore started again. But this time he could find no sheets at all; the candle was burning unnervingly near its socket; and for a moment he paused between irritation and discouragement.

In this pause his conscience stirred. If it was indeed true that his recent alarming experience was no more than a sympathetic response to some nightmare or even hallucination of Humphrey's was it not his duty to inform himself as to the boy's condition now? That Humphrey had raised no outcry was a fact capable of a distressing equally with a reassuring interpretation. Indeed, the fact that this abnormal experience had come to his tutor as some sort of message from another mind was surely an indication of that mind's having been perilously disturbed. And Mr Thewless had a sudden and vivid picture of the unfortunate child, prone to believe in sinister powers intent to shut him up in dark, confined spaces, lying strained and motionless in a bed round which he believed these powers to have gathered for a final onslaught. Humphrey's removal to another part of the house had not left him altogether happy – not because he judged Ivor Bolderwood other than in every way reliable, but because it was to himself, after all, that the boy had been confided, and it was he, again, who was best acquainted with the distresses to which he was liable.

There was, then, nothing for it. He must go at once and see how Humphrey was getting on. If the boy proved to be peacefully sleeping there would be no harm done. And Mr Thewless, taking up his stump of candle in his holder, opened his door once more. As he did so, he remembered *why* Humphrey had been moved out of his first room. It was because he had unfortunately been let overhear the elder Mr Bolderwood remark that it was haunted.

Had Mr Thewless been asked if he believed in ghosts, he would have replied at some length, and in a fashion altogether philosophical or scientific. But all this would have boiled down to the statement that he *did*. Supernatural appearances were for him, in theory, an essentially harmless and highly interesting class of phenomena, for long – most unfortunately – merely vestigial in human experience, from an intelligent study of which it might be possible to draw important conclusions on the growth and structure of the human mind. Thus if manifestations of this order lurked in Humphrey's late room; if it had been anything of the sort that had intruded upon himself; if, out in the corridor now, forces aside from the common order of Nature waited patiently for any move Mr Thewless might make: if these things were so the circumstance was to be regarded essentially in the light of a 'find'. A philologist who stumbles upon some substantial vestige of a dying language, or an anthropologist who peers over a rock and surprises some last rehearsal of the immemorial ceremonies of a vanishing tribe, presented – again in theory – a fair parallel to Mr Thewless's situation now. And yet he did not feel quite like this. Killyboffin Hall showed several aspects to the world, and if the one predominant among these was benign, being represented by the cheerful irascibility and muddle of its owner, there was yet another which was distinctly inimical to the easy poise of highly educated persons. The mere manner in which the winds blew through the place, and the diversity of odd acoustic effects they produced, were things in themselves discomposing. The recurrent washes of faint light through this upper story, like an infinitely distant reflection of the flicker and flare of some infernal bonfire, brought another sense into the service of unsettlement. And again – for by this time Mr Thewless had got himself fairly into the corridor – there was the powerful tide of suggestion that seemed to sweep in from the untenanted quarters of the house, from the vistas of shrouded objects – or, better, forms that every branching corridor and open door revealed. Into one of these – it was some piece of sheeted statuary which, unaccountably, he had not noticed before – he almost bumped as he turned left from his room and addressed himself to the task, not altogether simple, of making his way to Humphrey's new quarters.

There was a staircase to go down and presently another to ascend, with some stretch of corridor intervening and at either end. But he was now, he believed, thoroughly awake, and he set off confidently enough. If his wandering disturbed his hosts he might look a little foolish, but it was reasonable to suppose that they would accept his explanations sympathetically. And at least there seemed to be no possibility of a tiresome encounter with wakeful servants, since one of Mr Bolderwood's whims had effectively barred these from the main part of the building. He advanced, therefore, with his candlestick held before him, his free hand shielding as effectively as possible its uncertain flame. He had, he presently discovered, forgotten to bring his matches, so that an extinguishing puff of wind might be awkward unless he cared to go back and remedy the omission. But this he found himself obscurely disinclined to do. And the candle, for that matter, seemed not vital to him, for all along this corridor, and over the stair-head which he now glimpsed dimly before him, there still through sundry uncurtained windows played the intermittent gleam from the lighthouse – as also, he now noticed, a steady and yet more tenuous illumination which spoke of the waning moon as having emerged from cloud.

All this was almost cheerful. Nevertheless, Mr Thewless, his recent experiences having been as they were, would have been insensitive indeed had he not powerfully owned an impulse to peer warily about him as his bare feet (he had not paused for slippers or dressing-gown) felt cautiously over the expanses of worn carpet which he trod. First there was a line of large pictures so darkened that they might have been windows giving upon a starless night; his candle as he passed fleetingly conjured from their lower margins, above the dull gleam of tarnished gold frames, marble steps, the nether folds of flowing draperies, broken lances, and abandoned armour, here and there a human limb splayed out in some martial disaster or, it might be, voluptuous excess. These appearances were unalarming in themselves; yet their suggestion of violent matters transacting themselves just beyond his present circumscribed field of vision was not without its effect upon Mr Thewless, and irrational apprehensiveness would doubtless have gained upon him again even had it not been for the sudden appearance of the dog.

It was a creature that swept him back at once into that world of prodigies within which his railway journey had for a time submerged him; this less because of its evident ferocity as it stood suddenly and solidly before him than because of its unnatural size. It was a dog quite as big – and that in the sense of quite as *tall* – as Mr Thewless himself; and it seemed to have sprung from nowhere in this silent house and to be regarding the pyjama'd figure before it much in the light of a wholly unexpected nocturnal snack. In this crisis Mr Thewless's brain worked very well. From the size of the animal he concluded that it was extinct; if it was extinct it was stuffed; and a stuffed dog needs no collops. Nevertheless, the intellectual conviction that he was merely in the presence of a pretty museum specimen of the ancient Irish wolf-hound did not altogether end the matter. There was a glint in the creature's verisimilar glass eye that almost defied the reassuring voice of reason; and it was from the moment of this encounter that Mr Thewless looked not merely about him but *behind*. The stuffed hound remained harmlessly immobile, but it had done its work.

Mr Thewless looked nervously over his shoulder, and the motion bred the instant suspicion that he was being followed. This too was something against which reason's voice spoke loudly enough. Certainly there was no occasion to suppose that anything *physical* was following him, since he had concluded that, in the first instance, nothing physical had been involved. Moreover, the light was for the moment adequate for a careful inspection, and there was demonstrably nothing in the long corridor behind him except the now foreshortened pictures, and the stern of the stuffed dog, and a number of those sheeted objects – statues, armour, or whatever – which were pervasive about the house. Mr Thewless paused for a moment to convince himself of the folly of this latest feeling; then, without again turning his head, he marched on to the head of the stairs he must descend.

But now his ears were only all too open, and Killyboffin was suddenly alive for him with whisperings, soft footfalls, muffled groans, and all the hackneyed gamut – as he desperately told himself – of conventional supernatural solicitation. He had only, he felt, to allow credulity another inch to its tether and there would at once be added to these the final banality of dismally clanking chains. He was at the stair-head; a half-turn was topographically essential to his further progress; *one* more look behind, therefore, he might venture without too gross a capitulation to his own senseless doubts. Arguing thus, he looked – and the result ought to have been wholly reassuring. The corridor was empty still; only the same objects met his scrutiny. And yet he was at once – and as he had not yet been – alarmed. There was a sense in which this new trepidation could not be called baseless, since he was convinced that it was occasioned by some specific fact. But what this was he was unable to determine; turning face forwards once more and taking his first step downstairs, he was aware only of the uncomfortable fact of water creeping in a chill trickle down his spine. And at the same time there seeped into mind an anecdote of the most extreme inconsequence. It was that of the bishop who, glancing into a field, remarked casually that it contained a hundred and eight sheep – a circumstance presently verified by the computations of his curate. The point of the story, as Mr Thewless knew, lay in the fact that the number of objects that the normal mind can instantaneously enumerate is five. But if the point was tenuous the application was more so, and by the time that he was half-way down the first flight of stairs the mental image accompanying this odd reminiscence had been replaced by a melting succession of others, dredged up from childhood, in which, behind unfortunate persons benighted in dark forests, there peeped and crept maleficent goblin bands.

Almost, he saw himself presently in panic flight through the sleeping house; and it was as a rudimentary test of self-control that he now stopped by the staircase-window as if to look at his leisure into the night. But this pause was more definitive than anything that had happened yet, so absolutely was the sense it brought him of other entities pausing too. Yes, behind him *they* had stopped because he had stopped; and when he moved on *they* would move on too.

To allow his apprehensions to crystallize in this way around a pronoun so consecrated in a popular consciousness to expressing the menace of the unknown was, he very well knew, a step towards disintegration steeper than any he now trod again to reach the lower corridor. The wind – although he had a sense that, outside, it had almost died away – continued to prowl the house, and only the more eerily because now its operations were to be apprehended only by the tip of the senses. If the pattering footfalls were softer it was because, at some sinister crisis, they were approaching with additional stealth; if the breeze no longer flapped at one's pyjamas it was the more possible to feel it as the chill breath of some sepulchral phantom on one's neck.

Gaining the lower corridor, he found a deeper darkness. Here the sweep of the lighthouse was without effect, and only the faintest glint of moonlight percolated through a line of windows on his right hand. His candle, now all but guttering, had become vital to him; were it to go out he could only grope. For some yards he pressed forward rapidly – but not too rapidly, lest the little flame should be extinguished by the wind of his own speed. The corridor was much like that above, with the same embrowned paintings and shrouded statuary and ranged furniture along the walls. Once more he stopped and looked back. And this time it was as if he had caught the presences in the act, for his eye had surely glimpsed some suddenly arrested movement, some swiftly frozen gesture, in the short vista behind him. Again he thought of the bishop and the sheep, and this time the association tentatively explained itself. Had he – all instantaneously, with the speed of the unconscious mind – computed the number of the objects dispersed behind him, and found that they held no tally with a similar unconscious computation made upon his previous traversing of the ground? He was moving forward again before this speculation, in the circumstances highly creditable to his intellectual vitality, had fully formed itself in his mind; when it had done so he took some steps further and this time swung round with all the speed he could contrive. The issue of this manoeuvre, which precisely reproduced the ancient playground game of Grandmother's Steps or Fox and Geese, was at once successful and completely disastrous. It was successful because the shadowing presences did not on this occasion freeze into immobility with adequate speed – so that indeed, were the game being played according to the rules, Mr Thewless would have achieved the decisive stroke of returning them to their 'base'. What in fact he saw was two sheeted figures, entirely ghostly after the prescriptions of Christmas pantomime, hastily assume the postures appropriate to objects of statuary shrouded after the bizarre Killyboffin fashion. This untoward spectacle, as it were inverse to those which gratified Pygmalion and liquidated Don Juan, he had no opportunity to probe, for the disaster attendant upon his whirling round was as decisive as it was inevitable. His candle went out.

Were Mr Thewless's adventures in the hands of what is called an atmospheric writer, it might be possible to credibilize a fact which, as matters stand, can only be baldly stated. Killyboffin in the small hours had now wrought upon Humphrey Paxton's tutor to such a degree that, while retaining considerable power of rational thought, he was lamentably confused about the probable nature of the entities behind him; about the order of being, as it may be put, to which they belonged. Had he been convinced that they were human marauders, mere breakers-in such as his host was apprehensive of, the problem presented, even if uncomfortable, would have been comparatively simple. Correspondingly, had he kept clearly in focus the concept or theory of supernatural appearances, he would have been able to regain something of the poise of the open-minded, the speculative man. But all that Mr Thewless could now predicate of the forces behind him was this: that they stood for Danger.

But the peril was whose? For Mr Thewless, standing as he was in darkness and with his enemies creeping up behind, the achieving of this question was what the thoughtful reader will already have recognized it as being: a signal triumph of the mind. Were he being pursued with intent to silence him before an alarm could be given, this could have been done long ago – and with greater advantage while he was still substantially remote from the other occupants of the mansion. If, on the other hand, the constitution of his pursuers was such that they were without the power to command physical agencies, and must work their malign will by a mere operation of terror upon the mind, they would surely do better to bar the way between Mr Thewless and the moral support which he would gain by making his way to his friends. It seemed not their object, then, either to offer him direct violence or to lead or drive him into the prescriptive hazards of precipice, flood, or bog. They were, in the strictest sense, trailing him. They were, and with all the unobtrusivenes at their command, keeping him in view until his present pilgrimage through the house was completed.

In other words, Humphrey was the quarry. Mr Thewless did not, it must be repeated, at all clearly formulate the quarry of *what*; nor did he, standing with his extinguished candle while the house muttered and whispered around him, endeavour to relate this conviction to what had hitherto been his overriding sense of the total situation in which, with the boy, he had involved himself. He simply knew that it was the boy that was threatened. And he knew that this knowledge, held securely as gospel for the time, imposed upon him a complete reversal of his present plan. For it was a clear inference from what had been revealed to him that these sinister powers were without knowledge of where Humphrey was now lodged. They had penetrated to – or was it conjured themselves into apprehensible shape in? – the haunted room from which Ivor Bolderwood had caused him to be removed; failing to find him there they had taken a cast next door and so disturbed his tutor; they had now divined the injudicious purpose by which that tutor was at present actuated, and proposed simply that he should lead them where they wanted to go. There was thus for Mr Thewless only one course consonant with the safety of his charge. He must turn round in the darkness now enveloping him; march, or grope, straight past, or upon, his adversaries; and so return to his own room.

In this formidable posture of his affairs it would be ungenerous to say that he was frightened; what chiefly confronted him was the rudimentary business of getting his limbs to obey the entirely unequivocal dictates of his will. For in this episode of nightmare (and it did occur to him, indeed, positively to wonder whether he might not, in point of ultimately comforting fact, be at this moment simply if unsoundly asleep) – in this episode of nightmare he found himself for a struggling moment circumstanced as in certain veritable nightmares of long ago. In these, which drew their material, he had been accustomed to believe, from an early and soon exhausted interest in the mechanism of the homely 'tram', he had been wont to find himself, at sufficiently awkward moments, rooted to the ground as if by the agency of some magnet powerfully reinforced by electrical means. And this was his situation now. Neither his right foot nor his left was prepared to accept the hazard of detaching itself from the worn carpeting to which it was clamped. Mr Thewless, in the fullest sense of the slangy phrase, was 'in a fix'.

What came to his rescue was the decidedly chilly quality of the night to one attired exiguously for slumber. Mr Thewless sneezed. And at this the charm was miraculously broken. He found himself advancing, with what confidence was possible in a medium between the Cimmerian and the Stygian, in the direction that he wished to go. From the mere fact of this, unpromising though in some aspects it seemed, there was more than a grain of confidence to be extracted; and this less desperate mood was now reinforced by more factors than one. He had the impression that in the darkness in front of him his tergiversation was the occasion of perturbed conference; of a whispering suggesting that, whether his adversaries were creatures in or out of nature, his so decided move had, at least for the moment, 'got them guessing'. Moreover, it occurred to him that his candlestick, being of the massive and ornamental rather than of the utilitarian or dormitory kind, was by no means rendered entirely useless to him by reason of the temporary desuetude of its primary function. By reversing it in his grasp so that its heavy base was at a farthest remove from his hand, and exalting in air the makeshift bludgeon thus achieved, he could provide himself with what, for one without the opportunity of choice, was a fortuitously accorded weapon to be thankful for.

Mr Thewless, then, retraced his steps with some firmness, although to guide him he had now only the dim outlines of the row of windows on his left, together with a slightly more substantial radiance percolating down the staircase which he must climb. Nevertheless, it was in the nature of the transposition that had taken place that of anything of occult or other significance to be seen he should now have a substantial and unintermittent view. And in a moment he did become aware, upon the evidence of certain swiftly gliding silhouettes across the line of the windows just mentioned, that the enemy was in retreat before him. It was feasible, by rising only a little to the imaginative occasion, to frame it that he was now the hunter and these the hunted. And at this he felt within himself a certain mounting exhilaration which was yet not an index, perhaps, of any very reliable emotional tone. Indeed, Mr Thewless, had he known it, was approaching very near a point of complete nervous exhaustion. There would have to be but one further turn of the screw – the revelation, say, of a Parthian strategy in the apparent débâcle before him – altogether to upset such balance as, through the course of his trials, he had hitherto very creditably attained.

And of this now marginal and precarious nature of his resistance the passage of the staircase was an immediate index. He pressed up it boldly, but amid a physical distress having the effect of rendering each tread some two feet high. It was steep, it was gigantic, it was interminable; and, moreover, he acutely felt the possible advantage which, in point of any sudden assault, the retreating creatures might gain from their superior position on the incline. And again – and this assuredly was more ominous – he derived no satisfaction from the reflection that he was climbing steadily into a lesser darkness; into what was, comparatively speaking, a medium of light. It was clearly within our friend's recollection that the upper corridor upon which his own room lay admitted through some system of skylights considerably more of whatever mild moonlight lay without; and, moreover, that the periodic illumination from the lighthouse lent fleetingly to the scene a quality of which the only description at once compendious and fair would be one free of any hint of inconvenient tenebrosity. In this simple thought there ought to have been gratification enough. The entities which, whether preternatural or merely sordidly criminal, could scarcely be regarded as other than thoroughly sinister in their nocturnal intentions, and which, having – as he somehow fleetingly and all obscurely knew – assumed the protective covering of his own impudently ravished sheets, had pursued him far into the recesses of the mansion, he was now – by a mere assertion, it might fairly be said, of his own perilously stretched but yet supervalent will – pressing triumphantly back to what, at least for him, had been the very *fons et origo* of their existence. This was surely decisive success, and by its token he ought to have been eager for whatever final *éclaircissement* might now be achieved. But this was not at all the way in which Mr Thewless's mind found itself working. At any moment now there might indeed be something clearly to be seen. But Mr Thewless was with a definiteness unparalleled in his remotest recollection without the shadow of list to see it.

But now this curious episode in the Paxton affair, of which the present chapter has stumblingly attempted a rude chronicle, was nearing its term.

Mr Thewless had reached the topmost stair, and his knees were trembling. Nevertheless, he now attempted and achieved what he had not hitherto ventured upon: he ran. The door of his own room was open and visible before him; he had only to gain it, bolt it behind him, and tumble into a bed which, whether sheeted or not, offered a sufficiency of bedclothes of rougher integument to permit of his gaining the species of somewhat infantile security now with a quite resplendent candour uppermost in his mind. He ran – a swift glance having delusively assured him that the corridor was as void as he could hope. But even as the goal was within his grasp this assurance was betrayed, and one of the creatures of his long struggle – whether of design or through some hasty miscalculation of the line on which he stood – appreared hard before the doorway, barring his path. At this Mr Thewless perforce looked indeed – and what he saw was a shrouded figure hurriedly assume the posture, sufficiently hinted beneath an enveloping sheet, of some placidly posed Apollo of the Phidean age. It was a grotesque revelation beneath which Mr Thewless felt his nether limbs turning shamefully to water; and it is once more a mark of his quality that he now decisively acted in the very terminal moment in which action was possible to him. The candlestick which he still bore as a bludgeon he turned incontinently into a missile which he hurled with all his residual force at the figure before him. At this the figure gave a yelp of pain – a yelp swiftly overtaken in Mr Thewless's ear by a roaring as of great waters. Mistily he saw the figure stagger, the sheet drop away and then – for a brief flash, whether of revelation or hallucination – the swimming, melting, fading features of the man with the beard and the pebble glasses.

Even at this juncture he cannot altogether have lost consciousness. For, mingled with painful and massive auditory phenomena assuredly subjective in origin, he heard shouts, running footsteps, breaking glass, a violently closing door, glimpsed the elder Mr Bolderwood, red-faced and brandishing a revolver; glimpsed too the younger Mr Bolderwood, pale, swiftly calculating, similarly armed. These things faded, and he next knew that his head was being raised on a small, taut arm. He opened his eyes and saw that it was Humphrey who supported him – supported him much as in his dreams an interminable aeon ago. The boy was looking down at him with compunction, with amusement innocent of all malice. Mr Thewless felt that things had passed off not too badly and that he might reasonably go to sleep.

Chapter 16

While these simple passages of melodrama were transacting themselves at Killyboffin Hall, Detective-Inspector Cadover had been pursuing a plodding investigation into the murder in the cinema. He had failed to find any short cut to the identity of the dead man by way of the young lady with whom he was accustomed to dine confidentially at Smith's. For the degree of confidence involved in this particular satisfaction of certain of man's simpler needs had not extended to the communication of a surname and address; and when the clue of the casual letter referring to a scientist's son had failed him Cadover was no further forward than at the moment of his first glimpse of the young man's formidably anonymous corpse.

He had recognized this over his breakfast; recognized it with an insistence that spoke of his obscure sense of some special urgency in the affair. Nothing was less his inclination than to sit back and wait the event, even although his experience told him that this was now the course that the cinema case was most likely to pursue. His night's perambulations had been a sharp disappointment; in such subsidiary clues as remained to his hand he had very little faith; in all probability the next stage of the matter would be represented by somebody's turning up to claim the body. This always happened. It was remarkable – Cadover reflected over a somewhat inattentive communion with his wife at the breakfast-table – how hard it was in a civilized community to disappear without fuss. Taken in the mass, we have come to hold life extraordinarily cheap – far cheaper, surely, than any culture since something dimly Sumerian or Babylonian. We scrap a generation by violent and costly means, and very soon it is the cost and not the scrapping that troubles us. But let the loneliest old woman vanish from her garret and presently the local police station is besieged by a throng of her intimate acquaintance demanding an instant dragging of the local ponds. Only there is a time-interval in these disappearances; and one of the longest gaps, Cadover knew, is apt to occur between the disappearance of just such a person as his present corpse suggested and the emergence of a body of inquiring relatives. For young men of the sort either have, or by their mothers, sisters, or wives are apprehended to have, impulses liable to take them regrettably out of the family circle from time to time. The awkwardness produced by this – by the lurking suspicion that the missing man may, in the vulgar phrase, be enjoying a night, or series of nights, on the tiles – had often, in Cadover's experience, occasioned deplorable delay in the inquiries made by devoted persons into the disappearance of entirely blameless men. Human beings can be as inhibited by shyness before the very gates of death as before the door of a strange house to which one has been casually bidden to a party. About the young man of military appearance shot dead at the showing of *Plutonium Blonde* questions would almost certainly be asked. But they were unlikely to be asked for several days yet.

How, then, was Cadover to proceed? He summoned his available information – which consisted, in effect, of the scanty letter received by Miss Joyce Vane and the yet scantier entries in the dead man's diary. The picture to be built up from these documents was not remarkable for detail. The young man had engaged himself as a private tutor to take a boy to Ireland. The address to which they were going was unknown but might possibly incorporate the word – or fragment of a word – *Hump*. There was a substantial probability that it lay somewhere within the extensive area served by a series of wandering light railways of which the starting-point was the junction of Dundrane.

Next, the boy in question was the son of a scientist. This scientist was eminent either in the field of atomic physics or in some more or less related field which casual and uninformed reference might so name. Was anything else known of him? Cadover frowned. In the space in his new diary appropriate to Thursday – the day, that was to say, on which he had died – the prospective tutor had written the words *gun for boy 1.15*. This might, of course, refer to some quite inexpensive weapon – say, an air-gun of one of the well-known popular makes. But against this reading there had to be set one of the two entries immediately preceding; the one that read *N.I. police re guns etc*. The suggestion here of Customs regulations to be complied with, as also the season of the year, pointed to substantial designs upon the game birds of Ireland. The probability, then, seemed clear. The eminent scientist had delegated the new tutor to buy the boy a shot-gun.

Cadover reached for *The Times* – in the advertisement columns of which, at this time of year, there would certainly be a number of such weapons offered for sale. And presently he was confirmed in what he had supposed. Sporting guns were uncommonly costly in these days. Moreover, private tutors could not be altogether inexpensive. So here was something else that might reasonably be inferred about the unknown scientist: he was a person of some substance. And at this Cadover recalled Sir Bernard Paxton, whose style of living would here have fitted him so nicely into the picture. Unfortunately, Sir Bernard had proved a most abysmal blank, and in this he had been at one with two other comfortably circumstanced savants whom Cadover had interviewed on the previous night: Lord Buffery and Sir Adrian Ramm.

What more was there to go on? On the apparent eve of his departure, and at the seeming instance of his future pupil, Miss Vane's nameless friend had been persuaded to visit a cinema; and in that cinema he had been killed. Now, although many tutors, private or otherwise, are undoubtedly moribund, a positively dead tutor is of no use at all, and can certainly not be employed to take a small boy to Ireland. It seemed likely, therefore, that the particular small boy involved was not in Ireland now, and that inquiry at Dundrane or beyond would yield no very immediate result. For with the death of the tutor the Irish project had surely fallen through.

But where, then, was the boy now? This initial question raised a series of others of a complexity which, until now, Cadover had not quite fully realized. Had the boy left the cinema before his tutor was killed – or at least unaware that he had been killed? Was this scientist's son at home somewhere in London now, in a household merely perplexed by some unexplained hitch in a holiday plan? It was difficult to see any plausibility in this. Moreover, it took no account of another factor which now leapt at Cadover as of sudden immense significance.

The dead man's visit to *Plutonium Blonde* – there was his own word for it as given in his note to Miss Vane – had been something urged upon him by his new pupil. And *Plutonium Blonde* was assuredly the only film then in London during the showing of which a member of the audience could be shot, or otherwise violently despatched, without the risk of instant alarm; the only film, certainly, to combine a moment of absorbing suspense with an ear-splitting inferno of sound. Was the whole Irish proposal, then, bogus – the means, simply, of establishing a relationship whereby the unfortunate young man could be fatally lured into a certain cinema at a certain hour?

Cadover inspected this proposition carefully, and there came a point at which he had to boggle at it. That point was simply the proposed purchase, or acquisition, of the gun. If the boy was only a decoy, and the proposal to take him to Ireland a mere figment, this business of getting him a gun, Cadover felt, would simply not have happened; to have suggested it to the victim, and thus to have put him in the way, presumably, of inquiring after such a weapon, would be a useless bringing into the notice of sundry shop people a situation for which as little publicity as possible would be desired. Moreover, the whole supposition, further considered, seemed fantastic. To invent an eminent scientist, and provide him with a son who must be taken to Ireland, because it was for some reason necessary that a commonplace young man should be murdered, was a course of things too laboriously oblique to be sensible. And that an actual scientist of eminence should be involved in such a design, and should employ either an actual or a pretended son to further it, was surely a scheme of things equally fantastic. Cadover on the whole was disposed to believe in the scientist, in his son, and in the authenticity of some proposal to send that son to Ireland in the company of the man whose death he was now puzzling over. But from this it seemed to follow that it had been a boy innocent of any evil design who had accompanied – nay, persuaded – the doomed man into the cinema. On this supposition, how could any sense be made of what had followed?

There had been talk of two boys. And here Cadover got out his notes of the day before and propped them against the coffee pot. There had been talk of two boys – and there was some indication, moreover, that five persons in all had been in some degree involved in the affair in the cinema. Three seats had been booked together; to occupy the first of these a woman had arrived independently; to occupy the other two the dead man had arrived along with a fifteen-year-old boy. Subsequently, and before the discovery of the body, the woman and the boy had left unnoticed. But there was this to be remarked: that the boy upon his arrival had struck an usherette as being, in fact, not quite the sort of boy that he was holding himself out to be. This, of course, the usherette had announced only after the perpetration of an interesting murder. It would be folly to give weight to it. But it would be a graver folly to ignore it entirely.

Next, there were the remaining two of the five seats somehow concerned. From these, which had been booked independently, there had come out, apparently before the murder, and also before it was possible to have seen the main film through, a lad and a girl. The girl had been cross and bewildered; the lad had been hurrying her away. And the grand fact about the boy who was thus seen leaving the scene with a girl was a singular point of similarity he bore to the boy who was earlier seen to arrive upon it with the man who was killed. In an age in which many English public schools have dispensed with so much as a cap both the boys who had come under observation were sporting bowler hats. That the boy who came with the man was the *same* who had left with the girl was a hypothesis which, as soon as one peered into the matter, presented considerable difficulty. Suppose, then, there were indeed *two* boys. The identical style of their headgear was scarcely to be explained by the obvious supposition that here were two friends from the same school attending a cinema in each other's company, since it appeared certain that they occupied seats independently booked. On the other hand, it by no means followed from this last fact that the boys were in no significant relationship the one with the other. Coincidence might have brought them together with some immediate result thoroughly germane to the mystery.

It was after this fashion that Cadover's mind ploughed slowly forward as he presently made his way to Scotland Yard. In recognizing that the casual and the causal might have been bewilderingly at interplay in the cinema, he had an instinctive feeling that he was getting a first grip on the case. He knew comparatively little of what had happened at the Metrodrome, but it was enough to enable him to suspect that *too much* had happened; that the episode had taken on some complication it was not intended to bear. But along with this persuasion there grew up in his mind another to which he found himself equally disposed to attend. In any mental picture of the affair that he attempted to conjure up, or that came to him involuntarily as he essayed a more abstract dealing with it, he found that the predominant feature was the two boys with their several bowler hats. They balanced the composition like a pair of identical twins in comedy, dodging now one and now the other out of the wings to the diversion of a bewildered audience. Or, better perhaps, the evocation was of farce; of one character with a false beard impersonating another character with a real one. And surely that was it! Cadover, reaching his room at length and hanging up his own bowler hat, concluded that some element of impersonation would be found to lie near the heart of the mystery.

He knew what he had to do; what were the several lines, none of them particularly promising, that he must now take up. But for a time he sat doggedly driving his brain through any further inches of the thickening tangle that it could be made to go. Say that the dead man had arrived with the 'real' boy – with him on whom the bowler hat sat native and of right. And say that disposed hard by was some young criminal similarly provided and – it went without saying – similarly clothed *in toto* and of stature and feature colourably the same. Suppose that the genuine youth could presently be lured for a space from his seat, so that the other could then slip into it with the effect of the first returning to it. The intended victim, on whose other hand there already sat a woman already implicated in the affair, would then be nicely isolated between enemies.

Considering this, Cadover impatiently shook his head. It ignored far too much. It ignored that strong likelihood of some element merely coincidental in the situation suggested by the independent booking of the seats in groups of three and two respectively. It required, moreover, that the 'real' boy should not return to the seat he had vacated. In fact he must be supposed (unless, indeed, it was to be imagined that he, too, had met with violence) simply to leave the cinema and take no further interest in what happened there. Through this, by dint of certain rather fantastic propositions, it was possible in part to see one's way. For example, leaving his seat for a time, the boy might be given some urgent message, or confronted with some attractive proposition, which would indeed take him straight from the cinema. But – and Cadover glanced at his watch – yesterday's evening papers were now some thirty hours old and today's morning papers sucked dry on the breakfast tables. The murder at the Metrodrome was national news, and under that alliterative title bade fair to be a nine days' wonder. Unless this hypothetical innocent lad was also an uncommonly frightened one something ought to have been heard of him by now.

Patiently, then, Cadover retraced his mental footsteps to the point at which the theory of some impersonation had first opened before him. Take it the other way. Take it that it was the boy arriving with the dead man who was the impostor. And remember that this was a supposition sharply congruous with the social consciousness of the usherette who had believed herself to have detected something spurious about him! Cadover drew a long breath. Suppose that the tutor, perhaps newly engaged, had not in fact met his future charge until this visit to the cinema. There was nothing in the note to Miss Vane to conflict with that. Indeed, the note described the boy as 'sounding a bit of a handful all round'. At the moment of writing, in fact, he had *not* met the boy. And with a boy who was a handful – resentful or distrustful, perhaps, about the arrangements proposed for his holidays – might not going to a cinema together have been hit upon as a means, so to speak, of breaking the ice? The tutor, then, comes to the Metrodrome and thinks he meets his charge. But actually he meets an impostor, and presently he is seated between this impostor and a woman who is also in the plot. And meanwhile the genuine boy has been persuaded, say, to play a prank; to be present nearby in the company of a girl-friend. For a crime is to be committed and the genuine boy to be implicated. But just before the deed is done the genuine boy somehow takes the alarm, hurries out with his friend, and is now perhaps at home, panic-stricken, and explaining the disappearance of his tutor-elect in the best way he can . . .

Cadover's career would not have been the success it had did he not possess, mingled with qualities merely solid and reliable, a streak of genius that could, on occasion, run up such effective imaginative constructions as this. But equally – a fact of which he was abundantly aware – he would have come many more croppers than he had, had he not known with what extreme caution to proceed upon them. Moreover, any confidence he might have felt in his theory was in this instance conditioned by a troubled sense of something which he found peculiarly difficult to define. The notion of impersonation had really gripped him more than it should – or rather it remained in his mind as requiring attention which, in all this of the bowler-hatted boys, it had not really received at all. Already he had felt in this affair the haunting hint of some tenuous pointer by a hair's breadth fatally missed. And here was a similar feeling assailing him now. What the police detective chiefly needs is rather less a formidably developed power of inferential reasoning than the 'fine ear' upon which the successful physician also relies. And now Cadover's ear was just failing, or so he believed, to achieve some discrimination essential to the analysis of his problem.

He turned back to the dead man's diary. It was the point, after all, at which the criminals had slipped up. Potentially, it had been a very bad slip indeed, for had the diary been a little less new, a little more informative, their hope to prevent or delay identification of the body would have been frustrated from the start. And, even as it stood, the diary perhaps still represented the chink or crevice through which a first leverage could be obtained on the blank wall before him.

Smith's 7.30. That had led to Miss Vane, and Miss Vane, for the time, to a dead end only. He turned to the next entry:

> *Bolderwood*
> *Hump*

Here was something that could be investigated either swiftly or slowly. Within a couple of hours, that was to say, he could have a policeman on the doorstep of every known Bolderwood in Great Britain, Northern Ireland, and Eire, asking for any light they could throw upon the Metrodrome murder. But this might well be to sacrifice some virtue of surprise, and such inquiries should perhaps be precluded by confidential investigation in each case. Certainly the first thing to do was to hunt the directories for any Bolderwood in any way associated with a Hump; should such a one be discovered a very formidable battery would be turned upon him at once. Cadover pushed a button on his desk and spent some time delegating this task to assistants. And then he considered the two definitely Irish entries:

> *N.I. police re guns etc*

and

> *Light railway from Dundrane.*

Neither of these entries seemed very hopeful. The second appeared to be a mere memorandum, casually written, of how the latter part of the proposed journey was to be accomplished. One does not reserve seats, or book ahead, on an Irish light railway. There was nothing, then, in this, except a general pointer to a certain tract of country. Nor did the first of the entries suggest anything in the nature of preliminary correspondence; it was merely a reminder of certain formalities to be complied with – formalities, Cadover suspected, which, during a tourist season, might not be very strictly maintained. What the entry did give was this: that the 'Ireland' referred to in the dead man's letter to Miss Vane did in fact mean Eire and not Northern Ireland. It was for the purpose of taking guns into Eire – or rather of being permitted ultimately to take them out again – that some application was necessary or desirable to the Northern Ireland police. Here too Cadover set certain inquiries on foot. Then he turned to the final entry – the one which had already been prominently in his mind.

gun for boy 1.15

One did not note in quite this way an intention to *hand over* a gun; the reference must definitely be to *acquiring* one. And if the figures represented a time of day – as almost certainly they did – then there was surely some significance to be attached to them. A quarter past one is a slightly out of the way time to go buying an article the choice of which requires considerable deliberation. It means either an unusually early luncheon or an uncomfortably delayed one. But the fact that the entry was for the previous day suggested an obvious reason for this. The dead man's programme had been full. And if written out it would have read something like: *meet boy – quick luncheon – buy gun – Metrodrome in time for Plutonium Blonde – Irish boat train.* For the letter to Miss Vane, it had to be remembered, definitely named Thursday as the young man's proposed day of departure with his pupil. About this, of course, there might have been some later change of plan. But on the whole it seemed likely that about the entire affair this was the signal fact: the fatality in the cinema had taken place on the very eve of the Irish project.

Suppose, then, that a shot-gun had actually been bought round about one fifteen. What had happened to it? Where had it been, this last-moment purchase, while the people who had bought it were in the cinema? There seemed to be two possible answers. Either it had been sent to some private address in order to be put with other baggage, or it had been sent to a railway terminus to await the travellers there. And if Cadover was right in thinking that no journey to Ireland could well have taken place, then, in the latter eventuality, the gun might be in some railway 'left luggage' room still. There was a fair line of investigation in this, but it was one in which success would probably come more quickly at any other season of the year. Guns, in the second week of August, were decidedly on the move. It was true that King's Cross and Euston no longer presented the spectacle – astonishing to the itinerant foreigner caught in the whirl – of a whole social class equipped with such weapons, and migrating, together with an infinitude of crates, hampers, trunks, upper servants, and privileged dogs, to the remoter corners of the kingdom. Nevertheless traffic of this sort was still considerable, and a single gun would be hard to trace.

The occasion of purchase was a good deal more immediately hopeful. Considering it, Cadover indeed concluded that he had been taking too gloomy a view of the merely waiting part that might be imposed upon him. Again the season was a factor. The columns of *The Times*, for example, had shown him a good many people wanting to buy or sell sporting weapons, and the gunsmiths would similarly be doing a brisk trade. So again it was possible that a single purchase might take a little time to track down. Nevertheless, it could almost certainly be done, since one cannot walk into a shop and buy a shot-gun with the casual anonymity natural to the purchase of a pair of gloves or a packet of cigarettes. Indeed, Cadover, although not well versed in such matters, suspected that a good deal of ritual would accompany the acquiring of fresh property of this sort. He judged it likely that a man's gunsmith would hold something the same position – that of a species of paternal toady – as a man's tailor. But would the dead man *have*, in that sense, a gunsmith? He was not, presumably, a person of any great substance; nevertheless, this was one of the likelier points at which he would be tied on to the tail of privilege. He had looked just that type. *Gun for boy*, then, meant, most probably, his bringing some special knowledge or connexion of his own to bear; this more probably than his acting, namelessly and unnoticeably, as agent for the boy's father.

But would the gun, for that matter, be bought in a shop at all? Cadover was beginning to reach an age in which, every now and then, he had to hitch himself back into the present; and for a moment he had forgotten that nowadays neither gloves nor cigarettes nor shot-guns are simply to be had for the asking. Almost everything is in short supply at one time or another; and sporting equipment is particularly likely to be so at the start of the shooting season. But on this one could get assured information quickly. Cadover picked up his telephone and rang the first large firm of gunsmiths to come into his head. It was as he supposed. They took the gloomiest view of being able expeditiously to supply a weapon suitable for a boy of fifteen or sixteen.

Gun for boy 1.15. The man who made this confident note could not have been on any sort of waiting list for a suitable weapon, since his engagement to accompany a pupil to Ireland had not been more than a few days old. It was, of course, conceivable that he was somewhere the particularly privileged sort of customer for whom wanted articles are, in fact, produced. Alternatively, he might simply have chanced to know that some acquaintance of his own had an appropriate gun to dispose of. This second possibility Cadover eyed askance for a moment; it would be a circumstance that would pretty well destroy such hopefulness as there was in this approach to the case. But the tutor's likeliest manner of proceeding, after all, lay yet to explore; and Cadover sent for a file of recent newspapers. 'Articles for Sale' was his quarry, and he kept a particularly sanguine eye upon the personal column of *The Times* once more. The old agony advertisements, he reflected, were not quite what they had been when they delighted Sherlock Holmes; nevertheless, there must be a little drama, and a great deal of oddity, hidden behind some of them still . . . Every now and then he scribbled in his notebook, and as he did so his spirits rose. As he had anticipated, a substantial – yet not too substantial – body of people had been holding themselves out of late as having sporting guns to dispose of. To question them meant another pilgrimage much like that of the previous evening, and Cadover debated whether to put a team of men on the work. He decided once more to keep the matter in his own hands, thrust his notebook in his pocket, and reached for his bowler hat.

It will be recalled that the portion of our narrative now being offered to the reader is retrospective in cast. While Detective-Inspector Cadover is thus stepping out of Scotland Yard, with that heavy tread recalling his beat of long ago, the unknown boy with whom he is concerned, and the substitute tutor whose existence he does not suspect, are transferring to the light railway at Dundrane, with the greater part of their adventures yet before them.

Chapter 17

In estimating the course and tempo of the inquiry lying before him, Cadover had neglected a consideration that ought to have been sufficiently obvious. Persons with sporting guns for sale are commonly persons owning other sporting guns as well, and having a predisposition to put these into use in the second week of August. Working systematically through his list of advertisers, he found himself seeking a surprising number of people who were now out of Town. As he abandoned none of these until he had obtained from them by telephone or telegram, or through the agency of local police, particulars of anyone who had bought, or considered buying, the weapon they had advertised – and, moreover, as many of the replies received involved the instigating of further inquiries for which several assistants had to be briefed – the shades of evening had fallen as he drew towards the end of his list.

Now he rang the bell of a small flat in Hampstead. The house was retired and shabby, and its conversion into a dwelling adequate for several households had been carried out uncompromisingly on the cheap. A seedy retired major, Cadover speculated, who had felt a powerful urge to raise the price of a crate or two of whisky. The door opened before him. 'Does Mr Standage live here?' he inquired.

For a decayed sporty major, if such there was to be, was not yet visible;

Cadover found himself regarding, in a gloom not very convenient for precise observation, a sombrely dressed woman in late middle age, who appeared to look back at him with completely expressionless eyes. 'I am Mrs Standage,' she said; 'and I live alone. Will you come in?' She let him past and closed the door. 'This way, please.' And she led the way into a room on the left.

Here it was darker still and Cadover waited for his conductress to turn on the light. But the lady – she was emphatically that, and the more evidently in being a person from whom all other species of emphasis had drained away long ago – merely motioned to a chair and herself sat down with a straight back which seemed to speak uncompromisingly of a merely business occasion. 'I think I ought to tell you at once', she said, 'that I have had an offer. An offer from a clergyman.'

Cadover, who was weary, had for a moment a confused impulse to offer congratulations, as if what had been confessed to him was the prospect of some imminent matrimonial success. His perception of the folly of this left him just presence of mind to repeat, 'A clergyman?'

'For use in his parish hall. And I should, of course, be very pleased to think of the instrument as being employed for what would be, virtually, purposes of piety. Two of my uncles were archdeacons.' Mrs Standage paused, but not from any consciousness of irrelevance. 'Unfortunately the offer he was able to make was far from meeting my mind in the matter. Perhaps you would care to try the touch and tone.'

Glancing round the room, Cadover saw that what was being offered to him was the species of instrument known as a baby grand. 'It looks very nice,' he said politically. 'But I have not, as a matter of fact, come to buy a piano. I must explain to you that I am –'

'Then it's the rug.' Mrs Standage, who kept her eyes fixed somewhat unnervingly over her visitor's left shoulder, spoke with a shade of chagrin. 'Unfortunately, it is already sold – as was to be expected, I'm afraid. So fine a Persian rug would scarcely remain on – on the market long. But if a small Aubusson carpet would suit your needs equally well –' Here she broke off, as if aware of salesmanship of a somewhat too precipitate order. 'You may wonder why I should be anxious to dispose of things of such excellent quality – heirlooms, as they might be called. The fact is that I have had somewhat to contract my living quarters of late, and I am above all things fond of *space*. This is the sole reason for my having decided to part with something here and there.'

'I see.' Cadover barely did see, for the dusk was now deepening rapidly. But the room in which he sat, in addition to being faded, seemed already singularly bare; and by his head he could just detect a square patch on the wall from which a picture must recently have vanished. He was in the presence, in fact, of dire poverty in one of its most distressing forms. 'But you must understand', he said gently, 'that I have not come to buy anything you still have to sell. I am a detective-inspector of the police, and I have come to make inquiries about something you have already sold. I mean the shot-gun which you advertised about a week ago.'

Mrs Standage bowed, and it could be seen that a faint spot of colour had risen to her cheek. 'I beg your pardon,' she said stiffly. 'The misunderstanding was due entirely to my own carelessness. And any questions you have to ask I shall, of course, answer if I can. I hope I have not been culpable. It did cross my mind that formalities unknown to me might attend the – the disposal of firearms. The gun belonged to my late husband.'

'Quite so.' Cadover was infinitely soothing. 'But I don't think you will find us raising any questions of that sort.'

'It was taking up room.' Mrs Standage appeared to feel this a little tenuous and to cast about in her mind. 'And falling over. It made me decidedly nervous. I was not assured that the mechanism was entirely safe. So it appeared best to sell the weapon and be rid of it.'

'You acted very wisely, ma'am. Firearms can be extremely dangerous to those unfamiliar with them.' Cadover paused on this vacuous sentiment and then plunged decisively. 'And the gun suited the boy?'

'The gun suited the boy very well. He was delighted with it. It pleased me to feel that my husband's old companion was going to give such pleasure.'

For almost the first time in the cinema affair, Cadover felt a strong leap of hope within him. 'And the offer made – um – met your mind in the matter?'

'Entirely so. I had rung up my solicitor, an old friend with whom my husband used to go rough shooting, and he suggested a fair price.'

'I see. And that figure was –?'

'Thirty pounds.'

'The purchaser gave you that?'

Mrs Standage's curiously absent eyes appeared for a moment to waver. Then she smoothed out a fold in her dress. 'He gave me', she said, 'thirty-seven pounds ten shillings. I had to bear in mind that solicitors are conservatively inclined. They don't quite realize how everything goes up and up.' For a moment Mrs Standage's voice wavered as her eyes had done. 'And they *do* go up and up, as I have some occasion to know.'

'I am glad that you made a fair bargain. There might have been some danger of the gun's being too heavy for the lad. Perhaps its being just right persuaded the purchaser not to hesitate.'

'That was precisely the way of it. I know, as I have said, little of such things. But my husband was a small man – a *very* slightly built man, although full of fire and courage – and his gun was in consequence a light one. That was why the Captain bought it at once.'

'He was an Army man?' Cadover leant forward in his eagerness. 'His name was –?'

'He told me his name, of course – and his late regiment as well. But – do you know? – they have entirely slipped my memory.'

'My dear ma'am, this, I must tell you, is a matter of the utmost gravity. It is essential that I should learn this man's name at once. Did he not write out a cheque? Did he sign any sort of receipt?'

'Neither, I fear.' Mrs Standage was visibly distressed, and Cadover was convinced that it was not her intention to attempt any form of concealment. 'He was entirely a gentleman, and no record of the transaction appeared to be necessary. He paid me in cash.'

'I see. Now, in such a substantial sum there were no doubt Bank of England notes? Five-pound notes, for example?'

'He had only pound notes – Treasury notes, are they called? I remember his remarking that people are so reluctant to take larger notes nowadays – because of the Germans having forged so many, I think he said – that he never carried them.'

'That is most unfortunate.' And Cadover heartily cursed this further example of the dead man's circumspection. 'It means that, almost certainly, the money cannot be traced. Will you please make some effort to recall his name?'

Mrs Standage made a nervous gesture with her hands. 'I am ashamed to be so stupid,' she said. 'But it was so common-place and unmemorable a name! And, indeed, so was the young man himself – although entirely a gentleman, as I have said. Or was it *because* he was entirely a gentleman? There are so many ways in which a gentleman *should* be unnoticeable.'

'No doubt.' Cadover successfully concealed more than faint exasperation at this speculative social dictum. 'Well, what about the boy? Was he called anything?'

'Certainly. His name was Humphrey. And he addressed his companion as "sir". I conjectured that their relationship was that of pupil and tutor.'

'I think your conjecture was entirely accurate. But I should be better pleased to have the fellow's surname – better pleased by a long way.'

For several seconds Mrs Standage was silent. 'Do you know', she said at length, 'that I think it had something to do with rivers or boats?'

'That is something – indeed, it's a great deal. He wasn't just Captain Rivers, by any chance – Captain Peter Rivers?'

Mrs Standage shook her head. 'Decidedly not.'

'Or Captain Banks?'

'Not that either.'

'Shipton . . . Shipway . . . Seaman?'

'None of these.'

'*Steer?*' Cadover was irrationally hopeful. 'Captain Peter Steer?'

Mrs Standage oddly hesitated. 'No,' she said presently; 'his name was *not* Steer either. No doubt it will recur to me in time.'

'Well, for the moment let us take up another point. Did these two simply walk away with the gun?'

'No. They had some engagement that would have made that course inconvenient. The Captain asked if he might use my telephone, and he rang for a messenger, who came and collected the gun shortly after they had left.'

'I see.' For a moment Cadover gloomily confronted the blank wall that again seemed to have raised itself between him and his quarry. It was now almost dark in Mrs Standage's drawing-room. No doubt the lady's reluctance to turn on the light arose from a wish to conceal from her visitor the extent to which it had recently been depleted through the agency of public advertisements. But – perhaps under the influence of disappointment – Cadover's sense of delicacy in this matter had worn a trifle thin. He rose, switched on the light himself, and advanced upon the depressed gentlewoman before him, holding out a copy of the police photograph of the dead man. 'Will you be so good', he asked, 'as to tell me if this is the person who bought your gun?'

Mrs Standage did not move, and she appeared to ignore what was presented to her. When she spoke, it was very slowly. 'I am afraid, sir, that I cannot be of further help to you.'

'I realize that you have done your best. But please look at this carefully.'

'It is useless, sir. I must bid you good night.' And with even more dignity than she had yet shown, Mrs Standage rose and smoothed her dress about her.

'Useless –?' Cadover looked squarely at the lady, and the indignation that was in his tone died away upon his lips. For he saw that the woman who stood before him was blind. This was the explanation of the obstinately darkened room, and of what had seemed the absent gaze over his shoulder.

'I gather that you now realize my disability?' And Mrs Standage smiled faintly. 'And you will realize that I can give no description of persons who have never been visible to me. Let me show you out. I have – just at present – no servant in the house.'

There seemed nothing to say. Cadover stuffed the useless photograph into his pocket and walked behind his entertainer. His tread, he uneasily noted, was loud upon bare wood. Somewhere in the house an Aubusson carpet might remain. But from this room any floor-covering had disappeared – inch by inch, as it were, through the attenuated digestive system of the blind owner. With the help of the personal column of *The Times* she would nibble her way through what remaining possessions she commanded. And after that? Well, she might end up by being badgered by just such a conscientious constable as Cadover had once been for hawking matches in the streets.

Mrs Standage's shabby front door was opening before him. He was suddenly resolved not to let his commiseration and embarrassment stand in the way of a final effort. 'You say that the fellow's name calls up in your mind associations of rivers and boats. Well, what *are* your associations with such things?'

'It is difficult to say. I have never had anything in particular to do with them. It is an odd thing to have come into my head.'

'There must have been some associative process at work.' Cadover was obstinate. 'You sold him' – he barely hesitated – 'your husband's gun. Did your husband have anything to do with rivers and boats?'

'I don't think he did.' Mrs Standage's voice was strained and weary. 'And you make me feel it was wrong, indelicate, avaricious, to sell –'

'Nonsense, ma'am!' Cadover felt that to be brusque was to be kindly here. 'You must keep going – keep your end up – as you can. I admire you for it.'

'Thank you.' The voice in the near-darkness beside him trembled. 'And my husband, I say, had little to do with boats and rivers – or little since before I knew him, in his Cambridge days.'

'He rowed at Cambridge?'

'No. He was too light to row. But he coxed his college eight.' Mrs Standage paused. 'And that is it,' she said quietly. 'The name of the man I sold the gun to was Captain Cox.'

Captain Peter Cox. He was not in the London telephone directory. Although presumably a soldier, he was not, and had never been, in the Regular Army – and this, it seemed would mean an indefinite number of hours' delay in getting anything about him out of the War Office. He had, at least in his own name, made no booking of a sleeping-berth or the like between London and Ireland. He belonged to no London club. He had not recently been in any London hospital . . . Cadover, doggedly intent on beating to it, if only by an insignificant interval of time, the machine which would undoubtedly now disclose the dead man's history, found himself once more working into the night. At half past ten he was brought news that a certain Cyril Bolderwood was a substantial landowner at a place called Killyboffin in the west of Ireland. This opened a new line and what looked like a definitive one. Here was almost certainly the man whose name Captain Peter Cox, not many days before being shot in the Metrodrome Cinema, had confided to his pocket diary. And he was on the telephone . . . Cadover, haunted, as he had been from the start, by a feeling that in this obscure affair time was not to waste, let his hand hover over the instrument on his desk. But caution stayed him. Do that and – as he had discovered more than once – you can never tell what you may be giving away to whom. The case was beginning to move, and when that happens the first essential is that the movement should be controlled. Very obscurely, an imperfect pattern was forming itself in Cadover's mind – and cardinal in this was a notion of the species of crime into which his investigation had started to wind. And now there was no question of his holding everything within his own hand; of his plodding round on his own ex-constable's feet to peer at every point for himself. A whole posse was working under him. And other instruments of public order and security – robust infants merely godfathered by the venerable sage represented by Scotland Yard – must be asked if they had anything to say . . . At midnight Cadover went to get himself a cup of coffee.

The place never sleeps, for none would sleep securely in their beds if it did. Cadover brushed past two colleagues, their heads together over a plate of ham rolls.

'To me', said one of these, 'it sounded like *hump*. And the poor devil could get out nothing else.'

Memory tugged at Cadover. It brought him up with a jerk, like an actual tether. And as he thus stopped in his tracks the second of his colleagues spoke. 'It explained itself a minute later; if you'd stopped you'd have heard. *Humphrey*. That's what he was trying to say. Something nasty on his conscience, if you ask me.'

Cadover sat down abruptly. Coffee slopped in his saucer. He returned it carefully to the cup and stretched out a still trembling hand for a sandwich. 'Would you mind', he asked, 'sharing the joke?'

The first of his colleagues glanced up at him. 'Hullo, Cadover – hard at it keeping London pure? Poor old Hudspith was the chap for that.'

'Or solving horrid murders in ducal halls?' The second man chuckled. 'Appleby's mantle must fall somewhere, one supposes. And you, my dear Cadover –'

Cadover, holding his sandwich suspended in air, stretched out his other hand in a clutch suddenly as compelling as the ancient mariner's. 'Seriously,' he said, 'what was that about *Humphrey* and *hump*?'

'Certainly nothing by way of a joke to share.' The first man spoke soberly. 'I expect the poor chap's dead by now.'

'Nasty specimen called Soapy Clodd.' The second man put down his cup. 'Teen-age blackmailer, of all filthy trades. But he's got it now. Groaning in casualty. And any minute he'll be howling in hell. I hope it's hotter than the coffee they manage in this blasted cellar.'

Cadover, like one to whom has been granted a sudden mystical assurance of revelation, momentarily bowed his head. But, being economically disposed, he made the same motion serve for a gulp at his own coffee. 'Listen,' he said. 'There's something odd here. It sounds like linking up with an affair I'm busy on now. Tell me about it.'

'There's very little to tell. They'd been after this fellow Clodd for a long time, and at last they had enough for a fair chance of a conviction. So they picked him up. And then he bolted, made a run for it, and found himself underneath a bus. If you go up now – and if he's not, as I say, dead – you'll hear him moaning away about Humphrey Somebody – one of his victims lying particularly heavy on his conscience, I suppose.'

And Cadover went up. Tiled walls, glass shelves, chromium plate, the smell of ether and iodine: it was a chamber that had seen a large number of bad ends and a few surprisingly good ones. And, clearly, there was soon to be another end now. Soapy Clodd was a grey, contorted face on a pillow; a single skinny arm over which a police surgeon bent with a hypodermic syringe. His eyes were closed. There was the sweat of agony on his forehead; it collected in the wrinkles there and ploughed tiny furrows in the dirt.

'He'll have another period of consciousness soon.' The surgeon spoke impassively. 'And then he'll be out of it. He doesn't look as if life had enriched him, poor devil – or he it. Give me a call.' The surgeon went out. Cadover and an orderly were left together by the bedside.

Cadover stood motionless and absorbed. He remembered the coincidence of his driver's having remarked this wretched creature Clodd on the previous night. Was he really a fragment of the puzzle? If so, there seemed only one place into which he could be dropped . . . and yet it was a place into which he would not properly fit.

A long time passed and still Cadover waited, obscurely compelled to the conviction that he was not wasting time. And at length the dying man's eyes opened. Cadover sat down beside the bed. 'Clodd,' he said distinctly, 'what about this Humphrey?'

A faint indrawn breath was the immediate answer, and Clodd moved his head uneasily on the pillow, as if straining to hear something that came to him from very far away. Words formed themselves upon his lips – they were faintly blue – but no sound came.

'Humphrey,' said Cadover loudly. 'Speak up.'

'They're after him, the bastards.' Clodd's was a barely audible whisper. 'They're after my boy.'

'Your boy?' Cadover was disconcerted. 'You have a son called Humphrey?'

"E was *my* boy – not theirs.' Weak indignation breathed in the dying man's voice. 'And a fine lad, too. Couldn't arf write you a narsty letter, 'e couldn't – though I sez it that's a bit of an 'and at it myself. "Beware" – that's wot 'e wrote me. And just a kid with no proper eddikation. Couldn't even spell. "I'll 'ave yer put in goal", 'e wrote – just like that. A good one, that was. "I'll punch yer bleeding nose", 'e wrote. I tell yer, I didn't arf like young 'Umphrey. But I'd 'ave got 'im in the end, same as I've got lots with more spunk nor 'im. Then them blurry bashtards come along. What's their gime? That's what I'd like to know. Two lots of them, there were, and both up to something dirty over that poor kid. Made me sick, it did.'

'Two lots?' Cadover bent forward eagerly. 'You're sure of that?'

'I tell yer I was working that kid 'ard, and there wasn't much I didn't see. Two lots of crooks – narsty common crooks – up to something against that poor kid. And one lot 'ad a kid of their own. 'Opped out of a car, 'e did, and ran after the young chap was going to be a tutor or the like, and I'm blarsted if 'e didn't 'old himself out as 'Umphrey 'imself. And me listening down an area steps. Thought it might do me a bit o' good. "Are you my new tutor?" That's what the common little crook said, bold as brarse. Blurry himpersonation in broad daylight, that's what it was. I arsk you, what's the police coming to? Sitting back on their great be'inds while we pays taxes for them through the nose.'

'Who are these people? What is this Humphrey's other name?' Cadover spoke gently now, as if afraid that a vehement word might send Soapy Clodd a fatal second too soon to his last account.

And, plainly, the dying man did not hear. He lay quite motionless for a long time – only something, a sort of darkening or filming, was happening to his eyes. At last his voice came in a whisper even fainter than before. 'Hashamed of nothing I say or do . . . hashamed of nothing I say or do.'

It was, Cadover thought, a singularly strange profession for such a man. But a moment later he realized that it was quotation to which he was listening again.

'And there's not many as writes that, there ain't . . . "Hashamed of nothing I say or do . . ." And then a flourish, as you might call it, at the end . . . 'Umphrey . . . 'Umphrey Hedwyn 'Onyel Paxton.'

Cadover turned from the bedside and ran. Big Ben was tolling one of the small hours as he reached the open air and tumbled into his waiting car.

Chapter 18

Driving fast through deserted streets, Cadover at first asked himself the wrong question. Why should the eminent Sir Bernard Paxton wish to conceal the truth about his son's holiday plans? Had the boy, who had been for some reason regarded as a likely victim by the blackmailer Clodd, been involved in trouble so serious that his father had judged it necessary to safeguard his imminent escape from the country by telling a pack of lies? And had the trouble, in fact, been something very serious indeed – the sort of thing that might lead to a man's murder – and had there been an elaborate plan to baffle pursuit by creating a false Humphrey to lay a false trail? It was a hypothesis leaving a dozen questions unanswered, but it lasted Cadover through his brief dash across the West End of London and was in his mind still as he pressed the front-door bell at the top of Sir Bernard's stately steps. All patience had for the moment left him; the little button under his thumb was entirely inadequate to his feelings; he regretted that he could not prelude the stiff questions he was about to ask by tugging vigorously at a more primitive device calculated to make a much greater row. Probably, indeed, he would by this present means rouse nobody. And he was about to make night hideous by hammering loudly on the door – it would have pleased him to make with one of his stout boots a decided impression on that too pristine paint – when the offending barrier vanished before him and he found himself confronted by the butler whom he had encountered on the previous night. The man looked at him without visible surprise, and made no demur when he marched past him into the hall.

'I am Detective-Inspector Cadover. Rouse your master, please, and say that I must see him at once on a matter of the utmost urgency.'

The man bowed imperturbably. His dignity was by no means disturbed by his having just scrambled out of bed; perhaps – Cadover inconsequently thought – it was fortified by a dressing-gown entirely appropriate in its sombre splendour. 'Very good, sir. Will you please step into the library?'

It was, Cadover remembered, the Spanish room. He entered it and the door closed softly behind him. He waited.

He waited for perhaps five minutes, not displeased at having this interval in which to arrange his ideas and calm down. But presently he found that he was far from calming down; on the contrary, he felt an obscure pricking of impatience and even alarm. The house was quite silent. He listened in vain for a footstep, for the soft opening or closing of a bedroom door. He got to his feet and prowled. He stared at a picture confronting him from the end of the room. And as he did this there came back to him powerfully the first occasion upon which, tenuously but hauntingly, he had experienced the feeling of something eluding him that he ought to have held. Something that somebody had said . . . something that somebody had *failed* to say . . . a single word that had not been spoken . . .

Velazquez. That was it. The owner of this splendid thing had said it was there because of its likeness to his son. And then – as if by way of placing it – he had said that it was an old picture – very old indeed. It was a remark absurdly wide of anything that could, in its context, be uttered by a person of genuine cultivation in such things. And Cadover had missed it. He had missed the moment at which a monstrous and daring imposture had given itself away. And here was why the notion of impersonation had haunted him in some connexion other than that of the two lads with the two bowler hats. Sir Bernard Paxton, the owner of this august and sleeping mansion, was one on whom he had never yet set eyes. Sir Bernard had not told fibs about his son. Somebody else – having more colour as an eminent scientist than as an owner of Old Masters – had done that for him.

Cadover strode to the door and threw it open. The hall was in darkness. He brought out a pocket torch and let its beam play until it picked out the light switches. He flicked them on and an aggressively imposing world sprang into being around him. It was like one of those exaggeratedly spacious halls in the movies, with a great curving staircase on which female stars might display their gorgeous gowns or alluring nether limbs. Cadover glanced rapidly about him and discerned, among the numerous expensive and exotic objects displayed, one of homely domestic use, yet of proportions so noble as to be not inadequate to its surroundings. It was a gong – such a gong, it might be supposed, as had once thundered down the remotest corridors of some vast Tibetan lamasery. And Cadover, perhaps because his vanity was wounded at having been egregiously fooled, was prompted to have his moment of drama out of this plodding and harassing affair. He picked up the gong stick and plied it with a will.

The effect exceeded even his exasperated expectation. It was like being himself the stone cast into a still pool; great waves – and they seemed of sheer, quintessential energy rather than of mere sound – pulsed and beat outwards from him in widening circles. When he paused, laying a hand on the great bronze disc to still it, he was aware of numerous doors being thrown open, and of alarmed feet running, in some remote quarter of the house. That, no doubt, was the servants – or what was left of them. But he was aware, too, of something else. A light had flicked on at the head of the staircase, and a single tall figure stood there regarding him. And suddenly Cadover heard over again, on his inner ear, all the gloriously outrageous tumult he had just created. But it had shrunk to a tiny, foolish, and impertinent noise. *This* was Paxton. There could be no doubt about that.

'Who are you, and what the devil do you mean?'

The words were such as any indignant householder might have used. They were accompanied, moreover, by the thrusting forward of an object altogether familiar to Cadover's experience: namely, an automatic pistol. But for a full second longer, and as he laid down the gong stick, he preserved the simple sense of a unique event. He had never before looked straight at genius, and he might never do so again.

'I am a police officer, and I have taken the quickest means I could to rouse you to a matter of extreme urgency.'

For a split second the tremendous presence that was Sir Bernard Paxton wavered. It was, Cadover saw, unreadiness, irresolution; it was certainly no sort of uneasy conscience. And the impression was instantly gone. The tall figure half turned to some invisible corridor down which several pairs of feet could be heard hurrying. 'Go back to your rooms,' he said in a level voice. 'Tell the women that there is no danger of any sort. It has been' – and his glance came back to Cadover – 'a mere prank.'

The footsteps died away, and as they did so Sir Bernard came steadily down the staircase. He looked hard at Cadover, the pistol still in his hand. 'Your credentials,' he said briefly.

Cadover showed them. Sir Bernard looked at them for what they were worth. It was still the man he was sizing up. 'Please come into my study,' he said. Cadover followed him and was presently aware of light-coloured walls, Chinese paintings, glowing lacquers. Sir Bernard faced him squarely. 'Well?' he asked.

'I called here last night to interview you on a matter that might concern the safety of your son. I was shown into another room – I think, your library – and there I was interviewed by a person who purported to be yourself.'

'I see.' Very quietly, Sir Bernard Paxton turned aside and sat down. The movement, Cadover realized, covered the instant intellectual comprehension of a totally unsuspected danger. Because that danger touched his son, the man was shaken to the depths by it. But he was certainly not going to make an outcry. 'Jollard – my butler?' he asked.

'It was your butler who received me, who told me to come back at a certain hour when you would be available, and who then ushered me into the presence of the impostor. Afterwards, he showed me out.'

'And I came downstairs and saw him do so.' Sir Bernard spoke sharply.

'I called out to him and he told me I forget what. Well' – and he looked dryly at Cadover – 'you have not been the only fool.'

Cadover accepted this as it was offered. 'I was the bigger fool of the two. I ought to have got the hang of it before I rang your front-door bell tonight. As it is, your butler – Jollard, did you say? – has shown us a clean pair of heels. Have you had him in your service for long, Sir Bernard?'

'Six months.'

'And he has been in a position of some trust – or, at least, responsibility? He would be able to take, and appear to transmit, messages . . . that sort of thing?'

'Certainly. He appeared an efficient and reliable man, although I cannot say that I greatly cared for him. And now' – and Sir Bernard Paxton drew a long breath – 'if there is anything in all this that really concerns my son, we had better have it from the beginning, and at once.'

'Very well, Sir Bernard. I understand that you have an only son, Humphrey? And that you recently engaged a tutor to take him to Ireland?'

'I engaged a Mr Thewless, a most reliable and experienced man.'

Cadover took out his notebook and made a jotting of the name. 'Thank you. Did you, in the first instance, try to engage anyone else?'

'I engaged a Captain Peter Cox, who was highly recommended to me. Unfortunately, he has been prevented from taking up the post by an unexpected death in his family.'

Cadover stared. 'It would altogether surprise you, Sir Bernard, to learn that the unexpected death was his own?'

'It would, indeed. But all that I received was a telegram, which is no doubt evidence of the poorest sort. See for yourself.' And with some deliberation, yet with a visibly trembling hand, Sir Bernard Paxton fished in a drawer of the desk beside him. 'Here you are.'

Cadover took the slip of paper held out to him and read it grimly. 'Certainly', he said, 'it was a sudden death that disqualified Captain Cox. We seem to have a bit of a joker to deal with.' He thought for a moment. 'So when you received this you fixed things up with Mr Thewless instead?'

'Precisely so. And Mr Thewless and Humphrey consequently left together for Ireland late yesterday afternoon – or I should say late on Thursday afternoon.'

'This Captain Cox, Sir Bernard – did he ever, so far as you know, see Humphrey?'

'He did not. When he called on me, Humphrey chose not to show himself. He is a somewhat difficult boy.'

'Would it be possible that he was put up to not showing himself by Jollard – I mean by way of a joke?'

Sir Bernard looked surprised. 'It is not inconceivable. The man was at times a little too familiar with Humphrey. But I doubt if the boy liked him very much.' He paused, squaring his shoulders. 'Come,' he said. 'Let me have it, please. What has happened?'

'So far, I know only a little of what has happened, sir – and much of that is a matter of conjecture or inference. But I figure it out like this. When this Captain Cox left your house after accepting the post you offered him, he was accosted by a fifteen-year-old boy who gave himself out to be your son. The impression conveyed, I suppose, would be that your son, having been shy or coy while Cox was in the house, had now run out after him on a sudden impulse. Cox had no reason to suspect that anything was wrong, and he was probably rather pleased. And there and then, I suspect, they made two engagements. Humphrey, I think, was to have a gun?'

'Captain Cox suggested it, and I thought it quite proper. It was arranged that he should make the purchase.'

'Then I think he communicated this intention to the boy, and they arranged to meet some time after noon on Thursday. The second arrangement was that they should go on to a cinema, and after that set straight off on their journey. And now I have to tell you that the object of this extraordinary deception was an extremely sinister one. What further communication with you Captain Cox judged himself to have had, I cannot, of course, tell. Jollard and the telephone might account for a good deal there. But the final result was this. Cox entered that cinema – the Metrodrome – believing himself to be in the company of your son. And he never came out alive. He was shot, at close quarters, during the showing of a film called *Plutonium Blonde*. Meanwhile, you had been persuaded by this telegram that he had withdrawn from his engagement to you, and you arranged to employ Mr Thewless instead.' Cadover paused. 'It is clear, Sir Bernard, that this crime must have been designed to gain one of two possible objects.'

'Quite so.' Sir Bernard Paxton was now very pale, but it was evident that he had been thrown into no sort of mental confusion. 'The criminals may have wanted to ensure that Thewless should go with Humphrey, or they may have wanted to ensure that Cox should *not* go with Humphrey. And now I think we had better put through a trunk call to Ireland at once.'

'No, sir.' Cadover spoke gravely. 'I am afraid I cannot answer for that as being in the best interest of your son's safety. It is essential that we should try to get the whole matter clearer first.'

Sir Bernard Paxton, who had stretched out his hand to an instrument on his desk, let it fall again to his side. 'For the moment', he said, 'I will abide by your judgement. What can I tell you more?'

'Tell me, please, in just what circumstances your son did leave.'

'It was arranged that he should met Mr Thewless at Euston. His baggage was sent on there in the morning. I was extremely hard-pressed with work, and I said good-bye to him about eleven o'clock. He was to go to his dentist, he told me, in the afternoon, and then direct to the station.'

'I see.' And Cadover paused again, thinking hard. 'Tell me, Sir Bernard, has Humphrey begun to interest himself in girls?'

Sir Bernard Paxton looked startled. 'Why should you ask?'

'For one thing, your boy was apparently being pestered by a very unpleasant character called Clodd. And Clodd makes a speciality of blackmailing adolescents who can be persuaded that they have something shameful to conceal in matters of that sort. Incidentally, we must be grateful to Clodd, but for whom I should not be sitting here now.'

Sir Bernard Paxton's fingers drummed nervously for a moment on the desk in front of him. 'For some time I have had suspicion that Humphrey has formed a friendship with a girl – a girl, that is to say, who would not normally be within – um – his own circle of acquaintance. Indeed, it is a matter in which I have naturally felt considerable anxiety.'

'I see.' Cadover, although his ideas in the field now being discussed were certainly not lax, paused to reflect that Sir Bernard's evident habit of anxiety over Humphrey, and his equally evident inability to find time for joining in his son's occasions, made a combination about as fatal as could be. 'But there is another indication here. Tell me, sir – did Humphrey by any chance mention to you this film called *Plutonium Blonde?*'

'He expressed a wish to see it. I believe I discouraged him, although it was not a matter upon which I should wish to be coercive. From the reviews I had judged it to be a film dealing in a cheaply sensational way with what is, in fact, a shadow of unimaginable calamity impending over our civilization – and this, moreover, disgustingly glamorized through the super-imposition of crude sexual solicitations.'

Cadover made a sympathetic noise. These, decidedly, had been his own sentiments. At the same time he had a sort of sympathetic glimpse of the unknown Humphrey Paxton, subject to this polysyllabic disapproval when proposing an afternoon's mild excitement at the flicks. And this perception brought a touch of impatience into his voice now. 'I have some reason to believe that your son did not go to his dentist on Thursday afternoon, and never intended to do so. He took an unknown girl to see *Plutonium Blonde.* And, by an extraordinary coincidence, he found himself sitting next to himself.'

'I beg your pardon?'

'He found himself sitting next to the pretended Humphrey Paxton, or as near as made no matter. There was *himself*, and there was the Captain Cox who had sent a telegram walking out on you. Your son and his friend then left the cinema in a hurry, and just before Cox was murdered. And now, sir, a question about which I am very anxious indeed. Have you heard from Humphrey since?'

Humphrey's father took a deep breath. 'You appal me,' he said. 'But certainly I have heard – or rather I have heard from Mr Thewless. He wired to me late yesterday, Friday, evening, that he and Humphrey had arrived safely at Killyboffin.'

'You realize that this Mr Thewless, if he is indeed now safely with your son, is so only as the result of a criminal conspiracy that has involved deliberate and callous murder?'

For the first time during this strange interview something like helpless bewilderment showed for a moment on Sir Bernard Paxton's face. He passed a hand over his tremendous forehead. 'It is unbelievable!' he said. 'I cannot conceive of such a man – patently the most harmless of mortals, interested in Roman archaeology and other trifling branches of learning – being involved in complex conspiracy and atrocious crime. There is simply no sense in it, Inspector – no sense in it at all.'

'That is just what I want to be assured of.' And Cadover, in whose solidly buttressed veins a strong tide of excitement and anticipated triumph was beginning to pulse, leant eagerly forward. 'Your every instinct assures you that this Mr Thewless is, in fact, precisely what he appears to be: a reliable, conscientious, and entirely harmless – well – pedagogue?'

'I am seldom impressed by the promptings of intuition.' Sir Bernard, for the moment, appeared to mount some invisible rostrum as he spoke, so that it occurred to Cadover that he too, in the days before his present towering eminence, had owned to the pedagogic trade. 'I am simply offering you the judgement of considerable experience as digested by an obstinately rational mind. And I say that Thewless is no other than he appears to be.'

'So far, so good.' And Cadover nodded. 'Would you say that he would be a good man in a tight place?'

And this gave Sir Bernard Paxton pause – something, Cadover reflected, that had not happened hitherto. His extraordinary eyes – and Cadover had up to this moment scarcely noted *how* extraordinary his eyes were – seemed to shoot off into infinite space. 'I don't know. I am rather inclined to think that it would depend on the degree of tightness involved. In a *very* tight place I imagine that Thewless might be a very good man indeed.' And suddenly Sir Bernard smiled – and his smile was, after its fashion, as overwhelming as his most penetrating glance. 'But here we are landed with intuitions, after all.'

'We are landed with Captain Cox.' In Cadover's eyes too there was now a very respectable gleam. 'For remember our two propositions. If the crime was not a matter of *getting* Thewless, then it was a matter of *excluding* Cox. Now, why? What do you know about him? And what was your impression?'

'He was recommended to me by reliable friends as having a way with boys. His intellect was plainly negligible. He was commonplace and colourless. He had won the Victoria Cross.'

'I see. And would you say that that was the complete picture?'

'It gives us a line.' Sir Bernard was cautious. 'With Cox about, anyone openly threatening Humphrey's safety might have been assured of a broken jaw.'

Cadover pounced. 'You had reason to be anxious about Humphrey's safety?'

For a second Sir Bernard hesitated. 'I happen,' he said, 'to be a wealthy man – almost what passes for a very wealthy man in times like these. That is an accident of birth. And by another accident of birth, seconded by what

166

self-discipline I have been able to achieve, I myself happen to be a man whose work is vital to the safety of this country.'

'Quite so, sir.' Cadover was mildly confused. If it is possible without slight absurdity to remind a policeman that one is a genius, Sir Bernard Paxton had achieved the feat. But there seemed a slight indecency in obliging him to do so. 'Then it comes to this. The criminals with whom we appear to be concerned may have killed Cox because he was a person likely to be formidable to them. Not formidable in the sense that he had a penetrating intelligence, but simply as being of unflawed courage and possessing a powerful straight left. Does that seem plausible to you?'

'Not in the least.'

'Exactly, sir.' The genius, Cadover found himself absurdly reflecting, would make quite a promising detective-inspector of police. 'No criminal would undertake the immense hazards of murder to effect so tenuous a piece of insurance. So where are we now?'

'We are looking for something sufficiently evident.' Sir Bernard spoke a shade dryly. 'There must have been some more or less coincidental reason for Cox's being a particularly dangerous man. It certainly wasn't his brains that got him killed. And it wasn't even his V.C. It was something he *knew*. And that something it is desirable that we should know too.'

For a man whose only son was indisputably in some unknown but large danger Sir Bernard Paxton was putting up an uncommonly good show. Cadover warmed to him. 'We'll know,' he said stoutly. 'We'll know before the night's out.'

'It is almost out now.'

As he spoke, Sir Bernard rose a little stiffly from his chair and walked, a tall figure in a dressing-gown even more magnificent than that of his late butler, to a window heavily curtained in some ancient Eastern brocade. He pulled at a cord. And the dawn, bearing indefinably with it something ominous and urgent, slid into the too elegant, the obscurely vulnerable Chinese room.

Chapter 19

It was an hour later, and a coffee-pot now stood between the two men. Cadover glanced at it and saw again the scared face of the parlourmaid who had brought it in. The gong, the disappearance of Jollard, this mysterious matutinal conference in Sir Bernard's study: all these must be occasioning a fine whispering in the servants' quarters. The conjecture was doubtless that Master Humphrey had been kidnapped. And the conjecture was doubtless right. Cadover, thus gloomily concluding, glanced up at Humphrey's father as the latter set down the telephone receiver.

'Yes, Inspector, you were right about that. There can have been no question of Humphrey's going to his dentist on Thursday. Partridge is down with influenza. And I fear that his wife didn't thank me for the early call. The first step in the affair was my unfortunate boy's practising a foolish deceit.'

'You can put it like that if you like, sir.' Cadover saw no profit in the introduction of this particular moral note. 'He took the best means he had for securing a last meeting with his sweetheart' – here Cadover took some satisfaction at observing Sir Bernard wince at a word echoing, as it were, across a vast social gulf – 'before he was hurried off to Ireland. I don't see much harm in it myself. And it is possible that in going out with the girl again he was showing that he wasn't going to be scared by the abominable Clodd.'

Rather pathetically, Sir Bernard brightened. 'Yes,' he said, 'there may be something in that.'

'And there's another thing. It may be very important. If your son had not made this covert visit to the Metrodrome he wouldn't have sat beside himself – as he undoubtedly did. He must have been aware of it, you know. There is no other reasonable explanation of his leaving in the hurry that he did. Now, just think of it. He knows that Captain Cox (whom he may have had a peep at when he was here) has sent that telegram crying off, and that another tutor is to take him away. And now here beside him are two people addressing each other, no doubt, as Captain Cox and Humphrey, and indicating, maybe, that they are off to Ireland that evening. And at that Humphrey grabs his girl and bolts from the cinema. A very healthy bolt, I should call it. But what happens then?'

Sir Bernard took a moment to answer this. His eye, so apt to converse with astronomical distances, looked as if it might be discovering some unexpected horizon nearer home. 'What happened next? I don't think we know.'

'I hope we do.' And Cadover in his turn took up the telephone and made a call. Getting the number he wanted, he asked a brief question and then for the space of a minute intently listened. Then he put down the receiver. 'We've taken only half an hour to get hold of *that*.' He spoke with the satisfaction of a man whose organization has served him well. 'I've been a little anxious about that telegram from Thewless at Killyboffin. We've had one fake telegram already, after all. But I think it's all right. At least those two *set out* for Ireland. They picked up Humphrey's baggage at Euston, and there was some sort of little scene over the gun – the gun that Cox brought along with his bogus pupil, and that he had sent on to the station by messenger. It served to fix our two in the memory of a fellow in the Left Luggage . . . So there you are.' And Cadover paused, as with a decent sense of the magnitude of the moment. 'Your boy, Sir Bernard, went to Ireland. *That's* what happened next.'

Humphrey's father was at his most cautious. 'You judge that to be surprising, Inspector?'

'Come, come, sir. I take it that Humphrey is not a densely stupid boy?'
'Certainly not.'

'Nor abnormally phlegmatic?'

'He is abnormally sensitive and imaginative.' Sir Bernard's voice had risen a pitch. 'And of late he has actually been beset by obscure anxieties – by all sorts of baseless and fantastic fears.'

'And you have been anxious about this?'

'Certainly I have.'

'Would it be fair to say that you suffer from that sort of thing yourself?'

'I don't understand you.'

'Would it be fair to say that what you have called your obstinately rational mind would not in itself have taken you a tenth of the way you have gone; and that you are at bottom abnormally sensitive and imaginative; and that you pay for this by being frequently beset by all sorts of baseless and fantastic fears?'

Sir Bernard had risen to his feet, and for a moment Cadover thought that he was going to flare into anger. The great man, however, looked merely surprised – as he well might do at this sudden transmogrification of the policeman before him into a modish psychological inquisitor. 'What you say is of great interest. But I suggest that it is a little more speculative than is appropriate to the present occasion.'

'I think not. For we shall get at this most quickly, you know, by having some idea of how the minds of the people concerned are working. Now, sir, you have been fussing and over-protecting this only boy of yours – and particularly so, I should guess, since his mother's death. That is no more than to say that you have been letting your own hidden fears loose on him; that you have been using him as a channel for the discharge of your own anxieties. It is a considerable burden to impose on a lad.'

Sir Bernard Paxton had walked to the window and was staring out at a morning sky still darkly red in the east. 'Well?' he asked.

'The boy is aware of this situation – or say, rather, that he is sensitive to it. You are worried, scared; you plainly need support. Being your son, he feels bound to stand by you; to take on his own shoulders as much of the burden as he can. That, Sir Bernard, is the Paxton family situation. There's nothing occult about it. It must be evident to your parlourmaid or your knifeboy, if they have an ounce of brains and observation. And it is decidedly one of the facts in the situation confronting us.'

'You have a considerable power, Inspector, of succinct exposition.' Sir Bernard paused as if to inspect this defensive irony, and found it unsatisfactory. 'We get back to what Humphrey did on leaving the cinema.'

'Yes, sir. Imaginative boys know a hawk from a hand-saw, and he knew very well the difference between the insubstantial fears he obscurely shares with yourself and the tip of an actual, down-to-earth threat to your security.'

'To *my* security, Inspector? It would strike him essentially in that way?'

'Of course it would! The picture that emerges of him is of an extremely intelligent boy. He knows very well that, although enormously interesting to Humphrey Paxton, he is nevertheless only an unknown small boy, of no interest whatever to the great outer world. If anyone looks at him twice it is because he is Paxton's son. More than commonly, the father-image towers above him. At the same time, as you and I know, he has the job of giving that image a hand' – Cadover paused – 'of shoring it up, in fact, with whatever he can lay his hands on.'

Sir Bernard Paxton walked back across the room, peered into the coffee-pot, and rang a bell. He was, in a way, taking all this with flying colours. And now he turned to Cadover. 'So Humphrey came out of that cinema feeling the need of a stouter prop than usual?'

'He must certainly have had a more than usually urgent feeling that something must be done. But, chiefly, he felt the challenge in the thing.'

'Challenge?' Sir Bernard turned to the parlourmaid who had entered the room. 'Coffee,' he said briefly.

'Exactly – but excuse me for a moment.' The telephone bell had rung, and now Cadover grabbed the instrument. He listened for a moment. 'I see . . . I see. Well, I think we ought to have been told. They should never play that sort of lone game . . . Unofficial? – stuff and nonsense! And what name did you say? . . . Never heard of her. But it's better than nothing, I suppose . . . Yes, not later, I hope, than ten o'clock. And look here! – the Dublin people simply *must* be kept right. Go and get the Commissioner himself out of bed and make him telephone through . . . No; don't worry; he'll thank you in the end. The main point is that it must be quite clearly explained as something big, but quite without political colouring. Otherwise they may take fright, and hold us back while they hunt up their own big-wigs . . . Yes – ten o'clock.'

Cadover put down the receiver. 'I think it may be said we're starting to move.'

'I hope in the right direction.' Sir Bernard had returned to the window and was staring sombrely out at distant chimney-pots. 'What was that about a challenge?'

'Your son realized that, quite accidentally, he had been warned. What he had heard in the cinema said, "Ireland means danger." It must also have said, "Get home as quick as you can and tell Daddy" – something like that. But the boy decided to meet Thewless, all the same, and set off. He is seeing the thing through himself. I think it may be said that he is seeing to it that danger and you have the Irish Sea stretched between you. But we won't exaggerate. We'll put it simply that Humphrey has seen the chance of an adventure and has taken it.'

Sir Bernard Paxton made a non-committal noise, and as he did so the parlourmaid returned with the replenished coffee-pot. She set it down, retreated, hesitated by the door. 'If you please, sir,' she said, 'is it Master Humphrey?'

Her employer stared at her in surprise – altogether, indeed, as if something out of nature had transacted itself. 'You may go,' he said. 'And tell your fellows not to gossip.'

Beneath this displeasure, the girl trembled visibly. But she held her ground. 'It was only that, if it *is* Master Humphrey, there is something the policeman ought to know.'

Cadover, who had hardly supposed himself to have been identified after this manner, promptly took the matter in hand. 'In that case', he said, 'you had better speak up.'

'When Master Humphrey went away before lunchtime on Thursday he told us he wasn't coming back. He was going to Mr Partridge, he said, and after that straight to Euston. But he *did* come back. And he can't have been leaving himself very much time to catch his train.'

'I see.' The movements of the son of the house, Cadover realized, must be of considerable interest in the servants' hall. 'But was there anything very remarkable in that?'

'It was the *way* he came home, sir. It was only Mary saw him.'

'Mary?' Sir Bernard Paxton interrupted rather as if this was a particularly opprobrious name.

'Mary, if you please sir, is Evans, the second housemaid. She was in Master Humphrey's room, sir, taking down some curtains that were to go to the cleaners. And she saw a taxi stop at the end of the mews, and Master Humphrey get out and come up the mews and in at the back. And she says he was looking like a ghost, poor lamb.'

'That he was looking like a ghost is conceivable. But that he is reasonably to be described as a poor lamb is a proposition that we seem hourly more able to controvert.' And Sir Bernard, in whom paternal vanity, like almost everything else, seemed apt to take decidedly polysyllabic form, glanced swiftly at Cadover. 'You may, however, proceed.'

'Well, sir, there was Master Humphrey creeping into his own house no better than a thief. And for a while Mary waited, thinking that he might have been taken ill, and didn't want everybody to know it, and would be coming up to his room. So she went down, and through to the little door at the back, the one that isn't used even by the tradespeople any more, and there was Master Humphrey slipping out again. He gave a terrible start at seeing her. And then he gave her a –' The parlourmaid hesitated.

'Do you mean' – Sir Bernard was displeased – 'that Master Humphrey gave Evans a sum of money?'

'No, sir. It was a hug and a kiss, sir. And then he made her swear by all sorts of things that shouldn't rightly be mentioned that she wouldn't say a word about it to anyone.'

Master Humphrey, it seemed to Cadover, was not unpossessed of some knowledge of the world. 'And after that?' he asked.

'That was all, sir – only Mary and me felt we ought to mention it. Master Humphrey went straight out after that, and Mary heard him drive away in his taxi.'

'Thank you.' Cadover waited until the girl had left the room. 'Now, sir, what do you make of that?'

Sir Bernard considered. 'Perhaps he did mean to come home and tell his story, after all. His covert manner of entering may have been a boy's natural reaction to the atmosphere of melodrama in which he found himself. And then he may have changed his mind and decided to go through with it after all.'

Cadover shook his head. 'That leaves the taxi unaccounted for. I mean his apparently having kept the taxi waiting at the end of the mews. He *meant* to go off again. In fact, he came home to fetch something. And that something wasn't in his own room, since the housemaid, it seems, was there until she went down and found him leaving.' Cadover paused. 'Well, let us take up another point. The Bolderwoods – what about them? I understand that they are cousins of yours. Are they reliable people?'

'I have gathered that Cyril Bolderwood – who, actually, is only a distant connexion of mine – is a person of substantial means and considerable position. His interests have been mainly in South America. His son, Ivor, has called upon me. He appeared a very sensible young man.'

Cadover scratched his jaw. 'Does it occur to you –'

'Of course it does.' Sir Bernard, for the first time, was vehement. 'I have been criminally careless. The boy is a problem during the holidays. He and I are, at present, obscurely out of sympathy. This chance of dealing with a difficult period came along, and I snatched at it. I considered that if I found a reliable man to go with him – Cox or Thewless – then nothing could go radically wrong. But I acted rashly. I ought to have considered that these people's manners and morals were virtually unknown to me. I ought even to have taken into consideration the special risks – one may call them professional risks – to which my position might conceivably expose not only myself but my child.'

'Perhaps you ought.' And Cadover again scratched his jaw. 'By the way, Sir Bernard, to whom are you responsible for the work you are doing at present?'

'I am directly responsible to a committee of the Cabinet – that is to say, to the Prime Minister and three of his colleagues.'

'I see.' Cadover's lips formed themselves into what might have been the position for a low whistle. 'Do you think that, about that, they would mind if you told me a little more?'

Sir Bernard Paxton looked grim. 'I should certainly need permission before speaking another word.'

Cadover looked grim too. He pointed to the telephone. 'I suspect', he said, 'that they won't keep you waiting long at Number 10.'

Sir Bernard made the call. Cadover faintly heard first an unfamiliar and then a familiar voice; he heard, too, the tiny ticking of the watch on his own wrist – it suddenly suggested to him the remorseless effluxion of time in the heart of a delayed-action bomb . . . Sir Bernard explained himself.

The answering voice came incisive and faint, like a political broadcast almost tuned out. The watch ticked – but now there was a voice in it too. *Amorous-arrogant-armed, amorous-arrogant-armed*: the voice in the watch was an urgent and imbecile whisper. Vaguely apprehended masses formed themselves in Cadover's vision, took intelligible shape as a scantily-clothed female form, no more substantial than plywood but with the power to flex in a lascivious langour its grotesquely elongated limbs . . . Cadover jerked himself awake. He had hours of vigilance ahead of him yet.

Sir Bernard had rung off and was talking to him; his brain cleared and he was listening with narrowed eyes. 'I see,' he said; '. . . yes, I see.'

'And I collate the reports once a month, Inspector, and revise the plan in the light of them. The plan exists in a unique copy that stays with me. And when I have completed each revision I appear before the committee in person and report. It all requires, as you may imagine, a great deal of interpretation to the lay mind.'

'No doubt.' Cadover had turned slightly pale. 'But that sort of thing will require singularly little interpretation when one day somebody drops it out of a plane on London or Moscow or New York. The understanding of the lay mind will be instantaneous and complete.'

'May the world's cities be spared that understanding, Inspector.' Sir Bernard looked for a second so like a lost child – so like, conceivably, the missing boy – that Cadover almost repented the grimness of his pleasantry.

There was a moment's silence. 'Now – Cox,' Cadover said abruptly. 'We've got no nearer to why he was a threat against which such violent means had to be taken. He couldn't, in any way, belong to this world you have been telling me of?'

'Good heavens, no! The poor young man possessed, as I have said, only the most moderate share of brains. I had the impression, indeed, that he had been in on some queer affairs about the world – but definitely, I should think, as a reliable subordinate. Good physique, no nerves, and a straight eye.'

'He probably had no precise notion of the sort of work you do?'

'His ideas on that would almost certainly be of the vaguest.'

Cadover thought for a moment. 'And there is nothing – absolutely nothing – further of any significance about him, or about your interview with him, that occurs to you?'

'I think not.' Sir Bernard Paxton frowned. 'And yet – at luncheon, I think – there was something –' He broke off. 'There *was* something, and it just eludes me. And yet something, connected with yourself a few moments ago –'

'Something about me?' Cadover was surprised.

And suddenly Sir Bernard snapped his fingers. 'You offered a pleasantry – something about atomic warfare and the world's cities. It was not – you will forgive me – quite to my liking. Now, *that* was what happened with Captain Cox at luncheon. He said something that I took to be intended as a jest, and it displeased me for the moment. I judged it to be somewhat familiar and a little fatuous.' Sir Bernard paused, aware that in this there might be an implication not altogether polite. 'I need hardly say that in *your* jest it was not similar qualities that disturbed me. Yours, far from being fatuous, held a little too much salt.'

Cadover could still hear his watch ticking. But, even with his adored son's safety at unknown hazard, this august personage had his own tempo.

'I was proposing to give Captain Cox some sketch of the Irish household in which he would find himself, and I began – I recall the word precisely – by saying that the Bolderwood family was most respectable. Whereupon the young man said, "Ah, they wouldn't be the Bolderwoods I know." I supposed him to be making the facetious suggestion that he himself was without respectable connexions and moved only in rag-tag and bobtail circles.' Sir Bernard Paxton hesitated. 'I even suspected mockery of what I am aware of in myself as a certain stiffness of manner to which, by persons uncharitably inclined, the name of pomposity might be given.'

For perhaps the first time since he had seen Peter Cox's dead body, Cadover felt a momentary disposition to laughter. Genius apparently had its naïve side, and nothing could be more exquisitely pompous in itself than the complicated cadence in which Sir Bernard had framed this confession. He checked himself. 'But actually, sir, you think –?'

'It now comes to me that he may have meant exactly what he said. He happened to know some disreputable Bolderwoods, and he was dismissing the supposition that I could have anything to do with them. Viewed in that light, the unfortunate young man's observation was a perfectly proper one.'

'Perfectly proper. But I don't see –' Cadover broke off with a sudden exclamation. 'Could that fellow Jollard have heard all this?'

'Assuredly he could. He was waiting table at the time.'

'And after this happened Cox remained with you for a substantial interval? There would have been an opportunity, I mean, for Jollard to contact his associates on the telephone and arrange for the bogus Humphrey to waylay Cox when he left?'

Sir Bernard thought for a moment. 'I am fairly sure there would. We had coffee together, and then we spent about an hour in going over Humphrey's school reports.'

'That would certainly be time enough. And now I think we may be said to have got quite a long way.' Cadover paused. 'It would be nearly all the way, indeed, but for one thing. You remember, sir, my mentioning the blackmailer, Clodd? He hoped to make a victim of your son, and recently he seems to have had little that was more hopeful on his hands. As a result, he has had your household under pretty close observation. You might call it professional observation, so far as a knowledge of crooks and their ways goes. And Clodd – who is probably dead by now – came to the conclusion that it was not a matter of *one* gang or organization being interested in your affairs. He was convinced that there are *two*. If that is true, and if we now go all out in one direction, we may simply be leaving Humphrey – and in some danger, let us admit – farther and farther behind. And there is something else that I am uneasy about as well. You have spoken of this vital plan which you revise monthly as existing in a single copy that stays with you. Does that mean here in your own house?'

Sir Bernard raised his eyebrows. 'Good heavens, no! I mean simply that, so long as the present organization of things holds, nobody ever sees it except myself. It stays in a place of security – of quite fantastic security, I may say – to the innermost part of which I alone have access, and access that is very strictly controlled at that.'

'That sounds good enough.'

'But it is true that I do keep one file of highly confidential ancillary papers here in the house. It is an essential time-saving convenience when I am visited by any of the people with whom I am permitted to discuss – well, the project in general. That file tends to get known, quite inaccurately, as the plan. And it is important enough, goodness knows.'

'It might have been known to, say, Jollard as the plan?'

'Quite possibly. And he has seen it in my hands half a dozen times.'

Cadover considered. 'I think I should like to see it myself.'

'See the file, my dear Inspector? I hardly think –'

'I mean, see it in your hands – safe and sound. Where is it kept?'

'In a strong-room in the basement, which was put in for me by the Government during the war. It opens on a combination known only to myself, and I am given to understand that it represents about the last word in security available today.'

'Well, sir, I think I'll just ask you to make sure. Would you mind? And I'll stop here and make one or two more telephone calls.'

Without a word, Sir Bernard Paxton left the room. Cadover made two quick calls, and then walked to the window. Broad daylight had flooded this prosperous part of London long ago. The vista disclosed was unexciting, but it spoke of a security so massive as to be almost smug. Here and there one could perhaps spy signs that it was on the down grade; nevertheless, it was civilization's (as *Plutonium Blonde* was art's) supreme achievement to date. Taking civilization, that was to say, as meaning the commercial civilization built up in the nineteenth century. It had all, Cadover reflected, come out of the spout of James Watt's kettle. And the probability was that it would all dissolve again in some more extensive manufacture of steam contrived by Sir Bernard Paxton and his kind.

Cadover turned round at the sound of a door thrown violently open behind him. Sir Bernard stood framed in it, pale and trembling.

'It's gone!' he said. 'The strong-room was locked as I left it. But the file has gone.'

Chapter 20

Dawn had found Mr Thewless fast asleep. The regular pulse of light flowing over his ceiling had grown faint before the early approaches of the sun and then had ceased – the lighthouse-keeper having first turned off his machine and then betaken himself to slumber. The day promised to be calm and bright. From far below, the sea murmured its suggestion of just such another obstinate refusal to come awake as that of Humphrey Paxton's unconscious tutor; had one looked out at it, however, one would have judged it impossible that any sound at all could come from a sheet of silver so unflawed. No wind ruffled it, and in the little hamlet by its side the pale blue peat smoke was beginning to rise straight to the deep blue of heaven. No keel furrowed it, for the foreign trawlers were already gone from the harbour, and gone too was the motor-cruiser whose riding-light Mr Thewless had remarked in the darkness not many hours before. Only on the horizon the brown sails of outward-going fishing-smacks were already vanishing through the faint line between sea and sky.

This marine solitude at one distance was matched by a mountain solitude at another; indeed, the actual appearance of the sun had been delayed a full hour by the interposition, to the east, of a single peak, obtuse and massive, about the bare slopes and outcropping rocks of which clouds were still lazily disparting. Below this, where the white cottages in their invisible lanes glistened like sparsely-strung peals flung down upon a mantle of brown and green, more tenuous vapours drifted, broke, fragmented themselves to a point at which, mere fleecy wisps, they matched the nibbling sheep now moving slowly up the hillsides to meet them. Nearer still, from little valleys yet lost in shadow, diminutive figures in bright homespun or sombre black climbed to the potato fields or set out, a donkey beside them, on the long trudge to the turf. Another day had begun.

And about Killyboffin itself there was some stir of life. The poultry, perhaps indignant at having been so unjustly cast under a cloud in the estimation of their owner, maintained a constantly augmented volume of angry cackle; the half-Ayrshire and several of her fellows, sequacious of the milkmaid, mooed impatiently outside a byre; dogs barked; Billy Bone clumped noisily about a cobbled yard; and through the house itself sundry servants, presumably released by their employer from their nocturnal segregation, bustled amid floods of lively conversation. And still Mr Thewless slept.

When he was finally aroused, indeed, it was by olfactory rather than by auditory sensation. His eyes, prompted by some titillation of the nostril, opened upon a large and steaming cup of China tea. It was a composing sight; nevertheless, Mr Thewless sat up with a celerity that spoke of a clearly returning consciousness of something untoward in his situation. A glance about the room told him that he had a visitor. Cyril Bolderwood, in an ancient and unassuming bath-robe made of turkish towelling, was sitting in his familiar position in the window embrasure. And now Cyril Bolderwood, observing that he was awake, gave him a cheerful smile. 'Ah,' he said. 'Good morning, my dear fellow.'

Mr Thewless remembered with something of an effort that he was this genial person's guest – his dear fellow, indeed – and that Ireland and the Atlantic Ocean lay around him. He stretched out his hand, secured the handsome cup, and sipped his tea. 'Good morning,' he replied. He was aware of something circumspect – provisional, almost – in his own tone.

'A really nice day. In fact, I should say that we are in for a spell of fine weather. And in August, on the west coast of Ireland, that is something, I am bound to admit.'

Mr Thewless considered this – and also certain matters now returning somewhat confusedly to his mind. 'Um,' he ventured.

'And – what's more – I have some rather good news.' Cyril Bolderwood got up and obligingly tested the temperature of a jug of hot water standing in Mr Thewless's wash-basin. He shook his head disapprovingly, picked up the jug, and, not without splashing and accompanying imprecation, ejected it from the room. 'Gracie,' he bawled down the corridor. 'What good-for-nothing, idle, chattering chit brought this disgustingly tepid stuff to Mr Thewless? Don't they know what's due to a man of his great learning? Don't they know that in London there's but the turning of a shining tap and you can scald yourself like a milk-pail at will? Send up a great jug, now, that won't disgrace us all, you worthless woman.' And the master of Killyboffin, flushed and irate, banged the door to and returned to his perch in the window. 'Yes, indeed,' he pursued with instantly recovered equanimity; 'capital news. Last night, you know, I put my foot down. I made a real row.'

Mr Thewless remembered a row – and although it had begun in dreams he was tolerably confident that it had indeed been a real row in the end. 'Ah,' he said cautiously.

'The result is that at breakfast, I'm glad to say, there will be a couple of eggs all round. I was afraid, you know, that there would be nothing but champ.'

'Champ?' said Mr Thewless. The constitution of this dish was not one of the matters upon which he felt any urgent wish to be informed. But for the moment he was at a loss how to broach more relevant topics.

'Yes, champ. I won't say that I haven't had a very tolerable champ in the north – and particularly in County Down.' Cyril Bolderwood was judicial. 'But here in the south I don't recall anybody as being able to make it really palatable. They're too lazy, I should say, to pound it properly with the beetle. That means that it comes out sloppy. And nobody, you'll agree, could pretend to enjoy a sloppy champ.'

'No,' said Mr Thewless. 'Nobody could do that.'

'But I expect young Humphrey – a nice lad, I'm bound to say, although his father is said to be uncommonly stiff – I expect young Humphrey will enjoy his couple of eggs. If he turns up for them, that is to say.'

'If he turns up for them!' Mr Thewless set down his cup in frank dismay.

'He was off and away hours ago. Exploring, I don't doubt. There's a strong streak of wanderlust in Humphrey, if you ask me.'

Mr Thewless was fleetingly conscious that this suggestion – in which he saw no special cogency – had been made to him before. 'You think he will be all right?' he asked. 'I am bound to say I feel a little anxious for his safety.'

'As right as rain.' Cyril Bolderwood's reassurance was so confident as to have no need of being emphatic. 'Of course, this countryside is full of every sort of rascal, as I think I've told you. But they wouldn't harm a lad – and especially an English lad. It's astonishing how popular the English are in Eire. Just the same as in India, nowadays. Nothing too good for them. And all because they've climbed down and cleared out. Why, if it wasn't for the presence of yourself and Humphrey, it would probably be champ this morning after all – and that in spite of all the fuss I made yesterday.'

Mr Thewless had by this time finished his tea, got out of bed, and wrapped himself in a dressing-gown. It ought to have been pleasant to shave while enjoying the society of one so informally companionable as his host. But somehow he felt slightly intruded upon – he was growing old and secretive, he supposed – and in an endeavour to dissipate this churlish feeling he too moved over to the window. 'Ah,' he said; 'I see that the motor-cruiser has gone.'

'It has – and I don't think we'll see it again.'

'I don't see any sign of Humphrey.' Mr Thewless, dazzled by the morning light, was peering vaguely at the distant mountain, rather as if his charge might appear in infinitesimal silhouette on the summit of it. 'And I *am* rather anxious, I must repeat.'

'The boy will be quite all right, you may be sure.' Once more Cyril Bolderwood was soothing. 'As a matter of fact, I rather think that Ivor must have gone with him – or, at any rate, that Ivor has followed him out. They had some plan, you may remember, of going off early together.'

'Yes, of course.' Mr Thewless wished that he could be certain of just what he *did* remember. That the night had held wild doings he was well assured. But there might, he judged, be humiliating reasons for his preserving only a somewhat distorted recollection of them. 'I am afraid', he pursued, 'that – after last night, you know – I am in a decidedly nervous state of mind.'

'Last night?' Cyril Bolderwood looked momentarily puzzled. Then he laughed heartily. 'To be sure – and I am afraid you really had rather a bad time. It's not being used to nonsense of that sort.'

'I see.' But Mr Thewless was very certain that he did *not* see. 'Nonsense?' he queried diffidently.

'Atrocious and rascally criminals,' said Cyril Bolderwood. He spoke with the greatest good humour. 'Abominable and thieving ruffians, breaking in in the middle of the night. And yet one can't be angry with them for long. Children, my dear fellow – mere children. And, of course, you must remember their religion.'

'Ah,' said Mr Thewless. He was beginning to feel slightly unnerved.

'I've had them break in before. It's why I shut up so carefully at nights. But the tiresome villains managed to get in somehow. They were after the whiskey, you know – nothing but the whiskey. How could they tell that you and I hadn't left much of it, eh?' And Cyril Bolderwood laughed more boisterously still.

Mr Thewless's discomfort increased. He took his host's last reference to be by way of tactful reminder that any distorted picture of the night's adventures which he might cherish had its origin in potations which could not with delicacy be more specifically referred to. It was true that he *had* drunk rather a lot of whiskey – and, moreover, to Irish whiskey he was quite unused. Conceivably it had some quite special hallucinatory power. Yet by all this he was not, in his heart, quite convinced. 'My impression', he said boldly, 'was decidedly different. I thought they were after, not the whiskey, but Humphrey.'

'Humphrey? Good lord!' And Cyril Bolderwood delightedly chuckled. 'Why, that's just the sort of notion the dear, fanciful lad would think up himself.'

This was disturbingly true; it cohered absolutely with Mr Thewless's own obstinate reading of much in his recent experience. Nevertheless, he tried again. 'I have a recollection – really quite a distinct recollection – of these intruders dogging me through the house. I was convinced that they were trailing me to Humphrey's room.'

'Odd,' said Cyril Bolderwood easily. 'A very odd trick for the mind to play. But, of course, we must remember that you had been thoroughly fatigued.'

'And my recollection stretches further. I had, just before the general alarm, a direct encounter with one of the prowlers. He was wrapped in a sheet.'

'A sheet!' Cyril Bolderwood looked blankly at his guest.

'And I threw something at him. I think it was a candlestick. The sheet fell and I had a moment in which I recognized him. He had travelled with me on the train from Euston to just before Heysham.'

'Dear me.' This time Cyril Bolderwood was not amused. He was mildly embarrassed, as a man must be to whom a guest obstinately propounds fantasies that have come to him *in vino*. 'That is very curious, to be sure – very curious, indeed. But I must really leave you, my dear fellow, to finish dressing. Breakfast will be in a quarter of an hour. I think you may find that a cup or two of strong coffee may do you a world of good. And – don't forget! – champ is off and eggs are on. Now I'll go out for a stroll and try if I can see the others.'

And thus, with a smile of more than customary joviality, the master of

Killyboffin left the room. Mr Thewless, before turning to his shaving water, remained for some moments staring out of the window. He was browbeaten, bewildered, worried. He was also, had he known it, on the verge of being extremely angry.

The breakfast-table was generously appointed for four. But only the elder Mr Bolderwood and Mr Thewless faced each other across it. A massive silver contraption, which opened at a touch upon at least a dozen boiled eggs, emphasized the depleted condition of the company.

'Ivor', said Mr Bolderwood, 'must still be hunting Humphrey up. I took a turn in the grounds, but there was no sign of either of them. A bit odd, eh? One would expect two hungry young people – guns or no guns – to be waiting for the gong. I hope that egg isn't too hard for your liking.'

'It is quite excellent; a great treat.' Having made this eminently conventional response, Mr Thewless was silent for some moments. Then, rather abruptly, he spoke again. 'I suppose, sir, you will inform the police?'

Cyril Bolderwood looked mildly startled. 'You mean if Humphrey runs away? I hardly think so. It would be my inclination to get in touch with his father first.'

'I certainly mean nothing of the sort.' Mr Thewless was as emphatic as he was surprised. 'What I refer to is last night's housebreaking.'

'Oh, that!' Cyril Bolderwood's laughter – and with a quality now really irritating to his auditor – rang out anew. 'Yes, I suppose I better had. Yes, I must ring up Sean Cushin, and he must go round and give the horrible scoundrels a talking to.' He glanced at his watch. 'I could do it in about ten minutes.'

'Ten minutes?'

'When the girl opens the telephone exchange in the village for the day. At night, you know, we are quite cut off from the world. In all these ways, my dear chap, we are shockingly unprogressive here in the south. This ruffianly Government in Dublin dislikes anything it can't find an ancient Irish word for. Telephones must be included. For the purpose of getting news about the country those fellows would probably prefer beacons on the top of Slieve League and Ben Bulben.' And Mr Thewless's host, as he offered this political information, chipped the top off his second egg.

There was silence for a minute. Mr Thewless was conscious that he was listening with some eagerness for the sound of approaching voices. The vehement tones of Humphrey Paxton, even if raised in some tiresome chronicle of fictitious perils, would at this juncture have been music to his ears.

But *were* the perils with which Humphrey tortured or entertained himself indeed merely –? Mr Thewless, before the half-apprehended threat of something like a Copernican revolution in his thinking – or better, perhaps, of a return to the primitive, the monstrous, the Ptolemaic hypothesis, the Humphrey-centric theory, as it might be called, of his own first alarms on the Heysham train: Mr Thewless, confronted by this, wisely suspended speculation for a while and sought the material recruitment of another egg.

Cyril Bolderwood, too, ate silently. There was now a slight frown, as of the first dawn of anxiety, on his normally candid brow. He rose, walked to the window, and stared out at the limited prospect commanded from the ground floor. Then he moved to the door, flung it open, and fell to his familiar shouting to invisible retainers. His instructions, it seemed, were for some sort of search to be made for the late-comers. Then he crossed to a sideboard, poured himself out a second cup of coffee, and returned to the table. But immediately he was back at the window. 'Those foreign trawlers,' he said abruptly. 'Did you notice if they've sailed or not?'

Mr Thewless looked up in surprise. His host's tone forbade the supposition that this question was asked merely in a conversational way. 'Why, yes,' he answered. 'I noticed that they had sailed.'

'Um.' Cyril Bolderwood reached gloomily for the marmalade. 'And Ivor is usually so very discreet. If anything, he is a young man too much to the circumspect side. May I offer you the marmalade? I shouldn't have thought it of him.'

To Mr Thewless this was, for the moment, altogether mysterious. He possessed, however, very considerable intelligence – was he not eminently capable with capable boys? – and this fact (which conceivably had not become apparent to his host) did now result in a dim apprehension of being 'got at'. But at least the marmalade was excellent, and he helped himself to a little more of it.

'All that talk', pursued Cyril Bolderwood presently, 'about the North Cape and the Midnight Sun. Unwise, I fear, with so imaginative and restless a boy.'

'My dear sir' – Mr Thewless was suddenly impatient – 'I must say, quite frankly, that I judge you to be indulging a bee in your bonnet. For you are apparently apprehensive of Humphrey's attempting to run away to sea, or something of the sort. And it seems to me entirely unlikely.' Here Mr Thewless paused, abruptly visited by suspicion. 'But your anxiety *is* really about that? You are not attempting to divert my mind from the consideration of risks of a different order? For a number of things that have happened do make me occasionally feel –'

'Other risks?' Cyril Bolderwood interrupted with brisk incredulity. 'Of course not! Mere fancies, my dear fellow – like your odd notions about the whiskey-thieves last night. But about Humphrey's perhaps cutting and running I am a little anxious, I admit.'

At this Mr Thewless felt so exasperated that he paused before framing a reply. And in the resulting silence the sound of a telephone bell was heard shrilling in the next room. Cyril Bolderwood jumped to his feet. 'Ah,' he said 'that worthless girl has opened her exchange at last. And here's somebody been waiting to get through, I'll be bound, this last half-hour. Excuse me, my dear Thewless, while I take the call myself.'

Cyril Bolderwood hurried out. He was absent for a long time. Mr Thewless looked at his watch, looked out of the window, took another piece of toast. Could his host, conceivably, be right? His own acquaintance with Humphrey Paxton was brief – hardly sufficiently substantial, certainly, for the hazarding of any very confident opinion. But Cyril Bolderwood's acquaintance with the boy was briefer still; and there was no sign that of this distant connexion he had previously known very much by hearsay. Yet Cyril Bolderwood had been talking as one might do from a settled familiarity with Humphrey's character. There was surely something artificial in this; there was, as it were, a perceptible forcing of the pace . . .

Mr Thewless paused on this conception, and as he did so his host returned to the breakfast-room. He looked, Mr Thewless thought, oddly pale – and moreover it was visibly with a trembling hand that he now poured himself out a third cup of coffee. Could he have had some calamitous news, and was he now nerving himself to break this to his guest? Mr Thewless took another look, and was convinced by indefinable but powerful signs, that he was in the presence of a man in a panic. And at this, inevitably enough, all his own repressed anxieties surged up in him. Could Humphrey really have run away to sea in a trawler? He nerved himself to speak. 'Mr Bolderwood,' he said, 'I hope you have not had bad news?'

'No, no – nothing of the sort.' And the owner of Killyboffin Hall sat down heavily. 'The telephone call was about something entirely trifling. A mere matter of domestic economy, nothing more. I must really apologize for having left you so abruptly. But none of the servants is reliable with the telephone. The miserable rascals –' But here Cyril Bolderwood's voice trailed off, as if he had not the heart for entering upon one of his familiar imprecations. 'The fact is, I have been thinking.' He broke off again, and stared into his cup. It was, Mr Thewless thought, demonstrably true that his host was thinking very hard indeed – much as if, on the issue, his whole life depended.

'I beg your pardon. You struck me as rather upset.' Mr Thewless hesitated. 'For a moment I had a horrid feeling that you might have been right, and that Humphrey had really bolted.'

'Dear me, no.' In Cyril Bolderwood's glance as he looked up there was a momentary gleam that told of swift decision. 'To tell you the honest truth, my dear fellow, I have never really been afraid of *that*. In fact you were more or less in the target area a few minutes ago. I have anxieties about Humphrey that I was anxious to conceal from you. And being unable altogether to conceal my feelings, I rather played up the runaway notion.'

At this Mr Thewless set down his cup and presented his entertainer with an expression that was altogether new. 'Explain yourself,' he said sternly.

'Well, my dear chap, we must admit, to begin with, that you had a deuced queer experience yesterday afternoon. The more I think of it, the odder does that affair in the railway tunnel appear to be. And then consider last night. Consider the fellows masquerading as whiskey-thieves. I didn't want to alarm you, you will understand, and I made light of it as far as I could.

Still, it was a bit sinister, wasn't it? Trailing you like that in order to get at the lad. And one of the criminals having been on your train the day before. I don't like that – I don't like it at all. It is suspicious, my dear Thewless; positively suspicious.'

'Suspicious?' Mr Thewless would probably have recognized within himself a rising tide of indignation had this not been overtopped for the moment by bewilderment and dismay. 'You surely don't think –'

'Ivor and I noticed at once that your mind was quite at rest. The significance of your adventure had quite escaped you. And we were most anxious not to spoil your holiday. But we have ourselves been uneasy – very uneasy. It is why we shut up the house so carefully last night. But the criminals managed to break in. Had we not changed the boy's room – an excellent thought of Ivor's, since information of where he was first put no doubt leaked out through the servants – they would have got him, you know: they would infallibly have got him. Tell me – did anything else out-of-the-way happen on your journey?'

'Humphrey certainly told me a very odd story. The suggestion seemed to be that he had been kidnapped on the train, shut up in a dark, confined space, and then in some mysterious fashion rescued or released again. It seemed an extremely tall tale.'

'Not at all. It would be the fellow you saw last night, you know, when you made such an excellent shot with the candlestick.'

'I see.' Mr Thewless was a good deal put to a stand by this incontinent promotion to a secure reality-status of what his host had so lately aspersed as mere vinous imaginings. And now a thought struck him. 'Good heavens! I'll tell you rather a significant thing. The man who was with us in the carriage – a bearded man with glasses, whom I really *am* sure I saw again last night – left the train at Morecambe – the stop, that is, just before Heysham Harbour. He appeared to be a fisherman, and he had a rod and so forth with him in the compartment. But when he did get off, and I saw him on the platform, he had a case containing some enormous musical instrument. It seemed quite unnaturally heavy. It could almost –'

'Have held Humphrey!' Cyril Bolderwood, triumphant for a moment, paused perplexed. 'But it *didn't* hold Humphrey so how –?'

Mr Thewless answered this abrupted question as by sudden inspiration. 'In the luggage-van, when I come to think of it, as well as this double-bass or whatever it was, there was a weighing machine with a set of pretty heavy looking weights. So somebody –'

'Exactly!' Once more Cyril Bolderwood interrupted. 'Somebody could have released Humphrey – it would tally perfectly with the story he told you – and tricked your friend for a time by shoving in the weights instead. I don't like it – I don't like it at all. The whole situation that is revealing itself, that is to say. Here is responsibility that we ought positively not to have undertaken. Our invitation was ill-advised. And Bernard ought certainly not to have accepted it.' Cyril Bolderwood shook a severe and judicial head. 'The son of a man in his position, not only immensely wealthy, but doing secret work of the utmost national importance, ought not to have been sent off into the blue – not even to quiet relations like ourselves; not even under the guardianship of so responsible a person as you, my dear fellow. And I'm surprised – indeed I'm positively astounded – that the English authorities don't provide a lad in such a position with a bodyguard. Now, in South America –'

Mr Thewless had risen and taken yet another prowl to the window. 'Still nobody to be seen,' he said. 'Oh dear, oh dear!' He turned back again. 'I fear I have been extremely remiss.'

'And in this countryside, of all places in the world!' Cyril Bolderwood spoke from out of the deepest gloom. 'Full of lawless wretches, ready to cut your throat as soon as look at you. Danger on every side.'

'On *every* side?' Mr Thewless's alarm grew greater still. 'You think there might be more than one – gang, organization, or whatever it's to be called – plotting against Humphrey?'

'Oh, no – oh, dear me, no!' Cyril Bolderwood was more swiftly emphatic than he had yet been. 'That would be a most extravagant suggestion. *One* gang, my dear fellow, led by this abandoned desperado with the glasses and the beard. And quite enough, too, in all conscience. He probably had that motor-cruiser we saw in the bay. Any amount of resources, you know, agents of that sort have.'

'Agents?' Mr Thewless stared. 'You mean emissaries of a foreign power?'

'No, no – nothing of the sort.' And Cyril Bolderwood violently shook his head. 'Quite the wrong word. Straightforward kidnappers, I should say, out for a big ransom.' He looked at his watch. 'This is bad – really bad, is it not? I wish those two would come back. I wish I could contact Ivor and have his advice!'

Mr Thewless, for whom the excellent Killyboffin marmalade had ceased to have any savour, pushed away his plate and looked in sudden, perplexed speculation at his host. It struck him that in this last cry of the elder of the Bolderwoods there had been more sincerity than had sounded in anything uttered to him for some time.

Chapter 21

'I suppose you know,' Ivor Bolderwood had said quietly as soon as he and Humphrey had gained the open air, 'what those fellows in the night were after?'

'Oh, yes – I know. Look, Ivor – is that a kestrel?'

And Ivor Bolderwood had stared upwards at the small black shape poised above the dawn – but not before his glance had travelled curiously over the lad at his side. Humphrey, he thought, was in some uncertain stage of development, and ready to take a push either way. It would not, surely, take much to thrust him back into childhood and its helpless fears; correspondingly, it would not take so very much to make a man of him. 'A sparrow-hawk,' he said. 'It's looking for something small and defenceless to pounce on, and carry off, and deal with at leisure . . . I was talking about these men that are after you.'

But Humphrey was still looking into the sky. 'Did you ever', he asked, 'see an eagle fighting with a snake – high up, like that?'

'No, never.'

'Do you think Shelley did?'

'Shelley!' exclaimed Ivor. 'And what has Shelley got to do with it?'

Humphrey turned to him in surprise. 'Got to do with what, Ivor?'

'Why, this that you're up against. This situation.'

'Oh, that!' Humphrey's gaze went seawards. 'Are there any gannets?'

'Gannets? If we went along the cliffs we might see some now.' And for some minutes Ivor obligingly talked about gannets – and only the more coherently because he was aware of the unexpected appearance of something imponderable in the situation. Was it possible that the boy's fantasy life had led him to a point at which he was a little astray in his wits? Or – a totally contrary hypothesis – had somebody already been on that job of making a man of him? Ivor paused to fill a pipe. It was a disordered thing to do long before breakfast, but the last few minutes had made him feel oddly in need of steadying. Much more so than the mere fact that, as things had turned out, it was necessary to keep a revolver next to his tobacco-pouch, and to scan every hedgerow as he neared it. That sort of thing was part of the day's work with him; he had made his life of it. But this . . .

He let the subject of gannets, sufficiently explored, easily drop. 'You are fond of Shelley?' he asked.

'Yes.'

There was a silence. The subject seemed one upon which Humphrey was indisposed to be communicative. But for a moment Ivor kept it up. 'I don't know much about him,' he said. 'But I seem to remember that he once lay down on the bottom of a pool just to see what it would be like to drown. And, if somebody hadn't interfered drowned he would in fact have been. I suppose people do sometimes court danger even of quite a deadly kind just to know what it feels like.'

'Oh, yes – I'm sure they do.' Humphrey's reply was entirely ready. 'In fact, Ivor, I'd say you were rather the type yourself.'

'We go down this little path.' Ivor glanced first warily about him, and then with an almost equal wariness at his companion. 'But look here, Humphrey, would you like to go back? The truth is, you know, that we're courting danger ourselves, and I don't know that I ought to do it.'

'Do you think this might be gold?' Humphrey had picked up a stone and was pointing with childish *naïveté* at a streak of copper pyrites. With an inconsequence that was equally childish, he threw the stone away, and it bounded down the cliff they were now approaching. 'But you are armed, aren't you?'

'I certainly am. I have a revolver in my pocket.'

'Then I think we may perfectly reasonably go on. How green the sea is between the rocks!'

'Good. That at least means that you trust me.' Ivor paused for another of his wary reconnaissances. 'You *do* trust me, don't you?'

And at this Humphrey stopped. His glance – as a glance should do upon such a question – met Ivor's direct. It was wholly candid. 'Of course I do,' he said. 'I trust you as much as I trust any man.'

The reply had an oddly mature ring, and for a moment it held Ivor up. But Humphrey, he realized, did mean what he said. 'Good!' And he touched the boy lightly on the shoulder. 'Then we can face it out quite comfortably. Be careful at this next corner; there's a pretty sheer drop.'

'I don't mind heights. What I do hate is the dark. Sometimes it can make a kid of me at once.'

'Is that so?' For an instant Ivor might have been detected bearing the appearance of one who makes a useful mental note. 'Don't you like the headland straight in front? And there's a big cave beneath it. We might just have time to get to it now. You might as well see what you can *while* you can.'

'While I can?' Humphrey was startled.

'Well, you see, this can't go on. There has been an attempt to kidnap you, and that is a very serious thing. My father and I couldn't possibly take the responsibility of not letting Sir Bernard know at once; and Mr Thewless is certain to feel just the same. It will certainly mean policemen investigating, and that sort of thing. And I am afraid it is likely to mean the end of your Irish holiday as well.'

'I see. I'm glad I saw the gannets.'

Ivor received this with a glance askance; it was too like a remote irony to be altogether comfortable to him. But presently he spoke again. For the right ideas had to be injected, and moreover he was increasingly curious about this out-of-the-way boy. 'It all sounds more like America than England or Ireland, doesn't it? But there it is. You are the son of a very rich man. And somebody wants to kidnap you and extort, no doubt, a very large sum of money. You understand that that's it?'

'That's certainly it.' Humphrey paused, apparently in hopeful inspection of another ore-bearing stone. 'And *precisely* it, isn't it?'

A stone rattled on the cliff-path behind them, and Ivor swung round upon it. Nothing was visible, and its dislodgement must be a delayed effect of their own passage. But had something else startled him as well? 'We should hate to think of your father having to pay up some enormous sum,' he said.

'Yes – it would be too bad.'

Was there, for a fraction of a second, something like a secret smile about

Humphrey's mouth? Ivor was prompted to heartiness. 'Well, we jolly well won't let them get away with it.'

'No, they won't get away with it – whatever it is.'

'That's the spirit!' But, to a greater extent than before, Ivor was sensibly troubled. The peculiar confidence with which the boy had spoken might be mere childishness – but could it be something else? 'I'm glad you're quite sure of it, Humphrey.'

'Oh, I'm sure, all right. It comes of not playing the game.'

'Not playing the game! I don't think I understand you.'

'I suppose they've told you that I am a problem-child?' And Humphrey turned upon his companion a glance of which the innocent seriousness was decidedly baffling. 'It's been going on for some years – and, of course, one of the grand signs is that I don't play the game. If I get a hack at rugger I think they're being nasty to me, and I bite. If I'm bowled at cricket I say it isn't fair, and I throw the bat at them.'

'How very odd.' Ivor found himself quite unable to decide whether these shocking revelations were fact or fantasy. 'But I don't see what they have to do with –'

'Just that I've cheated this time too. They think I'm playing the game according to the idiotic rules they've thought up for it – the sort of rules that mean that they're bound to win. But I'm jolly well not. You see, I've kept the ace up my sleeve. Or rather –'

'Yes?'

This prompting word had escaped Ivor in spite of himself. Almost certainly, Humphrey was now delivering himself of no more than the meaningless boasts of infancy. And yet –

'Yes, Humphrey?'

It dried the boy up at once. 'Where's the cave?' he asked. 'Does the sea go right inside? Do you need a torch for it?'

'You'll see in a few minutes. But you were telling me how you were going to cheat them. I'm awfully interested. Do go on.'

Humphrey laughed. 'You would pluck out the heart of my mystery, Ivor.' He paused, suddenly frowning. 'Hamlet said that, didn't he? Who did he say it to? Was it a friend? Can you remember?'

'I think it was a thoroughly bad hat.' Humphrey, Ivor realized, was momentarily suspicious of him after all; some drift of association from Shakespeare's play – the false professions, presumably, of Rosencrantz and Guildenstern – had disturbed him.

'I know! It was one of the men that Hamlet thought was on his side, but who took him away to England to be murdered.' Humphrey had stopped on the perilous little track they were following down the cliff, and now he looked at Ivor with what really was swift distrust. 'Shan't we be late for breakfast?'

'Good gracious, no! We got up ever so early. But of course, if you like, we can turn back. Look! There's the first of the trawlers going out.'

'And the motor-cruiser's gone already. It's a terribly lonely sea. From up here it looks like a single toy steamer on an enormous pond.' Humphrey moved to the very edge of the track and gazed down. 'We're still tremendously high up. Like one that gathers samphire, dreadful trade.' He repeated the line, and his spirits seemed to rise. 'Come along, Ivor! Does the cave have an echo in it? Is it very cold?'

They climbed down steadily. The face of the cliff now screened them entirely on the land side. Below them, where first a line of tumbled rock and then a long, thin sickle of sand separated the base of the cliff from the sea, the prospect was utterly deserted at this early hour – and looked, indeed, as if it might commonly remain so all day. They walked in shadow; the rock face was cold as they pressed against it; with the smell of brine there was as yet only faintly mingled any of the awakening scents of heath and ling. But already the sea was a sheet of silver under the sun, its surface disturbed only by the long, lazy undulations in the wake of the vanishing trawler, or by the sudden plummet-fall of a gannet from the sky. Lesser gulls were wheeling above and below them as they walked, making the still air vertiginous to the eye, exploiting in shrill cries their power to evoke haunting suggestions of loneliness, desolation, pain. The path turned and for a few yards ran through the cliff like a cutting. Ivor, who was ahead, walked with one hand always in his jacket-pocket. His expression, as soon as his face was averted from Humphrey, had hardened into that of one whose senses are on the stretch for tiny physical things. And Humphrey too, when he ceased to converse, had a look not altogether ordinary. Sometimes his glance rested on the figure immediately before him, and in these moments a spectator would have found it readily interpretable, for it was the glance of one who sees, and would fain solve one way or the other, a known and finite problem. But at other times his eyes changed focus and glinted upon something very far away; his breath came faster through parted lips; his chin went up; he trod with a certain automatism the rough path beneath his feet. The swooping gulls, had they been anthropologically inclined, might have reflected that here was a stripling warrior advancing upon unpredictable rites. And thus this odd pair picked their way – having nothing of the appearance, to an intimate regard, of persons proposing a before-breakfast stroll to a place of local curiosity. They were almost at sea-level now, and could hear the flap and murmur of small waves stealing in from an ocean still half asleep – an ocean wholly and vastly indifferent to what transacted itself upon its verge. Ivor turned his head for a moment. 'It will be dark in the cave. Did you say darkness frightens you?'

'Sometimes I could follow it like a dream.'

Ivor was silent for a moment. He found Humphrey's unabashed – his positively monarchal – raids upon English poetry very little to his taste. 'And all this,' he said presently, 'doesn't that frighten you a bit?'

'This?'

'The fact of these desperate and unscrupulous people being on your trail.'

'It frightened me most terribly.'

They moved on again mutely, Humphrey with some obtrusiveness offering no elucidation of the tense into which he had cast this statement. Presently, however, he did speak: 'And I'm very glad I'm not taking this walk alone.'

There was a lurking appeal for reassurance in this. Ivor laughed. 'We certainly can't have you scouring the country by yourself just at present. That ambulance would roll up again, and away you'd go. They wouldn't bag the tutor instead of the pupil a second time.'

'It was odd they did that, wasn't it?'

This brought Ivor up. 'Yes,' he said. 'It *was* odd.'

'And I had another escape on the Heysham train that was odd too.'

'Did you, indeed?' And Ivor's eyes came swiftly upon his companion. 'Tell me about it.'

But again prompting proved to be a mistake. Something – it seemed three parts mischief and one part caution – held Humphrey back from pursuing the theme. Instead, he returned to a confidence of another sort. 'I suppose', he said thoughtfully, 'that some people are brave and some cowardly in a settled way. I mean the one thing or the other all the time. They're usually like that in books. But with me it's intermittent.' He paused on this impressive word. 'Last night, you know, when I heard old Thewless yell, and I grabbed my gun in the dark and ran out, I think I was more terribly scared than I've ever been before. There seemed to be no safety . . . anywhere. But then, when I saw that he'd had a rough time again, poor old chap, and I was afraid he might be badly hurt, and I got my arm round him and told him to cheer up, I just stopped being frightened without so much as noticing that I *had* stopped. Of course you and your father were about by then. That must have been it.'

'That must have been it. Mr Thewless is an excellent man. But I don't think he'd cut much of a figure in a crisis.'

'Oh, no – you're wrong there.' Humphrey's eyes went off into distance, so that he looked for a moment very like Sir Bernard conversing with the ether. 'You ought to be right, but I'm sure you're wrong. Perhaps he really –' Humphrey abruptly broke off. They had reached the bottom of the cliff, and beyond a strip of boulders, rock-pools, and shingle the long beach stretched before them. 'What wizard sands! I'll race you, Ivor.' And the boy went off at a bound.

For a second Ivor was irresolute, his eye on the firm, shining surface, printless save for the criss-cross tracks of gulls; he might have been a man recognizing in a situation some factor of which account ought to have been taken long ago. 'Stop!' he called. 'Come back at once!' And he himself advanced a few paces as if meditating pursuit.

Humphrey turned back in surprise. 'What's wrong, Ivor? You – you haven't spotted the enemy?'

'No, not that. But those sands are dangerous. We must keep along the rocks. Rather a shame, isn't it? This way! Look, the cave is over there.'

'Dangerous! You mean it's quicksand?' Humphrey's eye travelled swiftly over the long beach, and his intelligence was working swiftly behind it. 'Why, it looks impossible! I've seen –'

'Not all over, of course. Just in patches. And that makes it thoroughly treacherous.'

'Treacherous?'

The word, as Humphrey echoed it, hung upon the air rather longer than Ivor liked, making him wish that he had phrased his warning differently. 'But it's rather fun going by these pools. There are crabs, and sea-anemones, and some astonishing seaweeds.'

Perceptibly, Humphrey hung back. Perhaps it was merely that the proffer of these interesting marine exhibits struck too juvenile a note – as if the graduate in Biggles, the student of Captain Hugh Drummond, the explorer of the pastoral loves of Daphnis and Chloe had been questioned on a forgotten command of the creations of Miss Enid Blyton. Or perhaps it was something else . . . 'We'll be there in five minutes now,' Ivor said. 'You can see the opening. It's that dark patch just before the next headland.'

'It's going to be a long way back to breakfast. And I'm hungry. I'm tired, too.' The corners of Humphrey's mouth were dropping, and his mental age was clearly threatening to drop with them. For a moment he dragged one foot after another across the rock – a gesture very sufficiently childish. 'I want to go –' He checked himself, and was evidently confronting the fact that Killyboffin Hall was not precisely his native ground. His shoulders squared themselves. 'Then come on!' he said. 'But straight to the cave. Never mind the beastly seaweeds and jellyfishes.' And he scrambled his way forward, avoiding further talk – and also, perhaps, a little heartening himself – by whistling some altogether vulgar tune. But every now and then his glance went out across the empty sands, and his high forehead grew puckered under its crown of untidy black hair.

The gulls wheeled around them, crying out as if in some futile warning. The mouth of the cave, foreshortened to a jagged slit in the face of the cliff, lay in front – obscurely sinister, like an unsutured wound.

Chapter 22

Humphrey Paxton's doubts had grown as he walked. But when he entered the cave he knew at once that this was where the thing must act itself out. It was a cave such as adventure stories own – and must have owned, indeed, from the beginnings of story-telling, so familiar was it, so much part of the already existing furniture of the dreaming or day-dreaming mind. The low orifice; the vast twilight chamber, vaulted and silent, with further dark *penetralia*, forbidden thresholds, beyond; the deep waters flowing, mysteriously and excitingly, inwards: these were part of the archetypal cave, recognized at a glance. And orthodox too, if at a more superficial level, were the smooth ledges that ran, like narrow and sinuous quays, on either side of the darkly gleaming water. One of these, a resolute man might hold against a whole gang of smugglers, a whole nest of spies; from such a narrow footing, a well-directed blow might send some pirate captain, his cutlass helplessly flailing the air, sheer into his own element. Such fancies were the natural promptings of the place.

Such fancies, too, Ivor Bolderwood designed. Walking behind Humphrey, and glancing at his watch by the last clear light from the open sky, he saw that in just eight minutes' time the boy was to be kidnapped. His tutor – and the world, should it be disposed to inquire – might believe for a time that he had run away to sea. His father might guess the whole truth if he had a mind to. But the boy himself must guess no more than half of it – and, in a manner, events had conspired to just this end. Humphrey, returned crumpled and scared to the paternal roof in so many days' time – or weeks, if that were needed – must have no story other than that of his brutal snatching from kindly relatives in Ireland. The crux of the plan lay in that. And did not this unexpected complication of rivals at the game, although it introduced a fresh hazard formidable enough – marvellously second what was aimed at? Something had happened on the Heysham train; something more had happened on the light railway – yes, and something yet further at Killyboffin Hall in the small hours. And in none of these things was a Bolderwood implicated or implicatable. Decidedly it all went well. And Ivor smiled to himself in the growing darkness – unconscious of his father, at this very moment (the girl at the telephone-exchange having consented to begin her day's duties), listening to calamity on the line from London; unconscious of *Bolderwood Hump, of gun for boy 1.15*, of the fact that the late husband of the indigent Mrs Standage had once coxed an eight at Cambridge, of the outraged moral feelings of Soapy Clodd, of Detective-Inspector Cadover now grim and silent in a police car hurrying out to Croydon. There had been ticklish moments, as in a design so fantastically intricate there were bound to be. The strange chance of Sir Bernard Paxton's having chosen Cox for a tutor – Cox with whom he had had that uncomfortably revealing clash in Montevideo some years ago – that, as hurriedly revealed by Jollard, had required action swift, tricky, and nasty. But it had gone off very nicely indeed. There was great advantage in being after something really big. The resources one could draw upon were enormous.

'Have you seen *Plutonium Blonde*?'

The boy's question came out of the near darkness like a pistol-shot, and was followed to Ivor's ear by his own sharply indrawn breath, his own voice raised a pitch in too swift answer. 'What do you mean?'

'It just occurred to me to wonder . . . I say, Ivor, old man, I suppose you've brought a torch? Does the sea go right in? Is the air all right? Ought we to have a candle-flame to test it with?'

He knew by now Humphrey's trick of rapidly fired questions. They covered hard thinking. But this time they covered too his own first alarmed sense that, after all, there might have been some flaw in the design. It was simply impossible that this inconsequent question could be coincidental. Humphrey had framed it, hoarded it, and at last fired it off with what had been, perhaps, triumphant success. The boy suspected something – and that was bad. The boy, reported as immature, unstable, and apt for his part in the plan, proved to have a clear head and an ability to go on using it – which was surely worse. And Ivor began to wonder – as his father, had he known it, was desperately wondering now – whether there were not some alternative way of going to work that would better meet the situation as it had come to stand. But yet he must not exaggerate his misgivings – nor, in the boy, what were still, perhaps, no more than drifts of suspicion, forming only to dissipate themselves moments later, like the pockets of mist still at play on the hillsides when they had begun to descend the cliff. Moreover, the little drama about to be enacted ought to be convincing enough even to the keenest-witted boy, the more especially as it had, all unexpectedly and thanks to the bearded and bespectacled rival desperado – the immense advantage of kindred incidents affording an ample 'working up' of the sort of responses required.

Ivor became aware that he had permitted a silence, conceivably sinister in effect, to fall upon the tail of Humphrey's questions. 'A candle?' he said. 'No, we need nothing like that. I've been through here scores of times. It was my favourite hide-out when I was a boy. But here's a torch.' He let the beam play past Humphrey's bare legs. 'Straight ahead.'

'Am I to walk in front of you still?' There was a touch of resignation in the boy's voice.

'Yes – straight forward. It's a perfectly secure path. But, if you don't want a ducking, don't take too big a jump when anything startles you.' Ivor was gay. 'And one or two things *can* do that. Look' – and he flashed the torch upwards – 'the roof is stalactitic, as you can see. That means an occasional drop of very cold water on your nose or down the back of your neck. And do you notice how we have started whispering?'

'I certainly do.'

'It's because any noise multiplies itself quite astoundingly. For instance, fish swim right in, and sometimes they leap. The row is quite surprising. It might be the body of the murdered man going overboard in a sack.'

'I see.' Humphrey's tone acknowledged the perfect appropriateness of this image to the spirit of the place. He halted and peered down at the water a few feet below him. 'What I don't understand', he said, 'is why it *flows*. It's like a subterranean river.'

'It's the flow that makes a little current of air all through, and keeps the atmosphere pure. And it flows because the whole cave is in the form of a horseshoe, with a second, rather smaller, entrance at the other side of the headland. That the sea goes slowly through is some trick of the currents here.'

'Don't you feel that the whole place is a trick?'

'The whole place?' Ivor was again disconcerted.

'A *papier-mâché* cave in a fun-fair. You pay sixpence to drift slowly through in a boat, and there are all sorts of prepared surprises. Romantic views of Venice behind dirty gauze, and luminous skeletons that drop down from the roof. I don't think I'd feel it out of the way if we met one or two prepared effects here. It's in the air, as you might say.'

'I doubt the romantic view of Venice.' Ivor answered readily, but he was now more conscious still of the boy's power to set him guessing. He was relieved to think that in five minutes the present ticklish phase of the affair would be over.

'Well, I think I'd have more stomach for the skeleton not on an *empty* stomach. Do we turn back presently, or go right through?'

'I'm all for breakfast too. But it will be just as quick, now, to go right through, and up another track through the cliff. Only' – Ivor's voice was regretful – 'we shan't have time to look into any of the little caves.'

'Little ones?'

'They ramify out from this. We'll pass several entrances presently. Some are quite long; others are odd little places, rather like side chapels in a cathedral. You must never explore them by yourself, though.' Ivor delivered this caution with benevolent emphasis. 'Not all of them are safe, as the main cave is. Some have crevasses you can't easily see, with stalagmites like needles at the bottom. Others have deep pools, with smooth sides, like wells. And in some the roof is unsafe, and one might be walled up.'

Humphrey laughed softly. 'To be entombed in *papier-mâché* – what a horrid fate!' For the first time the boy glanced round. And Ivor, glimpsing his face, felt considerably relieved – for the boy's expression was not that of one taking matters so lightly as his mocking words suggested. He was – rather magnificently, Ivor acknowledged – keeping up a part: a part out of some favourite book, perhaps, in which the hero marched insouciant upon his fate. But he was as pale as a sheet in the torch's beam, and his lower lip faintly trembled. Better still, he was puzzled; he had found, in whatever conjecture he had formed, no absolute certainty. And, so long as his mind hung in the balance between one interpretation of his situation and another, the event now imminent could scarcely but take it down on the desired side in the end. Reassured as to this, Ivor could spare a little admiration for the boy's performance. And how superb the intuition of the *papier-mâché*, the factitious and contrived, essence of the scene!

But the cave itself – or rather the vast cavern that, in fact, it was – stretched sufficiently substantially around them. It had now taken in its course a turn entirely excluding the daylight, and the water flowing perceptibly through it, together with the unintermitted unfolding before their torch's beam of the gentle curve from which it took its essential form, gave it all the suggestion of some interminable subterranean river projected from the imagination of Humphrey's favourite poet. The rock face was damp and chill as they brushed it; and neither chill nor damp would wax or wane, whatever change befell external nature – for here the varying cycle of the year had no power to probe. Owning thus no pulse, no rhythm, the place was lifeless and ungenial, propagating only an unnatural and abundant brood of sounds. The waters that were now, as they climbed to a greater height, almost invisible beneath them, whispered ceaselessly like conspiring maniacs in some Tartarean bedlam. Single drops of water, falling from the fretted vault, exploded on polished stone with a strange resonance, like that of a distant harp string snapping in an empty house at night. And their very footsteps, as if each in alarm at the other's tread, fled before them and behind them in a constantly repeated diminuendo of frenzied escape. When they spoke their voices, like every other sound, were distorted strangely, so that it was as if they were beset by their own travestied images in some hall of misshapen mirrors. And above them, as perceptibly present as if some muscular effort of their own must hold it off, was the vast suspended burden of living rock, so that one could think up through it until at length, at what might be almost an aeroplane's elevation, one came upon sheep nibbling the turf directly overhead.

'Here's the first of the smaller caves.' Ivor's voice called Humphrey back to what was no more than a narrow slit in the rock face. The torch, thrust through at the length of an extended arm, played upon a blank surface only some yards ahead – the meagre aperture making it impossible to see what lay on either side. Ivor laughed softly. 'I haven't been in there since I was a kid – for obvious reasons! It's not exciting, though – just a small, almost square chamber, like a cell. I think you could just get in, although I certainly could not. If we thrust you in, Humphrey, and fattened you up on nourishing dishes, or just left you till you'd grown a bit –' He broke off, again laughing softly – laughter through which there for the first time incautiously sounded as it were the overtones of an unlicensed and sinister imagination.

'I think', said Humphrey, 'that we'd better go on.' They moved forward again. 'How soon do we see daylight?'

'I should say it's just a little more than as far again . . . Hold hard! Here's another one.'

This time the aperture was larger, and gave upon an oval chamber, low-roofed, down the longer axis of which the light of Ivor's torch led the eye to two further opening, set close together, that led apparently to further cavities or passages. And of this place the form was at once unreasonably alarming and mysteriously compelling or attractive; it seemed to tug at the very roots of the mind. 'And behind', said Ivor, 'there's a sort of maze of interconnected tunnels. One could bring a picnic and play hide-and-seek.'

'I still think we'd better go on.' There was now a tremor in the boy's voice, and he pushed forward even before Ivor had swung his torch back to the ledge – it was perhaps three feet broad – which had now climbed to something more than a tall man's height above the water below. He walked for some moments in silence. Then his voice came back – and this time it was once more level, but very serious, 'Ivor,' it asked, 'why have you brought me here?'

The direct challenge was curiously difficult to meet. There really seemed, for the moment, to be no colourable reason. And, because of this, Ivor, it may be, a little over-pitched his reply. 'Why? Because it's such tremendous fun!'

'Of course I see that.' Humphrey's reply was now not so much level in its tones as drowsy, and it was almost as if he spoke with some ambiguity he scarcely understood. 'I can see you find it that; I can see . . . the fascination. But it's . . . well, so decidedly underground and isolated.'

Ivor felt the torch twitch in his hand, felt indeed his whole body twitch as if a touch had been set to his main-spring. It was true that he had for long – and for no very pressing exterior necessity – found his fun in a world uncompromisingly subterranean. But now, blessedly, the definitive moment had come, and he could neatly enough introduce it by elaborating upon his reply. 'Rather fun,' he repeated. 'And at the same time quite safe for us in our present odd situation. Not that this wouldn't be rather a neat place for an ambush.' He let the torch play idly around them as he spoke. 'But it's only the local people who really know about the caves. The kidnapping crowd would never find their way in here.' He laughed lazily – injecting into the tone of it all the suggestion of unweariness, of relaxed vigilance, that he could. 'By the way, there's another little side-cave just here.' For a second his torch touched a dark concavity beside them. 'And it's here that there's an echo. If we stand with our backs to the little cave' – and he swung Humphrey round – 'we'll just catch it . . . *Cooee!*'

There was certainly an echo – although no very remarkable one, perhaps, in this home of echoes. They listened to it die away. 'Yes,' said Humphrey doubtfully. His voice was almost that of one who catches from the air some hint of defeated expectation.

'*Coo-ee!*'

In its turn, too, Ivor's second call ebbed away. There was a second of something as near to silence as the place allowed. And Ivor received it rigidly, his every muscle quivering. He turned – his motion was at once swift and indecisive, blundering – and strode into the small cave behind them. Humphrey – driven by darkness, led by curiosity and the full store of courage he had brought into these recesses – followed.

The boy followed – and it was as if he had dived head foremost into a maelstrom of violence whose buffeting made all mental process impossible, made observation as discontinuous, as phantasmagoric, as it was terrifying. Immediately before him was a flailing octopus-shape, uncertainly resolvable into the locked bodies of struggling men. From amid them Ivor's torch, as if in a clenched hand forced upwards, circled wildly on the dripping, gleaming roof. From some farther corner another torch was at play upon the scene, and through its beam Humphrey dimly glimpsed two further figures that seemed to be of men bound, gagged, and thrust out of the way, like supers whose moment was past in the advancing play. Then all his attention was swept to Ivor's face, sprung into fierce illumination, as by some searing light thrust hard against it. Desperation and rage glared from it, and with these emotions were mingled still the mere surprise of the wary man, betrayed against all expectations. His head went back, blinded; and from amid the confusion of pants, and groans, and blows driven hard upon a human body – grievous sounds multiplied and distorted into indeterminable agonies by the configuration of the place – Humphrey heard his companion's voice straining for a command of articulate words. 'They've got us! Run, Humphrey, r –' A fist came up hard against the working jaw. He saw blood spurt from Ivor's crushed mouth. The panting and groaning grew of heavier respiration more desperate.

For a moment Humphrey stood motionless – paralysed by his fear, paralysed by the vast injustice of the road his thoughts had lately been travelling. For here was revelation. Here was his cousin Ivor – whom he had monstrously suspected, whom he had even believed himself by cunning questions to have lured into self-betrayal – here was Ivor straitly beset by his, Humphrey's true enemies; here was Ivor literally defending him to the death . . . And Humphrey's legs, which for some seconds had been no legs at all, but clammy columns rooting him to the rock – Humphrey's legs became compact of nerve and muscle. Even his lungs obeyed him, so that it was with a shout of passionate anger, admirably calculated to wake the remotest echoes of the caves, that he charged into the fight, raining blows where he could.

And the struggling mass of heaving limbs and straining torsos gave for a moment under this fresh impetus, gave sufficiently for Ivor to heave himself partly free and snatch out his revolver. But they were upon him again in an instant, and it was without aim or any effective control that the weapon, twisted into air, now again and again spat fire – spat fire and vomited thunder, cataclysm, chaos as of the ruining down of the very pillars of the world. For this rapid succession of reports, which would have been sufficiently ear-splitting in itself, the caves in their farthest extension, their remotest and most intricate honeycombing, rose to nobly, as to a challenge. Second after second the uproar only grew, as if straining to some hideous consummation, some final shattering of the ear, the begetting of some last, all embracing Noise by which, as by the angel's terminal trumpet, all noises should be ended . . . It ebbed; hearing, exhausted, slept even in the midst of continued turmoil; another, and sluggish sense took over; the universe was all gunpowder and sweat.

Humphrey's arms were pinioned. There were shins before him and he kicked; there was some fleshly part, straining through stretched cloth, and he bit it – deep. He felt himself lifted bodily and pitched through space;

he might have been in mid-air still when his reawakening ear heard what was surely Ivor's last shuddering cry; he fell shatteringly on rock and for a moment lay still, knowing only that the pain he would presently feel would be deep and sickening in belly and groin. But the fight, he realized, continued after all; gasps and grunts attested it to his ear even while nothing but a swimming blackness hung before him. He staggered up on one knee, and as his eyes cleared saw standing before him, looking dispassionately down, the bearded man of the Heysham train. The man smiled at him – a sweet, evil smile, far more terrifying than any expression of ferocity could have been. The man smiled and then – expertly, with cold brutality – kicked the boy's raised knee, so that he tumbled again, as through a wave of agony, to the ground. His consciousness mercifully flickered; he was fadingly aware of the fight rolling out of the little cave to the narrow ledge beyond, and then of a reverberating splash, as of some inert body being pitched into the dark waters below. Instantly, as if it were his own fate, some cold element closed over him.

Ice-cold water deluged him. But it was not that they had thrown him in too; it was simply that they had found means to give him a good soaking by way of restoring him to consciousness. And at least it worked. His mind suddenly was very clear; he lay on his back and stared up into dazzling torchlight; beyond this hung the faces of his bearded enemy and two other men. They looked down on him in grim proprietorship, like people who had run some troublesome pest to earth. The bearded man spoke. 'He's cost us a good deal,' he said. 'But there he is. Bring him along.'

Humphrey was in great pain. In the attempt to smother it, he rolled over on his stomach. One of the men bent down and took him hard by the hair, dragging him up upon his hands and knees. Weakly, he began to crawl. The second man kicked him hard behind.

Had it not been for this last savagery it would all have been over with Humphrey, for he had believed himself – and with substantial reason – to be beaten. But in this there was sheer indignity as well as pain; it confronted him with obscure memories he had resolved never again to entertain; a flame of anger rose in him and brought him supernaturally to his feet; he saw the dark cave and the men around him through a milky mist. And he found that he had a weapon in his hand. It was no more than a short length of heavy rope, brought by his antagonists for their own sinister ends. But involuntarily he had grasped it – and now, straight before him, was the bearded man's face. He put all his strength into the lash; he heard a scream that went through his veins like wine. He swung round and one of the other men confronted him – surprised, straddled, vulnerable. Humphrey praised God for his stout shoes and kicked. The man went down howling. Humphrey jumped his body as it fell and ran out of the little cave.

He was in darkness and on the narrow shelf that led – but over interminable distances, as it seemed to his memory – to daylight and the possibility of freedom. A dozen feet below him, and flowing between walls of sheer rock, was the sea; and somewhere down there the dead body of Ivor drifted. Behind him were two ruffians recovering from an unexpected over-throw, and a third, uninjured, who must be coming hard after him now. They would have torches. He had only eyes which – from sheer necessity and the love of dear life – had at least some apparent power of distinguishing between the greater and the lesser darkness of rock and air. But this served him only as he stood and with concentration peered. Whereas his only chance – his only ghost of a chance – lay in the rapid flight that might gain him a flying start. He must race along this winding ledge in blind precipi-tance, with nothing to guide him but his finger-tips stretched out and brushing the rock face beside him as he ran. Yes, that was decidedly his single hope: to wring from his sheer desperation a speed more hazardously headlong than any his enemies, equipped with torches though they were, would willingly venture on.

It is not easy to run full-tilt through any pitch darkness; it outrages an instinct against which the will can scarcely urge the muscles on. Much less is it easy in the knowledge that ice-cold waters, through which a corpse is drifting, await one at the length of an extended arm. But Humphrey, having come at the intellectual necessity of running, ran. He remembered that the path, worn smooth whether by generations of smugglers or by the operation of the sea, had presented a reasonably level surface underfoot, so that there was comparatively little danger of a stumble. But in places, and even when he had been moving with care the other way, it had been too slippery for comfort; and in this there lay one of the dangers that he could afford now only to ignore.

For now they were after him. The cave was alive with their footfalls – footfalls that appeared to recede from him with miraculous speed, others that with an equal speed overtook him, but died away as they came. He was skilled to interpret this echoing confusion now; he knew that all three men were in the pursuit; and he knew that they were failing to gain on him as they ran. Hope in him grew suddenly strong. They could, of course, pinning him down in the beam of the their torches, shoot. But there was no reason to suppose that a dead boy would be of any use to them, and he knew enough of firearms to realize that only an exceptional marksman could, under such conditions, with any confidence fire only to maim. Certainly it was not unlikely that, if their pursuit failed them, they would shoot to kill rather than let him carry his story out of the cave. But this was simply another of the dangers about which nothing could be done.

His path was sloping downwards now, and an occasional glint from the water came up to him as he ran. His breath was coming very short and his heart was pounding; he had the swift, horrible knowledge that, unexpect-edly soon, his strength was going to fail. He had been pretty roughly han-dled in the little cave; his knee as he ran hurt in a fashion quite outside his experience, and it was this that took it out of him most. Hitherto, moreover, he had thought of his danger and this hideous, subterraneous place as being coterminous. But now he realized that there was only childish instinct behind this coupling of daylight and safety. He remembered the long beach, the long climb across the face of the cliff. Barring the unlikely chance of some sufficiently numerous assemblage of persons in that solitary spot, he had really no hope at all. He was simple giving the creatures behind him a run for their money.

Meanwhile, he was still heading them. But this start, after all, had been of the slenderest, and they were so close that, on rounding a bend, the torchlight they cast before their own feet afforded him, too, some illumination as he ran. And now one of them, realizing this, advanced his beam, for an instant let it rest on him, and then made it dance in rapid zigzags immediately before him. It was a cunning move, so bewildering as almost to take him into the water at once, and for the time he could only reduce speed so that he knew that they were gaining on him – so that he expected to feel, indeed, at any moment the hot breath of a pursuer on his neck. But still he ran, for the good reason that there was nothing else to do. They were not even the sort of urbane kidnappers who had frequently entertained him in fiction; if he was not to be booted and wrenched and tugged – treated worse than one might be treated at the most horrid of schools – he must keep out of their heavy hands. Particularly, he grimly thought, after having so gloriously landed that wallop with the rope's end, that extremely ungentleman-like kick . . . One of them had begun to shout. The sound, although in itself alarming, raised his spirits once more, since it seemed the distinctly futile expedient of an angry and baffled man. But this luxury he enjoyed only for a second; there was an answering shout from straight ahead, and the darkness was cut by a dazzling ray that leapt up and took him full in the eyes like a blow. It brought him up dead. And as the torches behind him advanced, and as the first blinding effect subsided, he saw enough to know that any faint hope of its being succour that lay ahead of him was vain. For here was simply another ruffian of the deepest dye.

The man advanced. The footsteps behind were now only a score of yards off. Only one resource was left to him: to take a header into the black waters below. But, even so, he could not swim *away*; he could swim only up or down, and most certainly not so fast as his enemies could run. They would only have to wait, and presently haul him out like a half-drowned rat . . . And now from in front and from behind they were upon him; their hands were stretching out to clutch, to wrench. Terror pouring over him, he cowered, shrank back against the face of the rock as if in very pity it might open and receive him. His shoulders were crushed as in a vice; he twisted, thrust, squirmed – and the rock *had* received him. He was *through*. In a fraction of a second's complete clarity he realized what had happened. This was the little cave into which Ivor had not been since he was a kid. This was the little cave through the narrow cleft to which no grown man could hope to penetrate. He fell on his hands and knees, and a strange new clamour was all around him. He listened to it with curiosity, but without alarm. It was, he discovered, his own wildly pealing laughter.

There was clamour from outside too, and for the moment it was merely bewildered. The speed of what had so unexpectedly happened had given to his disappearance all the effect of something out of Nature, and his adversaries were utterly at a stand. But his laughter had betrayed him; there was a shout of comprehension; once more torchlight was playing full upon him as he crouched. And like a minnow in a tank Humphrey started into movement and scurried to the most inviolate corner of his fastness. There he huddled, his heart pounding with the force of hammer strokes in his chest. Had Ivor's calculation been correct? Or could one of these men, if not too bulky, actually, fatally, squeeze through? There was a sickening sound from the aperture of successful heave and shove; then an exclamation of discomfort, of pain; there was a grunt as somebody freed himself from the constricting rock; there was imprecation, hurried and murmured talk. Humphrey waited, and this process repeated itself – again with no ill result. And at this Humphrey stretched himself out in utter luxury on the ground, his every limb relaxed. And as he did so the possibility of an ease yet more exquisite dawned on him. He could allow himself the extravagance of speech. 'Hullo,' he said. 'Hullo, you silly asses – won't you come in?'

At his words, the murmur outside stopped. He heard heavy and exhausted breathing, and realized that the condition of these great brutes was altogether inferior to his own; it was out of *them* that the headlong chase had really taken it. The knowledge went wildly to his head; his sprawled body curled itself like a spring; he was once more doubled up, dissolved, in helpless laughter. Through this he struggled again for speech, and presently it gloriously came – a torrent of childish mockery, rude epithets, snatches of verse, lavatory humour, farmyard imitations, puns. And when he had done himself this ease he was suddenly serious, practical, assured. There was a stick of chocolate in his pocket; he took it out and ate a piece with slow deliberation. Then again he spoke. 'Hullo, chaps – you still there?'

'We are here, Humphrey.' It was the voice of the bearded man; Humphrey remembered it as it had sounded on the Heysham train.

'Don't you think you'd better be cutting along, you great ugly, stupid, incompetent, clumsy brute? You've lost, you know – and that's that. If you hang about in this very unintelligent way you only increase your chances of an early appointment with the gallows.' Humphrey paused, pleasurably savouring this superior flight of rhetoric. 'The others realize that, you know. Just have a look at them; they're dead scared at what they've done – the dirty, murdering swine.' Exultation had suddenly left the boy; he was shaken from head to foot by what he realized was hatred and rage. 'You killed my cousin, you low maggots! You killed him when he was fighting to get me out of this. And if you *do* cut off now, if you bolt to the furthest corners of the earth, I'll never rest until I know that the law has brought you back and snapped your filthy necks.'

This speech was evidently not without effect. The murmuring outside was renewed, and this time it held a note of altercation. Presently, however, there was silence, and then the bearded man spoke. 'We are going to wait for you, Humphrey. We are going to wait until you come out.'

'And whatever is going to bring me out?'

'Thirst might, for one thing.'

'Never believe it. The moisture coming down these walls isn't even brackish. Besides, the idea's absurd. Ivor and I have been missed by now. And it's very likely that the racket those pistol-shots made has been heard over half the countryside. Look at your low friends again. *They* feel that. They'll be off without you, if you don't quit. And I'm not absolutely convinced that they won't put a bullet in you first – just for luck, you big stinker.'

'We can smoke you out.'

'Absolutely useless.' Humphrey was in command of the situation, and he knew it. 'I only got in with a tremendous effort and all my wits about me. Do you think I'd ever manage to get out again when half-stupefied? Besides, you sadistic moron, I'd rather die than fall into your hands. You know that – don't you? And it goes for shooting, too. Fire often enough into this little cave and, sooner or later, a ricochet would get me. But it wouldn't do you much good, would it? . . . Do I hear people coming?'

This last stroke was admirably calculated; it produced a moment's near-panic in the enemy. On the strength of it Humphrey had another piece of chocolate.

'Your only real chance is to clear out now and try again tomorrow. Or why not *pretend* to clear out now, and look somewhere for the innocent lad as he breaks cover and makes for home?' And Humphrey laughed comfortably. 'I expect you can answer that one. I'm not *going* to break cover; not until they've come down from the house to hunt for me. And not then either; not until they've sent for half a dozen armed policemen. I'm through with this as private fun, you great big ugly maggot. You've done something too jolly beastly. I'll have detectives and all the rest of it now. So be off, and crawl back into the woodwork. After the rotten show you put up last night, creeping all round Killyboffin and getting nothing but a clip on the ear from Thewless, I wonder you have the face to stay in business. And besides, you know, that feeble performance hasn't gone for nothing. It means that the police and the madhouse folk are out by now, scouring the country for a pack of half-wit, yellow, incompetent crooks.'

If there was much in all this of Humphrey's that was deplorably lacking in elevation of thought and dignity of tone, it was a speech nevertheless persuasively grounded in solid sense. The assistant ruffians were now audibly for immediate retreat; only the bearded man was obstinate – was, indeed, whipped up to fury. There was a moment's silence and then Humphrey was startled to hear the old heaving and straining begin again. The most formidable of his adversaries was having another try. But the boy was confident now. He crept up close to the aperture and substituted for his late loud tone a bloodcurdling whisper. 'Come on, old mole – work away! Do you know what I've got here? A really nice lump of jagged rock. And when your rotten head comes six inches nearer I'll pound and bash it into a pulp.'

There was a moment's stillness, followed by a sound of rapid extrication. The bearded man had given up. And Humphrey – who was undoubtedly behaving very childishly – had just begun to cast about in his mind for some further contumelious strain when the silence was cut, to positively electrical effect, by the shrill blast of a powerful whistle. The sound came apparently from that larger of the entrances to the long cavern by which Humphrey and Ivor had entered, but in a fraction of time its echoes were everywhere, so that it was impossible to tell by how many actual pairs of lungs the wild alarm was being sounded. By the ruffians without – whose morale, indeed, must have been considerably undermined by the implacable eloquence of their young antagonist – it was taken as a plain signal of whole cohorts advancing to the vindication of law and order. Humphrey glimpsed the torchlight through that blessedly narrow cleft waver and fade. Then he heard, first, a single, deep, panic-stricken curse; and, second, the sheer music of four heavy men taking to their heels. Again, and this time nearer, the whistle shrilly blew; and again echo wrought the same rich confusion of effect. With surprising speed the pounding footsteps – themselves augmented and distorted to render effects as of a whole herd of buffalo in stampede – faded and ceased. There was a second's silence and then, from the direction in which they had departed, the roar of a powerful marine engine starting into life. Perhaps, Humphrey thought, it was the motor-cruiser. They would have had it lurking at that farther opening of the cavern by which Ivor had proposed that they should themselves leave it.

Anyway, they were gone. And – quite suddenly – Humphrey felt queer; far queerer than he had ever felt in his life before. There was now only darkness round him, but it was a darkness that danced and sickeningly swam. He had believed himself to be standing firmly on his feet. But to his surprise – the dim surprise of an already fading consciousness – he found that he was really crumpled up in a deflated, a quite desperately small and weary, heap. He had an uncertain impression of light footsteps near at hand; of his own name being called, and called again, in a familiar voice. But his bruised and exhausted body had already curled in upon itself. He lay in a posture of infancy, a thumb stolen to his mouth. Perhaps he had fainted. Perhaps he was simply asleep.

Chapter 23

It was ten o'clock. Mr Thewless had retired to his bedroom and was finishing his unpacking. The operation was not exacting, and it need hardly
be said that he performed it in almost complete absence of mind. His chief
concern – apart from the almost intolerable one of simply *waiting* – was to
decide whether the situation demanded any immediate initiative on his own
part. By this he meant, say, action within the next half-hour. For it was
quite clear to him (and he marvelled, indeed, that it was not quite clear to his
host) that the sensational situation now admitted and to be faced decidedly
forbade the whole morning's passing without the taking of some quite obvious steps. He himself, he saw, had been extraordinarily obtuse; but he was
by no means now – as the elder Mr Bolderwood appeared to be – markedly
confused and dilatory. His initiation into the guardianship of Humphrey had been, thanks to the boy's seemingly bizarre behaviour at Euston,
a matter of wild and blundering suspicions; from this he had passed into
a phase of stubborn scepticism; and that phase his host, until not much
more than a few minutes ago, had sustained him in with what might appear,
to a scrutiny more leisured than that which Mr Thewless now commanded,
a positively mysterious answering obtuseness. But the events of the night
had constituted a fence stiffer than any reassuring interpretation could readily take. And Mr Bolderwood, after what appeared in the retrospect a merely
muddled endeavour to do so, had come round – dramatically and, to Mr
Thewless's recollection, upon no fresh presentation of argument or evidence –
to the view that Humphrey was, and had been, very startlingly in danger.
This being so, certain necessities were clear. The police must be told, and
their protection claimed – a proceeding that doubtless involved calling upon
forces considerably more substantial than the hamlet of Killyboffin could
provide. If there was likely to be delay here, the making of some immediate
appeal was only more desirable. And, again, Sir Bernard Paxton must
be communicated with at once. And this in particular, Mr Thewless
thought, was his own responsibility. Only it raised one issue the undeter-
mined nature of which would sound awkwardly on a trunk-line to London.
Was the threat against Humphrey merely impending still? Or had it accomplished itself?

The boy had gone out early, perhaps accompanied, perhaps only followed, by Ivor Bolderwood. And neither the boy nor the young man had
returned for breakfast. This, looked at squarely, was occasion for the blank-
est dismay; and the mounting irritation that Mr Thewless felt at something
obscurely equivocal in the attitude of his host was for the moment swamped
by an even larger tide of self-reproach. The very moment of his waking up
from the heavy sleep that had unfortunately followed upon his night's
adventures should have seen him hurrying to his charge's side, should have

seen him raising a hue and cry when the boy was discovered to have made off. Instead of which, he had allowed himself to be half cajoled and half bullied into some hours of passive spectatorship. What ought he now to do?

He was at the immense disadvantage, had he known it, of having never had other than the most respectable persons within, so to speak, view-halloo; and it was thus his instinct, when a rat was scented, to peer rather remotely at the horizon. He did this in sober fact now, crossing to his window for perhaps the twentieth time and gazing out as if in the expectation of discerning a band of cut-throats on the farthest hill-top. Suspicions alto-gether more domestic were, indeed, dimly awake in him, but they had as yet taken no effective grip on his mind. He knew simply that he was per-turbed by more than he could bring to the surface. He knew, for instance, that he had distinctly failed – had, unaccountably, over the last few minutes so failed – in taking some effective measure which it had been open to him to take. His inability at all sharply to focus this perception agitated him physically, and this agitation now had a small but fateful consequence. He let slip from his hands a small note-book which he had taken from his suit-case a moment before. And as it fell to the floor he was vividly reminded of an incident of the previous evening. Just so had Humphrey, while still occupying the room next door, dropped a note-book upon his tutor's enter-ing. But Humphrey had done something further. He had then kicked the note-book deftly beneath the carpet.

It might well be there still. And Mr Thewless – the tiny episode showing vaguely portentous in the light of subsequent events – resolved at once to retrieve it. He slipped into the next room, pulled back the carpet, and found that the note-book indeed lay to his hand. He carried it back with him, glancing at it the while. Why should Humphrey have been embarrassed when discovered having dealings with it? It was a plain exercise book such as one might buy for sixpence, with the name 'H.E.H. Paxton' written in a bold if inelegant hand in one corner. Presumably, Mr Thewless thought, it served as a private diary. He opened it gingerly at the first page and found this surmise amply confirmed:

DAIRY
(cont.)
Seecret!
Confidential!
Stranger, do not read!
H.E.H.P.

Mr Thewless frowned – partly at Humphrey's orthography, which was deplorable in so capable a boy; partly at the moral problem which he was himself confronting. But his perplexity lasted only for a moment and was resolved with great good sense. He opened the diary and scanned it rapidly.

*

While Mr Thewless was unpacking – slowly and in some absence of mind – his host, oddly enough, was engaged in the inverse operation – and if with an equal absence of mind certainly with much greater speed. This, he was reflecting, was it. To this his cherished and inimitable son, venturing at length too high a flight, had brought them both at last. In all probability there was nothing for it but a quick get-away and a going underground for good. One can, of course, engage in espionage and sundry related activities without cutting oneself off from the possibility of retiring, upon any discomfiture, to a number of pleasant asylums in one or another part of the civilized, or approximately civilized, world. But when one has been masterfully concerned in a murder in a London cinema one is almost certainly at the troublesome necessity of changing one's identity for good. The dubious South American magnate, the eccentric Irish squire, were both *personae* from which the last grains of sand were falling. Or so, at least, to the elder Mr Bolderwood it appeared. Ivor, when he returned, might yet contrive a more hopeful view of the matter.

But Ivor – such was the necessity of their plot – was not to return for a good many hours yet. Bloody but unbowed, he was to stagger in with the news of his own near-murder and the snatching away of Humphrey. And in the interim – such still had been the plan – the dimly perceptive Thewless was to have been put off with vague speculations of the boy's mere truancy – a truancy from which Ivor was to be represented as no doubt busily recovering him . . .

Thus did Cyril Bolderwood, nervously stuffing bank-notes and negotiable securities in a convenient grip, doubtfully recapitulate to himself the plot that had seemed so admirable so short a time ago. Abundantly wishing for his son's return, he yet felt with some misgiving that it might not be easy to justify his own deplorably abrupt and implausible change of front to the wretched Thewless hard upon the shattering telephone call from Jollard. Up to that moment he had played heavily (and in the light of the night's events even absurdly) on the 'run-away' theme which was to keep the tutor quiet for a vital twelve hours, and which was to be exploded only by the reappearance of a grievously battered Ivor. But when it had become apparent that the police of two countries must know enough to be moving against them now, and at the best they would find themselves faced with the closest questioning, it had appeared to him essential to drop at once an attitude that cool inquiry must inevitably brand as grossly irresponsible. Moreover, he had at last fully seen the advantage, the blessed hope of safety, resident in the fact that others besides themselves were 'after' Humphrey. *That* was the card that they should have played for all it was worth as soon as ever the truth of it was apparent to them. For its astonishing interlocking with their own design, its vast scope as both corroboration and obfuscation, surely by far outweighed the few hours' grace that the pretended belief in a mere truancy was designed to secure them.

But where were they now? Just how far did the news from London carry them? Was he perhaps precipitate in his feeling that all, or nearly all, was lost? And Cyril Bolderwood looked at the preparations for panic flight which lay around him with something like embarrassment. Conceivably this was just the sort of mistake that, in Ivor's absence, he was prone to make . . . He sat down to think it out.

Murder is always undesirable. And the fatal mischance that had befallen them was the necessity Ivor had discovered for arranging the liquidation of Peter Cox. The police had moved on that rapidly. They had identified the dead man. And they had traced his connexion with Humphrey Paxton.

And now Humphrey Paxton had been kidnapped while staying with his cousins, the Bolderwoods. That was by this time an accomplished fact. There was no going back on it. Even if they were to cry off now, and present the appearance of the boy's having been freed by his misdoubting captors, stringent inquiry would inevitably follow. That, of course, they had always envisaged; the whole elaboration of their plot was designed to withstand it. So – after all – were things so very much altered?

Cyril Bolderwood paused on this flicker of hope, and in a moment saw that it was delusive. Cox had been killed on the eve of his setting out with Humphrey for Ireland. The police knew this. And the police would ask *why*.

Perhaps it was to secure the boy's going with some other tutor, a tool of the kidnappers? Very little investigation of the blameless Thewless, Cyril Bolderwood grimly saw, would eliminate any such hypothesis as *that*. And only one other explanation was reasonable. Cox was killed because Cox must not go. *Why?* Because he would discover something. *What?* The crux lay here.

If the kidnappers were indeed persons working, as it were, from the dark, mere anonymous conspirators without identity, they would have no reason to fear anything that a particular man might *know*. And what Cox had known must be something at the very heart of the design; not something that some minor variation of it could get round. For – once more – murder is undesirable; one does not perpetrate it as a matter of minor convenience. What should it be, then, that Cox so fatally knew; what should it be but something compromising about persons who *had* identity; who, somewhere, stood, and were bound to stand, openly in the picture? And so (the police would say) we must cast about. What, to begin with, of those distant cousins in a remote and wild country, with whom the boy, so conveniently, had gone to stay? Is their respectability, their integrity, as unchallengeable as it seems? And is there conceivably some point at which their history, traced back, would be found to cross with the history, similarly traced back, of Peter Cox?

And Cyril Bolderwood, who in this analysis knew himself to have captured something of the cool intelligence of his son, once more reached for the bank-notes. For it *was* all up. This precisely, was the degree of investigation that they could by no means stand up against. So now –

At this point he broke off, hastily thrusting the so convenient and bulging grip out of sight. For his study door had opened and Mr Thewless had entered – very pale, very quiet, with a small note-book in his hand.

'It's much worse than we thought – or, at any rate, much more complicated.'

Mr Thewless, as he spoke, sat down and looked gravely at his host – looked at him, Cyril Bolderwood swiftly noted, entirely without distrust.

'They *are* after the boy, without a shadow of doubt. He is in deadly danger. But I judge that your son – if he is endeavouring to guard the boy – is in graver danger still. You see, Humphrey they must have alive. But about others – the rest of us – their ruthlessness would be absolute. Already there has been murder. And the thing is so – so *big*.'

'Murder, Thewless? Good God – what do you mean?'

'In a cinema. I can't quite make it out. But it certainly connects up. Humphrey, you see, has been keeping a diary. This is it.' And Mr Thewless held the little note-book up in the air.

'Good heavens! Let me look at it.'

But Humphrey's tutor, though apparently in no distrust, put it quietly in his pocket. It was still a private diary, after all. 'I think I can sufficiently explain. He went to a cinema. He went to see a film called *Plutonium Blonde*. There's a kind of irony in that.'

'An irony?' Cyril Bolderwood looked blank.

'You'll understand in a moment. The film is about atomic warfare – that sort of thing.'

'Well?' said Cyril Bolderwood. '*Well?*'

'And what these villians are really after – But I'll come to that. He went to this cinema just before joining me at Euston. And something disturbed him. Actually, he talked to me about it on the Heysham steamer, and I took it to be all moonshine. It must have been this mysterious shooting – probably you noticed it – that was reported in yesterday morning's papers. I bought one in Belfast.'

'But I don't see –'

'The point is this. What he saw, or heard, in the cinema gave him an inkling – it's not made clear how – that there *was* some plot against him; that in coming to Ireland he was walking straight into danger. And, all the same, he came.'

'What!' Cyril Bolderwood had paled. 'You mean that he came as a sort of decoy; that the police –'

'Not that at all.' Mr Thewless too was very pale. 'He came because he read it all as a sort of challenge, as a test of his power to control himself, to grow up. It's all in the last pages of this queer little book. But there was something else as well. He seems to have had some idea – not a very rational one, surely – that he was drawing the danger away from his father; that he was protecting *him*.'

'What extraordinary nonsense!'

'I don't know. Humphrey appears to have formed one idea in which there is a good deal of sense. Sir Bernard is extremely wealthy, as you know; and it would be natural to suppose that the kidnappers would be after money. But, of course, Sir Bernard is something else as well – one of the key men, at present, in the – well, in the country's power to wage war. And he has in his possession some sort of plan of an extremely vital sort. Humphrey has concluded that what the kidnappers would be after – privately, as it were, and beneath any more overt demand for money – would be *that*.'

Cyril Bolderwood, who had been standing rigidly before his guest, sank into a chair much as if his legs had been knocked from under him. 'The *boy* worked that out?'

'Why, yes – so it would appear.' Mr Thewless looked momentarily puzzled at the form this question had taken. 'And then there's a most remarkable thing. Humphrey – who must have been scribbling all this under my very nose, on that interminable light railway – Humphrey really has the queerest insight into character. He writes that his father, in his opinion, pays for his towering intellect in not having much guts.'

'Guts?'

'He appears to mean will-power, moral fibre – things like that. And he thinks that that was part of the calculation.'

'You mean that Humphrey worked it out that the – the criminals would rely –'

'Precisely. Humphrey himself is the one point at which Sir Bernard has an emotional life worth a tinker's curse. That, I may say, is the boy's very turn of phrase. He has, you know, streaks of extraordinary intellectual maturity.'

Cyril Bolderwood gave a sort of groan. 'If only we'd remembered', he said, 'that he was Bernard's son and Ivor's cousin!'

'I beg your pardon?'

'Nothing – nothing, my dear Thewless. I am becoming utterly confused. But, for heaven's sake, go on.'

'Humphrey judged that his father, secretly receiving unnerving threats as to what would happen to his kidnapped son, would simply crack up and part with anything he had – not with anything he had of his own, you understand, but with what he had, so to speak, of his country's. It was a thought unbearable to the boy. And he felt that he had to protect his father; that it was his job to protect him. He has the notion, you see, that *he* is the strong member of the family, and that he must always give his father a hand.'

'I wish to heaven Ivor were here!' Cyril Bolderwood, by an association of ideas not altogether obscure, came out with this with considerable vehemence. 'But I don't see – I can't for the life of me see – how it was going to help his father to – to –'

'To come to Ireland and put his head into the lion's jaws?' And suddenly

Mr Thewless brought out a handkerchief and mopped his brow. 'Well, it's here we come to the bit that's really grim; to a point' – for a moment Mr Thewless was vaguely magniloquent – 'where all these personal issues, Humphrey's fate and ours – are transcended. At this point the boy's faculties – terribly at a stretch, after all – seem to have broken down. He makes an obscure, rather childish note to the effect that he has cheated, broken the rules, taken some underhand way of baffling his enemies. What he means by that isn't quite clear, but I'm afraid it's something pretty appalling. He had access to the plan.'

'*What!*' Cyril Bolderwood was suddenly trembling all over.

'With some sort of child's cunning, and in the pursuance, one may suppose, of an innocent fantasy of secret service work and that sort of thing, he had possessed himself of the combination of a safe in which the thing is kept.'

'I can't believe it! It's incredible! You mean – simply in Paxton's own house?'

'So it would appear. And the boy resolved that, before coming to Ireland and running the risks of which he'd had so odd a warning, he would put it out of his father's power to comply with the demand that might be made on him. So he went straight home from the cinema, possessed himself of this vital document, and brought it along with him.'

Cyril Bolderwood made a choking noise in his throat, so that his companion positively thought for a moment that he had suffered an apoplexy. 'Do you mean that – that it's in this house now?'

'It may be, if he has hidden it cunningly. I have come straight from ransacking his room – I took that responsibility at once – and I could find no sign of it. He may simply be carrying it on his person. The diary, you understand, breaks off without being specific on the point. It is only apparent that as he sat opposite me yesterday in the little train, scribbling this astounding matter in his note-book, the document may have been somewhere within a yard of us. Or that is how I read the matter. And you see how catastrophic is the situation that confronts us.'

'Quite – oh, quite so, quite.' Cyril Bolderwood was staring with an almost glassy eye into space. The sudden, enormous hope in the thing had actually dazed him. What would the disappearances of the South American magnate, the Irish squire, matter if he and Ivor, in disappearing, took the thing with them after all – the whole speculative business of the pressure upon Sir Bernard short-circuited, obviated, by his son's crazy act? 'Quite – it's too terrible for words. But I still can't see why the child did it. It's quite mad.'

'I judge that he is not capable of thinking in terms of a nation's safety; that he has no realization of the vast public issues involved. His vision stops short with his father's honour. And he *had* saved that. If caught – and he was going to do his best *not* to be caught – he had the document to hand over and cry quits with. The thing then could not be charged against his father's weakness, but only against his own childish folly.'

'I see. I see.' Cyril Bolderwood was almost impressed.

'And *I* see too.'

The voice was a weak whisper. Both men turned in surprise. The study door was open. And just inside it lay Ivor Bolderwood in a pool of blood.

Chapter 24

With Humphrey the first flush of returning consciousness had been sheerly pleasurable, like waking up on his birthday. He had behaved in a heroical manner; he had been extremely clever; he had eluded, confounded, mocked his enemies. It was matter to compose a song about, full of thrasonical brag. Not Toad himself, when he had outwitted the barge-woman and sold her horse, was more outrageously pleased with himself than was Humphrey in these seconds during which his faculties were coming back to him.

But he was extremely cold, extremely bruised, extremely stiff. And there was something like a tiger gnawing at his right knee. Opening his eyes with some idea of investigating this phenomenon, Humphrey realized that it was dark.

Naturally it was dark. Lying quite still, he summoned hasty argument on the matter. This was the little cave – the one into which the entrance was a mere slit – and beyond that was the big cave; and of the big cave there was perhaps as much as a hundred yards before its gentle curve admitted a first gleam of daylight . . . So *naturally* it was dark.

But this, although it located him, orientated him, really helped very little. A box of matches, or the nursery nightlight for which he had never entirely shed a lingering regard, would have helped a great deal more. He shut his eyes once more – it was absolutely his only means of *dealing* with the darkness – and thought again. His pursuers, if they had been outwitted and adequately insulted by himself, had yet been finally routed by some exterior agency. There had been a police whistle which had sent them, already rattled as they were, pell-mell to their motor-boat waiting at the other end of the cave. But what had happened after that? Not – his recollection, although it was dim, told him – any massive irruption of the blue-clad (or here, rather, green-clad) forces of the law. And certainly no comfortable tramp of constabulary feet echoed in the cavern now. There were noises – and noises reverberating so that he by no means had to strain his ears to hear them. But they were only the murmurs and lappings, the dull explosions, the odd and muted musical notes, that the place contrived, as it were, on its own steam.

He must wait. Quite simply, he must do that. He had suggested to his enemies that their best chance was to retire a little and lurk – and might they not be doing so now? Whatever had disturbed them was apparently departed, and the possibility that they were themselves still a force actively in the field was at least something too substantial to take chances with. He had practically told them so, given his assurance that he would in no circumstances emerge until substantial and authentic succour had appeared. And it *would* appear; there could be no doubt of that. Let a man and a boy disappear in this district, and such a cavern as this would suggest itself as one of the first places to be hunted through. Even were he to fall unconscious again where he lay – or, worse, in that corner of the little cave inaccessible to inspection from without – competent searchers would not neglect the possibility. Ultimately, he was entirely safe . . . And thus Humphrey comforted himself, as he was so frequently able to do, by the slightly complacent exercise of his own good brain. Only, of course, he was neglecting the factor of the dark.

And it *was* dark. Here in the little cave the very most attenuated quiver of the sense of sight was absent. This was something he did not at all like. And in a flash he realized that there was still danger. Or rather there was a choice of dangers. Another five minutes here and he would have lost his nerve, would be battering himself wildly against the rock in a panic so catastrophic as to deprive him of all chance of finding and negotiating the narrow cleft leading to ultimate sunlight. That was one, and a very horrid, danger. The other danger, of course, was simply that they *were* waiting. He had said that he would die rather than fall into their hands, and he had abundantly meant it. But to die was one thing; to buffet himself into madness against invisible rock was quite another . . . He got to his feet – it was an action surprisingly difficult of accomplishment – and felt his way cautiously round the little cave. It occurred to him that there might be bats. He resolved to keep on remembering this, because a bat when one was *thinking* of bats would be rather less upsetting than, as it were, a bat from the blue. And, now, here was the narrow slit.

It was the worst thing yet. When he had come through it from without it had been in blind escape from imminent seizure; and, although bruised and breathless, his fund of nervous energy had been sufficient to honour the draft. Now he was stiff all over; danger lay on either side of the cleft; and danger lay, too, *in* it. Surely, surely, it was now narrower by far! He squeezed and strained himself to a dead stop, crushed in a brutal vice of stone, with nothing but his sense of touch to help him, with even that sense hopelessly crippled as his arms, his wrists, his very fingers seemed no longer to have an inch's play. Terror rose and lipped the threshold of his strained possession of himself. Panic *here* and he was done for. All that rescuers would find *here* – pinned in the rock – would be the wreck of a small boy, irretrievably insane. Or so it seemed to Humphrey, who was prone, as we know, to dramatic views. He gave a last shove – it would certainly mean one thing or the other – and found himself outside. He found himself, too, *seeing* something: the ghost of a glint of water. And this meant that he must be reeling crazily on the narrow ledge's verge, the sea flowing between its fatally smooth walls below. He took a step backwards and sat down.

At least the bearded man and his associates had not simply been lurking there, ready to pounce. And, if they were still lurking at all, would it not be here rather than in the open air beyond the cavern – a place which, however lonely, was yet within possible observation from the cliff, and from the sea, and by possible wanderers on the shore? Humphrey, taking fresh heart from this, got to his feet again and groped his way painfully forward.

It was incredible that along this ledge, that through this utter darkness, he had actually run headlong less, as it must be, than a couple of hours ago. Now, he could achieve nothing that could be called a walk, a crawl; he edged his way forward, fumbling and shuffling, as his very grandmother, similarly placed, might have done. And his heart was in his mouth throughout every instant of his progress. It was almost as if he were enjoying the luxury of manageable, of assessable fear.

And then he saw the light. Incredibly, alarmingly almost, like the first appearing sliver of the sun's orb after the long arctic night, it filtered in from distance and reached him; another moment only, and it distinguishably lit the remaining path before him. At this he paused, irresolution taking him like a strong hand. Would it not be best to wait at this spot – here, with the nursery nightlight comfortably glimmering in its corner? Then, should his enemies appear, he could retreat to the fastness from which he had just issued. But he had no sooner made this proposition to himself than he knew it to be nonsense; knew, that was to say, that he would never enter that little cave again. It had been the scene of his greatest triumph, of his most vulgar exultation. And it had been the scene of his life's most staggering scare. That, decidedly, was enough. Humphrey walked rapidly forward and out of the cavern.

The sea had been silver and now it was blue, a deep, deep blue; it had stirred into life, moreover, and there were little ridges of dazzling foam, whiter than any white thing had ever been before. The sky, too, was blue and brilliant; it was dressed with incredible clouds; gulls in enormous freedom cut it with their passionate geometry. Humphrey ran forward, let himself be received again into the abundant world, tumbled himself out upon its bosom with the tears streaming down his cheeks. Straight before him was the gleaming, empty beach. Across it – the only sign of change he could discern – a double row of footprints led to and from the cavern, traversing the lovely sand that poor Ivor had deemed so treacherous. And where they had gone Humphrey could go. He took them as a line and ran – a limping run with a stab of pain in every stride. He would have shouted – why ever should he not? – had he not preferred to keep all his breath for joyous speed. The footprints – they were as small, almost, as a child's – ended in a little eddy or sortie of others in a familiar spot. It was the place where he had himself made that brief dash across the sand before Ivor had called out to him to halt. And now before him there was only the path that slanted up the cliff. When he had climbed that the strange, the blessed populousness of rural Ireland would lie before him: tiny fields dotted with the bright homespuns of the labouring folk; dykes and hedgerows along which were strewn the same bright colours of the drying wool; white cottages with their open eyes and pricked ears; donkeys, sheep, goats; the absurd and suspect poultry of Killyboffin Hall.

He climbed, and that really hurt his knee badly. He braced himself against the pain by thinking, not very laudably, of the deep weal that must now lie across the bearded man's face. Perhaps that would help the police to nobble him. And perhaps the man whom he had kicked – Humphrey, wallowing in atrocious satisfactions, reached the top of the cliff. Everything was as he had imagined it, with one addition. At the end of the commanding headland to which the cliff here rose there stood the solitary figure of his friend, Miss Margaret Liberty. He took to his heels and ran to her as if she offered all the security of the Brigade of Guards. Then, becoming aware that this was a childish performance, he slowed down to an exaggerated saunter. 'Hullo,' he said – and his tone was extravagantly casual. 'It's a lovely morning, isn't it?' He paused, reading in her faint amusement an indication that this had been a little overdone. He gave a sudden incongruous sob. 'They've killed my cousin.'

But behind her moment's relaxation Miss Liberty had been grave. And at this, indeed, her gravity scarcely increased; it merely became shot with surprise, with the rapid recasting of some picture with which she was preoccupied. 'In the cave?' she asked.

Humphrey looked at her with answering surprise. 'You know about the cave?'

'I have been watching you come across the sands from it. Why didn't you answer me, Humphrey? Where were you hiding?'

The boy was now open-mouthed. '*You!*'

Miss Liberty smiled. But at the same time her eye was attentively studying the boy's battered condition. 'I took a walk quite early and noticed your cousin and yourself. Later I noticed your footprints where you had stepped for a moment on the sands. I followed the shore and came to the cave. And when I had gone a little way in I heard something that persuaded me it might be wise to do a little clearing of the air.'

'Clearing of the air?'

By way of answer, Miss Liberty took a small object from her bag and raised it to her mouth. And faintly, as for their private edification only, Humphrey heard the note of a police-whistle. 'It is', Miss Liberty said modestly, 'one of the prescriptive devices. We have often come across it, my dear Humphrey, in our common reading. And it certainly had an effect. But when the air *had* cleared, and I went further in to look for you, I got no reply. What had happened?'

'I'm afraid I had – well, gone to sleep. In a little cave in which they were besieging me.' Humphrey paused. 'Please, may I ask a question now?'

'Certainly, my dear boy. This is scarcely a cosy spot for a little chat. But it has advantages. We are in full view of a good many of the people working in those nearer fields. And if I stand *so*, and you face me – yes, just *so* – then you will be keeping an eye open *this* way, and I *that*. I think you scarcely need to be told by now that keeping an eye open in this part of the country is an *excellent* thing.'

'Indeed I don't!' Humphrey's tone was grim. 'But listen, please. I think it must have been you who rescued me on the Heysham train. And it was you who talked – well, so as to put guts in me. And it was certainly you – I see it now – who fixed it so that poor Mr Thewless found himself in the place meant for me in that ambulance. And then you turn up in a most frightful crisis, blowing a police-whistle like mad. And a police-whistle, after all, isn't a thing that old' – Humphrey blushed and stammered – 'that ladies commonly carry about with them. So – well, what I mean is, you're *not*, are you, just an accident?'

'No, Humphrey; I must admit to being distinctly intentional. You see, my brother, Sir Charles, has the duty of keeping an eye on certain most *important* matters; and he had grown a little uneasy. So when he found difficulty in the way of taking *official* action, he just asked me to come along – to keep half an eye, you know, on your little holiday.'

'Gosh!' Humphrey, round-eyed and awed, stared at his friend. 'It must be pretty hot when you get *both* eyes on the job.'

'Well, that precisely describes the position now.' Miss Liberty glanced at her watch. 'There doesn't seem to be much chance of your tutor's turning up.'

Humphrey could only stare again. 'Mr Thewless was to turn up here?'

'I endeavoured to convey to him a hint that he should do so – at ten o'clock. It seemed time that he and I had a *quiet* little talk. But he must have failed to take my implication. And now I think you had better tell me just what has happened this morning.'

Humphrey did his best. Miss Liberty listened with the steady and unstrained attention of a judge. 'And so', she said when she had heard him out, 'for a time you almost suspected your cousin himself?'

'I'm afraid I did.'

'But there can be no doubt of the fact? He *was* attacked – genuinely attacked, and overpowered, and thrown – dead, you think – into the sea?'

'There's no doubt of it. And the same chaps – at least the bearded man again and somebody else – raided us last night in Killyboffin Hall itself.' And Humphrey recounted the history of this too.

Miss Liberty listened and nodded, frowning slightly. 'The basis of success in this trade', she said, 'is to keep on suspecting everybody all the time. But, of course, there has to be a limit to it.'

'This trade? Is what you tell me about your brother Sir Charles not quite all the story?' Humphrey's wonder still grew. 'Have you been at it – often?'

'Ah, my dear Humphrey – we all have secrets in our past. I expect you have some that are quite dark to me still. Had you better tell me some of them – in so far, that is, as they may relate to this *exciting* affair?'

And Humphrey told – or told much. Miss Liberty, as she listened to these further disclosures, had moments of undisguised perplexity. 'And another requisite of success', she said when he had finished, 'is that one should recognize when the waters become too deep for one. But I think our next step is clear.'

'The police?'

'Decidedly the police. As a romantic adventure designed to exercise the faculties of Humphrey Paxton the affair definitely ended when your cousin went into the waters of that cave. And my brother's apprehensiveness has certainly been amply vindicated. We shall walk together as far as the Hall, still with our eyes *extremely* wide open. You must go straight inside. But you need not tell your uncle about his son's probable death if you feel unequal to it, my dear boy. For as soon as I have walked on to the village and made one or two telephone calls I shall come straight back, bringing the local police with me. And then we can have it all out while waiting for more substantial help to arrive.'

Humphrey nodded. 'Yes,' he said. 'That seems all right. And I don't think I shall too much mind telling. It has to be faced, after all.' He spoke with the sober confidence of one who had himself faced a good deal. They walked on for a time in silence, their senses alert to what was happening round about them. It was only when they had taken a cut through the ragged park, and were within hail of the front door of the house, that he spoke again. 'I suppose I *had* better go in?'

And for an instant Miss Liberty hesitated, caught by something in the boy's tone of which he was himself, perhaps, unconscious. Then she nodded. 'Yes; I think you had better go. The sooner the facts are spread beyond just our two selves the better. I shall follow you in less than a quarter of an hour.'

Humphrey watched her go – a slight, quick, upright figure glancing alertly from side to side as she walked. He noticed how she kept her right hand in one roomy pocket, much as Ivor had done on their walk to the cave. But at the thought of Ivor Humphrey's eyes misted with tears.

He turned and once more entered Killyboffin Hall.

Chapter 25

Cyril Bolderwood had at first viewed his prostrate son with considerably more surprise than alarm. He was immensely struck, that is to say, with the abundant quality of the verisimilar in Ivor's presentation of one who has, in the handy American phrase, been 'beaten up'. Ivor, indeed, looked, to the point of extravagance, a man who had been beaten *down*; he was now crawling across the room to prop himself, with a low groan, against the back of a chair. 'The boy!' he gasped. 'He's been kidnapped.'

The scene was taking place hours before it was due; and, thanks to the efficiency of the London police, it was taking place in a context the wider reaches of which were vastly other than had been planned. Apart from this, Cyril Bolderwood had no fault to find with it. 'Kidnapped?' he exclaimed. 'Good heavens – it is just what we feared!'

The tone of this – much that of Lady Macbeth's 'What, in our house?' – produced in Ivor a sort of weak gasp of strangled fury. 'By the people', he said hoarsely, 'who broke in last night. They got us in the cave before – before we had finished looking at it.'

And light dawned on Cyril Bolderwood. 'You mean', he shouted – a shade strangely to Mr Thewless's ear – 'that Humphrey has been . . . *kidnapped*?'

'Of course I do. And snatched from us, it now seems, with the plan – the vital plan – actually in his pocket . . . Get a bandage out of the cupboard there, will you? It's only a hack on the scalp, but it makes me bleed like a pig.'

Ivor's father did as he was bidden, but with the air of a man not at all knowing how to proceed. 'Thewless', he said suddenly, 'would you, like a good fellow, go up to the bathroom beside your room, and fetch some lint and sticking-plaster from the cupboard? We must do what we can until the doctor comes.'

Mr Thewless, although his concern was much more for the vanished Humphrey than for the injured Ivor, hurried away. When he returned it was to find Ivor sitting up in a chair. The young man, however, looked by no means better; he had turned yet paler and was breathing fast; it was clear that such intelligence as father and son had exchanged in the interval was far from having any composing effect. And one might, moreover, have formed the impression that something like a brief altercation had been in the air.

'Well,' Ivor was saying, 'these people have taken the boy, haven't they – after more shots at it than one? And the police must go after them for all they're worth?'

'Certainly – certainly.' Cyril Bolderwood, glancing rapidly at Mr Thewless now ministrant with the sticking-plaster, appeared to find difficulty in the easy expression of his feelings. 'The police *must* go after them, of course. And I'll telephone the moment we've fixed you up. The police, my dear boy, must investigate the *whole* affair from the start, you know; they must follow up whatever seems remotely connected with it. And they *will* do that. We can trust them, absolutely.'

Ivor received this for a moment in silence, and Mr Thewless took the opportunity to speak. 'I must get in touch with Sir Bernard at once. I feel about this quite terribly, since I was given his confidence in the matter. I wish to heaven the other man had been able to come. He would probably have been far more competent than I in such a disaster.'

Cyril Bolderwood pounced upon this. 'Another man?'

'Another tutor, who was Sir Bernard's choice in the first place. But he was prevented at short notice from taking up the post –'

'Now, that's just the sort of thing I mean.' Cyril Bolderwood, who had finished bandaging his son's head, drew back, fixed him with an urgent gaze, and proceeded in a sort of rapid gabble. 'Just before these plots begin – as a prelude to them, you may say – this other tutor suddenly drops out. Well, the police must go after that even, for what it's worth. Find him, you know, alive or dead – and find out all *about* him. They *must* do it. Exploring every avenue. Leaving no stone –'

'Yes, of course.' Ivor held up an impatient hand, and at the same time uttered what, since it could scarcely have been an imprecation, Mr Thewless took to be a muted exclamation of pain. 'The police are bound to go right through the whole thing. And – well, you'd better get on to them now.'

'Exactly.' And Cyril Bolderwood – obscurely, it seemed to Mr Thewless, as if he had carried some urgent point – turned to the telephone. Then he stopped. 'But, Thewless – I wonder if you'd make the call? I don't like Ivor's look; I don't like it a bit. I think I had better get out the car and drive him straight to the doctor's. Ivor, wouldn't that be best?'

And at this Ivor did unequivocally produce a murmur of weakness and agony. 'Yes, I think it would. I have lost a shocking amount of blood.'

'Good. I'll get it out straight away.' Cyril Bolderwood made for the door, checked himself, seized from beneath his desk a bulging leather bag. 'Brandy,' he said. 'And that sort of thing. Kept for an emergency. Get the police, Thewless, and insist on being put straight through to the county office. I'll have the car round for Ivor in a couple of minutes.'

Again he made for the door. But it opened before he reached it.

'Ivor!'

Humphrey Paxton, his face alive with amazement and joy, ran across the room and threw himself into his cousin's arms.

To Mr Thewless the sheer relief of this apparition was so great that it was a moment before he could identify in himself the further pleasurable sensation arising from the affecting nature of the scene; arising, basically, from all that was generous in his pupil's character. Twenty-four hours before Humphrey would not have known Ivor Bolderwood from Adam; but in the interim his cousin had fought for him against superior odds; and now Humphrey felt for the bandaged figure before him as Hamlet might have felt for a wounded Horatio. And at the sight Mr Thewless turned to Cyril Bolderwood, as if from an impulse to share with him something so decidedly worth sharing. What this movement brought into his field of vision was a state of affairs so entirely unexpected that an appreciable interval elapsed before it made, so to speak, any intelligible statement. His host was still standing by the door through which he had proposed to depart to fetch out the car. He had, however, laid down his bag – and what first dawned on

Mr Thewless, oddly enough, was the extremely unlikely appearance that this receptacle presented as the repository of a bottle of brandy. And in place of the bag Cyril Bolderwood was now handling something else. It was some small contrivance of gleaming metal. Mr Thewless placed it provisionally as being – what seemed in itself unlikely enough – a species of surgical instrument. But now Cyril Bolderwood was advancing it, pointing it, in the oddest way – in what was surely the most *threatening* way . . . Thus laboriously did Mr Thewless analyse out the wholly unfamiliar experience of finding himself covered with a revolver.

The boy understood first. His disillusionment, if even sharper, was almost instantaneous. He let his hand fall from Ivor's arm very gently and reluctantly, like a child who perforce abandons what he cannot, after all, 'take away'. And then he sat down on the edge of a chair. 'Yes,' he said. 'Yes . . . I see.'

And Ivor Bolderwood squared his shoulders – a man who had been roughly handled, indeed, but who by no means urgently required medical aid. His cheeks were faintly flushed. 'My dear father,' he said, 'I think you make it all rather unnecessarily dramatic. But, no doubt, we had better proceed to business.'

'We certainly better had.' Cyril Bolderwood kicked the door shut behind him. 'The police may be here in half an hour.'

'That is distinctly unlikely. But half an hour will be time enough, I don't doubt.' And Ivor turned to Mr Thewless. 'It's a great shame,' he said with a faint grin, 'but I'm afraid we shan't be able to show you that defensive earthwork at Ballybags, after all.'

'I think it very unlikely that either of you will be in a position to show anybody anything for a great many years to come.'

Ivor's grin widened, as if in amiable acknowledgement of the very proper spiritedness of this reply. 'That's as maybe – and I won't deny we take a risk. But you ought to be grateful to us, Thewless. We took much our biggest risk simply in order to ensure that you should come on this nice trip – or that somebody else *shouldn't* come. And things certainly haven't gone quite right. My father and I are obliged to quit these ancestral halls for good today. We certainly didn't envisage *that*. Nor did we envisage that the game of kidnapping this delightful Humphrey would become so deplorably popular with the underworld of which we are ourselves, so to speak, honorary members. I wonder who that bearded fellow is? And so you think that all *he* has been after is cash? That isn't *our* object, I need hardly say.'

'Not' – Cyril Bolderwood interrupted – 'that with things going well we mightn't have taken it out a bit in cash as well. Poor Bernard would have been in no position to refuse.'

Mr Thewless looked from father to son. 'You strike me as two singularly foolish, as well as two singularly wicked and contemptible, men. The bearded ruffian of whom you speak is, after all, a ruffian merely. He could not, in fairness, be described as basely treacherous. Nor has he concocted a futile and elaborate plot such as yours. He has simply tried to grab – and he has come uncommonly near being successful. The same cannot be said for you. And you don't cover the complete failure of your design by whipping out and brandishing a revolver. Your servants, who are as numerous as they are clearly innocent, must many of them be within hail. You haven't a card in your hand. My blindness has been great. But I can see *that*.'

'I don't think you have the situation quite clear.' Ivor spoke in a reasonable voice. 'Our boats are burnt, you know. And our strength lies precisely in that. By noon Cyril and Ivor Bolderwood will simply have ceased to exist. And the question is just this: Will anyone else have ceased to exist as well? For instance, there are Billy Bone and Denis. It seems most unlikely that they would regard anything you started shouting at them as other than the outcries of madmen. But if they did come in on your side, so to speak, it would cost us nothing to shoot our way out. It would cost us nothing, for that matter, to shoot our way out through the whole of Killyboffin.' Ivor paused. 'But I think it is with Humphrey that we had better do the talking at present. He strikes me, my dear Thewless, as having a much clearer head than his tutor can boast of. Come, Humphrey, are you ready to talk?'

Humphrey was still perched on the edge of his chair, like a very small boy uneasily present upon the fringes of a grown-up party. But he answered with a strange tranquillity. 'Yes, Mr Bolderwood, I'll talk.'

'Very well.' Ivor had faintly flushed again at this address. 'I think you and I can still be very good friends.'

'And I think you are almost as reliable a friend now as any I shall ever again be able to feel that I have.' Humphrey was tranquil still as he enunciated this rather complicated belief. And he turned to his tutor. 'Do you know, this must be what I came for, really? Not to discover if I could keep the stiff upper lip of a great big boy while being chased by thugs through horrible caves. But to see what I could salvage out of – well, of being utterly betrayed. And I do salvage something – although it's a very little something, I suppose. The power, you know, to take it quietly.' The boy paused, and for a moment he might have been thought to be anxiously listening. 'Well, Mr Bolderwood, talk away. You do it very well. Better, really, than you arrange bogus kidnappings in caverns. They had you caught out nicely, hadn't they? And – by the way – what happened to the chaps you must have had lurking and ready to go through their act? I seem to remember them now, uncomfortably trussed up in a corner. Did the rival gang pitch them into the sea as well; and did they have poorer luck than you?'

'The point is this.' Ivor had stood up rather unsteadily and now planted himself before the boy. 'We were going to have you held as by persons quite independent of us – were they not to have knocked me out in that cave? – and while there was the appearance of their demanding money from your father we were quite quickly and quietly going to get from him – well, something else. That has all broken down. And, as a result, we should have completely failed but for one fact. You yourself, with incredible folly, my poor child, brought that something else away with you from London. And so my father and I are in a position very nicely to retrieve our fortunes. You understand?'

It was evident that Humphrey understood. And in the little silence that followed Mr Thewless had his worst moment in the affair. 'Humphrey,' he said, 'it is my fault. I found your diary, and I felt, since you had disappeared, that it was proper to read it for the sake of any light it might give.'

'You were quite right.' Humphrey had flushed, but his eyes went straight to his tutor's. 'You did just what you ought.'

'Unfortunately, mistrusting nothing, I confided what I discovered there to the elder of these base men. And now they both know.'

'And now we *all* know.' Ivor's grin had returned. 'We all know precisely where we are. Humphrey has really been very fortunate. He does not need to suffer the inconvenience of being kidnapped, after all.'

'I should have thought' – Humphrey's voice, interrupting, was still curiously mild – 'that I am kidnapped *now*.'

'Not at all. It is simply the second day of your Irish trip, and we are having a friendly family talk. Before my father and I are unexpectedly called away. Kidnapping is definitely off. The circumstances of our retreat, I can frankly tell you, are such that a reluctant small companion would be definitely embarrassing. But there will be no objection to our taking a small sheaf of papers. And the only question is this. Have you, my dear Humphrey, actually got them on you now, or have you hidden them somewhere about the house?'

Humphrey was silent, again like one who listens for a distant sound.

'Come, boy, you must see how the thing stands. We win – at least your father falls into no disgrace. He cannot be held accountable for a disastrous domestic theft by an imaginative small boy. Everything, you see, really falls out quite nicely.'

'You are awfully considerate. But I think, you know, that these papers may be rather too important to be used as a sort of challenge cup in the Killyboffin annual sports.' Humphrey paused, evidently rather taken by this image. 'You win, and we all shake hands, and then it will go to the shop to be engraved "Cyril and Ivor Bolderwood". These papers – let's call them simply the plan – are quite unsuitable for that. And I've thought so, Mr Bolderwood, for some time. You just can't have the plan.'

Ivor shrugged his shoulders. 'You foolish child! Will you force us to give this talk a really unpleasant turn – to think of the really nasty things that might presently happen to you?'

It was at this point that Mr Thewless saw what seemed likely to become his necessary course of duty. That the Bolderwoods were utterly desperate and utterly ruthless he could see. And it might well be that their household would not be rapidly or readily convinced of their criminality. Nevertheless, some definitely criminal deed, if accompanied by sufficient uproar, would probably finish them; in such circumstances they would simply have to go while the going was good. It was his business to see that the uproar occurred; to sell his life if not dearly at least noisily. And no sooner had this thought come to him than he saw that he might have to hurry if he was to have the chance. For Ivor had walked over to his father, taking from his hand the revolver which he had been holding during these exchanges, and was now aiming it directly at his, Mr Thewless's heart. 'Listen, Humphrey.' Ivor's voice was now very quiet. 'We have got to have that plan. It means the difference for us between penury and a fortune. So we are not likely to boggle at a little bloodshed.'

'You can't have it.' Humphrey spoke stoutly, but with fear creeping into his eyes. 'It might mean far too big a difference for far too many other people as well.'

'We have got to have it, all the same – and within a few minutes now. Well, we'll make a very fair bargain. We'll swop it for poor old Thewless here.'

'What do you mean?'

'I don't, myself, think he's worth much. But it is possible that you think he is worth a good deal. I fancy he's been quite decent to you, and that you have grown rather fond of him. Well, unless you tell us at once where to find the plan –'

Ivor left his sentence expressively in air. And Humphrey looked piteously at his tutor. 'Do you think he means it?' he asked.

'Never mind whether he means it or not, Humphrey. This plan is much more important than my life. And it is my duty to tell you that it is much more important than your life too. You ought not to have taken it, and your notion that by doing so you might be protecting your father's integrity was a mistake. You made a bad mistake, even if an honourable one. And I have made equally bad mistakes at every turn. If we are to be killed, my dear, dear lad, we must put up with it. These villains must on no account be told where the plan now is.'

'As a matter of fact, I couldn't tell them, even if I wanted to.'

'What's that?' It was Cyril Bolderwood who spoke, and as he did so he advanced threateningly upon Humphrey. 'What's that, you horrible little rascal?'

'So that if you do any killing – of one or other of us, or both – it will be mere spite.' Humphrey paused; and it might have been evident that if he was facing death he was also, in a manner, enjoying his moment. 'Of course, I can tell you approximately where it is.' And he glanced at the clock on Cyril Bolderwood's mantelpiece. 'It must be somewhere between Preston and Crewe.'

Ivor Bolderwood cursed, and a dark flush overspread his pale face. 'You little brute! Do you mean you posted it back to London?'

'But of course! I only meant to hold on to it till I could *think*. And after what happened on the Heysham train I knew I hadn't much time. So I posted it back to London yesterday afternoon when we were changing trains at Dundrane. Only my diary hasn't got so far as to say so.'

'By heaven, we're back where we were!' Cyril Bolderwood was pacing agitatedly about the room. 'Bernard has the plan, and we have his boy. We must hang on to him. We must take him with us by hook or –'

'Oh, my *father* won't have the plan. I didn't post it back to *him*. Then we certainly *would* be back where we were.' Humphrey was looking from one to the other of his captors as if almost amused by the simplicity of their minds.

'You mean that you posted it to somebody else?'

'Of course I do. I wrote a little note – what they call a covering note, I think – and posted the thing off to the Prime Minister.'

'To the *Prime Minister*?' Cyril Bolderwood's voice held a strangled note.

'Why not?' And Humphrey looked mildly surprised at the sensation he had achieved. 'He is – don't you know? – a terribly nice man. He'll *quite* understand.'

At this Cyril Bolderwood, always inclined to display less finesse than his son, appeared about to hurl himself on the boy with a howl of fury. But in the same instant Humphrey himself gave a sudden shout. 'Danger, Miss Liberty! Danger! Run!'

But this call, if heard, was without effect. The door opened and Miss Margaret Liberty walked into the room. Her eye travelled briskly round it, and evidently told her much. 'Ah,' she said. 'Keep on distrusting everybody; I was remarking to Humphrey that it is the only safe rule. Mr Ivor, I see, has a revolver. Well, so have I, and that does just give us a chance.'

Chapter 26

To Cyril Bolderwood nothing seemed to occur in this exigency but recourse to vituperation. 'Why,' he exclaimed, 'you horrible old hag, what –?'

'Don't you dare to call Miss Liberty rude names!' Humphrey jumped from his chair, bounded across the room, and kicked his distant relative expertly on the shins. Cyril Bolderwood let out a howl of pain and grabbed at him; Humphrey dodged; the situation had all the appearance of being about to degenerate from melodrama into rough-and-tumble farce.

But Ivor was otherwise-minded. He put a hand on his father's shoulder and shoved him into a chair; he strode to the door, closed it and, weapon in hand, faced Miss Liberty. 'If you have a revolver, madam, you will give it up to me at once.'

'Don't madam me, young man.' Miss Liberty walked composedly across the room and looked out at the window. 'And, Humphrey, stop knocking people about.'

Humphrey blushed. 'They're quite horrid people; they've been wanting to kidnap me too, all the time; and they were going to shoot Mr Thewless in cold blood.'

'I have no doubt that some of their ideas have been *most* foolish. But now that they are in so tight a corner we had better leave their shins alone. Particularly as *we* are in the tight corner too.'

Mr Thewless, who had for some seconds found himself quite unattended to, had slipped over to the fireplace and possessed himself of the poker. 'Miss Liberty,' he said courteously, 'I suspect that these are matters in which you have some experience; and I should wish to defer to your judgement. But it appears to me that, if I were to make a resolute attempt to dash out this elder ruffian's brains, the younger would be constrained to fire at me with his pistol, and this might give you the necessary opportunity of bringing out your own. Shall we proceed after that fashion?'

'Dear me! You are even more bloodthirsty than Humphrey. But the position is not quite so simple as that. Our friends here appear to have forgotten that they are not the only pebbles on the beach. It has really been very rash of them to suppose that their rivals were routed beyond recovery when Humphrey made one of his alarming attacks upon them in the cavern. That is not so. They are altogether more resolute than that. And they are, in fact, coming back at us now.'

'I don't believe it!' Ivor Bolderwood spoke, but not with much conviction. 'A gang of common kidnappers like that would never dream of actually assaulting –'

'But that is precisely where you have gone wrong. You suppose that you and your father alone breathe the high air of international intrigue; and that all that these other people fly at is a few thousand pounds extorted by menaces. Nothing could be farther from the truth. Their employers, I suspect, are, at a remote level, your employers too. But theirs has been an altogether more sensible plot.'

Humphrey jumped up, round-eyed, from the chair on which he had once more perched himself. '*They* want the plan too?'

'Certainly not. They know that the plan as you call it – the real plan – is utterly inaccessible to them. The papers with which you walked off, my dear boy, are, of course, important. But the notion that they are in any sense the vital thing is a stupid misconception into which the Bolderwoods must have been led by some confederate in your father's house. You may be quite sure that the real thing is not, and never has been, in your father's uncontrolled possession. And, equally certainly, as soon as Sir Bernard Paxton's son was known to have been kidnapped, Sir Bernard himself would be very closely watched indeed. Your fear that he might be forced to part with something extremely confidential was quite groundless. And correspondingly' – Miss Liberty turned to the Bolderwoods – '*your* scheme was fantastic. But our bearded friend is after something altogether sounder. He knows just what he is going to have for sale as soon as Humphrey is in his hands and smuggled out of the country.' She paused. 'For I am afraid, Humphrey, that if *he* gets you, you are due for quite a long trip.'

'What will he have for sale?' Cyril Bolderwood, who had been staring in distrust and dismay at his son, now peered uneasily out of the window.

'Simply Sir Bernard Paxton's inactivity – his immobilization. With his son in those hands, he could neither be trusted nor could he trust himself. On the sort of work for which he is needed he would crack up almost at once. It has been the position, as you must know, with scores of scientists on the Continent whose families are in alien hands. *That* is what our friends are after. I have been watching them through binoculars' – Miss Liberty patted her bag – 'holding a sort of battle conference. Their zero hour will be in about ten minutes. And we have an hour or so in which survival is all our own affair.'

'An hour or so!' Mr Thewless was aghast. 'But surely the police –'

'The first thing I did in the village just now was to get through on the telephone to my brother, Sir Charles. He told me quite a lot. The London police have got entirely on the track of the affair, and one has been given permission to fly here direct. He is in the air now. Two senior officers of the Irish police are coming, also by air, from Dublin. And a local force, available about forty miles away, will be setting out any time by car. I had learnt just so much when I was cut off. The girl at the exchange investigated, and she says that the line must have come down outside Killyboffin. Well, we know what that means.'

'God bless my soul!' Mr Thewless tightened his grip on the poker. 'It means that we are completely cut off in this singularly isolated spot.'

'Exactly so. I went round to find the local *guarda*, for what his help might be worth, and discovered that he has been called away – no doubt on some fool's errand. The two cars one can hire have gone too. Your own car – it must have happened last night – has its tyres slashed to ribbons.' Miss Liberty had turned to Cyril Bolderwood. 'And, if you wonder how I managed to walk straight in, it was because your servants seem to have made themselves scarce as well.'

'The good-for-nothing rascals! The dishonest –' Cyril Bolderwood, about to launch upon his old star turn as the irascible squire, thought better of it. 'Ivor,' he demanded, 'whatever are we to do?'

Ivor said nothing, his brows knitted in thought. And Miss Liberty answered for him. 'It is *quite* fantastic, is it not? Here is your son pointing a revolver at me – and knowing that, through this convenient tweed pocket, I am pointing one at *him*. Here is Mr Thewless standing over *you* with a poker. And here is Humphrey, who has had a very rough time, with the light of battle beginning to show again in his eye. One possible way of proceeding is, of course, clear.'

'Clear?' said Mr Thewless.

'To our friends here, that is to say. They can try to do a deal with their rivals. Mr Ivor is thinking that out now. But you can see from his expression

224

that he regards it as not altogether promising. Earlier this morning they attacked him in the cave and pitched him into the sea as dead. It was not a good prelude to any relationship of confidence. He knows these people to be as treacherous and dishonourable as himself . . . I think, Mr Ivor, that that expresses the situation?'

'Certainly.' Ivor remained calm. 'It expresses it tactlessly, Miss Liberty, but accurately enough.'

'Whereas you know equally well that Mr Thewless and Humphrey and myself are fowl of another feather. We subscribe to the old-fashioned idea of keeping promises, and that sort of thing.'

'That is true enough.' Ivor was positively handsome. 'And the conclusion is that my father and I had better make our bargain with *you*.'

'Then I will make a proposal to you. Our interests are different, are they not? We, on our part, are simply concerned to hold on until help arrives. You, on the other hand, are anxious to go while the going is good. I suspect that your normal course would be to get away in your car to somewhere along this coast where you keep a sea-going boat. But your car is out of action, and you must take what other means you can. Well, my suggestion simply is that you set about it.' Miss Liberty was brisk, colloquial. 'In fact, that you clear out.'

'And you?'

'We shall endeavour to hold Killyboffin, or some part of it, until help does arrive. And we definitely don't want you as part of the garrison.'

Ivor considered. 'Just how are those people disposed?'

'They are assembling in surprising numbers in the village, where they have two large cars. And, of course, somewhere or other there is their motor-cruiser.'

Ivor Bolderwood's eyes for a moment sought his father's – but less for counsel, it appeared, than in command. 'Very well – we'll go. But we must have another revolver from the drawer of that desk, and also the grip that my father is pleased to describe as holding brandy.'

'Agreed.'

Mr Thewless, who was still grasping the poker, had listened to these exchanges with some reluctance. 'I am bound', he said, 'to express my heartfelt hope that you will both be in gaol before sunset. And it must be understood clearly that our engagement to let you go terminates two minutes after you leave this house. Thereafter we shall hold ourselves at liberty to assist in your apprehension and subsequent condign punishment by any means in our power.'

'Dear old Thewless, full of choice eloquence to the last!' And from beneath his bandages Ivor Bolderwood gave his last malicious grin. 'Well, you have about five minutes left to polish a period or two for our bearded friend. Good-bye.'

The door closed and they were gone. There was a moment's silence. 'I say,' said Humphrey, 'do you think they'll really beat it?'

Miss Liberty nodded. 'I think they will – as long as the son stays in charge.'

Mr Thewless demurred. 'It struck me as being the father who is in a panic.'

'Precisely. And it is he who might lose his head and senselessly turn and fight. Ivor is prepared to cut his losses and start life again elsewhere.'

'Life? It strikes me as a grave responsibility to let him loose again on what he calls that.'

'Our responsibility at the moment is towards Humphrey.' Miss Liberty was grim.

Humphrey produced a rather battered smile. 'I'm afraid', he said, 'that I have a grave responsibility towards *you*. I did start all this.'

'You must not be too hard on yourself.' Miss Liberty too smiled. 'After all, you were very young then, weren't you?'

'So I was.' Humphrey, offering this reply with perfect seriousness, crossed to the window. 'They *are* going. I think they're making for the shore. They're doubled up behind a dyke. Now they've vanished.'

'Capital.' Miss Liberty paused to consider. 'One revolver, Humphrey's shot-gun – and, no doubt, other sporting weapons if we have time to hunt them up. A large and rambling house to defend against at least half a dozen armed men. A hamlet not far off, but with a population chiefly disposed to keep out of trouble. Rescue on its way, but uncomfortably far off still. Those seem to be the terms of the problem.'

'Just so.' Mr Thewless too had moved to the window, and was scanning a prospect that already seemed wholly familiar. 'It might be called a problem that requires a little imagination in the solving. And that, of course, ought to be Humphrey's province. But do you know' – and Mr Thewless looked at his companions in mild surprise – 'do you know that, although my own mind is so desperately prosaic, I positively believe myself to have got there before him?'

Chapter 27

Ireland, a brilliant disc of many greens, circled, tilted, side-slipped beneath Cadover's eyes. The pilot had slightly altered course and was now pointing straight ahead. There, beyond the shoulder of a mountain and an arm of ocean, a tiny speck of white showed dazzling in the sun. It was the light-house. Cadover took a deep breath and a little relaxed the pressure of his toes on the metal bar beneath them. Like a lover in an overdue train, he had been absurdly employing his muscles to urge the aeroplane on. He peered downwards and, leaning forward, pointed in his turn. On a long white ribbon of road his eye had caught the dark shape of three large cars. A trail of dust behind them told of their headlong speed. That would be the Irish police.

The mountain melted on their flank and in its place he saw cliffs, sea, a village like a scatter of white pebbles on grass, a single isolated house. These all dipped and swung away; the mountain had taken their place and was charging at him; again the mountain vanished and his ears were singing. He glimpsed the house again, close beneath him, in a violent foreshortening capped by expanses of ribbed lead. Then his horizon contracted to a rushing river of green and he bounced gently in his seat. They taxied on grass, their wing-tip almost brushing a hedge. On the other side a flow of darker green slowed and took form. Fleetingly Cadover's mind essayed comparisons with the back garden in Pinner. They knew about potatoes; there could be no doubt about that. He clambered out. His pilot came behind him, tugging off gloves, pulling out a revolver. They had polished off queer jobs between them before now. But this time their wireless had told them of astonishing things. They ran. A blackthorn hedge was before them and they burst through it. The lane led straight to the village. Everything was very still. Far away they could hear the cry of gulls and a wash of waves. The sunshine was warm on the fields, hard and brilliant on the white cottages ahead.

The peacefulness of it sharply taxed belief as to what could lie in front. As to what *did* lie in front – for suddenly the air was torn by a rapid fusillade. Cadover gave a gasp of relief as he ran. They were holding out.

The village stretched out two lines of straggling cottages and received them. But it might have been a village of the dead. Its doors were closed; many of its windows were shuttered; it was as if the Troubles had come again and pacific folk kept indoors when the gunmen were abroad. And the nearer fields were deserted. Only on the farther hillsides, a mile or more away, scattered figures in their bright home-spuns were going about their rural tasks. This gave, as it were, the scale of the affair. And it was a scale formidable enough. And now – as if to enforce this – Cadover's companion grabbed him by the arm and drew him sharply into the hedge.

They had been told of astonishing things; they saw them now. At a turn of the lane before them two large grey cars were parked, and on guard beside them was a man armed with a revolver. But it was to something else that Cadover's pilot pointed. Close beside them, on rising ground, was a tall white barn. Straddled on its thatched gable a hazardously perched figure slowly swept the countryside through field-glasses. Below him, two more men crouched on stationary motor-cycles, like competitors at the start of a road-race.

Cadover felt himself tugged through a hedge, and heard his companion's voice in his ear. 'Can they have missed us coming down?'

'I doubt it. They saw the size of our plane, and feel they can still stick it out a bit.'

'And when the Irish chaps come?'

'It will be a score of men with tommy-guns and a wireless transmitter. They'll know they're done for then, all right. Listen! They're still fighting back from the house.'

Another fusillade had reached them. Stooping low, they pressed forward. The firing grew more rapid. But behind it now was another sound – explosive too, but accompanied by a low, deep roar, a dry crackling . . .

'It's on fire!'

They had pressed on regardless and scrambled through another hedge, so that Killyboffin Hall was full in front of them. From now one and now another upper window came an intermittent flash from some species of small arms; this was drawing an answering fire from various points about the grounds; and inside the house, too, there appeared to be shooting. But more startling was the fact that a large part of the structure was indeed blazing – whether as the consequence of accident or design it was impossible to say. One wing, indeed, was almost consumed, and showed as a mere glowing shell against which was oddly silhouetted a line of broken statuary which lined a terrace in front. The effect of outrage and mutilation was sufficiently bizarre to hold Cadover for a moment at a pause. And upon this new sounds broke: the roar of an aeroplane engine overhead, and an answering roar, scarcely less loud, of powerful motor-cars rapidly approaching the village behind.

'That's them! The police and the Dublin men too!' And Cadover leapt forward with an impetuosity quite beyond his years. His companion followed. Bullets sang about their heads; from somewhere a whistle blew shrilly; they ran up a flight of shallow stone steps and dashed into the house through a broken window. The place was full of smoke through which they could see several forms in rapid retreat. It was clear that all effective siege was already over. From somewhere quite close at hand came the crash of a falling beam. Cadover, his eyes smarting, blundered out into a long corridor. 'A staircase!' he shouted. 'If we can't get them down in five minutes it will be all up with them.'

They pushed along the corridor and found the smoke clearing; they passed through a baize door and found themselves in a part of the house not immediately threatened by fire. Presently they came to a narrow service staircase and climbed. They paused on a small landing, their eyes drawn to a window in which every pane had been shattered. Glass and splintered wood lay everywhere, and a white-painted chest of drawers, apparently tumbled down from some further floor above, lay sprawled before them, its drawers fantastically spilling a profusion of housemaids' aprons and caps. Cadover glanced out, and glimpsed a number of men disappearing round a group of outbuildings, shooting as they went; glimpsed too, advancing across the park, a grim sickle of green-coated figures – police or soldiers – with formidable automatic rifles in their hands. Eire, he reflected, had done the situation proud . . . And then he heard once more the crackle of flames and the roar of a ceiling coming down. Humphrey Paxton's kidnappers were a menace no more. The remnant of that astonishing organization was in flight. But another enemy, quite as lethal, was advancing fast.

He turned to mount higher – and suddenly paused, aware that he himself was in new danger. For the top of this further staircase was roughly barricaded with wardrobes, cupboards, upholstered chairs; and the place reeked of powder. Here the real battle had been fought out. And it seemed only too likely that the defenders would still shoot at sight. 'Hold your fire!' he shouted. 'We are the police.'

There was no reply. He heard instead only the crackle of the advancing fire, and the diminishing tumult outside, and his own voice strangely echoing in distant corridors.

'Answer!' he shouted. 'Answer – whatever you think. The place is on fire. You must get out.'

Again there was only silence – silence that bred a sudden and horrible suspicion. He thrust his revolver away and ran up the remaining stairs, his companion behind him. Together they heaved at the barricade, tore at it, broke the banisters, heaved cupboard and wardrobe pellmell down the stairs behind them. Cadover, straining to dislodge a chair, slipped and put down a hand to save himself. He looked at it and found it smeared with blood. Blood was trickling over the topmost tread and forming a little pool below.

But now they were through. Beyond a narrow landing two doors were open upon two small rooms. Their several windows showed beyond – and of these also every pane was shattered. A shot-gun lay on the floor of each. It was not to this, however, that Cadover's eye first went. Supine beside the barricade lay an elderly man, a revolver in his outflung right hand, his face blackened by smoke, blood welling in an ominous pulse from a long gash on his wrist. Cadover dropped on this like a plummet. 'Look after the others,' he called. 'I'll fix this.'

He busied himself with his task of first aid, for it was more urgent even than getting the wounded man out of the burning building. Intent on it, he heard sounds of rapid search around him. Then his companion's voice came for the first time since they had entered the house. 'The others?' it said. 'There aren't any others here.'

Mr Thewless opened his eyes, aware of the fresh air, of a cool breeze from the sea on his temples, of brandy sharp on his lips. He saw, first swimmingly and then coming into clearer focus, the face of a man of his own age, sombre in cast, crowned by close-cropped white hair. With considerable effort, Mr Thewless spoke. 'You look', he said, 'like an honest man.'

'And you have behaved like one.'

Mr Thewless made nothing of this. He felt very dizzy, very weak. 'The house,' he asked, 'is it burning?'

'It is burning to ashes. Nothing can save it.' The white-haired man paused to speak briefly to somebody behind him, and Mr Thewless was uncertainly aware of a background still of revolver shots, of shouted orders, of running men. 'But what about the others?' The white-haired man had turned to him again and his voice was urgent. 'What about Humphrey Paxton? What about Sir Charles Liberty's sister? Did they get the boy, after all?'

'I was extremely obtuse.' Words still came painfully to Mr Thewless, but he felt that this was an important point to make. 'I was a sadly inadequate person for coping with such a situation . . . although I did, to be sure, have this odd flash of imagination at the end. But even that was – well, literary and derivative. Poe . . . a very well-known story by Poe.' He paused, reading in the expression of the face before him that this was judged to be mere delirium. 'I think it is called *The Purloined Letter* – What's that?'

'That?' The white-haired man paused while the rattle of firing died away. 'There were a lot of them, you know – quite an amazing gang. And they're still rounding them up.'

'All of them?'

'Only the small fry so far. Apparently the leader –'

'The bearded man?'

'Yes, the bearded man. He turns out to be somebody pretty big. And he's got down to the shore – somewhere under the cliffs – so that they haven't got him yet. But I want you to tell me –'

'He has a motor-cruiser!' Mr Thewless struggled into a sitting posture. 'In a cave down there. If he is allowed to reach that he will get away.'

'The devil he has!' And once more the white-haired man turned and talked rapidly to someone behind him. 'We may get him, all the same. And I think we'll get the others.'

'The Bolderwoods? I most unfeignedly hope so.' And this time Mr Thewless did get firmly upright. 'For I must confess to grave misgiving, Mr–'

'Cadover. Detective-Inspector Cadover.'

'Ah. Now, what was I saying? But yes, of course! I was a good deal troubled by the morality of the bargain that Miss Liberty found it necessary to make with them. I should like to think that they had been laid by the heels.'

'They have a boat too – somewhere on the other side of the headland. But they have been headed off from it and driven back here. It is thought that they must be in hiding not far away. Perhaps they –'

Here the police officer called Cadover checked himself – and with an exclamation so startled that it brought Mr Thewless swaying to his feet. They had brought him, he found, a considerable way from the burning building, and he stared unbelievingly for a moment at the flames still licking through those upper windows from which he had fought his strangely epic fight. But this scarcely detained him. For all eyes, he saw, were elsewhere.

It was like a little battle station pitched near the edge of the cliff. Green-uniformed men were around him – one with binoculars, one crouched over what he conjectured to be a field telephone. Below them he could see a line of cliff, a segment of beach on which more uniformed men were running, a great splash of sea. And it was the sea at which all were looking. There, from behind the headland where lay the farther entrance to Humphrey's cave, a gleaming craft had appeared hurtling through the water, the roar of its engines reverberating still among the rocks. And it was impossible to mistake that curbed and leaping prow, that low-cut stern . . . 'It's him!' Mr Thewless cried. 'He's got away!'

There were bursts of firing from the beach below, and little lines of cascading water marked the path of the bullets. But the motor-boat held on its course, heading at a tremendous pace for the open sea. In a matter of seconds it would be out of range. And Mr Thewless felt his shoulder gripped by the man beside him, heard an altogether new anxiety in that level London voice.

'The boy, man! Where is he? Don't tell me he can have got him out there?'

'The boy? I hope –'

Mr Thewless heard his own voice drowned in a new clamour, in the roar of an engine yet more powerful directly above him. A shadow skimmed the grass beside him; a wind tugged at his sparse hair; he looked up and promptly ducked – ducked in fear of sheer decapitation by the aircraft passing overhead. From a field behind them there came shots and the sound of men shouting, running. And from close beside him came an answering shout.

'Great heavens, it's my plane!'

And the London policeman grimly nodded. 'We ought to have thought to set a guard on it. The Bolderwoods take the last trick.'

Mr Thewless gasped. 'The Bolderwoods . . . they're in *that*?'

'They've stolen it.' Suddenly the grip that was still on Mr Thewless's shoulder tightened. 'Look! I believe he can't –'

Cadover's voice died away. Steeply climbing, the little aircraft was now out beyond the cliffs; climbing more steeply still, it slipped, staggered, spun . . . There was a moment's complete silence, broken by a soft Irish voice from the man with the field-glasses. 'And no more he can, by all the saints! It's a mortal certainty he never held the controls of a plane before this fearful day.'

The plane rose again, for a second hung sluggishly in air, turned over, fell. It fell, Mr Thewless thought, much as a gannet dives . . . And directly beneath it was the hurtling motor-cruiser. There was a single blinding flash, a single deafening detonation. Mr Thewless shut his eyes. When he opened them the man with the field-glasses was crossing himself, was muttering a prayer. And the sea was utterly empty. Where the bearded man, where Cyril and Ivor Bolderwood, had been urging their flight a moment before, there was only a sullen and spreading pool of oil, circled by a single screaming gull. It was an end at once horrifying and grotesquely theatrical – as if some trap-door had opened and incontinently swept half the *dramatis personae* from the stage.

'Somewhere up *there*?' The officer with the field-glasses swept the hillsides before turning a puzzled face to Mr Thewless. 'We don't quite see how –'

'How *The Purloined Letter* comes in.' Cadover too had binoculars, and he spoke without taking them from his eyes. 'I think you *did* say *The Purloined Letter*?'

'Certainly.' Mr Thewless – rather to his own surprise – was biting hungrily into a sandwich which he held in his uninjured left hand. 'You see, the ruffians were advancing to attack us in force; and the only thing seemed to be to get the boy away – and, of course, Miss Liberty as well. But there seemed no chance that they could slip away *unseen*, since the gang would almost certainly have the countryside under observation just as you have it now. So it occurred to me that they must be positively obtrusive – positively *staring*, so to speak – and find a sort of invisibility in that. And that was just how the letter in Poe's story –'

The man with the field-glasses exclaimed softly, his instrument focused upon one of the highest fields beyond the village. 'And when you were after thinking all this, Mr Thewless – what then?'

'We had noticed how brilliantly many of the peasantry show up against the green grass because of the rich colours in which they dye their homespun cloth. You can see them there' – and Mr Thewless pointed – 'tiny splashes of red and blue right out on the mountain-side. So we hunted quickly through the servants' quarters and found a sufficiency of such things – for Miss Liberty a deep blue skirt, and for Humphrey some really brave claret-coloured trousers. Then Miss Liberty took a basket to balance on her head, and the boy a bundle for his back. Once they were a little beyond the house, and simply plodding openly across the fields, there was a good chance that they would be all right; that they would pass through whatever cordon the enemy had out. The danger was that the enemy might already have got into a position from which they were bound to spot them actually leaving. But it was necessary to risk that. And when they had gone – and I was never so glad of anything in my life – I prepared to give the effect of several people standing siege at the top of the servants' staircase. It proved to be excellently adapted for the purpose.' And Mr Thewless nodded with an assurance that almost touched complacency. 'I really believe I could scarcely have chosen better.'

Cadover and the green-uniformed man now both had their glasses fixed on the same distant spot. It was again the latter who spoke. 'Yes – to be sure! You'll be remarking, Mr Thewless, how they put out the long skeins of dyed wool to dry in the fields and along the hedges? Well, there's two folk at that up there now – and I'd say that one of them had claret-coloured trousers that are brave enough.' He laughed softly. 'Now, I wonder who he'd have persuaded to give him all that wool?'

Cadover too laughed – a short, deep laugh that spoke of a long strain broken. 'And he is entering into the deception with a will. He's laying the stuff out on the grass like anything.' he paused. 'Hullo! I'm blessed if he hasn't formed letters with it. *He*. Now, why should the lad want to write *He*?'

Mr Thewless smiled. 'Not *He*, Inspector. *H.E.*'

'You're quite right. And he's going on. *H.E.H* . . .'

'*H.E.H.P* . . . Humphrey has a string of names, of which he is inclined to be rather proud. It's his way of letting us know, you see, that all is well with them up there. I wonder if we can send some signal back? I believe he would be quite glad to think that things have gone not too badly with me down here.'

The green-uniformed man called out an order; there was a sharp report; a green Very light burst in the air. Mr Thewless watched it and judged it entirely beautiful.

'A capable boy,' he said. 'Really, a thoroughly capable boy.'

Operation Pax

Within the navil of this hideous Wood,
Immur'd in cypress shades a Sorcerer dwels . . .
And here to every thirsty Wanderer,
By sly enticement gives his baneful cup.

Comus

Note

It is proper to inform the reader that the internal economy of the Bodleian Library in the University of Oxford, as described with some particularity in the ensuing romance, is entirely the fruit of fancy. And, more particularly, those subterranean regions in which the climax is set, although frequently vouched for by reliable persons as bearing a general correspondence with what is here imagined, have never come within the purview of the author, whose common occasions have familiarized him only with that which lies above ground-level. He is very conscious of being seldom charged with any large adherence to the *actual*, and he begs acceptance of the postulate that, if there be (as assuredly there must be) a *real* Bodleian Library laid up in Heaven, its foundations unquestionably rest upon such immensities as are rudely figured in this insubstantial tale. And be it added that the author, contemplating his finished and fugitive performance and realizing one odd consequence of the Copyright Act of 1709, is constrained to murmur with a wholesome awe certain lines of old Samuel Daniel, similarly circumstanced three hundred and fifty years ago:

> Heere in this goodly Magazine of witte,
>   This Storehouse of the choicest furniture
> The world doth yeelde, here in this exquisite
>   And most rare monument, that doth immure
> The glorious reliques of the best of men,
>   Thou, part imperfect work, vouchsafed art
> A little roome.

1. Routh in an Infernal Region

> ...involv'd
> In this perfidious fraud.
> *Paradise Lost*

I

There was a wait in the bank. Routh's inside felt empty, flabby. His own patter nagged in his head. *No need whatever for a deposit to secure delivery. Our senior sales manager knows your standing in the community, madam.*

Routh shifted his weight furtively from one foot to the other. He glanced over his shoulder and through the gilded letters **MIDLAND BANK LTD** at the quiet street. The old Douglas two-stroke was just round the corner. He had to be careful that nobody following him out of the bank rounded the same corner and saw him mount it. Provided he worked each town quickly and left this one fault on his trail it was alright. You should say *All right.* Remember your education.

But just at present able to offer a few influential customers twenty per cent reduction for cash with order. Again his own glib phrases were spilling aimlessly over his mind. Perhaps that was what he would have to do in Hell: go on repeating these things through all eternity.

The man in front was paying in cheques and a lot of cash. The teller ticked off the amounts that were already filled in on a long slip. *Making only three pounds ten precisely, madam.* If only you had the guts for a hold-up. Smash and grab. Smash the teller's silly face and grab all that. Routh's right hand in his trouser-pocket – the one where the lining was only a big ragged hole – trembled as it touched the woman's mean, creased cheque . . . And all this for three pounds ten. *Uncrossed and made payable to bearer, madam, if you don't mind.*

It was here once more, the bad moment. The chap in front had closed his shabby leather bag, was having some fool joke, was going. Routh took the cheque from his pocket. The very paper was hot and clammy. He hated banks so, surely banks must hate him. At least they hated these small open cheques presented by strangers. Yet they would never really try a check-up – not then and there. Customers – the small sort that Routh chose for *his* customers – didn't like it. So it's all right, I tell you. Push it over. Remember you're a gentleman. Push it at him. Quietly, pleasantly. Good morning.

Routh saw his own hand tremble. He would remember afterwards – he always did – that it had been with anger, not fear. It was with anger at the pettiness of the thing, at all this for three pounds ten. He knew that, really, Routh was on a big scale, was a being cast in a large mould, would rise to the grand occasion when it came. And it would come. He would carry out a big thing as cool as ice, as cool as Raffles. And his heart then would not thrust against his ribs as it did now . . . The teller was looking at him.

But it was all right. The man's pen was poised over the signature to scribble. In a second he would say indifferently 'Notes?' and flick the petty amount off the orderly piles in his drawer. Don't say anything more. Wait. A normal commercial transaction. Routh repeated the phrase to himself. He found himself repeating it again and again. A normal commercial transaction. A normal . . . The teller had gone.

A big clock ticked on the wall. Its ticking queerly struck in at Routh's pounding heart, fought with it rhythm against rhythm. His knees went wrong, so that he had to lock them, to press them against each other. The bank swayed. All right . . . *all right*. It's happened before. Nothing to do with *you*. The woman has a shaky account, a tiny balance and no arrangement for overdrawing. She's been a nuisance for a long time, and now they won't even honour her cheque for three ten – not if the credit isn't there. That's what he's gone to see. Only hold on.

But what if it's something else? He tried to think about the woman and her cheque. It was the woman with the hare-lip, with the window curtains that had seemed more morbidly secretive than anybody else's in the drearily respectable little road. She had been one of those that open the door on the chain. With that sort, to get in is to triumph. *Our senior sales manager knows your standing*. In a quarter of an hour he had sold the non-existent contraption. *Making only three pounds ten precisely, madam*. Not, he had thought, the bank-account sort. Watching her write the cheque in her gimcrack parlour with its paranoid curtains he had been surprised. *Edges us round the quotas. Thank you.*

Of course she had swallowed it. Staggering, but they nearly all did.

Or had she?

Routh's breathing quickened. After all, one day you'd be caught out. One day you'd meet a trap. More often now you met a woman who knew, who tumbled. It was because of articles in the pocket mags, because of Scotland Yard programmes on the Woman's Hour. Then you had to smile yourself quickly out, make for another town, change for a time the thing you pretended to sell. And one day you'd meet some dim little woman who'd do better, who'd give you a cheque and then call straight round on the police. It might be the wife of a policeman. Come to think of it, there must be plenty. It might be the wife of a local detective sergeant. And perhaps the woman with the hare-lip was that.

There was a sudden cold sweat on Routh. He wrenched his eyes up from the counter. The teller had become the baldish back of a head, and blue serge trousers shiny in the beam of the bleak October sun. He was whispering into a sort of box or pen behind him. Routh heard the undistinguishable whispering and heard the tick of the big clock and heard still his heart that now had something slack and impotent in its throb like the sea idly pulsing in a cave . . . He knew with a quick rush of lucidity that he had lost his head. There was a sharp relief in knowing, in knowing that now he could only act out the logical consequences of panic. He knew that it was probably still true that the teller was debating whether to pay out three ten when there was only fifteen bob in the account. But he knew it was no use knowing that . . . And then he saw himself.

It sometimes happened with Routh. As if a great mirror were let down from heaven he would see himself as he there and then stood. It happened to him at bad moments, mostly. Backing off a doorstep with his mouth twisted in malice, beaten by a woman that wouldn't buy. Pawing a drab who disgusted him. Cringing in a pub before some drunken bully. And now.

The other Routh was standing beside him, sweat on his brow and with one cheek twitching, his eyes fixed in terror on a blue serge jacket shiny at the seams. The other Routh's left hand had gone to his mouth and furtively he was gnawing at a ragged cuticle. The boy from the good grammar-school hiding behind the second-rate public-school tie. The Army deserter with the Air Force moustache. The outlaw, the bandit, the lone wolf sweating into his soiled vest, having to battle with his knees, his breathing, his sphincter-control in order to bring off a seventy shilling swindle.

Rage and humiliation and naked fear swept over Routh. There was nobody on this side of the counter. He turned and ran from the bank, ran for the two-stroke round the corner.

2

Pulsing sturdily between his calves the worn old engine thrust the miles behind at a steady thirty-five. Suppose the bank rang up the police and told the story. That would be five minutes. The woman hadn't been on the telephone – he had noticed that – and it would be another ten minutes before they had one of their C.I.D. men on her doorstep. Another five and he'd have the type of fraud taped and his report back at headquarters . . .

But the familiar recital of dangers and chances that should have crossed and recrossed Routh's mind like a stage army, tedious and inescapable as a chain of cigarettes, was today reluctant to march. Riding blindly across country, he had to keep coaxing it from the wings. The raddled old thoughts that ought to have cut their routine capers effortlessly before his fatigued attention had gone shy like kids being smacked and cajoled through their first turn in panto.

Routh was frightened at this inertness of his fears. He knew that when his own arguing and reassuring voice left him other voices came at him instead – voices out of the past. Daddy's. Mummy's. Darling, darling Mummy . . . The throttle was full open already so if they came he couldn't get away from them that way. *Suppose the bank rang up the police . . .*

Around Routh, this morning of an autumn that had come early held shafts of sunlight through vapour, held dark rich ploughland backed by a dozen greens turning to russet and gold. Already there was a litter and soon there would be a mush of chestnut leaves on the macadam. A leaf caught in the spokes and flipped at the mudguard like the whirr of a flushed bird. Routh rode blind, deaf. What stretched before him was not a high road but a plank, slimy and supple, across a little weir. *Come on, old chap, have a go.* Routh felt Mummy's too quickly apprehensive hand tighten on his own. She could see how difficult the plank was, whereas Daddy's eyes behind their queer pebble glasses saw only the idea of it. Again Daddy was urging him. And he was hanging back. He was hanging back because already, secretly, he had attempted the crossing and had failed. Half-way he had turned giddy and fallen. In a second he had been down in the pool – down, down, suffocating and with a roaring in his ears, as if someone had pulled the plug on him, or let him out with the bath water. An old man pottering with a fishing rod had given him a hand to the side. Probably he had been in some real danger of drowning.

Come on, old chap. Over you go. We'll come round by the bridge and join you. His fear was irrational. He could only get bruised and wet a second time, could do no more than make himself ridiculous. But the thought of the first time – of the moment that was like a plug pulled – was too bad. He remembered the covert and dripping slipping home, round by the canal with street boys guffawing and in through the back garden . . . He took a great breath, and did it. He crossed the plank as his parents watched; and turned exalted. He expected them to wave, to move upstream to the bridge. But Daddy had laid his hand on Mummy's shoulder to stop her. *Now then back again, old chap.* Daddy shouted it as if Niagara were between them. It made him sound mad. Mummy had gone pale. She was wringing her hands, mute like a silent film. And a glint from Daddy's glasses, caught by the boy as he tried to brace himself, was like instantaneous intelligence flashed across a battlefield on a mirror. It wasn't the burden of his own funk he must carry over the plank again. It was Daddy's. And he knew that if he broke under it once he always would.

There had been a man in the next field, turning a machine that chopped up turnips. He had been looking over the hedge wonderingly when Mummy came and pulled him blubbering from the grass. Routh knew now that it would have been no good successfully making that second crossing. For there would always have been another one. That was Daddy's madness. But on the silent walk home, as he peeped snivelling from behind Mummy's skirts, he saw only Daddy's cheeks held two bright red spots. And that one of the cheeks was twitching.

240

3

It was a memory that Routh had come to fear as the entrance to a long tunnel of fantasy, worn mercilessly smooth by the constant cramped trans-passage of his straightened mind. The injustices, the deprivations, the slights, the cruelties leered at him from their niches. Routh cheated, scorned, mocked, ignored – he hungered after the endless images, but feared them more than he hungered.

Always this engulfing fantasy threatened to hurl him from his safety, from his rational mind's chosen vocation as a petty crook into some unguessable madness. To live by robbing obscure households of half a week's pay: it was the life of measure, of dangerous pride eschewed, of due and wary regard for the gods. Routh of the indomitable will, Routh the planning animal: the danger came when these were thrust aside by the long review of Routh the victim of circumstances, Routh doomed by Daddy, Routh spitefully beaten, Routh unjustly sacked, Routh demeaned and degraded in seedy travelling companies and troops of pierrots on the sands. And as Routh re-created in himself the sense of a whole society with cruel hand outstretched and eager to pull the plug, terrifying hints of hidden and dangerous volitions rose up through his weak anger. His whole body shook like a trumpery room given over to some obscure and vicious brawl.

It trembled now so that the Douglas left a wavy track behind it. The wash of fear that had swept over him in the bank and robbed him of three pounds ten was mounting, and as it mounted was meeting some strange new chemistry full of menace. He could no longer think about the number of minutes it would take for the police to begin inquiries there behind him.

Routh swerved at the side of the road and came jolting to a stop. There was now no dissociated part of him to control the machine. His eyes were misted with tears in which his anger, his resentment, his enormous self-pity welled up and out. That he should have been baulked of three pounds ten was a wrong deeper than any plummet of his mind could sound. At the same time it was a deprivation so squalidly insignificant that the spectacle of his own helpless anger at it was unbearable. The tears released by the sorry conflict had no power to assuage, afforded no relief to the weedy figure astride the old Douglas by the roadside. That figure in its pinched and manikin stature, was too vividly before him. It seared his vanity. To banish it, to vindicate in himself the generous inches that all the world had conspired to deny: this was the claimant need of his whole being . . . He looked ahead up the empty road and saw the figure of a woman.

She had overtaken and passed him regardless – a girl in breeches and leggings whom one would have taken at first for a boy. She was whistling. And her whistling picked out, as with a sudden strong accent, the stillness and loneliness of the place. As he looked, the woman turned to her left and disappeared down a lane. It could be distinguished as winding between high hedged banks to a hamlet nearly two miles away. Even more than this stretch of unfrequented secondary road, it seemed a place of solitude and secrecy. Routh slipped from the saddle and pushed the Douglas behind a near-by thorn.

He turned by the sign-post. It pointed to a place with a queer name – Milton Porcorum. He followed the whistling woman rapidly, exalted by the fierce purity of his intention. Beside him walked another Routh, a new and triumphant externalization, Routh gigantic and terrible. Routh the destroyer. He was ahead. Through this gap, as she came up with it, he would spring.

In fact, he slithered. It was less effective. But the woman pulled up, startled. She was older than he had thought – about thirty, with pale blue eyes and a thin, firm mouth. She was suddenly quite still. Routh gave a queer cry. At his first grab she quivered. At his second she vanished. The woman vanished and as she did so agonizing pain shot up Routh's left arm. It was such pain that his knees crumpled beneath him. He was kneeling in mud and his head was going down into mud. He struggled and the pain sickened him.

'Rub your nose in it.'

The voice of the woman from behind and above him carried to him inexorably his preposterous fortune. He put his face in the mud and moved it about feebly.

'And now in a bit of gravel.'

Throbbing to quickened pain Routh was kneed and twitched across the lane. Again his face went down.

'Rub it harder.'

The voice, mocking and excited, ended in a low laugh. Constrained by his agony, Routh did what he was told. He felt the skin of his nose and cheek go raw. He heard a quick controlled intake of breath, sensed skilled hands passing swiftly to a new hold, felt the earth drop away from him and swing back with shattering force low in the belly. For a long time he lay semi-conscious and helpless, deeper beneath his nausea than ever child sunk powerless in a chill brown pool. Through his ears passed waves of uncertain sound. It might have been the distant voices of street-arabs jeering at an abject small boy.

4

When at length Routh got to his feet it was early afternoon. His left arm was numb and his face felt bruised and scarified. He fingered over it tenderly with his right hand. His mind was an unfamiliar chaos. Staggering up the lane, he fumbled for a pocket mirror, and had to empty his pocket of slivers of glass. Into one of these, held up in a trembling hand, he peered apprehensively. At a first glimpse he felt a surge of mortified vanity, a fierce resentment. This was an outrage. He had been brutally assaulted. And not as in a clean row in a pub. There had been something dirty in it. What good were the police if they couldn't keep people like that behind bars?

For a moment longer Routh stood halted in the lane, his disordered body swaying slightly as he manoeuvred the now tiny scrap of glass before his face. The damage in point of fact was inconsiderable, for his subjection had been after all chiefly symbolical. Under the mud it looked like three long scratches and one raw patch over a cheek bone. He felt a flicker of returning conceit. Wily Routh. He hadn't rubbed his face in the gravel half as hard as he'd intended. There was some salve to injured vanity in that. But he needed water.

He realized that he was moving in the wrong direction. The two-stroke was up the lane, behind him. He was following the path that the woman must have continued on. He stopped, scared. She might come again and take him and twist him about. But something told him that the apprehension was unreal. He would not see her again. He went on, remembering that earlier he had passed no water for miles, and guessing that in a very little valley into which the lane presently dipped there would be a stream or spring.

He had come upon a high wall. Blank and curving, it followed the line of a concealed lane with which his own had now merged. It was no more than the sort of wall which, running perhaps for miles round a gentleman's park, speaks in the simplest picture-language of a vanished social order. The great house within would long since have been sold for a fraction of what it would now cost to build this massive outwork. And it would shelter a private sanatorium, an establishment for training bank clerks, an approved school. In all this there was no reason why Routh should feel himself in the presence of something indefinably sinister. Only the wall was very blank and surprisingly high.

And then Routh saw the man.

The appearance of this human figure, sudden and unaccountable, suggested a *coup de théâtre* for which the wall's sinister air had been a build-up deliberately achieved. At one moment the wall stretched unbroken before Routh, every foot of its well-appointed surface void in the bleak and shadowless sunlight. And at the next moment the man was there, an immobile and waiting figure some seventy yards away, with the unbroken stone behind him like a backcloth.

Routh's impulse was to turn and retrace his steps – to get back, muddy as he was, to the two-stroke, and chance finding water for a clean-up later on. His legs however carried him unsteadily and inexorably forward. The man made a very slight movement and a wisp of smoke floated upwards. He was smoking a cigarette as he waited. His immobility was hypnotizing. Against the clamour of his every nerve, Routh found himself quickening his pace.

The man was standing in front of an iron-sheathed, stone-coloured door set flush in the wall. His eyes took one sweeping glance up and down the lane and then settled themselves upon Routh. Tall and with square shoulders carried high as if in a frozen shrug, he was dressed in what Routh knew to be a high-class tailor's job in home-spun tweed. You could tell he owned whatever lay beyond that wall. But you could tell, too, that he was a townsman. His features were irregular and ugly, but they had the controlled mobility that tells of a mind schooled to work swiftly through complex issues. He belongs, Routh thought, at the top of one of the big-money professions – a leading surgeon, perhaps, or a successful K. C. Boss class. And a gentleman.

Well, that's what *you* are – see? Routh – muddy, dusty, torn, scratched, and with the toes hurting in his thin, pointed shoes – Routh braced himself to fill out the role. A gentleman taking an afternoon stroll in unfamiliar country. That was the formula. And better pass the time of day. *Good afternoon.*

The man made no reply. In his silence the uncertain flame of confidence that had leapt up in Routh flickered and went out. The man was looking at him steadily. He was putting two and two together about the shabby figure now sliding past with averted eyes. But at least, Routh told himself, you *are* past. He isn't really interested. Just keep on steadily. Only you'd better get back to the two-stroke another way.

'Come here.'

The words, quietly spoken behind him, had, in his already shaken state, the effect of a needle thrust into his spine. He knew that his only safety was to run, and chance making a race for it. But for the second time that day his legs were powerless, and nothing would race but his own heart. Oddly the world pivoted on him as he stood, and he found himself confronting the man who waited before the stone-coloured door.

The man beckoned, without again speaking. He beckoned, strangely, with a downward pointing figure – as one in a circus ring might beckon at a cowed and uniformly obedient brute creation.

Resentment rendered Routh articulate. 'Look here,' he said, '– what do you think I am?'

But his legs were carrying him back to the waiting man. The feeble truculence he had heard in his own voice gave him no encouragement to rebel.

'I think you are the ruffian who has attacked a girl in my employment.' The man was well over six feet, and he contrived to look down at Routh as at a cur. 'I suppose you know the sentence you'd get for a criminal assault of that sort?'

'She did it. She assaulted me.' Routh panted as he spoke. The absurdity and indignity of his words were only emphasized by the element of truth in them.

'Where do you come from? What are you?'

Routh took a quick, desperate glance about him. Somehow he had the impression that this scene was being watched, that the tip of his senses, whether of sight or hearing, had detected some presence that might succour him. But nothing he could now see gave any support to this fancy. So he must face it out. At least these were a sort of question that he could always answer after a fashion, and he judged it well to do so now. 'I'm a clerk, and out of work. I've come down from the north.'

'Do you think you're likely to get work in the heart of the country?'

'I'm going through to Reading.'

'Motor-bicycle?'

Routh blinked. Very faintly, as if some hatch had been opened deep down in his mind, cunning stirred beneath his rage and terror. There was something queer in the way that, underneath, the brute was interested in him. He resolved in a flash that he must at all costs conceal the existence of the Douglas. He plunged at it boldly. 'I'm walking. I've hardly any money left.'

'And no possessions?'

'A chap took my suitcase on a lorry. I'll pick it up at the station.'

'Let me see your identity card.'

'It's in the suitcase. And you haven't any right –'

For the first time the tall man faintly smiled. 'A deserter on the run – eh? Your people help you at all?'

He was softening. *Hard luck. Let the poor devil off. Give him a hand. A square meal and ten bob.* It was a stage in the well-to-do man's triumphant detection of petty crime that was familiar to Routh. Automatically he played up to it. 'I haven't any people. I'm an only child. My father's in a mental hospital and won't ever get better. My mother's gone to New Zealand with another man. I haven't heard from her for five years.'

Routh became aware that the tall man, whose hand should now be going to his pocket, was once more swiftly glancing up and down the lane, as if he too had a momentary sensation of being watched Then the man's eyes met his. Fear leapt anew in Routh. There *was* something queer about him. That he was softening was dead off the scent. On the contrary, there was some hard design in him. And it was only for a second that Routh thought he understood it. No, the man was looking at him simply as a carpenter might look at a plank which he would presently give himself the satisfaction of sawing into sections in the pursuance of some clearly apprehended design.

But even as Routh grasped this, the man's manner changed. Expression had come into his face. It was an expression of weighed or judicial contempt – a sort of judgement that had been impassively deferred until Routh in all his seediness, weediness and cowardice had been bared before him. He took a step forward and made a movement that Routh momentarily interpreted as the prelude to an iron handshake. Instead, he slapped Routh's face, paused, slapped it again back-handed. 'I don't know about your father being a lunatic,' he said, 'but I certainly believe that your mother –'

Routh sprang at him, screaming – groped for him through a red haze in which the external world had suddenly bathed itself. When he came to he was on the other side of the wall.

5

'I apologize.'

At first the words seemed to come to Routh from very far away. There was a burning sensation in his throat that ran deep down into his body. The words repeated themselves and the tall man swam into focus. He was standing over Routh with a brandy flask in his hand, and looking down at him with an appearance of whimsical benevolence. He screwed the top on the flask and thrust it away in a hip-pocket. 'A bit of a test,' he said. 'Don't take it hard, my good fellow. Something of a test – no more.'

Routh, helpless on the grass, wished that he had a revolver or a knife. But hatred and the brandy now coursing in him sharpened his faculties and he realized that he *had* a weapon. Trapped on the wrong side of that formidable wall – it was now a shadowed concavity towering above him and stretching around him – he felt obscurely and paradoxically in control – in control of a situation that as yet he didn't remotely understand. He had only to lie low, and never let his cunning sleep, and he would come out of this on top. He sat up. 'You can't do this to me,' he said, and his voice was shaky by necessity and plaintive by design. 'I don't care who you are. You can be gaoled for this.'

'Then it looks as if we are about quits, my friend.' The tall man laughed shortly and produced a cigarette-case. 'Smoke?'

Routh, although himself shaking like a leaf, observed with exultation a tremor in the tall man's hand. His irrational conviction grew that in the unknown game that had been violently forced upon him he would himself be a winner and take all. He had concealed the existence of the two-stroke, and to this for some reason he attached a vast importance. Then – mysteriously – the enclosing wall exhilarated him. He had got inside what hitherto he had always been kept outside of – the world where both honest man and knaves had large views and big chances. Yes that was it. For good or ill he had left the world of seventy-bob swindles behind him. *No need whatever for a deposit to secure delivery*. He would never say that again . . . Routh laughed aloud.

The tall man was startled. 'What's the matter with you?' he asked sharply. 'Want more brandy?'

Routh shook his head. He mustn't do anything unpredictable like that again. But his confidence took another leap. If only ever so faintly, his captor was unsure of himself. He was uncertain, standing there like an arrogant lout over a whipped cur, that he hadn't been precipitate, that he hadn't acted out of turn, in grabbing Routh as he had done. This uncertainty was tremendously important – but tremendously important too was the necessity that it shouldn't be let grow. Routh must be no more than the worthless and pliable lump of clay that the brute designed him for. The one thing that Routh must desperately conceal was any potentiality in himself for making a move or springing a surprise.

The tall man was holding out a match. Routh, swaying, managed to get his cigarette drawing. 'What do you mean – a test?' he demanded.

'I think I can put you on rather a good thing.' The tall man now smiled easily. And he took without a trace of hesitation the transition from country gentleman and outraged moralist to a world of evidently shady proposals and dubious confederacies. 'Only it needs guts. I don't mean that it's particularly risky – nothing of the sort – but it does need a *man*. I liked the way you came at me. It was damned plucky.' He paused. 'There's big money in what I'm thinking of.'

Routh felt his always facile resentment stir in him. He had evidently been graded as of very low intelligence indeed. And yet it *had* been a test. But of what? Whatever had flung him at this swine out in the lane, it hadn't been anything deserving a certificate for pluck. 'Big money?' he said – and managed to get quickened interest into his voice. He was certain that if there was indeed a gold mine in his present situation he himself would have to do all the digging. He remembered that at the moment his note was weak querulousness. 'And look here,' he added, 'who are you anyway?'

'You can call me Squire. And now, come along. We'll get up to the house.'

Routh got painfully to his feet. He began moving by the tall man's side. 'How do you mean?' he asked. 'Mr Squire? Or just Squire – of all this?' And Routh waved his hand at the park through which they were walking.

The tall man looked down at him slantwise. 'Whichever you please,' he said.

Routh bit his lip. The brute couldn't mask his contempt for a couple of minutes on end. It came into his head that he was going to be in some way enslaved, cast into thrall. Or that he was going to be killed. Very conceivably he was going to be killed in order to supply a body for, say, some insurance swindle. Routh's eyes widened on these conceptions as he walked, and his breath came faster than need be, considering the easy pace which his companion set. But still his mysterious and unaccustomed confidence failed to desert him. It was about him like a borrowed garment, unexpectedly bestowed and of surprisingly good fit.

He puzzled over the kind of racket that could support such wealth as he had stumbled upon. The park was large and there were deer in it. To encounter such creatures outside the zoo was, in Routh's mind, to be on the fringes of a magnificence positively ducal, and he stared in wonder at the creatures as he walked. He noted that Squire too watched the deer, but with a glance in which there was something faintly enigmatical – something of purely practical reference. No doubt – Routh thought – he eats them. No doubt he's deciding which to cut the throat of and get his teeth into next . . . And then it came to Routh that the manner in which Squire looked at the deer was precisely the manner in which he looked at *him*. For a moment his confidence dangerously flickered.

They had come to a halt before a tall wire fence. It was the sort of thing that runs round a tennis court to keep the balls in. Only this fence ran off indefinitely in either direction with just the same air of formidable enclosure as the high wall bordering the park. Squire had produced a bunch of keys on the end of a flexible silver chain and was proceeding to unlock a gate. Routh looked at the keys covertly. One of them had already been used on the stone-coloured door behind them. It looked as if the man who would get off Squire's property in a hurry must have that bunch of keys at his command.

'Short cut,' said Squire briefly. They went on, and he pointed to a grassy slope on their left hand. 'See anything moving?' he asked.

Routh looked. The slope had the appearance of a deserted rabbit warren. 'No,' he said, 'nothing at all.'

Squire nodded. 'No more are you likely to. Jerboa.'

'What d'you mean – jerboa?' Routh remembered again his scared, sulky note.

'The most timid mammal yet known on this earth. We'll go through here.'

Once again there was a high wire fence. But this one appeared to define a paddock of moderate size, across which Squire struck out diagonally. The ground here was uneven and there were considerable outcrops of rock. As they turned round one of these Routh stopped dead and gave a faint cry. There was a lion in the path.

There was a lion standing straight in front of them. For a second it was quite still except for a tail that waved slowly in the air. Then it turned round and made as if to slip away.

'Deilos – come here.' It was Squire who spoke. He spoke much as he had spoken to Routh in the lane. The result too was very similar. The lion turned again and reluctantly approached. As the beast came nearer the two men his belly came closer to the ground until he was creeping forward like a scared terrier. Presently he was lying quite still, his great jowl tucked between his paws, and a single eye looking slantwise upwards as if he expected a whip.

'The lion, you see, is prepared to lie down with the lamb.' Squire leant forward and tweaked the animal by the ear. 'So what about it?'

Routh stared at him. 'What d'you mean – what about it?'

'What I mean is quite simple. Get down.'

'Get down?'

'Certainly. But perhaps you don't believe that you are the lamb? I assure you that you are. The newest and most innocent of my lambs.' Squire smiled –

an odd, sweet smile that made Routh shudder. '*Lie down.*'

Routh looked from Deilos to Squire – from the unnatural animal to the unnatural man – and was by no means sure which was the more alarming. Was this mad freak before the tamed lion merely a whim or a cruel joke by the way? Was it, in fact, a sudden and almost meaningless fancy prompted by Squire's knowledge of his victim's earlier humiliation that day? Or was this sort of thing going to go on, and was the lion simply the first exhibit in a leisured sadistic joke?

Long before he had ceased confusedly asking himself these questions Routh found that he had in fact cast himself on the ground beside Deilos. The brute on this near acquaintance was rather smelly, but took not the slightest notice of him. Squire was looking down at them with his horrible smile. 'You must understand,' he said, 'that I am a magician. If I say "Abracadabra" Deilos will take no notice of you. But if I say "Abracadabra" backwards, he will at once change his nature and eat you. Wouldn't you like to be able to change the nature of a living creature at a word?'

Routh made no reply. He felt frightened and ridiculous, but still his cunning didn't cease to work. It worked the more desperately, the more he hated his tormentor. And by now he hated him very much.

Squire's smile vanished. He took a quick, almost furtive glance around him. He stepped forward and kicked Deilos hard on the rump – whereupon Deilos got to his feet with a yelp and padded away. Routh, without waiting to be kicked in his turn, scrambled to his feet. Squire brought out a handkerchief and dabbed his forehead. 'We must get on,' he said abruptly – and he strode forward. They passed out of the lion's paddock and moved downhill, through a stretch of sombre woodland. Presently, beyond a lighter screen of larches, the variously pitched roofs of a large and rambling house became visible.

Routh considered the simple proposition that his companion was insane. It was certainly the easiest way of explaining him. And Squire, if mad, must now be considered as harmlessly mad. For they were at length almost within a stone's throw of a house that must surely be too populous to admit even of a wealthy owner's engaging in vagaries of a markedly violent or criminal kind. On the other hand Squire had already behaved so strangely and unwarrantably to Routh that there was no likelihood of any further trouble being made about the affair with his employee in the lane. Whoever was more or less in charge of Squire would have to hush all that up. Otherwise there would be a row. For some seconds Routh gave himself up to the elaboration of a pleasantly novel fantasy. It would be high-class Sunday paper stuff. Out of the Lion's Mouth. The Frank Story of My Two Ordeals. Exclusive. By Alfred Routh.

The glowing picture faded. It wouldn't really do. For once the police had a grip on him they would uncover a dozen of the three-ten swindles while having him on remand. Still, the fact remained that if Squire were no more than a bit of a lunatic at large he, Routh, was invulnerable. There was so much of relief in this reading of his situation that Routh for some moments inclined to it violently. But if it ministered to the ease of his cowardice it correspondingly thwarted his cunning. There could be very little in it. A bit of bluster before a relative or a doctor, and he might get away with a five or ten pound note. There were far greater possibilities in the idea that Squire was involved in crime or racket in a big way, and that his keeping a pet like Deilos and using him to scare recruits was no more than a streak of casual nastiness such as a master criminal might very properly allow himself.

Or perhaps the suggestion of madness was a sort of blind. For Routh an interpretation of human conduct was always the more plausible if it embodied a large element of deception and fraud. With these ideals he was at home, whereas the notion of irresponsible madness was alarming and disagreeable to him. This being so, he had not gone another fifty yards before entrenching himself firmly in his first conviction. There was something very deep in the situation with which he had involuntarily become involved. And out of its depths Routh with all his wits about him might conceivably fish what, for him, would be fabulous wealth. He was proceeding to entertain himself with some details of this beatific vision when he and his conductor rounded the larch spinney and came full upon the house.

6

He had often enough seen such places from the road, but never before had he come so close up to one as this.

Squire's house – if it was indeed his – was very large, and Routh knew that it had grown up over the centuries. The chief architectural feature of the side at which he was directly looking was an affair of high Corinthian pillars running up past three storeys of windows to a blank entablature and pediment. All this, he saw, was not of stone but of some stuff that needs to be painted. It was, in fact, painted dead white, giving an impression that Routh was supposed to be American. But to the left of this was warm red brick enclosing mullioned windows and rising to a succession of gable ends behind which stood tall Tudor chimneys. Beyond this again, and running off at an angle, was a wing that had at some date been heavily Gothicized and that now lurked behind meaningless buttresses and groaned beneath improbable battlements. These vagaries accounted for about half the building, the rest of which was a solid Georgian.

Routh's awareness of all this was intuitive rather than technical. The effect, as of several houses backing awkwardly into each other, was for a moment as disturbing to him as some horror glimpsed in a doctor's medical journal in a railway-carriage, a monstrous birth of twins or triplets fantastically conjoined. But he told himself that once more he was unprofitably fancying things. All the more tangible suggestions that the condition of the place evoked were of prosperity, serenity and cheerfulness.

Well kept lawns and gravel walks, tall dark hedges trimmed to severe perpendiculars, a few broad beds of massed chrysanthemums: these seemed to speak of a taste in gardens that was mature and good. There was a wide shallow terrace now steeped in sunshine and serving as a promenade for half a dozen miniature poodles of expensive appearance and extravagant clip. Several french windows were thrown open to the air, and gave upon expanses of turf or paving so lavishly equipped with garden furniture of the elaborated modern sort, that the effect was of handsomely equipped drawing-rooms tumbling out of doors to breathe. Nor was the placid scene without its congruous humanity. A five-year-old boy, sturdy and flaxen-haired, was playing with the poodles. And on a lawn directly below Routh and Squire a company of ladies and gentlemen were enjoying a game of croquet.

A variety of impulses jostled in Routh. Here were half a dozen demonstrably sane persons, engaging in one of the mildest of civilized pleasures. Would it not be best to seize the chance of rushing forward, throwing himself upon their mercy, and claiming their protection from the abominable Squire? For whatever was the truth about Squire he was certainly dangerous, and the shadowy possibilities of financial exploitation which he represented lurked amid hazards quite out of Routh's common line.

But even as Routh debated with himself this course of action, he became aware of a further bewilderment in his situation. The croquet players puzzled and alarmed him quite as much as Squire did. The sharp *clop . . . clop . . . clop* of wood upon wood as a military-looking man with a grey moustache achieved a brisk break was obscurely frightening. If Squire was patently sinister and his house indefinably so, then this spectacle was like a calculated effect designed to enhance the fact. The croquet-players were disturbingly enigmatical. Routh didn't trust them. After all, in an environment which made the lion mild was it not very conceivable that a croquet-player upon being appealed to for protection might simply swing his mallet and dash one's brains out?

But on all this there was only a moment for reflection. Squire swung round a wing of the house and the croquet-players disappeared.

7

Routh now lost his bearings. Continuing to skirt the main building, Squire led the way into a walled garden and out again, using a key each time. Beyond this lay a kitchen garden, empty except for a bent old man culling cauliflowers, and they passed on to a sort of narrow alley of which one side was formed by a high beech hedge and the other by a long, low building of modern appearance and indeterminate length.

Presenting to the world nothing but a succession of frosted-glass windows, this building ran slightly downhill, so that the level dropped as by broad, shallow steps. And presently Routh caught a glimpse of its other end. It had been run out from the house as far as it could go – to the margin, in fact, of a small lake. In the middle of the lake was an island, seemingly entirely occupied by a large, blank and improbable temple. Although such fantasies were unfamiliar to Routh, he guessed at once that there was nothing out of the way in it. Much odder was the fact that this ancient absurdity was now directly linked to the new raw wing he had been skirting by a wooden bridge – a bridge lightly constructed but entirely enclosed, so that it was, in fact, a species of tunnel, relieved only by a few small windows.

But all this Routh only glimpsed. For Squire had stopped before a door near the end of the building, unlocked and opened it, and pushed Routh unceremoniously inside. He locked the door from within, while Routh took stock of a long, bleak corridor.

'Well, here we are.'

In Squire's voice Routh again caught a momentary note of uncertainty. He derived what comfort he could from it in a situation that he increasingly disliked. His isolation with the alarming Squire appeared to be complete. There was not a sign of life down the length of this narrow corridor. There was not a sound from the succession of rooms they were now passing. A modern monastery must be like this – the kind in which you take vows to keep your mouth shut. The unlikely comparison, floating through Routh's mind, increased his uneasiness, for there is a whole popular mythology of the hidden horrors of the cloister. Forty Months in a Flagellant Order. By the Author of A Short History of Torture (Illustrated). Momentarily overborne by these new imaginings, Routh looked about him in the expectation of seeing walls hung with scourges and a floor dripping blood. But the walls were pervasively blank, and on the floor of the long corridor was nothing more remarkable than a thick, green rubber that deadened every sound.

'And you can wait here.'

Squire was unlocking and opening a door. Routh looked at him warily. 'What d'you mean – wait here?' he demanded.

'There'll be an interview.'

The words were perfunctory, and Routh sensed that they were quite meaningless. He made to back away. Squire grabbed him, swung him effortlessly off his feet, and pitched him through the doorway.

'An interview with my colleagues, my dear fellow, quite soon. Did I say we were magicians? Alchemists would be a better description. You will no doubt make yourself as comfortable as you can.'

Routh picked himself up in time to see the door closing and to hear a key turn in its lock. It was his first confused impression that he was in a small kitchen, but in a moment he realized that it was a laboratory. He recognized it – as even the most ignorant can now recognize virtually any material creation of man – from the cinema. There was a bench, a sink, an affair with various gas burners and a small flue above. There were rows of bottles behind sliding glass doors. The only movable furniture was a high wooden stool. The room was lit through a large, barred skylight.

Routh surveyed the unfamiliar place. *Alchemy*. That was what Squire had said – that he and whatever confederates he had were alchemists. It meant chemists, scientists. A sense of vast illumination came to Routh. Now he understood.

He had puzzled and puzzled over the racket that could sustain a place like this. There had been a time – he believed – at which a really big operator on the black market could have lived like this if he had wanted to. But nowadays that line of country was said to be not nearly so good. No! Routh knew what he had found. He had found the people who forge the fivers.

8

Like Galileo in the dungeons of the Inquisition, resistlessly imagining the majestic pageant of the planets circling round their sun, Routh crouched in his odd prison and stared out, round-eyed, at the brave new world of his discovery. Not Cortez on his peak could have been more exultant. For in that criminal world upon the inglorious fringes of which Routh habitually moved no current conviction is more compelling than this: that every authentic five-pound note has its identical twin, the creation of forgers so scientifically skilful that all the answering science of the Royal Mint, the Bank of England, and other institutions and persons unspeakably august, is powerless to crush the racket. As far as five-pound notes go, there is twice as much paper money in England as there ought to be.

Routh leapt down from his stool. He, who had only that morning failed in the prosecution of a familiar seventy-shilling swindle, now brushed greatness. Not far away was a man who – although he had indeed knocked Routh senseless, obliged him to grovel in the dust beside a tame lion, and incarcerated him in an unattractive laboratory – was in all probability at the very head of Routh's profession. His instinct had been vindicated. Let him now but behave with sufficient ruthlessness and guile, and he might leave his baser self behind him for ever. All his frustrations, all his baffled hopes and cheated appetites were stirring. Those impulses which had led him into his inglorious exploit in the lane roused themselves again and roused themselves far more effectively, since they were now bent upon a design far more potent in its appeal.

Routh prowled his prison in a fury, convinced that just beyond its walls lay spread the power and the glory – an absolute command of wealth, and hence of all the kingdoms of the earth. Had he encountered Deilos again at this moment, the creature would certainly have taken him for a dangerous beast of prey.

He placed the stool on the bench, and from the shaky perch thus constituted he examined the skylight. Some of the panes opened outwards and upwards for ventilation. But the whole thing was securely barred and meshed. He went round the walls and cupboards, tapping and scratching; nothing appeared to give the slightest hope of escape. The innumerable bottles on the shelves fascinated and alarmed him. His ideas on chemistry were vague. He believed that if he mixed enough of these stuffs together on the floor there would certainly be an explosion that would blow the roof off. But what would be the good of that if he were himself maimed, blinded, perhaps killed? There seemed no resource but the poor one of making a row. That might frighten them so that they would turn him out. And then perhaps he could put some screw on them from safety.

Routh approached the single door of the laboratory, having now in his head no more than this inglorious notion of thumping on it. But as his eyes fell on the keyhole he stopped and stared. The thing was almost incredible. But there could be little doubt that behind that keyhole lay no more than a very common lock indeed.

From his earliest years Routh had been an amateur of keyholes. They constituted perhaps his nearest approach to a disinterested love of knowledge. And it so happened that this interest had broadened itself with the years. A keyhole had become for Routh not merely something to peer through or listen at; it had become something to fiddle with. And this substantial process of sublimation seemed likely to stand him in good stead now. Frequently he had beguiled the tedium of lonely nights in cheap lodgings by teaching himself, on the strength of such professional hints as he had picked up from inebriated cracksmen, to pick the simple locks that such accommodation commonly provided. And with such a lock, strangely enough, he was confronted now. He could confidently look forward to being on the farther side of it within ten minutes.

Routh fished from his pocket an innocent-seeming twist of wire. As he made his first exploratory thrust at the keyhole he felt the blood course more warmly in his veins. Reason would have told him that only the most slender of advantages was opening before him, and that in this inexplicable establishment he was likely to remain as helpless a puppet on one side of a door as another. But with the sense of power that had again leapt up in him reason had very little to do. The Tables Turned. Routh Hits Back. The theory which he had formed as to the nature of Squire's racket had stirred in him feelings that were avidly acquisitive and predatory. The treatment to which he had been subjected had filled him with malignity. Now his head was swimming slightly with the sensation of fresh scope given to these emotions. But his hand remained so steady that only a few minutes passed before he was standing, tense and listening, in the long empty corridor.

Close on the right, three steps led to a higher level. Much farther away on the left, several steps made an answering descent. He remembered the appearance of this long annex from the outside – how it dipped down as by several shallow flights to the level of the little lake. So the house lay on his right, while on his left the building ended in the odd covered bridge leading to the ornamental building on the island. Routh took a gulp of air, swung left, and walked rapidly and noiselessly forward.

Most of the doors leading off the corridor were open. But at this in itself he felt no alarm, since he was intuitively certain that at this hour the whole place was empty. Pausing to reconnoitre, he discovered that this long wing was given over to a series of laboratories, for the most part inter-communicating, and the majority being considerably larger than that in which he had been imprisoned. It occurred to him that there was more opportunity in these than in the corridor to lurk or dodge if anyone did, in fact, appear. He therefore made his way forward as much as possible by this route.

What he saw he saw only vaguely, since he was without a basis of technical knowledge to sharpen his observation. In one room the benches were crowded with complex units of glass utensils and rubber tubing and little bright sheets of metal connected by innumerable wires: these, articulated into a skeleton by sundry steel rods and clamps and brackets, had to his view the appearance of grotesque automata designed in mockery of living things. Another room looked like his idea of a telephone exchange. A third was given over to what seemed a huge pin-table – the kind on which valves light up and the score is progressively shouted at you as the meandering balls make and break one electrical circuit after another.

Routh had only such popular analogies upon which to draw. It was the more to the credit of his underlying astuteness, therefore, that a purely intellectual conclusion presently forced itself upon him. At a first blush these large evidences of scientific effort appeared abundantly to confirm him in the persuasion to which he had recently come – namely, that here were the people by whom the five-pound notes are made. But now a sense not only of the scale but of the variousness and elaboration of what lay around him suggested that even this impressive conclusion was inadequate. Or, if Squire indeed made the five-pound notes, he had some deeper and more grandiosely scientific plot or project in hand as well.

Routh's mind had just halted baffled before this conception when he became aware of voices somewhere ahead of him.

9

'I tell you he's no more than a little rat of a deserter living on his wits.'

Routh stopped dead. He recognized the tones of the detestable Squire.

'Very probably. But it's dangerous and unnecessary, all the same. This is something far too big to have you acting on these sudden impulses. What do you suppose the Director will say to such a story?'

'He ought to be damned grateful – and so should you. You know that I've brought in capital subjects before this.'

The voices were coming from behind the closed door of what Routh guessed must be one of the last rooms in the building. They were heard the more clearly because this door too had a keyhole. Routh's ear was pressed to it.

'And – what's more – you seem to be in an uncommonly foul temper.'

It was again Squire's voice. And Squire's voice had gone sulky. In a flash it came to Routh that Squire was by no means the boss of this mysterious place. He was talking now to somebody with whom he was on no more than equal terms – if even that. And they both had above them somebody called the Director. The word conjured up a vague image of striped trousers, a gold watch-chain, a silk hat.

'I'm certainly not feeling any too sweet. And in a moment I'll tell you why.' It was now the other man who was speaking – and his voice, Routh realized, was far more coldly formidable than Squire's could ever be. 'But first let me tell you this. We just can't afford the risk of people disappearing on our doorstep.'

'But you'd find him, I tell you, so devilish suitable. A craven little brute capable of moments of real fury. You've often said –'

'Never mind what I've often said. If I've said anything at all to you, the more fool I've been.' There was sharp anger in the second man's accent. 'And now go and turf the fellow out. He hasn't seen anything, I suppose?'

'Nothing at all. Or only poor old Deilos. I couldn't resist having a bit of fun –'

'I lose all patience with you, Squire. Something extremely serious has happened. And now you come in with this distracting nonsense. What have you done with the fellow?'

'Locked him up in number eight. Blue with funk. You can have him when you want him.'

'I don't want him. But no more do I want him going out and gossiping about what goes on here. Will nothing make you realize what we're on the verge of? Power such has never been wielded on this earth before. All the gold of the Incas wouldn't buy a tithe of it. And all that you –'

Routh started so violently that he hit his head on the door-knob and lost the conclusion of the unseen speaker's sentence. The astounding conclusion towards which his mind had already been unconsciously moving had flashed upon him in an instant. Alchemists don't make five-pound notes. Alchemists make gold.

All the gold of the Incas . . . Routh had read about them – a vanished folk in America whose very fish-kettles and chamberpots had been wrought out of solid gold. And the alchemists had wanted that sort of wealth. They had messed about, pretty well blindly, with chemicals and crucibles, hoping to make something they called the philosopher's stone – a substance that would turn to pure gold a million times its own weight of base metal. And now these people, substituting science for magic, were on the verge of doing just that . . .

Routh again pressed his ear to the keyhole. The missing of a single sentence, he felt, might be fatal to his own power to exploit the terrific possibilities now opening before him.

'Look here, Squire – you may as well know just how the matter stands. The stuff has gone inert again. I'm completely held up.'

A low whistle conveyed the invisible Squire's first reaction to this announcement. 'That's bad,' he said – and Routh thought that he heard malice in his former captor's voice. 'The Director won't like it at all.'

'It's not in the least out of the way, and the Director understands perfectly. I have command of almost nothing, you know, in a pure form. The position is just as it is with those growth-inhibiting stuffs they play about with. You, Squire, wouldn't make head nor tail of it in technical terms. But put it like this. Put it that you have a host of human beings, some tiny percentage of which constitutes a superbly efficient military force that you are concerned to cherish. All the rest are tiresome and irrelevant camp-followers who can never be the slightest use to you. *And you don't yourself know which are which.*'

A snort from Squire interrupted this exposition. 'It sounds damned nonsense to me.'

'It *is* damned nonsense, Squire. Unfortunately it is Nature's damned nonsense, not mine. Well, now – every now and then one of the camp-followers does something quite idiotic – stands on his head, say, or turns a somersault. And at that the morale of your unknown army mysteriously collapses and nearly all your work has to be done over again. My particular sort of chemistry has some very grand names, you know. But that is what you might call the low-down on it. And the present upshot of it is that tomorrow I go back to Formula Ten.'

There was a moment's silence during which it occurred to Routh to substitute an eye for an ear. What immediately became visible through the keyhole was not difficult to interpret. Near at hand a blurred but familiar form represented one of the oddly high and square shoulders of the man Squire. In the background was a green baize door in a wall lined with books. And in the middle-distance was part of the polished surface of a table or desk. On this there was nothing to be seen except a pair of hands issuing from the sleeves of a white coat – fine hands, powerful and with long square fingers exquisitely cared for.

'So you see that I have singularly little use for your tramp, my dear Squire. Formula Ten, I assure you, will occupy me very sufficiently for the next few weeks . . . By the way, here it is.'

For a moment one of the hands on the desk flicked out of Routh's field of vision. Then it was back again, immobile as before. But now between the two hands there lay what looked like a single folded sheet of quarto paper. The effect of this appearance was startling. Squire's shoulder disappeared. Squire's voice rose in something like a surprised and horrified yelp. The owner of the hands answered this with a low laugh. 'Yes,' he said. 'Here it is.'

'But you've no business to have it out like that. It's outrageous! If the Director . . .'

'The Director has some very odd ways, I admit. This, I really believe, is the only existing copy of Formula Ten. It is unique – and the basis of the whole effort. How lucky we are to have it! It was got out of Hendrik, I have been told, just before he succumbed to the persuasions that were unfortunately found necessary in his case. Am I right?'

'I know nothing about it.' Squire's voice was suddenly husky.

'Don't you? Then how much you must regret not having been present, my dear Squire, on an occasion so much in your line. But – as I say – we were lucky to get what we did. One knows people here and there about the world who would give millions for this, does one not? Or even – come to think of it – a kingdom? No wonder the Director will have it out only under circumstances of the most portentous security. I enter into your horror and dismay, my dear chap. But when I need Formula Ten I fetch it out and mention the fact afterwards.'

'I don't like it.'

'That reminds me. No more do I like your friend the tramp. I don't like his being brought here, and I don't know that I like his going away from here either. I think he had better be killed at once and the body incinerated. See to it, Squire, will you?'

It is difficult to hear something of this sort said about oneself and not suppose, for some moments at least, that one is simply listening to a rather tasteless joke. Had the full force of the words broken upon Routh at once he would undoubtedly have taken to his heels and run. As it was, he remained, misdoubting and stupefied, during the few seconds in which flight might have availed him. His eye was actually still at the keyhole when that orifice was obscured by what was patently the bulk of Squire advancing to open the door. And Squire, it seemed, was now to be simply his, Routh's, executioner!

That men so wicked as these could exist was at once incredible and most horribly plausible. And Routh realized that to be found crouching here would be fatal. It was not merely that the secrets he would be presumed to have overheard must absolutely seal his fate. It was also that in such a situation a passive role is fatal; that to turn the tables upon fortune at such a juncture only action will remotely serve . . . Routh opened the door before him and marched into the room.

Squire fell back with an exclamation. Squire's companion, seated still at his desk, quite feebly echoed it. Routh had undeniably caught his adversaries off balance. The sense of this enabled him to nod briskly at the seated man and to wave Squire casually back. 'Good afternoon,' he said.

The words came out with nothing of the anxious calculation that had marked his attempt at a similar greeting in the bank that morning. Had he not always known he would carry the big moment when it came? Routh glanced round the room with the easy command of an important person; with the sort of glance that makes enormous leather arm-chairs propel themselves forward, corks pop, syphons spurt, cigar-boxes fly open. 'Director not here?' he asked briskly. 'It's really with him that I'd better have a word.'

Squire and his companion glanced at each other. At length the seated man spoke. 'I don't know you from Adam,' he said. 'And apparently you don't know me. *I* am the Director.'

Routh again gave an assured glance round him. The room went some way to substantiate this false claim. The furniture was handsome, and all round the walls were the sort of heavily tooled books you see in expensive shop-windows in the West End. Over the fireplace was a high-class dirty picture: a lot of naked women lolloping around a pool. Underneath this a bright fire burned in an open gate. Routh walked across to it and warmed his hands. 'Nice place you have here,' he said. 'Plenty of books. Nice picture.'

'I fear I have not the pleasure of your acquaintance.' Squire's companion was a small man with a high domed forehead and almost no hair. His fine hands still lay passively before him. The rest of him was insignificant and even meagre, as if his body had no other function than that of providing a line of communication between that big brain and those long and powerful fingers. He had bleak grey eyes which he now turned from Routh to Squire. 'Presumably this is the gentleman whom you supposed that you had – um – accommodated in number eight?'

'Of course it is.' Squire, who had still by no means recovered his self-possession, stared at his late prisoner with mingled bewilderment and malice. 'But I can't think how he managed –'

'We learn that sort of thing very early in my crowd.' Routh put both hands in his trouser-pockets and chinked the few coins in the one without a hole in it. 'But you had no idea of that, had you, Squire?'

'Your crowd?' The white-coated man spoke sharply, and as he did so swung round upon Squire. 'Did I understand you to say that your encounter with this fellow was a perfectly casual one?'

Before Squire could reply, Routh laughed harshly. 'So your poor friend believed,' he said. 'Mind you, there's an excuse for him. The idea of attacking the girl and then hanging round until somebody appeared – well, it wasn't too bad, was it? Squire was convinced he had me where he wanted me. And so in I came. Not my own notion, I must confess. Quite a junior colleague's, as it happens.'

On the mantelpiece behind Routh's head, and just below the dirty picture, a clock was ticking softly. At any moment, he realized, it might begin to affect him as had the clock in the bank that morning; it might begin to pound like a hammer inside his head. And if his nerve went he was done for. For certainly the ice on which he was now skating was paper-thin. That he had fooled Squire from the start was a notion that might now take in

Squire himself. But could it conceivably take in this other fellow? Only – Routh saw – if it *attracted* the other fellow. If this egg-headed scientist disliked Squire enough to be willing to see him in a mug's role, then any cock-and-bull story having that effect might convince him for a while. The thing to do, then, was to make Squire look a perfect fool.

'Poor old Squire! Has he told you about my father in the asylum and my mother gone off to New Zealand? It would have made a cat laugh, the way it all took him in. Thought he was getting a waif and stray to keep under his thumb at some of your dirtiest work here. And all the time he was getting *us*.'

The clock was still behaving normally behind him. Squire was flushed and his shoulders had gone even more unnaturally high and square. The other fellow rose from his desk and walked away from it. 'Haven't you,' he asked, 'taken on rather a dangerous mission? The colleagues you speak of must be uncommonly obliged to you. It's a pity' – and with sudden dangerous sweetness the egg-headed man smiled – 'that they won't be in a position even to send a wreath.'

Once more Routh contrived a convincing laugh. 'If you ask me,' he said, 'it's your friend Squire here that's about due for a wreath. If he were with our crowd he'd have been taken for a ride long ago. But as for me – well, naturally I've taken my precautions.'

'It's damned nonsense.' Squire had taken a stride forward. 'The little rat's bluffing. He's simply making fools of us.'

'It may be nonsense. But it's a sort of nonsense that requires getting to the bottom of.' Egg-head turned his eyes slowly on Routh. 'You have a crowd,' he said. 'You have colleagues. You have come here by design. You have taken precautions to ensure your personal safety. If there is any sense in all this, I am quite ready to hear it.' He turned with a sudden flash of temper upon Squire. 'And as this whole piece of folly is your responsibility, you had better do so too.'

'I tell you, it's all –'

'Be quiet and hear the fellow out . . . Now then, what do you mean by your crowd?'

'I mean a crowd that knows about *your* crowd. All that science stuff.' He jerked his head in the direction of the long line of laboratories he had shortly before traversed. 'We know what it's about. We know what you're making. Valuable stuff, I'd call it. We think it needs protection. And that you need protection too.'

'Expensive protection, no doubt?'

'You mayn't like the bill, I agree. But it's probably very much in your interest to pay up, all the same.'

'I see.' The meagre man in the white coat again gave his disturbingly sweet smile. 'But suppose we are not interested? And suppose we are minded to give these precious colleagues of yours a little practical demonstration that they rather need protection on their own account? If they exist –

which is something I am by no means convinced of – we can certainly make you tell us where to find them. We could then return you to them – or return some significant part of you – just as an indication that we are not minded to do business with them. Don't you agree with me?'

Beneath the unfamiliar Routh a Routh all too fully known stirred uneasily. He knew that one falter meant that he was done for. Conversely, however wild his story, unflawed assurance might yet carry him triumphantly through. 'You just can't afford it,' he said. 'If our lot simply let the truth about you seep out, where would you be? The moment we simply *knew*, don't you see, we had you where we wanted you.'

There was a brief silence. Squire and his companion were once more exchanging what was a purely disconcerted glance.

'Perhaps you wouldn't mind telling us what you *do* know? Particularly if I admit frankly that there is a good deal of force in your proposition?' Egg-head spoke with a new mildness.

'Know? Why, that you have the means of making gold, of course.'

'Thank you.' For the first time Egg-Head looked really non plussed. He was staring at Routh as if considering whether here was something really very deep indeed. 'And Squire here is a sort of mad Midas? In imagining that he was luring you here it was his intention to transmute you into a full-size statue – the Golden Dustman, perhaps – and exhibit you at the Royal Academy?'

'I don't know what Squire was fool enough to think.' Routh spoke almost at random. Had he made some wrong move? Perhaps the concern of these people was not with gold at all. Gold, after all, had been no more than a clever guess. Quickly he endeavoured to retrieve himself. 'We'll call it gold,' he said. 'Perhaps we don't know for certain – and then again perhaps we do. But it's certainly something you can't afford to have talked about. And – mind you – I'm no more than a messenger.' Routh paused, displeased at thus having demoted himself. 'Or say an envoy – that's about it. And what I require now is simply this: a substantial sum on leaving as an earnest of good faith –'

'I beg your pardon? Of what?' Egg-Head had returned to his desk and sat down again.

'There's no need to be funny.' Routh's voice rose to a pitch. He realized that he was near the end of his tether, and that he must bring the thing off within the next few minutes if he was to bring it off at all. 'I'm to have a reasonable sum down. And after that my crowd will communicate with you by means that you will be told about later.'

'I see. Well, I think we can settle this matter almost at once. Only we shall first have to consult higher authority.' Egg-Head had a new note in his voice; it was almost a note of humour, and Routh was unable to find it reassuring. 'As you very acutely suspected, I am not the Director. Squire, will you slip across and explain matters? No, my dear fellow, you need not be apprehensive. I can keep a very sufficient eye on our friend. And although I dislike firearms . . .' Egg-Head's right hand vanished into a drawer of his desk, to reappear again holding an automatic pistol. 'Explain to the Director that we shall not occupy his time for more than five minutes.'

Squire's departure was by the green baize door that Routh had first become aware of when peering through the key-hole. There could be no doubt that the Director lived, or at least worked, on the island at the farther end of the enclosed wooden bridge. Supposing that there was no delay, Squire would presumably be back with him within five minutes. Meanwhile Egg-Head continued to sit at his desk, his back to the baize door, the revolver ready in his hand, and his eye never straying from Routh for an instant. A minute went by in silence, and Routh became aware that the clock behind him was beginning to misbehave. Looking at those two bleak eyes and the muzzle of the pistol, he found it, in fact, difficult to remain convinced that he commanded the situation. And no sooner was doubt admitted than it grew. Routh realized that he had shot his bolt. When a fresh mind was brought in – and moreover a powerful mind such as the Director presumably possessed – it would be all up with him.

Egg-Head broke the silence. 'Do you know, I think you have put up rather a good show? I no longer have the slightest inclination to believe your story, but as an improvisation it is thoroughly creditable to you. You are presumably just what poor Squire took you for: a mere vagabond that nobody is going to worry about, and regularly in some petty way on the wrong side of the law. That's it, is it not?'

Routh made no answer. He was chiefly aware that his stomach felt bad, just as it had in the bank.

'What I like is the way you really have tried to exploit the situation rather than simply wriggle out of it. I wish we could take you on, my man. You'd at least, one day, be more use than Squire. Unfortunately it's dead against the rules. So you see where you stand.'

Routh heard his own faint voice, speaking as if in the air above him. 'You can't do that! You can't do *that* to me!'

'Be very sure that we can. And look here – there's no need to drag it out. Take a rush at me, man. I can promise you that your death will be instantaneous.'

The room had begun to sway before Routh. Egg-Head's words had been altogther impassively spoken. It was impossible to tell whether compassion, or mockery, or the depraved wish for a moment's mortal excitement had prompted them. It was only clear that the game was indeed wholly up. He was to be murdered.

'You poor devil.' This time the accent came through. It really was compassion – compassion tinged with embarrassment at the mere sight of anything so miserable and so shabby and so helpless as Routh. And in Routh it lit a last desperate flare of rage. He felt, without any volition of his own, his whole body tauten to spring. If even with a burst of bullets in him he could get his dying fingers round that throat . . .

The baize door opened. A split second longer and he would have sprung. As it was he stared over Egg-Head's shoulder, fascinated. For the door had opened only a little, and what had entered the room was a cat. It leapt noiselessly to the back of a chair close to the man's back. He was totally unaware of it. If only . . . And then the thing happened. The cat took a further leap to Egg-Head's shoulder. It was evidently a familiar domestic trick – but for the moment it caught the man unaware and helpless. Routh sprang. The two men went down together with a crash, struggling for the weapon. Routh had it – and in the same instant became aware of Egg-Head's mouth before him, wide open and screaming. Routh thrust the muzzle in it and pulled the trigger. And the great domed head exploded under his eyes like a bomb.

Routh tried to rise. One of his knees, slipping from the body, grated painfully on a hard object on the floor. It was a bunch of keys, similar to that which Squire had used in coming through the park and gardens. Routh grabbed it and hauled himself to his feet. He must get out. The man who was to have killed him instantaneously he had himself instantaneously killed. The automatic as it emptied itself into the grey pulp of Egg-Head's brain must have alarmed the whole place. Within seconds not only Squire and the Director but everybody in the building – even the people whom he had watched playing croquet – would be about his ears. He had seconds to get out of this house; minutes to escape from this whole infernal region and reach the salvation of the hidden Douglas.

Routh turned to the door by which he had entered. As he did so he saw the cat once more. It was crouched on the dead man's desk with humped back and waving tail. He thought it was going to spring at him. But the cat remained immobile – a great honey-coloured creature with long curling white whiskers. Its two fore-paws lay on a folded sheet of quarto paper.

As if from very far back in time, the memory of what he had learnt about Formula Ten swam in Routh's mind. What lay there on the desk was something that Egg-Head ought not to have had access to except amid the most elaborate precautions for its security, something worth millions. Realization of his opportunity came to Routh like a great flood of white light. To snatch this paper from out of the paws of the cat might be to wrest unspeakable triumph from what had seconds before appeared defeat and death.

He took a step towards the desk. The cat hissed at him and bared its claws. Beside himself, Routh turned, caught a poker from the fireplace, and hit wildly at the brute, as if intent to mingle its bespattered brains with its master's. But the cat sprang aside and the poker crashed down on the desk. Routh grabbed the paper and ran from the room.

2. Routh in Flight

Who would not, finding way, break loose from Hell,
Though thither doom'd?

Paradise Lost

I

The corridor was deserted, and Routh ran for the door that gave on the open air. But even as he did so there was a shout from the room behind him. At the far end of the corridor first one door was flung open and then another; there was a chatter of excited voices; and several white-coated figures appeared simultaneously. Routh bolted through the nearest door on his right. He was back in number eight.

The room was empty. He realized that many of the adjoining rooms were now tenanted, and that his only exit was back through a corridor into which these people were peering or tumbling. But if his plight was desperate his mind was working clearly and swiftly. There was a white coat hanging behind the door; he snatched it from the peg and scrambled into it. From a corner of the bench he snatched a pair of horn-rimmed glasses – these he had noticed during his brief imprisonment – thrust them on his nose, and ran from the room.

The corridor held at least half a dozen white-coated figures, shouting and gesturing. Routh shouted and gestured too. At the same time he pushed his way towards the door he wanted. Squire had secured it behind them on their entry, but there was a chance that it was kept unlocked during the hours that all these people were at work. In a matter of seconds he had reached it and found that his calculation was justified. He flung himself through and banged it to behind him.

He knew that the respite thus gained could only be momentary. Fortunately the row of windows down the long corridor held nothing but frosted glass, and he could not be observed simply by a glance through them. In front of him was the high beech hedge that ran the full length of the long building, and Routh saw instantly that a gap to scramble through would not easily be found. His eye turned apprehensively to the door. It must surely be flung open now at any moment. Suddenly he saw that some half-hearted attempt had been made to embellish the bleakly utilitarian structure with climbing plants, and that up the wall on one side of the door ran a scrap of denuded wooden trellis. Routh grabbed at it and climbed. Within five seconds he was lying prone on the flat roof.

The surface was warm in the afternoon sunshine. Long and narrow, with its row of skylights down the centre, the roof was curiously like the deck of a liner. He was exhausted – so exhausted that he was suddenly afraid that he might go to sleep. But through the roof he could hear a mutter of voices, and presently the door by which he had bolted was flung open from within.

He heard louder voices and his body tautened in acute anxiety. It sounded as if two of the searchers were running down the path in opposite directions. Would another of them think of the roof, or spot the fragment of trellis?

The door was shut again, and in the immediate vicinity he could hear no sound. But now in more than one direction dogs were barking, and somewhere on the other side of the house a stable bell was being rung with a will. He knew intuitively that the strange establishment upon which he had stumbled had a well drilled response to such a crisis as had come upon it. In other words, against him, Routh, a whole powerful machine was being brought smoothly to bear. The two-stroke and freedom could not be more than two miles away. But he would have to fight his way out to them through the invisibly turning mesh of this formidable mechanism.

He raised himself cautiously. The first essential was to discover the extent to which his position was overlooked. Ahead of him lay the covered bridge and the island. These were alike invisible, and he was presumably immune from observation in that direction. On either hand was a scattering of tree-tops which represented very substantial protection; here and there were gaps through which, even when he was flat on the roof, he might possibly be spotted from the middle distance; nevertheless the hazard seemed small compared with some through which he had recently passed. He looked behind him – and found a very different state of affairs. As he ought to have remembered, this whole structure projected directly from a wing of the main building. And from the main building it was commanded by more than a dozen windows.

He saw that he must get off the roof at once and run for it. But he was reluctant to descend as he had come, and he therefore decided to crawl cautiously to the other side. In doing this he had to face the risk of making some sound that might communicate itself to people still in the laboratories below. On the other hand he had a strong impression that the farther side consisted of a single blank wall without means of egress from the building. And this seemed to represent one threat the less.

The bell had ceased ringing and the dogs had fallen silent. He guessed obscurely at forces now strategically posted and waiting; at the beginning of some systematic combing of the whole property that would be quietly efficient and final . . . Then he came to the edge, peered, listened, lowered himself over and dropped.

He landed among grass and pine needles, and picked himself up unhurt. It was as he had thought. The building was nothing but a blank concrete surface running off in either direction. In front of him was an indefinite extent of young fir trees. Among these he made his way at once, for they gave at least the sensation of shelter. In a moment he came diagonally upon a faint path. He wished desperately that he was armed. He wished that he had better understood the operation of the automatic. One bullet would have been enough for Egg-Head, and would have made a mess less likely to remain sickeningly on the memory. With the ability to kill and kill again he might be able to fight his way out. As it was, as soon as he was spotted he was helpless. He stopped, recalling that he still wore the white coat. He got rid of it, but without managing to feel any the more secure. The little plantation of pines was thinning out and merging with a ragged shrubbery. He left the path and ran crouching forward from bush to bush.

The shrubbery ended abruptly. It was bounded by a path which he had approached at right angles, and along the farther side of the path ran a six-foot wooden fence. He paused, hesitating whether to try scaling this, or to make what speed he could along the path in one direction or the other. And at this moment he heard voices behind him. He broke cover, ran to the fence, searched it for some foothold. There was none. He turned to his left and bolted along the path.

His heart was pounding yet more heavily. He realized that this was partly because he was running up-hill. If he had turned right he would have been making in the general direction of the little lake, and presumably of a stretch of park beyond it. As it was, he must be moving back towards the house. But to turn and retrace his steps required an effort of will that was now beyond him. He pounded on.

Somewhere beyond the fence on his right a whistle was blown. His fancy depicted a long line of men rising at its summons and moving forward, as if on a field-day. All sense of proportion and likelihood had deserted him; he thought of his pursuers in terms of platoons and companies; had a bomb exploded before him or a shell whistled overhead he would have felt no surprise, nor any appreciable increase of terror.

There was another shout on his left. He glanced in its direction as he ran and saw several figures break from the trees simultaneously. Then, as if he had been a train entering a tunnel, they vanished. A fence like the one on his right had abruptly risen up on his left. He was labouring along what was in effect a long corridor. If they caught him here he hadn't a chance. Not a bloody chance. If only he hadn't emptied that gun. If only . . .

The power of thought was leaving him, as if driven out of his body by the fierce pain of his breathing. If he could remember why all this was happening, it would be all right. If he knew where he was, or why he ran, so vast an accession of knowledge must infallibly save him.

Routh pulled up. There was some crisis and his brain had cleared to meet it. He was at a cross-roads – that was it. In front of him the fenced path ran straight on towards a huddle of buildings. To his left a transverse path led directly to the main bulk of the house. And to the right this same path, unfenced and bordered only by low box hedges, ran through an indeterminate stretch of garden to the park. That was the way he must go. He turned to run. As he did so a man with a gun appeared as if from nowhere some twenty yards ahead, leapt the hedge without looking towards Routh, and then moved slowly down the path and away from him, scanning the gardens on either side.

At any moment this new enemy might turn. There was nothing to do but go straight on, and make what he could of the shelter of the buildings before him. They were, he guessed, stables and places of that sort. The distance was scarcely greater than the length of a cricket pitch. Routh covered it without glancing behind him and found himself in a courtyard that was almost entirely enclosed. To his left was a wing of the house itself – the servants' wing, probably, and distinguished by a multiplicity of small, sparely draped windows. To face them was like a nightmare – the familiar nightmare of being on the stage of a crowded theatre, with no idea of a part and no means of getting off. On its three other sides the yard was a jumble of coach-houses, store-rooms, lofts and the like. The only entrance to it, apart from the narrow one by which he had come, was through a broad archway straight in front. Through this one would come, no doubt, to the main façade of the house. Should he dash straight through, and so make for that part of the park which was vaguely familiar to him? This question was answered even as Routh, with the slender mental concentration he had summoned back, addressed himself to it. Suddenly from beyond the archway came a sound that thickened and slowed his racing blood. He remembered Deilos and for a moment supposed that leopards or hyenas were at large in the gardens. Then he realized that he was listening to bloodhounds; that this appalling sound was the deep bell-note of which he had read in fiction. No living creature holds a more alarming place in the popular mind than does the bloodhound; and Routh was now reduced to sobbing with fear. At the same moment he heard voices and steps behind him. There was no more than the angle of a building between some group of his enemies and himself. He was within seconds of being captured.

The yard before him was an unbroken stretch of concrete, and it was quite empty. It looked like an arena cleared for some cruel sport. Routh had a fleeting fantastic vision of himself being driven hither and thither about it in abominable torment. His knees shook. He leant against the wall by which he was crouching, and his hands groped over its surface for something to which to cling. They found a small object, round and hard. It was like a cricket ball. Routh's mind was now scarcely more than a pin-point of consciousness, and he groped to understand the thing's function, to give it a name. But even as he did so it turned under his hand, and a door swung inwards behind him. He staggered back a couple of steps and fell. The door, just clearing his numbed body, swung to and closed. A great sheltering darkness had received him.

2

He lay curled up, his body inert but his limbs intermittently wracked by spasm. All his power of interpreting experience and devising responses to it had left him. He was on the two-stroke, and the smell of hot oil was coming up between his knees. Now between high wooden fences, and now over interminable ribbons of green rubber enclosed in the walls of frosted glass, the two-stroke was carrying him sturdily ahead of danger . . . *Bang!* Ominously the engine had back-fired. There had been trouble recently with the timing. *Bang!*

Routh stirred uneasily. *Bang!* What he now heard was the noise of a door being sharply closed. There were voices, foot-falls going up and down wooden staircases, the sound of more doors being wrenched open, banged to. They were searching the out-buildings all round the yard.

With his situation reconstructed around him, Routh struggled to his knees. The smell of oil was still in the darkness about him. He guessed that he was in a garage. But it was, he instinctively knew, a large place, and unusually lofty. It occurred to him that somewhere there might be a ladder that would take him to some obscure perch high up in the rafters. A flicker of confidence returned to him and for a moment he had a glimpse of the wily and undefeatable Routh, peering down from this fastness at his enemies vainly searching for him below. He got to his feet and felt about him cautiously. Vague masses, impossible to interpret, loomed around him. Garages, he remembered, often had the sort of pit used to get at a car from underneath. It wouldn't do to go straight into one of them.

Another door was slammed close by, and he heard footsteps more loudly than before. They were coming. Within the next few seconds he must hide himself. He took a further step forward, and stopped with a low cry. Directly before him, dim but distinguishable, hung a pale human face, its eyes on a dead level with his own. He drew back and the face drew back too. It was his own face reflected in a panel of glass. His hand went out and once more found itself on a handle – but this time it must be the handle of a car door. Even as he made the discovery there was a creak behind him and a finger of light shot through the darkness. He had only one possible resource left. He tugged open the door, flung himself through it, and drew it to behind him.

The finger of light was now a broad beam. He tumbled over the seat on which he was crouched and sought to flatten himself out to gain concealment. The thing was roomy. Conceivably it was a shooting brake, for there appeared to be no back seat. But there was some sort of tarpaulin sheet, carelessly thrown down; and under this he burrowed. Once there was an ominous clink of metal, for on the floor beneath the tarpaulin was what must be a heap of metal tools, loosely disposed. He lowered himself cautiously upon these and lay quite still.

There were now at least two men quite close to him. One was talking rapidly and the other was giving monosyllabic answers. It sounded like some sort of briefing. Routh was puzzled, for he got no impression that the place was being actively searched. The voices broke off and in a moment were succeeded by a new sound, impossible to interpret. A large door was being pushed back on rollers. At the same time light flooded through the chinks of the tarpaulin. Routh held his breath. An extraordinary possibility, alarming yet carrying with it a wild hope, had flashed upon him. Suppose that . . .

The two men were talking again, and this time he could hear snatches of what they said.

'Surely he can't get far?'

'Probably not. But the devil of it is, he got hold of some keys. So if by any chance he reached the ring fence before the current went on –'

'The current! You don't mean to say they've turned on that? They told me that was only for the greatest crisis of all.'

'Get in and don't waste time.' The floor beneath Routh lurched suddenly and there was the sound of a door closing. More faintly, the same voice continued. 'It *is* the greatest crisis of all – only not just as we've expected it. This fellow is the crack agent of something pretty big. And there's the point. He mustn't be killed. He may have hidden this thing already. Or he may simply have thrown it away. That's why we must have him back alive. Ready?'

'Ready.'

'Go out fairly rapidly and then come more slowly in again.'

Exultant and trembling, Routh hardly dared to breathe. There could be no doubt about the incredible truth. He was going to be driven straight out of this abominable place – yard, gardens, sinister ring-fence, park, boundary wall and all – he was going to be driven straight out of it in search of himself! The fools – the bloody fools! He lay absolutely rigid. Close to his fingers, he knew, was the heavy wrench or spanner that he would eventually raise to bring crashing down on his unconscious chauffeur's skull. And then, having pitched him into a ditch, he would drive the car himself hell for leather to London. Oh triumphant and all-powerful Routh!

The car was moving. It appeared to be coasting out of the garage. Lying on this hard floor, Routh thought, made the suspension feel funny. He had to brace his body more firmly still so as not to give himself away. But what did it matter if he was in for an uncomfortable ten minutes? Only provided –

The engine burst into life. For a full minute it appeared to race unbearably. Routh waited for the gears to engage, the clutch to be let in, the first swift acceleration that might send him lurching or rolling dangerously backwards. But nothing happened. The sense of something quite unapprehended in his situation possessed him. The whole movement was queer. And under his nose –

He stared again, and there was no doubt of it. Part of the flooring on which he lay was for some reason of a transparent substance – glass or perspex. He could see the road beneath him, studded with cats' eyes. Only the road was green – was as green as the rubber in that endless corridor . . . His eyes adjusted their focus and he saw what was really there. The two sides of the road were two broad green paddocks. The cat's eyes were the tops of white fencing posts dividing them. Routh, in fact, was suspended in air.

3

The discovery was a terrific shock. Nausea gripped him and for a horrible moment he thought that he must vomit. The line of posts slipped sideways across his field of vision. He stared below him in fascination. The earth had swung round like a compass-card and was now almost motionless. His tired mind, making a conscious effort of analysis, grasped the implication that he himself must be motionless too. In fact the craft in which he had hidden himself was a helicopter.

For a moment Routh closed his eyes. He was awed at the extent of his enemies' resources. But he himself had held out against them now – as it seemed – for hours. And he still had his astounding chance of triumph. He had nothing to do but rise from his lurking place, hit his unsuspecting pilot hard on the head, take charge of the machine –

But at this his nerve failed him. The thought of hanging high in air alone, with a set of unfamiliar and inexplicable controls between himself and disaster – this was something he found he couldn't take. In any case he had better wait. The fellow had been told to 'go out fairly rapidly'. That meant, presumably, outside the boundaries of the estate below him. He must bide his time until they were outside that formidable stone wall. The moment to act would be then.

The helicopter was moving again. It was passing directly over the house, and not thirty feet above the chimneys. The size and nondescript character of the place were now fully apparent. Routh was aware of a sprawling system of stone and tile ridges, irregularly disposed and alternating with broad, flat expanses of lead. His eye caught the long, low bitumen-covered roof of the building whence his flight had begun; and beyond he had a glimpse of the lake. Then the helicopter passed over the front of the house. Above the apex of the gleaming white pediment that had been his first impression of the place rose a flagstaff. Against this a white-coated man was steadying himself as he swept the nearer grounds with a pair of binoculars. The man looked up and waved as the machine passed over him. Routh drew back nervously, fearful that his lurking face might be discerned peering through the perspex. But already the roof had vanished.

Still he dared not move. He had to master a nervous impulse to get a glimpse of the pilot, to estimate from his manner of controlling the machine the chance of bluffing and intimidating him, to study the skull it might be desirable to fracture at a blow. Crouched still beneath his tarpaulin, he had already chosen his weapon for that – a heavy spanner, straight-ended and about a foot long. In his imagination he cautiously poised it, swung it in the air. His breath quickened at the thought of it. He realized, with a strange spasm of moral horror and a dark excitement, that there was a blood-lust in him; that he had killed one man and would willingly kill another. It was part of his new stature, part of the Routh by whom the seventy-bob swindler had been magnificently succeeded . . .

There was a queer sound in his ears. For a second he was puzzled, and then realized with terror that what he had heard was his own laughter. He had laughed aloud in a malevolent glee – and with the ear of his enemy within three feet of him. He realized a new danger – the danger that he might go light-headed, hysterical, mad. He lay still as death, biting hard at a wrist.

The fellow had heard nothing. He would have ear-phones, of course; for he was in some sort of short-wave contact with the people below. Indeed it looked as if he had received instructions to change his course of action. For he was not flying straight out of the grounds as Routh had hoped. He was moving gradually out on a spiral. There was no other explanation of the circular movement of the terrain below. And the helicopter was an incomparable machine to hunt with. It hovered at will. Several times it sank to within a few feet of the ground to investigate – Routh supposed – one or another suspicious appearance. Nothing, surely, could escape observation so miraculously armed – not Deilos, crouched among his rocks; not even the most timid mammal yet known on this earth . . . Routh frowned into the perspex, obscurely conscious of some unresolved perplexity deep in his mind. But at that moment he saw the ring-fence.

It looked something that a child could leap. But Routh knew how formidable it was. And if it really held some electrical charge as the conversation he had overheard suggested, then it was now insuperable. But the enemy was plainly reckoning with the possibility that he had made such good speed before the first alarm spread that he had actually got through it. Grabbing those keys had been a lucky move after all. But for that, they would scarcely trouble to send the helicopter beyond the fence and the wall.

And here *was* the wall. They were actually over and beyond it. Routh trembled at the full realization of how far he had got – of how tantalizingly near to safety he had come. The fellow was going to circle the park – perhaps to range swiftly over the scanty system of roads and lanes bounding it and running away from it. Nobody could stir on these without detection. While the helicopter was in the air only thick woodland would give secure cover to a moving figure. And of that there seemed to be comparatively little in these parts. Below, everything was bare, still, empty.

Routh's field of vision was restricted, but as the hunt progressed he realized that one suspicious object after another was being spotted, pursued, and then inspected at close quarters. It seemed impossible that so systematic a process would not ultimately succeed, and Routh presently recognized in himself a fresh anxiety so irrational that it appalled him. He was in a fever lest at any moment Routh should be spotted and caught. A swoop upon two lovers couched high on a haystack set his heart beating wildly; his mouth went dry as the helicopter casually followed and hovered over a school-child on a bicycle. Any one of the few figures animating this quiet countryside might be *him*. He bit again at his wrist, fighting this ghastly treachery to his own elementary sense of identity.

And then an astounding thing happened. Once more the ground had risen up to meet him – and this time it was coming nearer than ever before. There was a lane, a hedge – and protruding from the hedge a dark patch oddly like a human leg. It was this that was to be spied at – this and . . . The wild doubt lasted only a fraction of a second. What lay below was the Douglas. And the dark splash was one of the leggings he had kicked off when his first fatal madness of that morning had come upon him.

He was delivered from all madness now. He threw off the tarpaulin and rose. The pilot swung round and his eyes dilated. He threw up an arm and at the same time spoke rapidly into the wireless transmitter slung on his chest. Routh hit him and he crumpled in his seat. The helicopter was about twenty feet up. It suddenly looked a very long way.

Routh scrambled over the unconscious man. A wrong touch on the controls and he might soar again. He peered under the instrument panel and saw a tangle of thin cables and insulated wires. He thrust the spanner among them and twisted it – twisted it with all his might again and again. The engine raced, choked, faded out. The earth rose and dealt the helicopter a single shattering blow.

The machine had landed squarely on its belly in the lane. Routh flung himself on a door and tumbled into open air. He saw the Douglas not ten yards away and he gave a weak, exultant cry.

He turned back to the helicopter's cabin, in panic lest the pilot should have recovered, should be reaching for a gun. But the man was insensible. Routh stared at him and his exultation turned to senseless rage. He scrambled half into the cabin once more and with his bare hands pummelled the unconscious face. Then a revulsion took him. He clawed ineffectively at the body, striving to heave it into a position of greater ease. It was like lead. He dropped back to the ground and ran to the two-stroke.

4

The engine started at a kick. Its familiar rhythm steadied him and he found himself once more thinking clearly. There was acute danger still – and the more acute because he had made a bad slip. If only he had managed to rise behind the pilot quietly and get him unawares – or if, for that matter, the fellow had lacked the guts and presence of mind to make that quick revealing mutter into his radio – the position would be a good deal more comfortable. As it was, the enemy already had a fair idea of what had happened.

There was nobody in sight. But at any moment the situation might transform itself; he was, after all, no more than ten minutes' walk from that horrible wall. His first job was to get on an arterial road and merge himself in some southward-bound stream of traffic. Nobody, he recalled, was going to put a bullet in him from a distance. The swine were determined to have him alive . . . He shivered, and shoved the two-stroke across the grass verge to the road. His quickest route lay straight ahead. But that way lay the entrance to the fatal lane down which the girl had turned that morning, the lane to the abominable Milton – Milton Porcorum. He could see the mouth of it now. And up there, at any moment, might come some swift-moving reinforcement of his pursuers.

He turned the head of the Douglas and faced the helicopter once more. It lay like an enormous crippled insect, slightly canted over and with its rotor-blades quite still. As he opened the throttle and ducked he glanced sideways into the cabin. With a shock he realized that the pilot had come to. He was in the act of hauling himself up in his seat. For the second time his eyes – now glazed and painfully apprehending – crossed Routh's. Then he was gone. Routh cursed his own folly. He ought to have made sure of smashing the radio. Unless the fellow was too dazed to take in what he had seen, he would presently be reporting the direction in which the fugitive was heading.

Routh rode on, getting everything out of the old two-stroke that he safely could. It was still early afternoon. Yet the day had already stretched through aeons. His head swam and the wheel wobbled. He had to steady himself on the unfolding ribbon of time, steady himself on the unfolding ribbon of road. His breakfast had been a cup of tea and a scrap of toast. If he didn't get something soon he would faint. He had gone for several miles without seeing anybody – not even a distant labourer in the fields. But now a figure was approaching on a bicycle. Again Routh's front wheel wobbled. The figure approached and raised an arm. Routh ducked and shied. It was a clergyman, gesturing Christian brotherhood. *Major Road Ahead.* Thank goodness for that.

There was an A.A. telephone-kiosk on the corner, and beyond it a big sign advertising a road-house farther north. Close by this an old man was leaning on a gate, idly watching whatever traffic went by. Routh, remembering his senseless fear of the clergyman, glanced at him boldly. A shepherd or something of that sort, Routh thought – and rejoiced in the further proof that harmless folk existed. And here, going south at thirty yard intervals, were four lorries with enormous loads of bricks. He would let two pass and then cut in. The shepherd was looking at him with a mild, patriarchal benevolence. Routh gave him a condescending wave and swung in behind the second lorry. The shepherd had put a hand behind his head and was doing something to his stick, cocking it in air. The lorries were travelling fast. Routh opened the throttle. He had gone a mile or more before it came to him that if the old man were indeed a shepherd then he, Routh, was the sheep. The affair on the old man's back was a walkie-talkie. He was reporting on Routh's movements now.

Well, it was just another shock. His own speed, and the cats' eyes on the road, and the hundred telephone-wires overhead, and the thundering lorries that were his bodyguard, and the answering stream of traffic almost without intermission roaring, purring, rattling past on the right: all these things sang to Routh and exhilarated him. Let them lurk at cross-roads and jabber to each other over radios as they liked. They could do nothing. Already he had distanced them by nearly half a county –

Routh braked hard. The wall of brick in front was hurtling at him. The lorry, which had slowed apparently without warning, now swerved off the road and stopped. The lorry further in front had done the same. On a bare patch of ground a dozen commercial vehicles of various sorts were parked before a small architectural nightmare composed of a Nissen hut and three dismounted railway-carriages clustered round a mean central building of hideous yellow brick. Along the length of one of the railway-carriages, in white letters rudely painted on a black background, was the announcement:

GOOD PULL-IN FOR TRANSPORT
SNACKS DAY AND NIGHT

Routh hesitated only a moment. He must eat soon; otherwise he would pass out. And if he stopped now he could go on with the brick-lorries. Better risk it.

He dismounted, thrust the Douglas out of sight behind a trailer piled high with motor-car bodies, and followed the driver who had been in front of him inside. Two of the railway-carriages had been run together at an acute angle, and their point of junction had in turn been rammed like an arrow into the side of the Nissen hut. The whole place looked like the product of a ghastly accident. There were long narrow tables with benches clamped to the floor beside them. There were at least a score of men in the place. One was asleep and snoring, his head on the table and a straggling mop of hair trailing in a pool of spilt coffee. Most of the others were eating and drinking. In the main hut there was a counter with urns, ovens, and piles of sausage rolls and round doughy buns. Two slatternly girls dispensed the hospitality of the place, engaging in high-pitched and unintelligent badinage the while. It was hot and the atmosphere was horrible.

Routh wavered on the threshold. He hated it. It was dead common and everything looked dirty. It was the level of society he worked long hours, trudging from job to job, to keep himself from being submerged in. But hunger gnawed at his belly. He sidled in and sat down half-way up the carriage, beside the sleeping man. One of the girls was passing. He called to her. 'Miss!' She took no notice. He nerved himself and called louder. 'Miss, please!' She turned, looked at him with contempt and moved on.

He realized that the girls undertook only to clear away. You went up to the counter for what you wanted. He rose, stumbled over the legs of the man who was asleep, and went forward. 'A cup of coffee, please, and two sausage rolls.'

The girl whom he had addressed a moment before looked at him vindictively. She splashed coffee at random into a mug, her head turned towards her companion. 'My stars!' she said – and jerked an ear towards Routh.

Routh flushed so hard that the blood hammered in his head. Vulgar little sluts. If they only knew that he was Routh! If they only knew that less than a couple of hours ago he had blown to bits –

The steaming coffee distracted him. He grabbed the mug. It fell from his hand and smashed to pieces on the zinc counter. He stared at it stupidly. 'I'll pay,' he said, 'I'll pay for the mug. Give me another.'

The girl looked at him with suddenly much deepened contempt. 'Pay!' she cried; 'who cares?' She swept the fragments from before her so that they broke in further pieces on the floor. She gave the counter a perfunctory mop with a filthy cloth, thrust another mug in front of Routh as if he had been an animal, and turned to scream some greeting at an acquaintance who had just come in.

Routh took the mug and the sausage rolls and returned to his seat beside the sleeping man. Somebody had turned on a wireless. The hut and its tunnel-like annexes were filled with a metallic voice announcing the composition of next Saturday's football teams. Some of the men fell silent and listened. A few brought pool coupons from their pockets and studied them in the light of this fresh information. A man sitting opposite to Routh did this. He was a great brute with a shirt open nearly to the navel, and his chest covered with red hair. His thick fingers, hacked and grimed, fumbled clumsily at the creases of the closely-printed scrap of paper before him. Routh remembered the fine hands of the man he had killed.

He bit avidly into the second sausage roll. He ought to have got a couple of the buns to go in his pocket. But he quailed at the idea of going up to the counter again. It was a matter of physical size. He hated the thought that any man among them could take him and break his back across a knee, like a rabbit. He imagined it happening; the hairy man opposite taking him by the neck in a rough house; the slatternly girls, roused and bright-eyed looking on. One of them was flouncing past him now. She was actually carrying a big jug of coffee and a superior meat-pie, oozing gravy, to some favoured male. Other males, without animosity, shouted facetious remarks. The girl flung answers here and there as she moved down the carriage, brushing the close-packed men with her hips. A burly fellow in a boiler-suit slapped her on the buttocks and roared with innocent laughter. Routh hated it, it was so low. The place was full of the smell of human sweat, shot with the meagre smell of weak, stewed coffee. The sleeping man lurched over and a massive shoulder and thigh pressed on Routh. Routh took his last mouthful and wondered if he could keep it down. The carriage, he suddenly thought, was like a monstrous meat-pie stuffed with human flesh, with sweat and watery coffee as a gravy running over.

The man with the red hair on his chest raised his head and looked straight at Routh. It seemed to Routh that there was disgust and hostility in every line of his dust-grimed face. His mouth moved, as if he were collecting saliva with which to express himself. But instead he spoke. 'Heard what was last week's treble chance?' he asked.

'Ninety-eight thousand.' Routh heard his own voice automatically replying. 'A man and his wife in Swansea. Never filled in a coupon before.'

'Gor.'

The exclamation, Routh realized in a flash, was offered on behalf of both of them. It involved him and the hairy-chested man in a common response. There was a bond between them – that of their both being awed and disgusted also-rans. Routh felt a lump in his throat. Friendship. Pals.

The hairy-chested man brought from his pocket a tin of tobacco and a packet of cigarette papers. With these his blunt fingers fumbled in apparent hopeless ineptitude as he spoke. 'Nearly a hundred thousand quid! And Swansea!'

'They oughtn't to fix it that way.' Routh spoke spontaneously, firmly, from mature conviction. 'What's the difference between a hundred thousand and fifty thousand, I ask you?'

The hairy-chested man wrinkled his brow in thought. 'It's double,' he said.

'Don't you believe it. Not to the chap that wins it. Fifty thousand and a hundred thousand are pretty near the same thing to him.'

'How d'you make that out, mate?' An unshaven man with a battered peak cap had broken in from farther down the carriage.

'Think of the taxation when he's invested it. That's how. Super-tax he'd be paying, with a hundred thousand quid out at a good rate.'

'Super-tax! Well, I never thought of that one.' The hairy-chested man leant over to Routh. 'Fag?' He had contrived a grubby but reasonably efficient-looking cigarette. Routh took it gratefully and fumbled for a match. 'No,' said the man, 'I never thought of that one. And 'taint right. No – 'taint right, that isn't.'

'Have a light, mate.' The unshaven man was amiably thrusting his own cigarette at Routh. 'But it don't apply to them folk in Swansea. Man and wife, they are – and going halves.'

'If they're man and wife, they'll pay as one.' Routh was prompt. 'That's the law.' He drew at his cigarette. There was a little circle round him – friendly, attentive. The girl who had given him the coffee as if he were a pig had come up behind him and was leaning both her arms on his shoulders. Only the sleeping man was inattentive. 'So what I say is,' he went on, 'why not make it fifty and then ten fives?'

The hairy-chested man tapped his fingers on the table before him. He was counting. 'That's right,' he said. 'Give you a fair chance, that would.'

The second girl had now come up. She leant across Routh and brushed the crumbs solicitously from his part of the table. 'My!' she said, 'if you're not the one to tell us what to do.'

Popular Routh. Condescending Routh. The group grew. The discussion prospered. Routh steered it. The increasing babel of talk roused the sleeping man. His weight came off Routh's thigh and he sat up with a start. He was a lad of no more than twenty and he looked dead tired. The coffee dripped from his hair and trickled down his dusty cheeks. He put up a dazed hand to his head. Something queer and unaccustomed stirred in Routh and he brought out a handkerchief – the spare clean handkerchief that he always kept to put in his breast pocket before ringing a door-bell. 'Here,' he said, 'give it a wipe.' The boy flushed and took the handkerchief. Routh trembled with pleasure, and looked away.

Across the smoke-filled carriage he saw what made his heart miss a beat. The men driving the bricks were gone. And Squire was sitting in their place.

5

Vanity, for the moment, saved him. His prospective wealth as the proprietor of Formula Ten; his immediate personal safety as the man who had stolen it: neither of these seemed so precious to him as the esteem of the group of transport men around him, as the admiration of the two sluts now leaning on the counter. It was this that enabled him in a second to control himself – and that even stirred him to an act of sheer bravado. He caught Squire's eye through the haze, and gave him a brisk nod.

The man in the battered cap turned round and stared at Squire. 'Friend of yours?' he asked.

'Acquaintance.' Routh was off-hand. 'Commercial.' He paused to arrest sufficient attention. 'Travels in –' and Routh named something that produced a roar of mirth from the circle around them. The sluts tossed their heads in delighted disapproval, and fell to vigorously smearing ill-washed mugs with sopping tea-towels. Everybody turned and stared at Squire, who started to stand up, thought better of it, and sat down again.

But it was only for a moment that Routh was able to enjoy his enemy's discomfiture. The grimness of his situation rolled back upon him. Squire would have a car outside, and no doubt he had brought some of his confederates. How would he plan to capture the fugitive? A horrid possibility crossed Routh's mind. What if Squire said he was mad? What if he maintained to this uneducated crowd that he had escaped from an asylum? Might his pursuers not then simply drag him away screaming, without a soul lifting a hand to prevent it? Routh thanked his stars that he had got into the talk in the place; that he had held forth with such sanity and sagacity on football pools. But it had been a mistake to make that joke about Squire. They had all laughed – but it sounded a bit cracked all the same. And now Squire really was rising. He was coming forward to make his monstrous claim. He had pointed at Routh . . .

There was a sudden dead silence. Everybody was staring over Routh's shoulder at the main door of the hut. It framed two policemen in the flat caps of a county constabulary.

Just this situation Routh had dreaded for years. He had pictured it to himself with a hundred casual variations – but always in essence the same. The law had caught up with him. The bank had rung the police. The police had contacted the woman . . .

'Keep your seats, please. Licences first – and then a brake-inspection for all cars and commercial vehicles.'

The silence gave place to grumbles, routine profanity, and much fumbling in pockets. Routh gave a long gasp of relief – and then caught his breath as he realized not only the irrelevance of his first reaction but also the immensity of the issue with which this sudden and unexpected appearance of the embodied law confronted him. If he were captured by his enemies, they would first make sure of Formula Ten and then kill him. He was under no illusion as to that. And now that they had made contact with him again, did he really have the slightest chance of shaking them off? Except – and he looked at the two policemen – in one way? Powerful as they were, they were unlikely to get at him in a police cell.

He could give himself up. He could give himself up, here and now, as the man who had committed a score of petty frauds all over England. If Squire and his friends were indeed far on the wrong side of the law themselves, they could not then venture to come forward on their own.

The policemen were checking the licences of two men standing by the counter. Routh tried to think ahead. If he gave himself up he would be searched, and Formula Ten would be found on him. But it would be incomprehensible rather than suspicious, as likely as not. He could explain it as a system he was working out for playing the pools. His mind was made up. He would hand himself over.

He rose and took a step towards the policemen. The movement revealed to him that Squire had a companion – a burly man with a reddish beard, sitting half in shadow. In a flash it came to Routh that he had, after all, a chance worth taking. Probably there were only the two of them. However numerous his enemies, the hunt must have dispersed them thinly. Outside there could be nothing but an empty car . . .

He walked up to the policemen, his driving-licence in his hand. 'Mind if I get along?' he asked casually. 'I've only got a motorbike. Want to look at the brakes of that?'

One of the policemen, a sergeant, glanced rapidly at the licence, and shook his head. 'No need for you to stop, sir.'

He was in the open air – and free. Perhaps he could even – Routh glanced rapidly round the yard. There was a police-car, close to the high road. And there, its bonnet sticking out from behind a lorry, was what must be Squire's – a long grey, open Lagonda. The two-stroke was just beyond. He went rapidly forward, brought out his clasp knife, and as he passed the back of the Lagonda cut hard into the wall of a tyre, close by the rim. Then he ran the Douglas out into the road and in thirty seconds was heading south.

He must find another clot of steadily moving traffic. That was the next thing. It would at least give him breathing-space to think another move ahead. No good trying to make for London on the Douglas now – not with their knowing how he was mounted and which way he was heading. Better abandon it and get a long-distance bus for somewhere else. Once break the trail like that and he would be pretty safe. It takes the police to find a man who may be in any one of half a dozen large towns. And he had actually had thoughts of giving in! Indomitable Routh. Slippery Routh.

Going all out, he caught up with two furniture vans. As he slipped past the first in order to tuck himself between them he managed to glance into the cab. It contained just what he hoped to see – three hefty men. These two vans together were as good as a bodyguard. If the convoy held to the first decent-sized town he would be all right. He was on A 417. Wantage wouldn't be bad, but Newbury, if he could make it, would be better. Oxford, Reading, Basingstoke, Winchester, Salisbury, Bristol: let him only get on a bus for any one of these and he would be as good – or as bad – as a needle in a haystack, so far as Squire was concerned. It meant dropping the two-stroke – but what did that matter when he was on the verge of a fortune?

His mind began to work on the problem of Formula Ten. How could he find bidders for it when he really didn't know what it was about? He could do one of two things. Either he could seek out contacts who would know the right method, or he could take some means – newspaper advertisements, perhaps – of communicating safely with his defeated enemies, and simply sell back to them. This last was the cautious and moderate thing to do. Twenty thousand pounds, say, quietly handed over in one-pound notes compressed into a small suitcase . . .

The second furniture van was no longer close behind him. He twisted his head and saw it at a stand-still a hundred yards back. He could see, too, a puff of steam from its radiator. Presumably it had been obliged to stop and cool off. He faced forward again and saw that the first van was going steadily ahead. He had better do the same. For a couple of minutes he looked straight before him. When he again glanced backwards the stationary van was no longer in sight. It was hidden by a bend in the road – a bend round which there now swung a long, grey Lagonda.

They had lost no time in changing that wheel, or in their dealings with the police. His best chance was to get in front of the remaining van. He swung out – and as he did so became aware that the front van was now slowing to a stop. Presumably it was going to wait for its companion. Routh peered in as he swerved past. And his heart sank. Of this van – as if by some special malignity of fate – the driver was the only occupant. He was an elderly man who looked as if he would be of very little use. Routh had just made this alarming discovery when he heard the first throb of the car coming up behind him.

There was nothing for it but to accelerate in the hope of picking up some more effective protection before he was overtaken. He swung round a bend and knew that he was lost. Ahead of him was nothing but a long stretch of empty road. Within a couple of minutes it would all be over. They would simply force him into the ditch – perhaps send him into it with a nicely-calculated glancing blow – and then collect him.

Routh knew that he ought to stop and take to his heels across country. That would at least put the enemy and himself on more or less equal terms. But he couldn't do it. His muscles, if called upon for any such decided action, would simply not obey his will. The Lagonda was coming on very fast – far too fast, he suddenly knew, for the deft accomplishment of what it was after. The driver – whether Squire or his companion – had either lost his head, or –

A grey shape loomed for a second on his right. He was in the ditch with the world tumbling over him and the sound of a great crash in his ears. His consciousness, although momentarily reduced to a mere flicker, registered the knowledge that the crash represented some objective happening in the outer world, and that no impact upon either a human body or a single motor-bicycle could account for it. A second later he was sitting on grass, as if at a picnic, and staring past the buckled front wheel of the two-stroke at the Lagonda across the road. Only the Lagonda's back was visible. Its bonnet had gone through a substantial stone wall. Routh found himself laughing weakly. Squire had once more made an ass of himself. And this time, with any luck, to the actual destruction of himself and his companion.

Fear like a cold finger touched Routh between the shoulder-blades and ran down his back. He had heard a sound – it might have been a curse or a groan – from across the road. A second later first one human head and then another rose up behind the folded hood of the Lagonda. Squire and his accomplice were staring at him.

They weren't dead yet. But no more was he. Routh moved his limbs cautiously. He was bruised and shaken, and there was a cut across the back of his left hand – nothing more. And his pursuers, even if equally unscathed, had certainly derived no advantage from the crash. The odds were considerably closer than they had been a few seconds before.

Routh looked up and down the road. It was still quite empty. But it was a substantial high-road, all the same, and it could only be a few minutes – perhaps no more than seconds – before something came along.

But meanwhile Squire was making to climb painfully over the side of his wrecked car. Routh thought he had better get to his feet. But this took him longer than he expected. When at length he was standing on the road Squire and the bearded man were standing on it too. They were supporting each other like a couple of drunks. But they looked quite formidable, all the same.

Routh moved off. The effort to get on his feet had taken all his energy. He seemed to have none left to think with. But neither did his enemies. Routh shambled off down the road, and they shambled after him. Painfully his sense of the need to plan returned to him. They couldn't very well kidnap him here and now. The wrecking of their car had dished that. And until they knew that he hadn't cached Formula Ten somewhere on the route of his flight they couldn't bring out guns and shoot him. Or not to kill . . .

Something had happened to the sounds behind him. There was only one man running. He turned his head. Squire was down on one knee in the road. Routh thought joyfully that he had collapsed. Then he saw that Squire's left arm was up oddly before his face, and that there was something resting on it. A spurt of dust flew up beside Routh's feet. There was a sharp report. Squire had tried to wing him. They'd do that, fake him up as part of their car accident, and then manage somehow to smuggle him away – perhaps in a relief car of their own.

And still A 417 was wickedly empty. Squire was running again, but presently he would take another shot. The ditch on Routh's left had vanished, and in its place was a grass verge and a low stone wall. Beyond were trees. Routh stumbled to the wall and threw himself over; he blundered his way forward, staggering from tree to tree like a ball on a bagatelle-board. A bullet won't wind its way round a lot of bloody trees. He went on and on. There was silence all round him.

He stopped, not believing it. No pounding feet. His eyes were drawn down to his own feet, which ached beneath him. They rested on a thick carpet of pine needles. The enemy might be quite close, after all; they might be moving up on him in perfect silence. Nor was the cover so very good. This sort of tree was in too much of a hurry to reach the sun. It scrambled upwards with indecent speed, leaving nothing but a spare, business-like trunk behind it. Routh stood for a moment at bay, radiating futile male-volence upon the straight, still presences around him. He hated the wood. It wasn't natural – a place that was nothing but trees and silence. People shouldn't make such places. He longed for the street, for four walls and a roof, for a tough crowd that would see fair play.

Squire and the bearded man were close to him. The silence, as if retorting upon his dislike of it, allowed itself to be shattered by their voices. The sound seemed to be all around him. Wherever he moved it was in front of him as well as behind. If he turned half-left or half-right it was the same. Perhaps it was a trick of the place; perhaps among trees sound always behaved like that. Or perhaps – he thought in sudden horror – he was dying. Perhaps he was going to die of sheer long-drawn-out nervous tension. Perhaps this confusion of voices was simply the decay of the senses before death. He floundered on.

The trees thinned and vanished. In front of him stretched a low stone wall. Surely he had seen it before? What lay behind the wall, however, could not be the high-road, because he was looking directly at the roof and windows of a small, single-storeyed house. It was far from being a substantial refuge; nevertheless Routh saw in it his last hope.

But the wall was unexpectedly hard to surmount. His last vestiges of physical strength were leaving him. When he did get to the wall he could do little more than claw at it blindly. One moment it seemed an insuperable barrier; at the next he was lying along the top of it, his head swimming. The drop was steeper on the other side. He glimpsed a hard surface beneath him, and in front of him a pale wall, a blank window of the little house. And then he fell. He was aware of pain, of voices, of two obscurely familiar forms bending over him. Hands were laid on his body, and at their touch he fainted.

When he recovered consciousness it was to find himself lying on the floor of a small bare room. He was certain that very little time had elapsed, and he wondered how his enemies had conjured up this prison out of vacancy. His limbs were free; he flexed them cautiously and then, rolling over on his stomach, managed to raise himself to his hands and knees.

The place was tiny and smelt of fresh plasterwork; it had a single casement window, unbarred. Sudden hope leapt up in Routh. This was simply the tiny house in which he had hoped to find refuge, and it was not his enemies who were responsible for his being in it now. It was not *they* who had laid hands on him. He had been carried in here by a friendly, not a hostile power. But in that case his pursuers must still be close by. He got unsteadily to his feet. Why had his rescuers simply dumped him here? He must find them. He must explain the danger. Routh's eye, proposing to search the bleak little room for a door, fell once more upon the window. Squire and the bearded man were framed in it.

Without consciousness of the movement, he tumbled again to his hands and knees. And so he remained – looking up and out at his enemies, like a cornered dog. Squire's hand was on the window, and it was plain that he could force it in an instant. He was trapped. Only a miracle could save him now.

Routh prayed. He prayed for the miracle that would take him from these implacable men. And as he did so the faces of Squire and the bearded man moved queerly and unnaturally across the window – glided smoothly and laterally away. They were replaced by a telegraph post. And that glided away too. There was a tremor under Routh's body. The little house was moving. It was because he had been on his knees, he thought. *Darling, darling Mummy* –

This time he was unconscious for much longer.

6

Somebody was bending over him. It was the lad to whom he had given the handkerchief to wipe the coffee from his face and mop his hair. Behind him was his companion, the hairy man who had begun the talking about the pools. 'I wouldn't 'ave thought it of 'im,' the hairy man was saying. 'Law-abiding little beggar, 'e looks to me.'

'They might 'ave been crooks or they might 'ave been cops. But whichever they was, we didn't 'arf get 'im away from them nicely.' The lad laughed cheerfully; then, looking down at Routh, saw that his eyes were open. 'That's right, mate. Sit up and take a bit of notice. We must get you out before they check us in. No passengers allowed in these bleeding travelling Ritzes.'

Routh sat up. The hairy man stepped forward, fished the remains of a cigarette from behind his ear, and thrust it companionably in Routh's mouth. ''Ere,' he said, 'no 'arm in a puff of tobacco in the Louis Cans lounge.'

The Louis Cans lounge was the same bare little room in which Routh had lost consciousness. There was the window through which Squire and his confederate had peered at him. Routh got to his feet and staggered to it. He looked out on a landscape of trodden mud, dotted for as far as he could see with prefabricated houses. They were the kind that arrive in three ready-made sections which simply bolt together. He had seen these sections on the road often enough. And of course he was in one now.

The miracle was explained. Routh felt a momentary resentment against providence for not having, as he had supposed, suspended the natural order of things in his favour. 'What happened?' he asked.

The hairy man held out a match. 'We'd pulled up to fill in the log, mate, when you came tumbling over the wall like a sack. So we nipped out and took a look over, and there was your commercial gent coming after you with a gun, and a nasty-looking beggar with a beard beside him. So we bundled you into Buckingham Palace here, and carried you off under their bleeding noses.'

'How do I get away from this?'

'Straight down the Mall, mate.' The lad advanced to the window and pointed. 'There's a bus service at the other end.'

The hairy man had opened a door through which one could drop to the ground. Routh looked at the two men awkwardly. They looked back at him, benevolent and elaborately incurious. All words of thanks had for him connotations of insincerity, dislike, dishonest design. He could speak none of them. 'Hope you win that treble chance,' he mumbled. The lad gave him a hand down.

7

Workmen were tinkering at a score of prefabs on either side of him. There were acres of these, laid out in unbroken parallel lines. If you were in an aeroplane, and got your height a bit wrong, it would look like one of those awfully military cemeteries. Routh shivered. It would be horrible to live in such a place. It would be like annihilation. You would come to think that you were just like other people. There could be nothing worse than that.

At the same time he envied the workmen their anonymity. He realized that he looked queer among them, a hurrying figure with nothing to do with the place. As far as his eye could see, there were only these workmen, all geared into this ant-like, squalidly-impressive communal effort, and himself, a piece of loose grit in it – something lawless and on its own, slipping through the cogs to an irregular and problematical fate.

There was now a metalled road under his feet. And solitude around him. He stopped, alarmed. The workmen had vanished, because in this part of the new estate their work was done. He could hear their clatter behind him. And far ahead he could see different signs of life: patches of grass and flowers, a scattering of television aerials, washing fluttering on a line. Ahead of him people had already moved in. But round about him there was an intermediate stage in the growth of this mass building: rows of these little houses, blank, empty and unquickened. He felt, just because they were so empty, that anything might come out of them. He might turn his head for a moment and there, standing in each little doorway, might be one of his own hidden fears. It was another tableau that would build itself into his evil dream of the long tunnel.

The empty road in front of him was a regular chequer of sunlight and shadow. Each house cast its identical black cube of shade; and monotonously, just past this, was a shorter finger of shade from the sort of glorified dog-kennel provided as an out-house. He was near the end of the uninhabited block or belt – he could even see what looked like a main road ahead – when he found himself at a dead halt, quivering like a horse that has pulled up in its stride. For a second he was at a loss to account for his own action. And then he saw. Thirty yards ahead of him, the regular pattern of shade was broken. Between two of the cubes, instead of the expected blunt finger, lay an irregular mass of shadow, as if of something crouched low with an uplifted arm. He dragged himself forward, his breath shortening with every step. He read taut muscles, poised limbs into the enigmatical shape. He managed one more stride. Close beside one of the outhouses was the twisted trunk of an ancient apple tree. Its boughs had been lopped, but through some failure of energy it had not been grubbed out. A few shoots were springing from it. There was reason for it to cast a shadow instinct with life. It was the only thing left alive in all this wilderness.

Routh ran. He almost stumbled over a sticky-mouthed child on a tricycle – an intrepid explorer from the inhabited country ahead. There were voices – kids screaming, women gossiping, a baker's boy shouting at a horse – and gusts of music from the Light Programme. A few men, already at home from work or out of it, were pottering about their prefabs, obliterating what small patches of earth they had under useless little concrete paths and bird-baths. Routh spared them a glance of contempt as he ran. They took no interest in him whatever. Probably they thought he was running for a bus.

And so he was. For straight in front of him was a red double-decker, comfortingly urban in suggestion, waiting at its terminus – its side scrawled with a slogan exhorting the prefab population to National Saving. Routh put his last strength into leaping on the platform, and as he did so the bus moved off.

The upper deck was empty. As he swayed forward and slumped down he realized how done up he was. He realized too that he was still wearing the leggings he used on the Douglas. They made him look conspicuous now he was dismounted, and he hastily tugged them off and bundled them up as he heard the conductress climbing the stair.

'Fare, please.'

He fumbled in a breast pocket and brought out a ten shilling note. 'As far as you go.'

'Hey?' The girl seemed to doubt if she heard correctly. 'What d'you say?'

'I said "As far as you go." I can't say farther than that, can I?' Routh did his best to import an elaborate facetiousness into his tone.

'That will be one and ten. But you can have the Mental Hospital for a shilling.' The girl gave him a ticket, a handful of change, and a long stare. As soon as she had gone away he looked at the ticket. But it had only numbers on it, and told him nothing. He began to keep a look-out for a sign-post, a mile-stone, the indicator of a bus coming the other way. The bus might be bound for Witney, somewhere like that. It stopped in a hamlet and a number of people got on. Routh peered down at them anxiously as they mounted. It was three old women and a girl. At least it looked like that. He must suspect anyone, however unlikely, who took as much as a glance at him. It would be the same in a tea-shop or in the places one went for shelter: a cinema or a public library. He might feel the sudden prick of a needle. *Excuse me, my friend has fainted. But luckily I have my car outside.*

But perhaps that was only in stories. Perhaps they couldn't really get you with a drug like that. The bus stopped once more and its upper deck was invaded by a tumbling and shouting crowd of airmen. Most of them seemed no more than lads; they flung themselves on the seats, tossed each other cigarettes, called across the bus to particular cronies from whom they had been separated in the crush, craned their necks to study the conductress when she came up for fares. Here, Routh thought, was the best bodyguard he had found yet.

At last he glimpsed a road-sign and saw that they were running into Abingdon. The name conveyed almost nothing to him. He was sure it wasn't on any main line to London. Not that it mattered, if he had really broken the trail behind him at last.

They were in a market-place, and there was a lot of coming and going downstairs. He got large, vague comfort from the solid mass of laughing and shouting boys behind him. There were only two seats vacant up here: the one beside himself and the corresponding one across the gangway. The bus began to move, and then jerked to a stop again. There was some sort of flurry below. He peered out and saw, foreshortened with a queer effect of comedy, the hurrying figures of two nuns. They skirted the bus, one of them flourishing an incongruously secular-looking umbrella at the driver. Then they clambered on. The bus twisted its way out of Abingdon. Routh dropped into a doze.

When he woke up one of the nuns was sitting beside him, and the second had taken the other spare seat just over the gangway. Queer how they had to go about in couples. As if anyone would think of making passes at an old creature like that. Not that this one was necessarily old, since it was impossible to see her face. Pricked by idle and drowsy curiosity, Routh leant forward to take a peep. But still he couldn't see anything. The nun had an enormous white starched hood. She must feel as if she lived at the end of a tunnel. Routh wondered why such things had been invented. As blinkers, more or less, he supposed. See no evil unless it came at you head-on. That sort of thing.

He thought he might catch a glimpse of the other nun instead. When she turned to speak to her companion it ought to be possible at least to catch sight of her nose. But she showed no disposition to do this. Both of them sat perfectly still. Perhaps they were asleep. Or perhaps just staring straight ahead of them. Or again, they might be praying. But when they prayed didn't they go fumbling and clicking at a string of beads? Routh's eyes went to the hands of the nun sitting beside him. They were idle in her lap. Suddenly, and just as he was taking this in, she slid both hands beneath the black folds of her gown.

The bus was already airless and fuggy. Routh yawned. He remembered vaguely that giving way to sleepiness was a luxury in which, for some reason, he must not at present indulge himself. He yawned again – and jerked fully awake with a start that almost dislocated his jaw. He had experienced, against the screen of his closed eyes, a vivid image on the idle hands of the nun before she had slipped them out of sight. They were large and hairy hands. They were not a woman's hands at all.

The bus cornered sharply and Routh was flung against the inscrutably shrouded form beside him. What he seemed to feel, through every nerve of his arm and side and thigh, was an unyielding sinewy strength, implacably planted in his path to freedom, poised and ready to –

Like a train running into a cutting, the bus plunged out of clear sunshine and between two thickly wooded slopes. In the same instant the shrouded figures both rose and turned upon Routh. It was a moment of absolute horror. The voices of the young airmen behind him seemed to rise in diabolic mockery. Routh understood that he was in hell. In another instant the bus was again in sunlight, and the hooded shape that had been no more than a silhouette bending over him took on interior form and feature. With a tremendous effort Routh looked it in the face. He saw a wizened old woman with steel spectacles. She clutched an umbrella in one small, claw-like hand. With the other she had been steadying herself on the back of the seat close by Routh. But now, glancing at him and seeing something of what was in his face, she touched him lightly on the shoulder, murmured an indistinguishable phrase and went swaying down the gangway. The second nun was younger and went past with lowered eyes. The bus stopped. Routh glimpsed them a moment later, walking slowly up an avenue towards a conventual-looking building behind a high wall. And the shouting and laughing of the airmen was again entirely human.

Routh fell back in his seat, knowing that fear, unintermitted through all that day, had pushed him to the very verge of madness.

The bus swung right-handed round a corner and descended a hill. Routh found that he was looking down at a gas works. Beyond the gas works, mellow in the misted sunlight of a late afternoon in autumn, were the towers of Oxford. And from these, very faintly, there came the chiming of innumerable bells.

3. Routh and Others in Oxford

Turrets and Terraces, and glittering Spires.
Paradise Regain'd

I

Mr Bultitude stepped out of the main gateway of Bede's and looked about him in mild surprise. It was true that nothing had much changed since his performing the same operation on the previous day. Directly in front of him the Ionic pillars of the Ashmolean Museum supported a pediment above which Phoebus Apollo continued to elevate the dubious symbolism of a vestigial and extinguished torch. On his right, the martyrs Cranmer, Latimer, and Ridley, perched on their Gothic memorial, presided over a confused area of cab ranks, bicycle parks, and subterraneous public lavatories. To the left, and closing the vista of Beaumont Street, Worcester College with its staring clock kept a sort of Cyclopean guard upon the learned of the University, as if set there to prevent their escaping to the railway station.

All this was familiar to Mr Bultitude. But it is proper in a scholar, thus emerging from his cloister, to survey the chaotic life of everyday in momentary benign astonishment. Few, in point of fact, neglect this ritual. Mr Bultitude, having performed it punctiliously, turned left, rolled sideways to give a wide berth to a plunging young woman in a B.A. gown – Mark Bultitude was a renowned misogynist – and proceeded to propel himself laboriously forward. Mr Bultitude's form was globular and his legs were short; he had much the appearance of a mechanical toy designed to exploit the force of gravity upon a board or tray judiciously inclined; only he never seemed to enjoy the good fortune of facing a down gradient. In conversation with his pupils, indeed, he was accustomed to refer to Beaumont Street as 'that damned hill'; and to attribute to the fatigues and dangers attendant upon tackling this declivity his own indisposition to stir at all frequently from his rooms.

Witticisms of this water, reiterated over many years (which, in Oxford, can be a crucial point) had earned for Mr Bultitude a notable reputation as a University character. Freshmen would nudge each other in the street and intimate with awe that there was Mark Bultitude. If they were scientists they cherished hopes that their own tutors (who had proved to be insufferably dull) might be persuaded to arrange for their transfer to the care of this scintillating intelligence. If on the other hand they pursued more humane studies, but were sufficiently well-born, wealthy, good-looking or clever to have some hope of making Mark Bultitude's dinner-table, they importuned sundry uncles, godfathers, former house-masters, and others of the great man's generation and familiar acquaintance, to open up some avenue to this grand social advancement. Of all this Mark Bultitude approved. He valued highly his reputation as Oxford's most completely civilized being.

And an infallible index of civilization, he maintained, was simplicity of taste. His present expedition might have been instanced as evidencing his own possession of this quality. For his intention – as he had explained to a mildly astonished porter on turning out of Bede's – was to venture as far as the Oxford Playhouse, where he proposed later in the week to provide two of his favourite pupils with an evening's wholesome entertainment. They were to see a delicious old comedy by Mr Noel Coward. And he was now going to book seats.

Mr Bultitude, pausing only to pat on the head the youngest son of the Professor of Egyptology (a serious child who had been spending the afternoon in numismatic studies in the University galleries), moved steadily up (or, as it may have been, down) Beaumont Street, and presently arrived at the theatre without mishap. Having secured his tickets he emerged through the swing doors and stood, puffing gently as from healthful exercise, and contemplating with evident misgiving the toilsome hundred yards of his return journey. In this posture he was discovered and greeted by an acquaintance.

'Good afternoon, Bultitude. Like myself, you are taking a turn in this mild autumn sunshine.'

Mr Bultitude, who disliked having positive statements made about himself in this way, nodded curtly. 'Good afternoon, Ourglass. What some take, others give.'

'I beg your pardon?' Dr Ourglass was an obscure man from an obscure college, and understood to be wholly occupied with obscure speculations on Phoenician trade-routes. 'I don't follow you.'

'Then let us proceed side by side. I was suggesting that, in the vulgar phrase, you gave me quite a turn. You look wretched, Ourglass.'

'Wretched?' Dr Ourglass was dismayed.

'No doubt it is no more than a bilious attack – a passing error of the table. But to a stranger, Ourglass, your appearance would suggest dissipation.'

'Dissipation!' For a moment Dr Ourglass was indignant. Then some fuller light seemed to break upon him. 'You are gamesome,' he said. 'This is merriment.' And Dr Ourglass laughed conscientiously. Bultitude's high acclaim as a humorist had often been mentioned in his presence, and he understood that he was now in the experience of it. 'Evening is closing,' he said. 'But it might yet be possible to take a stroll in the Parks.'

Mr Bultitude soberly assented to this proposition – but with no sense of its bearing any application either to himself or his interlocutor.

'I mean,' pursued Dr Ourglass, rather feebly, 'that *we* might take a stroll in the Parks.'

The massive placidity and benignity of Mr Bultitude's countenance gave place to looks of the liveliest consternation and alarm. 'The *Parks*! and how do you propose, my dear Ourglass, that we should *get* to the Parks? Have you a conveyance? I see no sign of it.'

Although the University Parks might have been reached in some five minutes' leisured walking, Dr Ourglass was abashed. 'Perhaps it is rather far,' he said. 'And, you, Bultitude, are a very busy man.'

Mr Bultitude, although again disrelishing being thus dealt with in the present indicative, extended an arm more or less horizontally before him, and succeeded thereby in extracting a gold watch from his waistcoat pocket. 'Shall we walk,' he inquired courteously, 'to the farther end of Beaumont Street? Shall we even venture to turn for a few yards into Walton Street itself? . . . My dear Ourglass, you have taken to walking devilish fast – particularly up this damned hill.'

Dr Ourglass slackened his pace. 'Reverting to your jest –' he began.

'Ugh!'

Mr Bultitude's grunt might have been the consequence of unwonted exertion, or it might have been an exclamation of disgust. Dr Ourglass interpreted it in the former sense. 'Reverting to your jest upon my appearance, I am bound to admit the possibility of my not appearing quite in the – um – pink. You, after all, are a man of keen observation.'

Mr Bultitude continued to feel resentment at his companion's fondness for character-sketching. He contented himself, however, with what was virtually an imperceptible movement – that of coming to a full stop.

'And you may have noticed,' pursued Dr Ourglass, 'that I am worried. The fact is, Bultitude, that my nephew has disappeared.'

Mr Bultitude, although a man of various information and extensive views, possessed a discriminating mind. That Dr Ourglass had a nephew was information that he was disinclined to treat as momentous, and from this it necessarily followed that the nephew's vagaries could be of no interest to him. Nevertheless he looked at his companion as if in sudden naked horror. 'My dear Ourglass,' he said, 'were you present when this surprising phenomenon took place? And was any lingering appearance left behind? A smile, for example, as in the case of the Cheshire cat?'

Dr Ourglass took no offence at this. Possibly he supposed that Bultitude had entirely misheard his remark. Patiently he began again. 'I am speaking of a nephew of mine, Geoffrey Ourglass, who came up to Bede's last year to read Physiology. This term he has simply not appeared. You have, perhaps, heard his disappearance discussed at a meeting.'

The nethermost of Bultitude's chins contrived a caressing movement across his chest. It held the negative significance which a physically more reckless man would have achieved by shaking his head. 'So far this term, I have managed to attend only the wine committee. We discussed the disappearance of three dozen of vintage port. A graver matter, you will agree, Ourglass, than the mere evaporation of an undergraduate, however talented and charming. But have you yourself heard nothing from this young man?'

'Nothing whatever, although it has been his custom to write to me regularly when he is away. A friend, however, claims to have caught a glimpse of him some weeks ago in a place called Milton Porcorum.'

'It sounds, my dear Ourglass, as if your nephew, with all the generosity of youth, may be casting his pearls before swine. But let me set your anxieties at rest.' Bultitude, as he spoke, laid an arm on his companion's shoulder and exerted an encouraging pressure – with the consequence that Ourglass almost buckled at the knees. 'A young man who withdraws into the heart of the English countryside is most infallibly engaged upon one of two ventures. He is writing a play, or he is pursuing a woman. It is true that both activities are singularly futile, and that a young physiologist, oddly enough, stands no special chance of success at either. But at least the first pursuit is never, and the second is very seldom, dangerous. Whether it is a tragedy or a trollop, Ourglass, you may depend upon your nephew's turning up again as soon as he has completed the last act to his satisfaction . . . Dear me! We have got to the very end of Beaumont Street.'

2

Although expressed with some extravagance, the fact was undeniable. Like stout Cortez in the poem, Bultitude had now toiled to an eminence from which he could survey, on his right, the illimitable Pacific of Walton Street. He eyed it with disfavour, however; took out his watch once more; and then shook his head. 'I think,' he said, 'that we must abandon the more ambitious part of our design. For Walton Street, the hour is too far advanced. It is chill. It lacks colour. We will therefore turn left, Ourglass, and make a little tour of Gloucester Green. We will survey the buses.'

They walked for a minute in silence. 'This nephew of yours,' Bultitude asked abruptly; 'is he a schoolboy; or out of the Services?'

'Certainly not a schoolboy.' Ourglass beamed at this show of spontaneous interest. 'And Geoffrey was certainly in the army for a time. After that, he was engaged on some other government work, and his decision to come up to Oxford was quite sudden. I greatly welcomed it, I must confess to you. His abilities have always impressed me – and I hope not entirely as a consequence of – um – avuncular partiality. He might do very well. He might even prove quite a scholarly person.'

'Ugh.'

Bultitude's ejaculation was occasioned, Ourglass supposed, by the efforts of changing course in order to propel himself directly towards his confessed goal of the bus station. 'Or if not *that*,' Ourglass pursued with innocence, 'Geoffrey might at least enter politics with some chance of becoming a minister. There is our family connexion, you know, with the Marquis of Horologe.'

'Your connexion with Lord Horologe?' Bultitude looked at his companion with quickened interest.

'Quite so. Adrian Chronogramme – as you know, the present marquis – and I were Collegers together. The 1910 election. And Geoffrey's aunt, Clepsydra . . . But, really, I must not bore you with genealogies.'

'Not at all – not at all.' Bultitude appeared to make one of those rapid social reassessments which even the most finely intuitive Oxford men are sometimes obliged to in deceptive cases. 'I am most interested in your nephew. From all you tell me, I have no doubt that he has the seeds of scientific distinction in him. We must find him. We must bring him back. Milton Porcorum, after all, is not an *ultima Thule*. It would by no means surprise me to learn that there is a bus waiting to go there now. Come, my dear fellow – come along.' With altogether surprising vigour Mark Bultitude waddled quite rapidly forward.

Ourglass followed, apparently bewildered but much pleased. The celebrated Bultitude, he perceived, had begun to treat him with altogether higher consideration. Perhaps he had recalled that Ourglass was the author of that really very searching monograph on the Phoenicians in Spain. That must be it. And now he seemed disposed to take the matter of Geoffrey's worrying disappearance as a matter of personal concern. He had plunged among the buses like a bather resolved to breast the flood. Ourglass panted after him.

There is nothing exclusive about Gloucester Green. It bears no resemblance to Oxford railway station at, say 9 a.m., when an endless line of first-class carriages rolls in, to bear whole cohorts of the eminent to their learned occasions in the metropolis – nor to the same spot at six o'clock in the evening, when the same cohorts, exhausted by the implacable pursuit of knowledge throughout the day, are smoothly decanted into lines of waiting taxis, to be carried off to a refreshing bath before the ardours of dinner in hall and long hours of keen intellectual discussion in common-room. Gloucester Green is given over not to Heads of Houses but to mothers of families – massive women for the most part who, having been sucked in from the surrounding countryside by the lure of Woolworths or Marks and Spencer, reappear at this evening hour with bulging baskets, knobbly parcels, and jaded and vocal children brandishing glutinous confections on short sticks. For the more convenient reception of these hordes there has been erected a complicated system of tubular pens or runs, suggestive of arrangements whereby some race of gigantic and reluctant sheep might be driven to be dipped. And in and out between the pens rumble the big, red buses – extruding one horde, gobbling up another, and then winding themselves with altogether miraculous dexterity round several awkward corners before making for the open country. It was into the thick of this animated scene that Bultitude had now plunged.

Engines raced and roared; horns blew; across impenetrable masses of compressed humanity mothers separated from children, and children separated from lollipops, cried out in a dismal and surprising manner. It was a peak hour. The whole place throbbed like a mighty heart, governing with its deep pulsations the converging and diverging streams of red.

'Bultitude,' called out Ourglass, 'might it not be simpler to inquire at the office? I believe there is always someone –'

'No, no – nothing more fatal.' Bultitude was already forcing his way into the thickest of the crowd. 'To inquire there, my dear fellow, is invariably a labour *de longue haleine*.' The better to make himself heard he shouted this last phrase virtually in the ear of a large woman in front of him – with the satisfactory result that she gave ground in suspicion and alarm, and thus enabled him to press more rapidly forward. 'Always make your inquiries of the drivers – or of the conductors as second best. Particularly when it's a matter of connexions. Know the surrounding counties like the back of your hand.' And Bultitude continued to thrust through the press, peering up now at one bus and now at another. Ourglass, impressed by this superior *savoir faire*, laboriously followed.

'Now, here's Burford. I shouldn't be at all surprised –' With the head of his cane Bultitude tapped authoritatively on the windscreen of the bus before which he paused. 'Can you tell me,' he called up to the driver, 'if you connect with the bus for Milton Porcorum . . . yes. *Porcorum?*'

The reply was lost on Ourglass, but was presumably in the negative, since Bultitude again plunged forward. Ourglass made a great effort and caught up with him. The quays of ancient Carthage, he was reflecting, must have presented just such a bustle as this. The consideration afforded him mild comfort as he was bumped about.

A bus had just moved in beside them, and Bultitude sidestepped to peer at it. 'Abingdon,' he said. 'No good at all. Chipping Norton would appear to me to be much the most likely thing . . . Hullo! There's Kolmak – I wonder what he has been doing? You know Kolmak, our Research Lecturer?'

Ourglass looked obediently at the crowd pouring off the Abingdon bus. First came a small mob of young airmen; then a nondescript man, weedy and pale, and with a scratch across one cheek; then, following close behind, the person called Kolmak, whom Ourglass just knew by sight. But already Bultitude had lumbered off and was conversing with another driver; in a few seconds he was back, nodding his head in placid satisfaction. 'As I thought,' he said. 'The Chipping Norton driver knows the place quite well. And there is a connexion, should we care to go by bus.'

'Should we care . . . ?' Ourglass was somewhat baffled by the speed with which the physically inert Bultitude appeared to be taking charge of his affairs.

'Certainly. We will go out there, Ourglass, and investigate quite quietly. We may avoid scandal. Of course it may mean squaring the girl.'

'Squaring the girl?' Ourglass, who now felt himself being propelled gently out of the crush, looked helplessly at his companion. 'I am willing to believe that Geoffrey may be engaged in dramatic composition – although I have never suspected him of cherishing any literary ambitions of the sort. But your hypothesis – apparently your preferred hypothesis – of a *girl –*'

'Quite so. We must discuss it.' And Bultitude gave Ourglass a soothing – and again alarmingly flattening – pat on the back. 'And we might well consult Geoffrey's tutor – Birkbeck, would it be? – in a perfectly confidential manner. I think, Ourglass, that you had better dine with me. I believe Birkbeck is dining. We will plan out what is best to be done.'

'Really, Bultitude, you are very kind. But I fear the hour is somewhat late for your putting down a guest.'

'Not a bit of it, my dear man. At Bede's our arrangements in such matters are entirely domestic. Have you twopence? I said twopence. I'll slip into this box and give our kitchen a ring.'

And at this Mark Bultitude, much as if among his other angelic attributes was that of diminishing his bodily frame at will, contrived to insert himself into an adjacent call-box. He emerged again in a couple of minutes, appearing to dilate as he did so. All his fondness for slow motion had returned to him, and he made several majestic pauses *en route* to Ourglass, much as if the latter had been a beacon on a distant eminence. 'Well, that is capital,' he said. 'We shall meet –'

'I really ought to say,' Ourglass nervously interrupted his prospective host, 'that this – um – conjectural female –'

'Quite so, quite so!' And Bultitude raised a large, soothing hand – thereby causing Ourglass, now wary, to edge nimbly away from him. 'Seven-fifteen in my rooms, if you please. And remember that on week-days at Bede's we don't wash or change.' Bultitude paused for a moment to make sure that this parting witticism had sunk in. 'And now,' he said, 'I must address myself to that damned hill.'

3

Where Friars Entry narrows to burrow beneath the shops of Magdalen Street two women were edging past each other with prams. The wheels locked. *Zusammenstoss*, Kolmak thought – and then realized that the delay might be fatal to him. *'Bitte!'* he called out in his agitation. One of the women stared. He still hated that stare – the insular stare of the uneducated at any evidence of foreignness. But he smiled politely and swept off his hat. 'Excuse me . . . but my bus . . . if I might possibly –' The woman squeezed against the side of the passage – but without any answering smile. Perhaps taking off his hat had been a mistake. And he still hated all the mistakes, worrying over them far more than was reasonable in a man endowed with philosophic views, dedicated to liberal purposes . . .

As he feared, it made him just too late. He jumped for the moving bus and missed. The indignant yelp of the conductress chimed with his own exclamation of pain as he fell heavily on one knee. An undergraduate stepped forward and helped him to his feet, slapped at him in a friendly ritual of getting the dust off, was gone before he could be thanked.

Kolmak stood on the kerb, breathing fast. He looked up the broad vista of St Giles' and saw the bus disappearing. It was a Number 2. There wouldn't be another for ten minutes. His quarry had escaped him. Unless . . . He peered ahead to the cab rank – the one in the middle of the road, in front of the Taylorian. It appeared to be empty. Besides, you could not do such a thing in Oxford. You could not conceivably say to a taxi-driver 'Follow that bus.' It would be ridiculous. A group of students – of under-graduates – might do it. Then it would be what is called a 'rag'. But a *Docent* who acted in that way would be judged mad. Many of them, for that matter, *were* mad. But in their own English way . . .

Caught out by himself in mere dreaming, Kolmak jerked into movement. It was intolerable that he should be baulked in this way. Getting off the Abingdon bus, he had had the fellow virtually in his grasp. And now he was gone again. Was it worth while taking the next Number 2, going as far as the terminus, and then prowling a waste of suburban roads on the off-chance of once more picking up the trail? He joined the queue that was forming at the bus stop. No – it was no good. There was nothing to do but go back and report failure. As he slipped from the line of patiently waiting people he thought that several looked at him curiously. Perhaps it was 'bad form' to change your mind in such a matter. Kolmak walked rapidly off, clicking his fingers – an involuntary gesture to which he was driven when under some burden of embarrassment.

Threading his way through the crowd in Cornmarket Street, Kolmak thought of the Kärntner-Strasse. The jostling around him faded as he walked. He was in the Café Scheidl with a girl for a Dansing. Or – what was yet more delightful – he was there alone and had taken his favourite paper from the rack; had carried it, like a flag half-furled about its handle, to where his cup of coffee awaited him, dark and strong under its little mountain of whipped cream, and flanked by its equally delicious glass of the marvellous *Wiener* water . . . Kolmak thought of the Oxford water, chlorinated and flat, and he shuddered as he walked. Then once again his fingers clicked. He felt abased by this increasing tendency to weak, nostalgic reverie.

Kolmak pushed into shops that were almost closing; he bought food, and stuffed what he could into his brief-case. In the *Råthaus Keller* there had been a table prescriptively reserved for a group of *Privatdocenten* to which he belonged. If you kept to the unpretentious part things were very rea-sonable there. Why, Olli had liked to say, pay extra for a tablecloth? He remembered having been told that they had made Olli's death a very hor-rible one . . .

But it was no good thinking that. Undoubtedly the food in the *Rathaus Keller* had been excellent. And the place had been so snug in winter! Those tremendous Januaries, when the snow had been high along the sidewalks; when one envied the rich their great fur collars and the police the little muffs on their ears; and when he could watch, from his garret at the corner of the Otzeltgasse, the endless gyrations of the skaters on the *Eislaufverein!*

Kolmak found he had got blindly on his bus. It was really blindly, because there were tears in his eyes – tears of shame at all this weakness. ·As if he had not – great God! – something else to think about. And tonight he must go out and dine in the college. He had not done so for a week, and it would probably be accounted discourteous in him to stay away longer. Besides, it was a good dinner, and free. To save one's *Groschen* might make all the difference one day.

The bus was stationary at his own stop. He blundered out – apologizing too much, too little; he was uncertain which. In front of him a terrace of tall, narrow houses exposed the absurdity of its Venetian Gothic to a bleak evening sky. Kolmak thought it horrible. The dwellings suggested to him the remnant of some enslaved population, degraded in an alien place. Still, once more he had been lucky. There was, of course, the climb. But had he not a bath, even, at the end of it? And there was an empty room! If only Anna . . .

Kolmak bit his lip, turned from the road into a small garden, and paused under a steeply-pitched porch. This was supported on a massive, stumpy pillar which was just what it seemed to be: a sketch by John Ruskin retranslated into stone by some hand devoid of artistry or care. And you had to go under the porch dead-centre if you were not to bump your head against its trifoliations. What a fantastic race the Victorian English must have been!

Kolmak opened the door and went quietly through the hall. The house belonged to the Misses Tinker, ancient women who had owned some august connexion with the University very long ago. Kolmak believed that their brother had been *Rektor Magnifikus* – Vice-Chancellor – something like that. It distressed the Misses Tinker to have tenants in their attics. When they encountered Kolmak coming or going they were disconcerted; and because of this they would hold him in embarrassed conversation when it would have been mutually more agreeable to pass by with a smile. Kolmak knew that when he came in at the front door – or out of the little door that shut off the attic stairs – he ought to bang it loudly. For the Misses Tinker might then remain closeted in their own apartments and he would be able to go by unimpeded. But the bang invariably took more resolution than he possessed. He would close the door softly and tiptoe forward. And then one or other of the Misses Tinker – who since letting the upper part of their house had taken to going about nervously on tiptoe too – would bump into him in the shadows – shadows that were pervasive since the staircases were lit only by lancet windows filled with purple and blue and orange stained glass, and nervously converse.

It was the elder (as he supposed her to be) Miss Tinker who appeared on this occasion. She was carrying a bowl of chrysanthemums as withered as herself, and her form brushed against him like a ghost's as she came to a stop.

'Good evening, Dr Kolmak. Has it not been a delightful day?'

'It has, indeed, Miss Tinker. Have you cared to go out, at all?' Kolmak spread out the fingers of his free hand very wide, so that he would remember not to click them.

'My sister and I went out – on foot.' It was always an implication of the Misses Tinker's conversation that their pedestrianism was a healthful alternative to calling out their carriage. 'We walked round to Norham Road – the sunshine was really delightful – and called on Lady Bronson. You will be glad to know that we found her well.'

Kolmak bowed, and there was a faint click – but this time from his heels. 'I am most happy to hear it.' He restrained an impulse to edge away from Miss Tinker. Because she was a feeble and useless old woman she always conjured up in his mind the image of a gas chamber. It hung behind her now, a frame to the scant wisps of her silver hair. Kolmak tried shutting his eyes – an action which the shadows rendered indetectable. But at that his nostrils took up the evocation. Perhaps the chrysanthemums had a part in it. They ought to have been thrown out some days ago.

'But Lady Bronson's sister in Bournemouth has suffered an attack of bronchitis.'

'I am deeply sorry to hear it.' Kolmak felt that he might now with decency edge towards the next flight of stairs. Even when he had first come the Misses Tinker had been kind. But they had been relieved when he had become 'attached' – when Bede's, that is to say, had thrown some sort of mantle over him. Since then the Misses Tinker had lost no opportunity of introducing him to the other old ladies who constituted their circle of acquaintance. They had also put up the rent.

'And now I must rearrange these flowers. You will find your aunt at home, Dr Kolmak. Until a few minutes ago I believe she was at her piano. And how delightfully she plays! My dear brother used to remark that only Ger – that only the countrymen of Beethoven really know how to play the pianoforte.'

Kolmak backed upstairs, bowing. Did the old woman mean that Tante Lise's playing was a nuisance? He didn't know. Often he was helpless, not knowing whether in things said to him there was some underlying sense, some hint or warning or rebuke given under the form of irony. But at least Miss Tinker was retreating into her drawing-room. He had a glimpse of Morris paper, of spindle-legged tables and chairs, of blue and white china, and engravings after Botticelli and Luini. Probably the Misses Tinker had already begun looking after their brother while Walter Pater's sisters were still looking after *him*. Their drawing-room was in that style.

Kurt Kolmak, expatriate *Kunsthistoriker* from Vienna, climbed higher.

Now he had indeed to nerve himself. Whether or not Tante Lise was at her piano, he must confess this failure, this pitiable letting slip of –

For a moment he thought that he heard his aunt playing very softly. Then he knew that it was only the little Aeolian harp that she had insisted on hanging up on their 'landing' – the fragile contrivance of pine and catgut that he seemed to remember, all through his childhood, discoursing its alternate discords and harmonies at an upper window from which one could see, piercing the sky beyond the Hofburg, the great south tower of the *Stephans-Dom*. He opened the door separating his own domain from the Misses Tinker's and stood for a moment by the little instrument. A light breeze was blowing in through an open window and brushing the strings to a faint murmuring. He glanced out and saw – what never failed to give him pleasure – the fine lines of the Radcliffe Observatory, tranquil upon the evening. On its roof whirled an anemometer, ceaselessly propelled by the same force that was raising the low music at his side. If one looked at the anemometer fixedly, its four rapidly revolving hemispheres had the trick of appearing to slip instantaneously into reverse; to do this without stopping or even slackening the headlong speed of their revolution. And then as one continued to look they would have changed again: clockwise and then anticlockwise in an impossible alternation. It was an image of life, Kolmak thought – life that one so anxiously scans, and that cheats one ever and anon with some apparent sign of a reversal of one's fate, but that nevertheless bears one uninterruptedly –

'Kurt – you have news, *hein*?'

Tante Lise had appeared in the doorway. He went to her quickly, took her hands, and led her back to her chair. The room that she called her *salotto*, and that was all sloping ceilings and joists awkwardly placed for the head, was crammed with the massive birchwood furniture they had been allowed to bring away with them. Most of the pieces were so high that they had to stand far out from the wall, so that the room would have been a paradise for children to play hide-and-seek in. But, Kolmak thought, there were no children. The attics were as childless as was the faded elegance of the Misses Tinker's apartments below.

'I have little news, *Tantchen*. I had thought to gain a great deal. But I have been clumsy and it has come to nothing. See, though! I have been able to buy some *salami* – and a *bel paese* too.'

She took the food in silence and set it out on the Castel Durante dishes that were a relic of her childhood in Rome. Tante Lise's father had been the most distinguished *Kunstkenner* of his generation – that and an eminent medievalist, the friend of Winkelmann. These plates were her only material link with that spacious past. 'The police have been,' she said.

'The police?' Kolmak's hand trembled as he brought finally from his brief-case a bottle of cheap wine. 'For me?'

'*Aber nein!*' And Tante Lise laughed softly – as she used to do when, as a small boy, he had said some inept but charming thing.

'Then about . . .'

'No, no – not that either. Only about myself.'

'But it is intolerable!' Kolmak had flushed darkly. 'Do the ladies below, the Misses . . .'

'They know nothing of it. A most polite man came – an official of the police, but in ordinary clothing. I gave him *Fünf-Uhr-Tee*.'

'You gave him tea!' Kolmak stared at his aunt in mingled reproach and admiration.

'But certainly. Do not forget that I am required to report myself. This official's visit was to spare me that on this occasion. It was a courtesy, an act of consideration due doubtless to your *Stellung* – your new position.' And Tante Lise regarded her nephew with affectionate admiration. She had a high sense of what his abilities had gained him at St Bede's. '*Jawohl, Kurt, du bist nicht schlecht gestellt!*'

But he saw that her eyes were anxious and questioning, and he sat down heavily. 'I do not know that I shall keep the *Stellung*. It may be that I shall seek employment elsewhere.'

'Elsewhere?'

'With *them*.'

She sprang up. 'Kurt! What can you mean?'

'It may be the only way.'

'But you know nothing of them.'

He laughed wearily. 'That is the point, is it not?'

Tante Lise was silent for some moments. Taking the *salami* to the large cupboard in the eaves that served as her kitchen, she began to cut it into slices, paper thin. Kolmak rose, cleared a table of its litter of music, laid out mats and dishes. His aunt reappeared. 'But are you not dining with the *Professoren*?'

He put a hand to his forehead. 'I forgot.'

'You must go. It is advantageous to become more familiarly acquainted with the other *Professoren*. Moreover it is an intellectual stimulus such as I cannot afford you. Do not hurry home.'

Kolmak nodded obediently and went out to wash. It was something to have a bathroom. When he came back Tante Lise was standing before the empty fireplace – and so placidly posed that he suspected she had been weeping.

'Kurt, there are always the police.'

'No! Certainly not!' And he made a violent gesture. 'A hundred times no!'

'This man who came today. He was not courteous merely. He was kindly – understanding. He would not take a brutal view . . .'

'You do not understand. There is nothing personal in these things. It is all a machine. Your kindly and understanding man would do what some regulation commanded him.'

She sighed. 'But if there is real danger for . . .'

'We do not know. We cannot yet tell. Give me a little time.'

'And today? You hoped much of it.'

'I will tell you when I return. Perhaps I have taken too gloomy a view of its failure. Certainly there is one little thing that I have learnt. Yes, I will tell you what will surprise you!'

He was boasting – almost meaninglessly, as when he was a child. 'And I must go. They will be expecting me.'

'Of course they will.' Tante Lise was practised in providing reassurance at this moment. 'They looked forward – your colleagues – to your contributions to the discussions. They recognize your great authority in your own field. Remember to smoke a cigar. Whatever your ill-success today, you have striven hard, I know; and have deserved it. Shall you be speaking to Mr Bultitude?'

Kolmak looked at his aunt in surprise. 'To Bultitude? I suppose I may – though he is not always very approachable.'

'Then tell him about Uncle Nikolaus.'

'About Uncle Nikolaus! But why . . .'

'It is something that I observed about Mr Bultitude when we spoke together at your Provost's party. Remember I am a judge of men.'

Kolmak was uncomprehending. But again he nodded obediently. Then he turned to go.

'Kurt – you are forgetting your robe.'

'My gown, *Tantchen*.'

He smiled, kissed her on the brow, picked up the black M.A. gown from a chair and went out of the room, closing the door behind him. The Aeolian harp was still murmuring. He shut the landing window, for the breeze was now chill from the advancing autumn night. The music died away. He peered out, and could just distinguish the tirelessly turning anemometer on the Observatory. But the optical illusion would not work in the dusk.

Kolmak tip-toed downstairs. A door opened below. One Miss Tinker or the other would be there – perhaps, Kolmak thought, she would be remembering her brother, a young don with a gown over his arm, going out to dine with Walter Pater in Brasenose long ago.

4

Routh did not know where his new pursuer had picked him up.

He had thought of Oxford as a collection of colleges and a row or two of shops, and as a place where everybody went about in a sort of uniform, so that one might be awkwardly conspicuous in ordinary clothes. And he had somewhere read that there were officials of the University who might stop you in the street and ask your business, and who had the power to turn you out of the place if they didn't like you. He wished he had got to Reading, which was the sort of town he earned his living in and understood.

But the bus station reassured and comforted him. There was the sort of crowd in which no one could look at him twice. All the same, London would be better. He might get a long-distance bus from this very spot. He could get off as soon as it reached the network of the Metropolitan Railway – at Edgware, say, or Hendon. After that, and barring extreme ill luck, his safety would be absolute. There were half a dozen places where he could confidently go to earth.

First, though, he must get something to eat. He had been through more than any man could sustain on a couple of sausage rolls. If he had had something solid inside him he would never have let his fancy run away with him over those two nuns. Routh looked about him and felt that, except for his empty stomach, he was master of himself. He went over to an inquiry office and learnt that there was a coach to London in an hour. At the corner of the bus station he found a pub that was just right for him – unpretentious but putting on a square meal. He forced himself to eat slowly, and he drank no more than half a pint of bitter. Nothing had ever tasted so good, and as its warmth coursed through him his mind found release from its late tensions in pleasing fantasies. One of these was particularly satisfying; it presented a vision of Routh rubbing Squire's face savagely and repeatedly in gravel. But presently Squire's head turned into a lion's, and Routh was constrained to believe that he had been dreaming. For a moment of panic he thought he might even have missed his bus. His watch, however, reassured him that it could have been no more than a five minutes' nap. He paid his bill and went out.

He was still sleepy. The evening air had turned chill, so that he shivered. But it quite failed to wake him up. He looked around him, heavy-eyed. The broad expanse of Gloucester Green was now much less crowded, and his glance fell on a man standing near the middle of it and looking towards him. Routh had seen the man before; had seen him just as he got off the bus from Abingdon. There could be no mistake. The man was foreign-looking and noticeable. But of course it might be pure chance that he was still hanging about. Perhaps he too happened to be waiting for the London coach.

At least he could put the thing to test at once. He walked off and turned a corner. The façade of a cinema, islanded between two streets, was now before him. He rounded this, as if to stare idly at the posters with which the farther side of the building was plastered. And out of the corner of his eye he saw the foreign-looking man, now affecting to peer into the window of a confectioner's shop across the street.

Routh turned, and this time walked away as rapidly as he could. When he had gone fifty yards he looked over his shoulder. The man was just behind him.

Routh knew very well what he ought to do. He was still on the fringe of the bus station, which showed no sign of becoming denuded of drivers, conductors, policemen and substantial numbers of the public. He ought to stand his ground, get on his bus when it came in, and travel on it, as he had planned, to London. There, still moving with a crowd, he would get himself a taxi and vanish. But Routh, as all this revolved itself in his head, walked on. He knew he was being a fool. He knew that he was allowing himself to be driven off his own best line of retreat. But he was powerless to stop and stand. And suddenly the truth of his own position came to him. He was on the run.

They had got him on the run. The battle, essentially, was a battle of nerves – and he was losing. His mind flashed back over the afternoon and he saw the shocking significance of the clean break he had managed to make in the prefab, and in the bus blindly boarded for an unknown destination. If they pick up so swiftly after a check like that, if they could be on top of him like this the moment he set foot down in Oxford, his defeat seemed fated. They were invincible.

And once more the symptoms of fear began to operate upon Routh's body. The last enemy, he knew, would be sheer fatalism; would be a disposition to turn flat round and walk limply into his enemies' hands. Gloucester Green was now a nightmare to him, and he turned sharp out of it through the first means offering – a lane that narrowed before him and turned into a mere footpath between commercial buildings. From in front came a hum of traffic on what he guessed must be a principal street of the city. If he could dash out there and swing himself upon a moving bus . . .

He broke into a run, swerved between two women who were approaching each other with perambulators, and was on the street. There was only one bus. It was stationary. But the last of what had been a line of passengers were boarding it, and in a moment it would be moving. Routh glanced behind him. His pursuer was hard upon him, but seemed to be momentarily entangled with the prams. Routh ran for the bus and jumped on. As it moved off the foreign-looking man emerged and jumped for it too, but missed and fell. For a moment Routh had the happiness of looking down at him malignantly in the dust. Then the conductress pushed him off the platform and he tumbled into a seat just inside. For the second time within a couple of hours he was trundled off for an unknown destination.

Routh closed his eyes, the better to take stock of his situation. That he had once more shaken off his relentless pursuers seemed too good to be true. Nevertheless it was a fact. The foreign-looking man could hardly have had a car in waiting; otherwise he would surely have taken up the chase in it instead of jumping for the bus. So at the worst Routh had five or ten minutes' start. It was not much, but if he used it cleverly it would yet save him. And suddenly he knew what he would do. He would make no attempt to get back into the centre of Oxford. Rather he would keep a look-out for a suburban garage – the kind that is almost certain to have a car or two for hire. He would go in, take care to keep out of observation from the road, and ask for a car to take him straight out of Oxford. Hiring a car would be expensive, but he had the money and a bit over in his pocket, and it would be worth it. With his eyes still closed, Routh put his hand to his breast-pocket to feel the wallet in which he kept all his cash.

He seemed to go dead cold all over. The wallet was gone. He must have left it behind him when he emerged so sleepily from the pub where he had fed. There was nothing left in the pocket except the thin fold of paper that was Formula Ten. He had not even the twopence that would buy him a ticket on this bus.

Routh opened his eyes again. Planted opposite to him was Squire.

5

The double shock was too great. Routh gave a strangled cry. The effect of this was unexpected. Somebody sitting next to him took his hand and shook it warmly. And from out of a great darkness he heard himself addressed in a high and quavering voice. 'My dear Carrington-Crawley, how delightful of you to recognize me!'

The momentary black-out cleared, and Routh saw Squire leaning forward to listen, and at the same time gazing at him stonily. His hand was still being shaken – with surprising vigour in view of the fact that the person concerned had all the appearance of a centenarian. A second before, Routh had felt that he would never be capable of intelligent utterance again. But now words came to him from nowhere. 'But of course I recognized you, sir! In fact I was keeping a look-out for you.'

The centenarian gave a crow of delight. He had a spreading white beard, and his only other distinguishable feature was a pair of bright eyes twinkling behind steel-rimmed glasses. 'Splendid – splendid, my dear Carrington-Crawley! Perhaps you even might have time to pay a call?'

Routh took a deep breath. 'Thank you,' he said. 'That is just what I was on my way to do.'

At this the centenarian crowed again, dived into a pocket, and produced a shilling which he flourished in the air before him. 'My man,' he cried to the conductress, 'two fares, if you please, to Rawlinson Road.'

Routh took a sidelong glance at the centenarian, who was now counting his change. Presumably he was a professor, and in that case Carrington-Crawley had perhaps been one of his students. Anyway, that would be the best guess upon which to proceed. But Routh had the wit to realize that it was little use his calculating and planning the right things to say. He knew far too little about the ways of this place for that. He must simply proceed on impulse, and trust to the result's being as happy as his first two utterances had been. And impulse now prompted him to take the lead. 'By jove, sir,' he said, 'it's a great many years since we met.'

The centenarian nodded vigorously. 'My dear boy,' he chirruped, 'I think

I am enjoying my years of retirement. I think I know how to use them – to use them, I say, my dear boy – to use them!'

'I'm quite certain that you do.'

'But I look back on my final few years of teaching with particular pleasure, particular pleasure, particular pleasure. I look back on them with particular pleasure, I say.'

Routh wondered how much the old man was really off his rocker. His voice was shrill and commanding, so that several people turned round to glance at him. But none of them appeared to think him anything out of the way. Even the conductress, on being addressed as 'my man', had not shown any surprise. Perhaps he was a well-known character about the place. Or perhaps it was just that his sort were the regular thing here.

'And your own year, now – your own year, your own year. Some remarkable men – remarkable men, I say. Todhunter, for example. A most distinguished career – yes, a most distinguished career.'

'Ah,' said Routh, 'Todhunter – we all expected it of him.'

'Expected it, you say – expected it, expected it?' And the repetitive old person turned sideways upon Routh and stared so hard into his face that it appeared inevitable that all must be lost. 'Expected it?' The old person's voice expressed extreme indignation. 'Expected it of that shocking little drunk?'

Routh's heart sank. 'We thought he had it in him, all the same, sir.'

'You astonish me.' And the centenarian looked about the bus, as if this announcement ought to be of very general interest. 'You astonish me, Carrington-Crawley. But, no doubt, you knew each other best, knew each other best . . .' The old person's asseverations died away in a diminuendo, and for some moments he remained silent in what appeared to be a sombre reverie. Routh nerved himself to look again at Squire. The bus was crowded, but he judged it not impossible that his enemy might simply hold it up at the revolver's point and then hustle him into some high-powered car hovering behind. In that case . . .

'When did you last see Carrington-Crawley?'

Routh jumped. 'Carrington-Crawley?' he repeated blankly.

The centenarian nodded impatiently. 'Carrington-Crawley, I said, Carrington-Crawley. When, my dear Todhunter, did you last see Carrington-Crawley?'

Routh's head swam. 'I can't remember,' he said. 'But it was a good long time ago.'

'Precisely!' the centenarian was triumphant. 'Nobody ever sees Carrington-Crawley. Precisely, precisely, precisely.'

There was a silence in which Routh felt that something further was expected of him on this topic. 'Of course,' he said, 'Carrington-Crawley was always a retiring fellow.'

'Retiring?' The centenarian was momentarily at a loss; then he broke into a ghostly but unrestrained laughter. 'Very good, Todhunter, my dear boy –

very good, very good. Retiring, indeed! Tcha! Disagreeable young poseur that he was! But here we are, we are, we are. Come along, along, along, I say, along.'

At this moment, and while Routh's ancient friend was preparing to hoist himself to his feet, Squire acted. The seats facing each other at the rear of the bus each had room for three people, and beside Routh a place was now empty. Squire rose, slipped into it, leant across Routh, and addressed the centenarian – and at the same moment Routh felt something hard thrust into his ribs. 'Excuse me, sir, but you are mistaken in supposing this to be a former pupil of yours. He is, in fact, a friend of mine who has recently suffered a nervous breakdown, and we are getting off together at the stop after your own.'

'Rubbish, sir!' The centenarian had risen to his feet and was regarding Squire with the utmost sternness. 'Stuff and nonsense! Do you think I don't know my own old pupils? Do you think I don't know Rutherford here, of all men – a student who was genuinely interested in the *Risorgimento* – in the *Risorgimento*, I say, the *Risorgimento*?'

'You are quite wrong. My friend is nervously disturbed and extremely suggestible. And his name is certainly not Rutherford.'

The bus was slowing to a stop. Routh felt what must be Squire's revolver digging yet harder into his ribs, and he was frozen beyond the power of act or utterance. The centenarian, however, proved to have decided views on how this sort of thing should be met. He raised a gloved hand in front of Squire's face. 'Rascal,' he said. 'Are my grey hairs – my grey hairs, I say – to be no protection against public impertinence? I pull your nose.' And suiting the action to his words, he pulled Squire's nose – so hard that the latter sat back with a yelp of pain, to the considerable surprise of a number of people farther up the bus. 'And now, my dear Rutherford, off we get.'

Routh's ribs appeared to be no longer menaced. He got to his feet, and found it difficult to refrain from clinging literally to the centenarian's coat-tails – like a child to his mother's skirts when afraid of being left behind in some frightening place. But as he stepped off the bus his wits were working again. Would Squire follow at once? Had he reinforcements in a car or van just behind? These were practical problems. But Routh also wondered how Squire had found him, and why the foreign-looking man had leapt so desperately if he knew that Squire was on the job.

The centenarian had set off at a brisk pace down a long suburban road. Routh scanned it anxiously. It was quiet, but not too quiet. Three or four young men in skimpy white shorts and voluminous sweaters and scarves were congregated round a small sports car by the kerb. An elderly man was clipping a hedge. Farther along, a couple of men were high on a telephone pole, leaning back on leather slings as they worked at it with spanners. And scattered here and there were about half a dozen small boys in dark-blue blazers bouncing balls or circling idly round on bicycles. Routh glanced over his shoulder. There was as yet no sign of Squire or any other pursuer. If only he could gain the centenarian's house before –

'And now about the *Risorgimento*, Rutherford. What did you think of Count Fosco's book?'

'I'm afraid I haven't read it yet.'

The centenarian made a disapproving noise. 'Keep up your scholarship, Rutherford – your scholarship, I say, your scholarship. Busy as you senior officials at the Treasury always are, you should find time for your purely intellectual interests.'

Routh declared his intention of reading Count Fosco at the earliest possible moment. It was dawning on him that there were very considerable possibilities in this old man. Although not without abundant vanity, Routh had a tolerably accurate notion both of his own present appearance and of the social stamp he carried permanently about with him. He saw that anyone, however vaguely in contact with the external world, who took him for a senior Treasury official must be pretty far gone. He should have no difficulty, therefore, in continuing to deceive this old fool. There was money, for instance. He now desperately needed that. Well, the old fool probably kept a good deal in the house, and he ought to be able to clear him out of it without difficulty. Unless – And Routh turned to his prospective dupe. 'Is your household the same as ever, sir?' he asked. There might well, it had occurred to him, be unmarried daughters, or people of that kind – middle-aged folk still sufficiently in possession of their wits to see at once that there was something wrong.

'Precisely the same, Rutherford. My dear old sister and our dear old housekeeper. My sister is quite blind now, I am sorry to say; and Annie is very frail, very frail. A woman comes in during the morning and does most of the work, yes, most of the work, most of the work.'

For the first time for many hours Routh allowed himself an evil grin. This was better and better. If he failed to get what he needed by spinning a tale he could very easily clout the three old dotards on the head and take it. He was playing for high stakes, after all, and need not boggle at a broken skull or two. Particularly now that the stars in their courses had declared for him. Ruthless Routh. He looked behind him. There was still no sign of Squire.

The centenarian had stopped before a small detached villa lying behind a low brick wall from which the iron railings had been cut during some wartime drive for metal. As they walked up a short garden path Routh decided that the house was on the way to decay somewhat ahead of its owner. But what much more engaged his attention was the fact that he had gained its shelter without the observation of his enemies. For he was off the road and still there was no Squire.

'Come, my dear boy, come straight into my library – into my library, I say, into my library.' Routh was aware of a small gloomy hall, of a passage where his feet stumbled on an untidy rug, and of his protector throwing open a door at the end of it and beckoning him to follow. He was well into the room before he saw that it was entirely unfurnished. The centenarian stood by the single window, which was barred. He had thrown down his hat – and with his hat he had thrown down his beard as well. Routh heard a step behind him and spun round. Squire stood in the doorway.

6

'Put up your hands.'

Squire had him covered with a revolver – the same, no doubt, which he had covertly employed in what Routh knew now to have been a grisly comedy on the bus.

Routh put his hands above his head. He was caught. For a moment it seemed utterly incredible. For a moment the ramshackle structure of his self-confidence stood, even with its foundations vanished. And then it crashed. They had got him, after all. For behind him was a barred window, and in front Squire's square shoulders were like another and symbolical bar across the door.

But – oddly – he no longer felt fear. Somewhere in him was a flicker of anger – anger at the cleverness of the thing because it had been cleverer than the cleverness of Routh. Apart from this faintly stirring emotion the moment held a dream-like calm and an extreme visual clarity. He saw that his centenarian stood revealed as an elderly man with the air of a broken actor. He saw that the house was untenanted and indeed derelict. Paper hung in strips from the walls; there were places where the skirting-board had fallen away in tinder; the floor, which lay thick in dust, was loose and rickety from some sort of dry rot – it would be a good spot, he suddenly thought, under which to dispose of a body. But still he felt no terror. Far away he heard a bicycle bell and children's voices, and these mingled with the limp arabesques of the peeling paper and the sour smell of decaying timber in one complex sensory impression.

'Get the van round the lane at the back – at once.' Squire, without taking his eyes off Routh, snapped out the command to his accomplice. And the man went – keeping well clear of Squire's possible line of fire.

As soon as he was alone with Squire, Routh experienced in every limb and organ the flood of fear that had in the past few moments eluded him. For he recognized in Squire's gaze a lust deeper than the promptings of the predatory social animal and the gambler for high fortune.

It was something in the way that Squire's glance moved over him. He was studying the several parts of Routh's body in anticipation of the exercise of a sheer and disinterested cruelty. Routh felt giddy. He shifted the weight on his feet to prevent himself from falling. For a moment he thought that he was really going down – that the power of self-balance had left him. Then he realized that it was his footing that was unstable. A floorboard had given and sunk beneath his heel. And his senses, again preternaturally sharp, glimpsed a faint stirring in the dust immediately in front of his enemy. Routh was at one end of a loose board. Squire was at the other. And the board would pivot half-way between them.

But the revolver was pointing straight at his heart. Surprise must be absolute. And time was short. Routh wept. Without any effort, tears of rage and weakness and terror flowed from his eyes. 'You can't do this to me!' he cried – and his arms, still above his head, shook in helpless agitation. 'You can't – you can't!'

Squire smiled. He was beginning to enjoy himself.

'I tell you, you *can't* do it – you can't!' Routh was now no more than a terrified and bewildered child. He stamped with one foot – weakly. Then with all his might he stamped with the other. The board leapt up. Squire's evil face vanished within a cloud of dust. His revolver exploded in air. Routh sprang forward and with clenched fist and the weight of his whole body hit squire behind the ear. And then he ran from the room.

There would be the men working on the telephone pole, the man clipping the hedge, the group of athletes gossiping round the sports car . . . He was out of the house and had bolted into the road. Directly in front of him, one small boy was tinkering with a bicycle at the kerb. Otherwise, there wasn't a living soul in sight. It was disconcerting. Squire would be staggering to his feet at this moment, and groping in that blessed dust for his gun. Routh had seconds, not minutes, in which to vanish from the landscape.

Although the telephone men had disappeared they had left their equipment behind them: a ladder running half-way up the pole and a litter of stuff on a barrow. Sheer inspiration seized Routh. He grabbed the stout leather sling in which he had often seen such workers buckle themselves. Then he ran to the ladder – making a gesture as he did so to the small boy; a gesture that was an instantaneous invitation to complicity. He scrambled up the ladder, got the length of stiff leather round the pole and buckled again, and then mounted by the metal cleats to the wires. When Squire rushed from the house a moment later Routh was no more than legs and a bottom, a foreshortened trunk, and an arm working industriously as if at some screwing or tightening process.

Covertly, Routh peered down. It all depended on the boy. And Squire, glancing up and down the road, was talking to him now. The boy raised an arm and pointed. He pointed straight down the road in the direction which Routh and the false centenarian had been taking before they turned into that horrible house. And Squire at once set off at a run. Routh waited until he had disappeared; then he clambered rapidly to the ground. The small boy had placidly resumed tinkering with the bicycle. But as Routh came to earth he glanced up at him. 'Excuse me,' he said politely, 'but are you Dick Barton?'

'I'm Snowy. And thank you very much.'

'I wish I had my autograph-book with me.'

Routh realized that he was being addressed with irony; that the small boy shared, in fact, in the general queerness of the place. 'Look here,' he said urgently, 'how can I –'

The small boy pointed across the road. 'There's a narrow path between those two houses. My plan is that you should go down that. It comes out by my school. Hide in one of the form-rooms, if you like. There won't be anybody there.'

'Thanks a lot.' Routh gave an apprehensive glance up and down the road, and then began to cross it. 'You'd better get home, sonny,' he called over his shoulder. 'If he comes back he mayn't like you.'

'Oh, I'm not frightened of him, thank you.' The boy's voice, which held a muted and urbane mockery, was succeeded by the composed chinking of a spanner. Routh lost no more time, but bolted for the shelter of the path pointed out to him.

It ran first between two houses and then between long, narrow gardens. He saw the school, and hesitated. But instinct warned him against these empty rooms and out-buildings. Were he the hunter, he would be prompted to range through them at sight. So he went on, and presently found himself in another quiet suburban road. He walked down it, feeling his back immensely vulnerable. It became clear to him that he was fatally without a plan. His helplessness turned on the cardinal fact that he was penniless. There was now no possibility of hiring a car as he had proposed. He was so shabby that nobody would think of driving him a long distance without asking to see the colour of his money first. If he could get back to that pub he might with luck recover his wallet. And working his way back into the city would be no more hazardous than any other sort of wandering. Indeed, it was these quiet and unfrequented places that were supremely dangerous. Squire had probably begun a rapid scouring of this whole suburb in his van by now. And if that van came round a corner behind him at the present moment he would have hardly a resource left . . . Routh glanced nervously behind him. A small closed van had rounded the far corner. From the seat beside the driver somebody was leaning out and scanning the road ahead.

At the same moment a group of people emerged from a side-road just in front of him and walked down the road in the same direction as himself. They were elderly persons of leisurely movement, and they had an air of proceeding to some near-by social occasion. There was a silver-haired man in an Inverness cape and an elderly lady in clothes that were uncompromisingly Edwardian. To Routh, who by this time estimated all mankind simply in terms of potential resistance to armed aggression, they looked far from promising. And now they had paused by a garden gate. At the same moment he heard the van accelerate behind him. He found himself without the resolution to look round again and learn the worst. The group of elderly persons were moving up the path towards a large, ugly house standing in a substantial garden. Routh followed them. And at this the silver-haired man in the cape turned round for a moment and wished him a courteous good evening. He realized that the group was a heterogeneous one, and that not all its members were known to each other. Routh replied amiably, put one hand in a trouser pocket – the pocket that was no more than a jagged hole – and affected an unconcerned stroll. One of his new companions, a man of imposingly intellectual features, wore clothes very like a tramp's. His own shabbiness, Routh realized, was something that the conventions of Oxford rendered virtually invisible.

He heard the van stop and its door being flung open. Simultaneously the party to which he had attached himself turned away from the house and passed through a further gate leading to a garden on a lower level. At the end of this stood a large wooden hut. It was being used, Routh guessed, for some sort of entertainment. For on either side of a wooden porch attached to it stood a small girl in fancy dress, handing out what were evidently programmes. At the sight of this Routh's group blessedly mended its pace, as being fearful of keeping the show waiting. In another moment he was inside the hut.

The interior formed a single large room, long and low and bare. Islanded in the middle, something like a score of people had disposed themselves on forms and chairs. The farther end was shut off by an untidy but effective system of curtains. Routh slipped into a seat and glanced at the piece of paper which had been handed to him. It read:

DICK WHITTINGTON

PLAY

IN AID OF

DUMB FRIENDS

Routh turned from this to his neighbours, and his heart sank. It was true that nobody seemed disposed to question his presence. The gathering was one of parents and grandparents, uncles and aunts; and in various groups and couples they were animatedly discussing the schooling, athletic ability, artistic talent, physical health, nervous stability, feeding, clothing and disciplining of their own or each other's charges. They all spoke very loudly – this being necessary in order to make themselves heard above a hubbub rising from the other side of the curtains. But although an individual voice could be lost, an individual face could not. Anybody stepping into the hut in search of him would be bound to succeed in a matter of seconds.

'You *are* Martin's father, are you not?' A woman beside Routh had turned to him and was looking at him in friendly interrogation.

For a moment Routh stared at her in stupid panic. Then he nodded spasmodically, 'Yes,' he said, 'that's right. I'm Martin's father.' He might as well say one thing as another. It must be a matter of seconds now.

'I saw the resemblance at once. May I introduce myself? I'm Elizabeth's mother.' The woman laughed charmingly, as if there was a great deal of merriment in this fact.

Routh half rose from his seat. 'How do you do,' he said – and found even in his desperation a grain of satisfaction in having done the thing rather well. Polished Routh . . . His eye went past the laughing woman to a window close by the door through which he had entered. He just glimpsed, walking past it, the man with the red beard. So they were all after him. Probably the fellow he had knocked out in the helicopter as well.

'And in that case I have a message for you. Martin wants his part.'

'I beg your pardon?' Although still automatically the thorough gentleman, Routh was momentarily uncomprehending.

'It seems you have Martin's part. And he wants it to glance at between the scenes.'

'By jove, stupid of me – what?' Routh rather overdid it this time. But what did that matter? He was on his feet and dashing for the curtains. 'Give it to him now,' he called back. He was just vanishing through them when he sensed, rather than saw, the form of the man with the red beard darkening the farther doorway.

He had tumbled into a midget world of confused and furious activity. A horde of children, none of whom could have been older than thirteen, were making final preparations for their play. Close by Routh, a small boy in a boiler-suit was cautiously testing the cords that were to draw aside the curtains. At his feet a small girl, also in a boiler-suit, was banging at some invisible object with a hammer. In one corner several coal-black savages – presumably of the country which was going to be overrun by rats – were practising what appeared to be a spirited cannibal feast. A flaxen-haired girl in a ballet-dress waved a wand in the manner approved for the Good Fairy; another girl, dressed as a cook, was warming up at the business of banging a ladle loudly inside a metal pot; a boy with a sheaf of papers was rushing up and down shouting 'Where's Miles? Miles ought to be here. Has anybody seen that twerp Miles?' And in the middle of the floor Dick Whittington – who was a boy, not a girl, sat in austere distinction on a mile-stone, surveying the scene with the resigned condescension of a superior mind.

Routh took all this in very vaguely indeed. He had no doubt that the bearded man, as soon as he had satisfied himself that the fugitive was not in the audience, would come straight behind the scenes. One or two children were staring at him, but the majority were too much occupied to notice. He began to circle the stage, tripped over a welter of dangerous-looking electric wiring, and almost crushed a member of the boiler-suited squad who was crouched over a portable gramophone. He spied a door behind the backcloth and made a dash for it; as he reached it and slipped through he heard an adult voice behind him.

'May I just take a look round, boys? I am the inspector, you know, from the Fire Brigade. I go round all the theatres.'

There was a respectful hush on the stage. Routh ground his teeth and looked desperately about him. He was at an *impasse*. This room at the end of the hut was no more than a storage space; it had no other exit and was lit only by two small windows impossible to scramble through. The floor was littered with costumes and effects, and there was a square wicker basket in which some of these appeared to have been stored. Routh opened it with the desperate notion of jumping in. But he realized that even an incompetent searcher – and the bearded man would be far from that – would throw open the lid as he passed and glance into it. He was about to shut it again when he realized the nature of the single article left inside. He had worked in panto himself and had no doubt about it. If only he had the time –

From the stage behind him rose a clear, level voice. He guessed at once that it was Dick Whittington's. 'I think if you were from the Fire Brigade you would be in uniform.' The bearded man's answer was lost in a buzz of speculation. And then Dick Whittington was heard again, speaking very politely. 'If you don't mind, I think I would rather you saw my father.'

Already Routh had profited by the delay. His jacket and shoes were off. There was a minute of breathless struggle – the thing was, of course, far too small for him – and then he had bounded back on the stage on all fours, metamorphosed into Dick Whittington's cat. He miaowed loudly; a small girl screamed delightedly: 'Miles! Here's Miles!'; he went forward in a series of quick jumps, making his tail wave behind him. Through his mask he had a glimpse of the bearded man, confronting Whittington in momentary irresolution. Routh jumped at him, and rubbed himself vigorously against his legs. The bearded man cursed softly, looked quickly round him, strode into the inner room. Routh could hear him lifting the lid of the basket. Then he was out again and had vanished through the curtains. There was an indignant shout or two, and then everybody appeared to forget about him. The gramophone was giving out the sound of Bow bells very loudly.

'What are you doing in my cat?'

The mask was twitched indignantly from Routh's head. A red-haired boy stood planted before him in a belligerent attitude, looking him very straight in the eyes. 'I'm sorry,' said Routh. 'I thought it would be fun to try.'

'It's not Miles – it's a man!' The small girl who had been shouting before, now cried out in high indignation. A circle of children gathered round Routh and there was a hubbub of voices.

'I never allow anybody in my cat.' Miles, as he realized the enormity of what had happened, was going as red as his own hair. 'And you're much too big. You might bust it.'

'I'm very sorry.' Routh was inclined to think that he had escaped from the frying-pan merely to fall into the fire. He scrambled hastily out of the cat. 'I'd better be –'

'And who are you, anyway? And who was that other person?' This was Whittington's voice again, bringing its higher cogency to bear on the situation.

'Yes, who are you . . . Why are you spoiling our play . . . Dick's father should send for the police . . . He's bust Mile's cat . . .' The tumult of indignant voices grew, so that Routh was convinced that some of the grown-ups from the other side of the curtain were bound to come and investigate.

'Oh, he's all right. He's cracked.'

It was a new and tolerant voice – and a familiar one. Routh turned and saw that he was being inspected by the young ironist who had misdirected Squire when he himself was up the telephone pole. He was still in his dark-blue blazer. He even still carried a bicycle spanner.

'Stuart knows him . . . Stuart says he's cracked . . . Buck up . . . Tell Miles to get into his cat . . . Stuart's brought a man he knows . . .' And again there was a confused tumult. Some of the children had already lost interest in Routh.

'He works on the telephone-wires.' Stuart spoke loudly, being anxious to keep his own sensation in the forefront. 'But he's cracked, and thinks he's something out of Dick Barton.'

'Telephone-wires?' A new voice spoke from the background. It proceeded, Routh saw, from a worried boy in glasses, who was swathed in various coils of flex. 'If you understand electricity, will you please come and look at this?'

'Malcolm's electricity has gone beastly wrong . . . It's a man who's to help Malcolm with the lights . . . Get out of the way, you, and let the electricity man past . . . Shut-up all of you – far too much row . . . curtain should be up . . . wait until the man's done the lamps . . .'

Routh was hustled across the stage and found himself inspecting a complex piece of amateur wiring. The worried boy was asking him questions. With an immense effort Routh brought his mind to bear on them. 'You should do this . . .' he said. 'And *that* terminal should take *this* wire . . .' He had an elementary knowledge of what he was talking about, and the boy's fingers worked deftly at his bidding.

A hush had fallen on the stage behind him. Routh drew farther back in the skimpy wings. The electrician was muttering in his ear: 'I say, you can stay till the end, can't you?'

And Routh nodded. 'Yes,' he whispered. 'I can stay till the end.'

The curtains parted, rising as they did so. It was a neat job that had Routh's professional approval. He stayed his hand on the switch beside him just long enough to scan the little audience.

The bearded man, having drawn a blank, was gone.

7

Apart from Dr Ourglass, there had been only one guest at High Table at Bede's. As he had been brought in by the Provost, whose introductions were regularly unintelligible, nobody yet knew who he was.

'Provost, will you sit *here* . . . and place your guest *there*.' Elias Birkbeck, who as Steward of common-room had to determine the distribution of the company upon their withdrawing from hall to the privacies of the common-room, peered up from the card upon which he had earlier sketched out the most desirable arrangement. 'And, Mark, if you would put Ourglass here on my left, and on your other side . . . now, let me see.' At this stage Birk-beck, who was widely known among his fellow-scientists as a man of incisive intellect, fell into a muddle so licensed and prescriptive (for he had been known to avoid it only once, and that upon an evening when he and Bul-titude had found themselves at dessert without other company) that none of those now moved indecisively about as by a tyro draughts player was at all embarrassed. Or rather nobody was embarrassed except Kolmak, who unfortunately clicked his fingers. This produced a moment's disconcerted silence, in which everybody stared at him, including Birkbeck, who realized that he had forgotten him altogether.

Birkbeck's confusion deepened. He felt Kolmak to be the only man pres-ent whom it would be positively discourteous to slip up on. The further result of this was that he found himself unable even to recall Kolmak's name. His nearest approximation to recollection was first a toothpaste, and then a hair-cream; and the horrid possibility of actually uttering one of these by way of address to a colleague so much alarmed him that he dropped his card. Moreover he had already begun to speak, 'And if you . . .' he had said, with an intonation making it essential that some appellative should follow. Kolmak, very well aware of the difficulty, again clicked his fingers. At this Birkbeck had an inspiration. 'And if you, Doctor, will sit *here* . . .' It is always in order to address a learned Teuton as Doctor. Unfor-tunately Birkbeck's confusion was now such that he pronounced the word as if speaking German. And as everybody was now smiling encouragingly at Kolmak with the idea of being extremely nice to him he was left with the impression that some stroke of facetiousness had been intended. So Kolmak bowed, and clicked his fingers and heels, and sat down beside Bultitude. When he got home he would recount at some length to Tante Lise the fact that there had been a joke about himself which he had been unable to follow, and she would explain that incomprehensible jokes were an Englishman's way of showing that he wished to admit you to his closer intimacy.

Birkbeck was retrieving his card with the prospect of much further ma-noeuvring; the Provost had delivered himself of the long and heavy sigh which was his regular tribute to the futility of this part of the day's pro-ceedings; Kolmak was wondering whether anybody would introduce him to the Provost's guest, who was on his immediate left. But now a group of men who were undisposed of at the farther end of the table fortunately fell into hot dispute – and having done this forgot all about Birkbeck and his card, and tumbled into whatever chairs they could grab, arguing fiercely the while. Birkbeck, thus relieved of further responsibility, applied himself to the task of getting the port and madeira into circulation. The serious part of the evening had begun.

'Plain romancing,' one of the argumentative men was saying. 'But of course I made no suggestion that I didn't believe it. Children should never be challenged about their fantasies. Nothing more dangerous.'

'My dear Basil, how profoundly I disagree with you.' A second argumentative man, whose large, pallid face gave him the appearance of something normally kept in a cupboard, stretched out his hand for the madeira as it was about to pass him. 'If you really believe your son to have been romancing in this matter, and failed at once to admonish him, you have been watering that which had better wither. You have been conniving, my dear fellow, at the creation of poetry. I am surprised at you.'

'But *was* Stuart Buffin romancing?' The third argumentative man, who had the appearance of an elderly gnome, ignored the inquiring Birkbeck to challenge the table at large. 'Is not Basil Buffin making one of those rash assumptions for which he is so famous. Is there anything inherently improbable in what the sagacious Stuart reported?'

'Stuff and nonsense.' Stuart's father spoke carefully and without vehemence – but only because he was engaged in the delicate operation of draining a decanter of port. 'My Stuart's sensational report is simply the product of the cinema.'

'What's that about my friend Stuart?' The Provost, who had been talking to his guest, turned to the group at the other end of the table. 'What has Stuart been up to now, Basil?'

'It's like this, Provost. Just before I came into college, Stuart arrived home with a most absurd story. He claims to have been involved in an episode of melodrama somewhere in the heart of North Oxford. Something about one chap escaping from another chap by shinning up a telephone pole.'

'Dear me! Does he describe the chaps?'

'Certainly. The fugitive was a rabbity type, he says; and the pursuer was a tall fellow with high, square shoulders, brandishing a revolver.'

The Provost's guest looked up quickly, rather with the air of a man whose ear has been regaled in some unexpected way. Then he glanced at Kolmak on his right with a non-committal smile.

'And Stuart somehow assisted the first chap's escape. He's quite shockingly circumstantial about it all. The rabbity fugitive, he says, had a scratch across one cheek.'

'A scratch!'

Everybody looked tolerantly at Kolmak, whose limited understanding of colloquial English frequently led him into inept exclamations.

'I have no doubt whatever, despite Wilfred Wybrow here' – and Basil Buffin gave a casual nod at the elderly gnome – 'that Stuart has been going to too many cinemas.'

'And I have correspondingly none that there is another and equally tenable explanation.' The pallid man, who was a philosopher named Adrian Trist, reached for the walnuts. 'Stuart was not recalling a film *made*, but witnessing a film *making*. It's always happening in the streets of Oxford nowadays. Film units – or whatever they are called – descend upon the place several times a year. They consider that we provide a good *décor*. For my part, nothing of the sort would surprise me in the least. If I turned into Beaumont Street tomorrow and was an eye-witness of an atrocious murder, I should know that it was merely part of some horror being cooked up in Ealing, or wherever such things are coined and uttered.'

Birkbeck paused in the operation of dissecting a tangerine. 'If such an assumption were to become general,' he said carefully, 'there would surely be some risk of criminal elements actually perpetrating –'

'Quite so. But there is yet another possibility.' It was the gnome-like Wybrow who now spoke. 'What Stuart Buffin undoubtedly witnessed was an Initiative Test. It is something that the Army has lately thought up to give employment to otherwise idle warriors. Twenty or thirty young men wearing some distinguishing badge are set down, say, twenty miles from Oxford and told to reach the centre of the city without being spotted by a policeman. Naturally they behave in all sorts of *outré* ways, to the delight of the Stuarts of this world and the unspeakable alarm of sundry old women.'

'Both Adrian and Wilfred have given their censures with characteristic ingenuity.' Mark Bultitude, who had so far been concentrating on the consumption of a large slice of pineapple, looked solemnly across the table. 'But I am myself in favour of a real detective chasing a real criminal – or conceivably vice versa. After all, why not? There must be quite as many burglaries committed in this country as there are either films concocted or Initiative Tests carried out. Why should not Stuart have judged judiciously of matters which Stuart alone saw?' Bultitude paused to drink a glass of port, thereby refreshing himself sufficiently to tackle a second slice of pineapple. 'But perhaps there is more to tell? Perhaps the sagacious Stuart followed – "trailed" – would, I believe be the technical word –'

The Provost's guest looked up again. 'Shadowed,' he said.

Bultitude stared. 'To be sure – shadowed. Perhaps Stuart –'

'Your son followed this man with the scratch on his face – yes?'

Everybody again looked at Kolmak, who seemed this evening to be excelling himself in oddity. The usually retiring *Kunsthistoriker* was leaning forward and eagerly scanning Basil Buffin's face.

'Well, not precisely that. But Stuart claims to have seen the fugitive again quite soon afterwards. And where? Where, my dear Adrian, was this film actor spotted afresh? Where, Wilfred, had your otherwise idle warrior deigned to display his initiative? If we are to believe my Stuart the answer is *inside a cat*.'

Bultitude let a piece of pineapple fall on his plate. 'That,' he said, '*is* a little odd, one is bound to admit. And who would suspect a son of Basil's of possessing so abnormal a fantasy?'

'A cat?' Birkbeck repeated the word meditatively, as if particularly anxious to conjure up before his inward eye a substantially accurate representation of what it denoted. 'I don't know that such a statement makes sense.

In fact I am fairly confident that it does not. This boy must have been dreaming.'

'Not at all.'

Everybody turned in surprise. The speaker – the only person present who had hitherto been entirely silent – was Bultitude's guest, Dr Ourglass.

'Not at all. For your son, sir' – and Ourglass looked vaguely along the table, being not very clear as to which of the persons at its farther end stood in a paternal relationship to the problematical Stuart – 'your son is in a position to bring forward – if only indirectly and through myself – a significant piece of corroborative evidence. As I was walking into Bede's to enjoy an excellent dinner' – and Ourglass looked amiably about him, receiving a glance of large admiration from Kolmak, who judged this to be a particularly happy stroke of courtesy – 'as I was walking, in fact, down Bardwell Road I met a small girl of my acquaintance. Her name, indeed, is unknown to me, but we seldom pass without offering each other the time of day. As with all children – or so I should judge – her remarks are not invariably easy of interpretation. And on the present occasion she said something that I had to confess to myself at the time as leaving me wholly at a loss. But the very unintelligibility of her words only served – or so I believe myself able confidently to assert – to make them the more memorable, at least for the time.' Ourglass paused, having for the moment a little lost himself in the pursuit of all this precision. 'In short, what the child said was this: *"There was a man in Miles's cat."* The assertion is, I confess, a wholly mysterious one. But it does serve to corroborate the otherwise frankly somewhat unconvincing asseveration of – um – Stuart.' And Ourglass, presumably feeling that he had acquitted himself not ingloriously on this the first occasion of his dining in Bede's for a number of years, took a modest sip of madeira and followed this up by making careful approaches to a grape.

'There is very evident absurdity in this.' The gnome-like Wybrow, whose trade was English textual criticism, looked round the wine-table by way of carefully collecting attention for what he judged would be an annihilating stroke. 'No sense can conceivably attach to the proposition that there was a man in Miles's *cat*. Cats do not admit the reception of men. But you would be aware of no difficulty whatever, were I to inform you that there was a man in Miles's *hat*. For, even though it is admittedly true that a *hat* is no more capable of containing a man than is a *cat*, yet the idiom is a perfectly common and comprehensible one. I therefore judge, sir' – and Wybrow smiled blandly across the table at Ourglass – 'that your report must be the issue of imperfect hearing and insufficient reflection.'

The Provost's guest spoke. 'That won't really do. It misses out Stuart, who also said something about a man in a cat. If Stuart's father thought he heard the familiar voice of his son say *cat*; and if the last speaker, at that time knowing nothing of Stuart's statement, thought he heard a child with whom he frequently talks say *cat*, then the case for *cat* is a pretty strong one.'

It was in the slight pause induced by this speech, and before the textually-minded Wybrow had taken leisure to frame a suitable reply, that Kolmak turned with a polite bow to Bultitude. 'An inordinate love of cats,' he said carefully, 'distinguished my Uncle Nikolaus.'

8

This dauntingly inconsequent remark had the effect of bringing general conversation to a close, the majority of those present plunging hastily into *tête-à-tête* and leaving Bultitude to it. Ourglass took the opportunity of addressing Birkbeck on the subject of which he was preoccupied at this time. 'Bultitude,' he said 'was good enough to suggest a little conference about my nephew, Geoffrey. I am most distressed that he should not have returned to Bede's at the beginning of term. And that he should not have written to your Dean, or to yourself as his tutor, is quite incomprehensible to me.'

'A letter may have gone astray in the post.' Birkbeck, who judged it not easy to overestimate the typical undergraduate's capacity for negligence, was at the same time humanely anxious to say whatever might explain away the present unfortunate instance of this trait. 'Or your nephew may have been taken suddenly ill – not gravely ill, of course, but *suddenly*. I hope we may hear from him any day with an explanation that the Dean may be able to accept. He's the most promising pupil I've had in years.'

Ourglass's dejection was visibly mitigated by this praise. 'Bultitude has formed the curious notion that Geoffrey may be writing a play.'

Birkbeck considered this carefully. 'But,' he asked at length, 'might not a play be written in Oxford?'

'That is very true.' Ourglass was dashed again. 'As a matter of fact, Bultitude has an alternative hypothesis. He supposes that Geoffrey may be – um – preoccupied with a woman. Perhaps he will discount that suggestion, however, when he learns that Geoffrey is, in fact, engaged to be married. And the girl, Geoffrey will have told you, is actually up at Oxford.' Ourglass glanced across at the Provost's guest. 'And – do you know? – I could almost persuade myself –'

At this moment the Provost, who was generally accounted an amiable man of reserved manners, favoured Birkbeck with a ferocious grimace. There was nothing out of the way in this; it was his regular means of intimating that his enjoyment of his colleague's hospitality had now continued long enough, and that he would welcome a removal to the adjoining room for coffee. The move failed to abrupt Kolmak's confidences to Bultitude on the subject of Uncle Nikolaus's cats; indeed this appeared to be proving unexpectedly absorbing, since it was to be observed that Bultitude, with unwonted familiarity, had now draped a massive arm over Kolmak's shoulder. It occurred to Ourglass, seeing his host thus preoccupied, that here was a fitting opportunity to pay his respects to the Provost. Balancing his coffee before him, therefore, and making his way across the room, he found himself greeted with some urgency.

'Ah, Ourglass, how are you? I'd hoped that Birkbeck would have put us next to each other in there. Now – look – let me introduce my guest. But where is he? Ah – getting a cigar. John, come back here! This business of your nephew, you know, Ourglass – we must get it settled up. And John, as it happens – But here he is. Ourglass, let me introduce Sir John Appleby. John, this is Dr Ourglass, the young man's uncle.'

Sir John Appleby shook hands. 'How do you do,' he said. 'May I say how much I enjoyed your last paper in the *Journal of Ancient Geography*? It appears to put Cambremer's discoveries in quite a new light.'

Ourglass bowed, much gratified. 'I thought when we sat down in Hall that I recognized a likeness. Am I right in supposing . . .?

'Quite right, quite right!' The Provost, who had at all hours of the day a great air of being engaged in the rapid transaction of business, nodded briskly. 'Appleby, who is an old pupil of mine, is our young woman's elder brother. And he has come up because she has sent for him. It seems that your nephew's silence is now worrying her very much. And quite properly. It begins to look decidedly queer. But John, of course, will clear the matter up.'

Ourglass, while endeavouring to hint civil satisfaction that the brother of his nephew's betrothed was of responsible and presentable appearance, wondered why he should be regarded as having particular qualifications for finding the missing Geoffrey. But this enigma the Provost illuminated at once.

'A policeman, you know. Many of my old pupils have passed into the hands of the police, I believe. But Appleby is the only one who did so in the special sense of *becoming* one. And now he's gone back to the metropolitan people as an Assistant-Commissioner.'

'Dear me!' Ourglass, although impressed by this peculiar career, was somewhat dismayed. 'Does that mean what they call Scotland Yard?'

The man called Appleby nodded. He had a pleasant smile, but the nod was unnervingly incisive. It made Ourglass feel as if he were a short and simple communication that had been rapidly run over and snapped into a file for possible future consideration.

'I haven't met your nephew,' Appleby said, 'and I hope you will tell me something about him. Your view is likely to be a more objective one than my sister's.'

'I am as much worried on Jane's behalf as my own. If I may say so, she has stood up to this disconcerting and alarming incident very well. She appears to be a strong-minded girl, and I consider Geoffrey as most fortunate in having gained her affections.' And Ourglass, having discharged himself of this preliminary civility to his satisfaction, peered at the Assistant-Commissioner much as an anxious relative might peer at an eminent consultant physician straight from the bedside. 'Do I understand, Sir John, that you take a serious view?'

'I have insufficient information upon which to form a view either way. As a mere matter of statistics, there are two chances in five that your nephew has suffered a nervous breakdown with total amnesia, one chance that he is in gaol under an assumed name, one chance that he is concealing a course of conduct that is either illegal or immoral, and one chance that he is dead.'

'Dear me! Have you told your sister of these chances?'

'No, I haven't told Jane.'

Ourglass was confused. 'But of course not. You would naturally –'

'There was no need to. She will certainly have looked them up for herself.'

'Bless my soul!' Ourglass respected the instinct to look things up; he admired persons with the ability to do this in out-of-the-way fields. Nevertheless the thought of his nephew's chances of survival being investigated in this manner by a fiancée troubled him. 'This is very shocking,' he said vaguely, 'very shocking, indeed. But your sister is, as I say, strong-minded. There is some comfort in that.'

But this was a line of reflection in which Sir John Appleby appeared to see no special utility; he looked at his interlocutor in a silence that was presently broken by the Provost.

'I had young Ourglass to dinner in his first term. He didn't seem to me the suicide type – nor any sort of loose fish either.'

'Did it strike you that my nephew might want to write a play?'

The Provost ignored this incomprehensible interjection. 'Adventurous, I should say – and perhaps even rash. I got the impression that he had done a lot of courting danger in his time, and found difficulty in doing without it. That's a common enough type with us here at present. Not that he struck me as a common type. I had a feeling that he was rather remarkable.' The Provost's eyes fell on the elder Ourglass as he spoke, and some fresh aspect of the matter seemed to strike him. 'Odd – eh? But that's how he struck me.' He turned to Appleby. 'And he's not a boy, you know, John. Older than this young sister of yours by a good way.'

'I've gathered as much.' Appleby looked from the Provost to Ourglass. 'What was that you said about writing a play?'

'It was something put in my head – perhaps without great seriousness of intention – by Bultitude, there. We were taking – um – a stroll together this afternoon. And when I told him that Geoffrey had last been glimpsed in the country –'

'Now that's very important,' the Provost briskly remarked. 'That's the last thing about this young man of ours that we have to go upon. It appears that a friend of Ourglass's – *this* Ourglass, that is to say' and the Provost thrust a finger without ceremony into Dr Ourglass's stomach – 'saw the young man in a car –'

'In the back of a *large* car,' Dr Ourglass supplemented, 'and with several other men –'

'Driving rapidly through some small village called, I think, Milton Porcorum.'

'Precisely. If my informant is to be believed, Geoffrey was last seen in Milton Porcorum. And Bultitude suggested –'

'In Milton Porcorum!'

All three men turned round. The interruption came from Kolmak. He had been standing behind them in the somewhat perplexed reception of much affability from Bultitude. But evidently he had been paying more attention to their conversation than was in the circumstances altogether proper, and now he was staring at them in some obscure but violent agitation.

'Someone has disappeared – *nicht wahr*? And in Milton Porcorum?' Kolmak enunciated this last word in a fashion so Teutonic as to add substantially to the bizzare effort of his interposition.

'Well, yes. We were talking –'

But as the Provost, looking mildly surprised, began to frame this civil reply, Kolmak appeared to convince himself that he had behaved with marked impropriety. He flushed and rapidly clicked his fingers. '*Ich bitte mich zu entschuldigen!*' he exclaimed, and bolted from the room.

'Now, that's a most extraordinary thing.' The Provost contemplated his vanishing back in some astonishment. 'Kolmak is commonly a quiet, retiring sort of creature, very difficult to draw out. I sometimes think that his understanding of English is negligible, and that he puts odd misinterpretations . . .'

'But Kurt is a very good fellow, all the same.' Bultitude advanced, with a tread that made all the coffee cups in the room tinkle. 'I have become uncommonly fond of Kurt. Kurt's uncle –'

'Kurt?' The Provost was puzzled. 'I never heard you, my dear Mark, call him that before.'

Bultitude looked injured. 'Kurt Kolmak and I, Provost, have been on terms of increasing intimacy for some time. A very nice fellow, as I say. I don't know what bit him just now. Of course he had been through a great deal of stress. There was a period when, positively, he had to tighten his belt.' Bultitude, as he made this harrowing announcement, accomplished a reassuring exploration of his own waist-line, contriving with an effort that the tips of his fingers should touch just over his watch-chain. 'His people were liberals, and at the same time members of the old Hungarian nobility. Indeed Kurt's uncle Nikolaus, as I was about to observe, was the cousin of a very dear friend of mine, the old Gräfin Szegedin. Did you ever know the old lady? I recall her once saying to me . . .'

The Provost of Bede's assumed a resigned expression, and Dr Ourglass one of polite interest. But Sir John Appleby, less socially complacent, lingered only to give Bultitude a professionally analytical glance. Then, murmuring a word in his host's ear, he slipped from the room.

4. Bodley by Day

Many books
Wise men have said are wearisom.
Paradise Regain'd

I

A Complete Alphabetical List of the Resident members of the University of Oxford with Their Addresses is unquestionably the most useful publication of the multifariously active Oxford University Press. This work Sir John Appleby paused to consult in the Bede's porter's lodge; he then emerged into Beaumont Street and proceeded to move northwards at a leisurely pace. It was six minutes after nine o'clock. Christ Church, following its immemorial vespertine custom, was in the process of asserting its just hegemony of the lesser academic establishments clustered around it by the simple expedient of uttering a hundred-and-one magistral peals on an enormous bell. Abstraction grew upon Appleby as he walked. He was doubtful of the whole enterprise to which he had agreed to lend himself.

He was much attached to his youngest sister – only the more so because of the wide disparity between their ages. And Jane, very understandably, was in great distress over the disappearance of the young man to whom she had recently engaged herself. But Appleby had never met Geoffrey Ourglass, and he had a professional distrust of people who vanish. Follow up the sort of person who disappears and you will seldom come upon anything either very exciting or very edifying. Frequently you will be performing no kindness to those whom he has disappeared from.

And Appleby was equally doubtful about having come in upon the matter himself. Already, and from afar, he had seen to it that much in a quiet way had been done – so much, indeed, that the continued complete blank that Geoffrey Ourglass's fate presented had begun to take on an aspect of beguilement, of technical challenge, that he had, quite simply, found it very hard to resist. It had been reasonable enough to come up and stay for a night or two by way of fulfilling a promise to his old tutor, now the Provost of Bede's. And it was equally reasonable to employ the occasion for finding out a little more about Jane's young man. But he rather regretted the drift that the affair had taken in common-room that evening. A fairly substantial acquaintance with the academic classes had not altogether freed him from an early persuasion that dons are by nature so many gossiping old women. And he foresaw the Ourglass affair as possibly gaining more notoriety than he was at all inclined to welcome either on his sister's behalf or his own.

On the other hand – and now Appleby quickened his pace. For it was just possible that he had come upon something of real significance right at the start. It was just possible that this Geoffrey Ourglass was authentically the victim of something other than his own weakness or folly. For Jane's sake Appleby hoped that it might be so. And, after all, he had nowhere come upon any suggestion that the young man was either foolish or weak. These were not characteristics that would attract his sister. Moreover the qualities which the Provost had suspected in the young man had been those of adventuresomeness and rashness. It was perfectly conceivable that these might have led him to press into some situation more hazardous than healthy, and to do this from motives that were wholly reputable. And Appleby thought of a certain graph – one of many graphs in a file that never left his desk in New Scotland Yard. It bore a curve that required explaining. Perhaps he was walking in the direction of an explanation now.

And this must be the place. He had turned down a side-road, passed through a small garden and presented himself before a tall and narrow house of which the arched and carved windows were just visible beneath the night sky. He rang the bell. After rather a long wait a light flicked on above his head, the door opened, and he was confronted by a silver-haired old lady swathed in the faded magnificence of a large Paisley shawl. Appleby took off his hat. 'Is Dr Kolmak at home?' he asked.

The old lady found it necessary to give this question a moment's consideration. 'Dr Kolmak *came in*,' she said, 'a few minutes ago. But whether he is *at home* it is not, of course, for me to say.'

'Ah,' said Appleby.

'Dr Kolmak is my tenant. Or rather he is my sister's tenant. We had thought of a system of bells' – and the old lady made a vague gesture into the darkness – 'that would make the position *quite* plain.'

'An excellent idea. It would save you inconvenience.'

'Precisely.' The old lady appeared delighted with the perceptiveness of this reply. 'But tradesmen are so difficult nowadays. Lady Bronson has a system of bells. They were installed, however, by her nephew, who is interested in electricity and magnetism. I *ought* to have such an interest myself' – the old lady was apologetic – 'since my dear father was a close friend of Professor Faraday's.'

'That is most interesting.'

'Yes.' The old lady seemed a little doubtful on this point. Her communicativeness, it seemed to Appleby, was occasioned less by a preoccupation with the history of science than by uncertainty as to the correct technique for dealing with Dr Kolmak's visitors. It was to be presumed, therefore, that these were of comparatively infrequent appearance.

But now the old lady had an inspiration. 'The name?' she said interrogatively.

'Sir John Appleby.'

'Please come in. These things are a *little* difficult. Lady Bronson finds them *very* difficult. But then *her* tenants are *undergraduates*.'

'Ah, yes – a different matter.'

'Precisely. Dr Kolmak – who is of very good family – has recently been appointed to a lectureship at Bede's. We hope that he may be elected into a fellowship quite soon. There is *one* step.'

Appleby successfully negotiated the step and found a precarious foothold on the excessively slippery tiles of a dim, high hall. It was furnished with a number of impossible chairs designed to turn into suicidal step-ladders, and embellished with large photographic views of the Roman forum.

'The Kolmak domain – or should I say demesne? – is at the top of the house. Do you know that dear Frau Kolmak's pianoforte had to be taken in through the roof? She is an exquisite *artiste* and her playing is a great delight to us. Except, that is, when it clashes with my sister's Devotional Group. Will you please to come upstairs? I am afraid that the carpet is a little tricky in places. To be quite frank, there are *holes* in it, and no doubt it should be replaced. But my sister and I are too attached to our dear, shabby old things to be at all willing to part with them.'

Appleby contrived a murmur indicative of the conviction that such sentiments are the prerogative of highly-bred persons of fine tastes. 'The Kolmaks, then,' he asked, 'have not been with you long?'

'A *little* less than two years.'

'And besides Dr Kolmak himself there is just Frau Kolmak?'

'Just so. And you no doubt know that she is really a *Baronin*. But since coming into *exile* she prefers the simpler title. It is indicative of her exquisite *Gemütlichkeit*.' The old lady produced this word with a fine confidence which quite made up for its being not wholly apposite. 'We are even fonder of Dr Kolmak's aunt than of dear Dr Kolmak himself.'

'But you have never met other members of the family?'

'I have not had that pleasure. There was some question, indeed, of our receiving another member of the family – a female.' The old lady paused significantly. 'I must confess that my sister and I were a *little* anxious. The lady's relationship was, somehow, never very clearly *defined*. And with foreigners – particularly, I fear, *aristocratic* foreigners – one is never quite –' The old lady paused again, and evidently decided that this sentence had better be left in air. 'But the proposal seemed to "fade out" (as Lady Bronson's nephew is fond of saying) and I think some other arrangement must have been made. *One* more flight, and then I can simply *set you on your way* . . . But here is my sister.'

On a landing of modest proportions but lavishly medieval suggestion there stood another silver-haired old lady in another faded Paisley shawl. Appleby's conductress paused. 'My dear,' she said, 'let me introduce Sir John Appleby, a friend of Dr Kolmak's. Sir John, this is my sister, Miss Tinker.'

Miss Tinker bowed to Appleby. 'May I introduce you to my sister, Miss Priscilla Tinker?'

Appleby suitably acknowledged the propriety of these proceedings. The landing was small and cluttered on one side with an enormous carved chest and on the other side with a row of *prie-dieu*. These latter had something of the air of cabs waiting in a rank, and were no doubt brought into requisition during meetings of the elder Miss Tinker's Devotional Group. Meanwhile, they made things decidedly cramped. And this effect was enhanced by walls crowded with large Arundel prints themselves illustrative of uncomfortably populous fourteenth-century occasions. Perhaps it was the Gothic suggestiveness of the *décor* that gave Appleby an alarmed sense of the immateriality of the Misses Tinker. They were crowded up against him, and he felt that a single incautious step might take him clean through one or other of them. This would be interesting, but distracting – and he had better concentrate on the matter in hand. He therefore edged politely towards the next flight of stairs.

'I hope that you may not find Dr Kolmak unwell.' It was the elder Miss Tinker who spoke. 'He came in only a few minutes ago, and I happened to pass him on the stairs. We had not the few words of conversation that commonly pass between us. He appeared to be in some distress. I hope it is not an infection. There is not at present any epidemic in Oxford. But we heard only this afternoon that there is a great deal of bronchitis in Bournemouth.'

Appleby was now climbing. 'Please don't trouble yourselves further,' he said. 'I'll go straight up.' And he mounted, two steps at a time – aware of the Misses Tinker watching him still from below, like disappointed sirens whose singing has had only a momentary effectiveness. He realized that they would certainly be there when he came down again.

On the next landing there was a door apparently enclosing an upper staircase. Appleby knocked, but without result. He opened it and climbed higher. There was another doorway, at which he knocked again and waited. From within he could hear strains of music – a faint and uncanny music. If this was the *Baronin* discoursing on the pianoforte that had to be taken in through the roof then there could be no doubt that she in her turn would prove as ghostly as the old ladies below. The door opened and he was confronted by a handsome woman, old but very erect, who it was safe to guess must be the aunt of the man he was after.

'Good evening,' he said. 'Is Dr Kolmak at home?'

The woman eyed him steadily for a moment without reply.

Then she opened the door wider and in a manner that invited him to enter. The music came from an Aeolian harp set in a window.

'My name is Appleby, and I was dining in company with Dr Kolmak this evening. He left before I had an opportunity to talk to him, which I am very anxious to do.'

The woman inclined her head. 'My nephew,' she said, 'is unwell.'

'I am very sorry.' Appleby's tone was mild and conventional. Then suddenly he rapped out: 'You are alone with him here still?'

The unlikely shot went home and the woman's eyes momentarily widened in alarm. But she spoke composedly. 'If you will come into my *salotto*,' she said, 'we will talk together.' And she led the way from the tiny landing on which they had been standing into a massively furnished attic room. 'Please take place,' she said.

Nehmen Sie, bitte, Plaz . . . Frau Kolmak, like her nephew, appeared to preserve a good deal of native idiom. Appleby sat down. But his hostess for a moment remained standing. 'Are you, too, of the police?' she asked.

'Yes.' Appleby was startled, but saw no occasion for prevarication.

'Then, if you will excuse me, I must put on the kettle.'

'I beg your pardon?' Appleby supposed either that he had not heard aright or that, this time, Frau Kolmak's English had gone very markedly astray.

'Not on many days has one the pleasure of twice making tea for the English police . . . it is Mr Appleby?'

'Sir John Appleby.'

'*Ach!* This afternoon it was Detective-Inspector Jones – which sounds much grander, does it not? But you too shall have tea, Sir John.'

And Frau Kolmak applied herself to a spirit lamp. Appleby, unresentful of mockery, watched her composedly. She had considerably more address, he reflected, than her nephew. 'You are very kind,' he said. 'I shall be delighted to have tea.'

Frau Kolmak set a kettle on the lamp and turned back to him. 'It would be difficult to express to you,' she said, 'the charm of giving tea to a policeman; the charm – to put it in another way – of being in no expectation of being kicked by him.'

'I see.' Appleby looked at his hostess soberly.

'The officer who came this *Nachmittag* had a routine task. Unlike my nephew, I am legally of Hungarian nationality. It makes, at present, some difference in the formalities. But you, I judge, have nothing to do with that. You, who are of *die bessen Stände*, have come to control the police from the army, *nicht wahr?*'

'Oh, dear me, no.' Appleby was rather indignant. 'I joined the police as quite a young man, and right at the bottom.'

'That is most interesting.' For the first time Frau Kolmak looked faintly puzzled. Her urbanity, however, remained unflawed. It was, Appleby judged, too unflawed altogether. Frau Kolmak was really under considerable strain. Nevertheless her hands, as they busied themselves assembling what was evidently her formal tea-equipage, were perfectly steady. And presently she spoke again. 'Kurt talks very well – when his shyness is overcome, that is to say. So I am not surprised at your seeking his conversation. You, too, are interested in the art of the *trecento?*'

Appleby considered. 'It is an interest of my wife's,' he said conciliatingly. 'I'm afraid I myself know very little about it.'

'Nevertheless you have followed Kurt home for the sake of talk – knowing that he is *von grosser Unterhaltungsgabe?* What you have in mind is a purely social occasion?' Frau Kolmak quietly poured tea.

'I want your nephew's help in an investigation – a police investigation, in point of fact, although my own interest in it is personal and not official. It is a question of somebody's having disappeared.'

The small silver strainer which Frau Kolmak was manipulating tinkled against a tea-cup. 'Of a man's having disappeared?' she said.

'Yes, a young man – and, as it happens, an undergraduate at your nephew's college.'

'A young man from the *Studentenschaft* at Bede's? But how can Kurt –'

'*Guten Abend, mein Herr.*'

Appleby turned round. Kolmak was standing in the doorway – pale, and agitated to the point of being unconscious that he had spoken in German. Appleby put down his tea-cup and rose. 'Good evening, sir. I think you will recognize me, although we were not actually introduced.'

'Sir John Appleby.' Frau Kolmak had folded her hands in her lap and was looking at them. 'He has come to speak to you Kurt, about somebody – a man – who has disappeared.'

Kolmak bowed stiffly. 'I am afraid I can be of no assistance to you, sir, on that score. There must be a mistake.'

'That is perfectly possible, and if it is so I shall owe you, and Frau Kolmak, an apology.' Appleby judged it tactful to do a little bowing himself. 'Nevertheless I hope you will allow me to explain myself.'

Frau Kolmak's eyes travelled from her lap to her nephew's face, and thence to a chair. Kolmak sat down. 'I cannot well do otherwise,' he said coldly, 'to a guest of our Provost's. Please to proceed.'

'I think you overheard something of this matter in common-room just before leaving it – and although it concerns somebody at Bede's I believe that it was news to you. Very briefly, a young man called Geoffrey Ourglass, who ought to be up at Oxford now, has vanished. He is, as it happens, engaged to be married to my sister Jane, who is an undergraduate at Somerville. My own concern with the situation is solely on account of this connexion.'

Kolmak again bowed frigidly. 'We express our regrets,' he said. 'Our sympathy is extended to your sister.'

Frau Kolmak slightly flushed. 'Kurt,' she said dryly, 'you seem quite to have guessed that Sir John is connected with the police.'

'The police!' Kolmak appeared not, in fact, to have guessed the fact, for he now sat up very straight in his chair.

'Please remember that his colleagues have always been friendly to us as well as courteous.'

'Tante Lise, you do not understand the danger –'

'I have understood many dangers, Kurt, *liebling*, for now a long time. I shall say nothing more, but my advice to you is as it has been.'

During this enigmatical interchange, Appleby conveniently occupied himself with his tea. Now he tried again.

'About this young man's disappearance we have only one approach to a clue. He is believed to have been seen in a car, driving through a small village in the Cotswolds. It is so out-of-the-way that it is very tempting to believe that his destination must have been a local one. Inquiries, however, have produced no result. I have been prepared to believe that Ourglass was, in fact, passing through to a remote destination, or that the identification was a mistake.'

Kolmak had ceased to sit back stiffly on his chair. He had leant forward, and his head was now buried in his hands.

'And now, Dr Kolmak, I must be quite frank, and come to my sole reason for calling on you. This evening you heard the story. Or rather you heard the fact of somebody's disappearance associated with the name of this village – Milton Porcorum. You at once evinced sharper interest and marked agitation. You were so aware, indeed, of having betrayed a peculiarity of behaviour that you abruptly left common-room, and hurried home, feeling ill. Please understand that I should be lacking in my duty to my sister and to this young man – who may well be in some situation of great danger – if I failed to make the most earnest attempt to persuade you to an explanation.'

There was a long silence. Then Kolmak looked up abruptly. 'It is your sister's lover,' he said, '– her *Verlobter* – who has disappeared?'

'It is, indeed.'

Kolmak passed a hand wearily over his forehead. 'If you were but a private gentleman!' he exclaimed.

'If you have something to reveal, you ought to reveal it. Here is a young girl in cruel suspense and a young man in unknown danger.'

'As if I had no cause to feel it!' And Kolmak looked quite wildly round the room.

'I appeal to you, sir, as a scholar – as a scholar and a humanist.' Appleby too had stood up.

'Come back – come back tomorrow morning.' Kolmak appeared to be swaying uncertainly on his feet.

'Tomorrow may be –' Appleby checked himself. Out of the corner of his eye he had seen Frau Kolmak make him an almost imperceptible sign. 'Very well. I will call immediately after breakfast – say at nine o'clock. And, meantime, thank you for listening to me.' Appleby moved to the door and from there bowed to his hostess. 'And thank you, very much, for entertaining your second policeman to tea.'

2

The Misses Tinker were on the landing below, tiptoeing about with rubber hot-water bottles. Appleby sustained their conversation in some absence of mind. Their brother, it appeared, had been Junior Proctor some time in the eighteen-eighties and had been a distinguished advocate of higher female education in the University. Their father had visited Germany as a young man, returned under the novel persuasion that dons ought to engage in research, and in this cause conducted sundry heroic skirmishes against both the obscurantists of Christ Church and the utilitarians of Balliol. At a more convenient season Appleby would have derived a good deal of entertainment from ladies who appeared to regard themselves as contemporaries of Mrs Humphry Ward. As it was, he contrived to withdraw through the barrage with civil words. The elder Miss Tinker showed him out. As she opened the front door he fancied he heard Kolmak in colloquy with Miss Priscilla above. Perhaps he was explaining to her that he expected his visitor again at an unconscionably early hour.

North Oxford was already sinking into slumber. Appleby walked through the quiet streets lost in thought. The disappearance of Geoffrey Ourglass was linked – tenuously, it was true – with an unimportant place owning the picturesque name of Milton Porcorum. Between Ourglass and Kolmak there was virtually no reason to suppose any connexion whatever. Kolmak had nothing to do with the teaching side of life at Bede's, and he had not the appearance of one who cultivates the social acquaintance of undergraduates. Unless there were one or two historians of art among them – and young Ourglass's interests were certainly remote enough from that – they would be no more to him, in all probability, than vaguely recognizable faces. What had interested and agitated Kolmak was not the disappearance of Ourglass, but the linking together of the concept of *disappearance* and the name of *Milton Porcorum*. It was not necessary to stare at this fact for very long before forming a hypothesis. Only the most slender observation, it was true, lay behind it. Still, it was worth holding on to and testing out. *When people disappear, one hears talk of Milton Porcorum.*

Beguiled by this odd proposition, Appleby turned a corner. Why Milton Porcorum? It was a place without significance or marked attraction, offering no unusual facilities for either a life of anonymous beneficence or a period of covert vice. From the insignificance of Milton Porcorum could there be inferred – hazardously indeed but perhaps crucially – another conclusion? *Persons whose disappearance is associated with Milton Porcorum have not been attracted into the void. They have been pushed.*

Appleby had arrived so far in this decidedly uncertain ratiocinative process when his attention was abruptly recalled to the outer world. He was making his way back to the centre of Oxford by certain quiet roads which were very familiar to him, and for some little way he had passed nobody except a single elderly man belatedly exercising a small dog on a lead. But now another figure was approaching him – or rather (what was the occasion of abrupting his train of thought) had faltered in doing so and was rapidly disappearing up a side-road a little way ahead.

That falter was well-known to Appleby. He had encountered it often enough during the couple of years he had spent with a helmet and a bull's-eye lantern long ago. Instinctively he quickened his pace and turned the corner. Only a little cul-de-sac presented itself. And in this, dimly visible beneath a single lamp, a meagre and apprehensive man stood at bay.

Appleby was amused. It had never occurred to him that he might still give to a practised criminal eye the appearance of a plain-clothes officer on duty. At a guess, the man was a known burglar, with tools for breaking and entering now on his person, and in thinking to give Appleby a wide berth had taken this unlucky cast down a blind alley.

But at the same time Appleby was puzzled. If he carried his tools with him, the fellow ought not yet to be abroad. The night was still too young by far. Appleby took another look at him, and became aware of two facts. They were facts that fitted together. The man was not merely scared or nervous; he was in very great and naked terror. And he was Stuart Buffin's rabbity fellow with the scratched face. He had been up a telephone pole and – more mysteriously – 'in Miles's cat'. Stuart had not been romancing. He had veritably encountered a sort of museum specimen of that grand stand-by of the popular cinema, the hunted man.

Rather as if to repudiate the charge of craven orthodoxy in this role, the man in front of Appleby began to scream. It was an effect that Appleby did not recall having witnessed. The man did not, it was true, scream very loudly, being temporarily afflicted, it appeared, with some hysterical constriction of the vocal cords. Nevertheless the performance was extremely displeasing, and Appleby could see no better way of ending it than by turning on his heel and marching out of the picture. This simple plan he proceeded to put into effect.

But as he walked away he found himself uneasy on two quite distinct scores. The first proceeded from a habitual sense of responsibility for public order. This wretched little man was nothing to him; nevertheless he was either in some real danger or so far gone in lunacy as to be himself dangerous to others. Perhaps therefore he should be tackled and controlled at once, however much he screamed, and whatever indignation the proceeding aroused among disturbed residents in the district.

Appleby's second uneasiness was more obscure. He had a queer feeling that the man *was* in some way part of his direct concern. Yet he could assign himself no shadow of reason for this belief. Appleby snapped his fingers in vexation – and in the same instant was in command of the hidden connexion he sought. Kolmak! It was not once but twice that Kolmak had broken into other people's talk earlier that evening. The second occasion had been the notable one concerning Milton Porcorum. The first had been the mention of Stuart's rabbity fugitive as having a scratched cheek. And Appleby could now recall that both these interjections had possessed precisely the same quality.

He was on the point of emerging from the cul-de-sac. The man had stopped screaming. Appleby turned and saw that he was endeavouring to scale a wholly impossible brick wall. He watched him for some moments until he fell back panting and exhausted; then he spoke quietly down the length of the cul-de-sac.

'I'm not your enemy. Try to think. You are unarmed and helpless. If I want you, I've got you.'

The man had turned and was standing immobile, his arms spread-eagled against the wall. He was one, Appleby fleetingly thought, who had unconsciously a sense of style, an actor's instinct. It would make an effective shot.

'There would be no sense in my standing talking like this until, perhaps, the police came along and I had to clear out. So you can see you're in no danger with me.'

The man straightened himself, but said nothing.

'I do, as it happens, know something about you. You've been up a telephone pole. And you've been in Miles's cat.'

The man made a sudden dash for where, in the brickwork by which he was imprisoned, he had belatedly glimpsed a green-painted wooden door. He shook it furiously. It was locked. He turned again, and spoke at last.

'You're one of them.' His voice was at once high and hoarse. 'You're one of them, or you couldn't know that.'

'Nonsense.' Appleby got out a pipe and proceeded to fill it. 'One of the children told about it. The one that helped you. And look here: *he* knew about the telephone pole, but your enemies didn't. Isn't that right? If I was one of them, I wouldn't have tumbled to that yet.'

'They're clever enough.'

'And a lot too clever to stand jawing like this. Where are you trying to get to?'

The man hesitated. 'Into Oxford. But I lost my way. I want to get into a crowd.'

'Come along, then – we'll go together.'

The man didn't move.

'You're in a trap there, if this *is* a trap; and you can't make matters worse by coming out. Look, I'm crossing over to the other side of the road. You can come up here and see that there's nobody else about. And then we can go where you think it's healthy.'

Appleby suited his action to his words. The road was still quite empty. And presently the meagre man cautiously emerged into it. He looked about him warily but dully, and then crossed over. 'I wouldn't have believed that the old professor was one,' he said. 'But he was.'

Appleby realized that the man beside him was played out in both mind and body. Perhaps he needed food. And certainly he needed sleep. 'If we go by Walton Street,' he said, 'we can get a cup of coffee still at a place quite near this end.'

The meagre man was glancing swiftly from side to side as he walked, like a creature moving through the jungle. But Appleby doubted whether he retained much power to descry, let alone to ward off, danger. The dash down the cul-de-sac had been a pitifully feeble move. The man was approaching, in fact, a state of somnambulism. His response now, although designed as truculent, was ineffective. 'Who are you, anyway?' he said. 'Nobody asked you to come interfering with me.'

'Well, we do sometimes get what we don't ask for.'

A car went by, close to the kerb, as Appleby spoke. And the meagre man's whole body quivered. 'They've got a van out,' he said. 'And cars too. Smashed one great car, they did – and two of them ought to have broken their ruddy necks. But there's none of them dead yet, worse luck. None – see?'

'I see. None of them dead.'

'The law should get them.' Suddenly the meagre man's voice sharpened. 'What are you, anyway? That's what I ask. Are you the police?'

'Yes – I *am* the police.'

What might have been either a curse or a sob broke from the meagre man. He stumbled – lifting a knee queerly, as if he had made a wholly futile attempt to run.

'Here you are. Hot coffee, and a sandwich if you want it.' And Appleby steered his captive – if he was that – to a table in the small café he had had in mind. 'Your head will feel clearer, you know, when you've had that.'

He fetched coffee from the counter, glancing about him as he did so. There was nobody in the place except a sleepy woman presiding over the stuff stewing in urns, and a man and a girl in a corner, staring at each other in heavy-eyed misery. It was not very cheerful. But Appleby doubted whether a more festive atmosphere would much have encouraged his new acquaintance.

'Here you are. Sugar in the saucer.'

The meagre man took the coffee in two trembling hands, stirred, and drank. A couple of mouthfuls appeared to give him sufficient strength to take up matters where he had left them. 'I never had anything to do with the police,' he said. 'They've no call to come after me.'

'They haven't – not so far as I know.' Appleby put down his pipe and produced a packet of cigarettes. 'Smoke?'

The meagre man reached forward and took a cigarette as an addict might snatch an offered drug. 'Thanks,' he said. It was a word the enunciation of which appeared to afford him peculiar difficulty.

Appleby faintly smiled. With this customer he was on familiar ground enough. A little twister who could put up a genteel show among the simple, and get away with a pound note on the strength of one plausible tale or another. Appleby had often seen them, and often seen them scared – of six months, or two years, or perhaps a thrashing from some dupe's brawny husband. But he had never seen one as hard-pressed as this. Stuart's rabbit with the scratched cheek had been out in deep water. And he didn't like the feel of it.

'No,' said Appleby, 'I don't suppose the police have any call to come after you. But perhaps you have a call to go after them.'

The meagre man looked up quickly. 'I don't know what you mean,' he said.

'I rather think you do. The only way out of some tough spots is through the police station. It's a bit bleak. But it's as safe as Buckingham Palace.' Appleby paused. 'Even,' he said, 'if they keep you for rather a long time. Safety. Quiet and safety and all found . . . Safety . . . *safety*.'

The meagre man's head was nodding. 'You're a devil,' he whispered, 'a clever devil.' With an effort he looked straight at Appleby, raised his cup and drained it, let it clatter back into the saucer. 'See here,' he said – and his voice strove again for truculence. 'What sort of policeman are you, anyway? You don't *sound* to me like a policeman. Too much the bloody gentleman, you are. A bloody gentleman up to something dirty – that's you. Well, don't come to me.'

'Shall I get you another cup of coffee?'

The meagre man shook his head. His eyes were filling with tears of helplessness and rage. 'Policeman, indeed!' he pursued. 'How'd you like to come to the mucking station and see what they say? Oxford cop, eh?'

'Not Oxford. London.'

With the effect of some tiny mechanism starting into motion, one of the meagre man's cheeks began to twitch. 'You mean you're from the C.I.D.?'

'One of my duties is to look after the C.I.D.'

'Christ!' The meagre man looked at Appleby for a moment with all the sobriety of conviction. Then – totally unexpectedly – he smiled. It was not a very pleasant smile, but neither was it malignant. It was a smile, Appleby knew, of suddenly gratified vanity. The little twister endeavoured to square his shoulders in their cheap padded jacket. Then he leant forward. 'I'll tell you something,' he whispered. 'I'll tell you something to surprise your ruddy highness. I'll be bigger than you one day . . . bigger by a long way. I'll give your C.I.D. its orders – see? Yes, and the ruddy Government too.'

Coffee, fatigue and a little applied psychology, Appleby reflected, will sometimes do the work of large charges of alcohol. 'Well, why not?' he said. 'A man can always have a bit of luck.'

'You need more than luck. You need guts.'

'Ah – to grab what's there for the grabbing.'

'What d'you mean?' The meagre man made a spasmodic movement of his right hand towards his breast. 'I haven't grabbed anything. So you needn't think it.'

'Nobody said you had.' Appleby rose and went over to the counter for a second cup of coffee. In his jacket pocket the fellow had something he set store by – and something he had grabbed.

'I've lost my wallet.' The man spoke quickly and defensively as Appleby returned to the little table. He tapped his chest with a hand that trembled. 'Left it in a pub where I got some supper. Cleared me out.'

'Bad luck.' He had some command of his wits still, Appleby thought. He had realized the betrayal in that involuntary movement, and he had thought up this yarn to cover it. Only – what was rather odd – he had made the yarn sound as if it were true. Possibly it *was* true. 'You mean,' Appleby asked, 'that you haven't a penny?'

'Not a mucking farthing. And it's damned unfair.' The man's voice rose in a disagreeable but convincingly authentic whine. 'It means I'm helpless against them, just when it all looked like coming my way.'

'It sounds just too bad.' Appleby applied himself to stirring his fresh cup of coffee. When he looked up it was to see his companion glancing furtively and apprehensively first out into the darkened street and then at the lovers sitting glumly over their silent quarrel in the other corner. 'About that cat –' Appleby said.

The meagre man's head swung round as if at the blow of a fist. His face was ashen. 'What do you know?' he said hoarsely. 'It wasn't me! The cat got on his shoulder and he tripped. The gun went off –' He fell back in his chair, and both his hands went to his throat as if to choke words that it would be fatal to utter.

'There was a gun in this affair of Miles's cat?'

'You're making me mix things.' The voice was now no more than a whisper. 'It's not evidence. It's against the law. The judges don't allow it.'

'Never mind the judges, Mr –?'

'Routh.'

Appleby looked at his companion curiously. He was certainly pretty well through; he had handed over his name as if drugged. It was the moment for a shot that was wholly in the dark. 'Routh,' he asked sharply, 'when were you last in Milton Porcorum?'

It was a hit. The man calling himself Routh uttered a strangled cry and made a futile effort to get to his feet. 'You *do* belong to them,' he whispered. 'You must. You know.'

'I am a policeman. I know a good deal, but I am a policeman, all the same.' Appleby's voice, low, slow and clear, was like a hypnotist's addressing a man in a trance. 'The cats, Routh. Miles's cat. The other cat. They are both out of the bag. But you are safe with the police. Safe. We'll go to the police station and you can tell me just as much as you want to. Or they'll give you a bed. They always do, if you've lost all your money. A bed where the biggest gang of crooks in England couldn't get at you. Come along.'

And Appleby got Routh to his feet and out of the café. It was like handling a drunk. The night air was chilly but the man scarcely revived in it: his feet scraped and stumbled on the pavement; his head turned from side to side blindly in an empty convention of vigilance. He would be an unsuitable guest to introduce into the Provost's lodgings, for he would provoke too much curiosity on the part of anyone who set eyes on him. Yet Appleby was determined to hold on to Routh. In some undefined way the man was a link in the chain – tenuous but perhaps vital – that bound together Ourglass and Kolmak and Milton Porcorum. The police station, then, was the thing. If Routh had no great crime or misdemeanour on his conscience, then tact, a square meal, warmth, the law in its benevolent aspect of a powerful protector, would in all probability get his story from him. Alternatively, there was the fact that he was without visible means of support and had been loitering in a manner suggesting wrongful intentions; on the strength of this the poor devil could be charged, and his background and movements rapidly investigated.

But it was a considerable distance to police headquarters in St Aldate's, and Appleby remembered that there would still be cabs in the rank in St Giles'. He turned left down a side-street. 'Come along,' he said encouragingly. 'We'll cut down here and get a taxi.'

Routh hesitated. 'It's dark,' he whispered. 'And lonely. I don't like it. They may be waiting in it.'

The little street was certainly deserted and poorly lighted. Appleby took a side glance at the dim silhouette of his companion, wondering what queer adventure had reduced him to this state. 'I don't think we need worry about that,' he said. 'We're in Oxford, you know; not Cairo or Casablanca.'

He took Routh's arm and gently impelled him forward. The man moved on beside him, unsteadily, but without resistance. Appleby felt satisfied. This was an odd and unexpected evening's work. But he had an instinct that it was getting him somewhere, and that he had at least a fringe of his problem under control.

At this moment Routh gave a weak cry, and for a fraction of a second Appleby was aware of himself as surounded by figures that had sprung up apparently from nowhere. Then something was thrown over his face, and his head swam. He heard the engine of a car coming up the deserted street behind him. He smelt what he recognized as chloroform. He was fleetingly aware of having made a mistake – some ridiculous mistake. And then consciousness deserted him.

3

Like Pericles in the play, Appleby came to his senses to the sound of music. For what appeared an infinity of time it was a music of obscurely sinister suggestion. It set a problem with which his mind seemed to wrestle down long corridors. It reminded him of some careless and fatal error. For this he hunted through long stretches of labouring hours. And then it came to him. He had, through some absurd vagary of the mind, imagined himself in Oxford when he was, of course, in Cairo. This music witnessed to the sober geographical truth. It was like no music that is familiar to western ears. Rising and falling fitfully, it passed from harmony to discord and from discord to harmony . . .

Memory stirred abruptly in Appleby. He opened his eyes upon a small room into which daylight was filtering through a light-coloured blind. He was on a bed, partly undressed, and warm beneath a feather covering. Frau Kolmak was standing beside him with a coffee-pot. And from just outside came the low music of the Aeolian harp.

'Good morning, Sir John. I believe you are none the worse for your adventure – no?' Frau Kolmak set down the coffee, turned to the window, raised the blind, and appeared to take an appraising glance at the roofs of North Oxford. 'Kurt will be here *augenblicklich* – in a moment. He is shaving. The possession of a bathroom is a great satisfaction to him.'

Appleby sat up. 'Does your nephew commonly go about the streets at night, chloroforming people?'

Frau Kolmak laughed. 'You are confused. He will explain. I too am confused. It appears that Kurt has said something to the driver of a cab – something that in Oxford he judged it not possible to say. He is pleased.' Frau Kolmak lowered her voice. 'There are matters of which I hope he will speak to you.' She glided from the room.

Appleby sat up and drank the coffee. It seemed to him extremely good. But it always does, he reflected lucidly, when provided by persons with continental associations. Preponderantly, it must be a matter of suggestion. He looked up and saw Kolmak standing before him.

Kolmak bowed. In his prized private bathroom he had evidently shaved with the greatest nicety; he was dressed with some formality in a black jacket and striped trousers; this, Appleby conjectured was a civil tribute to the presence in his household of a high official of the police. 'Good morning,' Kolmak said. 'I hope, Sir John, that you are not too badly shaken –'

'I'm not shaken at all. Where is Routh?'

'Your companion of last night? He is in the little room' – Kolmak made some gesture indicating some far corner of his domain – 'and still asleep. I had not realized that he was your colleague.'

'My colleague?' Appleby stared, and then – a little painfully – smiled. 'Well, we'll talk about that presently. Will you tell me first how we got back here?'

'With the man you call Routh there was no difficulty. He is of slight build. I got him upstairs myself. But you, Sir John, presented a more serious problem.' Kolmak paused and clicked his fingers. He appeared confused. 'But how clumsy I am in expressing myself in English still! I do not mean to suggest that you are a *heavy* man. Your figure, if I may say so, might reasonably be described as a spare one – is not that the word? But your height –'

'Quite so. But do I understand that you really managed to haul me up all those stairs while unconscious? It's unbelievable.'

'The difficulty was not insuperable. My aunt helped. And the Misses Tinker too.'

'God bless me!' Appleby drained his coffee and swung himself off the bed. 'Didn't they think it a little out of the way?'

Kolmak nodded with some solemnity. 'I ventured to suggest to them that matters of state security were involved. They will be models of discretion. And discretion appeared to me to be the most important. I knew, Sir John, that your position in the police did not necessarily mean that you wished any of your colleagues to be officially associated with you at the moment. This consideration guided my course of action from the first.'

'I congratulate you.' Appleby looked at his host in some astonishment. 'And may I ask just what *was* your course of action from the first? So far as I can make the thing out, this fellow Routh and I were waylaid and kidnapped by an uncommonly bold gang of criminals. And now – here we are, hoisted up to your delightful flat through the efforts of your aunt and the Misses Tinker. If you feel at all like it, I should welcome an explanation.'

'By all means. When you left us last night I was agitated, I was uneasy. The thought of your sister's anxiety was very distressing to me. There are reasons why I should feel for her. After only a little hesitation I followed you downstairs, meaning to invite you back, or perhaps to have some conversation with you on your walk to Bede's. But one of the Misses Tinker held me in talk – it is the habit of these *Damen*, as you will have remarked – and by the time that I got out of the house you were some way ahead. I hesitated, and followed you irresolutely for some way. Then you disappeared down the *Sackgasse* – how do you say it?'

'The cul-de-sac.'

'*Aber!* How wise you English are to enrich your already expressive language from the French! In Germany our purism in such matters – But that is not the point. I waited and heard voices. I was nervous – unaccountably nervous – and I concealed myself. When you appeared again it was with this man. For a second I saw him clearly under the street-lamp. It was a shock to me. You must understand –' Kolmak hesitated.

'That you had had certain dealings with Routh already?'

'*Ja – wahrhaftig!* I was startled that you should be associated with him. It was something that put me at a loss. I followed you at a distance until you disappeared into the little café. I lingered nearby, wondering whether to join you. You will judge, Sir John, that my conduct by this time was quite irrational. But I continued in doubt, and when you came out I followed you again. It was thus that I was near by when the attack was launched upon you.'

Appleby smiled. 'It seems fortunate that they didn't chloroform you too.'

'I was much disposed to sail in.' Kolmak paused, apparently pleased with his command of this English idiom. 'But there were four or five of them, and it seemed unlikely that I could improve matters. It was very well timed, and they had you both in the van in an instant. No sooner had they done so, however, than there was the sound of a car approaching from the far end of the street. At once they scattered, and the van drove off. But now I come to the odd thing.'

'To what you found it possible to say to a taxi-driver?'

'*Ganz richtig!* What approached was a taxi – and empty. In Oxford – I cannot tell why – one may not hail all taxis, but only certain taxis. It is a system I do not understand. But this taxi I hailed. It stopped. I jumped in and said "Follow that van".'

'It was most resourceful of you, Dr Kolmak.'

'The man did so – without hesitation! We drove some way – I think it must have been down Little Clarendon Street – and were presently in St Giles'. I had a further thought. I said "Pass it before we reach Carfax". He was the most understanding man. He ignored the traffic lights at Broad Street – this, I hope, will not get him into trouble – and was well ahead as we approached the crossroads. I called to him to stop, thrust a note into his hand, and jumped out. My hope was that the lights at Carfax would be against the van. And they were! I was waiting as it drew up. I stepped into the road. There was nobody but the driver, and the window on his near side was open. I thrust in an arm, switched off the engine, and withdrew the key. He was immobilized.'

Appleby laughed. 'I am tempted to say that you have missed your true vocation.'

'There was a constable, as there commonly is, on the farther kerb. But I was uncertain of the wisdom of inviting official intervention. I therefore said to the driver "Get out and go away; otherwise I will summon the constable." He obeyed, for plainly he had no choice in the matter. I at once took his place, put back the key in the ignition, and drove on. The constable may have thought that the engine had failed – what is the word?'

'Stalled.'

'Thank you – stalled. But he was aware of nothing further. I took the route by Pembroke Street and St Ebbe's, and drove home.'

'You still have the van?'

'No. When I had broken into it at the back, and the two of you were safely here stowed in the flat, it occurred to me that the van might well betray your whereabouts, supposing that those people were prowling the streets again. So I drove it to the car park near Gloucester Green and left it there.'

Appleby was putting on his jacket. 'I am extremely grateful to you. And so should this fellow Routh be too. By the way, I think we'd better go and have a look at him.'

'You are sure that you are quite all right?'

Appleby smiled a trifle grimly. 'I've had to recover from worse knocks before now – and a good deal more quickly. Moreover I shall feel a bit of an ass until I've caught up with this whole queer racket. It comes back to me now that, seconds before they caught me out, I was paying myself smug compliments on getting along very nicely.'

'Like many of your countrymen, you surprise me, Sir John.' Kolmak moved to the door. 'In Germany – even in Austria – you would be a very strange policeman. I remember – Why, Tante Lise, *was ist's?*'

Frau Kolmak had entered the room in some precipitation. '*Was ist's?*' she repeated expressively. 'But he is gone – the other one! *Da liegt der Hund begraben.*'

Kurt Kolmak sat down on the bed and threw up his hands in despair. 'That I should not have thought to keep watch! And here has been Sir John complimenting me as one deft in such matters!'

'You mean that Routh has gone?' Appleby spoke sharply. 'They have got him?'

Frau Kolmak shook her head. 'He has gone – but freely. Nobody could have come to him. Our door was secured inside, and so was the house-door below. He too, after his adventure, slept through the night. An hour ago I took him coffee. Then, only a little after, I heard sounds of a door closing. *Leider*, I did not think! It must have been this man stealing out.'

'Then, for the moment, we have lost him.' Appleby smiled. 'He must have managed it uncommonly quietly to escape the conversation of the ladies below. Particularly after the excitements to which you introduced them last night. They must be all agog. Have you a telephone?'

'It is a thing impossible to obtain. But the Misses Tinker –'

'Then I think I will go down and beg the use of it. Your nephew was very wise to feel that we should avoid publicity. But this is now a matter for the local police, all the same. The fellow Routh must be found. So must that van. And one or two other things must be investigated as well. Then, Dr Kolmak, if I might borrow your bathroom and a razor –'

Kolmak beamed. 'But certainly! You will find the bathroom, for a household of this modest character, exceptionally well appointed.'

Appleby hurried out. The Aeolian harp was playing softly on the little landing. Through the open window it pointed at the Radcliffe Observatory on the sky-line, as if its operation depended on perpetual cupfuls of air tossed to it by the whirling anemometer. Appleby gave the instrument a glance of some affection as he passed. Cairo was well enough. But it was satisfactory to be back in Oxford.

4

The Misses Tinker were below, crowned with mob-caps and equipped with feather-dusters. Appleby much doubted whether their discretion would long be proof against the charm of retailing to Lady Bronson and their other North Oxford acquaintances of the same kidney the sensational events that had lately transacted themselves beneath their roof. By the time that his telephone calls were made and his shaving in the Kolmak bathroom accomplished, Frau Kolmak had provided in her *salotto* a breakfast for one, impeccably presented after the most orthodox English fashion. Appleby sat down to it very willingly. 'I got on to the Provost,' he said to Kolmak, 'and told him that I had domesticated myself here for the night. He remarked that my comfort could not be in better hands than those of your aunt.'

'Kurt has a communication to make to you.' Frau Kolmak spoke with a trace of nervousness, as if she could not be quite sure of her nephew's communicativeness until he was launched upon it. 'But I know that at breakfast the English have the custom of reading *The Times*. It is at your elbow, Sir John; and if we might perhaps leave you –'

'Decidedly not.' Appleby was emphatic. 'Quite soon I must go out and see my sister, and get going on a number of other things as well. It is most desirable that we should have this talk at once.'

'Then I will explain to you.' Abruptly Kolmak sat down at the opposite side of the table. 'My aunt has a daughter. Or rather –' He hesitated. 'How the English flies out when a little emotion, a little distress, come in! This daughter, this Anna, *verstehen Sie*, is *ein angenommenes Kind* –'

'I understand. An adopted child.'

'*Also!* Anna is a highly educated woman – an *Ärztin*, skilled in the treatment of children.'

'A doctor – a children's specialist.'

'*Ja doch!* And she herself has a child – a fine boy of five.'

'She is a widow?'

Kolmak hesitated. 'In fact and law, no. But, morally, yes. Anna's husband has left her. He too is a doctor, and he long practised in Breslau – a city to which some ridiculous new name has lately been given. Now he is in Leningrad, directing some *wichtig* – some important – medical research. But his wife and child he would not take with him, although it would have been permitted. His motive I shall leave undiscussed. It was not reputable. Anna, with her child, was stranded. We strove that they might come here. But there were difficulties.'

'Anna is legally this Russian doctor's wife?'

'Yes.'

'I see.' Appleby had a long and saddened familiarity with tangles of this sort – the private aftermath of Europe's public follies. 'Then there might certainly be difficulties, as you say.'

Kolmak nodded gloomily. 'And then the matter was taken out of our hands. You must understand that Anna was very anxious indeed to come to England.'

'She had some compelling reason?'

'But naturally.' It was Frau Kolmak who answered this, and in some haste. 'I had brought her up. She wished that she and the child might be with me here.'

Kolmak straightened himself in his chair. 'There was a further reason. We are deeply in love.'

'It seems a very good reason.' Appleby looked gravely at the man sitting stiffly before him. 'And then something decisive happened?'

'Anna came.'

'She managed to get to England in some irregular way?'

'She did. She was impatient – and she is resolute and able.'

'And the child?'

'She brought the child too.'

Appleby smiled. 'I think,' he said dryly, 'that Anna must be decidedly able. And then?'

'She was in London. We were much distressed. We hoped that permission might yet be gained, and that she could come to us here. But there seemed to be no way to begin. It was a *Stillstand* – an impasse.'

'Matters certainly weren't improved.'

'It was decided that she must leave the country as she had come, and that we must begin again. But it would be yet some weeks before that could be arranged. Anna, who knows English well, decided to go into the country. There were difficulties, you understand, about remaining in one place. So she bought a bicycle, with a little seat for the child, and with a rucksack she set off. She passed through Oxford, going west, and almost every day we had a letter. But the letters stopped. For a time we were not alarmed. A week passed, and we worried. But I had no means of making inquiries. Then, one day, I received this.'

Kolmak produced a pocket-book and from it drew something which he placed before Appleby. It was a plain postcard. On one side, written in a clear, foreign hand, was Kolmak's name and address. On the other, in the same hand, was the message:

Both unharmed. Do nothing. A

For a moment Appleby studied this in silence. 'When did it come?' he asked at length.

'Three weeks ago today. And it was dispatched, you will see from the postmark, in the little place called Milton Porcorum.'

'And without a stamp.'

'Yes, indeed. The Misses Tinker, who take in our mail, had to pay when it was delivered. That is one of the puzzling things.'

'Does Anna usually write in English?'

'No. But on a postcard she must have thought that it would be less noticeable.'

'Her English, you say, is good? It is good enough for her not to write "unharmed" when she meant, simply, "well"?'

'Assuredly.'

'When travelling, we sometimes send messages reading "Arrived safely". So there is a shade of difference between "Both safe" and "Both unharmed". She would be aware of that? You are aware of it?'

'Certainly. You must understand that, although our conversation is imperfect, our understanding of English is fully literary. "Unharmed" seemed strange to me at once. It was the reason of my venturing to disobey Anna's injunction. We were gravely concerned. Difficult as Anna's position was, there was nevertheless something altogether strange in this message.'

'You are quite sure that it is in her hand?'

'Both my aunt and I are certain of it.'

'How did you disobey this injunction? You didn't go to the police?'

'Certainly not. I was assuredly not entitled to do anything of the sort. But I went down to Milton Porcorum. It proved to be a small village with nothing remarkable about it. I felt that I must not so far disregard Anna's message as to go about asking questions. So I learnt nothing. In the afternoon I sought for aerodromes near by. The idea had come to me that Anna might have found at such a place a friend willing to fly her straight out of the country. But I was wasting my time, and I knew it. Anna's message did not – did not cohere with such a thing.'

Appleby nodded gravely. 'I agree with you.'

'So I returned to Oxford. Then evil thoughts came to me. It is painful to speak of them. Tante Lise, you must explain.'

Frau Kolmak had been sitting quite still by her piano – the same, Appleby conjured, that had come in through the roof. But now she turned to the two men. 'Kurt thought that Anna might be saying good-bye to us – that she might be shaking us off. He was ill with the strain of this anxiety, Sir John, and these ideas visited him. Some offer of security and affluence made by a powerful man – a protector, you understand? – had tempted her.' Frau Kolmak smiled gently. 'This was a most foolish notion, for my daughter is a very honest woman. It was a brief sickness of Kurt's, however, which we must mention, since it serves to explain how he came to make his discovery.'

'His discovery?' Appleby swung round on Kolmak. 'You *know* something?'

'Indeed I do. With these certainly foolish thoughts in my head, I went back to this little village several times, and I endeavoured to explore the whole neighbourhood. I took field-glasses. What I was interested in now was great houses – the homes of wealthy people of the kind to which might belong, I fancied, Anna's seducer. These are horrible words to speak.'

'But your discovery?'

'For a time I was almost mad, and I went about with my field-glasses like some unhappy man constrained to spy upon the privacy of others. And one house in particular tormented me, since it lies in the greatest seclusion. I came upon it, in the first instance, early in my search, since it is quite close to the village itself. It is, in fact, the historical manor house of both Milton Porcorum and Milton Canonicorum. There is a park surrounded by a high wall; and plantations and the lie of the ground make the house and all that lies near it virtually invisible from any public road. But my concentration was such that I found one spot – a small hillock to the west – from which

342

I could just bring into focus the corner of a formal garden. I studied it intently for a long time – perhaps more than an hour – and saw no one moving in it. Then something caught my attention in that part of the park that lay nearest to it. The park, I should say, is in places oddly subdivided by high wire fences, as if the owner, perhaps, keeps several species of animal that he desires not to mingle. What I was looking at was a small field so enclosed – do you not call it a paddock? – and lying, I judged, quite close to the invisible mansion. There were small animals moving in it. They might have been rabbits or hares. And a child was feeding them. It was Anna's child.'

Appleby drew a long breath. 'You are sure of that?'

'I am certain of it.'

'Let me remind you that you were a good deal upset. For an hour or more you had been concentrating with your binoculars upon what was scarcely a rational scheme of observation.'

'I know it. But there was no mistake.'

'And the little boy cannot, in the circumstances you have outlined, be at all intimately known to you.' Appleby was gently insistent. 'Can you be so certain that this was not an aberration? May you not have thought you saw what you expected to see?'

'I have asked myself these questions many times, Sir John. And, although the child vanished almost at once and did not reappear again, I am quite confident that it was Rudi.'

'Did you take any action as a result of this discovery?'

'First, I should say that I was for a time a little easier in my mind. Is not this a strange thing, now? The mere sight of the little boy through my field-glasses destroyed at once the bad thoughts which I had been nursing about Anna. And they have not come back to me. But I was, of course, anxious still. It came to me that Anna might have left Rudi in this place – perhaps some sort of children's home – the better to carry out some plan of her own. She is devoted to the child. But at the same time she is a woman of intellectual interests, deeply concerned by the world's political and social problems. When this possibility came to me I made inquiries about Milton Manor. It is not for children but for adults – a large, private *Kurort* or *Klinikum*. I do not know the word –'

'We used to say nursing-home or sanatorium. But we have started saying clinic too. Did you find out anything more?'

'Nothing, I still felt not at liberty to ask questions openly, or to pay a visit. And in secret it appears impossible to make any approach. There is this high wall; there are these fences. But the establishment is large and must employ many people. I have thought to disguise myself, perhaps, to seek an engagement –'

Appleby smiled. 'That is very resourceful. But perhaps the time has come for other measures.'

'There are yet two matters of which Kurt has to tell.' Frau Kolmak was sitting at her piano rather as if she proposed to provide a musical *coda* to these final revelations when they came. 'First, there is his adventure with the guest who has just left us.'

Appleby nodded and turned to Kurt Kolmak. 'You are aware of some connexion of Routh's with this place near Milton Porcorum?'

'*Wahrscheinlich!* But it is only from yesterday that this small piece of knowledge dates. Early yesterday morning I set out again on a further *Rekognoszierung* – a further spying. I walked all round the park. The circuit was almost completed, and with nothing gained, when I saw the *sogenannte* Routh approaching down a lane. He was staggering slightly, as if drunk or ill. There appeared to be blood on his face. I was very wary. It was not my wish to be seen by anybody at all at this prowling and spying. There was still Anna's injunction. Therefore I slipped behind a hedge and through my glasses studied this man. He turned along the road bounding this mysterious estate with which we are concerned. And then, as my glasses followed him, another figure came into view – one who had just appeared, it seemed, through a small door in the high wall of which I have spoken. I was excited. It was the first time that I had seen anybody appear from the place. And this figure – a man with high shoulders and of some presence – had an air of authority. His clothing was rural but elegant. He might have been the *Landjunker.*'

'The Squire?'

'*Also!* We ourselves employ the word. *Nun!* This man remained standing by his small door until Routh went by. No gesture, I believe, passed between them. But then he called Routh back. Routh appeared to hesitate, and then retraced his steps. The two engaged in conversation. It was my impression that there was some sort of dispute. And then I was interrupted. I had climbed a gate, you understand, and was in a field, crouched behind the hedge through which I was peering with my binoculars. Suddenly there was a farm-labourer in the field behind me, calling out to demand what I was doing. No doubt he suspected that I was a poacher or a thief or a deranged person, since my posture was not one that an innocent man would adopt.'

Kolmak paused, slightly flushed, and clicked his fingers. 'I see now my situation as comical. But at that moment I was humiliated and confused. I got up and ran away.'

'*Eine dumme Geschichte!*' Frau Kolmak laughed softly. 'But there is more of it to tell.'

Kurt Kolmak nodded. 'I gave no further thought to what I had seen. And this was because, when I recovered from my confusion, a new thought had come to me. Perhaps Anna was willingly a patient in this clinic. Perhaps she had suffered a nervous illness. She was, after all, virtually a fugitive – and one with a child to care for. Such a situation must involve great strain. She might, then, have found this place, where Rudi also could be, and have determined not to communicate with us – apart, that is, from this single card, written, it might be, in a disturbed state. What, in that event, was my duty? I found it hard to decide, and I spent the rest of the day tramping that countryside and endeavouring to wrestle with the problem. It thus came about that I returned to Oxford by a circuitous route, changing buses eventually at Abingdon. Imagine my surprise when I saw getting off the same bus at Gloucester Green, the man whom I had last seen in conversation with the owner, as it might be, of Milton. There was, of course, no mistaking him. This was the man whose face had been bleeding; the scratches were still visible on his face. I determined to track him to his destination. If I knew where he lived, then I might be able to take thought and find some means of gaining valuable information from him.'

'I see.' Appleby, who had finished his breakfast, was listening intently to this recital. 'You started to trail Routh. Did he seem scared?'

'Assuredly he did.'

'He had the appearance of a man who believes himself to be pursued?'

'That was my impression.'

'Before he had any opportunity of knowing that *you* were on his track?'

Kolmak considered. 'But yes! As soon as he got off the bus he made his way to one point and another about Gloucester Green – and always looking uneasily about him. This, I am sure, was before he ever set eyes on me. Presently he went into a small hotel. I waited. He was there long enough, I should say, to get a meal. When he came out, our eyes met. Very foolishly, I had waited directly in front of the place. I know that instantly he suspected me of spying on him. He proceeded at once to put the matter to the test. My following of him was very clumsy and obvious. And quite soon he got away from me, boarding a bus that I was unable to catch.'

'A bus coming out to North Oxford?'

'*Nun ja!* It was a Number 2. And here was an end of my playing the detective – the secret agent! Only how surprised I was, on going out to call you back last night, to find you conversing with this man.'

'I should much like to converse with him again. But there is still something further you have to tell me?'

'Yes.' Kolmak's face took on an expression more anxious than any it had yet worn. 'There has been another message from Anna. It, too, has arrived by post – this morning, while you were still asleep. You have it, Tante Lise?'

Frau Kolmak nodded, and rose from beside the piano. There was something in her movement that betrayed the fatigue of long anxiety; and Appleby saw that she was an older woman than he had supposed.

'Here it is, Kurt. I fear it occupied my thoughts to the exclusion of other matters. Had it not been so, Herr Routh would not have slipped away from us so easily.'

Appleby shook his head. 'Don't worry about that, Frau Kolmak. It may give him a chance to make some interesting contacts. Perhaps he will be found with them by my Oxford colleagues. Routh is decidedly their main interest at the moment, and they are a highly efficient body of men.'

'Sir John, here is Anna's second note. Again it is unstamped. And the material seems not designed for the post.'

'It certainly does not.' Appleby was looking at a slim piece of cardboard, about four inches by three. Medially on one of the longer sides, and near the edge, there was punched a small circular hole. 'It's clearly meant for use in a card-index. Addressed in the same way as the first, and posted in Milton Porcorum in time for the 4.15 p.m. sorting yesterday.' He turned the card over and read its message in silence:

Do not be hurt that I do not write. I am not a free agent, and there is danger in the attempt. Today or soon there is a crisis. Do nothing. But be by your telephone every day from 10 to 11 a.m.   A.

Appleby sat so long in thought before this enigmatic missive that Kolmak stirred uneasily beside him. 'Sir John – it suggests something to you?'

Appleby shook his head. 'This about the telephone. I don't understand it.'

'In my room at Bede's there is an instrument. And Anna has the number.'

'But of course – stupid of me.' Appleby nodded absently. 'What Anna enjoins upon you is rather a nerve-racking routine, I am afraid. But you had better be off to it. The time is nearly half past nine now. Incidentally, I must go down and make another call from the Misses Tinker's machine.'

Kolmak rose as if to open the door. 'That will be to your colleagues, arranging that my line in Bede's be tapped?'

'You are very acute – again the secret service agent in the making.'

'I am inclined to wish that I had told you nothing.' Kolmak was very pale.

'And that you had left me in that van?'

'*Aber nein!*' Impulsively, Kolmak took Appleby's hand. 'You judge Anna to be in danger?'

Appleby inclined his head. 'I do.' His voice was grave. 'She says so herself – and it appears that she is a level-headed and capable person.'

'She is indeed!' Frau Kolmak had come forward. 'My daughter has a good brain and great courage. Can you, Sir John, whose experience must be so great, form any conjecture as to her situation and Rudi's? If so, I beg of you to speak, however black the picture may be.'

'There is no scope for conjecture yet. Your daughter is almost certainly in some sense a prisoner. But she has been able at some risk to send you a couple of notes, and at a pinch she believes she can command a telephone. She might have stated her precise whereabouts and has refrained from doing so. Twice she has said "Do nothing". She has made no appeal for help, but at any moment she may do so. At the moment, that is about as far as we can get. Except, of course, for the parallel situation of Routh.'

'The parallel situation?' Frau Kolmak looked bewildered and rather displeased. 'Surely you see no similarity between my daughter and that man?'

'Certainly I do. Routh too, I suspect, has been in the hands of this mys-

346

terious organization. And Routh too has been fighting back. That is all to the good, since I suspect that we are very definitely in the presence of something to be fought against. But Routh and your daughter may prove to have something else in common.'

Kolmak was looking at his watch. 'Please do not speak in riddles,' he said. 'Please explain.'

But Frau Kolmak laid a hand on her nephew's arm. 'I think I understand,' she said quietly. 'I considered the little man with attention, and when I gave him coffee I exchanged a few words with him.' She was growing visibly paler as she spoke, but she stood very upright beside her piano. 'We will not go further into this now.'

Appleby moved to the door. 'There is, as you know, another person who must be fitted into the design.'

'The *Verlobte* of your sister – Mr Ourglass?'

'Yes. He too, from what I hear of him, would fight back. But, in that other particular, he offers no parallel to Routh and your daughter.'

Frau Kolmak considered. 'Might the young man be freakish, adventurous – and affect – what you have in mind?'

'That is a very shrewd suggestion. And now I must be off – and you too, Dr Kolmak, to that telephone.' Appleby turned back to his hostess and bent over her hand with some formality. '*Auf Wiedersehen, gnädige Frau.*'

On the little landing the Aeolian harp was still uttering its muted music. Appleby wondered what Routh had made of it. He wondered, too, what he ought to make of Routh.

5

Jane Appleby left Somerville College at nine-fifty, thus missing her brother by five minutes. It was her intention to proceed to the Examination Schools and there hear a lecture by the Stockton and Darlington Professor. In spite of her engagement to Geoffrey Ourglass, or perhaps because of it, Jane had now been, for more than a year, in general sequacious only of the more severe intellectual pleasures. This particular weekly occasion she invariably found wholly delectable. For many of her fellows it was an hour of furious inactivity – and indeed it has been calculated that more young women are constrained to buy fresh note-books after the discourses of the Stockton and Darlington Professor than after any other learned occasion whatsoever. Jane, however, was accustomed to sit in a still repose throughout. The substance of what the Professor had to say had, in point of fact, been bequeathed to her by an aunt who attended the lectures in 1925; and Jane was thus in the fortunate position of being able to sit as in a theatre and enjoy the finer points of the performance, without anxious thoughts of the likely bearing of such inactivity upon her examination prospects.

But now that Geoffrey's fate – or could it be behaviour? – had got her down (and to herself, at least, Jane now admitted that it had done this) Jane found herself, week by week, taking less and less delight in this particular facet of the pursuit of knowledge. The plain fact was that if she were not to be so miserable she must give her mind more active and tough employment than any that the proceedings of the Stockton and Darlington Professor could afford. She was very little disposed to sit and mope; she had been determined that her work was not going to suffer on account of the miserable and bewildering turn which her affairs had taken; and when she had come up at the beginning of term to an Oxford still devoid of Geoffrey she had signalized this determination by extracting from her tutor, for work in a college examination, the portentous mark known in Oxford as a pure Alpha. But since then she had been finding it progressively difficult to avoid making an ass of herself, and she had found that her best weapon in this struggle lay in the more stretching forms of mental exercise. It thus came about that, half-way down St Giles', Jane decided not to hear the Stockton and Darlington Professor after all.

If this decision was of momentous public importance (as may, indeed, presently prove to be the case) the public showed no consciousness of the fact. Around and about that secondary hub of Oxford upon one border of which stands the College of the Provost and Scholars of the Venerable Bede, and upon another the miniature churchyard of St Mary Magdalen, both Town and Gown continued undisturbed upon their familiar occasions. Regius Professors, visibly bowed down beneath their weight of erudition, pottered about, buying cakes and pies. Heads of Houses, upon whom even more evidently reposed heavy burdens of administrative care, absently exercised dogs or companioned their wives through a morning's brisk shopping. Outwards towards the Banbury or the Woodstock Road an unending stream of battered sports cars bore cohorts of male undergraduates, discreetly concealed amid golf clubs, shot-guns, and riding kits. Inwards towards the lecture-rooms and libraries of the University rode an answering army of young women on bicycles bearing large baskets bulging with massive volumes, as if they were the delivery service of a community given literally to devouring books.

It was as one in the main stream of this literary movement that Jane Appleby had now reached the lower end of St Giles'. On her right the reposeful statuary on the Taylor Institution – unknown whether mythological or symbolical, allegorical or historical – stared impassively across the hubbub to where Balliol, Trinity and St John's expire in a complicated embrace. Before her was the Martyrs' Memorial. To the right of this was Bede's. Jane took one glance at the college of her vanished beloved and decided that the prime need of the morning was arduous thought. She would make her way not to the lecture of the Stockton and Darlington Professor but to the upper reading room of the Bodleian Library, where there happened to be reserved for her a work of very sufficient intellectual difficulty.

She would wrestle with this until noon and then hunt up her brother. To this resolution Jane had come when she saw that somebody was waving an umbrella at her from the corner of Beaumont Street. It was Geoffrey's uncle, Dr Ourglass. She signalled her intention of joining him when she could, and presently threaded her way at some hazard across the street.

'My dear, I am very pleased to see you, and I was delighted to meet your brother yesterday evening. I was dining in Bede's as the guest of Mr Bultitude, whom I am glad to be able to introduce to you.'

It had been Jane's hurried impression as she dodged the traffic that Dr Ourglass was standing beside a large barrel awaiting delivery to the Bede's buttery. She now realized that she had been in error. The barrel was bowing to her with gravity. It was, in fact, the celebrated Mark Bultitude. 'How do you do,' he said. 'I am afraid we divert you.'

As Jane had been aware of an element of the ludicrous in the conjoined appearance of the gentlemen before her, she found this ambiguity disconcerting. 'Oh, no,' she said hastily, 'I wasn't going anywhere important; only to the Bodleian.'

Mark Bultitude directed a faint smile upon Dr Ourglass, as if calling upon him to remark the delightful fatuity of the young. 'In that case,' he said, 'we can make this small claim upon your time with a clear conscience.'

Jane, like most people of her age – and even a few quite mature ones – disliked detecting herself saying something silly. 'It's not wasted at all,' she said. 'One ought to meet the really interesting people.' She contrived to let her eyes rest, rounded in admiration, upon Bultitude. 'Yesterday I managed to talk to that funny old woman who peddles bananas.'

'You have the right instinct. You will end by collecting all of us Oxford worthies. We are a diminishing band, after all. For one thing, there are so few openings.' And Bultitude looked comfortably around him, as if seeking some enormous aperture through which he might edge himself.

Dr Ourglass thought it well to change the subject. 'It appears,' he said carefully, 'that Mr Bultitude is acquainted with a number of Geoffrey's – and my – distant relations; and he has become interested in this distressing thing that has happened. He is very anxious to help. He even suggests that he and I make an expedition.'

Jane received this communication with mixed feelings. She liked old Dr Ourglass, although she had no high opinion of his practical acumen. And she was spontaneously and instantly grateful to anybody – even this terrible great fat *poseur* – who expressed concern and a willingness to help in the horrible matter of Geoffrey's inexplicable and now long-continued disappearance. At the same time she hated figuring as the young woman who had mislaid a young man. She was well aware that all sorts of low, sinister, or facetious constructions could be placed on such a situation, and she was only the more sensitive to these because none of them had ever been even faintly obtruded upon her. 'Thank you,' she said. 'I am quite desperate, you know. Geoffrey simply *must* be found. He may be terribly ill – so ill that he doesn't even know his own identity.'

Bultitude nodded soberly. 'An able and well-connected young man,' he said. 'With everything before him here at Bede's – and a further tie of which I am now very well able to estimate the force. I am extremely shocked. Birkbeck ought to have been altogether more vigorous in the matter. He cannot, poor fellow, afford to lose good pupils right and left. Ourglass tells me that your brother is taking the matter up. I am sorry not to have had any conversation with him last night. But we shall meet. We shall undoubtedly meet. I have never, I believe, known anybody in the police. But my uncle Hubert once had command of the Yeomen of the Guard.'

Jane felt that the conversation in which she had become involved was somewhat lacking in direction. Dr Ourglass appeared to have the same feeling, and again changed the subject with unusual abruptness. 'Jane,' he asked, 'has Geoffrey ever shown any disposition to *write* – for example, a play?'

'I never heard him speak of such a thing.' Jane was puzzled. 'Geoffrey is simply a straight-out tip-top scientist. And they don't usually write plays. Of course Geoffrey is fond of acting, but that's a different matter. Why do you ask?'

'Mr Bultitude had a notion that a long-continued retirement and – um – neglect of one's friends is sometimes to be accounted for by absorption in a literary task.'

'I see.' Jane thought this decidedly a poor idea. Nor did Bultitude seem pleased at its being aired again. Perhaps Dr Ourglass was innocently labouring something that had really been one of his companion's obscure jokes. Anyway, she was not going to stand any longer at a street-corner gossiping like this. 'I think,' she said, 'I'd better go off and do some work.'

Bultitude nodded benevolently, as if here were another of the touching frailties of the young. 'Quite right,' he said. 'What sort of acting?'

For a moment Jane was at a loss. 'I beg your pardon?'

'What sort of acting is the young man fond of? Has he taken part in any plays here in Oxford?'

'Oh, I see. No – Geoffrey hasn't, I think, done any acting in a regular way since he left school. I just meant that he likes putting on turns. He can dress up a bit, and then pass himself off in a pub as pretty well anything. It's a sort of freakish amusement that he gets quite a lot of fun out of from time to time.'

'Impersonations, in fact.'

'I suppose it may be called that.' Jane found herself obscurely resenting the word. 'Only not of individuals, you see. Just of types.'

'Quite so. Impersonation, one might say, on the Theophrastan model. It doesn't sound a particularly dangerous hobby. The hazards ought not to extend much beyond a black eye.'

At this Jane felt really cross. 'You'd have to be quite tough, Mr Bultitude, to take to punching Geoffrey. He'd be back and finding a soft spot or two in no time.'

'Capital – capital. Young men are too neglectful of those manly accomplishments nowadays. Have you ever joined in these impersonations, Miss Appleby? And has the young man any favourite turns?'

Jane ignored the first part of this questioning. 'He can do dons. And bewildered foreigners. And – let me see – yes, young clergymen, and down-and-outs.'

'Young clergymen!' It was Dr Ourglass who spoke, and he was apparently a little shocked. 'I had no idea of this – and in a person of high academic promise!' He paused as if looking for a more reassuring view of the matter, inoffensive to his nephew's betrothed. 'Versatility,' he pursued, 'is a wonderful endowment. I am all too conscious of being sadly without it myself.'

But by this time Jane had turned her bicycle. A momentary break in the stream of traffic could be made the civil occasion, she felt, of a tolerably brisk farewell to her interlocutors. 'Sorry,' she said suddenly. 'Here's my chance.' And at that she darted away.

Although it had been accompanied by her best smile, Jane was not altogether happy about this manoeuvre. It was perhaps neither mannerly nor courageous; and she had only an obscure sense of why the encounter thus rather abruptly terminated had rattled her. When safely on the farther side of the road, therefore, she turned her head for a moment, intending to locate her companions of a second before and impart what cordiality she could to a parting wave. It was a movement involving her in a mishap which just escaped being serious.

Dr Ourglass and Mark Bultitude appeared to have moved off, and Jane's eyes continued to search for them a fraction of a second longer than was compatible with wary cycling. In the same instant a man stepped blindly off the kerb in front of her; there was a bump; and Jane found herself in the unpleasant position of lying flat on the road, with the wheel of a bus hurtling past her head.

She knew, however, that she was unhurt, and she scrambled hastily to her feet. It is bad to have been within inches of death. But, when one is young, it is almost worse to have made a fool of oneself, and to see a little crowd gathering, most of whom have just observed one come down hard on one's behind, and to expect at any moment a policeman, solemnly insistent upon making copious notes. Jane therefore hastily grabbed her bicycle and looked anxiously at the man with whom she had collided. He too, blessedly, was on his feet. If he were only unhurt and disposed not to make a fuss –

He was backing away through the little knot of people whom the incident had collected. Jane stared at him in surprise. He was a little rat of a fellow, shabby and unshaven, and – what was the odd thing about him – in a state of palpable terror. And it was not, Jane could see, what *had* happened that was the occasion of his miserable state; it was what *might* happen. The man as he tried to back out of the crowd glanced about him in vivid apprehensiveness; when he knocked into somebody he drew back as from a blow; his complexion was of an alarming pallor which emphasized his possession of one badly scratched cheek. That, Jane supposed, had been her fault – as must be also the sadly dusty and crumpled state of the man's attire. She moved forward at once, wheeling her bicycle. 'I'm most terribly sorry. It was entirely my fault. I hope –' Jane paused, disconcerted. The man's eyes had swept past her quite blindly; his unscarred cheek was twitching; his tongue went rapidly over his lips with an effect that was reptilian and repellent. Suddenly he turned, ducked, dodged, and ran. Jane was addressing her apologies to empty air.

Or rather she was addressing them to a small group of people uncertain whether to be puzzled or amused. The handlebars of her bicycle had got twisted, and to this a couple of undergraduates were attending with expressions so solemnly solicitous that Jane suspected them of concealing coarse amusement at the unlucky manner of her tumble. The one bright spot in the picture was the absence of any bobbing policeman's helmet. 'Thank you very much *indeed*,' she said. Her intention was to speak with an awful and freezing coldness. Unfortunately much of the breath appeared to have been knocked out of her body, and the words emerged with a panting effect proper to an adoring maiden chivalrously rescued from a ravisher or a dragon. She took the bicycle and thrust its nose not very gently into the crowd. Now, thank goodness, she was clear, and had edged into Broad Street. She mounted, settled herself rather gingerly in the saddle, and put this deplorable *contretemps* rapidly behind her. But the consciousness of having been vastly idiotic remained with her oppressively. The oddity of the terrified man's behaviour went entirely out of her head. So too did her encounter with Mark Bultitude and Dr Ourglass, and the latter's unexplained suggestion that they were going to make an expedition.

6

The upper reading room of the Bodleian Library is frequented in the main by persons occupying a middle station in the elaborate hierarchy of Oxford learning. In a university, as in the republic of literature, extreme longevity is a prerequisite of the first eminence; and in Bodley (as the great library is compendiously termed by its frequenters) those in whom extreme fullness of years and exceptional depths of erudition are thus naturally conjoined commonly inhabit studies, niches, carrels and (it may be) cubicles of superior distinction in other parts of the building – notably in what is known as Duke Humphrey's Library and the Selden End. These latter, although not places of the highest antiquity, are very, very old; and the pursuit of learning has for so long transacted itself within them as to have generated not only a peculiar aura but also an indescribable smell. As long as this smell endures Oxford will endure too. If its undergraduate population were dispensed with, Oxford would not be very much changed. If its bells, even, fell silent, something would be left. But if this smell evaporated it would be a sign that the soul of Oxford had departed its tenement of grey, eroded stone, and that only its shell, only its tangible and visible surfaces, remained.

It is normally only for the purpose of consulting the great catalogue of the Library that these ancients of the place repair to the upper reading room; and this they (and they alone) may do by means of a lift – a lift the nether terminus of which is a jealously guarded secret, and from which egression at its upward limit is almost equally mysterious, since none of the sages is ever observed actually stepping from it, being invariably first remarked advancing down the reading room with measured tread against a background of unbroken lines of books.

Nor do the young largely frequent the upper reading room, since for them, in sundry dependent libraries, judiciously selected books, independently catalogued, are provided in what, to their large innocence, appears inexhaustible abundance. It is only occasionally that – like those stripling cherubs who, in the first stainlessness of this terrestrial world, were drawn by curiosity to take a peep at Eden – undergraduate members of the university toil upwards to this unwonted sciential eminence. Those who do not take the lift to the upper reading room must mount a flight of sixty-four steps, involving twelve right-angled turns. It was to this that Jane Appleby addressed herself shortly after her misadventure hard by Bede's College.

There is surely something unique, if indefinable, in the atmosphere generated in the reading room of a great library. So many minds intently employed in divided and distinguished worlds; black men beside yellow men, and yellow men beside white; shoes and ships and sealing-wax all being studied in a row; the vision of the mysterious Goddess, alluring within the multitudinous and inexplicable folds of her sable robe, who at once unifies the spectacle and makes it possible: all these make a library a solemn place to an exploring cherub of twenty-one. No doubt Jane Appleby came in order to master a book that she knew to be confined here. But she came, too, for the smell of old leather and vellum and wood that permeated the approaches to the place; for the sound, strangely magnified in the stillness, of a fly buzzing on a windowpane, or for the muted clanking of the Emett-like contrivance which, behind the scenes, drew its continuously moving train of books up through the secular darkness from crepuscular repositories below. She came, in short – an unconfessed tourist disguised as a scholar of Somerville – for atmosphere. But if Jane came for sensations, she certainly did not come for sensation. She was not at all prepared for the spectacle that was presently to be afforded her.

The reading room appeared to be less frequented than was common at this hour. Nobody occupied the desk where Jane's book was waiting, and she settled down to it at once. Or rather she endeavoured to do this – and with no expectation of difficulty. Her mind was well-disciplined, and the constant sub-acute anxiety in which she now lived did not (as has already been remarked) seriously interfere with her working. And as for the upper reading room as atmosphere – that, she was convinced, was something that came to one most exquisitely as a faint wash of surface awareness when the greater part of the mind was plunged deep in its task.

But, this morning, Jane's mind proved reluctant to plunge at all – reluctant (as she told herself fretfully) even to wet its toes. Surface awareness turned out to be her sole stock-in-trade. She buried her nose in her book – which was a very big one – and peeped guiltily over its upper margin at the world about her. This, persisted in, was conduct so monstrous, that she positively expected some dramatic consequence to ensue. A bell might ring loudly, the little door magnificently labelled Protobibliothecarius Bodleianus open with an ominous creak, and hitherto unsuspected attendants, garbed in a Byzantine splendour congruous with that resounding inscription, seize her and bind her in every limb. She would be delivered into the maw of the Emett-like machine; that machine – unprecedentedly – would be thrown into reverse; and she would be conveyed to the icy embrace of some subterranean Oxford Bosphorus. Come to think of it, Oxford *did* have at least one underground river. Her brother had told her that, as an undergraduate, he had once traversed it in a canoe . . .

Jane felt a sudden chill. It was a feeling none the less horrid for being familiar – for being a sensation that gripped her whenever chance brought any occasion of danger into her head. She remembered now that just this thought had come to her half an hour before, when the rumbling bus had gone by within inches of her nose. Perhaps Geoffrey, having unaccountably strayed in the vacation to some outlandish place, had been inches less lucky. Or perhaps he had thought to make the solitary exploration of that hidden Oxford river, and his canoe had struck a snag, had pitched him –

Abruptly Jane emerged from the dark, dank tunnel into which her fearful imagination had carried her. Without her being at all aware of what it was, something in the actual and present world around her had plucked at her attention. It was not – deplorably – the printed page before her. It was not the neighbour on her right: a grey-haired woman copying from a book the size of a postage-stamp – barring Geoffrey, Jane thought, myself forty years on. Nor was it that picturesque Oxford figure, old Dr Undertone, on her left. For Dr Undertone, surrounded by eighteenth-century theology, had sunk, with closed eyes, into that species of profound cerebration, to a vulgar regard deceptively like simple slumber, which is not unfrequently to be observed in the upper reading room. It was neither of these people. It was, in fact the man with the scratched face.

He was still only on the threshold of the room. Subconsciously, she must have become aware of him the instant his pale – his curiously haunted or hunted – face appeared at the door. But, if Jane saw him, nobody else appeared to do so. Very few people in the upper reading room ever sit peeping over the top of their books.

The man had no business in the place. She was, somehow, quite certain of that. But he had not, apparently, been asked if he were a reader. This was not surprising, for it is only very infrequently that any official of the Library murmurs to anybody a courteous inquiry of the sort. Nor, really, did he look out of the way. He was shabby, but scholars can be shabbier than anybody else in the world. He was grubby, but that is not absolutely unknown among the learned. He was harassed to what is quite evidently the point of nervous collapse, and he had the appearance of one whose mind is bent with maniacal concentration upon the solution of some single, urgent and ever-present problem. But this is not uncommon among those who pursue the historical Homer or the origins of the Sabellian heresy, or who are hounded by urgent conundrums concerning the comparative phonology of the dialects of the upper Irrawaddy.

The man was completely at sea about the sort of place he had landed in. An unsensational explanation of his appearance would be simply that he had taken the wrong turning when searching for the picture-gallery. But if, to a gaze once bent upon him, he had not the air of a man concerned to read old books, neither did he very convincingly suggest any interest in old portraits. He was looking neither for knowledge nor for aesthetic delectation. He was looking for refuge.

To this conclusion Jane was, of course, assisted by recalling the man's odd behaviour when she had collided with him in the street. He had simply got up and bolted. Either, then, he was mentally deranged (which was the most likely explanation) or he was in actual fear of pursuit and apprehension. He was alternatively either a bit of a lunatic or a bit of a criminal.

Jane's mind reacted with no special interest to either of these notions. Although much given to reading – and over large mugs of cocoa discussing solemnly with her friends – the most recondite psychopathic aberrations chronicled by Freud or Stekel, her conviction was that at the casual sight of such distresses peeping out from some individual, good manners and natural instinct combine to make one look the other way. Nor did crime remotely interest her; she left that to her brother John. Despite all which, she now bent a steady but covert observation upon the fugitive. Between them, after all, was a common bond: they had lately almost delivered one another to death on the high road.

The man had now realized that he was in a library. He glanced over the rows of bent figures and made as if to sit down. But in the upper reading room every desk is commonly loaded with books reserved for one reader or another, and although it is the convention that one may take any place not actually occupied at the time, a stranger will always be likely to feel that there is standing room only.

For a minute or so the fugitive stood. In this there was nothing that was likely to call attention to him. The walls between the square Tudor windows are lined with books and bound journals supposed to be in common use, and before these, scholars will stand for hours on end, either running through the pages of one and another volume or simply studying their spines with an air of profound research. The man plainly hesitated to take a book from the shelf, but he contrived to let his eye run over several rows as if in search of some specific work. In this, even if it had been generally detected as a subterfuge, there would have been little to excite remark. For it frequently happens that scholars, seized suddenly as they are walking past by some irresistibly enticing train of speculation, and being brought to an abrupt halt thereby, avoid (what would be odious to them) the appearance of any singularity of conduct by going through just this conventional inspection of whatever shelves are nearest to hand. From these, nothing much distinguished the man with the scratched face save this: that every few seconds his gaze ran furtively along the stretching lines of books to the door of the reading room.

Several people wandered in, and Jane believed that she could see the fugitive quiver each time. The Emett-like conveyor belt behind the scenes emitted one of its faint clankings, and the man gave a sort of jump as he stood. Nevertheless he was demonstrably getting the hang of the place. He had now boldly taken a volume from the shelf, opened it, and turned round so that he could survey the room over the top of it – a technique, in fact, closely approximating to Jane's own.

Seen full face, he looked very tired as well as frightened. Jane remembered that free libraries of the municipal order are frequently the resort of the homeless, who will sit with an unmeaning book before them for the sake of shelter and a meagre warmth. Perhaps even this august chamber had been put to not altogether dissimilar use on some occasion or another. But this man was not minded to shelter from the elements. He was sheltering from his own kind.

At this moment somebody else entered the room. He was a man with high, square shoulders, and his appearance was eminently orthodox. His features held the mingled stamp of intelligence, authority and mild inquiry. His clothing was so quiet as to lend positive assertiveness to an extremely faded Harrovian tie. He carried a sheaf of papers yellowed with age, and under his arm was what appeared to be a mortar-board – more correctly known as a 'square' – and a crumpled M.A. gown. He was, in fact, the very type of the consciously busy don, dropping into Bodley to order a book before hurrying off to lecture.

The man with the scratched face had been scanning the readers with some particularity. And now the entry of the donnish person, from whom he was momentarily concealed, seemed to touch off in him a spring of activity. His eye had been on Jane. He thrust the book he had been holding back on the shelf and came straight towards her.

Jane experienced a second's ridiculous panic. There came to her an intuitive understanding of what the fugitive was about. He had recognized her. And – just because she was the only person in this strange reading room not absolutely unknown to him – he was going to direct at her some urgent appeal. Nothing could be more irrational. But the man had reached a breaking-point at which only instinctive responses were left to him.

And then he faltered. Jane wondered, with a quick compunction, whether she had shown herself overtly hostile to his approach. However this might be, the man halted not beside her desk but beside Dr Undertone's. He had been feeling in a pocket. Jane saw that he now held a paper in his hand.

The quintessentially donnish person was scanning the room. If it was the man with the scratched face he was seeking, he had not yet located him. And now the man was leaning over Dr Undertone's desk. Dr Undertone took no notice. Since his eyes were closed in meditation, and since he was ninety-six, there was nothing surprising in that. Nor did anybody else except Jane appear to pay any attention either. As books but not desks are reservable in the reading room it is necessary to do quite a lot of prowling round other people's property.

The man with the scratched face thrust the paper he was carrying into one of Dr Undertone's books and walked straight on across the room.

7

It was, as the vulgar say, a new one on Jane Appleby. And before she could decide what action, if any, was required, her attention was riveted upon the next act of the drama being played out covertly before her.

The donnish person had seen the fugitive and was advancing upon him. Between himself and this advance the fugitive was concerned to put a barrier. And one obvious barrier was available to him. Beginning at that end of the reading room which is nearest the door, and extending in two parallel lines down a substantial part of its length, run low, double-fronted cases containing the major portion of the great manuscript catalogue of the Bodleian Library. To move round these massive islands is to circumambulate a brief record of the entire intellectual and imaginative achievement of the race. And this was what the two men – pursuer and pursued – were doing now. They were playing a sort of hide-and-seek round this monumental guide to universal knowledge.

Jane watched, fascinated. It must, she realized, be some sort of symbolic comedy, arranged expressly for her benefit, although she had not the key of it. This weird ballet was being danced for a stake somehow commensurate with the tremendous character of its setting.

And nobody else noticed. For the strangest behaviour, Jane perceived, can pass undetected in the most sober places. To any one not persistently attentive to the whole sequence of events she was witnessing, nothing in the least out of the way had occurred or was occurring. That one man should be patently pursuing round the catalogue of Bodley another man who as patently fled, was a phenomenon offering in itself no difficulty whatever to a casual analysis. There are always in Oxford colleagues prone to engage with one at unseasonable times; there are always legitimate lengths to which one may go in side-stepping their approach. In Bodley the right-thinking greet only with the most distant nod (if at all) their fathers, mothers, sons, daughters or most intimate friends. But there are always those who default upon this convention: fellow-workers importunately desirous of learned communication, sociably disposed persons thinking to give (or receive) an invitation to dinner, deans and senior tutors allowing so exaggerated a regard to administrative affairs as to be willing even here to whip up a vote or debate a college by-law; there are all these, and there are plain bores as well.

Had the donnish man and his quarry positively broken into a run, or had the former offered to vault the long breastwork of enormous manuscript volumes standing in his way, this open breach of decorum would doubtless have been visited with the severest censure on the part of the assembled readers. But nothing of this sort was in question. The pursuit here in progress was a pursuit in slow motion. Presently it was to strike Jane that this was a very odd circumstance indeed. For the moment she was absorbed in watching it.

Half a dozen people were moving about the catalogue – lugging out a volume here and there, hoisting it by its leathern loop to the desk-like top of the long case, finding some desired entry and copying it upon a slip, replacing the volume and moving on to hunt for something else. Both the man with the scratched face and his pursuer were making some show of doing the same thing. Nevertheless their actual preoccupation was clear. The one was concerned to edge up and the other was concerned to edge away. This went on for some time. It was like some crazy sequence in a dream.

And that was it. There was an element of the hypnotic or the hypnoidal in the affair. And it was only in a minor degree that the donnish man was concerned physically to corner his victim. That, indeed, he had in a sense done already. What was now in question was an obscure battle of wills. The object of the pursuer was to compel the other man to leave the reading room, to walk quietly out of the library. And his weapon was this: that his person, or personality, was so repulsive to his victim as to make it physically impossible for the latter to bear any approach to contiguity. As the donnish person advanced, in the same measure was the man with the scratched face irresistibly obliged to withdraw. Watching the two of them at their covert manoeuvring around the catalogue was like watching some ingenious toy. Or it was like watching a child forcing one piece of magnetized metal jerkily across a table by nosing towards it the answering pole of another.

For Jane there was a moment of queer horror in this discovery of a sentient human being reduced to the condition of an automaton. And the donnish man was gaining in authority – was gaining in repulsive or expulsive power – as the unnatural game progressed. She wondered if her own collision with the fugitive had borne any part in the apparently fatal breaking of his nerve. And perhaps it was he who was presently to be dropped through a trap into some chilly Oxford Bosphorus . . . Jane jumped. Close to her, the door round which she had been building that foolish fantasy quietly opened. But no guard of janizaries was revealed. All that emerged was Bodley's Librarian – an elderly man with a high, domed forehead, quite bald, on which were symmetrically disposed several tiers of spectacles. Bodley's Librarian lowered one tier of spectacles to his nose and mildly surveyed the reading room at large; then he elevated these again, brought down another, and consulted his watch; finally he substituted a third pair, glanced at the people more immediately around him, and moved slowly down the room. Occasionally he paused to pat a reader benevolently on the back, for he took a fatherly interest in his flock. Among others he patted the donnish person as he edged along the catalogue – an attention which the donnish person received with every symptom of restrained and learned pleasure. He glanced into the apartment concealing the Emett-like engine – at which the engine gave a subdued clank by way of respectful greeting – and then drifted out of the room.

A long, low wheeze, as of air let gently out of a bicycle tyre, made Jane glance to her left. Dr Undertone had opened his eyes and was looking at her in great astonishment – rather as if, on returning to his immediate surroundings, he had discovered himself seated next to a studious walrus or erudite dromedary. This was disconcerting to Jane, but, upon reflection, not at all surprising. During a large part of Dr Undertone's reading life, it had to be remembered, women – and particularly young women – must have been an unusual sight in Bodley. Dr Undertone's eyes went back to his book – to that one of the small litter of books on his desk that lay open before him. He looked no younger than his years, and he seemed to Jane tired and ill. But he also seemed very dogged. There was a story that on his ninety-fifth birthday he had been discovered at his tailor's demanding to be shown a good, hard-wearing cloth. And now with a claw-like finger he was tracing out the words on the page in front of him. Jane wondered with what coherence and cogency they reached his brain, and what large labour of research he was embarked upon . . . She turned her head. Both the man with the scratched face and his pursuer were gone.

So now she could get on with her book. The comedy which she had been watching had come to the indecisive and obscure conclusion which comedies of real life – or for that matter tragedies either – are always likely to exhibit. But was it a comedy? If so, it had the quality of leaving its audience obstinately uneasy. Jane's book was no more attractive to her than before. The woman on her right – Jane forty years on – was unattractive. Dr Undertone was an uncanny old creature, uncomfortable to sit beside. The upper reading room, usually so dear to her serious mind, had gone spectral and insubstantial around her. What was important was not the slow march of intellect going forward invisibly but irresistibly at these rows of desks, but the physical pursuit of that wretched little man by a spurious don – a pursuit now, presumably, continuing below, or outside the building. Jane thrust aside her book and rose. Dr Undertone gave her a glance of grim satisfaction. She hurried as briskly as decorum permitted from the reading room.

The staircase upon which she presently found herself was deserted. Provided one has the agility necessary for cornering neatly as one moves, its shallow wooden treads admit of a considerable turn of speed. Jane found herself going down hell for leather. If her progress brought her full tilt into collision with the Vice-Chancellor, slipping upstairs to snatch half an hour's fearful joy from a book, it just couldn't be helped. It had come to her that she was involved, personally and deeply, in something very urgent indeed.

She reached the open air. It was now possible to take several routes. She might make her way by the entrance to the Divinity School – obscurely known as the 'Pig Market' – in the direction of Broad Street. Or she might move in the same general direction by way of the Clarendon Building. Or, again, she might take the little tunnel or passage on her right that gave immediately upon Radcliffe Square. She chose the last of these courses. And in a moment she knew that she had guessed right.

A small crowd had collected. It was very like the sort of crowd of which she had been the centre an hour before. Only this time there was a policeman. And this time the person who had drawn the crowd together didn't get up.

It was the man with the scratched face. He lay just off the footpath, supine on the cobbles of the square. As backcloth he had one of the great buildings of Oxford – the rounded magnificence of the Radcliffe Camera. In such a setting it would have been possible to feel the prostrate figure as something too insignificant for pathos – a mere piece of crumpled or deflated, of pashed and pounded, organic matter. But Jane's heart contracted as she glimpsed him. She shoved to the front. It wasn't difficult, for the crowd was no more than a knot of people – some standing, some doing no more than linger for a moment as they passed. Nothing sensational was happening. It was possible to suppose that the man was dead – dead of heart failure, or something of that sort – if one didn't notice that a cheek – the unscratched cheek – was twitching faintly. And he seemed to be lucky in having gained medical attention quickly.

For close by, at the corner of Catte Street, stood a large black car, with a chauffeur sitting impassively at the wheel. Out of this must have stepped the figure now kneeling, stethoscope in hand, beside the fallen man. He was dressed in a dark coat, and on the ground beside him he had laid a Foreign Office hat and a pair of immaculate yellow kid gloves. It looked as if, by some odd chance, the accident had attracted the notice of some very grand doctor indeed. And then this reassuring figure glanced up. In the same moment, af if his doing so had been a signal to them, all the bells of Oxford fell to chiming the hour. For Jane Appleby it was a moment of chaos, and she could not have told whether the jangling was inside her own head or out of it. For this dignified physician was the identical donnish person of the late drama in the upper reading room. He had in some degree changed his spots, but he was discernibly the same leopard. And he had made his kill.

Almost without knowing what she did, Jane pushed forward once more and dropped on her knees beside the hunted man. He had opened his eyes. Now he moved his head slightly and looked at her. She saw that he recognized her – or perhaps that he took her for somebody else. His lips trembled, but no sound came. Then his glance went to the man kneeling opposite, and Jane saw his eyes dilate. She knew that it was in terror. Something moved at his side. It was his hand, groping towards Jane. 'Mummy,' he whispered, 'darl –' His voice faded into a faint, thin wail.

Jane turned. She had remembered the policeman. But the policeman was briskly waving people to the footpath. To the accompaniment of an urgent little bell that had been quite lost amid the chiming all around, an ambulance had driven up, halted and backed, and was now standing with its open doors within a yard of the prostrate man's head. Attendants were getting a stretcher out. A sense of desperate urgency seized Jane. She scrambled to her feet and caught the policeman by the arm. 'Stop!' she cried, 'I want to tell you –'

But the policeman shook himself rather roughly free. 'Just a moment, miss,' he said brusquely. 'Plenty of time when we've got him in.'

The stretcher, with the man on it – the hunted man – was being lifted into the ambulance. 'You don't understand,' Jane cried. 'It's a trick! These people –'

From behind her she heard again the hunted man's thin wail. She was irresistibly impelled to turn back to him. He was just disappearing. Their eyes met. His head moved slightly in a sort of agony of impotence, 'No!' he whispered. 'You can't do it to me . . . not . . . not to Milton . . .'

The door of the ambulance slammed. The policeman was by the bonnet shouting to people to keep clear. The ambulance moved. The policeman opened the door beside the driver and stepped inside. In a second's swift acceleration the ambulance had swung out of Radcliffe Square and was gone. Jane turned round. The black car, with its spurious doctor, had gone too. The little knot of spectators was dispersing. To rush at one of them with a cock and bull story would be completely futile. It was the first downright adventure of her life. And she had been roundly defeated.

But there was something more than that. She stood where the hunted man had lain – stood fighting for recollection, for clarity, for what she knew was a single supremely important perception. She had a sudden irrational wish to be in open country, to be in a quiet room. All around her was a massive apparatus of learning: cliffs of books in the Camera, in the Codrington, in the Bodleian – and even beneath her feet, she knew, more and more learning, profound, unfathomable, in subterranean chambers deep down below the cobbles on which had been flung by some horrible and surreptitious violence the wretched little man who in his agony had called out to her as to his mother . . . Jane laughed aloud, in incipient hysteria. It was like being very thirsty on a broad, broad ocean. All that knowledge – and she wanted one single elusive fact alone.

She dug her nails hard into her palms. They were nails inadequately prepared to be very effective in this way, but she contrived to make them hurt. The man had whispered something just as he was whisked away. It was something idiotic, meaningless . . . something about a poet . . . *Not to Milton* . . . that was it. But why –

And then Jane understood. The sudden, full wash of lucidity over her brain was like a plunge into cold and reviving waters. Milton was not a man but a place. And the poor devil's last gasped word had been an agonized cry against being swept off to it.

And now he had vanished. And it was through a Milton – Milton Porcorum – that somebody had reported seeing another man being driven. Another vanished man . . .

For a moment her whole body felt very cold; it was as if she had indeed been plunged into icy water for a long time. But she knew she could run – and she ran. She ran through the Bodleian quadrangle, careless of its violated quiet, and through the gap between the Clarendon Building and the Sheldonian Theatre. There was no car for hire – as she had hoped there might be – in the rank between Turl Street and the gates of Trinity. But she had only to go on to the foot of St Giles' to be sure of finding one. She might have got there quicker on her bicycle, but she had forgotten all about that.

At the most, it would take little over an hour and a half . . . Struck by a sudden thought, she stopped and turned, panting, into the Broad Street post office. She was out of it within three minutes and running up Magdalen Street. It was just here that she had had that idiotic collision. But not so idiotic, either. She would never have noticed what was going on in the upper reading room had she not earlier knocked the man down in the street. And she wouldn't have done *that* had she not been in such a hurry to get away from poor old Dr Ourglass and that ass Bultitude. So even fat and famous dons had their utility . . .

She tumbled into a waiting and reasonably powerful-looking car. The driver, a young man in an enveloping duffel-coat, received her instructions with unobtrusive respect – with a respect *so* unobtrusive, indeed, that Jane took a second look at him. If the morning's events had not made her sensitive to the notion of imposture, she would probably have held her peace. As it was, she spoke out baldly and with frank suspicion. 'Didn't I use to see you at lectures?'

The young man's eyebrows raised themselves slightly in mild reproach. 'Madam,' he said, 'must I always be reproached with my past?'

Despite the turmoil of her thoughts, Jane still had some area of her mind available for the sensation of feeling a fool. 'I'm sorry,' she said. 'It just surprised me. Will you please –'

Her speech was cut short by a sudden and astonishing commotion all around her. It was rather like being incontinently in the middle of a flock of starlings. This commotion wheeled on the car as on a pivot and disappeared down Beaumont Street. The young man was startled too. 'That's odd,' he said. 'What on earth can the little creatures –' Then it seemed to occur to him that a taxi-driver should be a man of few words. He shut the door on Jane, jumped in front and took the wheel. The car moved smoothly off down Magdalen Street and the Cornmarket. It had turned at Carfax and was nearing the railway station when the young man spoke over his shoulder. 'I know fares sometimes don't like it,' he said, 'but do you mind if I make an observation?'

Jane compressed her lips. The world – or certainly the world of Oxford – is full of tiresome young men. 'Not in the least,' she said coldly.

'Well, it's about those lectures. I was carried away by presumption. It wasn't me you saw. Your question prompted me to claim a higher station in life than I am rightfully entitled to. I hope you will forgive me.'

'Stuff and nonsense. It was certainly you. You came from Balliol.'

The young man gave a low moan. 'Then it has happened again – this humiliating, this intolerable confusion.'

'I don't know what you're talking about.'

'It was my brother.'

'Your brother?'

'My *legitimate* brother, Herbert. I'm just 'Enery.'

Jane lost patience. 'For goodness sake, shut up. And get a move on.'

The road ahead was clear. The young man who was pleased to call himself 'Enery cast a swift backward glance at his passenger. 'In a hurry?' he asked.

'Yes.'

There was that in Jane's voice that the young man took a moment to digest. 'Life or death?'

'Quite honestly – just that.'

The young man thrust at his accelerator so that the car seemed to punch Jane in the back. 'If I lose my licence,' he said, 'and – mark you – it's all that stands between a poor bastard boy and the gutter, I am wholly yours. They say these things will touch eighty.'

Jane set her teeth. 'Then,' she said, 'touch it.'

8

The play had been timed for the eve of the half-term holiday. This avoided complications over home-work. And the play had been quite a success. But this served only to lend the morrow a tiresome air of anti-climax. Stuart

Buffin, having improvidently made no arrangements whatever for its expenditure, felt this with peculiar force. The sensation, however, was pervasive throughout North Oxford that morning. Had this not been so, things might have turned out very differently. To begin with, Jane Appleby and her driver 'Enery would not have experienced that startled moment at the spot which has now for some time been the hub of our narrative: that corner, to wit, of St Giles' and Beaumont Street the dominating feature of which is Bede's College.

Stuart's sense, moreover, of having brushed adventure on the preceding evening was another important factor. And – further to this again – was his indignation that this sense of having brushed adventure had itself been brushed rudely aside. His father, lingering for a few moments in benevolent if absent contemplation of the frugal family supper before going off to dine in Bede's, had received the story of the hunted man without enthusiasm. He had even made a derogatory remark about the effects of too much Superman – a quip that had offended Stuart as much by its *passé* quality as by its injustice. The world, Stuart considered, was not so pervasively dull and securely ordered a place as long years of comfortable dining in Bede's and similar establishments led elderly persons to believe. Things *did* happen. Only, when they began to happen, authority was prone to take one firmly by the ear and lead one into inglorious security. That was what had occurred during the war, when substantial numbers of future Tigers had been bundled off to America. It was what had happened when the gym caught fire and they had been indecently herded into the middle distance much as if the fire-engines had been a force of hostile tanks. *They* would always nip in and cut you out of things if given the chance.

These and other dark thoughts had disposed Stuart Buffin to make a most belated appearance at breakfast that morning. They disposed him, when he realized that his mother wanted to get the table cleared, to sit owlishly over the repast, nibbling his way through toast and marmalade at the steady rate of one slice every twelve minutes. This recalcitrance, however, was visited with its just penalty, and Stuart found himself implacably roped in to help with the washing up. By the time that this tiresome operation was accomplished and he had emerged into the hall the clock was striking ten. He wished that he had fixed something up with Martin or Miles or Dick or Malcolm. As things were, he addressed himself gloomily to climbing the stairs, being persuaded that nothing lay before him but a morning's communion with his stamp collection. And stamp collecting, he was rapidly coming to feel, was a nauseating practice . . . It was at this moment that the telephone bell rang.

Stuart's mood being not at present cooperative, he at first felt disposed to ignore the instrument. His father had already left the house. If his mother had to hurry in from coping with the hens in order to answer the thing, or if Mrs Sparks emerged from her soap-suds to deal with it and got the message hopelessly muddled – well, that was just too bad. Stuart, however, was really a child tolerant of – indeed, amiably disposed towards – those with whom fate had directed that he should live. Partly because of this, and partly because the call was probably from one of his father's pupils, tiresomely wanting to change the hour of a tutorial – in which event Stuart would give himself the satisfaction of replying to the great lout with the most awful and freezing courtesy – he decided to answer the summons after all. He moved over to the telephone and picked up the receiver. What he heard was a low voice with a foreign accent. What he believed this voice to say was 'Stuart, is that you?'

'Yes.' Stuart growled this reply with a good deal of moroseness. He had jumped to the conclusion that some silly ass of his acquaintance was having him on.

'This is Anna.' The voice was really a woman's – and it was tense and vibrant. 'The place is called Milton Manor, near Milton Porcorum. The danger is now too great. And it is to the boy.' The voice grew suddenly yet more urgent, so that Stuart felt a queer pricking in his spine. 'Come at once, Kurt. Bring –'

And then the voice broke off. It broke off with a sharp, interrupted cry and a smothered gasp: it was as if powerful hands had closed round the speaker's throat. There was a thump – a very horrid thump – and then the click of a receiver being set down. The line was dead.

Stuart . . . Kurt. It had been a wrong number – they were always happening – and he got a message not meant for him. Stuart Buffin found that he was trembling and wet all over, as if he had tried to break the record in the school quarter mile. He found that he had sat down – and it was only because of this, he realized, that he was not rushing to his mother for all he was worth. For he was not in the slightest doubt about the kind of thing with which he had been in contact over some unknown distance. It was violence . . . danger . . . evil. And suddenly his eyes rounded. It was more even than that. It was the proof of what he had known: that things *happen*. He took a deep breath. He glanced in quick stealth about the hall, listened for footsteps, for any sound in the nearer rooms. There was nobody about. He picked up the telephone again and swiftly dialled a number. And when he got an answer his voice was as urgent as the woman's he had just heard.

'This is Stuart Buffin; please may I speak to Miles? . . . Miles, it's Stuart. Ring round and get everybody to your place *now*. I'm coming straight across . . . *Everybody* . . . Miles, it's something sticking out . . . it's tremendous . . .'

He banged down the receiver and dashed upstairs, taking the steps three at a time. When he came down again a moment later he was wearing his dark blue blazer with the crouching tiger on its pocket and its peremptory injunction: *Symmetry*. In the pockets were his purse, his torch, his big clasp knife.

Stuart's mother, returning from her hens, was just in time to see the boy disappearing on his bicycle. For a moment she was sharply anxious. But he

365

was safely past the cross-roads – the quiet one which she was convinced could be so treacherous. Thank goodness, she thought, Stuart seemed to have found something to do. It had looked like being a sticky half-term.

9

Miles never did things by halves. There was a formidable gathering of Tigers in the hut, and soon debate ran high. The red-haired Tigers – known throughout Oxford to be the most temerarious and terrible – were on the side of Stuart, and of Miles, who was their natural leader. But (as in the great consult in Satan's Pandemonium) there were other voices that urged caution. Of these the first was Dick's – that cool intelligence who, as Dick Whittington, had maintained so lofty a port amid answering confusion the evening before.

'I think it's too far,' Dick said. 'We *could* make it. But look at that hilly terrain.' His finger went down with a staff officer's decision on the map spread before him. 'It might take up to three hours.' He shook his head sombrely. 'A good many of us would never get back.'

'I don't see why not.' Miles was obstinate. 'Coming back, a lot of it will be downhill.'

'I know that, idiot. But we'd have a head-wind against us.'

'A head-wind!' Miles was rash and eager. 'How can you tell that?'

Silently, Dick moved his finger first to the pocket compass by which he had set the map, and then to a window through which it was just possible to see a neighbouring weathercock. Everybody was impressed. Stuart saw that things were going badly. 'But the wind's sure to change,' he said. 'It nearly always does, in the afternoon.'

'That's right!' Several Tigers, mostly red-headed, immediately took up in all innocence this mendacious statement. 'Stuart's right. The wind always changes. Ask Malcolm. Malcolm knows.'

And Malcolm, the scientifically minded child who had been somewhat overborne by the complexities of theatrical lighting the evening before, nodded gravely. 'Of course,' he agreed. 'It has something to do with the cooling off of the central land mass. But I'm not *quite* sure about the details.'

'I bet you're not.' Dick was angry. 'And there's another objection. We'd have to leave some sort of word. We can't all just go off. And if we once let parents and people know –'

But this was a mistake, and was at once cried down. 'Rot!' 'We can all go off till supper time.' 'That's only the kids.' 'Just say it's a picnic.' 'And so it would be if we took some sandwiches.' 'Leave some sort of message to be found later.'

'Very well. I agree we could go – if we could make the distance.' The lucid Dick was quick to abandon an untenable position. 'But there *is* the distance. And there's another thing. I think it more important. Stuart says this may be frightfully serious. That means we ought to speak out about it. Probably to the police.'

'And what good would that do?' Miles advanced into the centre of the assembly. This delay infuriated him, and his face was growing increasingly pink beneath its mop of red hair. 'Everybody would say that Stuart had been dreaming – or sogging himself in flicks. One never *does* get things like that believed.'

'Here, here!' 'Miles is right.' 'They'd laugh at it.' 'They'd laugh at it – and then keep an eye on us.' 'No good.' There was now clamour from all over the hut, and most of it was in the form of a demand for action. A crowd was milling round the map, disputing fiercely. Dick walked away from it moodily – rather as Napoleon might have withdrawn himself from the burdensome society of a group of excited marshals.

'Why not go by train?'

Everybody turned and stared. There were several girl Tigers in the gathering, and it had been a small and very red-headed one who spoke. Dick turned round. 'Nonsense. Go and look at the map, Marty, I've been through this Porcorum place by car. It's miles from a railway station.'

The girl called Marty thrust her way close to the map, and with some difficulty got her nose above the level of the table. 'I thought so,' she said. 'We can put our bikes on the eleven twenty-five, and be in Bourton-on-the-Water an hour later. And from there we can *strike*.'

There was a moment of awed silence. Of Tigers it is particularly true that the female of the species is more deadly than the male. The small person called Marty was challenging the gathering with flashing eyes and dilated nostrils. Dick was clearly wavering. But a new and solid point occurred to him. 'And what about the fares?' He ran his eye over the assembled crowd. 'It would be an enormous sum. And bicycle tickets, too. We wouldn't have anything like it even if we pooled all we've got.'

'We've got the money for the Dumb Friends from last night. It came to pounds. Martin has it. He was treasurer.'

Again there was a hush. Before this female ruthlessness the predominantly male assembly was momentarily speechless. Then a serious-looking boy spoke from the back. 'Isn't that,' he asked, 'what's called embarrassment?'

Yells of mirth from the better informed greeted this unhappy malapropism, mingled with urgent demands for Martin and the money-box. Dick, like the Homeric hero hither and thither dividing the swift mind, and seeing that the issue was in fact decided, instantly took the course necessary to maintain his predominance not only of the gathering as a whole but of the insurgent and triumphant faction of the red heads. 'All back here with bikes in fifteen minutes,' he shouted. 'Sandwiches, chocolate, macs, compasses, and all useful weapons. Proceed by Banbury Road, St Giles', and Beaumont Street. Roll-call at the station, and Martin and I buy all the tickets. Nothing to be said at anybody's home except that it's a picnic.' He raised his voice against a chorus of excitement, 'And I hope – you silly twerps – you won't make all that row if we have to go into action. You might be a crowd of howling Chinese.'

Without paying much attention to this tart remark, the crowd hastily dispersed. Stuart Buffin and his crony Miles, wild with joy at having carried the day, dashed for their bicycles. But before they could leave the hut they were cornered by the unremittingly clear-headed Dick. 'Look here,' he said, 'trying to talk sense to these silly asses is no good at all. But I'd better tell *you*.'

'What do you mean – tell us?' Stuart was suspicious. 'This is jolly well my affair. It's for me to be telling you.'

'Forget it.' Dick frowned at hearing himself drop into this vaguely transatlantic expression. 'All I want to say is this. Before that train goes out I send a telegram from the station – see?'

'Who do you want to send a telegram to?' Miles was quite as wary as Stuart.

'I couldn't care less.' This time Dick seemed to take satisfaction in the raciness of the expression. 'The police, your father, my father, the Prime Minister: you can take your pick. But to somebody I send back word of just where we're going. No reason why we shouldn't keep in touch. We're not bandits, you know. We're part of the law.' He took a quick glance at Stuart and Miles, uncertain whether he had hit on a line that would appeal to their childish intellects.

'Very well.' Miles was pink and furious. 'But if we find a couple of country bobbies at this Bourton-on-the-Water place, told off by telephone to pack us off home, I'll – I'll scrag you.'

'You're welcome.' And Dick went briskly out. A little Secret-Service Boy stuff, he was reflecting, had its amusing aspects. There was no harm in giving the young a day out with Biggles – provided that one kept, for one's own part, the realities of the situation in mind. Riding off to collect his sandwiches, he began composing his telegram. It looked like being a long one.

But presently, and as he furiously pedalled, his serious air relaxed. There was nobody to see him. He grinned broadly. For even this serious child had a proper streak of fantasy. He looked forward to the confusion at the railway station when a small army arrived with bicycles and insisted on loading them on the sleepy little train for Bourton-on-the-Water. After that, there might, or might not, be adventure in the thing. He had an open mind. He always had.

5. Nemesis at Milton Manor

And they, so perfect is their misery,
Not once perceive their foul disfigurement.
Comus

I

Appleby made a final jotting on the pad in front of him. 'Thank you,
Superintendent. The facts seem to be pretty well as I remembered them.
But there's one thing more – about the place Milton Manor . . . Yes, I know
it's that. What I want is something much fuller. Get on to the General
Medical Council. These concerns must be registered, and you can get a bit
of a line through that. Who sends people there, and why – you see? . . .
Yes, of course they're often sticky. If there is delay, ask the Commissioner
to be good enough to tackle somebody high up at once. But remember the
time factor. I don't want a bulging file next Friday; I want what you can
get by noon . . . And – Superintendent – one more thing. You've spotted
this place on the map? Good. Well, if you don't hear from me between two
and three o'clock, carry out Instruction D . . . You needn't sound so surprised . . . Yes, I *did* say D . . . Thank you – that's all.'

The Provost of Bede's knocked out his pipe into the comfortable fire
glowing in his study, and waited until Appleby had put the receiver down.
'Well, well,' he said; 'and to think that all those meditative essays you used
to read to me were leading to this . . . You are become a very brisk fellow,
my dear John.'

'They weren't meditative; they were merely thorough.' Appleby smiled
rather absently, and walked across the long room to stare out of the window.
'As for briskness, since you became the Head of a House, you are a model
of it yourself.'

The Provost reached for a decanter. 'I attribute the still comparatively
unclouded state of my faculties to the observance of one single rule. I have
taken to nothing but solitary drinking. Drink does no harm if you are in
a position to give your mind to it. Moreover the habit is very inexpensive.
Two glasses of brown sherry – or, for a change, of light hunting port –
consumed slowly between 11 a.m. and noon: I do all my work on it.' The
Provost raised the decanter. 'But, for this once, I will have somebody join
me. Perhaps I may convert you.'

Appleby took the glass held out to him, and shook his head.

'The prescription is useless to me. My hours of labour are not so agreeably
contracted. Frequently I work right on into the middle of the night – only
to be hit on the head in a quiet Oxford road and carried away in a van. If
many of your guests are served in the same way, it will positively give the
place a bad name. I think you ought to take the matter up with the Proctors.'

'It will be simpler, John, that you should take it up with the criminals. And that is just what you have rather the appearance of being engaged in.' The Provost took the poker and gave a vicious thrust at a sluggish lump of coal. 'Look here – I wish you'd tell me what all this is about. Is this tramp, or whatever he was, that you hit up with last night – Routh, did he call himself? – really connected with our missing undergraduate?'

'I think there can be small doubt about it.' Appleby's voice was grim. 'For my sister's sake, I wish it wasn't so.'

'You think the young man was once hit on the head and put in a van, too?'

'No, I don't. Because I don't think Routh's adventures began that way either. Nor Miss Kolmak's.'

'Miss Kolmak? Who on earth is she?'

'Well – that's not, come to think of it, her name. She's Mrs Something-or-other – some name with a decidedly farther-side-of-the-iron-curtain twist to it, I imagine. And she is the adopted daughter of your Kurt Kolmak's aunt. She, too, appears to have been kidnapped, together with her small son.'

'God bless my soul! Do you mean to say, John, that such outrageous things happen in this country?' The Provost, who had been about to set down the poker, appeared to think better of it – much as if a handy weapon might be needed at any moment.

'It seems they do.' Appleby made a wry face. 'Unexplained vanishings do from time to time occur. And lately some have occurred in a way that has set us thinking.'

'You mean that this queer and disgraceful business here somehow hitches on to a situation you have been investigating already?'

'I think it just possibly may. And, while I'm waiting for a little more data, I propose to tell you about it – just as I used to bring you philosophical problems that were too tough for me.'

The Provost, while receiving this analogy with evident scepticism, abruptly put aside the poker and sat down. 'Good,' he said.

'Well, then – here is the first problem I'd put to you. Suppose, Provost, that you are to all appearances a law-abiding Englishman – one engaged, indeed, in some wholly beneficent profession –'

The Provost grinned. 'You always did begin, my boy, with some wild hypothesis.'

'Don't interrupt. Suppose that, although your way of life is entirely blameless, you yet keep a Minotaur in your back yard. This creature must have its regular tribute of youths and maidens. Not a vast number, for this is a small and abstemious Minotaur. Still, its appetite is steady, and must be satisfied. How would you do the catering?'

The Provost considered. 'I should keep an eye open for the *filius nullius*, the *filius terrae* –'

'While avoiding the *filius honesto genere natus*. Precisely! In other words, it would be foolish to make away with persons of established position so long as you could conveniently find waifs and strays.'

'I see what you are getting at.' The Provost stretched out an arm for his second glass of brown sherry, appeared to think better of it, and thrust the decanter out of reach. 'But it doesn't seem quite to fit last night's proceedings. Assistant Commissioners of the Metropolitan Police are neither strays nor waifs.'

'That was a different matter. My guess is that they were endeavouring to recover an escapee, and that they just had to take me while they were about it. Although there may well have been another reason, too.'

'Are you going to tell me who "they" are?'

'I wish that, with any certainty, I knew. But let me stick to a proper order. Some time ago there was a curious case of a fellow who was released from prison after serving a long term on account of a big robbery. He hadn't a relation or acquaintance in the world, and he took to drifting about, getting a labourer's job from time to time in one town or another. Nobody ought to have the faintest interest in either him or his movements. But – as it happened – the Bristol police had. There was stuff that had never been recovered, and they thought that eventually he might make for it. So an eye was kept on him, without his knowing it. He vanished.'

'Smart of him, I'd say.'

'Perhaps. But there have been one or two other cases that have come, you might say, within the same general category. Waifs and strays who turned out to be not quite absolutely *filii terrae* after all. They vanished and – what nobody would have suspected from their circumstances – were inquired about.'

The Provost frowned. 'Interesting, no doubt. But, unless the numbers were quite considerable, I don't see that you could build much –'

'They grouped on the map.'

The Provost sat up abruptly. 'And this place we keep hearing about – Milton Canonicorum –'

'Porcorum.'

'This ridiculously named place is well in the picture?'

'It is. Not plumb centre. But decidedly there.'

'And it's dawned on you that you now have a new crop of relevant disappearances?' The Provost had suddenly assumed an expression of sombre melancholy, suggestive of a rational being condemned to pass long hours in the society of more primitive forms of mental life.

Appleby smiled. 'You haven't altogether lost your old touch. And the point's fair enough. But remember that I came up thinking simply of this young man of my sister Jane's. And he's a bit out of series, as you probably already see. But there's the first fact: people have in a mild way been tending to disappear within a certain area. People like this chap Routh.'

'A tramp?'

'Routh is not in the least a tramp – and, I'd say, nothing like half as honest. But he is definitely a lone-wolf type. Probably he's proud of it, so that it would emerge pretty well at a first brush with him. Well, I think he went to feed the Minotaur.'

'And was disgorged again?'

'And escaped from the labyrinth. I'm not sure it wasn't with blood on his hands. And he certainly carried something that he believed valuable off with him.'

'Not an Ariadne?'

'Something much more portable than a young woman. He had it in the inside breast-pocket of his jacket.' Appleby had risen and was pacing the room – his eye, every now and then, straying expectantly to the telephone. 'Well, he got away. Then they got him again, plus me. Then we were both rescued by this astonishing Kolmak of yours, about whom I must ask you presently. Then, in the early morning, and while I was still oblivious, he beat it.'

'And is now?'

'I only wish I knew. And I have my fears, as you can guess. The local people have a net out for him – but I don't much like the way the half-hours are going by without news . . . Where in Oxford would you hide, Provost, if you felt yourself to be a fugitive both from lawlessness and the law?'

'In Bodley.' The Provost had no doubts about it.

'I hadn't thought of that. Do you think the local men –'

'It certainly won't be quite their first thought either.'

'Well, we must give them a little more time. Now, consider the woman. Her name is Anna, and she has managed to smuggle both herself and her child into England. Her position was irregular, and her past was no doubt a long history of senseless persecution. Probably she was inclined a little to dramatize her predicament. She and her boy were fair food for the Minotaur.'

The Provost stirred uneasily. 'I begin to believe in it. And I don't like it – particularly the bit about the child.'

'Quite so. But here we come to an odd thing. It is quite clear to me that this woman, with her little boy, was carried off and put under some sort of constraint. But not an absolute constraint. She twice managed to elude the vigilance of her captors – I think we may call it that – and communicate covertly with Kolmak. On each occasion she could have declared her whereabouts. And on each occasion she deliberately refrained. The second message spoke of danger, and of the possible need to send an urgent telephone summons for help. That second message was sent off yesterday afternoon. Kolmak is waiting beside his telephone now. And, of course, it is being checked. If his number is called, any conversation will be recorded.'

The Provost, who had been sitting with closed eyes, momentarily opened them. 'What about a wrong number?'

'What's that?' Appleby was startled.

'Suppose this woman's danger is suddenly precipitated. She's in a great hurry to send out a telephone-message – secretly. Quite likely, you know, to get through to the wrong number.'

Appleby frowned. 'Then it will depend upon a time-factor. The County people will be arranging to tap the telephone – or telephones – in this Milton place. But, technically, it will be a bit of a job.'

'Just an idea.' The Provost's voice was so vague and apologetic that Appleby found himself grinning a most juvenile grin. He remembered very well what this meant. The old boy was really thinking.

'My impression is this. The woman called Anna feels that she is on the verge of discovering something. She judges it so important that it is her duty to continue courting danger – danger not only for herself but for her boy. She didn't want Kolmak, the police, rescue, and so forth. What do you make of that?'

'Has she a profession?'

'She's a doctor.'

'Would you say, John, that Minotaurs find female physicians particularly toothsome?'

'I think I'd say that her profession made her something of a special case. Perhaps there was some idea of making her less a victim than an attendant.'

'And correspondingly, her professional knowledge would give her a special interest in – and perhaps penetration about – the activities of the establishment.'

'Quite so. And now to come to young Geoffrey Ourglass. He is clearly to be bound in somehow. He too vanishes – long before either of these other two – and is last seen being driven through Milton Porcorum. But at once – or almost at once – his uncle, his fiancée, his tutor, and no doubt plenty of other people too, start inquiring about him. So you see what I mean by his being out of series.'

The Provost nodded. 'The point is hardly an obscure one. Far from being a *filius terrae*, this young man is highly prized by the world and shortly due to scoop the pool: a First in Schools, a secure and probably highly distinguished career, an admirable wife and an irreproachable brother-in-law –' Abruptly the Provost's eyes came open again, fixing themselves on Appleby as if he suddenly felt obliged to verify this last statement. 'But – great heavens! – now that I come to think of it –'

The telephone at the farther end of the room gave a low purr. Appleby leapt to it. 'Yes,' he said, 'yes – I am Sir John Appleby. . . . An accident? . . . I see . . . And what about that van? . . . Thank you.' He put down the receiver and turned to the Provost. 'Routh was still in Oxford just after ten o'clock. A constable saw him bolting down Broad Street.'

'Saw him! Then why the dickens didn't he go after him?'

'Because it was only when he got down to Carfax that the word about Routh was passed to him by the next man. You must remember they've been on the job only a couple of hours. But seeing a fellow rather the worse for wear making off down the street, the constable took a good look at him.

And a passer-by told him there had just been some sort of accident with no great harm done – this fellow having bumped into a bicycle, or something of the sort. But, so far, a hunt in that district has produced nothing more. Incidentally, the van that operated so drastically against Routh and myself last night, and that was driven away and parked by Kolmak, has vanished. The enemy must have retrieved it.'

'Enemy seems the right word, John. I get the impression that you are confronting quite a crowd. But there was something I was going to say. It's a story about young Ourglass that Birkbeck told me, but that didn't strike me as relevant until this *filius terrae* business sprang up. To begin with, Ourglass, as you probably know, isn't really so very young. He's in the last batch of our actual war-service men, and he must be a good many years older than your sister.'

Appleby nodded. 'He's twenty-seven.'

'Well, the point is this. Although not a *filius terrae* in actuality he did on one occasion put up a very good show of being one. And the story is so much to his credit that I am sorry it didn't reach my ears earlier. I don't very effectively get to know our men before the end of their second year, and I'd have been glad to make this fellow's acquaintance earlier. But perhaps you know about him from your sister?'

'I know very little. Jane has been rather close about the engagement, and so far today I've failed to contact her.' Appleby glanced quickly at the Provost. 'You know, the more I've thought about this business in the last few hours, the grimmer the view I've been inclined to take about the young man's chances of survival. The mere length of his disappearance looks pretty bad. But I'm not sure you're not going to tell me something hopeful.'

'I hope I am. At least young Ourglass appears to be – or to have been – a person very able to give a good account of himself. The facts are these. He has a flair for acting of sorts. Character-turns and sketches – and an ability to take on the colouring of the people he's living among. Moreover, he's a bit of a linguist. Well, in the last couple of years of the war he was spotted doing that sort of thing – simply to amuse himself and his friends – in Italy. He could do an Italian peasant to the life. So he was parachuted either into Germany or German-occupied territory – I'm not sure which – and managed to get himself rounded up as a D.P. worker and clapped into an armament factory. Before the show ended, it seems he got one or two pretty useful bits of information out. A pretty gallant job. And I've an idea that his subsequent delay in getting up here may have been due to some rather similar assignment. It might be part of your picture – eh?'

'It might, indeed. And it's odd that nothing of this came through to me. The young man must be even closer than Jane.'

'Presumably he is. I had this from Birkbeck only after you left common-room last night.'

'And from whom did Birkbeck have it?'

'From Bultitude.'

Appleby frowned. 'Bultitude! You mean your fat scientist?'

'That is a very cavalier way, my dear John, to speak of Bede's only celebrity. Bultitude had it from somebody terribly high up in something. He likes altitudes, you know.'

'So I gathered.' Appleby was silent for a moment. 'Great carcass of a man, isn't he? How did they use him in the war – as a barrage balloon?'

'Biological warfare.'

'Sounds horrid.'

'Quite unspectacular, I believe – or at least the parts of it that ever got going. Thinking up insulating materials that wouldn't be devoured by bugs in New Guinea and Malaya . . . Would you care for that second glass of sherry?'

'No thank you. Nothing more for me until luncheon in Milton Porcorum.'

The Provost nodded. 'I wondered when you'd be going out there.'

'I'm leaving at noon. But first I want to catch Jane, and also get more reports from the local people and the Yard . . . Ah, there they are.'

The telephone had purred again, and Appleby sprang to it. 'Hullo, is that – Oh, I see . . . This *is* Sir John Appleby speaking . . . Yes, go ahead . . . What's that word? . . . s-u-a? . . . I've got it. Go on . . . Thank you. Yes, send the confirmatory copy to me at the Provost's Lodgings.' He put down the instrument and turned to the Provost. 'Well, I'm dashed.'

'Telegram from London?'

'No. It was from Jane, here in Oxford. Listen.' Appleby glanced at the note he had made. 'Man weedy scratched face first observed upper reading room now being taken non sponte sua in ambulance to Milton stop left Radcliffe Square 11 a.m. stop am following in hired car investigate.' He threw the paper on the desk. 'And it's signed "Jane". What do you think of that?'

'That your sister has the rudiments of the Latin tongue. Though why she should break into it –'

'She felt that to say in English that a man had just been carried off against his will from Radcliffe Square might provoke questions and hold her up. Well, these people have got Routh again. And they may presently have this impetuous sister of mine as well. I'd better be off.'

'I agree.' The Provost rose. 'Does it occur to you that they must know that you *know*?'

Appleby nodded grimly. 'It certainly does. Of course the only positive fact they have is that I have talked with Routh, and they probably suspect nothing of our having tumbled upon other evidence pointing their way. They may reckon now on extorting fairly reliably from Routh just what he did tell me. But – unless we have the whole picture wrong – Milton Manor now contains a large and quite ruthless criminal organization, who have been up to heaven knows what, and who now confront a state of emergency. In fact, they are preparing to pack up. And that's what I don't like.'

'I don't see why not. It means that, even before you know what their game is, you've got them on the run.'

'No doubt. But people driven to hurried packing sometimes decide to travel light. They even scrap things.'

The Provost pursed his lips. 'I hope you return in time to dine, and if you bring back our missing undergraduate – well, his dinner too awaits him – such as it is.'

2

Just short of Witney, it occurred to Jane that the young man styling himself 'Enery might eventually find her behaviour odd. She had very little to go upon. Indeed, all she could do was to poke about Milton Porcorum inquiring for an ambulance. And that must be a proceeding that would strike anyone as a little out of the way. She had better, therefore, do some explaining. On the other hand it would not do to explain too much. If she announced that it was her aim to track down and interview a number of men who had just carried out a highly criminal abduction, he might suppose her to be mad or at least unwomanly. He would probably suggest applying to the police. But she had done that – she was sure in the most effective way possible – by sending John the telegram; and now it was a point of honour to push straight in herself. If the ambulance led to Geoffrey, and to piercing the dark veil that had made a nightmare of her life week after week for what seemed an eternity, she must follow it at any hazard whatsoever, and with all the speed that a hired car could muster.

Jane determined to reopen communications. She therefore leant across the front seat. 'May I explain a little?' she asked.

'Does a romantic secret cloud your birth too?'

Jane ignored this. 'What I'm looking for,' she said, 'is an ambulance.'

'Isn't that a trifle pessimistic? I'm quite a careful driver – although you *are* making me go at a fair lick.'

'It's impossible to talk to you.'

'Not a bit. I'm attending. And I'll find you an ambulance if I possibly can. Any particular sort?'

'I want to *trace* an ambulance. It left Oxford – Radcliffe Square, to be exact – at eleven o'clock, and I think it's going to this Milton Porcorum, or to somewhere near there. There is somebody in it that I want to keep in contact with. Only I wasn't told just where it's bound for.'

The young man received this in silence. But he had the air of giving the matter a good deal of thought. When he did speak, it was with some appearance of irrelevance. 'My name is not 'Enery.'

'I didn't think that it was for a moment.'

'My name is Roger Remnant. I *was* up at Balliol. And doubtless you and all your acquaintances *did* see me at lectures. I didn't think much of them.'

'I'm sure my acquaintances would all be very much upset if they knew.'

'Not your acquaintances – the lectures. That was the trouble. I didn't manage to see much in the lectures, and eventually the chaps giving them weren't able to see much in me. Fair enough. But I thought I'd like to stop about Oxford for a bit, so here I am. Who are you?'

'My name is Jane Appleby. I'm up at Somerville.'

Roger Remnant bowed gravely towards the wind-screen; he was driving much too fast to take his eyes even for a moment from the road. 'How do you do.'

'How do you do.' Jane judged it discreet to comply with this fantastic observance of forms.

'Our association is now on an entirely different basis.' The late 'Enery made this statement as if he wholly believed it. 'And we had better get back to this ambulance. You say it left Oxford at precisely eleven o'clock. We left at eleven-ten. There would be a point at which it was no more than two miles ahead. But it would increase that lead when it got into more or less open country and we were still nosing out of Oxford. An ambulance can get away with a lot. I'm afraid we are not likely to catch up with it. And, of course, it may have gone out of Oxford by the Woodstock Road. I reckon Witney and Burford to be best, but I can see that there's a case for Chipping Norton and Stow-on-the-Wold.'

'I see.' Jane was impressed by this professional clarity.

'So it looks as if our best course will be simply to inquire for it when we get into the neighbourhood you think it's making for.'

'That's what I think.' Jane was relieved. Roger Remnant appeared disposed to take it as all in a day's work.

'Is it really an ambulance, or is there something queer about it?'

Jane jumped on her swaying seat. She hadn't expected this swift perspicacity. 'It – it's something queer.'

'I expect we'll find it. Do you know the country?'

'Not very well.'

'There are some maps in the pocket on the door on your left. You'd better sit back and do a bit of work on them.'

The map that looked most hopeful was an ancient one on a scale of eight miles to an inch. Jane learnt what she could from it. Finding the area involved, she ran to earth, despite the jolting of the car, a small black point marked 'Milton'. Towards this, and from a secondary road some miles away, an unobtrusive scratch moved indecisively before petering out. The place must be decidedly in what is called the heart of the countryside. She looked about her and saw that they were already in rural solitude. There was an empty road before them, with nobody in sight except two trudging women with rucksacks. It was good walking weather. The autumn day was like a great cup of sunlight. She thought of the wretched little man shut up in the near-darkness of the bogus ambulance, of the sinister power that had edged him out of the security of the upper reading room, of the alarming efficiency with which he had then been dealt with in what could have been no more than a few seconds free from public observation. And she suddenly felt cold. The Cotswold air, perhaps, was chilly despite the clear sunshine.

The drive seemed endless. But eventually she was aware that they had left the high road, and were plunging down what was no more than a lane between high hedges. The proximity of these magnified her sense of the speed at which the car was travelling; sometimes a projecting branch whipped its sides with the effect of a momentary hail-storm; she wondered what would happen if they met a farm wagon, or a straying horse or cow. Roger took a right-angled turn almost without slackening pace, so that the racing wheels and strained chassis gave a squeal of protest. 'No call for alarm,' he said. 'Tyres just a trifle in need of air . . . Here's another one.' They cornered again by a small half-obliterated sign-post that Jane failed to decipher. It had a look of local enterprise, and suggested recesses of the region so obscure as to be beyond the interest of any county authority. They rounded a bend and a scattering of cottages appeared before them. 'My guess,' Roger Remnant said, 'is that this is it.' And he brought the car to a halt.

The place consisted of no more than six or eight cottages. Jane jumped out. The car had been travelling so fast that her feet for a moment felt unsteady under her.

'There doesn't seem to be much life.' Roger Remnant too had got out and was surveying the hamlet. 'And we're too early for tea – or too late by about twenty years.' He pointed to a board, depending by one remaining nail from the side of the nearest cottage, which forlornly announced the presence of this facility. 'Not a tourist centre. Nothing ye olde. But there's a school farther down the lane. That means there are probably other little places like this round about.' He sniffed. 'It *smells* of pigs.'

Jane moved to the side of the lane and peered into the garden of the cottage with the superannuated sign. It was a wilderness of weeds from which protruded, like wrecks in a fabled Sargasso sea, the rotting remains of a few home-made tables and benches. 'It's a sort of shop,' she said. 'And a post office as well. I'll go in.'

'Give a shout if you want help.' Remnant spoke humorously – but Jane, looking at his eyes for the first time, saw that they were grey and serious. 'Now or later.'

'I will.' She walked to the front of the cottage and pushed open the door. A small cracked bell feebly tinkled. There was a little room with a counter, and a surprising variety of wares exposed for sale. These latter all contrived to look thoroughly dreary. The place was so dismal that it was possible to feel the dismalness seeping even inside the tins. And there was still a smell of pigs.

The bell had been without effect. The little shop was untenanted. Jane tapped on the counter. Presently there was a response to this from some interior recess: the sound of an unwieldy body moving low on the ground, accompanied by a loud and displeasing snuffling.

Jane had a moment of panic. Milton Porcorum . . . Perhaps she was really in the middle of a nightmare, and it had brought her to the land of the pigs. The whole hamlet would prove to be veritably inhabited only by Pigling Blands – by little pigs going to market, and little pigs staying at home. She would find nothing but a dumb and bestial rout . . . mute inglorious Miltons with trotters and curly tails. Or perhaps she had come to the land of Circe and her swine . . .

'Yes?' The old woman who had appeared in a doorway was lumbering and stout; she snuffled; and she had a mottled and unwholesome complexion, definitely suggestive of a Gloucester Old Spot. But at least she was endowed with speech.

'Is this Milton Porcorum?'

'It be.' Any faint suggestion of cordiality that might have been read in the old woman's expression decidedly faded. 'You'll have lost your way.' She spoke with sombre conviction, born, no doubt, of many similarly unremunerative tinklings at her bell and tappings on her counter. 'Just go straight on.'

'But,' said Jane, 'if you don't know where I want to go –'

'Go straight on.

It was like something particularly exasperating in *Alice in Wonderland*. Jane tried again. 'I'm not quite sure of the place I want. But it's where the ambulances go.'

'I never heard of any ambulances. We're all healthy here.'

'I'm sure you are.' Jane hastened to disclaim any reflection upon the salubrity of the Milton Porcorum air.

'It's at Canonicorum you'll find folk going sick. They've an ill wind at Canonicorum.'

'Canonicorum?'

'Milton Canonicorum.' The old woman enunciated the words with perceptible distaste.

'I see. But I'm thinking of ambulances that bring people – patients – from quite a long way off. Is there some hospital –'

'There's nothing of the sort here. Canonicorum's the place for carryings on. There's talk of a cinema.'

'You don't happen, in the last hour or so, to have *seen* an ambulance? An ambulance with –'

'You'd better try Canonicorum.'

Jane decided it was hopeless. 'Very well,' she said. 'I *will* try Canonicorum. But how do I get there?'

'I've told you, haven't I? Go straight on.'

The old woman turned and vanished – snuffling, as she had come. Jane had for a moment the disordered fancy that she heard a rustling of straw.

3

She left the little shop and the bell tinkled behind her. She was baffled, and for a moment felt discouraged to the point of hopelessness. The ambulance had vanished; there was no more to it than that; and she might as well return to Oxford. But at least she could go to Milton Canonicorum first. Not that she had any faith in it. Just as Milton Porcorum contained nothing but porcine old women, so would the answering village be populated exclusively by monkish and uncommunicative old men. They would have nothing to say – except that there was an ill wind at Porcorum, and that she should go straight on.

She returned to the car and reported her lack of success to Roger Remnant. He listened attentively. 'The old lady sounds a rich type,' he said. 'If you don't mind, I'll have a go at her myself.' And he walked over to the shop.

Jane looked about her. She ought to make her inquiry of anybody she could see. But Milton Porcorum seemed the next thing to a deserted village. The few remaining cottages constituting it were unpromisingly blank and silent; the only sound was a distant, shrill shouting from the school some way on; the only wisp of smoke, even, was from a farmhouse a couple of fields away.

Remnant was back again. 'She'd farrowed,' he said.

'Don't be absurd.'

'Nothing but a small, fat, sucking-pig of a child. She said that granny had been taken poorly. The shock of doing no trade with you has sent her to her bed. But I did a bit of trade myself. It's all I got out of the place. A much better map. The one-inch Ordnance Survey.'

Jane took the map and they climbed into the front of the car together. 'We'd better try Canonicorum,' she said. 'And I'll have a squint at this as we go.' She spread the map out on her knees. 'What a tremendous difference this makes. One feels one could really find one's way about with it.'

'If we knew where to go, Miss Appleby, it would take us there in no time. As it is, we'll try Canonicorum, as you say. They may have quite a line in ambulances, after all.'

'It's about three miles ahead, and this lane curves right round to it, skirting a big green patch.'

'That's a wood.'

'Only mixed up with the green there's a lot that's uncoloured, and dotted with little circles.'

'Park and ornamental ground. There ought to be a seat in the middle.'

'A seat? Oh – I see. And so there is. It's called Milton Manor.'

'Milton, thou shouldst be living at this hour. But, actually, it will be quite dead – or dead so far as the old squirarchal spirit is concerned. Here's the wall bounding it. Pretty formidable, isn't it? But there'll be nothing inside except a district headquarters of the Coal Board, or perhaps a high-class loony bin . . . That wall would keep anybody in.' The car was now racing past a seemingly interminable curve of masonry. 'Look at that sinister little door.'

'Stop!' Sudden and unaccountable certainty had flashed upon Jane. 'It's the place.'

Remnant threw out his clutch and applied his brakes. 'The place where the ambulance has gone?'

'It must be.' Jane was peering at the map. 'But go on. I've seen where there must be gates and a drive. In about a quarter of a mile. A black spot and then a double line of fine dots through the park.'

'That will be a lodge and a drive, all right.' The car moved on again. 'Are we going to pay a call?'

'Yes.'

Remnant said nothing. But he was frowning slightly.

'You don't mind, do you? I don't expect I shall be long.'

'I don't mind a bit. But, you know, you've managed to import an atmosphere of melodrama into this. Yet you don't look a romancing type. It seems to me you may be running into something uncomfortable . . . Here we are.' The car had stopped again at a point where the high wall was pierced by double iron gates. 'I wish you'd tell me what this is about, and how it began.'

Jane hesitated. The gates were flanked by massive stone pillars supporting eroded and obscure heraldic animals; there was a lodge immediately inside; and from it a well-kept drive curved away through a gloomy belt of woodland. She had never supposed herself to be very sensitive to impalpable things. But even the outer defences of Milton Manor had an atmosphere she greatly disliked. 'Well, as a matter of fact, it began – or more immediately began – in the Bodleian this morning.'

'The Bodleian!' Remnant's tone might have been elicited by a mention of something as remote as the Taj-Mahal. 'You mean the place where they keep all the books?'

'Precisely, Mr Remnant.' Jane looked at the young man suspiciously. But his innocence appeared entire and unflawed. 'I don't suppose that your occasions ever drew you there.'

'Not at all.' Remnant was indignant. 'I once took an aunt of mine there. She wanted to see something called King Alfred's Jewel.'

'Don't you think that was the Ashmolean?'

'Aren't they the same thing?'

It was borne in upon Jane that the young man, although doubtless not of a studious temperament, was decidedly not a fool, and that idiocy was his way of expressing a profound scepticism as to her proceedings. That this wild goose chase was authentically the consequence of anything that could have happened in Bodley was really too much for him. And small wonder,

Jane thought. But she could hardly sit back and try to tell him the whole story now. 'Look here,' she said, 'do you mind if we just get out and nose around? Perhaps I'll try explaining presently.'

He jumped out, came round the bonnet of the car, and opened the door for her. 'Very well,' he said impassively. 'Provided we nose together.'

They crossed the road and peered through the high iron gates. The lodge showed signs of being tenanted, but there was nobody stirring. Jane shook the gates cautiously, and tried turning a large wrought-iron handle. They were certainly secured. 'What does one do,' she asked, 'when visiting the gentry? They don't seem to demean themselves by having any sort of door-bell.'

'Blow the horn, I suppose – and wait for the vassals to come running out, touching their forelocks.' Remnant's distrust of their proceedings seemed to have increased, and his voice for the first time held a hint of impatience. He really *did* believe – Jane thought resentfully – that she was a romancing type, after all.

She spoke almost at random. 'It can't be empty,' she said. 'Everything's very tidy.'

'Except for a bit of litter outside.' Remnant had stooped and automatically picked up a scrap of crumpled paper from just beside the gates. He seemed to be summoning resolution to speak his mind. 'Now, look here . . . well, I'm damned!'

Unthinkingly he had smoothed out the piece of buff paper in his hand. It was a blank book slip from the Bodleian.

4

'He saw people filling in slips from the catalogue. And he pretended to be doing the same thing – so as not to attract attention.' Jane spoke absently. She was still staring, wild-eyed, at the small oblong of paper.

'For goodness sake, woman, explain yourself. Who did?'

Jane paid no attention. 'And he must have had this one, crumpled in his hand – when it happened. And then – well, when the ambulance stopped for those gates to be opened, and he knew he was on the threshold of the place, he managed, somehow, to thrust it outside. In the desperate hope that it would act as some sort of sign . . . And it has.'

'I can see that it is a sign all right. Do you mean that somebody has been taken in here against his will?'

'More than one person. I'm sure of it now! This wretched little man that I saw for the first time this morning, and – and somebody that I know much better . . . who is very important to me.'

'Nothing to do with – with being quite lawfully taken charge of by doctors who believe – rightly or wrongly – that they are insane?'

'Nothing to do with that.'

'Good!' Roger Remnant spoke with decision. 'Then the whole thing is simplified. Here they are. We're morally certain of it. And now we have just got to get them out again. We go straight in, Miss Appleby.'

She turned to him gravely. 'You mean that? You're helping?'

He answered her gravity with sudden extreme merriment. 'My dear young woman, *you* are helping. Bulldog Drummond is on the job – but of course you can stand in the corner and hold the sponge and towels. Incidentally, unlike the bone-headed Bulldog, we don't go *quite* straight in. That might be unhealthy. We send some word of our intentions into the outside world first. That's sense. *Then* we go right in. That's what, in the circumstances, a chap – and even a lass – must do.'

This judicious admixture of prudence and personal honour was something that Jane found she highly approved of. 'As a matter of fact,' she said, 'I've done that already. I sent a telegram to my brother before I picked you up.'

Remnant grinned. 'Do you always telegraph your brother before you –'

Jane was mildly confused. 'Don't be an ass. And he'll have got it by now. He's in Oxford.'

'An undergraduate?'

'No, he's much older than I am. He's a policeman.'

'Excellent. We now approach something like social equality.'

'He's an Assistant Commissioner at Scotland Yard.'

'Snubbed again.' Remnant's cheerfulness, however, suffered no appreciable diminution. 'And that suggests something. How do we stand to one another when we do barge in? Great lady and her chauffeur?'

'You don't look a bit like a great lady's chauffeur, Mr Remnant.'

'I'm not very sure, for that matter, that you look like a chauffeur's great lady. What about brother and sister?'

'Very well.'

'And what's our business?'

Jane hesitated. She hadn't considered this. 'We should really know', she said, 'what the place *is*. I mean, what it *pretends* to be. They must know in Canonicorum. Shall we drive on there first, and ask?'

'Certainly not. I wouldn't call that going right in. Come on – into the car, face the gates, and sound the horn like mad. Childe Remnant – and faithful page – to the dark tower came.'

'And trust to luck?'

'We haven't much else to trust to, have we?'

Jane said nothing, but climbed into the car.

Remnant backed, swung round to face the gates, and gave a blast on his horn. It was a very loud horn – or here in the silence of the country it appeared so – and he made prodigal use of it.

'I say,' said Jane, 'perhaps you'd better not be so –'

She stopped as she saw the door in the lodge open and a man come out.

He walked briskly but without hurry to the gates, and immediately unlocked them and drew them open.

Remnant drove in and stopped. 'Sorry to make such a row', he called cheerfully, 'but we've got an appointment, and we're a bit late.'

The man had every appearance of respectability, and might have been a retired N.C.O. in the employment of his former colonel. 'Yes, sir. With the Medical Superintendent or the Assistant Director?'

'The Medical Superintendent.' Remnant's voice held not a hint of hesitation.

'Very good, sir. Will you drive straight up to the house?'

'Right – thank you.' Remnant prepared to let in the clutch.

'One moment, sir. Have you been here before?'

'No. This is our first visit.'

'Then I'd better mention, sir, that there's an inner fence right round the park. It's because of the animals, sir; and as some of them are very valuable, the gate across the drive is kept locked. I ring through to the house, and a man comes down at once to open it. You won't be delayed more than a couple of minutes, sir.' The man stepped back smartly – the air of the old regular soldier was now unmistakable in him – and turned to close the gates.

They drove on. 'We're in,' Jane said.

'We're in – and that reliable retainer is now locking the gates behind us. Presently the same thing is going to happen at an inner barrier. It's not hopelessly out of the way – but it's not quite what I'd call natural . . . Well, we now know that the establishment is a medical one.'

'That it *pretends* to be one.'

'Nothing on this scale could be a hundred per cent bogus. You just couldn't get away with it. We'll find this in a perfectly pukka sanatorium, or something of that sort, with the dirty work neatly confined to the back stairs.'

'Perhaps so. And I don't in the least know what the dirty work is. I only know that they kidnapped a helpless looking little man from the heart of Oxford this morning, and that weeks and weeks ago they kidnapped somebody I'm going to marry. And he's not at all helpless.'

'Then they're crazy.' Remnant still spoke with the same composed decision. 'Listen. We may find ourselves up against what looks like a very formidable set-up indeed. I don't know – but it's a guess. Master criminals. Some deep design. A powerful and ramifying organization. The whole bag of tricks – see?'

'Yes.' But Jane wasn't quite sure that she saw.

'But it will be paper-thin. We just have to put a fist through it and it goes. Just remember that we approach the job in the light of that knowledge.'

'Very well.' Jane didn't at all know whether she was listening to wisdom or folly. But she realized that Roger Remnant was a heartening companion.

'Here's the fence – and the valuable animals.'

The fence, constructed of a stout wire diamond mesh, ran off on a convex line on either side of them, and in that arc of it which was visible, the gate now immediately before them appeared to be the only aperture. Just beyond it, a herd of deer, unfamiliar in appearance, was peacefully grazing. The park behind them was dotted and streaked with clumps and groves of trees, amid which there was still no sign of a house.

They were silent for some minutes. The man at the lodge seemed to have underestimated the time they would have to wait here. And the wait was unnerving. Knowing what they did, they were bound to look somewhat askance at the sort of large zoological enclosure into the sinister security of which they were about to deliver themselves.

'Have you got a plan?' Jane found that she had uttered the words spontaneously and without premeditation. They seemed to represent a very definite handing of what was, after all, entirely her affair to the young man beside her.

'Certainly not. Nothing could be more hampering. And you're not going right in if you have a plan.'

Jane found the *mystique* of this difficult. 'You mean you just charge head down?'

'Nothing of the sort. I mean that it's only useful to think of the current move. Try thinking ahead, and you only clog your mind with preparations for situations that are not, in fact, going to turn out at all as you imagine them . . . Here the fellow comes.'

'I don't know at all about that.' Jane eyed rather apprehensively the figure now hurrying towards them from the farther side of the fence. 'For instance, there's this. We told the man at the lodge that we had an appointment. Probably he has reported that on the telephone. And we *haven't* an appointment.'

Remnant chuckled unconcernedly. 'If there's anything in all this at all, my dear woman, we shall meet rather more considerable embarrassments than that . . . Good morning. We're very sorry to trouble you in this way.'

'Not at all, sir. Sorry to keep you waiting.' The man now throwing open the wire gates was as respectable as his fellow. 'It's this particular herd, sir. We have orders to lock up when it's grazing in this section of the park. Very rare, I understand these deer to be. It makes things awkward for visitors. But it's better than having the deer stolen for a black market in venison. You'd hardly believe it, sir, but it's happened here two or three times.'

'Kidnapping – eh?' Remnant shot out the question abruptly.

'Exactly, sir.' The man was certainly not disconcerted. 'Will you drive straight on? You can't miss the house. And the entrance to the clinic is by the main door, under the portico.'

They drove on. Remnant gave Jane a triumphant nod. 'There,' he said, 'you see? We pick up the facts as we go. Our visit is to the Medical Superintendent of a clinic. What *is* a clinic?'

Jane considered. 'I think it's becoming a fashionable word for a grand sort of nursing home – the sort that has one special line. If the rich want to slim, they go and live on roast beef and orange juice in the appropriate clinic.'

'Perhaps that's it. Perhaps that's what the deer are for. One vanishes into the kitchens daily in the interest of a high-protein diet.' Remnant swung the car round a bend in the drive. 'Here we are.'

A large house had appeared before them. Its form was irregular and rambling, so that it might have been very large indeed; but the aspect which they were approaching was dominated by a graceful white portico, now glittering in the sun. They looked at this curiously. 'It must take an awful lot of paint,' Jane said.

'About as much as the Queen Elizabeth. I suppose it gives the right effect: cheerfulness and antisepsis hand in hand. There's a garden over there with quite a lot of people.'

'They must be ambulatory patients.'

Remnant slowed down. 'You do have a fine stock of words.' His glance was moving swiftly over the whole scene. 'What sort of patients are they?'

'The sort, oddly enough, that don't need an ambulance.'

'Well, they certainly don't look as if they had been kidnapped in one. Do you think we drive under this portico affair? I think we do. Nothing like a confident approach to the dark tower.'

'Yes, drive right in.' Jane found that her heart was beating much faster than usual. But it was only sensible, she reminded herself, to feel a bit scared. Unless she had made a colossal ass of herself – and that would really be almost worse than anything else – they had embarked on an enterprise of very actual danger.

They got out in front of a short flight of steps and mounted to a door painted in brilliant vermilion. There was a large brass bell-pull, brightly polished, and a small brass plate, equally brightly polished, on which both their glances fell at once. It read:

MILTON MANOR CLINIC
REGISTERED OFFICE

As Jane read this she was aware of a first twinge of mere misgiving as momentarily replacing her alarm. The little notice was somehow both unobtrusively and monumentally respectable. She had a vision of imminent fiasco – of a reception at first puzzled, and then successively amused, annoyed, frigid . . . But Remnant appeared to have no doubts. His hand had gone out unhesitatingly and given a brisk tug at the bell-pull. This proved to be attached to one of those genteel contrivances which simulate a miniature carillon. They stood for a moment listening to the brief cascade of musical notes releasing itself somewhere inside. Before it had died away – or, Jane reflected, they could turn and bolt – the door opened.

They were aware of an interior that was all cool, clear colours and polished floors. Standing before them was an immaculate nursing sister. 'Good morning,' she said.

'Good morning.' Roger Remnant, in his old duffel coat, Jane noted, had somehow taken on the appearance of springing from the most privileged and opulent class of society. 'I am Lord Remnant.' He paused as if this must be a very sufficient announcement in itself. The nurse seemed suitably impressed, but her features contrived, at the same time, to suggest the need of further information. Remnant's eyebrows elevated themselves slightly. 'My sister and I have an appointment with the Medical Superintendent.'

'With Dr Cline?'

'I'm afraid I have no idea. His name hasn't been given to me. The appointment was made by my aunt – or at least she intended to make one. But it is just possible she failed to ring up. She is very distressed – has been very hesitant about the whole matter.'

'I *quite* understand.' The nurse's voice might have been described as oozing comprehension. 'Will you please come in? I am afraid that if there has *not* been an appointment you may have to wait a little. Dr Cline is having a terribly crowded morning. But I will let him know at once.'

They entered a large hall with panelled walls and a broad staircase, all of which had been enamelled in light greens and greys. At one end was a bright fire, vying with the sunshine that poured in through tall windows giving upon some broad court at the back. The other end was a mass of chrysanthemums disposed behind and around a small fountain. Two silver-haired old gentlemen of distinguished appearance were coming down the staircase, surrounded by a group of spaniels. As they reached the bottom a man-servant appeared and encased them in hats and coats. They turned down a broad corridor, apparently intent upon a stroll in the gardens. Jane had an enhanced feeling that it was all too true to be good – to be at all good for what was surely the utterly extravagant hypothesis she had formed. High blood pressure, or chronic disorders of the liver, looked like being the only sinister revelation Milton Manor had to offer.

They sat down to wait. By way of intellectual beguilement there was a choice between *Country Life* and *The Field*. It was all too depressing for words.

The wait, however, was brief, for the nurse returned almost at once. 'Will you come this way?' she said. 'The Superintendent can see you now.'

They were led for some way through the house and shown into a room of moderate size, furnished with consistent sobriety as a study. Dr Cline was a rubicund man of buoyant manner who came forward with a frank smile. 'Lord Remnant?'

Roger Remnant bowed. 'My sister, Lady Jane,' he said gravely.

'How do you do. I understand that your aunt – But I am afraid it is a little chilly here – and really a little gloomy as well. I suggest that we go out to the sunshine of the terrace.' And Dr Cline led the way towards a pair of french windows. 'After all, there is much to be said for a cheerful atmosphere when discussing these things. Whether the Clinic is efficient is a matter of statistics. But that it is a reasonably gay sort of place you will presumably see for yourselves.'

The Medical Superintendent, it was evident, had no hesitation in getting briskly down to sales-talk. And he had all his wits about him. Jane had a sudden and horrid conviction that, before admitting them, he must surely have made a grab at *Who's Who* or *Debrett*. But of course, for all she knew, Roger Remnant might really be a lord. He might even have a sister called Lady Jane . . . They had emerged on a flagged terrace. It was liberally provided with garden furniture, but untenanted. Perhaps it was reserved for the Superintendent's private use. For on a second terrace, immediately below, was a scattered group of some half-dozen people. They were for the most part elderly, and engaged in reading, conversing, or simply gazing into the gardens. An air of waiting, somnolently but pleasurably, for what could confidently be anticipated as an excellent luncheon, was pervasive among them. The only pronounced activity visible was on the part of a small boy of about five years of age, who was wandering restlessly from individual to individual . . . At this small boy Jane, as she sat down, took a second look. And it flashed upon her that he represented what, so far, was the only discordant note about the place. For he did not look at all a gay or cheerful child. On the contrary, there was something strained and tense about his whole bearing. And when he glanced towards the upper terrace for a moment it was with eyes that it was not at all comfortable to become aware of.

But Roger Remnant was talking – and with the most complete assurance still. 'You will understand, Dr Cline, that this is an entirely tentative inquiry. And my aunt – who is naturally very distressed – has felt quite unequal to coming down herself. She is afraid that –'

'Quite so, Lord Remnant, quite so.' The Superintendent was eminently willing to meet this half way. 'There is always the dislike of talk – of gossip. But I assure you that it is a matter which we handle with a good deal of acquired skill – of *finesse*, I may say. Residence at Milton Manor can be *entirely* confidential. Take correspondence, for example, from the patients' private friends. That can go to an address in London, from which it is brought down daily by private messenger.'

'That,' said Remnant, 'is very important.' He smiled amiably at Dr Cline. 'It makes one begin to see one's way more clearly.' And his eyes, although quite expressionlessly, moved fleetingly to Jane's.

'Precisely.' Dr Cline looked understandingly at his visitors. Then – and rather as if it were something that had just come into his head – he suddenly assumed an appearance of mild professional reserve. 'But I must point out,' he said, 'that, in the first instance, it would have to be your – um – uncle's personal medical adviser –'

'We perfectly understand that. But I must repeat how tentative this is. Nothing has been suggested to my uncle, and his doctor is not yet really aware of – er – how bad the position has become. What has happened is simply this. My aunt confided her anxieties to Lord Polder, who is a very old friend.'

Dr Cline, at the mention of this most august of medical names, bowed gravely.

'And Lord Polder mentioned the possibilities of the Milton Clinic. He, rather than the family doctor, you know, would be the best person to take on the difficult job of broaching the matter to my uncle. They regularly shoot together. And of course they are constantly meeting in the Chamber.'

Jane wondered whether the Chamber was really what very grand people called the Lords. Anyway, it sounded well. It all sounded incredibly well, indeed. And this fashionable little medical parasite appeared to be eating out of Remnant's hand. She speculated on what atrociously disreputable disease the noble peer under discussion – whether real or imagined – was about to be plagued with by his ruthless nephew . . . But now Remnant had gone off on another track.

'There is one thing that makes my aunt rather uneasy. She has been told about the research. Of course, my sister and I understand very well that research is always carried on in a leading institution of this character. But my aunt would want to be assured that there was no risk –'

With a gesture perhaps a shade more theatrical than professional the Medical Superintendent of the Milton Clinic raised two protesting hands. 'But quite so! And I can assure you that nothing of the sort would at all impinge upon your uncle during his residence here. The research is, of course, of the utmost importance. We are making constant gains from it on the therapeutic side – constant gains. But, of course, nothing is embodied in our regular treatments that has not abundantly proved itself when employed in the case of – um – patients otherwise circumstanced. The research establishment, indeed, is entirely separate. The Director and I, needless to say, are in the closest cooperation – the most intimate scientific touch. But the two establishments have no contact, so far as patients and – er – inmates are concerned. The inmates – who come on *very* reduced terms and who are *most* helpful to us – are a completely detached community. We have fixed them up very pleasant – yes, *very* pleasant – quarters in the old stables.'

Remnant looked much relieved. 'I see,' he said. 'Guinea-pigs, what?'

Dr Cline did not let his wholesome respect for the aristocracy prevent him from looking slightly shocked. 'It might be better, my dear Lord Remnant, to express it –'

But Remnant had turned to Jane with an air of brisk decision. 'Well,' he said, 'I think that just about settles it – don't you, Jane?'

Jane nodded, and spoke for the first time. 'It all sounds very satisfactory – and hopeful for poor uncle. And, for poor aunt Emma's sake, I shall be so glad if it puts things right.'

'Quite. Well, we must book the poor old boy in, and then get Polder to apply the heat.' From this slangy excursion, proper in addressing a sister, Remnant turned with renewed gravity to Dr Cline. 'You could manage it at any time?'

'Well, hardly that – hardly that, I fear. But the wait would not be long. And it will, of course, be perfectly correct that Lord Polder rather than a family physician should refer your uncle to us.'

'I think we'd better have a firm date, if we can. Nothing like going straight ahead once these things are fixed upon.' And Remnant looked firmly at Dr Cline. It was evident that, for his distinguished family, waiting-lists simply did not exist. 'In fact, I think it had better be Monday.'

'It is just possible that it could be arranged.' For Dr Cline, seemingly, this was a game that had to be played out according to the rules. 'But I shall have to take a look at the book. And as my secretary is away for the day, it will be necessary to go across and consult it in the other wing. Will you excuse me?'

And Dr Cline bowed himself off the terrace. Roger Remnant took a long breath. 'And now,' he said, 'now, my dear sister Jane – where do we go from here?'

5

Jane was watching the small boy. He had been becoming increasingly rest-less and irritable. In fact he might have been described as trailing his coats, for it was his evident desire to make himself sufficiently tiresome to the elderly people around him to stir them into drastic action. It must, Jane thought, be a poor sort of life for a child amid these comfortable invalids or valetudinarians. They did not appear to take much interest in him, but what interest they took was wholly benevolent. Children need an occasional rumpus. They find an adult world that never turns aggressive on them extremely frightening, for it makes them feel their own aggressive impulses to be something wicked and out of nature. The small boy – he appeared to be a foreign small boy from fragments of his speech that drifted to the upper terrace – was decidedly in this state. He was longing for a clip on the ear. And nobody seemed at all disposed to give it to him . . . Jane turned to Remnant. 'Where do we go now? It depends on how much we feel we've really found out. What is this place, anyway? What is it going to cure our uncle of?'

Remnant chuckled. 'Obesity, I should say – to judge by that great fat man who appeared a minute ago.'

'A fat man? I didn't see any fat man.'

'He simply popped round the corner of the terrace for a moment and vanished.'

'Probably he was one of the doctors – grown sleek on the job. I don't think it's obesity. It may be rather comical to be fat, but it's not indecent. And apparently to make it known that you're taking the cure at Milton Manor just isn't done.' Jane's eyes went again to the people below them. 'Besides, just look at that lot. You can't say that their garments are beginning to hang loose upon them. Rather the reverse, if anything.'

'True enough. And, in point of fact, I don't think we need be in any doubt about the place. Our poor uncle's danger is D.T.s. And this clinic – ostensibly, at least – is nothing more than a high-class drunks' home. The alcohol habit cured in six weeks. Utmost privacy assured. Fee, five hundred guineas.'

'And something else goes on behind?'

'Something else goes on behind.' Remnant paused. 'Unless, that is, we're barking up the wrong tree.'

'You think I'm making a fool of both of us?'

Remnant shook his head decidedly. 'I certainly don't think that. But you must admit that, so far, there's precious little evidence of dirty work behind the curtain. If only – Good lord, look at that little boy!'

The boy's desire to plague his companions had increased yet further. He had gone up to an elderly lady apparently engaged upon a cross-word puzzle and insufferably snatched her paper from her. The lady had merely smiled and made a small, resigned gesture. And at this the boy had lost control of himself. Darting forward again, he had dealt her a stinging blow across the face. And – once more – the lady simply smiled.

This was the startling incident that had attracted Remnant's attention. But it was not concluded. The boy had drawn back. He was very frightened. He looked from face to face of the people scattered around him. Some of them had seen his act; others were preoccupied. But nobody made any move. He gave a choking cry and rushed at a tall man with a pipe in his mouth who was sitting in idle contemplation of the garden. The boy knocked the pipe to the ground and clawed, battered at the tall man's face. The man smiled, slightly shook his head, got up and moved to another seat. Most of the people were now watching. They watched as if nothing abnormal was occurring. But this was itself the only abnormal thing about them. They conversed, smoked, looked up from or returned to their books with every sign of reasonable mental alertness. The boy threw himself down on the terrace and sobbed. At this the lady whom he had first struck rose and bent over him solicitously. Others showed a similar kindly concern. And then from a door farther along the terrace a nurse hurried out, picked up the weeping child, and carried him away. The whole incident vanished. Everybody was completely composed. It was like seeing a wet sponge being passed over a slate.

Remnant had got to his feet. He and Jane looked at each other wide-eyed. Without a word passed between them, they knew that they were agreed. They had witnessed something unutterably shocking. A child's temper-tantrum had betrayed the presence of abomination – there, in the clear sunlight, only a few yards away. It was something obscure, and at the same time instantly clamant. They had witnessed the fruit of some horrible violation of human personality.

Jane heard Remnant catch his breath and saw him move in half a dozen swift strides to the lower terrace. He looked quickly round the people assembled there and picked out a man in a somewhat different category from the others. He was younger and of fine physique, with a strong mouth and jaw; he might have been a professional soldier. Remnant stepped up to him and slapped his face hard. The man jerked back his head. Remnant could see pain – perhaps two sorts of pain – in his eyes. Then he too smiled, rose, walked quietly away.

Remnant returned to the upper terrace. He was very pale. At the same moment the nurse who had carried off the boy returned with a second nurse somewhat older than herself. They moved about among the group of people, speaking to them briefly. Each of those so spoken to nodded, smiled, rose, and moved off. They betrayed no consciousness of awkwardness or discomfort, but went off in a group – either conversing placidly or glancing still at their open books. Within a few seconds the lower terrace was empty.

Jane was aware of something wrong with herself. She realized it was a sense of brute, physical nausea. But she could just trust herself to speak, and she opened her mouth to do so. Then she became aware that Dr Cline had come back. He was carrying a large diary.

'I see that we can just manage it.' He sat down, glanced at the empty lower terrace and then at his visitors. 'Ah,' he said, 'I am afraid that you have been obliged to witness one of our little hitches. I assure you that they occur very infrequently. And I think I had better explain the system to you.'

Remnant nodded – and Jane noted with admiration that he did so very pleasantly. 'Yes, Dr Cline, we should very much like to hear about the system.'

'Our patients are divided into messes – into progressive messes. It is rather like the successive forms in a school. You must realize – and it is the reason why our treatment sometimes has to be of rather long duration – that alcoholic addiction is merely one form of addiction to drugs. It cannot be broken at once. The process must be gradual. Consumption is reduced in stages – stages, of course, that go hand in hand with the progress of our psychiatric and other treatments. And here let me emphasize that what we aim at eventually is *total* abstention. Experience has compelled us to conclude that a return to moderate indulgence is psychologically impracticable. It is a thousand pities – for, after all, a glass of wine is both a civilized and a wholesome pleasure.'

'But with former addicts it doesn't work?'

'Precisely!' Dr Cline tapped the book on his knees with measured and impressive emphasis. He was well launched on his sales-talk once more. 'Our patients go out drinking *no* alcohol – and our figures show that in eighty-seven per cent of cases the cure is permanent and absolute. Perhaps –

on the psychological side – the decisive factor is this: that we never antag-onize them. There is a positive transference from the first.'

Dr Cline paused on this weighty technical term. His smile was amiable, Jane thought, but his eye was wary. Remnant broke in smoothly. 'I see. The patients, in fact, just love all they get?'

Dr Cline appeared gratified by this interpretation of the tenor of his remarks. 'I think I can say that they are very well contented from the first. And now, about the messes. On arrival, most patients go into – well, what one might term the Lower Third.' Dr Cline permitted himself a mild laugh-ter at this scholastic pleasantry. 'It is, of course, entirely a matter of the amount of wine and so forth served at table. In the Sixth – shall we say among the prefects? – there is none at all.' He paused admiringly. 'Not even a light cup; not even a glass of cider!'

'Remarkable.'

'I think I may say that it is. But of course it is necessary that intercourse between the various messes – and I need not tell you that each has its own dining-room – should be minimal. Otherwise a certain amount of friction and jealousy is apt to be engendered. The people we saw just now belong to a mess that ought not to be in this part of the grounds. Some mistake had been made. But I need hardly say that – such unfortunate slips apart – nobody here has ever the slightest feeling of being dragooned, of being ordered about . . . And now I will just mention some details about the fees, and so on. But perhaps we might go into that more conveniently indoors. And no doubt you will wish to go over the Clinic, so as to be able to give your aunt a full description of it.'

Remnant nodded. 'We should certainly like to see,' he said, 'whatever can be seen.'

'Which is everything!' And Dr Cline smiled quite brilliantly as he led the way back to his study.

6

It seemed to Jane Appleby that matters were now at something of an *impasse*. They might be shown a great deal of Milton Manor Clinic. But nothing more would transpire that was at all to their purpose. They could get away, and then think again. Or presumably they could get away. For the Medical Superintendent appeared not in the least to suspect their *bona fides*, and there was no reason to suppose that the respectable and respectful persons who had unlocked gates upon their arrival would not unhesitatingly perform the same service for them when they signified a wish to depart. Yes, they could clear out – and consider themselves thoroughly lucky in doing so. Perhaps their account of the very odd thing they had seen would be sufficient immediately to procure a radical investigation of the whole place. But meantime she had seen or heard nothing of the fate of Geoffrey – which was the single and overwhelming concern with which she had come. She had seen only a brief, enigmatical horror which filled her with the deepest fears for the man she loved. And to go away hard upon that sinister and imperfect revelation seemed to hold something craven in it that she did not like.

The Medical Superintendent had sat down comfortably at his desk, opened his large diary, and produced a beautiful gold fountain pen. 'I am bound to say that you are very wise,' he murmured. 'In these cases quite a short space of time may be important. Monday, I think you said, Lord Remnant? Excellent! What can be more satisfactory than decisive action?'

'What indeed?' And Remnant, leaning across the desk, slapped Dr Cline hard across the right cheek.

The man scrambled to his feet and staggered backwards, his mouth feebly working. It did not appear that he was either a very courageous or a very quick-witted person. He stood staring at them helplessly with watering eyes. Then he made a dive for a drawer in his desk, emitting at the same time the enraged snarl of a cornered animal.

But Remnant was before him, and slung him across the room. 'Reactions very poor,' he said. 'Definite signs of resentment. Needs a spot of the cure himself.'

Cline regained his balance and dashed for the fireplace, his hand stretched out in front of him to press a bell. Remnant stepped forward and hit him on the jaw. Cline made a half turn on his heels and dropped to the floor. He struggled to his hands and knees and rose, staggering. His mouth was streaming blood. He opened it and let out a feeble attempt at a yell. Remnant hit him again. He went down and lay quite still.

These were proceedings that Jane Appleby had never before witnessed except in the cinema. She stared at the inert body of the Medical Superintendent and felt her head swim. Remnant had stepped to the closed door and was listening. 'No sound of alarm,' he said.

'Is he dead?'

'Good Lord, no.' Remnant looked down impassively at the figure supine on the carpet. 'But it's not a bad knock-out. Do you know, for a moment I thought I had mistimed it? Getting a bit rusty, I'm afraid, at this sort of thing.'

Jane's head began to clear. 'I suppose you *haven't* mistimed it? I mean, it was the best thing to do?' She was far from clear what their next step could be.

'I told you, didn't I? When you meet a thing like this, you put your fist straight through it. And it's obvious enough now. These people are kidnappers, just as you said. And they use their victims – the little man you saw today, those people outside, your own young man if they've caught him – for some filthy sort of experiment. The only thing to do is to keep on hitting them hard.'

'I see. Well, whom do you hit next?'

'I'd say that this just about concludes our concern with the clinical side. It's not of much interest, and I expect that this precious swine hasn't all that importance in the set-up of the place. What we're looking for is the research . . . Will you do something?'

'Whatever you say.'

Remnant cheerfully grinned. He was reflecting, perhaps that these were not words which this young woman frequently addressed to her male contemporaries. 'Then cut out to the car. Don't be in a hurry to offer explanations to anybody you see about. Remember you belong to a class of society accustomed to going its own way unquestioned.'

'Thank you very much.'

'Yank up the front seat. There's a leather bag, and there's a bottle. Empty the bag, put in the bottle, and bring it back here. I'll give you four minutes. Then, if you're not back, I'll change plans and come and find you. Understand?'

'I think I do.' Jane took a deep breath, opened the door, and walked out of the room.

The broad corridor was deserted. So was the hall with its foolish little fountain and its massed chrysanthemums. But in the vestibule was one of the manservants she had seen earlier. She fancied he looked at her curiously. Jane walked to the front door and halted – with the air of one who very seldom has occasion to open doors for herself. The man jumped to the door-handle and let her out. 'I'm returning,' she said briefly, and walked across to the car. She managed to do as Remnant had instructed her – and probably, she judged, without the precise nature of the operation being observed. She turned and mounted the steps, the bag in her hand. The man was waiting, with the door held open. He bowed impeccably and closed it behind her. She thanked him and walked on.

Remnant was sitting on the Medical Superintendent's desk, examining a revolver. He looked up quickly as she entered. 'Good girl,' he said. 'Now we can get cracking again.'

Jane looked about the study. 'Where's Cline?' The Medical Superintendent had vanished.

'I've lugged the guts into the neighbour room.' As he delivered himself of this stray fruit of his former frequentation of the lecture-halls of Oxford, Remnant slipped the revolver into his pocket. 'This is what he was making a grab for in the drawer. I don't like the things. Noisy. But you never know what will come in handy.'

'Mayn't he recover quite quickly?'

'I've tied him up, gagged him, and put him in a cupboard. Useful that they taught us all those dirty tricks. Got the bottle?'

'Here it is.' Jane set the bag down on the desk. 'What are you going to do now?'

'About Milton Manor?'

'Yes – of course.'

395

'Burn it to the ground.'

'Burn it! You can't –'

'Never believe it.' Remnant had brought out the bottle. 'Capital stuff, petrol. And this room is pretty well ideal. Panelled walls, bookshelves, massive desk, all those curtains – give us a splendid start, believe me.' He uncorked the bottle. 'Just pass me that big waste-paper basket, will you?'

Jane gasped, but did as she was told. 'But what about Cline?' she said. 'Didn't you say he's in a cupboard?'

'Cline? Oh – I see what you mean. Well, they say it's not really bad. The suffocation knocks you out before the actual roasting. Quite humane, really.' Remnant was going composedly about his fire-raising operation.

'But – but it would be murder.'

'Just stand back a bit, will you?'

Jane's head was decidedly swimming again. 'You don't know what you're doing! You can't murder –'

'Much worse than murder going on here, if you ask me. Whole place overdue for the everlasting bonfire. I say, what an anticlimax, my dear woman, if I haven't got a match.'

'I devoutly hope you haven't.'

'Here we are – box of Vestas. I think you should have the fun of starting it off. Your show, after all.'

'I'll do nothing of the sort. I think you must be –'

'Just one lighted match, please. Into the waste-paper basket. And then we go out by the french window.'

Jane glanced unbelievingly at Remnant. He was looking her straight in the eyes. He might be crazy, but he was certainly not mad. She took the box, got out a match, and struck it. It was like being a hangman and giving a tap or a pull to whatever worked the drop. She threw it into the waste-paper basket and there was a great leap of flame. Remnant grabbed her and they bolted through the window.

Remnant chuckled. 'I never had a girl commit murder for me before. You mayn't believe it – but it's the honest truth.'

Jane's head was still misbehaving, and she felt that at any moment her knees might misbehave too. 'Look here', she said, 'couldn't we just – just get him out of that cupboard and drop him into a flower-bed?'

'How pity runs amok in gentle heart.' Remnant was looking rapidly about him. 'Or have I got that one wrong?' Abruptly his manner changed. 'I say,' he said, 'I'm sorry. As a matter of fact the whole place isn't going to burn down – worse luck. A fire started in the night like that might get sufficient grip to do it. But not now. Your match hasn't started much more than a pretty good diversion. And that's what we want.'

Jane gave a long gasp. 'Then let's make the best of our chance.'

'Capital. Excellent girl. You know, until we winkle out this young man of yours, and until I get back to my wife and twelve kids, you and I make not a bad team.'

Jane became aware that they were hurrying with considerable purposeful-
ness along the terrace. 'Where are we going now?'

'It's like this. I reckon that in the excitement of our little fire, you and
I will be forgotten for a bit back there. And that gives us our chance of
finding the other side of the place.'

'The research side?'

'Exactly. The real devilry is there. What we want is the boys in the back
room. I expect there will be quite a number of them. And – for that matter –
I expect they're really at the back. Did you notice the structure of the
place as we drove up? There seems to be a lot of new building – much less
dressy than all this – stretching out behind . . . Round this way.'

They turned a corner of the main façade of the house, and as they did
so heard shouts behind them. Jane quickened her pace yet further. 'Are
they after us?'

'Not a bit of it. They're after the fire. No doubt in a remote place like
this, with a big staff, everybody has a job when it comes to fighting a blaze.
That means that we turn their own efficiency against them.'

'I see. And I'm not really surprised you didn't care for those lectures.
You must have found the don's wits a bit on the slow side.'

'Steady on. There's a chap coming.' Remnant laid a hand on her arm and
brought her to a leisured walk. 'New patients – understand?'

Jane nodded. The man approaching them was clearly some sort of servant
or attendant about the place. He had almost the look, indeed, of what might
be called a guard, for he had the measured pace of somebody on a regular
beat. Remnant raised a hand and beckoned him forward. 'The sort of
patients we are,' he murmured, 'don't mind mentioning a disastrous fire in
passing. But they preserve a lofty demeanour, all the same.'

The man had quickened his pace and was eyeing them suspiciously. 'One
moment,' he said; 'are you residents in the Clinic?'

Remnant frowned. It was evident that he was one very little disposed to
be questioned in this way. 'Certainly, my man. But I signed to tell you that
you are needed at the front of the house. There appears to be a fire.'

Audible corroboration of the truth of this was now available. Somewhere
on the other side of the building a shrill bell was sounding; there was shouting and a calling of sharp words of command; it was even possible to hear
an ominous crackle of flames. The man hesitated, took a bunch of keys from
his pocket, made as if to turn round, and then hesitated again. 'Not through
the red door, please,' he said sharply. 'Some of the Director's animals are
out, and they're not to be disturbed.' Again he looked them over in quick
scrutiny. Unlike the servants they had so far met, he had only the most
perfunctory semblance of a respectable bearing. The shouting increased,

and this appeared to convince him where his most urgent business lay. He went off at a run.

They resumed their brisk pace. 'You see?' Remnant said. 'They always hand you your next move on a plate. We find a red door and go straight through. It looks as if he's meant to keep it locked, but thought he was hardly going to move out of sight of it . . . How peaceful all this is.'

Jane was not very confident that she agreed. But she had come to recognize that with Remnant one had an exhilarating sense of going just where one wanted to go. There was now nobody near them. Only on somewhat higher ground on their left, and beyond the formal gardens, a scattering of people – patients presumably – were strolling and pausing before what appeared to be a series of enclosures cut into the slope of the hill. Jane glanced at these as she hurried forward. 'It's very odd,' she panted, 'but it looks rather like a zoo – a private zoo.'

'Nothing more likely. All guinea-pigs needn't have only two feet. And that fellow said something about animals through the red door . . . How this place goes on and on.'

They were still skirting the main building on their right. But it had now changed its character, and presented a long line of mullioned windows separated by heavy buttresses which had nothing much to support. There was something decidedly uncomfortable upon passing each of these in turn, for they seemed almost constructed for the sake of affording lurking places.

'But here we are.' The mullioned windows had given place, for a score of paces, to blank walls. And now, between two of the buttresses, they came upon a wide archway, so high that one could have driven a double-decker bus beneath it, and closed by vermilion-painted double doors. Inset in one of these was a wicket. Remnant gave this a thrust and it opened; they went forward as if through a short tunnel, and presently emerged in a broad courtyard. On their right was some sideways aspect of the main building. The three other sides of the court were formed by a miscellaneous but continuous jumble of stables and offices.

'Quick!' Remnant took Jane's arm and drew her like a flash behind the shelter of half a dozen piled bales of hay close by where they had emerged. There were three or four men on the farther side of the courtyard, hard at work trundling a small fire-fighting wagon from a shed. They brought it across the yard at the double; the doors beneath the archway were flung open; they disappeared towards the front of the house.

'Another riddance of bad rubbish.' Remnant drew Jane from their hiding-place and glanced around. 'Nobody else in sight – and no animals. We'll go through there.' He pointed to a narrower passage-way that seemed to afford an egress from the courtyard immediately opposite where they stood. 'And I think we'll go at the double too.'

They dashed across the yard and up the passage-way. When they emerged it was to run full-tilt into a man standing stationary in the open air at the farther end. He stepped back, at the same time whipping something from his pocket. It was a revolver. This time, there could be no doubt whatever about what they were in contact with.

'Come on, then!' Remnant had shouted over the man's shoulder – and with so convincing an urgency that the elementary trick worked. The man spun round apprehensively and Remnant sprang at him. In a second he had gone down with the same sort of thud as had the Medical Superintendent. Remnant knelt beside him, and then glanced up at Jane. 'Go on,' he said sharply. It was a tone of command more absolute than any he had used before.

She walked on. She felt a sudden fierce excitement – and at the same time wondered how much more of this she could stand. He was with her again within seconds. She saw that, once more, he was very pale. It was a moment to hold her tongue, but she was physically unable to do so. 'What did you do to him?' she asked.

'Nothing pretty. He'll be the worse of it for weeks. But it gives us the time we need. He's behind a bush . . . And there are the animals.'

They had continued at a run along a narrow lane between high wooden fences. On their left this fence continued to shut out any view but on their right it now turned off at a right angle, and their path was bounded instead by a plantation of fir trees. Among these a number of small pig-like creatures were routing. Jane recalled her queer thoughts at Milton Porcorum. They seemed, somehow, less queer in this setting. It was possible to believe that these snuffling and grunting little creatures had lately been small boys and girls – and that they were themselves approaching the very hall of Circe . . . She brought her mind back to what Remnant had been saying. 'What time *do* we need?' she asked.

'Not much. If we manage anything at all, it must be soon. Within an hour or so the whole place will be packing up.'

She looked at him incredulously. 'Packing up?'

'Certainly. Keep a clear head. Didn't I say that one had only to put a fist through an affair like this and it crumples? No matter how cleverly the sinister side of the place had been insulated and hidden away, it is almost absurdly vulnerable. Whatever it is, it's a thoroughly top-heavy piece of villainy, and the chaps who run it must be prepared to fade out at very short notice indeed. And the moment they discover I slugged that fellow behind us, or that I punched poor old Cline on the jaw, they'll know their hours are numbered. You see, they won't dare to reckon we broke into their filthy hide-out without leaving a word or two behind us. Presently they'll be on the run. We want to trip them up in the first hundred yards . . . There seems to be a building through the trees. We'll make for it.'

They plunged into the little wood. The small pig-like creatures scurried out of their way. Jane thought of the forbidding outer wall, the high wire fence, the men who seemed to prowl the place with guns, the sinister suggestion of inner recesses of the building given over to the perpetration of unspeakable things. She remembered the terror of the little man in the upper reading room . . . But Remnant treated the whole impressive structure as so much papier-mâché. She hoped he was right. The plantation was no more than a narrow screen of trees, and they now found themselves before a long, low, blank building that ran off indefinitely on either hand. Remnant glanced to his right. 'Seems to run out from the back of the house. Lit by skylights let into the flat roof. All the windows and doors – and perhaps a corridor – on the other side. Much what we're looking for, if you ask me. Let's see if we can get round it on the left.' They turned and hurried along the blank surface of the building. It would not be a pleasant spot to be brought to bay against. 'Well, I'm blessed!' Remnant had come to a halt. Before them was a sheet of water, and into this the end of the building dropped sheer. 'Take a look at that.'

Jane looked. Before them was a small lake, its banks thickly wooded. Near the centre was an island, almost entirely occupied by a large circular temple of somewhat bleak design. The walls of this were entirely blank, and recessed behind Doric pillars supporting the curved architrave; above this was a somewhat inelegant and incongruous dome. But the odd feature of this not very successful ornamental venture was its being joined to the building they had been skirting – and joined by a drab and utilitarian enclosed wooden bridge. It was like a Bridge of Sighs run up in a drearily functional age.

'Quite a strong-point, in a quiet way.' Remnant was looking at the temple with a sort of reluctant admiration. 'Ten to one, it's the nerve-centre of the whole bit of voodoo we're inquiring into.' He glanced at Jane, and she saw that his face was set in new and grim lines. 'All hope abandon, ye who enter here.'

She felt herself turn pale. 'You think it looks horrible?'

'Well – my guess is that it would do with a little airing. And now we go up this apple tree.'

Jane stared. Here at the edge of the little lake there was the ghost of an orchard, and one gnarled and sloping old tree grew close to, and overhung, the building beside them. 'You mean we get on the roof?'

'Just that. Then we can either drop down on the other side, where there may be doors and windows, or take a bird's eye view of things through the skylights. I'd like to know just how the ground lies in this long building before we tackle the island and that temple. We'll do our final clean-up there, I don't doubt; but we'll just have a look at this first.' Remnant was already on the flat roof, and in a moment he had hauled Jane up beside him. 'It's rather raked by the windows of the house. But that can't be helped.' He walked to the nearest skylight, knelt down, shaded his eyes and peered in. 'I can't see the whole room. But it looks like a small bedroom – and not exactly luxurious. We'll move on to the next.'

They were unpleasantly exposed, Jane thought, to anybody who was prepared to take an interest in them. But excitement sustained her; she felt a mounting certainty that they were really coming nearer to Geoffrey; and if he, and others, could be rescued at all, Roger Remnant seemed very much the man to do it. He had dropped down beside another skylight. 'Different cup of tea,' he said. 'Rather like Cline's study over again. Leather chairs, handsome books, bathing belles by some lascivious old Italian over the mantelpiece. What about its belonging to Cline's opposite number on the research side? . . . Move on to the next . . . Looks like a lab. It *is* a lab . . . And so is this one. As far as I can see all these rooms intercommunicate – and they open on a passage on the far side as well. The set-up is pretty clear, wouldn't you say?'

Jane too was peering into a laboratory. 'Well, it looks like research, all right. But as for the set-up –'

'The main building, as we've seen, is pukka clinic. Wealthy drunks faithfully attended to. Perhaps used as guinea-pigs at times, but only in a quiet way. Move a bit in this direction and you come to the research outfit. Has all the appearance of being pukka too. Inquiry into the physiology of alcoholic addiction, or some such rot. Some advanced drunks, perhaps, as cotcases. You can always be a little bolder in experimental treatment with "no-hope" patients – particularly if they come from the humbler classes of society. Move a little farther and perhaps you come to more fundamental research. But by that time, if you ask me, you're over the bridge and on the island. And just what you keep isolated there, the world simply doesn't know. Suppose a high-class patient, strolling in the grounds, hears some rather nasty noises from that direction. Why, our talented research scientists are doing something useful to one of those dear little pigs.'

Jane found her breath disposed to come and go in shaky sobs. 'If half of what you're imagining is true, it's –'

'Quite so. But don't forget it now has only about half an hour to go. We're right on top of it.' Remnant stamped his foot on the flat roof. 'And now we drop.'

'Five minutes is too long. If we can drop, let's drop quick. But how?'

'If we dropped down on the other side, we might be able to force a door or window giving on the corridor. But this' – and again Remnant stamped – 'is still, remember, no more than outworks. We want to get straight at the brain-centre. And the dividing-line, I'd say, is that handsome room with the bathing nymphs. Beyond that, there's a change of atmosphere – that little bedroom, for instance. A more honest word for that would be a cell. And close after that there's the bridge. I wonder if one could get along the top of it? Let's see.'

They retraced their steps. Jane stopped by the first sky-light at which Remnant had paused, and herself peered down. She drew back her head hastily. 'There's somebody there.' she whispered. 'A woman. She's lying on a little bed.'

'She must have been in another corner when I looked.' Remnant in his turn peered down. 'Seems the moment to take a chance.' He put his foot through the skylight.

The crash of splintered and falling glass seemed terrific. But Remnant thrust at the thing with his foot again and again. Within seconds the skylight was a wreck. The woman below had sprung up and was staring at them. 'Friends,' Remnant said. 'We're breaking up this whole racket. Sorry to startle you.'

'*Aber!*' It was less a word than a hoarse cry. 'You are truly friends? *Gott sei Dank!* You may be just in time. They have taken my boy. They have taken my boy to the island. Never have they done that before.'

'We'll have him back to you in no time.'

'But you cannot get in! Look – between us still there are these bars and that strong mesh.'

Remnant knelt down. The skylight had been as flimsy as such things commonly are. But there remained, at the level of the ceiling of the cell-like apartment below, a barrier of the sort the woman had described. Remnant nodded. 'I see. But don't worry. You couldn't do much with it from below. But from up above it may be a different matter. Please stand right back.' Remnant rose, retreated a dozen paces, and ran. A yard before the shattered skylight he leapt high into the air, and then went down with his feet rigid under him. There was a resounding crash. Jane ran forward and looked down. Remnant was on the floor below, scrambling to his feet from amid the debris of twisted bars and tangled wire netting. He looked up. 'Did I say you put a fist through it?' he called. 'A foot's even better. Now then, down you come. Imagine you're making one of those thrilling midnight climbs into college.'

With what she felt was a dangerous approach to hysteria, Jane laughed loud. Then she scrambled over the edge and dropped. Remnant caught her. 'Good girl.' He turned to the woman. 'We know a good deal. Explain about yourself. As quick as you can.'

8

'I am Anna Tatistchev, a doctor.' The woman's eyes were wild with anxiety, but her speech was collected. 'I was persuaded – it is now a month almost – to come here with Rudi, my small boy. I was to be shown work of medical interest in which I might assist – living quietly for a time, as it was necessary for me to do.'

Remnant nodded. 'You mean you were hiding from someone?'

'From the English police. Rudi and I ought not to be in England. So I came. For a time the work seemed indeed interesting and honourable. Then I suspected. There were patients – experiments too – that I did not understand. Or not at first. Then my position was difficult. They had chosen well. An outlaw is helpless.'

Remnant had walked to the single door of the room. He held up his hand for silence, and listened. He shook his head, came back, and smiled. 'Isn't "outlaw" pitching it a bit steep?' Anna Tatistchev looked at him uncomprehendingly. 'Never mind. Go ahead.'

'I found that my so-called employment was almost imprisonment. I have known prisons, but this, for me, was a new kind. But I came to know that it was that. Twice only I found a way to send out a message to my friends. I did not yet wish them to come, for I believed that there was much evil here of which I might discover the secret. Evil so great that my own safety must not be counted. No – and not even that of my boy. Twice I slipped notes deep in a pile of letters that I knew would be taken, without more examination, to the *Ortspostant* – the little post office. And there was a telephone from which I believed I could send a call for help if some crisis came. And yesterday – it came.'

'And you managed to telephone?'

'This morning – yes. And I hoped that my message got through. But I was detected as I was speaking. So my imprisonment was made strict in this small room.'

'They know that you got this telephone message out – giving the address of this place?'

The woman nodded. 'They know that.'

'Then they must certainly be packing up. But why did a crisis come yesterday?'

'It is obscure. But there have been several misfortunes – calamities. One is very technical, and I have been able to find out little. But some preparation of great intricacy – one vital to what goes on here – has become impure, and so is nearly all gone inert. The little that is left will be similarly useless in a day or two. And there is even some hitch in starting the long process of synthesizing it again. I suspect that some – how would you say? – *entscheidend –*'

'Crucial.' Jane pounced on the word at once.

'– that some crucial formula is not available. Then, there was a death. One of the Assistant Directors – the only one with whom I have had dealings – died. It is my thought that he was killed.'

'Capital.' Remnant nodded briskly. 'One less to deal with.'

'And the man who first persuaded me to come here – a man called Squire – has been in trouble. I believe it is thought that more than once he has acted rashly in finding people who might be obliged to stay here – to stay here and to submit to things. And I think too that there was an escape. It may have been an escape of such a person.'

'It sounds a pretty full day. And the result is that something is being hurried on?'

'I fear that it is so. There are to be two or three swift experiments. It is a matter of using quickly, and while it is still potent, the substance –'

'I understand.' Remnant was dragging a small table to the middle of the room and perching a chair on it. He was clearly determined that action

403

should begin without delay. 'But what *are* these experiments? What does the whole thing aim at?'

'It is a scientific conspiracy. They call it Operation Pax.'

'Operation Pax?'

'The aim is to find a means of neutralizing the combative – the aggressive – component in the human personality, and perhaps of spreading this, like a disease, through whole populations. They call that the General Pacification.'

Remnant received this in silence. But Jane spoke up at once. '*Would* that be a bad thing?'

'It is the question I asked. At first it seemed to me that here was something perhaps of great benefit to mankind. I soon saw that it was the intention of these men to use their achievement in evil ways. They planned the means of making whole peoples – whole nations – helpless, impossible to arouse. These would be mere cattle – mere sheep – while others would remain wolves, lions, beasts of prey. And they would sell this instrument of power. More – they would *be* this power. For somewhere in this organization, in some inner circle to which I have not penetrated, there is a lust for power, an unlimited ambition, that is very terrible.'

Remnant was testing his means of climbing again to the shattered skylight. 'Certainly a very considerable project,' he said. 'What we call a tall order, Dr Tatistchev. But, only half an hour ago, we have seen it under way ourselves. Now we're going to stop it.'

'But surely –' Jane hesitated. She was struggling for clarity amid the fantastically vast issues which had suddenly opened around her. It was like being a swimmer unexpectedly submerged deep in a whirlpool to escape which it was vital to strain every nerve and muscle. 'Surely it is like the other great discoveries of science – very powerful for either good or evil? Surely it is a matter of how it *would* be used?'

Anna Tatistchev nodded gravely. '*Fräulein*, so I too thought. But it is not so. *Gar nicht!* For the process is not a modification, but a destruction. It would create not another sort of men, but something less than men.'

'Quite right. It's pure devilry.' Remnant spoke absolutely. He sounded not at all like a man whose intellectual vigour had been inadequate to support the discourses of the Stockton and Darlington Professor. 'Every creature born into a world like this needs every scrap of aggressiveness, or whatever you call it, that he can summon up. Most of us might use it better than we do. But the thing itself is ours; it's a need and a birthright; and the chap who'd steal it must have it turned against him overwhelmingly. That, as it happens, is our job now. I haven't over-much of it myself, but –'

Jane again found herself laughing. But this time it was not in the least hysterically. 'What you have will do to be going on with. And we'd better *be* going on with it. Let's climb out.'

'Then out we go. But there's something more to find out first.' Remnant turned to Anna Tatistchev. 'Do you think they have other places besides this?'

'I think they have.'

'Well, now – they must be packing up, you know. They simply must. That escape, your telephone-message, things we've done this morning if by now they've discovered them: these things are their marching orders. But you think the active villainy is going on still?'

'I am sure it is. There are two reasons. One is the using to the best advantage of what little remains of the substance of which I have spoken. And that is why I fear for Rudi. It was only early yesterday that I came to suspect this of a child's being required. It is believed that with a child certain effects may be more lasting and complete than any achieved so far. And they have taken my boy to the island! I beg that you and your friends should act quickly.'

Remnant nodded in brisk reassurance. 'As it happens, we haven't any friends here yet. But we, ourselves, are going to act now.'

'*Got sei Dank!* Then you will be in time. It was only within this half an hour that they took him. And they will have to put him to sleep. There is a certain harmless drug which must act – I think for perhaps an hour – before the thing is done . . . But you must hasten very much, because of the other.'

Jane caught her breath. 'The other?'

'A young man. For him too I think they intend the injections. And then, if they had to abandon this place, they would take them both away. For these are crucial experiments. And it might be a long time before the substance is prepared again.'

'Have you seen this young man? Do you know his name?'

'His name – no. He has not told it to me. But I have seen him and two or three times spoken. He is tall and fair, and his complexion – I do not know the word –'

Jane was trembling all over. 'You mean –'

'It is *sommersprossig.*'

'Freckly . . . It's Geoffrey!'

The little prison-like room swam round Jane, and she sank down on to the bed. Remnant strode across to it and gave her an uncompromising shake. 'Steady on. This is the best news we've had yet. The chap's alive. And we'll have him joining in the kicking in no time.'

Anna Tatistchev too had come over to Jane and taken her by the hand. 'He is your husband?'

'He is going to be.'

'Nothing has happened yet. He is well. His danger too is great, but your friend will save him.'

'It's horrible – abominable!' Jane sat up straight. 'He has been kept here for weeks in this frightful peril, and nothing has been done.' She turned to Remnant. 'For God's sake put your fist through the rest of the place – quick!'

'Come along, then. Up we go.'

Jane climbed on the table. She hesitated. 'You spoke to him? Did he speak of how he came here, or of – of things outside?'

'I was told that he was a very bad dipsomaniac, segregated here, and for whom there was little hope. Then I suspected that he was really imprisoned. Several times we spoke through a door before I had a glimpse of him. He told me that he had come here disguised, and for adventure – pretending to be homeless and friendless – because he had stumbled on the suspicion that the clinic was criminal. And they held him. I told him of how my own suspicions had grown, and of how I too now knew all the evil. We have talked hurriedly – secretly – of the danger, and of some plan. But then they took him to the island.'

Remnant jumped on the table. 'Well we're going there now.' He picked up Jane as if she had been a child, mounted the chair, and gave her a vigorous hoist that sent her scrambling out on the roof. He turned to Anna Tatistchev. 'I think three may be too many at the moment. Is anybody likely to come in on you here?'

'I think not.'

'Then, just for a time, you'd better stop. We've started a distraction at the front of the house that must be keeping the bulk of these people busy. With luck Miss Appleby and I can break in to this place on the island and take whoever is on guard there by surprise.'

'You are brave people. Have you arms? . . . Yes? Then go. I will wait, since you ask me. But there is one other thing of which I was to speak. It is the second reason why they will press on with what they have wished to do, even if they feel that soon they must abandon this place. It is the active evil spirit . . . I do not know the words for it.'

'I think I see.'

'Since yesterday I believe it has become a madness, a fury. Such a plan as theirs aims at wealth and power. But it springs simply from an illness of the mind, a compulsion to destroy. And if things go badly, and their ambitions are checked, then they will destroy blindly, rather than not destroy at all. So they are very dangerous.'

Remnant nodded. 'In fact there's a strong case for getting in on a little destruction first. That's just my notion.' He put his hands up to the shattered skylight and heaved himself to the roof. 'We'll be back in no time.'

Anna Tatistchev nodded. '*Gott gebe!*' She sat down quietly on the side of the bed.

Jane Appleby was already at the extreme edge of the long roof. Remnant hurried after her. Fortune, he thought, had thrown him up against two very good sort of women for an affair of the sort on hand.

9

Jane was staring at the temple. It had a sufficiently forbidding look. 'Ought she not have come with us? She's the child's mother, after all.'

Remnant shook his head. 'For the moment, only business considerations count. We've got two guns – the one from Cline's drawer, and one I took from the chap I slugged . . . Got a pocket?'

'Yes.'

'Ever fired a revolver?'

'Quite often. But only at targets, I'm afraid.'

Remnant grinned. He seemed to have leisure to regard this as a capital joke. 'Good enough. Here you are.' He handed Jane Cline's weapon. 'Right shoulder if you want to be humane. Tummy if you're feeling nasty.'

'I see.' Jane shivered slightly. 'I can imagine circumstances in which I shall feel very nasty indeed.'

'They won't happen. We're a step ahead of all that. Things are going along quite nicely. It's a matter of impetus, you know. First thing they teach you about assault.'

'And I can imagine other circumstances in which I should find you insufferable, Mr Remnant . . . How do we go?'

'Straight across the bridge, Miss Appleby. Take your shoes off.'

Jane obeyed without asking questions.

'Good woman. We go across the lid, so to speak. And it's tin. Don't want to make a row. Twenty fires in that highly respectable drunks' home wouldn't draw the whole high command away from this affair in front of us. So follow me, and don't speak until you're spoken to.'

Jane compressed her lips. There were moments when she found Roger Remnant very hard to take. His own shoes were off and strung round his neck. From the roof on which they stood to the upper surface of the tunnel-like bridge was an easy drop, and he made it in absolute silence. Jane dropped down beside him. They went forward on tiptoe. The surface was of corrugated iron. Walking delicately, it was not easy to keep a sure balance. But in less than a minute they had reached the other end.

Remnant came to a halt and stood quite still, frowning. Jane saw that the next problem was a hard one. On either side of them the sheer wall of the temple went off in a blank, smooth curve, and below them it dropped clear into the water. Remnant's voice came softly in Jane's ear. 'No good taking a swim. Bad splash. Bad for the guns. We don't know what's on the other side. This is perhaps the only entrance – and it may be sheer like this all the way round.' He paused, rapidly appraising again the whole situation. 'Have to go up.'

Jane looked up. The proposal seemed blankly impossible. What confronted them was a steeply pitched pediment – presumably an ornamental feature crowning the doorway now concealed by the bridge – which rose until it almost touched the curved cornice of the building. Remnant put out his hand to it. 'That or nothing,' he murmured. 'We can just get on the outer face of the pediment; it's not too steep to crawl up – at least I don't think so. How to get off it and on top of the cornice is the headache. But there isn't sudden death below; only a filthy ducking. I think I can take you. Follow me.' He edged himself on to the pediment, belly downwards, and crawled up its smooth incline. 'Not bad,' he whispered back. 'Pediment projects beyond the cornice a good six inches. And there's a lightning-conductor to help. We can do it. Come on.'

Jane came on. Her head was clear, but her recollections immediately afterwards confused. Somehow they had done it. They were lying in a sort of broad lead gutter behind the cornice. Beyond this again the curve of the dome.

'We're perfectly hidden here. Lie still. I'm going right round.' Remnant breathed the words in Jane's ear and set off at a crawl. He had become, she realized, suddenly very cautious. He disappeared round the curve of the dome, keeping wholly prone in the gutter. His progress in this fashion could not be rapid; to Jane it appeared an age before his head and shoulders emerged from behind the answering curve of the dome on her other hand. She thought inconsequently of Sir Francis Drake, home after circumnavigating the world.

'The temple doesn't cover the whole thing. There's quite a bit of ground on the other side, and the island runs out in a little tongue, with a much smaller temple at the end of it. That means there's probably another entrance to this big one, facing that way. But, ten to one, it's pretty massively locked up. I'm going up again. Better do it from the other side, where there's less chance of being seen.'

This time they both crawled half round the dome. Peering over the cornice, Jane presently saw the vacant stretch of island that Remnant had described. The second temple was very much smaller: an oblong affair, again with Doric columns. Jane, a severely educated child, at once saw that it was a miniature version of the Theseion at Athens. But Remnant was paying more attention to what was above him. 'Only a step up to the drum', he said. 'But the first part of the dome's more difficult. However, it's ribbed. I'll go up and have a look.' He rose, spread-eagled himself between two of the ribs to which he had pointed, and worked himself upward. As the ribs converged and the pitch lessened the going got easier. Presently he set himself astride a single rib and kneed himself to the top. Within a minute he was sliding down a rib and had come to rest beside her again. It was an expert roof-climber's job, and Jane guessed that if he was unfamiliar with the lecture rooms of the colleges of Oxford he was tolerably familiar with their towers and pinnacles. 'Any good?' she whispered.

'What have you got on under that skirt and jersey?'

By this time Jane was schooled into finding nothing that Roger Remnant said at all odd. 'Nylon.'

'A lot of it?'

'Well quite a lot.' Jane was apologetic. 'It's getting on in October.'

'Stockings?'

'Nylon too.' This time Jane was yet more apologetic. 'Economical, really.'

'I want the whole lot.'

'The whole lot?'

'Listen – it's as I thought. The lantern up there screens a circular opening at the top of the dome.'

'An eye.'

'Very well – an eye. And it looks straight down on a sort of small circular hall –'

'A cortile.'

'– with rooms opening off all round. I think we can make something that will take me down.'

'If you mean out of my nylon, then I'm going down too.'

'We'll see about that. Look – I'll nip round here a bit and see what I can contribute.' Remnant grinned. 'Not that I can really compete. But a pair of braces will give us a final useful three or four feet.'

He was gone. It was not a commodious spot in which to undress, but Jane made no bones about it. The garments when lying in a heap at her feet seemed absurdly tenuous. She picked them up and crawled with them farther round the drum. The sensation of a skirt and woollen jersey next to her skin was mildly disconcerting. Remnant was waiting for her. He took the things one by one. 'Absolutely splendid. Marvellous stuff. Take an elephant. Unfortunately it needs a bit of time. You can fill it in by finding your way about that gun.'

Jane obediently found her way about the gun. Remnant worked with concentration and extraordinary care. Every drop of impetuosity seemed to have evaporated from his personality. She suddenly knew that her confidence in him was complete.

He had finished. 'You saw how I went up?'

'Yes.'

'Could you do it?'

'Yes.'

'Then up you go first. If you slip, go slack and spread-eagle. You won't come really fast, except right at the end here. And – listen – when you do get up and peer over, the floor will seem the hell of a long way down. But it isn't as far as it looks.'

'I understand that.'

'Then off you go.'

The woollen jersey tickled horribly as she sprawled and kneed her way upwards, and the scratching of the tweed skirt was worse. But the climb itself was a good deal easier than she had expected, once the first thrust of the dome was conquered. In a few minutes she was under the lantern with which this freakish building was surmounted: and a moment later Remnant was beside her.

'A bit conspicuous up here, so we don't want to waste time. And there won't be much of this admirable rope to spare, so we mustn't waste that either . . . But here's the lightning-conductor again. Saves us a couple of feet. There – it's fixed. You can go up and down ropes?'

'Yes.'

'Then you may follow as soon as I've touched down. If it bears me it will bear you.'

'In that case wouldn't it be better –'

'Be quiet. The stuff's all right. It's the knots. But I've worked each one just all I know how. Well, this is the dangerous bit – see? Every way the dangerous bit. After this the clean-up will follow.'

'I believe you. Go ahead.'

Remnant swung himself over the eye. 'As it happens, I go down a bit fancy. But you come plain – feet, knees, both hands. No bright girl of the gym – understand?'

'Agreed.'

Remnant drew the revolver from his pocket. He still had his appearance of extraordinary concentration. And then he was gone – so quickly that whatever was fancy in his method quite eluded Jane's analysis. Whatever it was, it took him down the improvised rope like an express elevator, and with the revolver poised ready in a free hand. He was safely on the floor – a marble floor, Jane suddenly saw – and standing quite still. He did not look up. That, she realized, would have made this yawning and suddenly horrible chasm seem somehow much deeper. He would betray no anxiety about her. His attention was absorbed in studying the circle of closed doors surrounding him. A gentle draught of air came up. It was a very chill air, and it stirred the crazy dangling thread that, minutes before, had been no more than a thin and diaphanous sheath round her own body. It looked now as if it would scarcely bear the weight of a small plummet at the end of it. But it had borne Remnant. She realized that it was now or never – both for this, and for ever looking herself in the face again. She went over and down – hand over hand, carefully, as she had been told.

She had done it, and the marble floor was very cold on her bare feet. Remnant's hand came out and touched hers. It was a gesture commanding absolute silence. The little cortile, with its cupola and lantern above, could be a dire acoustic trap. A mere whisper, incautiously pitched, would echo and re-echo round it, until the reiterated and amplified sound was like surf breaking on a beach. Jane strained her ears. She could hear only a low, intermittent sighing, now rising towards a whistle and now sinking to a moan. It was the wind, she thought, playing through the lantern and washing round the chill concavity of the dome.

Remnant moved his other hand slightly. It was the one holding the revolver. She understood, and drew out the weapon in her own pocket. She gripped it firmly, imagining the clatter it would make if it fell. She looked downwards. The marble was white and faintly veined, like her own feet that rested on it. She looked around. There were five closed doors. Two of them were symmetrically placed on either side of a vaulted passage leading, she guessed, to the main doorway and the bridge, and the fifth was directly opposite this.

She heard her own heart. Remnant's left hand let go of hers and described a small circle in air. She understood him instantly. It was like having a twin brother with whom no speech was necessary. He disliked the way the closed doors surrounded them. Let the wrong one open, and for a fatal second they could not help being taken unawares. His finger moved, and she knew that they were to stand back to back. With infinite caution he took a step sideways. She did the same. It was like ceasing to be man and woman, and becoming a monstrous crab. They moved towards the vaulted passage, holding the doors covered on either hand. She still heard faintly the sob and wail as of invisible wind. They had traversed the breadth of the marble floor. It was patterned in concentric circles, and their slow progress had been like that of a pawn on an unfamiliar board. The open archway was now above their heads. The length of the corridor on which it opened must correspond to that of the surrounding rooms.

She was touched lightly on the shoulder. It was her job to stand guard alone. Remnant had gone. A moment later she heard the first sound that either of them had occasioned. It might have been the scrape of iron on stone. Remnant was back and standing beside her, his revolver in front of him and his glance circling warily from door to door. His left thumb went over his shoulder. She was to make the same inspection that he had just carried out. The passage proved to be no more than eight paces long. At the far end were massive double doors, sheathed in bronze, and with their handles gripped in the jaws of bronze lions. A key stood turned in a powerful lock. And a stout steel bar, pivoting at the centre, had been swung round and engaged in niches in the surrounding stone. It had been the sound of this forced home that she had heard a moment before. Remnant had made very sure that they would not be surprised from the direction of the bridge.

So they were shut up with the enemy, lurking in some or all of the surrounding rooms. Jane thought of those gruesome pictures, beloved of persons who fabricate history-books for the very young, depicting martyrs in the arena, awaiting the release of the wild beasts from their cages. She returned to Remnant. He was not – as the analogy might suggest – engaged in prayer. Nevertheless he had something of the same rapt quality. And he appeared to be listening with all his ears. It came to Jane in a flash that there was something ominous in the silence of the place. Remnant had been very sure that this whole hideous organization must be aware its hour had struck. What if it had already vanished to some other lurking-place, some emergency headquarters – taking its crucial victims with it? There was nothing but dismay in the thought. A thousand times better than that would it be for every one of those five sinister doors to open simultaneously and pour the whole filthy gang upon them. Which means – thought Jane dispassionately – that at least I haven't got cold feet . . . But that wasn't true in a physical sense – for now both her feet and calves felt icy at the creeping chill of the marble.

Remnant signed to her to stay where she was. He began to move – more rapidly now, but with absolute noiselessness – round the circumference of the circular hall. She was unable to follow him continuously with her eye, for it was her business to keep all five doors under observation. And this was the best position from which to do that. The curve of the building put even those most immediately on either hand all but simultaneously within her vision. She wondered if she was to shoot at sight. The revolver was perfectly steady in her hand, and she knew that at this range she could do what damage she was minded to . . . Remnant was stopping at each door, intently listening. She had a sense that he was inwardly perplexed . . . perhaps even that some doubt was growing in him. He paused longest at the door directly opposite. He crouched down by it, and she saw that he was licking his left hand. For a moment the effect was weirdly feline. Then she saw that he was passing the moist hand close to the floor, and then at a right-angle up the edge of the door. . . . Presently he moved on and completed the circuit. She glanced swiftly at his face as he came up to her. His eyes seemed to have gone darker. There were beads of sweat on his forehead. He pointed back at the door straight ahead of her. She knew that they were to go through it.

They moved straight across the floor, brushing as they went past it the tatter of nylon that had brought them here. Remnant paused, pointed to himself, raised one finger; he pointed to Jane and raised two: he stepped for a moment in front of her and made a gesture from his back to the space on his left. She understood that he was to go in first, and that as she followed she was to place herself on his left hand.

He was reaching for the handle. He must be proposing to take a chance that the door wasn't locked. The faint sob and whistle she had already heard was louder. Perhaps the wind was rising . . .

Remnant flung back the door. It was of abnormal thickness, and bedded in rubber. What Jane had heard through this insulating medium was a human voice, screaming in agony.

10

Something whined past her ear and smacked against a wall far behind her. She knew that it was a bullet: that with formidable swiftness of response the enemy had met the assault in its first moments. Then she realized that she was again on the wrong side of the door. At that first shot Remnant had thrust her back and half closed it on her. Her impulse was to thrust at it furiously. But his shoulders were hard up against it, and she saw that to push might be to endanger rather than help him.

The screams of agony had mercifully ceased. Or perhaps they had only disappeared behind a curtain of more deafening sound. So confounding was the uproar that for a second she lost all clear understanding of its occasion. She recovered herself and knew that it was a gun-battle. The number of shots actually fired was not, perhaps, so very many all told. But the reports chased each other wildly round the domed hall to which she was still, infuriatingly, confined, and the noise was so great as to shut out every other sensation and perception. She looked quickly round to see if anybody was emerging from the other rooms. If reinforcements did come from these she would have a part to play yet. When she turned again Remnant's shoulders had gone. She had a horrible fear that he had been hit; that he would be lying crumpled on the floor. She pushed at the door. It swung back freely and she entered the room.

The place reeked of powder, and of queer smells she could not identify. There was one further shot. She saw a white-coated figure in the middle of the room dive head foremost to the floor like an acrobat and lie still; and in the same instant she was aware of two similar figures dashing through a door straight in front of her and slamming it behind them. Remnant was on his feet still; he leapt at the door through which the figures had retreated, and locked it. Then he turned round and saw her. 'Go out,' he said.

She found herself trembling with anger as she looked at him. 'I'll never forgive you – never!'

'Go outside.' His voice was low – but it fell on her like a strong hand. She turned and walked unsteadily into the circular hall, her temples hammering. Things that she had momentarily glimpsed and instinctively refused to acknowledge the meaning of swayed before her inward vision, and she felt, like an actual physical thing, an icy and invisible hand on her heart.

'Jane – please come back now.'

She turned again and re-entered the room. 'I'm sorry,' she said.

Remnant raised the ghost of a smile. 'We're getting on pretty well. I think the child's all right.' And he pointed to a corner of the room. Jane took one look and ran to it. Rudi Tatistchev, the small boy whom they had already glimpsed once that morning, was lying there, curled up, his face stained with tears, and apparently in a deep sleep. She knelt beside him and took him in her arms – with a surge of deep feeling such as she had never known.

'He really is all right. They hadn't got going on all that.' Remnant had come up beside her. 'They were busy instead with your poor devil from the Bodleian.'

'They wanted to experiment –'

'No – not that.' Remnant's voice was quiet. 'They were trying to get something out of him. He's been pretty filthily handled. That was why I pushed you out the second time. I wanted to tidy him up a bit. He'll be quite all right – in time. I've put him over on that bench.'

Jane set the sleeping child down gently and turned round. The battlefield – for it was like that – was a large wedge-shaped room that had been turned elaborately into an operating theatre. It was lit by sundry impressive electrical contrivances, and the only daylight – as presumably with all the rooms in the temple – was from shallow windows high up under the architrave. There was blood now all over the place. In the middle of the floor, huddled on his side, the man she had seen fall there lay in a pool of it. He was alive; his body was spasmodically twitching; when it did this it emitted noises that were not human but merely mechanical or hydraulic; and his face was hideously grey behind a neatly trimmed red beard.

Her eye passed swiftly on, very fearful of what it might next see. But there was now only one other figure in the room: the little man into whom she had so fatefully bumped upon leaving Dr Ourglass and the inquisitive Mark Bultitude. Fate had decreed that he should be one of Nature's meaner and more insignificant creations; man had lately seen to it that he should be much less even than this. He half lay, half sat on a bench by the wall where Remnant had shoved him, wrapped in a sheet patched with blood. His eyes were open, but it was impossible to tell if they saw.

'Stay here and keep an eye on things – and particularly for anybody coming to monkey with the door.' Remnant was moving across the room again. 'I'm going to make sure there's nobody lurking – of his own will or otherwise – elsewhere in the building.'

She watched him go out, understanding very well the meaning of his move. They had rescued the little man she had seen kidnapped in Radcliffe Square – or at least they had rescued what was left of him. And – what would have been worth crossing the world for – they had rescued the little boy. But of her lover whom she had set out to seek there was still no sign . . . She looked at the shambles about her – the product of the heat of battle and partly of madness and cold cruelty – and her whole body shivered as if in ague. The resources of the desperate people amid whom destiny had brought her appeared endless. Perhaps about England, about Europe, they had half a dozen places like this; and perhaps they were already hurrying to one of them now, bearing Geoffrey with them.

Remnant was back. The chill of the ghastly place seemed mitigated as he entered. 'Nobody and nothing,' he said. 'On one side a room rather like Cline's but grander, and with a laboratory next door. On the other side a bedroom and a slap-up bathroom. And there's a surprisingly dry cellar used as a store.'

'I see.' Jane's voice trembled. Her eye fell on the bearded man on the floor. 'Can we do anything for him?'

'Unfortunately he's past getting anything *from*.' Remnant's tone held a momentary savagery that startled her. 'He's going to die.'

'Do you think that Geoffrey –'

'Your young man? Don't worry. I'm afraid they're holding him still. But he's in no danger. Or in no danger of – this.' He glanced round. Jane saw that, beneath his reassuring manner, he was fighting mad. 'We've smashed all that for good.'

'They may have the means of starting it up elsewhere.'

'Don't be dismal. And they've got something coming to them yet.' He looked at the locked door that gave on the farther end of the island, and frowned. 'Only we've got to think . . . I wonder if the poor chap over there can tell us anything.'

They both crossed the room. Jane's bare feet were like metal dragged at by some powerful magnet under the floor. With an immense effort she looked straight at the man and walked on. His eyes were still open. And as they reached him his lips moved.

'Others . . . there was a kid.'

Remnant spoke clearly. 'The kid's all right. He's over there. Was there anyone else?'

'The little place beyond this . . . I didn't see it the first time.' The man's face contorted itself with the effort of speaking. 'They put me in there first . . . a young chap . . . prisoner –'

'Yes?'

'Asked –' The man gave a deep groan. 'But I didn't –' His eyes turned to Jane. 'Bicycle', he murmured, with a queer inflexion of recognition. And his eyes closed.

Jane looked at Remnant. 'He means the little square temple?'

'Clearly. A couple got away there when they'd had enough of the shooting game here. And there might be one or two more. You sent a telegram to this top-ranking policeman brother of yours?'

'Yes.' Jane looked at her watch. 'And he must have got it well over an hour ago.'

'Of course they don't know about that. But it seems they *do* know that Anna What's-her-name got out a telephone call. So they can't reckon on much more grace. On the other hand, they can no doubt communicate with the rest of the gang – those that are real in-on-the-thing accomplices, I mean – who are now milling round our fire. They may have found poor old Cline in his cupboard.'

'I suppose those people in the other temple can get away if they want to?'

'Good Lord, yes. The lake would be no obstacle to them at all. Ten to one, they're gone by now. They've got precious little motive not to quit. Unless –' Remnant frowned. 'I think we'll try a little experiment.' He moved across to the door leading to the open air and studied it. 'Metal-sheathed too,' he said. 'So there's not much risk. Come over here.' Jane joined him. 'Now, listen. While I –'

A high, hoarse scream from behind them froze the words on Remnant's lips. They whirled round. The savagely manhandled figure, who a minute before possessed scarcely the strength to whisper, had flung off the sheet enveloping him. Bloody and almost naked, he was staggering across the room. In an instant they saw why. The bearded man had got on his knees and was crawling along the floor, clutching in one hand a short, gleaming knife. He glanced side-long as he moved – and Jane, catching his eye, saw that in his last moments humanity had left him and he was become a beast.

'Not the kid!' The little man, as he screamed the words, flung himself upon the insane creature on the floor. Rudi Tatistchev, in his deep drugged sleep, lay no more than a yard away, and the bright surgical knife had been poised in air. There was a second's violent struggle as Remnant rushed forward. The two figures on the floor were a tangle of flailing and twitching limbs. Then there was a single deep groan. Remnant took the bearded form by the shoulders and flung it aside. It lay quite still. The little man turned over on his back with a low wail. The knife was buried in his breast.

Jane dropped down at his side. He opened his eyes on her and his lips moved. 'Your kid', he whispered. 'Your kid's safe . . . across the . . . weir . . . They can't . . . can't pull the plug on him. . . . Dar –' His lips became motionless, and his eyes closed.

Remnant moved from one inert form to the other. 'Both dead.' He looked down at the torn body of the little man whose name was unknown to them. 'I don't suppose he ever got high marks as a citizen', he said soberly. 'But he wasn't a bad chap.'

It was an unexpected epitaph on Albert Routh.

I I

A mile short of Milton Manor, Appleby overtook and cautiously passed a small horde of children on bicycles. Almost immediately afterwards, and as he turned into the side-road on which the entrance to the estate must lie, he just saved himself from head-on collision with a powerful car swinging out at a dangerous pace. The two vehicles came to a stop, bonnet to bonnet, with a scream of brakes. Appleby was preparing to speak in his frostiest official manner when he became aware that the driver of the other car was known to him. It was the fat Bede's don, Mark Bultitude.

Without attempting to back, Appleby climbed out. 'Good afternoon,' he said. 'We nearly did each other a good deal of damage.'

For a second Bultitude, who had not stirred from his wheel, stared at him blankly. Then his face broke into a smile. 'Dear me,' he said. 'Sir John Appleby, is it not? I was sorry not to have some conversation with you last night. We are undoubtedly here on the same errand.'

'Except that I am coming and you are going.'

'Precisely. You remember Cumming who was always going, and Gowing who was always coming? Too few people now read that immortal diary . . . You are looking for news of the young man Ourglass?'

'At the moment, I am looking for my sister. It is she who is looking for him – with some rashness, possibly.'

Bultitude raised his eyebrows. 'I was being introduced to your sister a few hours ago in Oxford. If I may say so, I thought her a delightful girl, who never says anything silly, and who looks particularly charming when she thinks she has.'

'Thank you.'

'It was meeting her that put this expedition into my head . . . Good gracious – what a mob of brats!'

The children on the bicycles had swept past. They were shouting and arguing hotly as they disappeared in a cloud of dust. Appleby watched them absently. 'It was through meeting my sister that you came out here?'

'Actually, I had suggested to the young man's uncle – I think you met him when he was my guest last night – that we should come and do a little exploring together. But he finally excused himself. Not that he isn't genuinely anxious about his nephew. But I believe that I offended him deeply – although almost, perhaps, without his conscious awareness – by making one or two unfortunate facetious suggestions when he first told of the matter. Anyway, I came straight out myself.'

'I see.' Appleby, who a few minutes before had been in a tearing hurry, produced a pipe and filled it slowly. 'You've become interested in this young man?'

Bultitude considered. 'It appears,' he said gravely, 'that this Geoffrey Ourglass is an *Ourglass*. I had no idea. One is naturally interested in a well-connected youth.'

'Naturally.' Appleby looked hard at the fat man. Bultitude, he thought, must have had a motor-car body more or less built round him.

'And if in addition to that he has brains – as this Geoffrey apparently has – then he is a *rara avis* indeed. No exertion should be too great if he can be brought back to Bede's.'

'A very proper collegiate feeling.' Appleby lit his pipe. 'And you came out this way simply because you had heard the story of young Ourglass's having been seen driving – or being driven – hereabouts?'

Bultitude's arms began to flip about his person with something of the helplessness of the wings of a penguin. It presently appeared that he was in search of a cigarette-case. Appleby produced matches. When this exigency had been adequately met Bultitude picked up the conversation as if it had not been interrupted. 'No, Sir John. I had a further reason – an acquaintanceship in these parts.'

'At Milton Manor?'

'My dear Appleby – if I may so address you – how thoroughly on the spot you are. At Milton Manor, as you say. A certain Dr Cline, who runs the place. Or who runs one side of it.'

'That is most interesting to me, Bultitude. A close acquaintance?'

'Dear me, no. My intimates, such as they are, move in other classes of society. A former professional contact – no more. But it struck me that it might be worth while consulting him.'

'How very odd.'

Bultitude pondered, as if resolved to accord this response fair consideration. 'Yes,' he said. 'I agree. It *was* odd. It was a queer idea. Less an idea, indeed, than an intuition.'

'A successful intuition?'

'Unfortunately not. At first Cline was engaged, and then they couldn't find him. Moreover there was a fire. By now the whole place may be burnt down.'

'Burnt down?'

'Would it be so regrettable?'

This time Appleby looked at Mark Bultitude very hard indeed. 'Am I to understand that you have formed an unfavourable opinion of this clinic?'

Bultitude smiled his most brilliant smile. 'I should conceive it – upon reflection, but quite recent reflection – to be highly dangerous and probably highly criminal . . . Dear me – how late it is! I really must be pushing on.'

Appleby seemed not altogether disposed to take this hint at its first offering. 'It seems likely,' he said grimly, 'that my sister is in this highly dangerous and probably highly criminal place now. I shall be there myself in five minutes –'

'I am delighted to hear it. The matter – if I may be allowed to say so – will be in most competent hands.'

'And unless certain coded instructions are given to the contrary, there will be a very considerable force of police there – well, a little later on.'

'How much I wish I could stop. Unfortunately, most important business calls me back to Oxford . . . *most* important business, my dear Appleby. And now, if perhaps I were to back a few yards –'

'That is most obliging of you, Bultitude. It is really my car that ought to be moved.'

'Not at all, dear fellow – not at all.' By what was, in him a remarkable acrobatic feat, Bultitude contrived to raise an arm in a condescending and dismissive gesture. 'By the way – was it just the old story of Ourglass's being seen hereabouts that has brought *Miss Appleby* out this way?'

'Far from it. Last night – although she knows nothing of this – a thoroughly desperate gang of criminals were hunting a small man with a scratched face about Oxford. They captured him. They captured me too.'

'That was indeed an achievement.'

Appleby smiled. 'If I were confronted with them, I would be the first to offer my congratulations.'

'It would be handsome of you. But proceed.'

'We both escaped – or rather were rescued. Then this little man faded out. My sister saw him this morning in the upper reading room in Bodley.'

Bultitude raised his eyebrows. 'How very interesting. It is true that highly criminal proceedings are frequently conducted there – but on what must be termed, conventionally, the intellectual plane.'

'Then she saw him being kidnapped from Radcliffe Square, and somehow learnt that the destination of the kidnappers was Milton.'

Bultitude's engine started into life, and his car shot alarmingly backwards. It then advanced, clear of Appleby's mudguards, and stopped again, with the engine ticking over. The bulk of Bultitude deflected itself by some inches from the perpendicular. In a common man the attitude would have been that of leaning affably out to bid a friend farewell. 'This has been a most enlightening conversation, Appleby. I have missed a luncheon party, but I am really very glad that I came out, all the same. There are times when one must cut one's losses – in the interest, of course, of greater ultimate gains.'

'Yes, indeed. It is a generalization one must bear in mind.' Appleby stepped clear. 'I hope your important business in Oxford will go well.'

'And I, in my turn, am most anxious about the issue of yours, here in Milton. And who knows' – Bultitude let in his clutch and his car glided smoothly forward – 'that we may not meet and compare notes later?'

'In your common-room tonight?'

Bultitude smiled. 'I wonder,' he said – and drove on.

12

The cyclists had not got far. Appleby passed them again round the next bend, scattered over a grassy knoll in a sort of irregular bivouac. Some were eating sandwiches or apples; some were disputing hotly; the greater number were listening to an impassioned harangue by a small, red-haired boy. Perhaps they were unable to agree on whether their expedition had taken them far enough. Appleby was not inclined to give the matter much thought. He had other things to think about.

At the lodge of Milton Manor he was nearly involved in a second collision. The gates were open, and a couple of heavy covered lorries were just swinging out. Drawn into the side of the road with his engine running, Appleby eyed them grimly. Then before the gates could be shut again he drove through them and stopped. A respectable-looking man at once hurried up. 'I'm very sorry, sir. But no visitors today.'

Appleby shook his head 'I'm not a visitor. I'm a fireman.'

The man looked startled. 'Sorry, sir. My orders are –'

'Don't you know the place is on fire?'

'Yes, sir. I've had it on the house telephone. But my –'

'Then don't be a fool, my man.' Appleby was suddenly brusque. 'I always come out ahead of my brigade, as you very well know. The engines will be here within a minute. Leave these gates open, and see that nothing gets in the way.'

'But you won't get through the fence.' The man was puzzled and worried. 'And I've orders –'

So there was another barrier. It was something, Appleby thought, that one might have guessed. 'But surely,' he said, 'you keep a key here?'

'No, sir. I telephone up to the house.' The man was apologetic. 'It's the animals, you see. Very valuable, they are.'

'No doubt. And I suppose the house itself is of some value too. And it's burning. See that you telephone at once.' Appleby let in his clutch again and shot forward. As he did so he fancied he heard, far off and faintly from behind him, the chiming of a great many bicycle bells.

Driving fast, he rounded a bend and saw a tall wire fence in front of him, running away on either side of equally tall gates of the same material. If he waited, perhaps somebody would come and unlock them. Or perhaps somebody would not. No buildings were as yet visible, but from beyond a belt of trees a thin column of smoke was rising. It did not look as if the fire reported by Bultitude was in fact very serious. He took his foot from the accelerator, meaning to slow down and consider his best course of action. As the roar of the engine died, he thought for a moment that he heard the crackle of flames. Then he realized that the sound was of rifle or revolver fire. He compressed his lips and peered ahead, trying to estimate from a distance the strength of the barrier before him. There really was no help for it. He pressed down on the accelerator hard. The car had still been travelling at a good pace. He felt in his back the sudden thrust of its eight roaring cylinders. One did this in the circus. Only there the barrier was of paper, and the vehicle a discreetly cantering horse . . .

The gates went down with a crash – and with a flash of brilliant blue flame. Appleby's body tingled all over; there was a queer sensation in his scalp; for a moment an unaccountable smell of singeing filled the car. By the time he had taken a guess at what had happened he had rounded another bend and glimpsed Milton Manor straight before him.

There was a crowd of people out on a lawn – patients, he supposed, because several nurses appeared to be attending on them. At a little distance from these a man in a white coat was lying back in a deck chair, with the appearance of being assisted or revived by two more nurses. Farther on, he could see a red fire-tender and a tangle of hoses. He cut off his engine and heard another shot. It came from somewhere beyond the house. The drive forked and he swung left. It curved towards the house again, and in front of him he now found a tall archway that appeared to lead into a courtyard. He drove straight through.

'And now for our experiment.'

Remnant was coolly stripping a strip of cloth from the white linen coat of the corpse with the red beard. Some yards back from the door that pointed towards the tip of the island he had already built a formidable double breast-work out of the stainless-steel equipment with which the place was lavishly provided. Now he advanced to the door with his improvised rope – the second he had constructed that day – in his hand. He tied it to the handle, unlocked the door, and retreated, gun in hand.

'You'd better be inside this too. And bring the boy. It will be the safest place if there really is shooting and things begin to ricochet.'

Jane Appleby did as she was told. 'You think they're still there?'

He grinned. 'I'll be pretty surprised if they are. But we'll take no chances . . . Ready?'

Jane nodded.

'If anything does happen, take your time. I got the lie of the land pretty well from the roof. They've no chance of rushing us, even if they've been reinforced from the house. And – by that same token – we have no chance of advancing against them . . . *Now!*'

Remnant pulled firmly at his rope and the door swung open. In an instant a bullet rang past above their heads.

Jane's heart leapt. They were still there – which meant that Geoffrey was still there too. 'Roger Remnant,' she murmured in her companion's ear. 'His first bad guess.'

Remnant's reply was lost in a second rattle of fire. The bullets ripped harmlessly overhead. She heard a click of metal beside her. Remnant was fiddling with a long forceps and a couple of mirror-like stainless-steel plates. 'First-rate periscope,' he said. 'Keep down, whatever you do. I'll give you a full report in a tick.' He shoved up the forceps with one plate gripped in it, and manoeuvred it to an angle. 'O.K. Perfectly clear. Temple has pillars all round. And a couple of fellows are lurking there to keep us back. I'll just touch them up a bit. Show them we're quite lively.' He suddenly thrust out an arm and fired.

'Perhaps they can't get away?'

'Unless we already have friends on the spot, I don't see that that's possible, worse luck. They must have a punt beyond the temple – or something of that kind. I'd say they're holding what's a strong position until they get a car round from the house. Then they'll be off all right.'

'I wish John would come.'

'That your brother? So do I. We could do with every Appleby – male and female – your family can raise.' Remnant's voice was not, Jane considered, altogether convincing. He's a vain creature, she thought ungratefully, and just loves it being all his show. He'd like to beat them off his own bat. And I wouldn't put it beyond him . . .

Her thought was scattered by the sudden roar of an engine starting into life somewhere beyond the square temple in front of them. Remnant scowled. 'There they go,' he said. 'But keep down still. I'm going to have a proper squint . . . Hullo – what's that?'

From somewhere out in the park a new sound came to them: that of racing cars, a low, almost continuous penetrating horn, and behind that a single urgently-chiming bell.

Jane gasped. 'It's John . . . it's the police – and an ambulance . . .'

Remnant had got on his knees. He fired a couple of shots at the farther temple, waited a second, and stood up. 'Gone,' he said.

The engine beyond the temple was still roaring. Suddenly above they heard a single shrill call – a call for help. The sound brought Jane to her feet in an instant. 'Geoffrey!'

For a second she saw nothing except a row of Doric pillars and a dark doorway beyond. Then a single figure emerged flying – the figure of a young man in ragged trousers and a torn shirt. His hair was matted and his face was a dead white streaked with grey. Two men – one in a white coat – pounded after him.

'Jane – Jane!' It was a cry like a child's – and as he uttered it the young man thrust out blindly, gropingly, an appealing arm that seemed bruised and blackened in its torn sleeve. 'Help!'

She took the breast-work at a bound and ran. She heard Remnant curse and leap after her. There was a hail of bullets, and she heard Remnant give a cry, spin round and fall. But she herself was untouched. Geoffrey was no more than five yards away. She was nearly there. She was nearly touching him – Suddenly from the lake on her left a dark, dripping figure rose up, took her in a flying Rugby tackle and then, with almost no loss of impetus, went rolling with her across the narrow tongue of land and into the lake on the other side. The water closed over her head just as she heard another fusillade of shots.

For a moment she thought that she would never come up again – that she was down at some great depth in the grasp of a drowning man. Then – ludicrously, tragically – she found that she was struggling upright in some four feet of muddy water. Her head was out; she shook it; her eyes cleared – but in her ears there was still a great roaring. The square temple was straight in front of her. And above it hung something monstrous, out of nature: a vast and hovering insect. She shook her head once more, and knew that the roaring noise was not inside her own brain. The noise came from the insect. The insect was a helicopter . . . Even as the realization came to her the machine climbed, hovered again, and moved off on a lateral course.

'They certainly seem to keep a trick or two up their sleeve.'

She swung round. The man who had carried her headlong into the lake was standing breast-high in the water beside her. It was her brother John.

She was sitting on the bank The skirt and jersey that had been her only garments lay heavy on her in sopping folds. Her hair was soaking. The shoes still slung absurdly round her neck were two small buckets of water. Only her eyes were dry – dry and bitterly angry.

'John, why did you do it – *why?* It was Geoffrey – he's alive!'

'Which is more than you would have been in another five seconds.' Her brother, who was binding up Remnant's right arm, spoke grimly and without turning round. It dawned on her that he was quite as angry as she was. 'Do you think, sir' – he was addressing Remnant – 'that this was a proper affair in which to involve my sister?'

'Yes, I do – or I wouldn't have done it.' Remnant in his turn was angry and uncompromising. 'She has what it takes – and I don't know that there's any other test.' He smiled wanly. 'Besides – if I may say so – she rather involved me. I apologize, all the same.'

'How dare you apologize!' Jane had jumped to her feet, at once dripping and blazing. 'I think –'

'Easy, easy.' Her brother was now smiling at the two of them. 'I apologize too. We needn't quarrel. After all, we're doing pretty well.'

Jane felt the blood going to her head. 'Doing pretty well! With Geoffrey –'

'Use your head, Jane.'

She gasped for breath. John was every whit as intolerable as Remnant. 'I *do* use my head.'

'Very well – just consider. Those people in the helicopter are some sort of criminals I haven't got the hang of. Perhaps you two have. Something pretty bad, no doubt. But, likely enough, nothing can be proved that would positively hang them. But if you hadn't gone in the lake, my girl, you'd have gone in your coffin. And then they *would* have been murderers – every one of them, regardless of which did the actual shooting. You'd have gone. And your young man would have followed.'

'By jove – that's right!' Remnant, struggling with considerable pain, looked up sharply. 'As it is, he's tolerably safe. The devilry's over; we cooked that goose. And if they're not murderers yet, they're unlikely to commit gratuitous murder now.'

'It's what the man with the red beard meant to do.' Jane still spoke hotly. 'Sheer gratuitous killing of that child.'

'He was off his rocker. But the fellows who got away like that' – and Remnant jerked his head skywards – 'have all their wits about them still. If you ask me, they'll land young Geoffrey in the next county –'

'He's not young Geoffrey. He's a lot older than you are – and very much more –'

'Be quiet, Jane.' Appleby had stepped to the edge of the island and was scanning the park. 'By and large, your friend is right . . . Now, where have all those police come from?'

'Those police?' Jane opened her eyes wide. 'Aren't they yours?'

'Quite impossible. I did arrange for something of the sort in certain circumstances. But a good deal later in the afternoon . . . And what the dickens is all that yelling?'

'I shouldn't be surprised at a bit of yelling.' Remnant spoke dryly. 'This place is on quite a big scale. Jane and I have more or less smashed it. But you'll find, sir, that there's a fair amount to clear up.'

'I find no difficulty in believing you there.' Appleby was still scanning the grounds. 'It isn't . . . it isn't by way of being a children's home? I could swear those were children's voices.'

'Dear me, no – nothing of the sort.' Remnant had got to his feet. 'I see you haven't got your bearings at all. But if I may lend a hand –'

'Thank you – I think I can manage.' Appleby was still inclined to treat with some asperity the confident young man whom he had found involved with his sister in a shooting match. 'You came here by car?'

'By taxi. I am a taxi-driver.'

'Then I hope you drive, sir, with rather less impetuosity than you fight.' Appleby frowned, seemingly feeling that this had come out with rather more of complimentary implication than he had intended. He turned to his sister. 'Can *you* drive a taxi?'

'I don't think, John, that I have the right sort of licence.'

'Bother the licence. I don't think that that wound's serious. But it had better have medical attention at once – and not precisely the sort they seem to keep about here. Put this young man in his cab and drive him to Oxford at once.'

'But, John, couldn't we –'

'*At once.* Drive straight to Casualty at the Radcliffe. When you've got him comfortably settled, dispose of his precious cab where you please. Then go back to Somerville and stay there. Perhaps you can find some dry garments in this barn of a place as you go. I shall.'

'*Couldn't* we –'

'Listen. I shall bring you definite news by midnight. That's a promise.'

'Visitors can't come in after –'

'Don't worry. I'll get in, even if I have to rouse the Principal from her bed. Now, get moving, or you'll catch a chill. I'm off to get a line on all this uproar. It needs calming down.'

Remnant pointed to the big circular temple behind them. 'If you go through there –'

'Thank you. It will be quicker to go as I came.' And Appleby took a shallow dive into the lake and vanished.

Hard after riding through the shattered wire gates the expedition split up, obedient to tactical dispositions laid down by Dick. Stuart Buffin found this an excellent plan; it meant that he and his friend Miles were on their own with a small group of like-minded Tigers, and that they could forget Dick and his unremittently asserted High Command. Piling their bicycles, they had made a wide detour to the left of the drive. Now they had climbed to the brow of a low hill, and the chimneys of the house could be seen below them.

'It *is* on fire!' A lanky boy ahead of the others pointed dramatically to the dark column of smoke rising from the house.

There was an immediate babel of voices, not very conformable with the idea of a military force moving up to a surprise attack. 'The place is on fire ... It's burning down ... Rot – that's a potty little fire ... Anyway, there's a fire-engine ... Only the kind people keep themselves ... It's the crooks ... Why should the crooks burn down their own place, you silly twerp? ... I don't believe there are any crooks ... Shut up and come on ...'

'Listen!' Stuart's voice asserted itself above the hubbub. 'I hear something else. Be quiet.'

The chatter dutifully stilled. Round the part of the building that was on fire orders were being shouted, and on a lawn at the side of the house a collection of elderly and harmless-looking people were huddled in a group talking. But over and above this there was certainly another sound. It was like the sound that an axe will make across a valley in frosty weather. Only this sound came in short bursts, with nothing of the regularity of axes being set to a tree.

'It's shooting.' Stuart spoke with sudden conviction – and also considerable relief. 'I was right. They *are* crooks.'

'Crooks don't spend their time shooting.' A sceptical voice spoke from the back. 'In this country they don't often shoot at all.'

Stuart swung round. 'Well,' he demanded, '*isn't* it shooting? Don't you know the sound of a gun going off, you idiot?'

'Probably somebody out after rabbits.'

The confusion of voices grew again. 'The crooks are shooting. ... There's a man out after rabbits ... They're shooting at the crooks ... Somebody says there's shooting ... What rot ... Listen, I tell you ...'

'Look!' Miles's arm had shot out. 'Those buildings in the middle of the lake. You can see the flashes. It's a battle. Come *on*, you asses!'

'Here's the fire-brigade!' The cry was raised by a shrill voice on the flank. 'Golly, they're coming at a lick.'

'That's not a fire-brigade. All fire-engines and things are red.' Stuart was staring down at the drive. 'These cars are blue.'

'The fire-brigade's come ... It isn't the fire-brigade ... There's a bell ... That's an ambulance bell ... Rot ... I tell you it is.'

Stuart was frowning. 'The cars have something on their roof.'

'It's the police!' Miles gave a shout of excitement that was quickly echoed by everybody. 'It must have been to the police that Dick sent his telegram. They'll join the shooting, with any luck. Run!'

The whole party tumbled downhill. Suddenly the lanky boy, who was still leading, dug his heels hard into the ground, slithered, and came to a stop. He had almost hurtled over the lip of a small precipice. The Tigers halted beside him, and stared down unbelievingly. What lay below them was a sort of den, gouged out of the side of the hill. And it contained half a dozen tigers.

'It's a zoo . . . There are tigers . . . It must be Whipsnade . . . And lions farther along . . . Masses of wild animals . . . You large idiot, Whipsnade's miles away . . .'

'It *is* a zoo – a sort of private zoo.' Stuart had begun to skirt the upper edge of the series of dens. 'They're all barred in front, and then there's a terrace to walk along. Let's get down.'

'Wait a minute.' Miles did not approve of the way in which the adventure looked like degenerating into a mere visit to the zoological gardens. 'I can just see something going on in a sort of yard behind the house. Chaps loading a lorry in a fearful hurry. I expect –'

'There's a helicopter going up!' It was the young scientist Malcolm, who eagerly called attention to this new sensation. 'Look – from behind that square temple, where they were shooting.'

Everybody stopped and stared. 'It's going up . . . It's moving away . . . Why does its nose point down? . . . Why has it got a little propeller too? . . . That's because of the torque, idiot . . . It hasn't much speed . . . Yes, it has – wait and see . . .'

'Look out!' Miles's voice was urgent, quelling the chatter. 'There's a man coming up that path on a motor-bike. What a lick! and he's coming this way. He's coming along the terrace with the dens . . . Take cover.'

They flung themselves on the ground. The motor-cycle had screeched to a stop at the end of the line of dens and the rider had leapt off. He was in a tearing hurry; and as they watched he began to run along the terrace, stopping every twenty yards and doing something that resulted each time in a heavy metallic clang.

'He must be the keeper.' Miles was whispering in Stuart's ear. 'He's opening all the doors between the dens and turning them into one.'

'It's the crook!' Stuart's voice was tremulous with excitement.

'What?'

'The crook I saw chase the little man out of the house.'

'The little man who was in my cat?'

'Yes, you idiot. The little man shinned up the telephone-pole, like I told you, and this fellow came running out after him. With a gun – I saw it. He's got queer shoulders. I'd recognize him anywhere.'

'They must be all the same crooks – that lot and the people holding the woman who got the wrong number – who wanted somebody called Kurt— *He's letting them out!*'

The children all sprang to their feet. For there could be no doubt of what the man with the queer shoulders was now up to. He was heaving back a gate in the last den of all – a gate that opened on to the bare hill-side. And in the den were lions.

Miles picked up a flint and hurled it. His aim was perfect, it took the man on the side of the face, and he staggered back. Miles and Stuart charged down the hill. The other Tigers, very little aware of what was happening, charged happily after them, whooping joyfully. The man looked up and saw the racing children; he hesitated, and then dashed for his machine. Some of the lions were roaring, and this was taken up by the other wild beasts farther back – beasts that were now padding and leaping into each other's dens. As Miles reached the terrace the first lion emerged and paused uncertainly, waving its tail. The children behind, still unknowing, gave another yell. The lion retreated just inside the den and crouched. Miles flung his whole weight on the gate and it shut with a clang in the instant that the lion sprang at it. The creature fell back with a snarl, and then there was a moment of complete silence. The Tigers stood, solemnly staring through the bars at a congeries of beasts of prey that would have done credit to Noah's ark.

'Do you think they'll fight each other?' Malcolm, always intent upon natural knowledge, glanced mildly round his companions. 'They are usually aggregated, after all.'

'Segregated, you silly stinks-merchant.' Some more lettered Tiger spoke with proper scorn from the rear. 'Let's poke them up a bit and see.'

The man who had attempted to free the wild beasts was gone; they could just hear his engine in the distance. There being no prospect of pursuing him, the suggestion just made had clearly considerable attraction for the younger and less responsible Tigers present. But at this moment there was a further diversion.

'I can see the others.' It was Stuart who spoke, and he pointed across the park. 'Better join them. It's different, I expect, now the police have come. And the shooting's stopped.'

'They've got hold of something.' Miles's face under its mop of untidy red hair lit up at the prospect of further excitement. 'Come on. Let's cut across and see.'

They ran the length of the terrace and out across the open park. The group approaching was certainly in some commotion; and it was contriving to make even more noise than their own group had done. It dropped on to a path as they drew near it; and in doing so it parted and revealed what was occasioning its clamour. In the midst of the children padded a large, tawny beast. Stuart gave a gasp of horror. 'It's one of the lions!'

'We've got a lion! We've got a lion!' The small red-haired girl called Marty was walking beside the beast, her arm plunged deep in its mane, and she was shouting at the top of her voice. 'We've got a tame lion – it's just like Miles in his cat!'

The lion was not, in fact, so very like Miles in his cat – for the simple reason that it was not nearly so aggressive. It shambled uneasily amid its new companions, looking now to one side and now to the other in a sort of amiable self-disparagement. It looked a very unhappy lion.

The two groups had begun to shout questions at each other, and were on the point of merging, when the motor-cycle engine was heard again. They turned and saw the machine hurtling towards them. The man with the queer shoulders had failed to get away on the path he had planned. Now he was having another shot – and it was evidently a desperate one. He rounded a bend at suicidal speed and very badly – he did not appear to be a good rider – and as the Tigers scattered they could see his eyes glaring and his mouth working convulsively. Hastily they scrambled to safety on either side of the path. But not so the lion. The lion turned and lumbered off down the path in front of the motor-bike. It behaved just like a rabbit caught in the head-lights of a car at night – without the wits to get off the path on one side or another . . .

It was all over in a flash. The man was almost up with the lion. The lion, increasingly terrified by the roar of the engine, slightly changed direction. The man swerved – far too wide and uncontrolled a swerve for his purpose – and the lion tried to turn. The front wheel struck the lion a glancing blow on the flank; the machine staggered; and the man went over the handle-bars. The machine tumbled over and over, and came to rest with its front wheel spinning. The man lay quite still, with his head tucked oddly under him. The lion lay down at his side.

Some of the children moved uncertainly forward – including Dick, who had returned from some foray or reconnaissance ahead. But as they did so a man appeared before them as if from nowhere, for they had been so absorbed by the accident that none of them had seen his approach. His clothes were dripping wet. But he stopped them in their tracks with a single gesture of authority. 'All right,' he said. 'Stay where you are.' He walked over to the motionless figure of the man with the queer shoulders, stopped over it for a moment, and then came back, looking them swiftly over.

'Can we help, sir? Can one of us take a message?' It was a subdued voice speaking from the middle of the group.

The man in the soaking clothes shook his head. 'No,' he said gently, 'you can't give any help here . . . Anybody in command of your lot?'

There was a moment's hesitation, and then some shoving and pushing. A boy rather taller than the rest stepped forward. 'Would you please,' he said politely, 'say who you are?'

'I am Sir John Appleby.' The man looked gravely at the children as a group, but addressed the tall boy. 'I belong to the Metropolitan Police. I come, that is to say, from Scotland Yard.'

There was a moment's silence that spoke of absolute awe. Even the tall boy appeared to have to think twice. But when he spoke it was with com-posure. 'My name is Richard Martin,' he said. 'How do you do?'

'How do you do.' Sir John Appleby was looking at their blazers. 'You all come from Oxford?'

'Yes, sir.'

Sir John Appleby turned for a moment and looked at the house, now cordoned by police. 'And is one of you responsible for this remarkable turn-out of the County Constabulary?'

Richard Martin answered without hesitation. 'Yes, sir. I sent a telegram.'

'I see.'

'I hope, sir, it was all right.'

'It saved the situation.' Appleby's eye had again strayed in a certain wonder to the mass of blue uniforms in the middle distance. 'It's an effect that I doubt if I could have achieved myself. You must be a natural master of the electric telegraph.'

This time Richard Martin violently blushed. But his voice maintained its composure. 'I gave the wording some thought,' he said.

'Always a good thing to do.' Sir John Appleby smiled, and glanced over the whole group. 'Thank you,' he said. 'The police are much obliged to you all. And now you had better cut off home. Can you get a train part of the way?'

'Yes, sir.'

'Good. You might meet a head-wind.' Appleby nodded briskly. 'Good-bye.'

'Good-bye, sir.'

Appleby turned away, and the Tigers moved off obediently in search of their bicycles. But a moment later a voice spoke at Appleby's shoulder. 'Sir, may we ask a question?'

Two of the boys had remained behind. One was red-haired and his eyes were still shining. But it was the other who had spoken.

'Go ahead.'

'My name is Stuart Buffin.'

'I've heard of you. And I begin to understand. But what's the question?'

'May we talk about this?'

Appleby appeared to consider this question with a good deal of grave deliberation. 'Even if you don't,' he said, 'I suppose the younger ones would be bound to?'

'I don't think so, sir. We have them pretty well in hand.'

'That's an excellent thing.' Appleby smiled. 'But I think you can talk. Everyone his own story at tea. It's a good part of the fun, after all.'

'*Yes, sir!*'

Wreathed in smiles, Stuart Buffin and his companion hurried off after the other Tigers. Appleby walked back down the path. The lion was still lying close by the man. They were covered with the same dust. The brute looked at Appleby apprehensively, and sheepishly licked its paws. It looked a very harmless lion. Nor would the man now couched with it ever do any harm again.

6. Bodley by Night

Unwounded of his enemies he fell.
      Samson Agonistes

I

Roger Remnant's headlong drive to the demesnes of Milton Porcer et Can-onicorum, involving as it had done much fast cornering, resulted in trouble during Jane Appleby's much more cautiously conducted return journey. A tyre blew out just before Eynsham. And as Jane took some pleasure in debarring her companion from attempting to assist her in any way, and laboriously but effectively contrived to substitute the spare wheel herself, it was nearly five o'clock when she reached the Radcliffe Infirmary. There she handed over her charge, answered such questions as the mildly sensational nature of his wound made necessary, and then drove back the few yards to Somerville. Such clothes as she had hastily commandeered from Dr Cline's deplorable clinic by no means became her, and the frailty of her sex obliged her to get out of them at the earliest possible moment. She changed quickly, resisted the conversational attempts of several interested friends, and returned to the car. It was her intention to return it to the rank where she had so·fatefully picked it up, and then to retreat hastily into college without answering any questions. There she would await news from John with whatever patience she could muster.

The first part of this project went smoothly. She drove down to the end of St Giles' and saw that there were no other taxis waiting in the rank. This was decidedly to the good. Remnant, presumably, had colleagues, and if one of these was about he might prove tiresomely inquisitive. She had just swung the car round to bring it out of the line of the traffic when she heard a vigorous hail from the pavement opposite. 'Taxi!' Since it did not occur to her that she herself might be the object of this shout she paid no attention. '*Taxi!*' This time the shout was a bellow. She looked up and saw, first the silver knob of an elegant cane being brandished peremptorily in air, and then – beneath it and spread out far on either side, the massive figure of Mark Bultitude.

Jane was feeling both exhausted and grim. She had been the occasion that day of at least two notable acts of deliverance from evil; and these she regarded with deep and honest satisfaction. But the one thing that she had set out to accomplish – the one act of deliverance that lay nearest her heart – she had failed in, and her final desperate attempt to achieve it had resulted only in the wounding of a total stranger who had stood by her that day like the staunchest friend. Geoffrey had been snatched from her – almost literally from her grasp – with what had been in effect the maximum of cruelty. The situation now was worse than it had ever been, since she at last knew the quality of the people who held her lover in their hands. And despite her long-standing faith in her brother, and her almost equal faith in Roger Remnant, she found it very hard to take comfort from the reassurance they had tried to give her. That John would very quickly run to earth such of that evil gang as yet remained alive – that she would indeed receive news of this before the end of the day – she certainly believed. But she had been at too close quarters with the horrible madness underlying the criminal conspiracy she had uncovered to have anything but the direst forebodings as to what might be Geoffrey's fate if he was no longer of any utility to it alive.

All this being so, Jane had very little use at the moment for any further encounter with Bultitude. She had come to the conclusion earlier that day that he was a foolish and rather offensive figure, who had displayed a purely impertinent interest in her troubles. So now she let her gaze pass him stonily by, and prepared to step quickly from the car and march off without explanation.

This, however, proved to be impossible. Bultitude had recognized her; for a moment his features expressed extreme but seemingly genuine astonishment; then he launched himself into St Giles' with all the resistless momentum of a hippopotamus taking to the water. A Number 4 bus swerved violently away from him much as it would have done, Jane thought, upon the sudden materialization before it of a Centurion tank. And a moment later Bultitude was at her side.

'Excellent!' he said. 'Excellent! In the morning the keen young student off to Bodley, and in the afternoon the resolute and emancipated bread-winner. But – my dear Miss Appleby – have you had the Proctor's permission to follow this laudable avocation?'

Jane, who hadn't thought of this one, eyed him askance. 'I am putting it away for a friend,' she said. Her tone was icy.

'Then the misfortune is mine. I had hoped to hire you to take me to Trinity.'

'To Trinity!' Jane could have thrown a stone into the nearer precincts of this venerable place of learning from where she sat.

'Certainly. I missed a luncheon party there and had intended to present my apologies to my host. However, that can be deferred.'

'I expect there will be other taxis turning up presently.'

'No doubt. But not other young ladies with whom I have a strong impulse to converse.'

Jane, who could think of no polite reply to this – and who was determined to be polite, since she suspected that earlier in the day she had been rather rude – said nothing.

'I have already had some conversation with your brother, Sir John – on my way back from Milton.'

'From Milton! You mean that you made your – your expedition, as you called it?'

'I went to Milton Manor, decided that it was a very shady place indeed,

431

and came back to think about it. Probably I should have decided to contact your brother in any case. I am not fond of policemen investigating the vagaries of Bede's undergraduates, and I had – indeed, still have – some notion that I might clear the business up myself. Would you advise me to try?'

'No – certainly not.' Jane still spoke coldly. But Bultitude's more direct manner of speech was making her look at him with new interest. 'We have discovered that it was full of criminals, practising abominable scientific experiments upon people kept there by force.'

'I must confess, Miss Appleby, to being not altogether surprised by what you tell me.'

'I don't see how you can know anything about it. And, if you did, it was your duty –'

'It is the business of scientists – those few of them who are *not* engaged upon experiments abominable in one way or another – to put two and two together as rapidly as may be whenever queer appearances come their way. And that – since yesterday – is what I have been doing. And I may say I mean to have Geoffrey Ourglass back at Bede's.' Suddenly Bultitude looked Jane very straight in the eyes. 'Where is he?'

'They have him still. They got away with him at the last moment.'

Bultitude gave a moment to studying the silver knob of his cane. 'I'm sorry,' he said.

'John thinks they are unlikely to do him any harm now. Perhaps they will let him go.'

'I see . . . I wish I could help.' Bultitude tapped his cane on the ground. 'And perhaps I can. The scientist sometimes remembers the importance of very simple things. When did you last have a meal?'

Jane stared. 'Why – well, it was at breakfast.'

'Then come and have some tea.'

Jane hesitated. She was coming to believe that she had misjudged Mark Bultitude. 'Thank you very much. But John said I was to go back to college and wait.'

'He hopes to have news?'

'Yes – before midnight.'

'That is rather a long time off – and tea can be consumed with a moderate approximation to civilized custom in something less than half an hour. I should like to hear a little more of your day's adventures – and tell you a little more of my own. Incidentally, I have some quite good Orange Pekoe.'

Jane decided to go. Bultitude puzzled her. He seemed to have his own slant on the affair. Perhaps if they pooled what knowledge each possessed something really helpful would emerge. It was a long shot, but a shot worth taking. And the invitation was certainly an entirely harmless one. It was also subtly flattering. For Mark Bultitude was commonly reputed not to care for young women at all. 'It's very kind of you,' she said. 'I'd like a cup of tea.'

'Then come along. There is only the breadth of Beaumont Street to negotiate, and we can walk straight into my parlour. I need hardly tell you that the rooms I keep in Bede's are on the ground floor. My philosophy of life, such as it is, is nothing if not *ventre à terre*.'

2

The apartment into which Jane was presently ushered by her host would have been described by an unfriendly critic as overwhelming. It was large, and everything in it had the appearance of being very valuable. Bultitude, dispensing his Orange Pekoe from an equipage that had appeared with miraculous speed, gave his young guest a charming smile. 'I see,' he said, 'that you are looking at my Battle of the Centaurs.'

'Oh – yes.' Jane was not aware that she had been looking at anything in particular.

'It is, in fact, a Caravaggio. I bought it off the Gräfin Szegedin – you know the dear old Gräfin? I was speaking of her to somebody only last night – a good many years ago. It gave the poor old dear a helping hand.'

'That was very nice of you.' Jane took her tea and spoke without much enthusiasm.

'And the little hunting scene is by Uccello. Dear Bernhard – you know Berenson? – prefers it to the one in the Ashmolean. The Rembrandt was picked up for me by Bredius – or was it Borenius? I really forget – just before the war.' Bultitude looked about him with what was either complacency or a good imitation of it. 'Nothing but odds and ends, of course, but I think they hang together not too badly.'

'I suppose it's a very nice room.' Jane, who was much depressed again, realized that this was not altogether a happy choice of words. 'I mean –'

'They tell me that my pupils call it Toad Hall. Undergraduates have an extraordinary faculty for hitting the nail on the head.'

Jane stared. Bultitude, she divined, was rather a complex person.

'And the name is the more apposite since I bought a very large car. Perhaps it was the pleasure of driving it that really drew me out to Milton this morning.'

He plunged back to the point. For some reason it was not easy for him. He was pausing, as if searching for words, and Jane had suddenly the impression of being in the presence of some large, masked anxiety. 'But you really knew something,' she asked, 'before that?'

'I wonder if I did?' Bultitude frowned. 'But won't you have a muffin?'

Jane suspected that the fat don was going to be evasive, after all. His attitude was coming to puzzle her very much. There was something baffled in it – as if he was helpless in knowing where to begin with her . . . But now he was trying again.

'This place in Milton is in the hands of the police?'

'Yes.'

'So far, so good. I suppose you already know the things your brother told me?'

'John said very little. Our talk was hurried – no more than a scrap. I think he was anxious to get me out of the place and begin clearing up in a professional way. I'd meddled, I'm afraid.'

'If you did, the circumstances make it very natural.' Bultitude had one of his odd drops into simplicity. 'Then you don't know – no, your brother told me you didn't – that last night this gang of criminals was hunting a man – a little man with a scratched face – about Oxford?'

'I know that they were hunting him this morning. I saw them at it in the upper reading room, when I was reading there.'

'Sir John told me something of the sort. Who else was working there at the time?'

'I don't think I noticed them, very particularly. But I was sitting between old Dr Undertone and Miss Butterton.'

'They actually chased him about the reading room? It seems unbelievable. Surely they'd have been stopped?'

Jane shook her head. 'It wasn't quite like that. There was only one man in chase. The little man kept edging away from him. He came quite close to me. And then his pursuer seemed to force him out of the room by something like sheer will-power. It was rather horrible . . . But not so horrible as what happened later, at – at Milton.'

Bultitude laid down an unbitten muffin and again frowned. He appeared to have less and less liking for a conversation which he had himself insisted on initiating. 'That happened . . . to the same little man?'

'Yes. They got him, you know. And – and I think he knew something they wanted to know. When I arrived there – with the young man to whom that taxi really belongs –'

'A young man?'

'His name is Remnant. I don't really know him. He's in the Radcliffe. He got hurt – not badly. He's just had to go to Casualty. But I was saying that when we got there, and broke in –'

'You broke in?'

'Well, this Mr Remnant did, and I followed. We found that these people had – had maltreated the little man very badly. He's dead now. But that's rather another story. He saved a child.'

'Saved a child – from these people who were conducting abominable experiments?'

'Yes.'

Bultitude – who did so many things with ostentation – slipped a handkerchief from his pocket and gave a covert dab at his brow. 'I can see,' he said, 'that everything has been worse even than I thought. It is quite wrong to make you talk about it so soon. I apologize.'

'That's all rot.' Jane did not know at all whether she was grateful or impatient. 'And I thought perhaps that you had something to tell me?'

'There are one or two things that I can mention.' Bultitude – and the action, it occurred to Jane, was as incredible as that of the man in the circus who ties himself into knots – Bultitude had stooped down to the lowest of an elaborate system of trays by which he was flanked and grabbed a plate of excessively creamy cakes. But the action had not absolutely excluded from her view a look of swift calculation such as she imagined herself to have seen on his face before. He raised himself, puffing and blowing. 'Won't you have one of these?'

Jane took a cake. She was young, and could eat automatically and unknowingly when her body required it. 'You can mention –?' she prompted.

'I can mention – well, that during the war I had a good deal to do with one or two rather special lines of inquiry. The physiology – and also the psychology – of fear and bravery, endurance and the liability to crack up, aggressive and passive responses to stimuli – things of that sort. For instance, I knew a man called Cline. Later I heard that he had taken a place in the country and was developing new ways of treating drunks. It was a laudable but not very exciting activity. And it didn't quite fit in with what I remembered of Cline. Naturally, I didn't think much more about it. Then I gathered that he had associated with him – ostensibly in this blameless species of social medicine – several people whom I knew. The question of why they came together again as crusaders of scientific temperance was a real one, which I found myself turning over from time to time . . . Those little ones with the cherry on top are excellent.'

'No more, thank you.' Jane had set down her cup and was leaning forward on her chair. 'And then?'

'I believed myself to have found the explanation. It was an explanation which meant that the whole affair was no business of mine. And so I put the matter out of my mind. It was only yesterday, when the sinister nature of your fiancé's disappearance was brought home to me, and I learnt from his uncle that he had been seen near Milton, that I saw I must make a crucial inquiry. As you have doubtless heard' – and Bultitude gave a brilliant if rather strained smile – 'I have a great talent for knowing all the right people. I rang up a friend in town and learnt confidentially that my explanation of the holding-together of Cline and his group was wrong. I had supposed that they were doing work on a secret list; and that the drunks' home, and the researching into alcoholism and so on, were genuine and reputable activities serving at the same time as measures of secrecy – secrecy dictated by national security. Now I learnt that nothing of the sort was in question. What they were up to, they were up to on their own account. And I didn't like it. For some of them had quite patently been persons of altogether impaired moral perceptions.'

Bultitude as he produced this orotund phrase again mopped his brow –

but this time openly. There was a moment's silence. 'And . . . about Geoffrey?' Jane asked. 'Can't you say anything about him?'

'I can say this – that as soon as his uncle said something connecting his disappearance with Milton Porcorum I recalled an element in the conversation of one of these people I have been talking about.'

'Cline's friends?'

'Yes. He was not a scientist but an administrator; an able – and yet again in some ways rather stupid – person, called Squire. This fellow used to praise' – Bultitude hesitated – 'used to praise those civilizations, if they are to be called that, which delivered over felons, captives, slaves and the like, alive, to the uses of science. He used to say that it was the way to get results. And there were others who used to back him up. I thought of it as idle talk without substance. But now we must –'

'Mr Bultitude – tell me.' Jane had sprung to her feet. 'Were they – when you knew them – mad as well as bad? If things go wrong with them, and their plans crash, and there are – are people who are no more use to them, will they . . . would they –' Jane found herself unable to finish her sentence.

'No.' Bultitude had also risen. 'In my opinion – not.'

'They won't . . . kill Geoffrey?'

He looked at her strangely, and for a moment was silent. She suddenly saw that he, too, was indeed a scientist. The fat *poseur*, the University Worthy, the celebrated snob had all faded out of him. Instead of these – little estimable but yet human and intimate – there was only something aloof and very cold. He made as if to speak, and then hesitated again. She believed that – out of the sheer instinct of the scientist – he was seeking for words which he could believe an exact representation of the truth as he saw it. 'Miss Appleby, Geoffrey Ourglass is in grave danger. It would be foolish to pretend otherwise. Yet I think I see something which would mean that he is safe from them. But I may be very, very wrong . . . You must go?'

Jane nodded. She was very pale. 'I think I'd better go. John may come.'

Bultitude bowed, moved to the door and opened it. 'Thank you for coming to tea,' he said gravely. 'I hope you will come again – not alone, but in very much happier circumstances. Let me walk with you to the lodge.'

'No – please no!' Jane was agitated. 'I am going to hurry. I mean –'

Very faintly, Bultitude smiled. 'And hurrying is not my line? But you are perfectly right. Good-bye.'

'Good-bye.' Jane stepped into the open air, and turned to reach the lodge. As she did so, her eye went uncalculatingly to the window of the room she had just left. Level evening sunlight was pouring into it, and in this illumination she had a final glimpse of her late host. He was in movement – very rapid movement – across his gorgeous room. Then he stopped. She saw his face unnaturally large, framed in the centre of Caravaggio's struggling Lapithae and Centaurs. He was talking urgently into a telephone.

3

There was no message from John. Jane took from the shelf that notebook in which her aunt had bequeathed to her the lectures of the Stockton and Darlington Professor, efficiently abridged. But this afternoon the volume had no charm. Recognizing that she was unable to work, she fell to pacing her room. But this was not very satisfactory either; there were too few paces to take, and too many things to step over in taking them. Presently she discovered that her restlessness had a more specific cause than the general anxiety under which she lay. In her encounter with Mark Bultitude there had been something missing. He had failed to say something that he ought to have said. Or *she* had failed –

One of her immediate neighbours was giving a polite tea-party to relations and dons. The murmur of talk from this reminded her that she had been invited. She paused, oddly seized in the midst of her grim situation by purely social dismay. It was frightfully uncivil to have forgotten all about the thing. She had better still appear, with whatever apology she could think up . . . As she moved to the door she remembered – remembered something which, either by inadvertence or some wholly obscure design, she had not told Bultitude. And as she remembered this she forgot about the tea-party; it vanished into the oblivion from which she had fished it a moment before. She left her room and once more hurried out of college. She had told Bultitude something of the affair in the upper reading room which had been the first occasion of her adventures that day. But she had missed something out – and until a moment before she had missed it out of her own thoughts too. The little man who now lay dead at Milton Manor had *hidden* something in the upper reading room. He had thrust something into a book on old Dr Undertone's desk. And what he had there hidden must surely be what his captors had sought. Moreover, there was something further that could safely be said. The hidden paper – for it had been that – if it at all came into the picture in this way, was important. The unrelenting manner in which the pursuit of the hunted man had been carried out was surely proof of that. Only the fantastically rapid series of events in which she had been involved could have made so significant a point slip her mind . . . Emerging into the Woodstock Road, Jane turned right and set off hurriedly for the Bodleian Library. The paper, whatever it was, must be retrieved and given to John. As she gained St Giles', she almost broke into a run. It had become her accustomed way of moving, that day. But Oxford people are often in a hurry, and nobody paid any attention to her. Had they done so, they might have remarked that something like a procession was involved. An unobtrusive person was, in fact, following Jane Appleby down the street. But this was not all. A second unobtrusive person was following the first.

4

In the upper reading room the long day's task was almost done, and learning had turned to packing up for the night. The unashamed were yawning, the reflective were finally sorting out their musings, the industrious were gathering up sheaves of notes. In its hutch in one corner the Emett-like conveyor-belt moaned with a suggestion of weariness stoically borne; in another corner Bodley's Librarian was amiably assisting an Ethiopian to decipher a manuscript, and for this purpose he superimposed three pairs of spectacles each upon the last. A broken light still struggled through the broad Tudor windows, and sent long, soft shadows exploring across the littered, or ordered, desks. The people continuing here and there to get up and go were commonplace and familiar; at the same time it was possible to feel them as growing shadowy and insubstantial – a race of middle spirits, grown half ethereal with long feeding on books, and presently to be succeeded, as the dark came down, by other spirits wholly transmuted – the veritable ghosts to whom the tremendous place most truly belonged. Bodley at midnight, Jane thought, must be the strangest of all places ever reared by mortal hands.

Miss Butterton – Jane Appleby forty years on, Jane Appleby as she would be if the transmuting years were to wash over her here – was gone; her tiny duodecimo and decimo sexto volumes were marshalled into disciplined ranks, as if waiting to stand guard through the night. And Dr Undertone was gone too. But his desk was empty.

Jane paused for a moment, disconcerted. Then she turned away and retraced her steps down the reading room. There was an assistant sitting at the table near the great catalogue. She went over and spoke to him. 'Has Dr Undertone finished with all his books, do you know?'

The man nodded. There was nothing out-of-the-way in the inquiry, for in Bodley people are always mildly hunting one another's volumes. 'Yes. As he went out at lunch-time he said that he would need none of them again. So they were cleared.'

'Simply all put back on the shelves?'

'Yes. Dr Undertone spoke quite decidedly – in fact curiously so. I'm afraid it will be too late to get anything back for you now.'

'Thank you.' If Jane had been disconcerted before, she was now nonplussed. But she asked one more question, although she already knew the answer to it. 'There wouldn't be any record of the books he's been using?'

'Oh, no.' The man was surprised. 'The books go back on the shelves and the slips are destroyed.'

'Yes – I see.' Jane moved away. An understanding of the extreme queerness of what had occurred came to her fully as she walked towards the door. If in all the wide world the little man had sought an inviolate hiding-place for his scrap of paper he could scarcely have found a better than he had done. For the paper now lay between the leaves of one among several million books. If old Dr Undertone's present studies were markedly off a beaten track – and with so immensely learned a person they almost certainly were – it might be a generation, or even a hundred years, before – quite fortuitously – the thing was again held in human hands. It was Dr Undertone alone who could now abbreviate this process.

So struck was Jane by this strange consideration that she stopped dead in her tracks – thereby just avoiding, as it happened, being bumped into by a hurrying figure now entering the reading room. She stood aside, gave the figure an abstracted glance, and saw that it was Geoffrey's uncle, Dr Ourglass. Her heart sank a little. He was certainly the most harmless of men. But – just at the moment – she had no list for a further colloquy with him. In a moment, however, this apprehension turned out to be groundless. Dr Ourglass had not noticed her. He hurried down the reading room with a purposeful air not altogether common in him. No doubt he wanted to verify a reference before the place closed. When Jane last glimpsed him he had stopped, disconcerted, before an empty desk. So he, too, had been balked of some book . . .

It had been Dr Undertone's desk. Jane was half-way down the sixty-four steps, and had taken six of the right-angled turns, when this fact confronted her. Her head whirled – much as if she had been taking the right-angled turns much too fast. Then she turned and ran upstairs. When she reached the upper reading room again it was to find Dr Ourglass departed. Exercising some lofty privilege, he must have gone down in the lift.

5

Jane came downstairs again – slowly, this time – and in the Bodleian quadrangle stopped to think. One or two readers came out and passed her; a nondescript man was examining the Pembroke statue; another nondescript man was staring at the effigies on the ornate East Tower. Jane turned to her right and emerged into Radcliffe Square. It was just here that they had got him . . .

Again standing still, and absently watching through the great arched windows of the Camera young persons for the time more studious than herself absorbed in the reading of law or of English literature, she firmly dismissed the behaviour of Dr Ourglass as coincidental and distracting. Old Dr Undertone was her quarry. She knew that he was a Fellow of St Gregory's. And, almost certainly, he was a bachelor and lived in college. Even at ninety-six, only a bachelor could have looked at her quite as he had done that morning – as if she had been a camel or a crocodile. And, remembering that look, Jane hesitated. Better leave it to John. Dr Undertone might decidedly not welcome the visit, close upon his dinner-hour, of a beast of burden or a creature of the mud claiming the status and consideration of a member of the University.

But Jane Appleby – at this late stage of our narrative it can, like some other things, no longer be concealed – was a girl of impetuous and even headstrong disposition, lightly disguised by an air of learning. She ought to have been in Somerville; she had been told to remain there by an admired brother greatly senior to herself; nevertheless her legs were now taking her rapidly in the direction of St Gregory's College. There are no long distances at Oxford, and in five minutes she had passed through the gates. 'Can you tell me,' she asked the porter, 'which are Dr Undertone's rooms?'

'Number five staircase in the next quadrangle, madam.' The man had hesitated before replying. Probably the inquiry was unprecedented; in all Dr Undertone's seventy-odd years at St Gregory's no female had ever inquired for him before. But Jane marched on. The second quadrangle was small and high and dark and damp; its walls – like many stone walls in Oxford – tattered and peeling; evening mist was beginning to thicken in it and lie in almost palpable folds, as if nature were concerning herself with the weaving of a shroud.

Jane found number five staircase. The stone treads were worn and hollowed; the walls were grimy and flaking; there was an indescribable smell – the smell of centuries of food and wine and polished leather. Dr Undertone had rooms on the first floor. Jane climbed. The whole quadrangle was very silent.

She stopped on the landing and listened. There was no sound. Dr Undertone's oak was not sported and she knocked at the door. There was no reply. She knocked again, without result. Perhaps he was a bit deaf. Indeed, he might well be. And he would have several rooms, and perhaps be in a farther one . . . Jane knocked a third time and waited. Perhaps she should go down again and find the scout who worked on the staircase. Probably Dr Undertone kept a personal servant who might be discovered in some dungeon decanting port or counting claret . . . Jane gave a fourth and perfunctory knock, opened the door and peeped in.

The room was large and lofty, and completely surrounded with books. The only light was from a single candle, set in a candle-stick with a reflector to it. This had probably been a bold innovation of Dr Undertone's in the eighteen-eighties. He must have turned conservative before the spread of gas or the invention of electricity. There was a dull glow from an open fire which had been allowed to go almost out. It played upon the surface of a large, shabby desk, piled with disordered books and papers. Everywhere the books overflowed from the walls into the room; they were piled on chairs, on occasional tables, on decaying horse-hair sofas, on the threadbare and ragged Turkey carpet. On other chairs – since there was no wall-space for them – pictures were propped with the air of having been set down there many decades before: photographs of athletic groups fading into mere yellow stains, as those they represented must, for the most part, have already crumpled into dust; photographs, equally ancient, of dead and buried St Gregory's dons assembled round dead and buried royalty; copies of Raphael Madonnas and Murillo saints such as mothers used to give to undergraduate sons with injunctions to attend the sermons of Dr Pusey. Over the mantelpiece was a portrait of Archbishop Tait, and directly under it a small shield displaying the arms of Rugby School. On the desk, in a silver frame, was a photograph of an early Victorian lady. All Dr Undertone's life was concentrated in this room. But Dr Undertone himself was absent.

To go farther would not be decent. She must try – Jane decided – to find a servant and inquire when Dr Undertone might be able to receive a visitor. But as she was about to close the door softly, and explore the situation downstairs, another door opened at the far side of the room. It was a manservant. Perhaps he had heard her.

Jane took a step forward. 'Is Dr Undertone at home?'

'Yes, miss.' The man closed the door behind him. 'Never more so, if you ask me.'

Jane hesitated. 'Do you think he can see me?'

'Yes, miss.'

'Then will you tell him –'

'I can't tell him anything, miss. He's dead.'

6

Jane felt rather queer. She was seeing and hearing too much of death today. 'Dr Undertone has died – this afternoon?'

'Just after luncheon, miss. When he came back from the Bodleian he wasn't looking at all well. And I think he knew it was coming, for he ordered an extra chop.'

'An extra chop?'

'Yes, miss – for his luncheon. "Finch," he said, "two chops" – just like that. And he ate them.' The man paused. 'Ate them right down to the bone, the Doctor did.' He spoke with a good deal of pride.

Jane considered. 'I hope I shall be able to do that.'

'That's right, miss.' The man nodded approval. 'And he drank a couple of glasses of burgundy. Then, when I came in to clear, he flew into a terrible rage.'

'A rage?'

'A terrible rage, miss. It was fearful to watch. "You rascal," he said. The Doctor often addressed me like that, miss. He was a good honest-spoken gentleman of the old school. "You rascal," he said, "when did you uncork that wine?" And he stood up, all swollen and purple in the face. "How often have I told you," he said, "that burgundy must breathe?" And then, miss, he fell dead. It was what you might call a very peaceful end.'

'I suppose it was.'

'I've seen worse, miss, by a long way. For instance –' The man checked himself. 'But such talk isn't proper to a young lady. I don't expect, miss, that you'd ever seen death?'

Jane smiled rather wanly. 'I have – as a matter of fact.'

The man's serious face lit up. 'Then perhaps, miss, you'd care to view the body? Very fine it is. Just like a baby.'

'Thank you . . . but I think I'd rather –' Jane scarcely knew how she got out of the room and into the air, now turned more damp and raw, of the little quadrangle. It was still very silent, and this time she knew why . . . From somewhere on the other side a wafer of eaten stone detached itself from the wall and fell with a dull, small explosion. Change and decay she thought, in all around I see. And she hurried from St Gregory's. Nothing, she was sure, would ever bring her back there.

Moreover she should be in college. A sense of urgency so possessed her that she took a taxi, pausing only to scrutinize the driver. He was elderly and uninterested.

A telephone message was waiting for her. It said simply 'Ten o'clock – John.' Which was something – but she disliked its brevity. She looked at her watch. In a few minutes she would have to go into hall and dine with some two hundred of her kind. The prospect rose before her as unusually depressing. Her mind had ceased to work, either anxiously or eagerly, on the problem of Geoffrey's peril, the chances of saving him, what John would prove to have done. She felt simply that she had come to a dead stop, that all the wishes and fears left in her were very small and very futile, that life was bad and Oxford worse. But her body was shockingly tired, and perhaps it was only for a time that it was dictating this craven line of thought. The only sound resource was to find the next thing to do, and do it. But there wasn't anything . . . And then she remembered that there was. She had a duty to walk round to the Radcliffe Infirmary and inquire about Remnant. Perhaps they had been able to send him away. On the other hand, they might have had to clap him into bed.

She ran into him under the archway by the lodge. After the manner of Oxford males preparing for a foray into unknown regions, he was making a cautious survey of Somerville in the gathering darkness. His arm was in a black silk sling. But he had managed to change, and was now dressed in an immaculate dark suit, like a fashionable undergraduate prepared to go up to town. The effect needed only a hard hat and an umbrella to be complete – and it was disconcerting. Jane felt that he was a stranger, after all. But Remnant smiled, and she realized that she had guessed wrong. 'Come along,' he said. 'We need dinner badly.'

'Are you all right?'

'Perfectly all right, thank you. But hungry – as I say.'

'And do you often dress like that?'

Remnant nodded his head seriously. 'Only change I have. That and a pair of pyjama-trousers. Everything else gone up the spout to support the wife and little nippers . . . Any news?'

'Yes and no. No news from John – nothing about Geoffrey. But I have found out something queer myself.'

Remnant looked at her, she thought, with momentary apprehensiveness. 'Something to tell?'

'Oh, yes. And John's coming to see me at ten.'

'We can eat quite a lot by then. Where would you like to go? Mitre? George?'

'If the family is right down on the bread-line like that, Mr Remnant, you oughtn't to be thinking of going anywhere at all.'

Remnant made no reply to this. Argument indeed was unnecessary, for they were already walking down the Woodstock Road. 'The Radcliffe's not a bad place,' he said. 'I got a cup of tea and bun.'

'And I got Orange Pekoe and some out-size cream-cakes from Mark Bultitude.'

He gave her a quick sidelong glance. 'Like him?'

'I don't think I know. But he's in on all this in some queer way.'

'He's the enormous great fat man at Bede's?'

'Yes.'

'Well, listen.' Remnant hesitated. '*He* was the fat man that I caught a glimpse of on that terrace when we were waiting for Cline.'

Jane nodded. 'That doesn't surprise me a bit. He told me that he'd been out there this morning, doing a little quiet investigating. He'd been suspicious about the place for some time.'

'I see.' They walked for some way in silence, and when Remnant spoke it was abruptly. 'Here we are. In we go.'

Their dinner at first showed some signs of being rather a laboured affair. But Roger Remnant made no attempt to be more entertaining than the continued crisis in Jane's personal affairs warranted. He was hungry as he had said, and he managed to make Jane feel hungry too. As she ate and drank she ceased to find a good deal of silence burdensome. She ceased, too, to feel that her sallying out like this had perhaps been in rather feeble taste. Remnant now had the manner of a civilized business man, with matter of substance to come to that must yet wait until dining is over. And thus they arrived in decent comfort at coffee and cigarettes. He eyed her gravely. 'What is the queer thing you have found out for yourself?'

'It's not so much something I've found out as something I've remembered. And you'll think me an utter ass for not remembering it before. When the little man was in the upper reading room this morning he *hid* something – a paper.'

'And has anybody found it?'

'Almost certainly not. And now it seems possible that all chance of finding it is gone. It's like this.' And Jane told the story of the late Dr Undertone and his books.

Remnant heard her through in silence. 'Good riddance,' he said at last.

'Of poor old Undertone?'

'Lord, no. He sounds a decent stick. But of that paper. If it was something your little man had stolen from our Milton friends, then, ten to one, it's better vanished. Some secret trick of their dirty game – that's what it must be.'

'Yes – I think it must be that too. But it hasn't disappeared in any absolute sense. Some other reader in Bodley may come on it tomorrow.'

Remnant was frowning across the room. He started, 'Sorry! I was just thinking there was somebody over there that I've knocked up against not long ago . . . Whatever it is, your new reader isn't likely to make head or tail of it. He'll chuck it in the waste-paper basket – I suppose there are such things in Bodley? – and that will be that.'

'I think it's important.'

He looked at her curiously. 'It's hardly the centre of your problem, Jane.'

'It might be. It might be the key to it.' Jane, who less than an hour before had been feeling that she had no more fight in her, was again quick and eager. 'To begin with, it must be important to *them*. They did so much to get it back that –'

'I agree. But still I don't see how, directly, it's going to help.'

'If *we* had it, it might be a card in our hands.'

'You mean a bribe, a bargaining point, a hostage – something like that?'

'That against Geoffrey.'

He looked at her with yet fuller gravity. 'These people can't be bargained with. They are outlaws. It would be futile, immoral, illegal. You couldn't give them back –'

'Of course I know that. But if we had it the thing might be a bait, a trap, *something*.' Jane's voice was suddenly urgent and appealing.

'Very well. The thing, whatever it is, would certainly be better in our hands than simply lost. It may be the key to something that has potentialities for good as well as evil. But how do we get it?' Jane could see that Remnant's mind was beginning to work swiftly and in a way she knew. 'You are sure nobody could have spotted the actual book the little man thrust it into? What about the person on Undertone's other side?'

'There wasn't anybody.'

'Then on *your* other side? Somebody might just have got a squint from there.'

'That was Miss Butterton. She might conceivably have seen that the little man was fiddling with Undertone's books. But she couldn't have seen that it was this particular book or that.'

'Certain?'

'Absolutely.'

'Then we come back to the start. There's only Undertone himself. Short of a seance, we can't ask him . . . What was his line of country?'

Jane considered. 'He was an ecclesiastical historian . . . no, that's wrong. I remember! He retired ages ago from the chair of Pastoral and Homiletic Theology. And he's been compiling an enormous history of that ever since.'

Remnant grinned. 'Remember,' he said, 'that I stopped off from all that lecture-stuff. Do you mind telling me just what that rigmarole means?'

'It means something more impossible than I can say. His work in Bodley consisted in reading all the sermons that were ever published.'

'And have a lot been published? I don't think I've ever seen any.'

Jane laughed a little desperately. 'Far more of them than of anything else in the whole world.'

'Well I'm blessed! I'd never have thought it.' Remnant stared at her with the utmost *naïveté* – but his next question was sufficiently shrewd. 'Do you think Undertone would have a collaborator – work hand in hand with some other old person who would share the burden?'

'I'm pretty sure he wouldn't. Part of his legend is his extreme aloofness and isolation.'

Remnant had paid their bill. 'Up you get,' he said. 'We'll take a walk on this. It needs thinking out.'

There was now a thick mist shrouding Oxford – the Thames Valley mist which is not quite a fog, but which gets in your throat and eyes all the same. Jane thought walking through this a poor idea and not likely to clear the brain. But she had got in the habit of obeying Remnant. They set off. Tom, the great Christ Church bell, had not begun the tolling that would announce five past nine. She still had plenty of time in hand if she was to be back in college with half an hour to spare before her brother's arrival.

'I suppose we couldn't get in?' Remnant's voice spoke from the uncertain darkness beside her. 'I mean into this old man's rooms in Gregory's?'

She was rather shocked. 'The body's there. They'll have sported the oak by now to leave it in decent security. And we couldn't possibly ask.'

'You can't think of a story that would get us in? Nephew and niece? Illegitimate but sorrowing children hurrying to Oxford at the news?'

'Of course not! I think you are the most unscrupulous person I've ever known. And – anyway – it wouldn't be the least good.'

Remnant said nothing. They continued to walk in silence. Either their footfalls were producing a queer echo in the mist or somebody else was walking this inclement evening behind them. Jane lost her bearings. Presently Remnant spoke with an air of casual surprise. 'This *is* Gregory's,' he said. 'Never been in it. Have you – before today? Low college.'

'We can't all go to Balliol.'

'True – true. And we can't even, all of us, stop there when we make it. They're very keen, at Balliol, on a chap's going to those lectures.' Remnant's voice was extremely absent. 'Where about are that poor old chap's rooms?'

'Number five staircase in the second quad.'

'Well, I believe this is the second quad we're skirting now . . . On this side?'

'Yes – on the first floor, at the corner. You can't see in this stuff – or I can't. But they must be those rooms just above our head now.'

'Interesting.' Remnant did not sound as if he was at all interested. 'Mind if I just step behind this archway to light a pipe?'

'Not a bit.' It was a chilly night, Jane felt, to hang about. But she owed Remnant a good deal more than permission to smoke. She waited. Suddenly – and utterly without rational occasion – she felt panic grip her. It was as if danger had suddenly reached out hands at her in the dark . . . 'Roger!' Her call was low but urgent. There was no reply. *'Roger!'*

'Yes, Jane?' The mist was playing odd tricks with sound. His voice seemed to come from straight overhead. 'Don't worry. Keep quiet. Even with only one arm it's pie. I'll be back in two ticks.'

She understood – she understood and trembled. But she did not call out again. Aeons passed. Once she was certain that she heard whispering in the darkness – an angry and dissuasive whispering. There was a further efflux-ion of almost infinite time. She knew that – for the first occasion in her life – she had lost her nerve and her wits. So she must keep still. If she only kept still nobody – not even Remnant – need ever know. More time went by – enough time for whole solar systems to emerge from mere vapour, spin, and perish . . . Suddenly her right hand was taken in a strong clasp. She knew that she could scream. Fear sometimes kills the power to do that – but with her it had not done so. She kept silent. Remnant's voice spoke in her ear. 'Good girl.' He took her arm and moved her forward through the mist. 'A bit more walking. Say as far as Magdalen bridge. This still needs thinking out.' They went on in silence. It seemed incredible that only a minute of two before she had been scared out of her wits . . . 'I say' – Remnant's voice was unwontedly diffident – 'what would *perlegi* mean?'

For a moment she was puzzled. Then she understood. *'Perlegi?* It's Latin for "I have read through".'

'I guessed as much.' The voice was now triumphant. 'Then we've got it.'

'You actually got into Undertone's rooms?'

'Quite easily. I went up the rustication and in at the bedroom window. Roof-climbing used to be one of my things, rather.'

'I see . . . You said the *bedroom* window?'

There was a quick chuckle in the dark – and then Remnant's voice, swiftly repentant. 'I'm sorry if it shocks you. I've had times that rather blunt one to all that . . . And he's dead, all right.'

'You . . .'

'I made sure. This is so queer a business that you can take hardly anything on trust . . . And then I got it – this *perlegi* business. A fairly fresh piece of paper on his desk, with a lot of book-titles in Latin and French – and then after all but the last two this word *perlegi* and a date. The last date was today's. Oh – and there were a lot of letters and numbers against each book. I copied them down too.'

'The case-marks.'

'What are they?'

'Where the books live on the shelves – all over Bodley. They're very complicated, and only the Bodley people understand them. You copy the case-mark from the catalogue, and that tells them where to find the book for you.'

'Don't you go and get it yourself?'

'Of course you don't, you idiot. But I suppose you're pulling my leg.'

'No, I'm not.' Remnant sounded aggrieved. 'Just not been my line. If you roof-climb, and that sort of thing, then you just can't expect to sit in libraries too and have people bringing you books. It wouldn't be reasonable. You must see that.'

Jane was silent. She knew by this time that when Roger Remnant talked such ineffable nonsense as this his mind was likely to be hard at work in its own effective way.

'Aren't there a tremendous lot of books underground?'

Jane started. She had been thinking that she again heard footsteps. 'I believe so – although, of course, readers don't go down. I've been told that it's quite tremendous – miles and miles of it. But of course that must be an exaggeration.'

'Well, now – don't they arrange the books in a sensible order – alphabetically, or something like that?'

'My dear boy, you just haven't got the scale of the thing. There are *millions* of books. Some are kept together in great collections, more or less as they were given to the place. Others are arranged I just don't know how. The commonly needed books – the sort of book *you* would ask for if you ever went in – are kept together and handy; and a lot of them are on open access. But the sort of stuff old Undertone revelled in is probably all over the place. And the catalogue – or those case-marks you've copied – is the only clue. And it's only a clue, as I say, to one of the library people.'

'I think it's quite absurd.' Remnant was honestly exasperated. 'You mean to say that you and I couldn't find these things? That if we broke into this Bodleian place –'

'Broke into Bodley!' Even although she knew she was being absurd, Jane's voice was stiff with horror.

'Why ever not?'

'You just don't understand. Besides, you're talking nonsense. We've found what we want. The thing is certain to be in one of those books. And it's certainly safe there till tomorrow. John must see about it.'

'I hate to say it – but I think John might be a bit behind the times.'

'John is never behind the times.'

'Well, we don't need to argue about that. I'm sure he's a good sort of stick.' It was evident that Sir John Appleby's manner at Milton that afternoon still a little rankled. 'The point is that I'm not at all sure about the thing's being safe there till tomorrow . . . Did you think I took rather a long time over my burglary?'

'Well' – Jane was cautious – 'yes. I did.'

'It was because I had to join in the queue.'

'Whatever do you mean?'

'There was somebody before me, jotting down those books. I had to lurk in the bedroom quite a bit.'

'It's impossible! I'm sure nobody in the reading room understood what was happening, besides me . . . Did you see who this person was?'

In the darkness Remnant seemed just to hesitate. 'Yes.'

'Somebody we know?'

'Yes. At least you know him. And I know him by sight.'

Jane gave a gasp. 'Was it Mark Bultitude?'

'No. It was your young man's uncle, Dr Ourglass.'

'Dr Ourglass! He's the most harmless –' Jane gave a little cry, and groped for Remnant's arm. 'But that's what I said to myself when I saw him – I forgot. I haven't told you. I saw him in the upper reading room this evening, peering at Undertone's empty desk – just as I had been doing myself. I thought it could be no more than a queer coincidence.'

'Well, it wasn't.'

'Surely old Dr Ourglass hadn't climbed –'

'Good lord, no. He had plainly been brought into Undertone's room, as official as anything, by some great panjandrum at Gregory's.'

'I can't understand it.'

'No more can I. But it doesn't make me feel that this needle in your absurd haystack of a Bodleian is particularly safe . . . Hullo – I wonder where we've got to?' They had been walking seemingly at random, and now Remnant was peering about him in the dark. 'How very odd. Do you know, it looks like Radcliffe Square?' Suddenly he turned his head, as if listening.

Jane's heart sank. She had experienced just this technique a little too recently to have forgotten it. 'Now look here, Roger Remnant. I simply will not –'

Reaching out in the darkness, Remnant suddenly put his fingers on her lips. She fell silent – and found that, like her companion, she had frozen into immobility. The mist was now very thick, and the few lights in the Square made little impression on it. One could see no more than the vaguest outlines even a couple of yards ahead. His voice was in her ear. 'Sorry, young woman. Getting into melodramatic habits. But I've had a feeling that there's somebody interested in us.'

'So have I. I had it when you were doing your climb into Gregory's.'

'Well, we're old hands at all that. And it's probably imagination anyhow . . . We'll scout round here.'

They were somewhere out in the Square, for she could feel cobbles under her feet – the identical cobbles on which the little man had been lying before they bundled him into the ambulance. Then she lost her bearings. Far away she heard a train hoot, and nearer at hand there were some young men calling to each other in the mist. But the voices might have come either from Brasenose or from Hertford, and her sense of disorientation was complete. The street lighting was going dimmer and more yellow. Straight ahead of them, nearer the ground, they saw a dull red glow. Remnant moved towards it. She realized that he was reconnoitring the terrain of some proposed operation. Again she felt misgivings. She ought to be back in college, waiting for John . . . The red glow came from a charcoal brazier. Some building was going on, and in a little shelter before the fire a night-watchman was settling in to his job. They went on, and were presently in complete darkness. Again Remnant spoke softly in her ear. 'About roof-climbing –'

'I'm not going roof-climbing, and neither are you. You can't possibly – not with that arm.'

'Listen – and don't be so quick to make irrelevant remarks.' Remnant's tone held its old assurance. 'It's a principle of Oxford roof-climbing that there is no natural feature known to climbers of which there is not a pretty fair artificial equivalent in the buildings of this city. And the principle has been worked out very fully.'

'I haven't the slightest doubt it has.'

'Do you know about the Mendip caves?'

A dim and horrid light began to dawn on Jane. 'No – I don't and what's more –'

'They form a very extensive system of underground caverns which it is possible to get into here and there – with a very tight squeeze. *Really* very tight. Not a game, for instance, for your friend Bultitude. Well, like everything else in the world, the fissures that take you down there have their equivalent here in Oxford. Or rather have *one* equivalent. You're standing beside it now.'

'You mean –?'

Roger Remnant laughed, very softly. 'I mean that you and I, Jane, are about to enter the world's greatest library.'

7

Somewhere at her feet Jane heard a muted clang, as of a metal plate or grid forcibly displaced. For a fraction of a second a torch flashed on in Remnant's hand, and she had a glimpse of what appeared a very small circular aperture flush with the ground. Then the darkness was again entire and Remnant was once more whispering.

'Listen carefully. This is important. As it happens, I've never made this expedition, for a reason that I can tell you about later. But I have the facts. First, there's your clothes. People commonly strip.'

'Thank you – no. I've lost quite enough perfectly good clothes today already.'

'Good enough. But they absolutely mustn't bunch up. Can you grip your skirt between your knees?'

'Yes.'

'That should do. Your measurements are pretty fair.'

'Thank you very much.'

'You go down feet first – legs together, hands palm downwards on your thights, wrists in the pit of your tummy, all quite rigid. Can you feel your heart beating?'

'Yes.' Jane was tart. 'I can.'

'Let it count five for you as you go down. Then begin to pull up. That means you jack-knife ever so slightly. Behind down and knees up. You may lose a bit of skin. But it's perfectly all right, unless you start slowing down too suddenly and too soon.'

'What happens then?'

'The confidential character of our mission fades out. I fetch the police, the Fire Brigade and the University architect. Sappers are sent for from the nearest garrison town.'

'I see. I don't think it's a thing to think about very much.'

'Then down we go – me first. Don't worry. It's not half as bad as that crazy nylon rope.'

'I'm not worrying. I just want to say –'

Remnant had vanished. For a moment Jane thought he had stepped behind her. 'Roger,' she said softly.

There was no reply. Her sense that there was any longer somebody near her must have been illusory. He had really gone – had vanished down that small hole that now lay invisibly at her feet. He probably has the disadvantage, she suddenly thought, of not having the sort of heart that makes itself heard . . . For a second she hesitated. What she had meant to say was that her appointment with John made this underground proposal impossible. And he had known it well enough. His cutting her short like that – his simply vanishing like the bad fairy in pantomime – had been typical Remnant unscrupulousness . . . Jane found that she had sat down on very chill stone – and that, as once before that day, her legs were dangling in nothingness. The shaft, chute, or whatever it was, felt quite desperately narrow, and she had a sudden vivid sense of what it must be like to be the lead in a pencil. But Remnant had gone. And his shoulders must be far broader than her hips. Jane went too.

She certainly lost some skin, but there was more of indignity in the thought than painfulness in the sensation. Her brain worked with extraordinary speed. As she fell she guessed what the particular hazard of this journey must be. The chute must have a kink in it, or must somewhere flatten out like a section of a big dipper. If you gained too much momentum there would be a nasty crash at the end. If you checked it too soon you simply came to a stop in a spot too tight for wriggling. She felt that she had never had a nastier thought . . . She was suddenly in empty space, and Remnant had caught her and set her on her feet.

Her knees were unsteady, and she felt the need of something to say. 'It was absolutely horrible. Miles worse than the nylon rope. But just your cup of tea. Why have you never done it before?'

'Because I like shaving at half past seven and having breakfast at eight.'

'What has that to do with it?'

'Well, of course it's one-way traffic. You couldn't go *up* that, could you? There's a bit of Latin I once knew –'

'*Facilis descensus Averno* – quite so. I knew some spark of learning would be struck out of you sooner or later, Mr Remnant. But I don't see –'

'And there isn't any *other* way out. The whole place is locked up at night as strongly as a bank. I suppose the books must be valuable.'

'I suppose they must.' Jane was alarmed and angry. 'Do you mean to say that we have to stay here till morning? John –'

'Bother John.'

'I won't bother John.'

'Bless him then. The normal situation is this. Chaps coming down to the Mendip caves simply have to lurk until the place is opened up, and then dodge their way out. The few people who have made the attempt have got away with it so far. But –'

'Of all the perverted and idiotic uses to which to put –'

'– a great library? I'm quite sure you're absolutely right. But, as I was saying, to slip out when things open up is desperately difficult. Sooner or later, somebody will be caught, and there will be a fearful row – far worse than over roofs and towers and things – and the Mendip caves will just cease to be a feature of Oxford life. Which will be a great pity, in my opinion.'

'Can't we get up to ground-level?

'I think not. We're inside a vast, well-ventilated safe. Look at it that way.' Remnant fell silent for a moment. They were standing in complete darkness. 'I have got an idea, all the same. When we've found this paper –'

'I don't believe we can possibly find it.'

'Don't be dismal, girl. When we've found this paper, it occurs to me that we might rustle up a telephone. The place must be stuffed with them, and one of them may be connected with the city exchange. In that case, we'd just ring up the old boy who runs this place –'

'Bodley's Librarian?' Jane, who thought that she had already touched the uttermost verge of horror, felt her blood curdle in her veins.

'I don't see why not. He could come along with a key and let us out. Glad to assist in the course of justice, and so on. I'd ask him to keep dark about the caves, of course.'

'To keep –' Jane found herself speechless. At last, with a struggle, she found words. 'We'll tackle that problem when it comes. At the moment, the point is that we don't in the least know how or where to find this batch of books. Particularly as we're in pitch darkness.'

'A point well taken. But here you are.' And Remnant snapped on his torch.

The beam fell on books. This, at least, was reassuring; Remnant had not been wildly out in his calculations and landed them in a sewer. Jane remembered the old fantasy she had indulged that morning of being precipitated through some hidden trapdoor into dark and subterranean waters, deep beneath the foundations of Bodley. It had been, she decided with interest, a clear case of dream-like precognitive thinking. One's actual dreams were said to be full of distorted images from one's own future . . .

Her eye was following the sweep of Remnant's torch. It was a powerful torch, and its beam had now moved laterally far into darkness. But it was still playing upon books. It swept back, and then off in the other direction. The books ran off, apparently to infinity, in that direction too. It struck her that she had seen something like this not long ago. For a second she was puzzled. And then she knew of what she had been reminded. It was the high and interminable boundary wall of Milton Manor. But that had appeared to lose itself in distance because it was a single great curve – what the old writers on aesthetics liked to call an artificial infinite. The books marched on and on in straight lines.

'I had no notion of this.' Remnant – for the first time since she had known him – seemed impressed. He also seemed puzzled. 'Do they keep all the *old* ones?' he asked.

Caught unawares, Jane laughed aloud. And her laughter pealed and rolled through vaulted immensities, to come echoing back to her, deepened to a sort of stage thunder. 'They didn't always,' she said. 'At one time they had rather a knack of selling things. But not much goes out of the place now.'

'It's very depressing.' Remnant's reaction was decided. 'I've never before been made so powerfully aware of life's utter futility. All those chaps scribbling away, persuaded that fame and immortality were just round the corner. And now nobody so much as remembers their existence, except this old fellow – what do you call him? – Bodley's Librarian. It's the sort of thing that makes one look round for a drink. Sorry to be such a barbarian.'

'You're not terribly singular. A great library made Dr Johnson feel much the same . . . But now you see that it *will* be rather difficult finding what we're after.'

'It's just a matter of time. And we've got all night for it.' Remnant was dogged. 'Good lord – look at that!'

He had turned the torch upward, seeking the roof. But as its beam climbed and climbed it still met books – although books now in part obscured by open-work cat-walks of cast iron, by vertical ladders and spiral staircases, and by criss-cross of supporting girders. Jane felt slightly giddy. But she managed to speak firmly. 'Try downwards.'

The beam swept down. They were standing on just such a cat-walk as they had been observing high above their heads. Below them was another infinity of books.

It was like something, Jane thought, by Piranesi – a dream, architecture cunningly devised to suggest at once the reach and the impotence of the human mind. But Remnant's response was now severely practical. 'It all seems reasonably orderly. You made it sound, you know, quite cock-eyed. But there are all the books –'

'Nothing like all the books. This is just a place that was dug out forty years ago to hold a million or thereabouts. There are stacks and stacks elsewhere: in Bodley itself, in the New Bodleian, in the basement of the old Ashmolean –'

'I see. Well, this will do for a start. But the point seems to me to be this: the more books there are, the more efficient must be the system of running them to earth. All that case-mark stuff can't be the absolute abracadabra. What sort of people actually find the books?'

'Quite small boys, I've been told – although one hardly ever sees them. Some people say it has to be either boys or dwarfs, so that they can wind their way between some of the stacks. Rather like children in the coal mines long ago. But that's unreliable.'

'Any ponies? They have them in mines.'

'No. I think it's a matter of mechanization having been brought right up to the face, so to speak. There are said to be conveyor-belts and pneumatic tubes, and all sorts of gadgets like that.'

'But the crucial point is those boys. No doubt they're bright lads, but they can't all be little Einsteins and Isaac Newtons. The job must be organized so that they get a grip on it fairly easily. There may be this collection and that collection, as you say. But there must be overall order, and a key to the whole thing. We can certainly puzzle it out in time. The trouble is' – Remnant hesitated – 'that there may be others on the scent who understand the system already. I expect most dons do.'

'Dons?'

'My dear girl, we can't ignore the fact that we know two of them to be mixed up in this affair in a rather unaccountable way.'

'But we're in and they're out.' Jane felt very clear-headed. '*They* can't get in until Bodley opens up. If we could find the telephone you spoke of and put up a sufficiently convincing show, we could make sure that those likely books were searched before anybody else was allowed to lay hands on them. And surely that's our best plan.'

'Good girl – *fairly* good girl.' Remnant had begun to move cautiously forward, shining his torch before them. 'But about others getting in – getting in any time now – well, I just don't know. Think of that Gregory's business. I got in there just as we have got in here. And there was old Ourglass already, almost scooping the pool. And – mind you – I expect the sort of people who run places like this are pretty guileless. Other-worldly, and all that. Suppose a plausible and unscrupulous colleague hurried in on this Bodley's Librarian as he was flooring his fourth glass of port –'

'I think you have distorted ideas of life among senior members of this University.' Jane paused. 'Still, I see what you mean.'

'It comes back to this: that the best thing will be for us to win out now. And first, we want lights.'

'Isn't that risky?'

'I don't see how it can be. We might be at the bottom of a mine, for all anybody in Oxford can know about it . . . And – by jove – here we are.' Remnant's hand had gone out to a cluster of switches; he flicked at them rapidly one by one. Clear light sprang up everywhere. What they had hitherto only glimpsed piecemeal they now saw in its entirety. Thus displayed, the vast storehouse was not less impressive than when Remnant's torch had been exploring it. It was this, partly, as being another world from the Bodley that Jane knew. There, the buildings and its furnishings were heavy with immemorial associations and rich in intrinsic charm, so that the books were no more than an element in the total effect. But here, everything was modern and bleak and functional; the single use of the place was to range in an accessible manner as many books as could be crowded in. There were three main levels; they stood now on the second; and this and the level above them were no more than a system of girders supporting the stacks and the narrow lanes that ran between them and at intervals intersected them. Thus visibly on every side of them, and above them and below them too, were hundreds of thousands of books. It was a striking spectacle, but it was an uncommonly oppressive one as well. The narrow lanes were mere slits or canyons between the interminable and towering cliffs of leather and cloth and vellum. These went so monotonously on and on that one was constrained to fancy some illusion – one, perhaps, whereby a spectacle of less credible proportions was merely magnified by a cunning arrangement of mirrors. Nor, whether one looked up or down, did the eye and mind gain any relief. For the first time in her life Jane felt that she had some inkling of what it must feel like to be a neurotic suffering from acute claustrophobia. Living in a submarine must be something like this – a Jules Verne submarine as cramped as a real one but as big as a grand hotel. She would have given anything for space to swing a cat.

Remnant was busy with a pencil and paper against the side of the nearest stack. 'There you are,' he said. 'One copy for you and one for me, since we may find it quicker to split up. Title and casemark of the four likely books. They're as complicated as you said. But I've noticed something about them. They're in pairs. These two differ only in the last couple of figures on the line. And it's the same with those. So we have just two rows of books to find, all-told. There's a start in that.'

Jane doubted its being much of a start, but she said nothing. Certainly Remnant's observation was accurate as far as it went; in two several places in the Library they had to find a couple of books that would be shelved almost side by side. But in the *Library*, she reminded herself grimly; not necessarily in this single vast chamber hollowed out under Radcliffe Square. She looked at the stack nearest to her – one of a thousand identical units in the place – and frowned. 'Why is it so broad?' she asked. 'Books don't require all that depth.'

'I've always been told that some are very deep indeed.' Remnant seemed to take considerable satisfaction in this little joke. He was peering at the stack. 'Actually, it's pretty cunning – a space-saving arrangement. I wonder if the old boy thought it up himself.'

'You have a very primitive notion of the functions of Bodley's Librarian. But how does it work?'

'Can't you see? They all move on rails. That allows you to mass four tiers of books without any space between. It's simply two double-fronted bookcases that move parallel to each other and almost touching. And in every long row of them there's one gap. You just find your place, and, if what you want is behind, you give a shove and get the gap where you want it . . . Like this.' Remnant, as delighted as a boy with a new mechanical toy, gave a thrust at the case beside him. It rolled away, traversed the gap to which he had pointed, and came to rest with a dull thud against the case beyond. 'Isn't that enchanting? You could have your gap in the same place on both sides and be able to dodge through.' He grew enthusiastic. 'You could have a sort of perpetually changing course, and think up a sort of dodging game with rules. I wonder if the old boy –'

'For pity's sake get to work.' Jane was exasperated. 'If we have to shove a lot of these things about it easily doubles the job . . . I wish I had a notion where to begin.'

'Haven't you? Look down at your feet.'

Jane looked and was abashed. She had noticed that the ends of each stack bore casé-marks. She now saw that at every main intersection the floor was painted with a system of arrows and symbols designed to show what further case-marks must be sought in one direction or another. She studied first this and then the paper in her hand. 'I don't think we're burning hot,' she said, 'but it does seem to me that we may have had the enormous luck to begin not altogether cold . . . I believe all four really will be in this place, after all. Look – you hunt the two "*perlegi*" ones and I'll hunt the two others.'

8

It was perhaps twenty minutes later that Jane knew she had progressed from warm to hot. Not only the case-marks but the titles glinting on the old leather spines told here as much. She had come to that wide field of learning upon which the late Dr Undertone had turned himself out to grass in his ripest years. *Sure Sanctuary of a Troubled Soul . . . Preces Privatae . . . An Explanation of the Grand Mystery of Godliness . . . Bowels Opened . . .* The ancient hortatory voices seemed to murmur endlessly on the shelves, as they must have come to murmur ceaselessly in the ear of the dead scholar.

She was on the ground floor of the vast chamber. Remnant's quest had taken him higher, and into a remote corner. They were like Adam and Eve in the Garden, when they had separated the more efficiently to cultivate its fruits. Jane's mind, drawn to this analogy by the Biblical cast of the acres of old print around her, for a moment elaborated the fancy. It was by taking advantage of that rash isolation of our first parents that the serpent –

Suddenly she knew that she was uneasy. But that was foolish. There could be no serpent in Bodley. She brought her mind back to her task. *An Apologetical Narration . . . The Sinner's Mourning Habit . . . A Buckler against Death.* She halted, and gave a low cry. The first of the books she sought was there in front of her. *God's Terrible Voice in the City.* She stretched out her hand to take it from the shelf. The hand trembled, so that she could hardly hold the volume securely. It was the excitement of the discovery, she told herself, that made her tremble. The book was quite small. She opened it, shook it, ran through the pages. There was no lurking paper.

And now for the second book, which she knew could not be far away. Peering at the shelves, she moved along the stack in front of her. *A Large Theatre of Divine Judgments . . . Enthusiasmus Triumphatus . . . The Religion of Protestants a Safe Way to Salvation . . .* Her excitement must be mounting, for now she was trembling all over. *A Treatise Concerning Eternal and Immutable Morality . . .* It was not excitement that had taken command of her. It was fear.

It was the same fear that had reached out and seized her in the dark when she had been left alone outside St Gregory's. And it was fear of something very evil and very close to her. Her senses, she knew, had brought her no report of this presence. But her certainty was entire. She fought against it. She forced her eye to travel over two more books. *Joy in Tribulation . . . An Examination and Censure of False Devotion . . .* She could hardly breathe. She looked at the next book, and put out her hand to it with a gasp. Then her senses did speak. One of the iron platforms above her had creaked, vibrated. She turned her head, and something moved on the very fringe of her vision. She looked up. Danger threatened her – not as she had irresistibly felt, close at hand, but from high on a remote gallery. There, framed at the end of a vista of stacks, a man had appeared. He was looking at her directly and fixedly, and she saw that it was not Remnant. The platform creaked again beneath the weight of the man standing on it. He was Mark Bultitude.

At least she must have the book. She grasped it and pulled it from the shelf. Bultitude was raising an arm as if to point at her. She remembered that she could shout.

'Roger!'

As if she had spoken a magic word, the books immediately in front of her moved. Thrust at by an unseen hand on its farther side, the stack glided away on its rails. And in the gap stood a man – a man with a pale, freckled face.

'*Geoffrey!*'

As once before that day, she stretched out a hand to her lover. And Geoffrey Ourglass too stretched out a hand. But it was not to her. It was to the book.

The movement was a blinding revelation – instantaneous and final. The foundations of Jane's world had crumbled as in some fantastic spectacle on a stage. She gave one protesting cry, and then acknowledged the truth. Geoffrey took a step forward and with horrible dexterity, like a low thief on a racecourse, drew the book from under her arm. He stepped back and the stack moved again. In a fraction of time she was once more confronting only a wall of books. She heard a woman's voice calling for help in a strong, clear voice. It was her own.

The place was suddenly full of voices: her brother's, Remnant's, Bultitude's – and another, elderly and authoritative, that she knew to be that of the Bodley Librarian. At the end of the long lane of books in which she was standing she glimpsed one and then another hurrying figure in uniform. The police had come. Over the dark surface of the great horror that Jane confronted, a tiny and momentary horror rippled. It was very shocking that the Bodleian should be turned over to this sort of thing.

There were now other sounds as well as the shouting: a low rumbling, at first intermittent and then rapidly becoming almost continuous: a succession of dull thuds, with now and then a clash of metal, as one massive and buffered rampart of books came up hard against another. It was Roger Remnant's grotesque game come true. The place had become a vast maze, through which Geoffrey fled and the mustered forces of society pursued. But it was a moving, a protean maze, a kaleidoscopic or mutable labyrinth, changing its form from moment to moment as, now here and now there, one or another gap opened or closed between the stacks. It was like a chase through a surrealist nightmare – a chase down endless corridors in which every yard of wall could become at any moment an opening valve, a sliding door . . .

They were closing in. They were driving him towards the centre of the great, dimly-vaulted chamber. Jane moved towards the centre too. She had no awareness of what she was doing. Her lover had been a criminal. And now he was become a hunted man.

In the middle there was a small clear space – a sort of well up one side of which a spiral staircase climbed through tier upon tier of books. Geoffrey had leapt out of hiding and was at the foot of it. He started to climb. The book was still in his hand. He went up with incredible speed, so that as her eye followed him the surrounding books seemed to take on a spiral motion of their own. There were two figures pounding after him. He was high –

457

very high. Not far above his head must be the cobbles of Radcliffe Square, where the other hunted man had lain . . . From somewhere on a lower level she heard a shouted summons, and in an instant two further figures had appeared at the head of the stair. Geoffrey saw them, ducked under the rail, and leapt perilously on the top of a stack. He swayed, steadied himself, prepared for another leap. In the split second before his taking-off the book dropped from his hand. His foot caught on it and he fell.

He fell sheer – and into a great darkness that now flooded up over Jane. But for a second yet her inward eye could see him – plunging down through a million books, rank upon rank of books, armies of unalterable law.

9

'Thank you.' Bodley's Librarian took the book from Appleby, laid it on his desk, and examined it carefully. 'The joints are cracked, I fear. But, on the whole, we must congratulate ourselves on getting off fairly lightly.' He turned to Remnant. 'I suppose,' he asked mildly, 'that you came in by the Mendip cleft?'

For the first and only time during the events here chronicled, Roger Remnant was staggered. 'Yes, sir – we did. But surely *you* don't –'

'My dear boy, I first enterd Bodley that way myself. It was what first drew my interest to the Library. So it is very possible, you see, that one day this room will be your own. I had supposed, I confess, that the Mendip cleft had long since passed out of mind. Otherwise, no doubt, I should have felt constrained to have something done about it. As one grows old, you know, one becomes very cautious and curmudgeonly.' Bodley's Librarian picked up the book again, adjusted his system of spectacles, and again examined it. 'This is now something of a bibliographical curiosity, Sir John. It cannot be often that a book has proved lethal – in a direct physical sense, that is to say. Curious, too, that it should be *this* book. You have looked at the title?'

Appleby shook his head.

'*A Thunderbolt of Wrath against Stiff-Necked and Impenitent Sinners* . . . Whether the young man was indeed impenitent at the last it is not for us to say. But his persistence in crime certainly suggests that he was stiff-necked.'

Bultitude was turning over the leaves of the book. 'Not a neck stiff enough to stand that drop. It was broken and he died instantly . . . And here is what it was all about.' He drew from the book a folded sheet of quarto paper, smoothed it out, and laid it on the desk. For a few seconds he studied it silently. 'Interesting,' he murmured. 'And extremely complicated – in fact, quite beyond me.'

'There is much that is beyond *me*.' Bodley's Librarian was courteous but firmly curious. 'You say that this young man had actually succeeded in becoming the directing mind behind a formidable scientific conspiracy?'

Appleby nodded. 'He was known to have been a first-rate scientist – as brilliant as we now realize him to have been unscrupulous. His adventures during the war had brought him into the way of conspiratorial activity. We don't know how he uncovered this organization, or how he managed, within no more than a couple of months or so, to force himself to the top of it. But I suspect the key to his sinister success lay simply in his being very clever. A man may be both able and brilliant without being that. Young Ourglass held all three of these cards.'

Bodley's Librarian elevated one pair of spectacles to his ample brow. 'In what,' he asked, 'was this cleverness instanced?'

'Notably in the measures he took to retrieve the mistakes of less intelligent colleagues. There was a fellow called Squire who was inclined to take the bit between his teeth in the dangerous business of kidnapping people or luring them into Milton. Ourglass, who kept himself quite aloof and concealed, had a wary eye on that. Three times he met, or tried to meet, critical situations of the sort by exploiting the flair he had for character-acting. Squire brought in the foreign physician, Dr Tatistchev, thinking that she might eventually be corrupted into a valuable member of the gang. When Ourglass gathered that she might be unreliable, he put himself in her way as a victim of the place and endeavoured to find out where she stood. Again, Squire brought in the little man Routh, and then let him escape again, with this paper in his possession, and with a corpse, it seems, to his credit. That was the grand disaster. Before Routh was recaptured, he had hidden the paper – as we now know, in *A Thunderbolt of Wrath*. Before licensing more brutal methods, Ourglass seems to have tried the same bogus-prisoner trick. But his most brilliant – and blackguardly – application of it was on the island, after the fight. There was a matter of minutes left to him if he was to get away. And he thought it likely that Routh would have parted with his secret to his rescuers. So he put up a show of making a desperate bid to escape. He knew, you see' – Appleby's tone was grim – 'the sort of person my sister is. And he'd have had her – and any secret she possessed – if I hadn't myself nipped in just in time. As it was, he failed – and simultaneously gave the whole show away.'

'He almost gave the show away to *me*.' It was Remnant who spoke. 'You see, I'd rigged up a bit of a periscope and caught a glimpse of the fellows who had been shooting from behind the pillars of the little temple. And I had the impression – no more than that – that the fellow who rushed out as a fugitive had been one of them. It put me in a very wretched doubt. But I don't see how *you* could have known.'

'It was no great feat of detection.' Appleby smiled. 'He came running from the place, you remember, in a ragged shirt, and holding out his arms.

His right arm was blackened right up to the elbow. In other words, this supposed helpless fugitive had been firing with a revolver in a confined space. There was smoke on his face too.'

Bultitude began flapping about his person, produced a cigarette-case, caught the eye of Bodley's Librarian, and hastily stuffed it away again. 'So you, my dear Appleby, had certainty. I had only suspicion. It was born the moment I heard of this able young scientist's being seen in the neighbourhood where Cline and his queer lot were working. But it was not a nice thing to speak up about until one was sure. I was feeling very cagey – I believe that is the word – when we met this morning. Later, when your sister came to tea and I heard about the incident in the upper reading room here, I saw that I must get all the information about it that I could. I got hold of Miss Butterton on the telephone. She had noticed a little man, and seen him doing something at old Undertone's desk. It was not difficult to guess what he had been up to. Not being of a very active disposition – a fact, Appleby, which your sister has very frankly pointed out to me – I enlisted the help of young Ourglass's uncle. If my suspicions were correct, he was going to suffer a great family humiliation, and I judged that it would be easier for him in the end if he could look back upon having a little helped in the cleaning up. Eventually, and in our own way – much less spectacular than Mr Remnant's here – we got a list of the books in which the secret, whatever it was, was likely to be hidden. I then sent old Ourglass home to bed – things might well begin to happen which would not be fit for him to witness – and contacted Bodley's Librarian and yourself.'

Remnant was frowning. 'I don't understand how young Ourglass got after us.'

'No difficulty about that.' Appleby shook his head. 'He still felt that you might have got the whereabouts of the paper from Routh. And he was, of course, desperate about it. Without it, apparently, nothing could be retrieved from the ruins of his organization at all. Well, he got out of his helicopter – I don't yet know where – in time to have Jane trailed in Oxford. Later, he joined in on that himself, and went down your so-called Mendip cleft after you . . . Only, of course, *I* was having Jane trailed too.'

'*You* were!'

'Certainly. I know my sister pretty well. And I didn't quite trust her to stop in Somerville.'

Remnant rose. His face had gone very still and grave. 'You say you know Jane well. Will she . . . get over it?

'In time she will.' Appleby looked at the young man swiftly. 'But I think I understand what you mean. I don't know. Perhaps.'

'Ought I to go away?'

Bodley's Librarian too had risen. 'I take it, Mr Remnant, that you are not a married man?'

'No, sir. I put up a bit of a yarn to Jane about the missis and the twelve kids. But I'm not.'

'The other side of the world. For a year.'

'Write?'

'Picture post-cards every three weeks. A letter from time to time.'

'Then I'll be off.' Roger Remnant moved to the door. He had the habit of not wasting time. 'I suppose, sir, they'll let me out?'

'I am sure they will.' Bodley's Librarian dropped a pair of glasses on his nose and smiled. 'But I doubt whether they will let you back again.' He advanced and shook hands. 'If, when you do return to this country, you are minded to pursue your studies here at irregular hours, will you please ring me up? I have a telephone beside my bed. Good-bye.'

The door closed. Mark Bultitude looked at his two companions with a light of sudden speculation on his face. 'A very good boy,' he said. 'I wonder, by the way, if he's a *Remnant*? It hadn't occurred to me.'

Bodley's Librarian had moved over to a window and opened it. 'I don't know how you people feel. But to my mind there's been a good deal in this that needs blowing away with a breath of fresh air.'

They crossed the room and stood beside him. A wind had risen and dispersed the vapours shrouding Oxford. Before them were the spires and towers of the city. They looked up, and could distinguish a few stars. Directly below the window there was a dull red glow. It was the night-watchman's brazier, and the night-watchman was sitting beside it, stuffing a pipe. He glanced up at the sky – an old man, unambitious and serene.

The wind was blowing hard, and licked the charcoal to a fuller glow. A puff of it blew through the room; there was a flutter of papers behind them, something white floated past their heads into the open air and drifted down towards the ground. Before they realized the significance of what had happened it had come to rest, close by the old man's feet. He stooped to it. Appleby leant out, prepared to shout – and stopped as Bultitude murmured something in his ear. The old man picked up the scrap of paper – it was simply the first thing to his hand – folded it, thrust an end into the brazier, and lit his pipe. Then he tossed the remaining fragment into the flame. He drew at the pipe and again looked at the stars. His face appeared yet more serene than before.

Bodley's Librarian closed the window. 'We can go to bed,' he said. They left the room in silence, and in silence walked through the immemorial place, empty and yet so tremendously thronged. 'I'm fond of Bodley,' Bodley's Librarian said casually. 'And particularly of Bodley by night.'

The Man from the Sea

Chapter 1

The beginning of Cranston's adventure – the real adventure, not the intrigue – seemed as sudden and grotesque as a queer twist in a dream. The night was very still, and the empty sea as it rose and fell gently under a great low moon sighed like a woman half-awake – sighed and then stretched out cold fingers of surf to the young man's naked body sprawled on the cold sand. He told himself that he wanted to be very cold; that this was why he lingered. Lady Blair – for in his own mind he still involuntarily called her that – had disappeared among the rocks, so the hide-and-seek which was now prescriptively the next phase of the affair was due to begin. She had a childish love of it, and part of the two nocturnal hours they could risk together went regularly to a sort of ritual enactment of the game. Tonight these hours were already running out. But Cranston still lingered. Prompted to give himself a reason, he recalled – conscientiously and from all the luxury of his large new knowledge – that to start with chilled limbs was additional fun. Lingering still, he turned over on his belly in the last feeble ripple of a wave. But the movement plucked obscurely and disturbingly at his mind, edging towards the light a very different reason for delay. And at that moment the thing happened.

What had appeared to be a clot of seaweed floating in with the tide became the head of a swimmer. The swimmer dropped his feet to the sea-bed and started to wade ashore. He was stripped except for a belt about his middle and a wisp of fabric round his loins. Under the sudden unnatural weight of a body long supported in water, and with the staggering movement of a clumsily constructed ambulatory toy, he lurched forward foot by foot. Seeing that he was exhausted – that he might fall on his still streaming face at any moment and drown in eighteen inches of water – Cranston scrambled up and ran towards him. The man from the sea stopped dead. It was a reaction which for some reason made Cranston stop too. On this unfrequented strip of Scottish coast in the small hours, the two confronted each other like wary savages. And then the man from the sea turned his head – turned it in the direction from which he had come. He was listening.

What the man from the sea had heard Cranston caught a moment later. It was the throb of an engine. Already that night he had heard something of the sort. Lady Blair – Caryl Blair – had been frightened by it. She enjoyed fear in a way that fascinated and repelled him. It was at its prompting that she had made this the manner of their meeting; it was what lay perhaps at the bottom of their relationship. She had insisted that the sound was from a car on the coast road; that it was her husband; that it meant discovery, confusion. And she had clung to him. He had known very well that the sound came from offshore, that it was the pulse of turbines in some steamer moving down the coast. And then it had stopped and she had been reassured. It had seemed to *stop* – he now remembered – rather than to fade into distance. This new sound, although also from the sea, was very different. It was the rapid throb of a motor-boat. And it was coming nearer.

The man from the sea took a great breath and stumbled forward once more. It was when only his ankles remained in water that Cranston hit on the truth about him. He was a fugitive.

He was a fugitive. That was why the engines had ceased. The man had swum from a steamer out at sea, and it had stopped and sent a launch in pursuit of him. The discovery drew from Cranston a confusion of responses. Here was something vexatious, frustrating – perhaps dangerous. His meeting with Caryl – their assignation, in the dark word that still excited him – was suddenly a mess. This encounter had ruined it, and presently they must manage to scramble out of its mere embarrassment and indecency as he himself must scramble into his shorts. For a moment he was aware only of what he was going to miss, and he felt his body tremble in what he took to be indignation or rage. But it wasn't that – or not wholly. Even as he stared at the other naked man he recognized within his own physical response a thrill of pleasure. What had risen from the sea was some harsh male predicament to which he responded as to a release.

The throb of the motor-boat was louder, as if the craft had rounded some point near at hand. And the man from the sea turned upon Cranston with an urgent and commanding gesture. The little sandy bay, pale as a bleached bone tossed against the dark cliff, was flanked at either end by a tumble of dark broken rock, and into gaining the shelter of the nearer of these refuges the man was now throwing his last energies. But he had also managed this imperious wave. Cranston was to go into hiding too. The motor-boat, if it appeared, must find only an empty beach.

This much was clear – and so was the proper immediate response to make. As Cranston ran for the rocks he felt again the flush of unreasonable pleasure. A problem had bobbed up from the blue – literally from that – and this time he knew the answer. Of course the man must be given a chance to explain himself. Even if some lurking risk were involved, he must be given a chance. To wait for the motor-boat, to haloo at it, would be treachery. It was surprising to Cranston that he should have this clear bit of knowledge, and surprising too that in the hurry and huddle of this strange flight it should rise up in his mind as a fact that was lucid and important. Moreover, it had so risen up without any visible basis in reason. The fellow now by chance at his side had no conceivable claim on him – and it was long odds, too, that he was simply some sort of commonplace wrong-doer. Treachery meant the breaking of a bond, and here no bond could possibly exist. Then why . . .?

They had made it. Their feet lost the firm sand and slipped on slime, trod painfully on barnacled rock. It was necessary to climb, but even some way up there was no more than bare cover for the two of them, and as they crouched down together in a shallow cup of darkness they had to press so close that each for a moment could hear the other's heart. Then the sound of the motor-boat drowned this and their rapid breathing. Cautiously Cranston moved his head a couple of inches to peer round a boulder. At the same moment the engine stopped. The boat had entered the bay on a long curve and was coming directly towards them now. As many as three or four men were crouched aft, and another man stood poised in the bows, sweeping the shore through night-glasses. For perhaps half a minute he scanned the farther rocks. Cranston remembered Caryl. She must have heard the engine, and presumably she was lying low there at the other end of the beach. He wondered what would happen if she lost her head and made a dash for his protection. He wondered what this boat-load of mysterious searchers would make of that surprising appearance.

The man with the glasses swung them round and appeared to focus straight on Cranston. Instinctively the young man drew back his head and shoulders, and the movement caused him to jostle his companion. Caught off balance, the man from the sea swayed and was about to tumble over the lip of the narrow depression in which they cowered. Cranston grabbed at him and caught first a naked shoulder and then an arm. For a moment the two men clung together, steadying themselves, and for the first time their eyes met directly. Here in the rocks they were in near-darkness, and what Cranston was aware of was no more than a fleeting intent gaze in a featureless face – a mere glint of light, no more, upon dilated pupils. But he knew that a signal, a sort of recognition, had passed. It declared a union which, if quite impermanent, was for the moment primitive and absolute. Neither had spoken a word, had so much as attempted to whisper. The whole adventure, so far, had happened in silence. But now there were voices. They came from the boat.

At least three of the pursuers were talking. Their words came clearly over the water but were completely unintelligible. They were speaking in a foreign language unrelated to any of which Cranston had a smattering. Yet it was clear to him that they were arguing, and with the same caution as before he took another glance round the boulder. The man in the bows was pointing towards the rocks and seemed to be urging a landing. It was about this that there was a dispute. And now, almost at once, the man in the bows prevailed. The boat had not yet entirely lost its momentum, and at a touch on the tiller it turned slowly and glided towards the beach. And Cranston found himself reacting swiftly. His mind took a leap to the backdrop of this obscure drama in the line of cliff overlooking the bay. There were a dozen places where it could be negotiated, and lately he had come to know them well. One of them lay almost directly behind this hiding-place. If the man from the sea could be guided up that at once – and in the moonlight there was no great difficulty – his chances of finally escaping would be good. Cranston had put out a hand to tug gently at the fugitive's arm when he was arrested by a fresh sound.

'*Dick-ee!*'

It was Caryl calling from the farther rocks. And her voice held nothing of the fright that might have been expected of it. It held only what, heard ten minutes before, would have sent him racing across the sand with a swimming head. Now it did something queer to his stomach instead.

'*Dick-ee . . . where are you?*'

Cranston heard the man beside him catch his breath. Perhaps it was at the new hazard that this irruption brought into the affair. Perhaps it was an involuntary male response to what Caryl could put into that sort of call. And the young man felt himself deeply flush, so madly incongruous with that summons was the new drama into which he had been caught up. Then he tried to think. It seemed incredible that Caryl should not have heard the motor-boat and the voices. But nothing about her was quite incredible; nothing could be quite incredible about a woman so astoundingly –

His mind stopped, astonished at itself. The important thing was to get the hang of the new situation, and act. And once more he peered out. The men in the boat had all turned and were gazing at the farther rocks. They had certainly heard that unexpected call, and now there could be little doubt that they were glimpsing the caller. Impatient of delay, Caryl had emerged from hiding. Where they had supposed solitude and their quarry there was suddenly this untoward vision. That they were disconcerted was evident at a glance. And in a flash it came to Cranston that they were no more within the pale of the law than was the man they were hunting. There was a very good chance that they could be stampeded.

And Cranston shouted. '*John . . . Harry . . . David! Here's a boat, chaps! Come along down!*'

He made the rocks ring with it – and was aware that the man from the sea had caught the idea and was lustily shouting too. The success of the stratagem was startling. The engine of the motor-boat leapt into life, and the craft first turned in a whirl of foam and then tore out to sea. Within a minute it had vanished.

'*Dick-ee!*'

This time there was no doubt of Caryl's fright. The note of it touched off in him the strong positive response that had been so singularly lacking a few seconds before. His sense of himself as her lover seemed to slip over his head and slide down his body like a shirt: he was startled at the queer aberration which had presented him with her image as astoundingly stupid. But she did get easily confused and scared. It was rotten luck that having been so generous, so marvellous, she should be caught up in this bewildering assault from the sea. He felt protectiveness rise in him – an easy, obliterating emotion. He rose to his feet and called across the bay – called out in urgent, robust reassurance. 'Darling . . . it's all right!'

'Dick-ee, come quickly!'

'All right, Caryl. I'm coming. But stay where you are. There's a man here . . . a stranger.'

There was silence – stricken silence – and he turned to scramble down the rock. The poor darling. The poor old darling. He was about to call out again when, for the first time, the man from the sea spoke.

'Where are your clothes?'

Cranston stopped, startled. From the moment that he had heard the voices in the motor-boat he had been taking it for granted that the fugitive was a foreigner. And he had jumped to a conclusion, too, about his class. He must be a common sailor, a steward, somebody of that sort, involved in unknown shady business turned suddenly desperate. It was on the basis of these assumptions that he had felt his unaccountable impulse of solidarity with the man. But now the man turned out to be an Englishman – and an Englishman who might have been at his own school. For Cranston the consequence of this discovery, strangely enough, was an immediate distrust, expressing itself in a quick backward step. Both men were now standing up, and the stranger was in full moonlight down to the waist. Cranston's recoil completed the movement he had begun to a lower level of the rocks, and he was now looking at the man from the sea as one might look at a picture skied in an old-fashioned gallery. The effect was, in the old exact sense, picturesque. The background was of jagged rock and the empty vault of the night, sparsely pricked out by a few pale stars. Against this the man was posed naked in a symbolism that might have been Leonardo's: the flesh – enigmatic and evanescent – framed in the immensities of geological and astronomical time. Moreover, in his own figure he sustained the comparison. He was a common man neither in the sense that Cranston had assumed nor in any other.

'Where are your clothes?' The man from the sea repeated his question impatiently, as if he seldom had to ask for information twice. He was in his early forties – and the fact that he was old enough to be Cranston's father increased the young man's new sense of distrust. He experienced a strong instant persuasion that this was the wrong sort of person to come tumbling out of the sea on an obscure wave of melodrama. But there was something more – a further and somehow yet more disconcerting perception to which he was helped by his own very respectable cleverness. He was in the presence not simply of another clever man, far more mature than himself. He was in the presence of a strong capacious intellect.

'My clothes?' Cranston heard the words jerk out of himself. 'They're no distance away – what I've got. I've been bathing.'

'So have I. And we couldn't have chosen a better night.'

The joke – if it was meant as that – held for Cranston no reassurance. For the first time there came home to him what the pitch of the fugitive's desperation must have been. The channel was a long way out. Even from the cliff, steamers following it were hull-down on the horizon. The man had done a terrific swim. And he was next to naked. Clothes were his first necessity. And in the pool of shadow in which he still stood there was probably quite a number of small handy boulders lying about. Cranston realized a sombre chance that, when he turned away, the man from the sea would grab one of these and hit him on the head.

'If you want clothes, we'll have to do some talking.' Cranston heard himself with surprise – both for the words, which he had not premeditated, and for the tone, which was calm. The discovery that he could command a decent poise before a man who was disclosing himself as formidable brought back to Cranston the start of pleasure which had been his first response on tumbling to the stranger's plight. 'But you'll have to wait a bit.' The better to assure himself that he really had some grip of the situation, Cranston for the second time looked straight into the stranger's eyes. This time, the features surrounding them were distinguishable, and for an instant he imagined that they stirred at something in his memory. 'You'll have to wait.' He repeated it briskly. 'I'm going across to those other rocks. There are things you've rather upset.'

'So I gather.' The man from the sea was impassive. 'But you should get them straight, I think, inside ten minutes. I'll expect you back then.'

'I'll come back when I can.' Cranston stiffened under what seemed a threat.

'Thank you. I realize I'm not your only pebble on the beach.' The voice was ironic. 'But don't forget me altogether and clear out. It would be disconcerting if I had to follow you like this . . . back to civilization.'

Cranston, without replying, began to climb down to the beach. He did so slowly, since he felt it prudent to keep an eye on the other man still. 'Stay just where you are,' he called back.

'Certainly – for a few minutes.' The torso of the man from the sea slipped down into darkness until only his head and shoulders showed in the moonlight. He had found something to sit on. 'But you needn't, my dear young man, think I'm going to slug you. I value you too highly for that. And doesn't the mere suspicion make you out a rather fickle fellow? We were like blood-brothers, you know, only five minutes ago.'

Again Cranston said nothing. But he felt irritated – partly at having his years condescended to, and partly from acknowledging the truth of what the man from the sea had divined. He completed his scramble, and felt his feet on the sand.

'I wonder why?' The voice of the man from the sea came to him now from above only as a meditative murmur. 'I wonder . . . can *you* be getting away with something too?'

The last throb of the motor-boat had faded, and the sea lay dim and empty on either side of the broad bright causeway thrown across it by the moon. When half-way down the beach Cranston swerved and ran for the cliff. The shorts and gym shoes which were all he had set out in on this warm night lay at an easily identified spot; within seconds he had them on and was running to the farthest rocks. 'Caryl?' His voice was carefully without anxiety. 'Come out . . . it's quite all right.'

She appeared instantly – jumping a small rock-pool in her urgency and tumbling into his arms. 'Dicky, Dicky – what is it? I don't understand. It isn't Alex?'

'Of course not. Nothing like that.' He took her in a quick embrace. Her body, slim beneath the slacks and thick sweater into which it was huddled, trembled not with the excitement familiar to him but in simple terror. He felt for her a sudden enormous pity and compassion, holding no proportion either with the degree or occasion of her distress. He held, caressed, soothed her – murmuring all his private endearments, secret names. It was something he had been constrained to do before, and he had skill at it. Out of the force of his solicitude he strained that skill now, exploited it with all the resource of his quick brain. And suddenly the very effort of this produced, without a single premonitory flicker in consciousness, a complete revolution.

He *was* so skilful only because it was all – the whole damned thing – happening through his brain. In this infernal theatrical moonlight he was like an actor who has been sunk for a space in his part, but to whom detached consciousness has returned, so that he must simply get through his scene with what deftness rests in him. The very largeness of his emotion of seconds before had spoken of its instability; and all that he now felt was a sharp impatience. That – and the shocked sense of everything being in process of becoming different, as if experience had incontinently, treacherously turned upon him its other face. But for the moment at least he could shut out its new enigmatical lineaments and look only at the practical problem confronting him. 'It's all right,' he whispered, '– quite all right. Only something's happened that rather ditches us for tonight. A man from the sea.'

'A man from the sea?' She was bewildered.

'Escaped from a ship – and swum ashore. That motor-boat was after him. It's gone. But the man's on my hands still. He's over there in the other rocks.'

'What sort of a man? What's it about?'

He shook his head. 'I don't know. Smuggling, perhaps. I believe various up-to-date varieties exist.'

'But how stupid!' Her confidence was returning. 'He must go away. You must send him away.'

'I don't know if I can.' He hesitated. 'And I want to know about him.'

'But he has nothing to do with *us*!' It came from her as if proving that he had said something strictly nonsensical. 'Please, please, Dicky, go and get rid of him . . . I've only a little time. I must be going back.' Her voice had gone husky, and she moved in his arms – with calculation, some new perception told him, so that through the thick wool her skin slid beneath

471

his fingers. 'Or can't we just slip away – into the field above the cliff?'

'I've got to find out about him.' He saw that she was surprised as well as puzzled, and it came to him humiliatingly that here was the first indication she had ever received that he had a will of his own. He was prompted to add: 'And get him clothes.'

'But he may be a criminal!' Caryl was horrified. 'And you would be breaking the law. Dicky – do, *do* let us clear out.'

Cranston let go of her and stepped back. She was at least tolerably secure again on her own pins. 'I don't know that we could if we would. He's keeping an eye on us, I suspect. And he's prepared to make trouble if we don't toe the line.'

'Make trouble?'

She was scared again – so that instinctively he put out a hand to her once more. 'He's an educated man, and nothing escapes him. He sees that we wouldn't care for a lot of shouting.'

'Why should we be afraid of it?' Abruptly, as if to enhance his sense of some horrible disintegration, she was spuriously bold – dramatic on a note that was wholly false. 'I'd take it – with you, Dicky. I'd take *anything* with you. But I have to think of Sally.'

It was the first time that she had spoken the name in weeks. He said very quietly: 'Look – *you* can clear out. That will be the best thing, and at least it will cramp his style. Slip through the rocks to the cliff-path by the groyne. Then double back along the top to your bike and go home. I'll stay and deal with the chap.'

For a moment he could see her waver. When she spoke it was with a queer desperation. 'No. Not unless you go too.'

'But surely –' He stopped – having caught suddenly at a fantastic truth. In her incredible head Caryl had fudged up some crazy suspicion. Perhaps it was to the effect that he had been prompted to conceal a second mistress at the other end of the beach. More probably what had peered out in her was without definable content – a mere irresistible wash of undifferentiated sexual jealousy. And at this, under a sort of cold inner light flicked on by the absurd discovery, Cranston starkly realized the simple truth over whose contours his mind had been intermittently groping for days and nights. It was as if his fingers had slid beneath a delusively seductive garment and come on ice.

He was crazy himself. For weeks he had been indulging in a bout of madness. A casual observer – and now there was one – would see in it no more than a run-of-the-mill indignity of late adolescence. But it wasn't that. It wasn't remotely just what one might feel elated about or ashamed of according to one's mood. It was entirely different. He wondered if it was unwittingly that Caryl had touched the unbearable quick of the matter only a minute before . . .

He caught himself up. Their situation demanded action and not reverie.

Something prompted him to turn his glance back along the beach. 'Well,' he said, 'it's too late, anyway.'

'Too late, Dicky?'

'He's grown tired of waiting. Here he is.'

Chapter 2

'But he's naked!'

She spoke in a quick prudish alarm which ought to have been funny. But again what Cranston felt was impatience. 'He's not – for what it's worth. But he certainly can't get far dressed only in the ghost of a pair of pants.' He paused, perplexed. 'What can his plan have been, going overboard like that?'

'He hadn't one, I suppose. He was just escaping from some foreign ship. They do often pass quite close.'

Cranston was silent. The man from the sea would never be without a plan. His mind was of a sort that made such a state of affairs impossible. Cranston was sure of this, even while realizing that he could give no rational account of his certainty. He watched the man come straight across the beach, and it occurred to him that in this light he ought to look slightly unreal, uncanny. For the moon takes the weight and substance out of things, and relieves them of intent and relatedness. But the man was quite real and very purposive. He might have been a golfer – a professional golfer – marching after his ball in the cold concentration of an important match. And now he was up with them and speaking.

'I thought it better to come across. It can't be very long till dawn. And you are probably anxious to get home.' He had looked first at Cranston, as if to an acquaintance by whom some ceremony of introduction should be performed. But when nothing came of this he turned with brisk ease – with what might have been an acknowledgement of the happy propriety of a less formal note – to Cranston's companion. 'Although', he added, 'it's a perfect night on which to be out.'

For a moment Caryl Blair said nothing, puzzled by the flat conventionality of his tone – by its lack of the impertinence or urgency she had expected. But she was still afraid, and when she did speak fear made her forthright. 'Who are you? Why are you here? Why were they hunting you?'

'These are very reasonable questions.' He was looking at her steadily. 'And the first brings me at once to something rather astonishing. We have, as a matter of fact, met before.'

'Oh no! I'm sure we haven't.' Caryl's voice came to Cranston as pitiably scared. 'There's no possibility –'

'But indeed we have . . . Lady Blair.'

She gave a gasp and shrank towards her lover. 'Dicky,' she whispered, 'take me away . . . take me away!'

'But not in circumstances which would cause *you* to remember *me*.' As if unaware of her reaction, the man from the sea continued on the note of polite talk. 'A mere introduction – but I was far from likely to forget it.' He looked at her directly again, and his voice carried the precise intonation that the urbane compliment required. 'And I met your husband too on the same occasion. But not, I think' – and he turned to Cranston – 'your son.'

There was a blank silence, and then Cranston heard Caryl draw a long shuddering breath. It was oddly echoed by a tiny wave breaking on the beach. The man had hit upon a pretence at once deft and cruel – something before which she was helpless, like one suddenly offered an insulting charity. And Cranston, determined that this make-believe should get no further, broke in. 'You may as well know –'

'At something of the Royal Society's, would it have been?' The man from the sea ignored the interruption. 'Certainly it was some rather grand affair, at which I was surprised to find myself. You were wearing diamonds. That interested me, I need hardly say.'

'My diamonds interested you?' Caryl had sufficiently recovered her nerve to tumble into vacuous curiosity. 'I don't see why they should.'

The man from the sea smiled. It was not, Cranston thought, a real smile. Indeed, nothing that he said or did was quite real; only his presence – his enigmatical presence – was that. And now for a fraction of a second he seemed to hesitate, as if debating some disclosure that it might, or might not, be expedient to make. When he spoke again, there was for the first time the hint of some concession to the dramatic in his voice.

'You were wearing uncommonly fine diamonds. But nothing like so fine, Lady Blair, as I am wearing now.'

Again it should have been a funny moment. Caryl Blair, although she had all the careful modesty of an unchaste woman, looked the almost naked man up and down, round-eyed. '*Wearing* diamonds?'

He tapped his waist, and Cranston was once more aware of the belt he had first noticed as the man rose from the sea. The belt was bulkier – and the man himself more youthfully slim about the tummy – than had become apparent before. 'You mean you *carry* diamonds?' Cranston asked.

The man from the sea nodded. 'It's my trade. I work at this end of some rather large-scale I.D.B.'

Cranston could see Caryl's eyes grow yet rounder. It struck him – and simply as one further confounding revelation – that her facial expressions were all conventional muscular manoeuvres, picked up from plays and films, imagined from books. But her interest was genuine, and it was clear that this mysterious talk of diamonds held for her the same sort of fascination that an actual outpouring of gems themselves would have, were the stranger to tumble them out before her, all ice and fire beneath this ghastly moon. 'I.D.B.?' she asked.

'Illicit diamond buying.' The man from the sea, it seemed to Cranston, might have been saying 'I work at the F.O.' or even 'My job's with I.C.I. – no reason why you should have heard of it, but it has to do with chemicals and things of that sort.' He was entirely bland. And now he spoke again. 'I'm afraid that tonight you've come up with – well, somebody doing what's scarcely expected of him.' He gave Cranston a swift sardonic glance. 'You mightn't believe it – but it does happen from time to time.'

There was another silence – but not because Caryl made anything of this. Chinese would have meant no less to her. She turned to Cranston. 'Then it *is* just smuggling? Not anything criminal?'

'Perhaps it can be put that way. But, if we help our friend here, we are certainly liable to be put in gaol – and after a picturesque joint trial. Can't you see us side by side in the dock?' He stopped – astonished at himself and suddenly ashamed. He had never before spoken to her meaning to hurt, and it seemed to him incredibly mean. For he was clinging to the cloudy notion that she had made for him some enormous sacrifice, and that he ought to be her man to the death. Yet there she was, a woman of about the same age as the stranger beside her, dressed in a sweater and slacks, and with an empty head. He glimpsed the terrifying fact that one creates and uncreates as one goes along; that one cannot help it; that fatuities and disenchantments and treacheries are regular byproducts in the queer chemistry of living.

'I'm afraid that is perfectly true.' The man from the sea struck smoothly in, like a skilled family friend sensing domestic friction and unobtrusively pouring oil. 'Fortunately, detection is unlikely. Indeed, it's scarcely an exaggeration to say that it hardly ever happens – at least as long as one's brains continue to work.' He was mildly humorous. 'And I think ours will do that.'

'Was your brain working when you jumped overboard in your skin?' Cranston turned on him swiftly. 'Is it your regular technique? Do you reckon to crawl gasping from the sea and stumble straight upon people like – like ourselves, every time?'

'That would be to expect too much altogether.' The stranger's humour was a shade broader. 'You weren't in my mind at all.'

'Then what was in your mind? You seem to me to have done something quite desperate.'

'There was a decided emergency. A matter of three or four friends of mine being suddenly prompted to cut my throat. It happens – in I.D.B. I jumped.'

'With any plan?'

'Dear me, yes. One can't set out to swim an unknown number of miles in a lounge suit or a dinner jacket. But, once ashore, I was sure I could find a bathing-beach in time. And there I could lie about unregarded all day in next to nothing – and until somebody proved a little careless of their clothes. Everything would be simple after that. I have plenty of money.'

'Then you had better carry on. We won't stop you.' Cranston hesitated. 'Or say anything, either.'

'That's right.' Caryl joined in eagerly. 'Go at once. And we'll say nothing. On our honour.'

'Ah – on that.' The man from the sea looked at Cranston inscrutably. 'I wonder whether you – or your mother – can think of a better way in which I might get hold of some clothes?'

'I'll get you clothes.' Cranston spoke coldly. He knew the man from the sea to be under no misconception about his relationship with Caryl, and his continued affectation in the matter was part of what appeared his pervasive falsity. Even his diamonds were surely false – and whether false or real they belonged to some small world of low criminality. Cranston felt that the man from the sea had in an indefinable way let him down. Nevertheless – if yet more indefinably still – there remained between them something that Cranston felt as a bond. He would have liked to break it – and now he was trying to see it as some sort of measurable obligation. Let him hand over so much, and he would be quits. Let him get the man from the sea inside a suit and walking upon leather – and that would be the end of him. 'I'll get you clothes,' he repeated. 'I'll take you home and fit you out at once.'

'But Dicky – you can't!' Caryl had grabbed him by the arm – and now, absurdly dragging him a few paces away, she fiercely whispered. 'Dicky, it's too risky . . . the village . . . your people . . . you mustn't.'

'It can't be helped, I'm afraid.'

'We must take him the other way – mine. It's far safer. I can go ahead and get some of Alex's things. He'll never miss them. I'll leave them in the summer-house – the one by the cliff. Follow with him – and when he's dressed get him away. And meet me, Dicky – meet me tomorrow night.'

'Very well.' He knew it at once to be the better plan; that on a sober calculation it involved her in less ultimate risk than did his own. And he turned to the man from the sea. 'We've fixed it up. Within an hour you'll be clothed – and gone.'

'I mean to go ahead – but only to get things ready.' Caryl added her explanations. 'And I'm quite good at men's clothes. You can trust me.'

'I'm sure I can, Lady Blair.'

'Then I'll go.' She had winced again at his knowledge of her name, as if feeling that it vastly increased his power to harm. 'And we won't breathe a word. Only there must be a bargain.'

'A bargain, Lady Blair?'

'Never mind.' Before his polite blankness she was confused. By tomorrow, Cranston thought, she might be believing that they really had been taken for mother and son out on some innocent nocturnal skylarking; that no bargain had been in question; that they had helped the fugitive out of the bounty of their own romantic felings . . . And now she was still lingering. She still had something to say – and such was his pained sense of a large new knowledge of her that he was surprised at having no notion of what it could be. She was looking almost shyly at the man from the sea. 'Will you show them to me?' she asked.

For a second it left Cranston merely wondering. The stranger was not at a loss. 'I wish I could. But they are rather particularly sewn up, you know.' Once more he tapped his belt. 'And you couldn't tell them from pebbles.'

'Pebbles?' She was naively astonished.

'They look no more than that – until they're cut.'

'I see.' She was like a child whom some prosaic fact betrays in the legitimate expectation of pleasure. 'Where do you take them to?'

'Hatton Garden. All diamonds go there.'

'So they do.' She accepted this sagely. 'But they will come back to you later – I mean the same ones?'

'Yes, I shall have further dealings with them later on.'

'They'll be for sale?' She hesitated. 'I could perhaps buy one or two – just by way of remembering this funny night?'

'It could be managed. Perhaps we might meet and discuss it some time.' The stranger's tone continued to be conventional – so that Cranston supposed him quite unsurprised. Cranston himself felt his head swimming. He had good reason to know that Caryl's mind could very queerly veer about. But this freak was unbelievable. Or was it? She was silly about gems, and there was a bit of an explanation in that. Perhaps – he found himself considering this quite dispassionately – she was inevitably silly about men who rose gleaming from the sea in the small hours or presented any similar bizarre interest. But of more certain relevance was the fascination she found in funk. The man from the sea was frightening, and there was a good nine-tenths of her which this whole encounter prompted to mere flight. But some tiny remaining component wanted to stay and dabble . . . like this. Here on the familiar beach she had enjoyed her fill of one sort of delicious apprehensiveness. And now – perhaps without awareness of what drove her – she was reaching out to the man from the sea for another.

And Cranston's impatience was suddenly acute. A pair of diamond cuff-links would make a nice Christmas present for Alex. He heard the low pleasantry enunciate itself inside his head; and although he had no impulse actually to speak the words he flushed at them. It was true that everything had turned abominable. For a moment he believed that his consciousness of this was affecting him physically – had set a pulse throbbing at his temple. Then he realized that he was hearing, once more, something far away. The throb was from a steamer out in the ocean-channel. And it had begun quite suddenly. The engines that had stopped half an hour ago were in action again.

The sound cut Caryl short. Perhaps the image of the invisible ship, variously manned and purposively moving, brought the outer world in its threatening aspect more sharply home to her. She turned away from the man from the sea – and a last quick scrutiny of his stripped body was perhaps only to tell her which of Alex's clothes would fit. 'Dicky,' she whispered, '– till tomorrow!' Then she vanished among the rocks. A minute later there was a glimpse of her – all tight slacks and voluminous sweater –scrambling clear of them and making for the cliff. The two men were quite silent. Only when the slow sea gave its next soft sigh their eyes met. They might have been acknowledging something appropriate in the sound.

'We'll give her twenty minutes.' Cranston spoke prosaically. 'For time, I think, isn't a worry. The nearest railway-station is about five miles up the glen. And there will be nothing odd about your strolling up to it in time for the first train.'

The man from the sea nodded. 'Nothing at all – provided the clothes are a reasonable fit.'

'Blair's things will fit you, all right.'

'Blair? Your –?'

'Drop that, please.' Cranston was surprised to hear his own voice tremble with anger. 'You understand what – what you've seen, very well.'

'I don't altogether understand *you*.' The man from the sea spoke soberly. 'Are you, I wonder, just a very great young puritan? Or is there something more?'

'I don't know what you mean.' Even as he uttered the words, Cranston realized that they were the first lie he had spoken that night. And on this it came to him, as a linked and answering discovery, that the man from the sea had lied a great deal. 'Let's stick to what's on hand, please. We've already made one slip.'

'A slip?' The man from the sea was curious rather than alarmed.

'Shaving things. You won't look right in Blair's classy clothes and a day's beard. Perhaps –' Cranston stopped. His glance had travelled to the face of the man from the sea. Even by moonlight, it was possible to distinguish it as perfectly smooth.

'That's all right.' The man was laughing softly. 'I shaved before I jumped.'

'While your friends were trying to cut your throat?'

'Precisely.'

Again they were silent. The throb of the engines was fading. From what sounded almost as far away, a gull called and called again. Intermittently the sea, as if tired of a vain whispering in the ear of night, heaved itself into a larger wave which splashed on the pale beach like the smack of a drowsily amorous hand. A light breeze, faintly chill, was now blowing in from the ocean; it could be felt flowing past them – now fading to a breath and now growing to a small wind that would bend Jamieson's corn and Neil Clark's barley, that would rustle in the grasses of the old glebe where Sir Alex Blair's men might be mowing in the morning. It was strange to Cranston that in the familiar terrain he should suddenly be jostled by so much that was alien and inscrutable. The man from the sea was that. He presented indeed a front that was comprehensible enough – that was as dull as greed and as small as cheating. But behind him – Cranston perfectly knew – was some large hinterland of darkness. And it had been Cranston's immediate intuition of this that had given him the first sick sense of another vista. The affair with Lady Blair – so bewilderingly exciting and yet so finite as to be measurable in terms of mere minutes and inches – had its incalculable hinterland too. To put it bleakly, he had made a shocking mistake.

Cranston shivered – and if it was partly at his own train of thought it was nevertheless substantially because of what the breeze was doing to his skin. The night – all this succession of Scottish nights – had been incredible. His limbs had moved in an unreal medium, more balmy than any actual air, as if he had slipped into some travel advertisement in a glossy American magazine. But in the small hours there came an honest northern chill, and it was licking at him now. He had emerged cold from his short wallow in the sea, and nothing had happened at all to warm him up since. At twenty-two, such sensations resolve themselves into simple and immediate impulse. Cranston knew that he wanted to run. He wanted, if possible, to race. Almost theatrically, his world was darkening round him – but nevertheless he wanted the blood to be moving faster in his veins. He looked at the man from the sea.

He remembered that the man *was* from the sea. He had been in it for a long time – had in fact been very near never coming out of it. He, far more than Cranston, should be shivering now. But if he even felt the chill he gave no sign of it, and his naked poise was that of an athlete, despite his middle years. 'What about a run to warm up?' Cranston asked.

'That's quite an idea.' His idiom was Cranston's own, and as he turned lightly on his toes and glanced down the beach he might have been an undergraduate lazily ready for physical expression. He pointed to the other end of the beach. 'There and back?'

'Yes.' Cranston restrained himself from adding: 'And I'll give you fifteen yards.'

The man slipped off his belt and dropped it carelessly on the sand. 'No point', he said, 'in carrying weight. Will you give the word?'

'On your marks, get set, go?'

'Right.'

For a moment more they parleyed over the form of the thing. They were like two boys from different public schools, rather warily meeting in the holidays and making their arrangements with punctilio. Then they were off. Cranston could tell at once that the man had been a sprinter. His own best distance was the half-mile. He gave himself to the serious business of running as fast as he could – thinking about his breathing, trying to avoid spots where the sand looked too soft to thrust from with the ball of the foot. The man from the sea was actually heading him; they were level at the turn by the farther rocks; Cranston led all the way back, but at the finish would scarcely have cancelled the fifteen yards' handicap he had rashly thought to offer. For some moments they stood panting. For a further second they turned to each other, laughing – as if experiencing again, less tensely, the odd intimacy that had surprised them as they lurked in hiding. And then the man from the sea stooped quickly, picked up his belt, and fastened it round his middle. He glanced down as he did so, making sure of the buckle. And something pricked at Cranston's memory.

Once already he had experienced the sensation of near-recognition. This time it prompted him to speak. 'You know,' he said, 'I don't believe a word of your story.'

The man from the sea made one further movement, settling the belt about his waist. And then he stood quite still – and for so long that Cranston had the sense of having uttered unwittingly the words of a potent immobilizing spell. They had been words prompted, at least in part, by the obstinate irrational feeling that the man from the sea had something to share with him. They had borne – or been intended to bear – the character of an approach to confidence, an appeal for candour. But they were also the product – Cranston was conscious – of some piece of crucial knowledge hovering just beyond his power of recollection. Perhaps it was the nature of this – he suddenly found himself rather urgently feeling – that now gave them, retrospectively, the sense of being highly injudicious.

'What's wrong with my story?' When he did speak, the man from the sea spoke gently. At the same time he took a couple of steps away from Cranston, so that the rocks received him partly into their shadow and he became once more like a picture cast in bold chiaroscuro. 'You interest me,' he said mildly. 'Just where does my story strain credulity?'

'It's not your story; it's yourself.' The race had not only sent Cranston's blood coursing more swiftly. It had quickened his brain. He had lately experienced novel pleasures – but now an old one had with unexpected suddenness returned to him. It was the clever schoolboy's pleasure in his own powers – when only lately discovered and still felt as a wonderful springboard to the world. He remembered that his wits worked well – and at the same time realized that for days, for weeks, they had hardly been working at all. But they were coming back to him now, and with them the power of lucid speech. 'Or rather,' he said, 'it's the lack of adequate correspondence between the one and the other – between your story, you know, and *you*. You're the wrong man for it – quite the wrong man for that diamond-smuggling yarn. If I'd thought to pick up that belt and hand it to you – and why in the world *didn't* I think of it? – there would have been nothing like the feel of gems beneath that webbing. It isn't even heavy; it didn't fall as if it were. Papers, perhaps, or banknotes well waterproofed. But *not* diamonds destined for Hatton Garden.' He paused. 'That's one thing.'

'There are others?'

'I don't think you jumped into the sea because some chaps were then and there going to cut your throat. You jumped on a predetermined plan – and it included the efficient little detail of shaving immediately beforehand.'

Cranston paused. He was the schoolboy in the middle of a model construe. 'You seem so efficient that I'm surprised you didn't get overboard more quietly, or in circumstances that would allow you more grace. Being chased up so quickly was, if you ask me, a poor show.'

'It was a very uncomfortable one. Anything else?'

'No. But the point, I think, lies there. This diamond-smuggler in a professional way that you conjure up – he might well choose that desperate swim if there was really a knife at his throat. But he wouldn't plan it, have that tidy shave, and then jump in cold blood. It's a different order of person who'd do that. It's other motives that drive men to tricks of that sort.'

'Is that so?' The man from the sea paused. It was something that he, too, knew how to do. 'Would it be terribly impertinent to ask your age? This blending of the severities of logic with a ripe human wisdom makes me decidedly curious.'

Cranston flushed. 'I'm twenty-two,' he said shortly.

'Twenty-two? So wise so young, they say, do never live long.'

'I beg your pardon?' Cranston was startled.

'Something that an extremely sinister person was prompted to say about a very bright small boy. The story ended in the Tower of London. I hope neither yours nor mine will do that.'

'There you are.' Cranston made a bold bid for recovery. 'Diamond-smugglers don't gabble Shakespeare.'

The man from the sea nodded. It was his first movement for what seemed a long time. 'It's not a bad point . . . Are you just down from Oxford?'

'Cambridge.'

'Then let me say that your intelligence does your college credit. Your morals appear to be another matter.' The man from the sea produced his softest laugh. 'And how, my dear boy, you feel it!'

'My affairs aren't really the question, are they?'

'Do you know – I believe *that* a little remains to be seen?' The man from the sea stepped forward again – and contrived to make the action suggest some marked drop in tension. 'By the way,' he said, 'isn't it about time we were going after those clothes?'

'More than time.' Cranston took a last glance at the empty beach and then turned towards the rocks. 'It's a bit of a scramble in places. I'll go ahead.'

For some seconds they moved in single file through deepening shadows. When the man from the sea spoke again it was on a practical note. 'Do they have dogs?'

'The Blairs? They have several. But I don't think they'll make a row.'

'I suppose they're used to a certain amount of nocturnal traffic.'

Cranston said nothing. He hated the joke – and hated himself for having no right to resent it. And he felt that it was not made for its own sake. The man from the sea didn't really have any humour in him. But he had plenty of subtlety. If he irritated you, it was by design.

'Is it a large household?'

'No – quite small.' Cranston answered without turning his head.

'There isn't what I so tactfully tried to take you for – a grown-up son?'

'No.' Cranston felt his anger mounting.

'Ah – childless. That's where to look for a maternal mistress.'

Cranston stopped and swung round. 'She's not childless, blast you. There's . . . a grown-up daughter. Hers – not his.'

They had emerged from the rocks, and the moonlight fell full upon the face of the man from the sea. He said nothing, and his features remained entirely impassive. But after a moment he gave a slight nod – as a person might do who has solved some very simple problem along expected lines. The two men looked at each other – it was another of their odd exchanges – and then turned and walked side by side towards the cliff.

Chapter 3

The attack came seconds later and took them both utterly by surprise. Cranston was not to know the man from the sea so caught unawares again. Even so, he acted very quickly – taking Cranston to momentary safety in a rugger tackle as he went down himself. It was in the hollow of dry loose sand immediately below the cliff; they lay prone in it as the second batch of bullets kicked and spat about them or whined over their heads. In the sudden unbelievable crisis Cranston found his mind working fast. Apparently fear was like a wound, and took time to make itself felt. It had got no grip yet. But in a matter of minutes – if he *had* minutes – it would be humiliatingly at work on him. Meanwhile the initiative was his. He knew the ground. 'Are you all right?' he asked.

'Yes – but can we get clear?' The voice of the man from the sea was calm. 'They must have landed somebody before making off back to the ship. Silly to think there's magic in British soil. But my guess is that it's only one chap.'

'It's one chap, all right – and with some sort of tommy-gun out by the point. If we can make the cliff we've a chance. The path cuts through it so that there's nearly always at least a foot or two of cover from down here.'

'Good. We'd better make the dash now. If we stop, the blighter has only to walk up to us and blow our brains out. On your mark?'

Cranston heard himself laugh – and distrusted the sound. 'Get set,' he said. His finger-nails were digging into his palms, and it was with an effort that he flattened his hands on the sand to get better purchase for a spring. He drew up one knee beneath his belly and tensed his whole body. From behind him he fancied he heard the scrape of booted feet on rock.

'Go!'

They were up and running – and instantly the bullets were spitting and singing again. The man from the sea went down and rolled in sand. There was another burst and he gave a sharp cry of pain. The fear Cranston had been expecting pounced. It came as a sickening physical clutch at his bowels and reins. But he found that he had stopped and was trying to heave the man from the sea into cover that was now only a few yards away. There was another spray of bullets which for some reason flew wide. The man from the sea was on his feet again and running. There was something odd about him, but he was making it. They had both made it. On one side of them was the main face of the cliff and on the other an almost continuous breast-work of rock, to keep in the shelter of which they had barely to stoop. Cranston thrust the man from the sea before him. 'Up you go,' he said. 'You can't miss it.'

They climbed – but to Cranston's mind too slowly. 'Speed up,' he whispered. 'But quietly. It's only if he wastes time finding the path that we've a chance.'

'Get ahead of me, will you?' The voice of the man from the sea was still calm. 'It was a graze on the ankle that brought me down. But the real mischief's my eyes.'

'Your eyes?' As he scrambled ahead Cranston felt a queer chill.

'One of those bullets spat sand into them far too hard to be comfortable. I can't see a thing. But I can follow you well enough.'

Suddenly Cranston felt himself rebel – rebel against the grotesque destiny that a brief hour had brought upon him. If he stuck by the man from the sea he was almost certainly going to be killed – and without so much as knowing why. It was true that in some brief span of months or years any one of a variety of horrible deaths might come to him. His whole generation walked day by day in the consciousness of that. But death in battle would be death with others of his own sort – and in a cause at least approximately definable, so that there would be a sort of meaning in it. In this there was no sense at all. It was going to be like a street accident. And he was going to be dead. Dead at twenty-two. Because of having got mixed up with some sort of crook . . . Cranston looked at the cliff-face on his left. He could turn aside and scale it. The light was quite good enough. He would be out of this nightmare just as quickly as he had been in. And the man from the sea could settle his own account.

Suddenly he was shivering from head to foot. It was as if these thoughts were equivalent to finding himself out on the verge of the cliff in a great wind, with his balance swaying. For a second the image held him paralysed. And then, oddly, it prompted him to think ahead and to speak. 'Listen – there's only one dangerous place. It's about fifty yards in front of us and half-way up. The path takes a turn on an overhang, and for perhaps a dozen feet it curves round with no protection on the outer side at all. But I'll face round and keep a hand on your right shoulder – and you'll keep your left dug into the cliff. All right?'

'All right.'

They continued to scramble. Again Cranston thought he heard the scrape of boots, and from almost directly below. His heart sank. If they could gain a sufficient start there was a chance that they might successfully go to earth somewhere on top. But if the fellow found the path and sighted them before they were clear of the cliff, then they were certainly done for. At the top he would have them in a narrow cleft and with the moon dead ahead. A single burst from that gun would settle the matter.

And now they had come to the ugly bit. The natural parapet on their right had vanished; for four or five yards the path ceased to be through the cliff and wound on a steep curve sheer across its face. Cranston turned round and dropped on all fours. The man from the sea was already crawling. Working backwards was not difficult in itself, but it was less easy when he had to keep one guiding hand almost constantly on the other's shoulder. And suddenly their pursuer made himself unmistakably heard. He was on the path and coming up rapidly. Their plight was hopeless.

Cranston looked to his left and down. They were out on the over-hang, and the moon-blanched sea lay directly below. He wondered what would happen if one took a dive from a height like this. Probably one's body would lose all control of itself and hit the surface in a fashion that would immediately kill. Anyway, there were rocks. He could see them just beneath the surface, like green veins in a milky marble . . . They went on crawling. He avoided looking directly into the face of the man from the sea, because even in this horrible situation there was a further horror in the thought that the man was perhaps blinded. Once, the man's right knee slithered under him on some treacherously worn patch of the path, and Cranston thought that they were both going over. Then a shadow loomed behind his own left shoulder. It was the parapet again. Their death wasn't to be by water.

But now their pursuer was upon them. He was somewhere just short of the hazard they had so painfully negotiated. And they were utterly helpless. He was again in the position that the man from the sea had crisply defined. He had nothing to do but walk up and blow their brains out.

The path was less steep and they had got to their feet. There were at least a few more paces that they could take, and it seemed a point of honour to take them. Cranston had the man from the sea by the hand. And suddenly he realized that they were in almost complete darkness.

It was the point at which the path turned again sharply into the cliff – and its direction was such that, for no more than a matter of feet, the clear moonlight made no impression on its shadows. But in another couple of yards there would be no shadows at all. Cranston stopped, turned, and took a couple of backward paces. As he edged past the man from the sea his mouth was close to his ear. 'It's the only place,' he whispered

'To fight?'

'To have a shot at it.'

'He's more likely to have several shots at us.'

'Ssh!'

From quite close to them there had come the rattle of a pebble displaced on the path. Cranston took one further backward step and had before him a panel of moonlight and a strip of sea. It was the last few feet of that hazardous curve. If the man with the gun could be stopped anywhere, it was decidedly here. Cranston turned to claw at the cliff-face for a loose stone, a clot of clay. And as he did so the man appeared.

The moonlight fell upon him as for a photograph. He had rounded the curve and was standing still, so that for a moment he was like a dummy in a tailor's window. And the first thing noticeable was his clothes. They were absurdly urban to have come direct from ship-board. Moreover, the man himself had the same suggestion. He was plump and pale – and he was peering into the shadows through rimless spectacles and from beneath a trilby hat. The whole appearance thus presented was so incongruously mild that Cranston for a moment felt almost persuaded that there must be some bizarre mistake. Then he saw that the man really had a gun. He was raising it now. He knew just where his quarry lurked. He was making his kill.

Something came free under Cranston's fingers. It was about the size of a cricket-ball. He looked fixedly at the man's spectacles glinting with a sort of treacherous reassurance in the moonlight and tried to imagine them a pair of bails. The distance wasn't much farther than from cover-point. He raised his arm. The movement must have betrayed him, for in the same instant the man levelled his gun – a glinting short-barrelled affair. There was no time for a more careful aim, and Cranston threw. The stone – for it was that – had scarcely left his hand when he knew that it was going wide. And he would never have a chance to reach for another. The stone was flying wide of the spectacles by eighteen inches – by a couple of feet. And then he saw the gun magically flicked from the man's hands, and in the same instant heard a sharp crack. The stone had taken it on the muzzle and it was spinning in air. A fraction of a second later there was a tiny splash. The weapon was in the sea. The enemy had been disarmed.

'Can we go for him?' It was the man from the sea who spoke. Whether or not his sight was coming back to him, he appeared to know perfectly what had happened. 'Could we chuck him into the water?'

'I could take him over with me – like Sherlock Holmes with Dr Moriarty.' Cranston was moved to sudden sarcasm. 'And then you could just carry on. Shall we try that?'

'Or have you a knife?' The voice of the man from the sea was quite level. 'Could we collar him lower down and cut his throat?'

'He looks as if he'll just clear out. Won't that do?'

'I'd rather we killed him.'

Cranston was silent. He realized that the man from the sea meant precisely what he said. And this realization, more than the deadly danger he had himself been in seconds before, brought home to him the queer fact that he had dropped into an utterly unknown world. It occurred to him that the man with spectacles might have another weapon – perhaps a revolver –

and that it was of this danger that the man from the sea was thinking. But there was no sign of anything of the sort. For a further couple of seconds their late pursuer held his ground – harmlessly and irresolutely, like a pedestrian become aware of being in the wrong street or meditating a cautious encounter with a stream of traffic. The circumstances of the affair seemed to require from him a grimace of rage, a howl of baffled fury. But all that the man with the spectacles did was to clear his throat as if about to address the darkness. No words came – and the commonplace sound was followed by a gesture yet more uncannily commonplace. The man produced a handkerchief, removed his trilby hat, and mopped his forehead. Then he replaced the hat, stowed away the handkerchief, turned, and walked off down the path. In a second he had vanished; for some seconds more they could hear his composed retreat; and then that was the end of him. Cranston was alone with his first and equally problematical companion.

'I can see the moon – or at least I'm aware of it.' The man from the sea was moving forward cautiously, his hand on Cranston's arm. 'But that's all. It presents a complication.'

'In getting to Hatton Garden?'

'We've agreed, I think, that Hatton Garden is a fiction.' The man from the sea produced his accurately contrived yet spurious effect of humour. 'I can't expect you to believe that diamond-smugglers go to quite the lengths we've just been witnessing.' He paused. 'I wish that fellow hadn't got away.'

'He can do more damage – arm himself again?'

The man from the sea shook his head. 'He can contact . . . others. Again, it's a complication.'

'There's the house.' Cranston pointed, momentarily forgetful of his companion's condition. 'We skirt this wall, and then go through a gate to the summer-house. The clothes will be waiting. And that will be a start. It could be an end, as far as I'm concerned, except for this business of your eyes. If you want more help, you must tell the truth.'

'My dear young man!' The voice beside Cranston had taken on a tone of mock alarm. 'That might be stiff, you know – very stiff, indeed. Patricide, fratricide, and all unmentionable crimes may be on my hands.'

'I'm bearing that in mind.' Cranston spoke grimly.

'My advice to you is to give me more help – just a little more help – while asking no questions. It will be more comfortable . . . all round.'

'Is that a threat again?'

'I suppose it is.' The man from the sea paused. 'Would you have Sir Alex Blair know?'

'Blast Blair.'

'Or . . . the daughter?'

There was a long silence. Cranston was waiting for the blood to stop hammering in his head. 'Aren't you,' he asked carefully, 'a pretty great blackguard?'

'I am what you knew me to be in the first minutes of our meeting. The right word for it is desperate. Do you know what it is to be desperate?'

'I'm learning.'

The man from the sea had paused in his halting walk. Now he moved on. 'One can talk to you,' he said unexpectedly. 'You're beyond your years.'

'So wise so young –?'

'You'll live long enough, so far as I'm concerned. It's not all that catching.'

Cranston looked sharply at the man treading carefully beside him. But he could distinguish no play of expression accompanying this odd speech. What the moonlight did sufficiently reveal was the fact that the man's face was a mess. He must be in considerable pain – but after that first sharp cry he had given no sign of it. If he was a blackguard he was other things as well. And his real life – it came to Cranston – lay far below any facet of himself that he had yet revealed. He had come naked out of the sea – but in an impenetrable disguise. There was nothing about him that one could be sure of – except some underlying intensity of purpose, some dark obsession, which it was impossible to define. There was that – and there was this last queer little speech. It had seemed to slip up, eluding the vigilance of some censor, from a hitherto hidden stratum of his mind. But even of that one could not be certain. The man from the sea was subtle and formidable. His most spontaneous-seeming utterance might be a premeditated and planted thing.

'We go through here.' Cautiously, Cranston eased open a door in the high stone wall. 'I hope I'm right about those dogs. Better take my hand again. There's a winding path to the summer-house. I can just make it out. The moon's going down.'

'And that means dawn in no time. We can be clear in half an hour?'

'We could be. But it all needs thinking about. And what's possible depends upon the truth of your situation, you know, and the risks you may actually have in front of you.' Cranston was briskly practical. 'That's why it's just no good keeping me in the dark.'

'I wish I could keep myself there. Is this summer-house we're making for safe?'

'No one comes near it, day or night. It's perfect for –' Cranston broke off, and he knew that his cheeks had flushed as at a monstrous recollection. 'The house is a quarter of a mile away. It's got enormous grounds.'

'Of course Blair is wealthy as well as scientifically distinguished.' The man from the sea had turned on his note of irony. 'I remember how your friend's diamonds proclaimed the fact at that reception.'

'Did you say the Royal Society?' Cranston scarcely knew why he asked the question. But even as he uttered it he acknowledged that it was significant – that his mind by means of it was taking a dive at some submerged memory.

The man from the sea made no answer – perhaps because he had almost stumbled at a turn of the path. When he recovered himself it was to speak in a tone of impatience. 'Aren't we nearly there?'

Cranston in his turn was silent. The garden was warm and scented and very still. The breeze from the sea had either dropped or was here deflected by the sweep of the cliff. The scents were the unique mingling he had known from childhood in such rare northern gardens as this: lavender and roses and sweet briar and night-scented stock shot with the sharpness of the sea and the tang of the surrounding pine and heather. It was a heady mixture. Eden, it queerly occurred to him, had been eminently aromatic – and but for that Eve might never have eaten her apple there. His own apple – Cranston caught himself up. With an appropriateness that was sufficiently broad, the familiar summer-house had loomed up before him. 'We're there,' he said briefly. 'I don't know about risking a light. We'll see when we get in.'

They mounted the little flight of steps and passed across the broad verandah. The summer-house was an elaborate and expensive affair, commodious but without appropriateness to its situation. There was a large dark central room that might have been intended as a refuge from tropical heat, and from the shadowy corners of which it was possible to picture the emergence of exotic persons in the tradition of Conrad or Somerset Maugham. And there was such a presence now – a vaguely defined form in white, that stirred and rose as they entered, and then stood still.

Cranston was startled. 'Caryl! You've waited? We've been –'

The figure in white took a single step forward, and spoke very quietly. 'I'm not Caryl. I'm Sally.'

Chapter 4

'Mother sprained an ankle coming up the path. She could hardly get as far as the house.' Sally Dalrymple continued to speak from the darkness. Her voice was slightly tremulous and slightly hurried, as if she were determined not to be interrupted before she had declared herself. 'So she tumbled me out of bed. She'd had one of her bouts of sleeplessness, she said, and had gone to walk on the beach. And she'd run into you, Dick, with a friend in some sort of fix. It wasn't very clear – but I was to bring these clothes. Is that right?'

There was a silence – a silence that Cranston knew it was his business to break. But his mouth had gone dry, and he felt as he had sometimes felt when half awakening from a ghastly dream. In the dream he had done he hardly remembered what. But it could never be undone. *Never*. And its aftermath was dread and dereliction and dismay.

'The clothes are right, at least!' It was the man from the sea who spoke – striking in with the hateful urbanity he could command. 'From my point of view, they are the important thing. I have to be dressed in them.'

'Then I hope they fit.' Sally's voice was cold, and Cranston knew that she had instantly disliked the stranger. She distrusted him – and for the same reason that Cranston himself had felt a sudden distrust earlier. He was the wrong age to be in a fix with innocence, with any attractiveness as of mere escapade or extravagance. She had been trying to accept the situation as her incredible mother had launched it at her – and that meant a Dick Cranston involved in some hazardous silliness with a contemporary. Poaching, perhaps – or swimming out to Inchfail to play some prank on old Shamus in the lighthouse. But this smooth middle-aged man was inexplicable.

'I'm sorry about Lady Blair's ankle.' Cranston spoke these words simply as being no worse than any others. Anything he said to Sally must be abominable. He realized – and his realization was like a further turn of the screw – that he had no notion what Sally felt or believed. It seemed incredible that she shouldn't know the truth. But perhaps a girl like Sally was like that – incapable of conceiving evil, or that sort of evil. At least she must be on the brink of knowledge. And Caryl had put her there deliberately; had put her there with the particularly ugly deliberation of the unconscious mind. No doubt Caryl *had* sprained an ankle. But it was, at this moment, the ingenious thing to do. It had enabled her to play what he now understood to be her morbidly compulsive fear-game; to wake Sally with a story as thin as paper. Perhaps – for he felt his new view of Caryl becoming fuller and fuller – perhaps there was a sort of cruelty in it. Perhaps she enjoyed the thought of constraining her daughter desperately to repel what could be to her only a vile suspicion.

'Can I do anything more for your friend?' The girl asked the question carefully as if she were an agent only, involved in this nocturnal huggermugger simply because of an order that had come to her.

'He isn't a friend.' Cranston swiftly spoke the truth where it could be spoken. 'He's a stranger straight out of the sea, and he has a cock-and-bull story about smuggling diamonds.'

'But I'm not sticking to it.' The man from the sea spoke with an air of easy candour. 'I don't smuggle diamonds.'

'Then is it some sort of joke?' Sally turned towards Cranston in the darkness. 'Or is he mad?'

'If he's mad then others are mad too. You didn't hear a racket?'

'Not that firing?' Sally spoke swiftly, so that he remembered with ignoble fear how intelligent she was. 'It didn't sound like the usual stuff out at sea.'

'It wasn't. It was a chap with a gun. And he tried it out on us.'

For a moment she was silent. 'Honour bright?'

It was an old challenge between them, and now he hated it. 'Honour bright,' he answered. 'He ended by losing his gun. But he did some damage first.'

'To you?'

His heart leapt in a sort of dreadful joy at something in her voice. 'Not me.'

'He got my eyes.' The man from the sea had been very still in the darkness, and Cranston knew that he was making it his business to gather all he could of the relationship at play before him. But his speech was almost casual. 'Only, I think, to the extent of bunging them up with sand. I hope I can get rid of it. For I have to get south, you see – and it will have to be done unobtrusively. Is there any water here?'

'I'll fetch water – and an eye-bath and lotion if I can find them.' Sally became brisk and moved at once towards the door. She had her sex's instinct for practical action in any obscure exigency. 'But I shall be at least a quarter of an hour. You can work out your plans together.' She had given an edge to this – but now as she passed Cranston she whispered to him on another note. 'Dick – are you really involved with him?'

'In a limited way, yes.' This time he felt merely awkward. 'But I know absolutely nothing about him.'

'Then I don't see –' She checked herself. 'And it's something that has to be kept from . . . Alex?'

She had made the little pause before her step-father's name by which she commonly seemed to distance him. He knew that for some reason she didn't find Alex Blair easy to take. 'Yes,' he said. 'I think it better had be.'

'Very well.' She was suddenly indifferent. 'There are cigarettes and matches on the table, if you want them. Although I can't think who put them there.'

He was silent. Caryl and he had smoked three or four. It was a small squalid moment as in some low stage-play of adultery.

She turned away. And then suddenly she had turned back again and put out a hand. It touched his arm, his chest, and then without haste withdrew. She was laughing – innocently and genuinely amused. 'Dick – have *you* no clothes on either?'

'Precious few.'

'I'll bring something – a pullover.'

'Alex's?'

'No!' He was startled, bewildered by the sudden passion in her voice. But she laughed again. 'Something of my own. It won't be too bad a fit.'

She was gone. For a moment he saw her as a mere white blur in the last faint moonlight filtering into the garden. But he saw her too in a sharp interior image, dressed for the moors – wholesomely broad at shoulders as well as hips. It was true that she could bring something that would fit well enough.

From behind him in the summer-house the man from the sea spoke composedly. 'So far, so good. For me – and, I hope, for you.'

'I'd have thought your chances were pretty thin.' Cranston spoke more from irritation than from any sense of a secure grasp of the affair. 'You must be some sort of outlaw, I suppose, or you would already be taking steps to contact the police. And a helpless outlaw, too, as long as your eyes are out

490

of action. What you have found, for the moment, is a very insecure refuge, indeed.'

'One must look on the bright side.' The man from the sea was quite invisible, but he appeared to have found somewhere to sit down in the darkness. 'Not that realistic appraisal is not always valuable. Were you ever under fire before?'

'No – except for field-days. And with blanks.'

The man from the sea laughed. 'Then you did uncommonly well. But so, for that matter, did I.'

'Have *you* never been under fire?'

'Decidedly not. You mustn't form, you know, too romantic a picture of me.'

'I don't find you in the least romantic.' Cranston spoke with conviction. 'My guess is that you're some sort of paid spy.'

'It sounds ugly. And yet I suppose all spies get pay. Is it your idea that the chap with the gun was from – what is it called? – M.I.5?'

'I don't know. And I don't know why he went off in that commonplace fashion.'

'Because he wasn't – for him – doing anything very out of the way. He could take no further effective action against us. So he simply passed on to the next thing.'

'Which would be reporting failure? Would he go back to that ship?'

For a moment the man from the sea made no reply. When he spoke again his voice was slightly muffled, and Cranston caught a gleam from his naked shoulders unexpectedly near the floor. He must be sitting on some low bench or stool, with his head buried in his arms, and probably his eyes were hurting him badly. 'The ship? I don't think so. It wouldn't linger. He was simply shoved ashore from the motor-boat before it went back to the ship, and told to do what he could. The people he will have to contact are now in this country.'

'Doesn't that give you time?' Cranston felt for something on which to sit down himself. 'I find it hard to believe that he can whistle up a whole like-minded gang out of the Highlands.'

'It's an encouraging point.' For the first time, the man from the sea let something like weariness tinge his irony. 'But how boring this is. All about me. Let's talk about you – and the girl.'

'Let's do nothing of the sort – and damn your impertinence.'

Cranston took some satisfaction in coming roundly out with this. But the response of the man from the sea disconcerted him. 'I'm sorry. I oughtn't to have approached it – or not in that way. But you've been rather a good show, you know, so far as I'm concerned. You've given me the deuce of a leg up – and for no earthly reason that I can see. So I didn't mean impertinence – only sympathy.'

'I don't want sympathy.'

'No more you do. I talk like an idiot. All long-distance swimmers are probably idiots.' The man from the sea produced his phonetically perfect laugh. 'But I think you might want – well, an objective appraisal. Are you in a mess?'

'You can see that I'm in a mess.'

'Talked to anyone?'

'No.'

'You love the girl?'

There was a silence. 'Yes.' Incredulously, Cranston heard his own voice ring out the word. 'Yes. I do.'

'She turned you down?'

'She turned me down. She had a right to, hadn't she?' He spoke savagely. 'As a matter of fact, she was horrified.'

'My dear lad!' The man from the sea appeared to be soberly unbelieving. 'You can't mean horrified. It doesn't make sense.'

'It had to make sense – to me. There it was. I'd thought – I'd thought it might be all right. And there it was – a ghastly flop. It must have been the last way she was prepared to think of me. And yet it wasn't . . . or I thought not.' Cranston stopped, aware of his own incoherence. 'That gun shook me, I suppose. I'm crazy to tell you this.'

'Did you ever think to make love to a girl before?'

'No – I didn't.'

In the darkness the man from the sea laughed softly, so that Cranston felt his cheeks suddenly burn. 'My dear boy, I won't say of the virgin approach that it's a terrible mistake. But it invites disasters – and it's a matter of luck whether they turn out comic or tragic. You were utterly at sea. You hadn't a clue. And you missed out whole volumes in folio.'

'I don't believe a healthy girl wants volumes in folio. But I expect I was' – Cranston hesitated – 'clumsy enough.'

'That was the whole thing.' The man from the sea spoke with unemphatic conviction. 'Think about her here – about her tone to you – a few minutes ago.'

'I can't – I won't.' It came from Cranston like a cry. 'There can't have been a mistake – a misunderstanding. There mustn't. It would make it worse, far worse, unbearable.'

'About the mother?'

'Yes.' It took Cranston seconds to utter the word, and he did so tone-lessly. 'I turned cynical, vicious, crazy – and I went for her.'

'What utter nonsense.'

It was the man from the sea at his quietest, and it pulled Cranston up. 'What do you mean? Do you think we haven't –? Do you think I'm boasting, telling some filthy lie?'

'I think you're flattering yourself.' The man from the sea was amused. 'About that access, I mean, of vicious, cynical activity. You were thrown off balance and the mother seduced you. It came to no more than that. You're about the age she goes for, I'd say. And if she virtually raped you from her own daughter – well, that was additional fun.' He paused. 'You know all this. You possess an active intelligence which has certainly got you straight about it by this time.'

'Do you think you're being comforting?'

'I certainly hope so.' The man from the sea sounded genuinely surprised. 'It's the first stage with a problem – isn't it? – to get the terms of it clear. And yours is not a very complex problem, you know. Ten minutes has served to see it as it is. Now you work out the solution. I wish my own conundrum were as simple.'

'You talk as if it was all science.'

'Of course it's all science. Anything in which the mind can establish causality is science – and nothing but science. And the solution of your problem is simple – as simple as a right-about turn.'

'I just have to try again – and on some convenient future occasion tell Sally that once upon a time I was an ass?'

'In essence – yes.' The man from the sea was still confident. 'Of course, I'm not discounting emotional complications in what is itself an emotional matter. You must work out how to deal with them. Particularly the magical side.'

'I don't know what you mean.'

'The really primitive response in your situation, I imagine, is a kind of tabu response. You are inclined to imagine an absolute inhibition. The idea of first the mother –'

'For God's sake shut up!' Cranston found that he had been crouched on a wicker chair, and that now he had sprung up and was pacing the summerhouse. A faint grey light was seeping into it, and he could distinguish the few pieces of neglected furniture scattered about. 'Didn't Sally say there were cigarettes?' He fumbled at a table. 'You can say that a feeling like that is magical, primitive, pagan, uncivilized. It's probably unchristian too, for all I know.'

'It's certainly that.' The man from the sea spoke with undisturbed authority. 'Although there other and difficult concepts come in. Repentance, penance, expiation –'

'But that's not how my mind works.'

'Isn't it? It's not always easy to be sure. But I think I know the ideas your mind does feed on. Cheapness, humiliation, disgrace.'

'Nothing of the sort.' Cranston was impatient. He had found the cigarettes and was about to light one. But before he could strike a match, something further burst from him. 'The dishonour!'

The man from the sea had been fumbling for the cigarette packet in his turn. But at this he stopped and was strangely still. 'Dishonour?' he asked unemotionally. 'It's the same as disgrace, isn't it?'

'No.'

The man from the sea laughed – but his laughter had no effect upon an indefinable sense of crisis that had built itself up in the summer-house. 'I should have thought that it was only in rather deeper waters that one learned that.'

'What do you know about it?'

'Didn't I come from them – before your eyes? Let me have the matches, will you?'

Cranston pushed the box across the table. 'It's dishonour when you have to say *never*. Never, never, never.'

'When I was stripping for that swim, I lost my watch. I took it from a pocket, meaning to transfer it to this belt. But I was at the rail, and my hand slipped.' The man from the sea paused. 'It's a habit it has.'

'Your hand?' Cranston was puzzled.

'Never mind. That's another story. My hand slipped, I say – and the watch had vanished in an instant. Honour – dishonour: is that how you see them?'

'Yes. Never, never, never . . . You are going to say one can dive.'

'I am. But – my dear boy – it has to be to the very bottom of the deep . . . My eyes are still smarting like the devil, but I don't see that I need deny myself a cigarette.'

There was a moment's silence in the summer-house, and somewhere in the distance Cranston heard a cock crow. Sally had been longer than she reckoned. He tried to remember the time of the single early-morning train down the branch line. Then, at the spurt of the match, he glanced at his companion. The small intense flame lit up the face of the man from the sea. It was evident that he could see nothing. But his attitude was of one glancing downward. Once already – but less clearly – Cranston had glimpsed him in that pose, and had felt his memory obscurely stir. It stirred again now – and to such an effect that he cried out.

The man from the sea raised his head. His eyes, horribly bloodshot and almost closed, were directed for a moment sightlessly before him. And then he blew out the match. 'Did you speak?' he said.

'I know you.' Cranston took a deep breath. 'You're Day.'

Chapter 5

'Yes – I'm Day.' The man from the sea struck another match and lit his cigarette. 'But we never met before tonight?'

'Photographs. There were no end of photographs when – when it happened. No wonder you know about Alex Blair – and remembered meeting his wife at some grand scientific do.'

'If you recognise me from a photograph, other people will be capable of doing the same thing. It's part of my problem, as you can guess.'

'No doubt.' Cranston had gone to the door of the summer-house and was peering into the garden, the nearer outlines of which were becoming faintly visible. 'As I now know that you're John Day I'd better say that my name is Richard Cranston. But it's not a very equal exchange of information.' He swung round. 'What made you do it?'

'Go – or come back?' The man called John Day got to his feet, and as he did so put both hands across his eyes. 'Curse this stuff! Has something gone wrong, do you think? The girl ought to be back by now.'

'I think she ought. But we can give her a few more minutes before worrying.'

'And go on talking? Now, what was it about? Honour and dishonour, I think – and diving to the very bottom of the deep. That's why I've come back. It's my dive. As for why I went – well, I believe people have written books about it.'

Cranston was silent. The dimensions of what he was involved with were coming home to him. When John Day had taken a holiday in Switzerland, vanished, been glimpsed in Vienna and vanished again, Cranston had still been at school. He remembered hysterical stuff in newspapers. And he remembered his senior physics master, uncommunicative but grim. Two years later there had been a particular sort of explosion in the heart of the Asiatic land-mass. Instruments in North Africa, in California, in New South Wales had recorded it. One man's deciding to differ from his immediate fellows could mean that – could even sway the balance, perhaps, in which hung the fate of nations. And now here was John Day in the Blairs' summer-house. He had just conducted a good-humoured inquisition into the momentous matter of a young man's having developed a morbid sense of guilt in consequence of mucking a love-affair.

Day had found his way across the summer-house and was fingering – like the blind man that he momentarily was – the heap of clothes which Sally had left on a bench. 'Let me be quite plain,' he said, 'that what I called a moment ago my problem is a purely practical one. The larger issues, you see, I have got entirely clear.'

'Was the solution as simple as you say mine is – as simple as a right-about turn? Is that what you're doing – turning?'

'Turning my coat again, I think you mean? I suppose it might be put that way.'

'You have plans?'

'I have a very simple plan.'

'But not so simple that you don't require help?'

'It's possible that I need only a bowl of water – in addition, that is, to what are clearly these admirable clothes. If I can get rid of this sand and reasonably see –' Day broke off – and a moment later uttered in a strange voice a single word. 'Harris!'

'What's that?' Cranston was startled.

'This jacket – or whatever it is. Harris tweed. I suddenly got the smell of it – and smell's a damned queer thing. It's four years since I've had decent – since I've had western clothes in my hands. Clothes are damned queer too, by the way.'

Cranston made no reply. Sally's delay was disturbing, but nevertheless he hoped now that it would last a little longer. If he said nothing Day might fall silent – and then he could think. He desperately needed to. He was aware that some great responsibility had descended upon him, and that he must put himself the right questions and find himself the right answers. When Day – as a mere unknown – had come a fugitive from the sea Cranston had prided himself on finding one right answer at once. In his own private affairs he had guessed very badly – had behaved very badly. He had been becoming aware of it. And the ability suddenly to decide rightly about the fugitive – to acknowledge that he must be given simple human solidarity until he had a chance to declare and explain himself: this ability had brought him its odd comfort for a time. But how was he to act now – suddenly caught up by the necessity not for some merely private decision but for a decision very conceivably involving vast public issues?

His first duty was to remember his years. He saw this at once – and felt a faint flicker of intellectual satisfaction, of intellectual pride, in so seeing it. At least he still had a clear head. There was a sense in which he had the largest confidence in himself, and of this not even his having so mucked things could substantially rob him. But at the same time he knew that here was something which he ought not to be taking on alone. He paused on this. Where did such an acknowledgement lead? Ought he to leave the summer-house, affecting perhaps to search for Sally, and go straight to the house and rouse Alex Blair? And, if he turned this suggestion down, ought he not to be very sure that his reason for doing so had nothing to do with the privately disastrous disclosures that would almost certainly follow?

For a moment it seemed to him that here *was* the obvious course. Blair was the nearest person of standing and of mature judgement. More than this, he was himself an eminent scientist, already knowing something of Day both as a man and as a physicist.

Cranston extinguished his cigarette and walked out to the verandah. Day did nothing to stop him. The sky was faintly luminous and there was a bar of orange in the east. He fancied that he heard peewits crying very far away. He couldn't go to the house. Abruptly he knew this absolutely. But he was unable to find the reason. Only he thought it wasn't funk about Caryl. He turned back into the summer-house and found that there was at least a line of inquiry in his head. 'The police,' he said boldly. 'This must mean the police for you, sooner or later. Why not now?'

'The police? No. They're no part of my plan.'

'I don't understand you. You've come back as the only way of – of recovering your watch. You can't expect a reception by the Lord Mayor of London. And if you really believe that the fellow off the ship will presently be raising a whole hunt against you – well, I'd have thought you might as well get yourself safely locked up sooner rather than later.'

'You'd like me safely locked up?'

'I can't be sure about you. Suppose your eyes clear up with a little bathing, and you are able to get along by yourself. Ought I just to let you disappear? Oughtn't I to be more – more suspicious of you than that? You left this country meaning mischief to it, and it seems very possible that you've come back to it meaning more. If it isn't your intention to contact the authorities, oughtn't I to be very suspicious of your story indeed? If you can be said to have produced a story at all.'

'You'd like to listen to the confessions of a penitent traitor? My Life of Disillusionment behind the Iron Curtain – that sort of thing?'

'Not that. But you mayn't be at all as you represent yourself. For instance, it seems very queer that you should just arrive like this. I don't see how you can have done it. You must have been quite tremendously a marked man – watched and guarded right round the clock. How on earth could you have smuggled yourself on a ship due to skirt the Scottish coast?'

'I couldn't – and I didn't. I wasn't any sort of a stowaway, my dear chap. I was the star turn on board. We were on a little scientific cruise.'

'Scientific?' Cranston reached for another cigarette. 'You mean some sort of devilry?'

'Just that. You can guess the sort of thing.' Day was ironic. 'Call it doing something sinister to the Gulf Stream. Or perhaps the Sargasso Sea.'

'Rubbish.'

'Quite so. Still, the motive of our cruise was simple enough. Forty years ago its equivalent would have been, say, charting the other fellow's mine-fields. Nowadays one noses out other things, and the job requires far higher technical skill. Not that I didn't have the deuce of a time getting the assignment.'

'Because you were any number of cuts above it?'

'Just that. But I persuaded them that I had a valuable and intimate know-ledge of the terrain. So they sent me. And then they let me slip. You are still sceptical?'

'I don't know that I can be – just about that. What I came in on didn't look like a put-up show. But wasn't it pretty feeble of them?'

'Perhaps so. But it was outside their expectations, outside their very comprehensive system of suspicions. An act of sudden individual initiative, proceeding from an entirely private and personal – what shall we call it? – movement of the spirit. It's what sometimes takes people their way, you may say. But they're slow to realize that it can be a two-way traffic.'

'What did your movement of the spirit prompt you to stuff in that belt?' Cranston paused – and thought that he sensed Day stiffen. 'The inner secrets of the Kremlin? Chats on nuclear physics?'

'Money – dollars and francs and pounds sterling.' Day's familiar laugh was at its easiest. 'In quite astonishingly large amounts – which I had the devil of a job getting together. If you care to hit me on the head and bury me in the garden, you can set yourself up on the proceeds handsomely.'

For a moment Cranston said nothing, and the ugly little joke hung in air. 'Money?' he asked presently. 'Do your simple plans need such a lot of it? You'll have free keep in Pentonville or Brixton.' There was a further silence, and he realized that this, too, had been ugly enough. 'I just want to make sense of you,' he said.

'I hadn't much idea, you see, where my break-away might happen. Or who might have to be bribed to do what. I envisaged a great many possibilities. Science, you know, trains one to that sort of thinking ahead.'

'It doesn't seem to have trained you to think sufficiently ahead in the first instance.'

'We can all get things wrong.'

They were back, Cranston felt, where they had started. He went again to the door and listened. Sally's absence was now alarming. He turned round. 'It would be easier, wouldn't it, if you could bribe me?'

'Very much easier.' Day spoke whimsically. 'But of course you are incorruptible – in matters of this sort. And I don't think you are to be blackmailed either – which is a suggestion I rather carelessly made to you. It is awkward about Lady Blair and so on. But it would no longer count with you.'

'It certainly wouldn't. Not now that I know who you are.'

'But what does still count is the fact that we've both mucked it. My chance seems to be to trade on that.' The words came softly to Cranston with the effect of cards dropped deliberately on a table. 'Each of us has let himself down.' Day broke off. 'Surely it's growing light? What's the time?'

'Dawn is certainly coming. But I can't tell you the time. I haven't –'

'You haven't got a watch either. And your word for the condition is the precise one. Dishonour. And, just because you have let yourself down, you won't now let me down – until you're certain that I'm no good. Until you're certain that my deep, deep dive is bogus. Isn't it queer? Isn't it extraordinary that, staggering at random from the sea, I should run straight into a full-blown young romantic idealist?'

'She's coming!' Cranston had moved swiftly to the door. Now he was back again. 'Can't you speak out – straight? What are you going to do? What's this plan you talk about?'

It was perhaps because Sally's footsteps could already be heard on the path that Day replied in the softest voice he had yet used. 'I've told you that my plan is very simple. It's the simplest of all plans.'

'The simplest –?'

'Ssh!'

Chapter 6

The girl was in the doorway. She carried a bowl and a large jug, and there was a basket over her arm. 'It's no good', she said, 'trying to beat the dawn at this time of year.'

Cranston took the jug from her. 'As a matter of fact, you've been rather a long time. It wasn't . . . your mother again?'

'I've no doubt Mother is asleep – ankle and all.' Sally put down the bowl and basket composedly. 'Alex.'

'Alex!' He was startled.

'I thought your friend would at least be dressed.' She turned to Day. 'You're not a doctor – or anything like that? You have no special knowledge of what to do? The water's warm, and with boracic. I'd simply try opening your eyes in it. And I've brought some of the dark stuff – argyrol, isn't it – and a dropper. Will you come over here?'

She was as impersonal as a nurse, and Day submitted to her. Cranston watched from a corner. There was still no more than a pale grey light in the summer-house, but objects and actions could be distinguished. Certainly there could now be no question of getting away under cover of any approximation to darkness.

'Sally,' he said, 'you mean that Sir Alex knows?'

'Knows what, Dick?'

The cool question seemed to him like a flash of lightning on what Sally herself must now know. But he went through with answering steadily. 'About this chap – and what we're up to.'

'I'll empty out this water. And then you can try again. Do you want a towel?' Sally made various dispositions at the table before she turned again to Cranston. 'I'd just got into the house when there was – Alex. He was up and prowling. I can't think why.'

'The shots, perhaps. If he heard them he'd know at once it wasn't aircraft practising.'

'No doubt. It was awkward.'

'I'm frightfully sorry, Sally.'

'Really?' For a second she was rather coldly mocking. 'It was one of those occasions on which one has to risk a great deal of the truth in order not to give away the whole of it.'

There was a little silence. The words, quietly uttered in the fresh young voice, seemed to hang oddly in the air. It was Day who spoke. 'Did you feel that you had so much truth at your disposal?'

She made no reply to this. It was as if she was determined to have only the most businesslike relations with him. Instead she turned again to Cranston. 'I told him that it was you – here in the summer-house, Dick. I told him that you had awakened me by throwing gravel at my window, and that it was a question of some poaching exploit gone wrong. You and a friend had been guddling Lord Urquhart's trout – and had lost nearly all your clothes and come by a great many scratches. Of course I'm sorry to have represented you in rather a juvenile light. You're the last person I'd really think of as – getting into mischief. But I had to consider what would amuse Alex – amuse him without really interesting him. I gather you don't want him out here.'

'I don't think we do.'

'If he does come out it will be in the most good-natured way in the world – a matter of what he calls jollying you up.' She spoke with her flicker of fastidious disdain. 'But you can bank on his laziness, no doubt.'

Day raised his head from the big bowl. 'Is Sir Alex Blair so very lazy?'

'If he weren't wealthy and lazy he'd be in the very top flight of British scientists today. And he knows it, I imagine.' Her voice was indifferent. 'Has all this helped?'

'It has made me much more comfortable. But I still can't really see.'

'Hadn't we better get a doctor?'

Day shook his head. 'My guess is that time, and only time, will clear it up. A doctor would do no more than produce reassuring talk and a roll of bandages.'

'I haven't any talk. But I can produce dark glasses. I slipped some into the basket. Also a flask of brandy, a packet of biscuits, and a block of chocolate. And, Dick, here's the pullover. Canary, I'm afraid – but it won't go too badly with your tan. I shall go in now – and leave you to evolve whatever further adventure you have a mind to.'

She was gone – before Cranston could speak. But he strode after her and caught her on the verandah. 'Sally –' He broke off, confused and finding himself without words.

They were facing each other. He had a sense that – inexplicably – she was trembling all over. But for the moment they stood confronted, her gaze at least was perfectly steady. 'I know how you feel,' she said. 'At least . . . I know how you feel.'

She had turned, run down the little flight of steps, and was hurrying through the dimness of the garden. He found himself repeating the banal words as if they had come to him charged with impenetrable mystery.

'A capable girl.' Day was opening the brandy flask.

'Yes.'

'Knows just what she is about.'

For a moment Cranston was silent. These last words – he strangely and intuitively knew – were not true. Perhaps Day was deceived. But Day was a liar. He had to remember that. All the stuff about diamonds: the fellow would have persisted in it if there had been a chance of sustaining that particular deception . . . 'Shall we get back to business?' Cranston asked.

'Brandy, biscuits, and chocolate are decidedly part of our business at present. Would you pour out? It's a thing the blind find tricky.' Day paused only for a moment. 'Do you play rugger?'

'Yes.' Cranston poured – and drank.

'Three-quarter?'

'Yes. But I don't see –'

'That we're getting back to business? But we are, you know. You had fumbled a pass. How unforgivably, you were just coming to realize. And you remember the next stage? An absolute determination to take the ball cleanly next time. Well – I'm the ball. I think that was about as far as we had got.'

'And I think you've laboured all that long enough. I'm prepared to admit that it's not precisely nonsense. But taking the ball cleanly mayn't at all mean anything that you greatly fancy.' Cranston reached for a biscuit and paused to munch it. 'Your story may be full of psychological interest. Your wanderings – physical and spiritual – among the nations may open up all sorts of fascinating vistas upon the dilemma of modern man. Everything of that sort. High-class thriller stuff, in which recurrent chapters are devoted to an anatomy of the soul.' The small swig of brandy, Cranston realized, had gone straight to his head. 'But the fact remains that you are almost certainly even more dangerous than you are interesting. Taking *you* cleanly ought perhaps to mean putting you inside as fast as the job can be done . . . I've halved the chocolate.'

'Thank you – and of course you're right. There's a presumption, I mean, that I'm far too dangerous not to jump on. But suppose it's otherwise. Suppose I can convince you that – well, that all that's over and done with. Suppose you wanted to help me – to go on helping me, I ought to say. Could you do it?'

'Could I help you?' Cranston was disconcerted at being thus abruptly placed once more in the position of the challenged party.

'Just that. For there's not much point in my telling you anything more – opening any of those fascinating vistas you're so neatly ironic about – if in fact your neat undergraduate wit is altogether in excess of your practical capacities. I'll admit you cut a pretty good figure, my dear young man, in the matter of the fellow with the gun. But are you resourceful? And are you your own master at present from day to day? Could you get a blinded man from here to London – perhaps against desperate opposition? There's more to a good wing-three-quarter, you'll agree, than just taking the ball cleanly. He has to carry it over the line.'

'I think you have the most frightful cheek.' Reduced to this rather juvenile sentiment, Cranston picked up another square of chocolate. Brandy, he had decided, was an unsuitable sort of refreshment at dawn.

'Alex Blair, I take it, is the grand person hereabouts – the laird, and all that. We're now in the grounds of the big house.'

'It's a castle, as a matter of fact – Dinwiddie Castle. And I'm not sure that "laird" is quite grand enough for our host. Not that he wouldn't be perfectly pleased with it.'

'And you? It's plain that you are on terms of intimacy – varying degrees of intimacy, shall we say? – with the grand folk. But who are you? And where do you come from?'

'I'm the doctor's son – and from three miles away. But my parents are very respectable.' No doubt because of the brandy, Cranston was unable to refrain from further sarcasm. 'Our family connexions are, if anything, superior to the Blairs'. So if you're wondering if I qualify for your –'

'And you can come and go as you please during your holidays – your vacation? You can go home this morning and simply announce that you will be away for a week?'

Cranston flushed. 'Of course I can.'

'Borrowing a car?'

'I've got a car.'

'But this is capital.' Day took another biscuit. 'You are decidedly worth converting.'

'To those plans?'

'Precisely.'

'The plans that you say are so simple?'

'My dear young man – yes, indeed. My plans *are* very simple. I am going to die.'

For a moment the small, bleak statement held the air unchallenged. Then, from somewhere far down the garden, a dog barked and a man's voice was heard calling. Other dogs joined in. The man's voice rose again – cheerful, commanding, but of no effect amid the clamour of terriers.

'It's Sir Alex.' Cranston had no doubts. 'He makes a thorough nuisance of himself at times, I've been told – fooling around long before breakfast with the Cairns.'

'He'll come up here?'

'Very probably he will, now that he's in the garden . . . What do you mean?'

'Just what I say – that quite soon I shall be dead. It's a great simplification of things . . . But can't we get away?'

'There's nothing behind this summer-house except a high wall and then the cliff. And if we go down the garden we shall simply walk into him. But need you worry? It must be a simplification in the matter of new acquaintances too. If you are going to be dead, I mean, virtually before you need return Sir Alex's call.'

Day laughed – but low and cautiously. 'I see you don't believe me – yet.'

'How do you know I don't believe you?'

'You wouldn't make just that joke. Your feelings, you know, are at present superior to your morals.'

'Will he recognize you?'

'What's the light like? I get the impression of clear daylight.'

'It's pretty well that.'

'Then I suppose he will.'

They were now whispering. The voice in the garden was raised in song, and the Cairns were responding with a more frenzied yapping. Cranston moved to the door of the summer-house. 'I'm sure Sally did her best,' he said. 'But she over-estimated his laziness and under-estimated his curiosity.'

'Not, with most scientists, an easy thing to do.' Day, Cranston saw, had got to his feet and was contriving to peer painfully about the table. 'Didn't she say something about dark glasses? Ah – here they are.'

The singing was quite close, and the terriers could be heard scampering. Sir Alex Blair's voice broke off in the middle of a stave and then raised itself again in robust speech. No doubt it was what Sally had called his jollying manner. 'Dick, my boy, come out and declare yourself! Don't forget that I'm a magistrate, sir. Come out, I say, or I'll send the hounds in.'

Day slipped on the glasses. 'The question', he murmured, 'was of your resourcefulness. Say, the quickness of your wit.'

Cranston turned and walked out to the verandah. It was outrageous that he should be thus challenged. He moved to the top of the steps, and as he did so ran a hand through his hair. The gesture told him at once that he was on a stage. It went with an engaging grin. 'Hullo, Sir Alex,' he called. 'Did Sally peach?'

'She had no choice, poor wretch. I caught her red-handed.' Blair had at least come to a halt. Clipped and brushed and polished, florid and well-dieted, dressed in a faded kilt and carrying the shepherd's crook he commonly affected when at Dinwiddie, he was glancing up at Cranston, facetiously severe. 'And you too, you young scoundrel – what have you to say for yourself?'

'Nothing at all, Sir Alex. As usual – nothing at all.'

'And so I'd suppose. Still – deeds sometimes speak louder than words – eh? What have you brought me for breakfast, my boy? What have you brought the corrupt old capon-justice of Dinwiddie?'

Cranston grinned – and for good measure again put on the turn with his hair. 'I'm sorry to say, sir, we didn't get a single fish. They were on top of us far too quickly.'

'Not a single one of Urquhart's trout?' This time Sir Alex's severity appeared genuine. 'I wouldn't have thought it of you, Dick – I wouldn't indeed. And what's this about the other fellow having to cut and run without his clothes? Guddling for grilse in the deep pools, eh?'

'It was pretty bad, sir – a thorough rout of the anti-Urquhart forces. The less said about it the better.'

'Very well, very well – I'll leave you both to your shame. If you recover face in time, join us at breakfast.' Turning away, Sir Alex fell to whistling up his dogs. Then he turned back. 'But – just in case you don't – I'll come up and be introduced to the chap now. Only civil, eh?'

'Steady on, sir.' Cranston discreetly lowered his voice. 'Aren't you taking something for granted?'

'What's that, Dick? What d'you mean?'

'Well, sir, about its being . . . a chap.'

Sir Alex stared. 'But Sally said —'

'I'm sure Sally would say the right thing, sir.'

'Well, I'm damned!' Sir Alex lowered his voice. 'One of those madcap McGilvrays – eh, Dick?'

'Tales out of school, sir.'

'Quite right, quite right. You may rely on me, my dear fellow.' Sir Alex dropped his voice to a robust whisper. 'And left in her pelt . . .? You young dog!' He burst into a loud guffaw, checked himself, and turned away with a quick wave. 'Come over and see us soon, my boy. Sally likes it.'

Cranston watched his retreat down the garden. Once more he had been obliged to choose. And he had chosen instinctively. He knew that he could have taken no other course. He knew too that it had been, this time, a real burning of his boats. Sir Alex represented the established order of things. He was, as he had humorously remarked, a magistrate – and much else besides. And Cranston had stood on his verandah and lied to him. He had lied to him by way of concealing and protecting John Day.

He turned back into the summer-house. It was still shadowy there, and for a moment he distinguished little after the clear morning light. And then he saw that Day had sat down again at the table. He was oddly posed, with his hands stretched out before him, palm upwards. Cranston took a couple of steps towards him and stopped. He found himself staring at the palm of Day's right hand. And Day knew what he was doing. 'Look closer,' he said – and after a pause: 'You've never seen anything like that?'

'No – I haven't.' Cranston felt an uncertain sensation in his stomach. 'Is it . . . important? I'm not a – a pathologist.'

Day closed his fist. 'I think I mentioned – didn't I? – a bad habit of mine?'

'About your hand slipping?'

'Yes. This is something that began happening when my hand slipped – not very long ago. It was then, you know, that I decided to come . . . home.'

Chapter 7

'It's how you know you're going to –?' Cranston hesitated.

'Yes. It's as certain as the tokens that used to tell people about the plague. Interesting, don't you think? Your father would be fascinated. And lucky, too – if he could get hold of me. A unique case, you know. Nothing like me in these islands today. Of course, in Japan –' Day, who had followed Cranston back to the verandah, broke off to stretch himself lazily in the morning warmth that already seemed to be breaking over the garden like a wave. It was a gesture, the young man realized with a shiver, of simple luxury in the sense of being alive. But Day's tone continued ironical. 'Would you be inclined', he asked, 'to see in it the operation of what they used to call poetic justice?'

'No.' Cranston put out a hand and guided his companion to a seat on the steps. Then he sat down beside him. They might have been two friends on some idle holiday, lucky in the weather, and up at sunrise with no very definite plan in their heads. 'It doesn't prompt me to any fancy thoughts at all. Or even' – he was awkward – 'to say anything much.'

'Then tell me about the view.'

'The view? Well, there's a screen of pine trees beyond the garden, and one just gets a glimpse of the battlements and turrets of the castle.'

'It's a real castle?'

'Basically. But it's been cobbled up a great deal, and a lot of Abbotsford Gothic added on. The main turret is quite bogus. Incidentally, there's a flag being broken from it now. Blair is a great stickler for that sort of thing. He inherited unexpectedly, you know, when he was a professor of physics in some dim university.'

'Do you notice the scents?' For a moment Day had been inattentive. 'They're changing. They're no longer those of the night. I suppose it's the sort of thing one becomes sensitive to when really blind.' He paused. 'Any other sights?'

'The flag is just fluttering. That means there's a light breeze blowing offshore. And dead above it – I mean what looks dead above it – there's a kestrel hovering . . . Is it really – just that?'

'Just –?'

Cranston glanced almost furtively at Day. He was still stripped – experiment with Sir Alex Blair's clothes was something he appeared willing to defer – and his spare body showed itself in clear daylight as much an athlete's as it had done when glinting beneath the moon.

'Is it really true that – that you have come home like a sick animal –?'

'To die in my own hole? Perhaps it is – a little. But chiefly I want to see my wife.' Day's voice had gone suddenly expressionless. 'And sons.'

There was a long silence. It might all be lies. And if it was true, then its background was an experience upon which Cranston could have no proper comment at all. Yet it seemed wrong not to say something – and something as directly relevant as he could reach to. 'Are you sure', he asked, 'that they want to see you?'

'I don't suppose they do. But I want to apologize. It was rough on them, you know . . . my doing what I did.'

'Thoughtless?' Cranston asked the question with what he felt as a sudden irrepressible enormous irony of his own.

'Yes.'

Day's voice was again utterly without expression. It occurred to Cranston to wonder whether his experiences – or perhaps the first working inward of his mortal malady – had unhinged his mind. 'You'll feel better', he asked, 'when forgiven, and assured that by-gones are by-gones?'

'Nothing like that. Don't you remember? *Never*. Never, never, never.'

'But you have had to come, all the same?'

Day answered obliquely. 'It was difficult to do.'

'The escaping?'

'Yes – and leaving my work. Particularly with only a few more months chance of it.'

Cranston had an impulse to jump up and run for the castle – the impulse of a small child venturesomely bathing, who suddenly knows that the next breaker may go over his head. 'You don't make things any easier,' he managed to say. 'You don't make it at all clear where you now stand.'

'Not on any particularly rational ground.' Day had put on the dark glasses, and as he turned his head towards Cranston he had the appearance of scrutinizing him seriously. 'To come back – through difficulties, as I've said – and tell her that I had been wrong: well, it has seemed the only thing to do.'

'Wrong, as they say, ideologically? You've lost faith in –?'

'Not particularly.' Day's voice was indifferent. 'But then I don't know that, particularly, I ever had it.'

'Then why –?'

'I wanted recognition, facilities, a different sort of sense of power.' Day's voice was suddenly vibrant. 'To run my own show. To be clean at the top.'

'And by going over to them you got there?'

'No.' With what Cranston obscurely sensed to be an immense effort of will, Day spoke flatly again. 'I got higher. But not right up.'

'Surely you might have guessed as much at the start?'

'Yes, indeed.' Day was now blandly acquiescent, persuasive. 'I was rationalizing, no doubt. Indeed, eventually I proved it to myself. I got at a deeper motive – by a sort of auto-analysis. Chiefly, it all had to do with my father.'

'Your father?'

'He died when I was twelve – but he remained my great problem, all the same. Acute father-eclipse. That, basically, was what sent me to Russia.'

'I suppose that's Freud or somebody? I had a notion your late friends don't much go in for that sort of mythology.'

Day shook his head. 'No more they do. I had to get it all out of books. And that was partly what made working out the whole thing so difficult. But I got it clear in the end.'

'I see.' Cranston uttered the words mechanically. For it seemed to him that this was flabby talk, not easily to be reconciled either with that desperate swim or with what he continued to sense of concentrated purpose in the man before him. 'It all comes to you as a private matter?'

'Absolutely. That is where the only real treacheries lie – in the sphere of personal relations. That is where dishonour comes. Don't you know it?'

Cranston was silent – somewhat in the fashion that he was silent at home when his father or mother made what he thought of as a completely 'period' remark. There was nothing that could usefully be said. But he might ask one further probing question. 'You feel that your slip-up was in the shame and so-forth you brought on your wife and children? It's a social response to your action that has made you regret it, and not the emergence of a conviction that it was inherently wrong in itself?'

'How charming is divine philosophy.' Day was suddenly mocking. 'And catching, too. Didn't your tutor think up questions like that?'

Cranston stood up. 'You can't escape – a person with your history can't escape – having a public self. And it's the only self the world at large is going to bother about. You're the man who has carried enormously valuable information, I suppose, to a potential enemy. And now you've turned up out of the sea, disposed to conversation about your wife and children. It may be true that nothing now seems important to you except getting square with them – except making some sort of symbolic gesture to them and then packing up. But it can be done in gaol. I believe they arrange these things decently enough nowadays. And why shouldn't you accept that? If what you say about – about your health is true, then it's no more than an extra penny for you to pay . . . And there's another thing –'

'I hope there are several.' Day smiled, and the smile seemed less artificial than his laughter had done. 'Do you know, you make me a little wonder if I'm off my head? And you intoxicate me, too.'

'Intoxicate you?' Cranston was disconcerted.

'You see, you're the first person for a very long time to whom I've talked anything but physics or political claptrap. Imagine, my dear chap, spending your life in a lab – certainly a splendid lab – and leaving it only for an eternal Rotarian lunch or Primrose League tea-party. Think how delightful, after that, a nice lad from Cambridge must be.' Day paused. 'But I interrupted you.'

'I say there's another thing. What you carried in one direction, you are now carrying back – and with interest, I don't doubt – in the other. Willy-nilly you are doing that, since the stuff must all be there in your head. I believe everything you say now about the chap who came at us with that gun. He's rousing every fellow-spy in the country. And that ship is sending out coded signals like billyho. And here you are, stranded and helpless in Scotland, with no resources but a nice lad from Cambridge – if you can catch him.' Cranston allowed himself to pause briefly on this shaft. 'Hours are slipping by – and you're getting nowhere. But those people certainly are. It seems to me that if you want that meeting with your wife – and I don't pretend to comment on it or on what it means to you – your only real chance of it is to send me to find a copper. Or Blair. He'll call out a territorial regiment, or raise the clan if you've a fancy for it. That's where security lies – not in a crazy dash for London.'

'*Your* security?'

Cranston felt himself flush. 'Yes, damn it – *my* security. And my country's, if that's not something too unimportant to mention.'

'It's a reasonable point of view at least in a layman. But one of the troubles, you know, of my line of business is the melodramatic light in which the public is inclined to regard it. Still, I wish I could fall in with your plan. Unfortunately it wouldn't be at all the same thing. My wife coming and taking a peep at me – no doubt after having my arrival and arrest tactfully broken to her by a smooth old person from the Home Office? No, no – it's just not what I see.'

'Isn't what you see itself a bit of melodrama – and not perhaps very considerate of the other people involved? The essence of it is walking in – just freely walking in – on your family?'

Day nodded. 'Yes. Is it very queer? It may be – as I've said – that I'm a bit off my head. On the other hand, it might seem less queer – mightn't it – to somebody –'

'Less immature and inexperienced and so forth than myself?' Cranston took this up quite seriously. 'I suppose so. And yet it isn't just a blank to me. You are telling me about a sort of *idée fixe*. And I can see a person in your situation genuinely having it. There isn't *really* any return to that domestic past of yours. It's a matter of never-never-never, all right. And so there is only this gesture. It doesn't at all make nonsense to me. But whether it's genuine in *you* remains rather an open question.' Cranston rose. 'I'll think about it as I walk home.'

'That's what you're going to do?'

'Yes. You'll be all right here – and conversely, I don't see that you can take matters much into your own hands at present. And I'll be back.'

'With your mind made up?' Day, too, got to his feet. 'Very well. But perhaps you'll give me a hand into some of those clothes before you go.'

'Certainly.' Cranston moved back into the summer-house. 'Not that you're likely to have visitors.'

'You don't think Blair will come back?'

Cranston shook his head. 'I'm pretty sure he will keep tactfully away – and tactfully mum. He really does believe that I've been fooling around with some –' Cranston broke off, confused.

'With some madcap girl from among your neighbours – whereas it was really with his wife?' Day might have been offering this in a spirit of mild humour. 'And he isn't even wondering whether he's been told a lie.'

It came as an enormous relief to be alone, and halfway down the garden Cranston stopped and took a deep breath. There was a large tumbling shrub of damask roses beside him; he put his head right into it and took a deep breath of that too. It was like the action of a man escaped from a charnel-house, and it told him how vivid his sense of John Day's condition had been. The man was really carrying his death about with him: there was no question – Cranston seemed to know it instinctively – of a lie there. And yet the horror of it did not mean that Day repelled him. When he had helped the blinded man to dress he had felt no trace of bodily revulsion. The simple physical sympathy that had established itself when Day had come lurching out of the sea and they had instantly gone into hiding together still existed. It was in itself something altogether unremarkable, and yet Cranston knew that in his present strange situation it counted for a great deal. It helped on – that was it – the insidious and surely wholly irrational sense of identification with Day which a rather sketchy correspondence in their situations had given birth to. Cranston frowned and walked on. The question was whether he would let Day down.

Or was it? If he allowed himself to put it that way, could there be more than one answer? Must he not acknowledge that he was indeed romantic – or, in a more modern and less flattering idiom, that he was some sort of compulsion-neurotic in the making? Probably he wasn't fit for the sort of experience that Caryl Blair had brought him – and certainly wasn't fit for such experience with a married woman. All that he got out of it – or all that he got out of it except on the most short-term basis – was a pathologically devious sense of guilt. And just when that had been about to break the surface of his consciousness Day had walked up out of the sea. So what had happened was perfectly clear. He had instantly identified himself with one whose occasions were patently unlawful. And then had come a revelation exquisitely calculated to tune up to its very maximum of driving-power this bizarre mechanism of the mind. From the point of view of society Day's guilt had revealed itself as enormous; there was enough of it to satisfy the more inordinate demand for self-punishment. That – Cranston told himself as he halted before the door in the garden wall – that was the way the machine ticked; that was what gave him his large vague sense of implication with the man from the sea. And probably it was a quirk of the mind that grew on one, became obsessive, ended in a total divorce from sober reality. His only chance was to cut out of it at once. He could, at a pinch, tell the whole story to his father. And yet were things so desperate? Could any mind so clever as his own – so swiftly lucid as this admirable piece of self-analysis showed it to be – stand in any substantial danger?

Asking himself this, Cranston opened the door in the high wall and took a step outside. As he did so – as he cast no more than an absent eye on a scene which should have been wholly untenanted – the whole airy fabric of his painful yet intellectually satisfactory ruminations vanished in an instant. In their place stood objective reality – in the person of the man with the trilby hat.

Cranston stepped backwards and softly closed the door. He was almost certain that he had not been seen. The man was standing within a few paces, but his head had been half turned away.

There were two stout bolts on the door. They looked terribly rusty, but it was possible that if cautiously handled they could be fairly silently pushed home. He had no reason to suppose that the man with the trilby hat had managed to arm himself again. But the possibility had to be faced. Had he picked up in an out-house as much as a pruning-knife or a sickle he would be formidable. Or even a hammer. A hammer or a sickle . . . Cranston checked himself and got to work on the first bolt. It slid into place with scarcely a creak. The second was more difficult. As he eased it forward he felt sweat upon his forehead. It astonished him that this fresh encounter with the enemy should so key him up. He supposed it was once more a matter of delayed reaction. He hadn't liked that gun. Perhaps he wasn't made for gun-play any more than for –

A faint sound behind him made him whirl round, taut and trembling. It was Sally. She had approached to within a few feet of him and was looking at him in cool astonishment. He suddenly felt a fool. But he kept a sufficient sense of the reality of the situation to raise a finger swiftly to his lips. Then he turned back to the bolt. When satisfied that it was secure he straightened up, beckoned, and walked off down the garden. Sally followed. From the instant of his making his gesture she had been very quiet. He walked far down the garden, but to a point from which he could command a view of most of the wall he had just left. Then he stopped. 'It's the chap who had the gun,' he said. 'He's hanging around.'

'This is something you've got mixed up with quite by chance?'

'Yes.'

'And that you haven't really got the hang of?'

'I've got a good deal of it now.' Cranston looked at Sally cautiously. She must have returned to the garden for the purpose of talking to him again, but now she had an air of waiting for him to take some initiative. 'It's very queer.'

'You seem to have thrown Alex off the scent. But isn't it a little hard on whichever of the McGilvray girls he –?'

'That was simply a conclusion he jumped at. I didn't mean to put into his head any particular – particular girl.'

'I'm sure you are thoroughly thoughtful of female reputations.'

She had forced herself, he felt, to come out with this hard stroke. And now she had gone pale and her eyes were on the ground. He felt desperate. 'Look,' he said, 'it's no good pretending. I know it's all been too rotten –'

'All?' she seemed strangely startled – even frightened. And then she was cold again. 'Don't let's start on heaven knows what. Isn't this man of yours enough to be going on with? And he seems to be on our hands as well as yours. What does the other man want to do? Kill him? Carry him off?' Sally paused. 'And who or what is he, anyway? Do you know *that* yet?'

'He's John Day.'

Cranston had spoken on impulse, but vehemently. And it seemed to be the intensity of his words, not their content, that surprised her. 'Day?' She shook her head. 'Somebody well known?'

He saw that it meant nothing to her. And he guessed that it was only the skin of her mind that she was contriving to give to this whole aspect of what the ghastly night had produced. But his understanding of her went no farther than this. He had for a moment the sense of some veiled element in their disastrous relationship. 'Don't you remember?' he asked. 'A scientist who bolted to –'

'Dick?' She had interrupted round-eyed. 'He hasn't come here because of . . . Alex?'

'I'm sure he hasn't. It's pure coincidence that he's now hiding in the summer-house of a fellow-scientist. And he hasn't come back to Britain because of that sort of thing at all. He's a dying man. He had an accident with what was, I suppose, some sort of violently radio-active material. He wants to see his wife.' Cranston paused. 'Or so he says.'

She was puzzled. 'But surely a man who has gone off like that can't simply –?'

'Of course not. He's virtually an outlaw. And the people he's deserted are after him too. That's the explanation of the chap outside. Do you see now that it all makes a sort of crazy sense?'

'I suppose I do.'

'Could you guard Day – just for an hour?'

Sally looked at him in astonishment. 'I don't know what you mean. I'm not a daft McGilvray.'

'I'd only ask somebody I could trust.' Cranston hesitated. It occurred to him that she might answer 'I might do it for somebody *I* could trust.' But she was silent, and he saw that her pallor had given way to a faint flush. 'You see,' he said, 'I am in a way mixed up with him quite a lot. It's because of something I feel.' He stopped again, wondering if she could conceivably guess what he was talking about. But that was too tall an order, since he didn't really understand it himself. 'You see,' he said again, 'I've made up my mind to something. I did it the instant I caught another glimpse of that chap outside. I'm going to take Day to London.'

'Is that right? Oughtn't you to speak to Alex? He's amazingly . . . enlightened and tolerant.'

He shook his head – and wondered at the same time why her words sounded so very little like a testimonial. 'I couldn't do that and then ask Sir Alex to back my plan. He has responsibilities that I don't have. If I miscalculate and am disgraced it doesn't much matter. But you – you people must be kept clear.'

For the first time Sally gave a small exclamation as of pain. But her voice was hard again. 'No scandal at Dinwiddie?'

Cranston made no direct reply. She was entitled to come out with these cracks. And yet there was something queer about them. 'Shall I explain about you guarding him?' he asked. 'I want to go and get the car – and at the same time cook up some story for my people at home. I can't be certain of doing it in less than an hour – perhaps longer. And meantime there's this chap outside. I suspect that he's merely guessing that Day has gone to earth somewhere round Dinwiddie. But it's conceivable that he successfully sleuthed after us in the night. Anyway, he's almost certainly awaiting instructions and reinforcements, and is simply keeping an eye on things meanwhile.'

'He's very strategically placed.' Sally's tone showed that she had been thinking quickly. 'The garden wall runs right to the cliff, and in the other direction he can watch the castle road all the time.'

Cranston nodded. 'That's true. Of course I can get away by going down the cliff on the other side. Arriving back with the car is a different matter. I'll have to think it out. But my point at the moment is that he just might try to climb in. He's lost his gun, but he may have something ugly in the way of a knife. And as Day seems to be really almost blinded for the time being, he couldn't put up much of a show. So could you get a gun, and plant yourself where you could keep an eye on the summer-house?'

'I can always get a gun. But the garden's an odd place to be found taking it to.'

'Perhaps a carrion crow, or something like that?'

'No doubt I can think of a suitable lie.' She looked at her watch. 'But it probably won't be necessary, and if we hurry we can put the whole thing through before breakfast. But must you go down the cliff – and the awkward way?'

Sally had spoken with sudden unconcealed anxiety, and this was so over-whelming to him that he had to make an effort to answer calmly. 'I think it's my best plan. I doubt if that fellow saw me a few minutes ago, and his suspicions about Dinwiddie may at present be quite vague. But if he did see me leaving the place he would know at once that he was really hot on the scent.'

'Very well. I'll get the gun – my own gun – now, and go straight up the garden with it. You needn't waste time after that. Get over the wall and down the cliff as soon as you see me. And I'll stick on the job until I know that you're back on it.'

He watched her go. She seemed to draw all his vigilance and all his thought after her, so that for the moment the whole violent and actual adventure into which he had been precipitated appeared shadowy and insubstantial when set beside the mere unfulfilled intention which must be the only memorial of his relation with her. And if he had now a little involved her in the doubtful drama of John Day, it was only partly because the momentary logic of the affair had appeared to require it. He was unwilling to let Sally go, and rather than do so he had brought her into the affair as if she was a boy ready for an escapade. It could hardly be maintained that he had assigned her a post of danger, since she could summon both her step-father and his men-servants readily enough at need. But he wondered whether he ought to have done it, all the same . . .

There she was – so quickly that it almost seemed as if she must have had the gun ready hidden. She gave him a wave and they moved swiftly on converging paths through the garden, so that when he climbed the wall where it gave directly on the cliff she was no more than twenty yards away. He waved to her in turn and allowed himself to drop.

He was on an outcrop of rock. He had remembered the precise spot where the thing could be done. The wall here was in places part of the outer ward of a former castle, and there were points at which it rose sheer from the cliff. This rendered impossible any walking round it on the outer side, nor could a view of it here possibly be commanded by the lurking man with the trilby hat. It was a climb – at least it was decidedly not a walk – down to sea-level, and the state of the tide meant that he could then do a quick scramble along the rocks until he gained the beach. And there he would recover his bicycle and be home before breakfast was on the table.

If he didn't break his neck . . . It was trickier than he remembered – particularly at the start – and dropping the first thirty feet required absolute concentration. When he had accomplished this he paused and looked upwards. Sally was perched on the wall almost directly above him. She was attending to her job, for he knew it to be a spot from which there was a clear view of the summer-house. But for the moment she was looking down at him. And he could distinguish – it was as if his senses were tuned to some state of hyperaesthesia by his task – the expression on her intent pale face. There was only one way of describing it. Despair.

Despair . . . It was by quite a long way, he now realized, that this descent was trickier than he had supposed. And perhaps Sally realized it. Perhaps she was convinced that his chance of avoiding disaster in the next few minutes was very small. And perhaps she –

Cranston made a tremendous effort to thrust out of his mind all speculation on how Sally might, after all, care. The surest way to end up pulped and broken on the rock below was to let his mind wander an inch from his business. And perhaps that was the way that a woman – any woman – would look if she saw a man – any man – in what she judged to be mortal peril.

He gave a reassuring wave, examined the state of his gym-shoes and their laces carefully, and started on the next bit of the drop. When he reached the bottom and looked up again it was no longer possible to see Sally. But her image was still vivid to him. He could see that expression still. Almost, he felt that it might haunt him.

Chapter 8

It was the memory of Sally's pallor, perhaps, that made Cranston find the appearance of the girl hiker so startling. The girl's face was red and shining, and high on her rucksack there was sewn some species of red flag. The effect, from a little distance, was alarmingly Janus-like; approached from front or rear, she would equally present an appearance as of the blazing sun. The sun indeed was suggested by everything about her. Her hair and her khaki shorts and shirt were alike bleached by it, and her limbs – which her garments did not much obscure – were burned brown beneath a glint of fine golden hairs. If one put one's nose to her skin and took a good sniff – Cranston supposed – one would know at last just what the sun smells of.

But Cranston had no thought of this experiment. He had come up with her only a couple of hundred yards from his own garden gate, and he would have skimmed past her rapidly enough if she had not turned and given him a hail. She waved a map as she did so, and it was clear that she was seeking directions. Cranston jammed on his brakes and dismounted. It was something he was unable to do very graciously, for he was both in a great hurry and increasingly burdened by a sense of hopeless stupidities past and problematical actions to come. Nevertheless, as he asked whether he could help he summoned up some sort of smile. The girl had the legs of her shorts rolled up to the thigh, like the awful little trollops who scour the countryside on bicycles at week-ends. Moreover, her accent was of neither of the kinds that Cranston had been brought up to regard as socially acceptable. He had remarked this – and was attempting to square it with the fact that her shoes were sensible and her fingernails unpainted – when the girl spread out her map in a businesslike fashion over his handlebars. 'Will you just show me,' she said, 'about where I am?'

'The village straight ahead of you is Easter Dinwiddie.' Cranston put a finger on the map. 'And you're just here.'

'Thanks a lot.' The girl looked up at the sky and then frankly at Cranston, so that he had a sensation of seeing his own features reflected on her shining cheeks. 'I suppose', she said, 'that it will be another regular cow?'

'I beg your pardon?' He was bewildered – and anxious to push on.

'The day – really hot.'

The girl had dropped her rucksack at her feet. He saw that the red flag had a Union Jack and the Southern Cross on it. 'I'd have thought', he said, 'that you wouldn't mind heat. You're rather my idea of a salamander.'

For a moment she looked puzzled, and he was sorry to have said something unintelligible and therefore unmannerly. 'I mean –'

'But of course. We're thrice colder than salamanders in my part of the world. Fires of Spain and the line mean nothing to us. But we don't expect to be grilled when we come to Scotland.'

'I suppose not.' Cranston felt with his left foot for the pedal of his bike. She had squashed him and he could get on. But if salamanders were not mysterious to her, and she could bandy Donne or whoever it was, why had she looked puzzled? Suddenly he realized that it was because she had noticed his pullover and recognized it as not designed for his sex. This annoyed him. 'It's certainly going to be hot,' he said, and slung himself over his bike. 'But you've made an early start.'

'I was glad to. I spent the night in rather a hole. Bed and breakfast. But I didn't stop for the second after sampling the first.'

'The bed was a regular cow?'

She looked at him quickly, and it was possible to conceive that she had flushed. Then she picked up the rucksack. 'You can't', she asked briefly, 'tell me where a Dr Cranston lives?'

'Just down there, on the left. You can see the drive.' And with obscure misgiving he added: 'My name is Richard Cranston. I come from there.'

'Richard!' The young woman's effulgence seemed to increase – as if, so far, she had after all been shining through a light morning mist. 'I'm George,' she said, and held out her hand.

'How do you do.' He was just in time, he decided, by alertly exerting considerable muscular pressure of his own, to avoid having his fingers badly crushed. 'We've been wondering when you would turn up.'

Again she gave him her quick look, and when she spoke it was with a shade of defensiveness or distrust. 'I only wrote to your mother once – and quite vaguely.'

'Yes – but even the off-chance of a visitor is something we do a lot of talking about here.' Cranston, who did recall his mother recently murmuring about some itinerant Australian cousin, spoke with decent heartiness. He was sure that an antipodean sun-goddess called George was not at all his style, and the girl's arrival at just this moment was going to complicate his getting briskly away from home. Still, he couldn't do other than welcome her. 'Come along,' he said. 'We're both in time for breakfast.'

'Beaut!' George slung her rucksack – which was enormous – lightly on her shoulder. Then, seeing him put out a hand for it, she resigned it without comment. 'Do you often go for an early morning spin?'

'No.'

He had spoken abruptly, and for a few moments they walked in silence. It occurred to him with a sort of surprise that he still had a natural instinct for telling the truth. The last few weeks, indeed, had given him a sharp schooling in lies, but he was subject to constant dangerous relapse. Perhaps he should have assured George that he went out at crack of dawn quite frequently. He glanced at her cautiously. She seemed to be exactly his own six feet, but to possess an even longer stride. They were covering the ground briskly enough – but she had put her hands in the pockets of her shorts and had the appearance of gently strolling. 'I don't really know about your family,' she said. 'But have you got a sister?'

'No, just one brother – and he's in Germany.'

'I see. Do you often arrive home early in the morning in your own pants and somebody else's jersey?'

'No – I don't.' He was astounded at this casual frankness – the more so because it couldn't be called, in its manner, either flippant or offensive. 'I was doing some nocturnal bathing; and various things happened; and I borrowed this when it turned a bit chilly.' He increased his own pace. Sooner or later the lies would have to begin. He might be better at them after a solid breakfast. 'Is it so very obviously', he asked, 'a woman's jersey?'

'Haven't you a nose?' George was amused.

'A nose? Oh – I see.' It was true that the scent of some expensive stuff clung to Sally's pullover and that he had failed to be aware of it. 'Here we are.' They had walked up the short drive and the uncompromising square house was before them. 'Do you find Scottish architecture a bit grim?'

'It does rather hit you – on the Border. But up here it either isn't quite so bleak or you get used to it. Do I walk straight in?'

He nodded. The front door was open and they walked into the square tiled hall. 'At least I can smell coffee,' he said. 'It's something slightly exotic, insisted upon by my father. But everything you see around you is authentic to the region: chocolate-coloured paint, ground glass in as many of the windows as possible, stags' heads, steel engravings depicting striking incidents in sacred history. Do you like it?'

'I like it very much.'

George was emphatic, and he realized, without much caring, that she misinterpreted and disliked his tone. Moreover, she seemed suddenly slightly awkward. Perhaps she was afraid of melting something or of setting the whole place on fire. But conceivably the awkwardness was really his own. Leaving things at the castle as he had done, he felt that every minute had to be counted. But he could scarcely now simply scribble a note for his mother, grab a couple of rolls, get out the car, and vanish. If only –

He became aware that George was expecting something, and he took an inspired guess at it. Her mind would work in terms of a tradition of unquestioning hospitality. 'Look,' he said, 'nobody seems to be about yet. But you'll want to go to your room. I'll show you.'

She nodded and he led the way upstairs. Fortunately there always was a room in decent order. He would shove George into it. And then – it came to that – he would rapidly plan his escape.

His mother was in the kitchen, so he knew there would be scrambled eggs. On this simple dish Mrs Cranston held strict views, and she seldom allowed it to be prepared by other hands. He had laid a fourth place at the table before she entered the breakfast-room. He kissed her. 'The Australian cousin has come,' he said. 'I was out early and met her. She had slept goodness knows where. I put her in the spare bedroom. She'll be down any minute.'

'Then you must have yours boiled.' Taking her son's news very much in her stride, Mrs Cranston turned back to the kitchen. 'Elspeth, boil two eggs for Master Richard. And make a little more toast and add one cupful of boiling water to the coffee.' She returned to her son. 'I felt Georgiana might just turn up. I shall be so pleased to meet her.'

'She's not Georgiana. She's George.'

'How very amusing! And is she charming?'

'Charming?' It was one of his mother's period tricks to take it for granted that one must develop a sort of moonstruck interest in any fresh girl on the horizon. 'She's quite terrible – enormous and roasted and toasted and without a pure vowel in the –'

'You should be ashamed of yourself. She's your father's cousin and she's in my house.' Mrs Cranston could be briskly formidable.

'Yes, I know. And I'm sorry. I daresay she's a nice child. Only she does make you want to grab a fire-extinguisher. She burns with a hard gem-like flame.'

'I very much wish that you had gone to St Andrews, Richard, where you would have enjoyed the society of gentlemen, and not to that dreadful –'

'Ssh! I think she's coming down. And you mustn't be shocked.'

'Shocked? If you don't shock me nothing will. What's wrong with her?'

'George is dressed like a boy scout. Or rather she protrudes from garments of that –'

'Be quiet.'

There was a step on the staircase and George came in. Mrs Cranston, before advancing, allowed herself a withering glance at her son. George was in a frock, miraculously uncreased. It was true that she remained more like Aurora than a mortal girl, and that the comparatively small areas of her person now exposed put to shame the toast which was presently carried into the room. But this was far from offending Cranston's mother – and it plainly delighted his father when he appeared. Indeed, it was presently plain to Cranston that George was going to be a great success. Mrs Cranston gave her a rapid sketch of the families in the neighbourhood, with particular emphasis on the young men. Dr Cranston inquired her age, height, and weight and was accurately answered. George herself, without a glance at Cranston, remarked that she liked the simple Scottish ways. At home, Mum would let none of the boys sit down at table without a collar and tie.

Through all this only his real anxiety and a sense of the ticking clock preserved Cranston from merely childish gloom. The fact that the girl was a pure menace – and that she probably by now much disliked him as well – by no means made it any easier to drop his uncivil bombshell into the proceedings. But presently he did so, nevertheless. He had made unexpected arrangements on the previous night, he declared, and he was motoring south immediately after breakfast.

But the announcement fell flat. The fact came to him in what he knew to be a thoroughly foolish mingling of relief and resentment. If his mother thought his conduct outrageously rude, she dissimulated it in the distraction of calling for a fresh jar of marmalade. And presently she was sketching out picnics and tennis-parties designed, it seemed, to spread over a long vista of coming weeks. Gavin McGilvray would make an excellent partner for Georgiana; he was even taller than Richard and his backhand had become far better controlled. Dr Cranston inquired about golf. It was clear that, as an entertainer, he saw no difficulty in stepping into his son's place. He had his busy times – he had been out on an emergency and had had to call a county ambulance that very morning – but then he had his easy times too . . . Cranston was breathing freely, and had already bolted a second cup of coffee preparatory to rising and saying good-bye, when George abruptly succeeded in achieving what he had so notably failed at. She announced, amid general consternation, that as Richard was motoring south she would take the opportunity of travelling with him. This had been only a dash to Scotland, and she had heard of friends whom she must presently meet in London. But, if Mrs Cranston allowed her, she would come back for a proper visit. And on this she was so specific, and prepared so unhesitatingly to name dates, that dismay was transformed into approval within five minutes. Mrs Cranston saw great advantages in the proposal. Later in the summer, Richard would, of course, be at home to take her about, and numerous parties could be arranged well in advance.

Cranston listened in absolute dismay. The girl was outrageous. His sense of this – although in fact it rather lacked conviction – emboldened him to try something like blank refusal. 'I'm frightfully sorry,' he said, 'but, you see –'

'You're not going alone? You haven't room?'

'Of course I'm going alone.' He stopped. It was his first blank lie, and for a second he looked at her uncertainly. She was deplorable, without a doubt, but she didn't remotely mean any offence or aggression. The proposal had come into her head as absolutely licensed and, so to speak, graced by their vague cousinly relation – or perhaps just by some antipodean canon of normal human feeling. Nor, he realized, were his parents remotely within hail of thinking any evil of a plan which would send him off into the blue with a virtually unknown young woman. Their period sentiments were always shot with a large innocence. It was a fact of which he had become remorsefully if conveniently aware during the last few sultry weeks. He turned to George. 'I meant that I'm afraid you wouldn't – you won't – be very comfortable in my terrible old car.'

It was a remark which could only, in the circumstances, be received with mirth and jollity. George disappeared to get her rucksack and Mrs Cranston to cut sandwiches. Cranston was left to the company of his father and the contemplation of an entirely new predicament to which he had committed himself. The real mischief, he saw, was the element of danger. Here at his mother's breakfast-table it had become hard to believe in. But it was there, all the same. A couple of miles away Sally was still doing duty with a gun, John Day was sitting helpless in that summer-house, and the man with the trilby hat lurked outside the castle – a figure of ruthless violence with incalculable forces already perhaps mustering behind him. All Cranston could now do was to set off with George and then in some way get rid of her. For instance, he could insult her. There were decidedly things for which he was sure that she wouldn't stand. He could –

Cranston's mind worked doubtfully forward in a series of displeasing images. He found that they were so displeasing as to be in fact impracticable. It struck him that he had better tell George the truth – or enough of it to convince her that he must go off on his own. But he could do this only after they had set out. To enter into the matter at all was now impossible.

His father was composedly reading *The Scotsman*. Something that he had recently let fall echoed oddly in Cranston's head. 'Daddy,' he asked, 'what was that you said about an ambulance?'

'Yes – but too late. Dead, poor old soul.' Dr Cranston, absorbed in the London letter, answered concisely.

'It's gone back?'

Dr Cranston glanced up briefly. 'Not yet, I think. I arranged for the fellow to get some breakfast at the Dinwiddie Arms. An old friend of yours – before your expatriate period.' Dr Cranston was mildly caustic. 'Be civil to this girl, by the way – even if she isn't a baronet's step-daughter and educated at Girton.'

'Yes, of course.' Cranston gave what he knew was a juvenile scowl.

'The Australian Cranstons have the high distinction, my dear boy, of sharing a great-grandfather with yourself. And he was a younger son of –'

'Bother the Australian Cranstons . . . You don't mean Sandy Morrison?'

'Certainly I mean Sandy Morrison. He left his uncle a year ago and has been driving the ambulance for some time.'

'I think I'll go across and look him up.'

'To be sure.' Dr Cranston, because pleased, spoke as if in marked absence of mind. His feelings about great-grandfathers he found very easily reconcilable with others of a democratic cast, and both his sons had started at the village school. 'Have you got enough money? I don't know what are the conventions when a young man gives a hitch to a hiking girl cousin.' He chuckled. 'But I imagine you might without offence offer to pay for a meal. Not that the Australian Cranstons aren't extremely prosperous, I understand.'

'Is that so?' Cranston in his turn was absent-minded. 'I think I've got enough cash.' He rose. 'I'll just say good-bye to Elspeth.'

'Say good-bye to Elspeth?' This time Dr Cranston was genuinely astonished – indeed he eyed his son rather narrowly as he left the room. Then he returned to his newspaper. Curiosity however pricked him – he was after all a man of science – and presently he found himself going on tip-toe to the door. He was edified by a cautious whispering from a back passage.

'Master Richard – for shame! I'll do no such thing.'

'Come on, Elspeth – there's no harm in it. Just for this once.'

'No harm, indeed! It would be clean daft – and no' decent, foreby.'

'If you don't, I'll tickle you till you scream – and leave you to explain to Mummy.'

'It's outrageous, Master Richard. If you ask me, you just weren't enough skelpt as a bairn.'

'I wasn't skelpt at all. Quick now – I'm in an awful hurry.'

There was a sharp giggle – at the sound of which Dr Cranston withdrew to his seat. When five minutes later his son returned to the room he looked at him somewhat doubtfully over the top of *The Scotsman*. 'Really,

Richard – have you been taking it into your head to woo your mother's mature Abigail for busses?'

'I don't know what you mean.' Cranston grinned. 'Or, alternatively, you're a shocking old eavesdropper.'

'And so I am. Your disease has a learned name, my boy.'

'Rubbish.'

'Gerontophilia, or sexual passion directed towards the aged. Think better of it, sir. There are maidens in Scotland more lovely by far, who would gladly be –'

'All right, Daddy – all right.' Cranston heartily wished himself in a better position to relish this liberal paternal fooling. 'But I wasn't, as a matter of fact. Kissing her, I mean.' He hesitated. 'I was borrowing something.'

Dr Cranston was alarmed. 'Not a ten-shilling note? You used not to be above it. But you've just said –'

'No – not that. Something else. Will you promise me something?'

'Perhaps.'

'Don't make a joke of it with Elspeth. Don't ask her when I'm gone.'

For the first time, Dr Cranston's brow clouded. There was something in this that lay outside the family conventions, and he was obscurely disturbed. 'Richard,' he asked, 'is there anything in the wind? Have you been making a fool of yourself? Or are you up to something dangerous?'

'Both.' Looking at his father, Cranston said this quite suddenly. 'I have made a fool of myself. And I am up to something that's possibly dangerous – by way of getting clear.'

'By way of getting clear of – a mess?' Dr Cranston put *The Scotsman* down on the tablecloth. 'You don't mean you're bolting from the consequences of some idiocy?'

'No. But I'm perhaps doing something a bit queer. It's by way of getting square with myself.' He felt himself blush furiously. 'A kind of debt of honour.'

'And that's why you were so awkward about this girl? Shall I head her off – insist that she stop a bit?'

'No. I've got that fixed.'

'I think I hear her coming downstairs with your mother now.' Dr Cranston reached again for his paper. He was contriving a gallant appearance, his son saw, of having found their conversation satisfactory. 'And I shall hold no converse with the outraged Abigail, my boy.'

'Thank you.'

'Drop me a line – if you feel prompted to, that is.'

'Yes, Daddy.'

'You can send it to the Infirmary, you know, if it's something with which you don't want to worry your mother.'

'Yes – I see.'

Dr Cranston had risen and walked to the window. 'Nice day for the run,' he said. 'Even in an awful car like yours.'

Chapter 9

Cranston pulled up in the village. The ambulance was still outside the Din-widdie Arms. 'I want to have a word with a schoolfellow,' he explained. 'Do you mind waiting?'

Without raising her eyes from the map she was studying George shook her head. She was still in her frock – a deep yellow frock, so that she had the appearance of a portentously enormous sunflower. 'I'll be seeing you,' she said.

'He drives that ambulance.'

'I see.' For a second she took it as unremarkable. Then she looked surprised. 'Didn't you go to Eton or somewhere?'

'I went there.' He pointed across the village street.

'Where it says "Infants"?' George was impressed.

He nodded. 'Yes – and so did Sandy Morrison. I'm going to introduce him to you. We're all three going to do something together.' He glanced cautiously at George. 'At least I hope so.'

'You didn't say anything about this at home.'

'No more I did, George.' He used her name for the first time. 'But when I said I was going south alone I was fibbing.'

She was disconcerted. 'But, Richard, I asked if I was butting in.'

'You're not. You're going to help. You see the castle on the map? I'm going to smuggle somebody out of it, and make hell-for-leather for London.'

'Do you mean that I'm going to help at an elopement?' George spoke coldly and the effect struck him as so ludicrous that he had to smile. 'I thought the Gretna Green business happened the other way on.'

'It's a man, George – not a girl.' He paused. 'It's John Day.'

'The scientist who disappeared? And he's now in Dinwiddie Castle?'

Cranston's estimate of the possible usefulness of George shot up. And that was how he had come to regard her. She was a great Amazonian creature who had blundered in, and she must take her chance. He would shove her out of the affair if real peril threatened. Short of that, she was expendable. After all, he hadn't scrupled to involve Sally – whom he had already wronged in ways that Sally might or might not know. So why not exploit this monster of a cousin? But he had been taking it for granted that the monster was shock-headed. Now he knew that he was wrong. Her way of taking the thing was in some indefinable way indicative of intelligence. 'Yes,' he said. 'The scientist. He walked out of the sea and into my arms in the small hours of this morning.'

'You mean that you were waiting for him? Is this Cold War stuff – with you active in it . . . on one side or another?'

'It was pure chance. And the Cold War aspect of John Day is over. He's a dying man. And he wants to see his wife.'

'You're making it your business that he should?'

'Just that. He happens to be temporarily blinded, which makes things difficult. Will you help?'

'No.' She looked at him seriously. 'Not unless you convince me that you have to.'

'I don't know if I can do that.' Cranston paused – and as he did so it came to him like a revelation that he could tell this Amazonian intruder the whole thing. Or almost the whole thing. It might be brutal. He had the sense to know that a girl may not be the less maidenly for calling herself George and striding about the countryside in inconsiderable pants. He had not the slightest disposition to believe that Britomart herself had been more virginal. So if he told her she might hate it. But at least there was nothing between them that could be damaged by revelation. 'Listen,' he said. 'It's simple, really. Day feels he acted unforgivably towards his wife, and that he has some sort of gesture – and no more than a gesture – to offer her. Well, he tumbled into my arms last night only because I was out fooling with a married woman. And it wasn't just fooling. There is something – I needn't go into it – that makes it vile. Mine's another unforgivable thing. And *my* gesture is to risk something, seeing this chap through.'

George had gone very still, and for a moment he thought she was going to say nothing at all. And when she did speak it was with painful constraint. 'I can't say I didn't ask for it – your story. Which doesn't mean that you should have told it, all the same.'

'I'm sorry.'

'Or am I being a fool? Probably I am . . . And what do you mean by risking something?'

'Being killed, for one thing. There was shooting last night. The chaps to whom he's given the slip are out for his blood – and that of anybody holding in with him.'

'Very understandably, I'd say.'

'Yes. But there's another risk, less easy to express. If Day had murdered somebody, or was a wicked blackmailer, or a defaulting financier or something of that sort, I'd only be risking – and inviting you to risk – being uncomfortably packed off to gaol. But behind Day – and willynilly all around him still – the issues are tremendous. He may have vitally important information which some Cabinet Minister, or old colleague, or efficient policeman could show him he ought to come out with. I may keep him away from these people only to see him successfully hunted down and killed by his former employers. And there are other possibilities – I'm risking – well, having to admit that I've been an irresponsible ass in rather a big way.'

'It's an awkward situation, Richard – I agree.'

'It's a regular cow, George.'

She faintly smiled. 'We'd better get on. What do I do?'

'Could you impersonate a Scottish housemaid?'

'Better, I suppose, than I could impersonate a Scottish countess. But I couldn't manage the accent.'

'That won't matter. You'll only be talking to a foreigner – and then no more than a few words.'

'Don't housemaids in this part of the world dress in a particular way?'

'I've got the proper clothes in the back. I borrowed them from our maid at home. Only I'm afraid they'll be on the small side.'

'But I'm used to giving rather skimpy effects?' George was amused at the discomfort this thrust occasioned him. 'Do I have to do things with your Sandy Morrison?'

Cranston shook his head, and climbed out of the car. 'No. But if I can't nail him to do his own turn we'll have to think again. Sit tight. I'm going in to try.'

'Hullo, Sandy.'

'Good morning, Mr Cranston.'

This was unpromising, and Cranston took cautious stock of his erstwhile fellow scholar. With one hand Sandy was frugally rotating a crust in the last of the bacon fat on his plate, while with the other he drained a large mug of tea. They had dressed him decorously in some approximation to uniform for the purpose of driving the ambulance – but he was discernibly Sandy Morrison still. He was freckled and snub-nosed and tousle-haired, with a dour pious expression and a glint of dangerous mischief in his eye. Cranston contrived to look at him insolently. 'Is that the way they've taught you to talk, you silly loon?'

Sandy set down his mug. 'It isn't often that we have the pleasure of seeing you in the north, sir.'

Cranston advanced and towered above him. 'I could take you by the lug', he said, 'and haul you behind the kirk, and hammer you till you were roaring like a two-headed calf, Sandy Morrison. And that would learn you good morning and pleasure of seeing you in the north.'

Sandy got to his feet. 'And could you that?'

'That I could – as I did the first day that ever I had sight of your ill features – Sandy Snotnose.'

'Then come awa' – Dickie-Big-Doup.' Sandy was breathing wrathfully.

Cranston sat down. 'Sandy,' he whispered, 'are you for a splore?'

'The devil take you, Dick.' Sandy sat down too. His expression was now less pious than sanctimonious, but the glint in his eye was correspondingly wilder. 'Can't you see, man, that they've turned me respectable? The ambulance is probation. If I pass I'm to have the hearse.' He paused and dropped his voice. 'Is it salmon?'

'Nothing of the kind. It's just to drive your ambulance up to the castle and through the gates. And to bide there a while not much noticing things. And then to come away again.'

Sandy looked apprehensive. 'Is it something to dae wi' a quean?'

'It is not. I'm not one that goes after women.'

'It's no' to dae wi' her leddyship there?'

'No.' Cranston had a moment of panic. His madness – his late madness – must have become gossip already. 'I want to smuggle a man out of the place, Sandy – and without some that may be watching knowing it.'

'I'm to be back at the Infirmary in the forenoon.'

'And so you shall be.' Cranston rose. 'I've got my car – and somebody in it who's helping me. I'll drive to the head of the glen and park in the quarry. Do you follow in five minutes, Sandy. After that, the whole thing won't take half an hour.'

'It's clean skite, Dick Cranston, and I canna thole such daftness.' Sandy rose resignedly. 'When I drive in, what am I to tell the creature Patullo at the lodge?'

'You're to tell him it's an emergency, and then drive on past the first turn in the drive. Then you stop, and I get out and fetch the man I'm speaking of. He's in the old garden now. And then we drive away and go back to the quarry.'

'And Patullo when he lets me out again?'

'You're to say it was all a mistake, and that it's not Dinwiddie you should be at, but Dindervie.'

'And what o' Sir Alex? Suppose he's up and ploutering, and syne finds an ambulance in his drive. Won't he be dumbfounded?'

'You must scratch your head, Sandy, like a regular daftie, and have nothing sensible to say of yourself. He'll do no more than turn you out, and make a great joke of your gormless wandering . . . But now listen. Later today, or perhaps tomorrow or the next day, strangers may come checking up on you, asking what took the ambulance to Dinwiddie. You'll say it was an emergency call for the cook there, and that the poor soul is now in the Infirmary having her appendix out. You're to say that, and nothing more or other, to any stranger or foreign creature that asks. Because somebody else is going to be telling the same story.'

'It seems there's a muckle o' falsehood being required o' me for auld acquaintance sake, Dick Cranston.' And Sandy shook his head gloomily. 'We maun hope your foreign creatures don't do their speiring on the Sabbath.'

Sally's vigil had lasted rather longer than he had intended. But at least he had turned the general awkwardness of the morning to positive account. Or he would have done so if this plan worked. To get Day away from the castle unobserved so that the man with the trilby hat would still be left guessing, would be an unexpected gain. And now the success or failure of his stratagem was imminent. The ambulance had swung out of the glen and the castle was straight ahead. Cranston glanced across at George. 'You understand your instructions?'

She nodded – and then frowned at what must have been an incautious grin. 'I'm a tremendous figure of fun?' she asked.

He allowed the grin cheerfully to grow. 'Do you remember whether Phoebus Apollo had a sister?'

'No – I don't.'

'A *big* sister? Well, if she existed, and was banished from Calydon to Caledonia, and took service in a manse, succeeding to attire which the minister's wife had judged suitable and adequate for some merely mortal handmaiden –'

'Shut up!' He believed she was really angry. 'I don't mind the cap, or even this idiotic starched apron. But these black woollen stockings I pretty well can't stand.'

'They scratch? You must just thole them, as Sandy there would say, for ten minutes more.' Cranston peered out. 'And now, George, get ready. We'll be stopping between the gatehouses while old Patullo opens up. That means that for a minute we'll be quite cut off from any possibility of close observation. So when you nip out and stroll down the road, you'll appear to have come out from the castle. You've got the letter?'

'Here.'

'The pillar-box is at the foot of the hill. The castle folk don't really use it, but the chap won't know that – just as he won't know that Melbourne and not that manse framed your accents.'

'You think he'll really come?'

'It's a pretty good bet . . . Watch the gates as you walk back, and try not to reach them until they're opening again. Ten to one the chap will have strolled away a bit after pumping you, and you'll be able to slip back in here quite undetected. If Patullo sees, he may think it a bit queer, but he's a stupid old boy and will have a dim notion you're a nurse.'

'We're slowing down. Is this it?'

'Yes.' Cranston put a hand on the door of the ambulance and pushed it open. '*Now!*' he said.

She was gone. He closed the door. There was a murmur of voices – Sandy blathering and Patullo havering, he thought – and then the ambulance moved forward again. Presently it turned a corner and stopped. He thrust the door wide open and jumped out. Sandy was looking round at him apprehensively. 'Dick,' he said, 'what if that dreich auld Patullo telephones up tae the castle and doon comes the laird? They'll never gie me the hearse if –'

'Turn round, Sandy. And dinna fash. I'll be back with my man in five minutes.'

Cranston turned and ran. The old inner ward was the awkward stretch, because parts of the modern building commanded it. After that he had the cover of the ruined shell-keep until he had gained the garden. What would he do if he bumped into Sir Alex – or even into Caryl, limping about with her martyred ankle? But he was all right for the moment – safe in the garden and making full tilt for the summer-house. He glimpsed Sally – she was sitting precisely where he had left her – and saw her wave. 'Day,' he called, 'are you ready? We'll be away in no time.'

'I'm glad to hear it. I've been wondering.' Day's voice was conversational and unreproachful. 'I still see damned little. But I'd no longer run straight into a tree.'

'Then, come along. But better take my hand to make sure. I've arranged a private departure for the south.'

'Splendid.'

The return through the garden was less rapid, but without disaster. Sandy had turned the ambulance and Cranston thrust Day into it. 'Right!' he called. 'But don't forget the girl.'

'The girl?' Day was instantly questioning. 'The step-daughter?'

'No, no – not Sally. Somebody else I've had to bring in to help. I'll tell you later. Keep quiet.' The ambulance had stopped. He could hear Patullo grumbling. He was a surly old brute. But this held one advantage: to any stranger's questioning he would be unlikely to offer any response at all.

They were through the gates. He could hear Patullo banging them to. The ambulance was crawling. He opened the door. George tumbled in. 'Can I take them off?' she asked.

Cranston laughed aloud. 'Elspeth's stockings?' He felt an extraordinary exhilaration in the sense that Dinwiddie was behind them. 'This minute, if you like. And the whole outfit, as soon as we get back to the quarry.' He took a deep breath. 'May I introduce John Day? Day, this is my cousin Georgiana Cranston from Australia.' He turned to her. 'Did it happen?'

'The encounter? You're telling me. But it wasn't a Slavonic gentleman with a trilby hat. It was an American lady with field-glasses and a camera.'

'Oh!' Cranston was disconcerted. 'Perhaps there was nothing in it. Perhaps it was just chance.'

'I don't think so.' George had sat down on a species of stretcher and was composedly rolling off the offending stockings. 'In a casual way, she was much too much on the spot. Was this romantic pile Dinwiddie Castle – and did I work there? There wasn't much in that. But she wanted to know about the ambulance. So I told her your story about our poor cook. I said that the letter I was posting was to poor cook's married daughter in Glasgow telling her that her mother had been taken poorly. Was taken poorly right?'

'Not bad.'

'I didn't forget to call her madam. And then she asked if we had a lot of visitors, and if any had just arrived. So I said no, I was sure nobody had. And then I turned shy and came away.'

George, who had delivered all this with some complacency, glanced at her now bare feet and then tucked them away beneath the stretcher. Cranston turned to Day. 'What do you think?'

'That they could muster one or two agents pretty quickly . . . and any number quite soon. My guess is that it wasn't just an idle tourist.'

'I'm sure it wasn't.' George, although she was studying Day with attention, spoke crisply. 'I left her and walked back up the road. But just before I turned into the gatehouse I took a look round. She had climbed a bank and was scanning a high stone wall – is it the garden wall? – towards the cliff. And then she put up a hand and waved. It wasn't – well, one tourist's wave to another who has gone astray. In fact, it wasn't a wave at all. It was a signal.'

There was a moment's silence in the swaying ambulance. Sandy Morrison was driving fast. George, Cranston thought, had no particular flair for the dramatic. Nevertheless, her last words had touched an ominous note. And it was Day who spoke. 'Could you say what sort of signal?'

'It was a slow horizontal movement with one arm. I'd say she was giving a negative report.'

'And so far, so good.' Cranston nodded confidently. 'They're left quite at sea about what has happened in the last seven or eight hours. All the same, we mustn't waste time. It looks as if, even in that quarry, we mightn't escape observation for long . . . And here we are.' The ambulance had stopped. Cranston braced himself. 'Listen, George. You've been wonderful. And now Day and I will hop out, and you can change into your own things.'

'No, you don't.'

He was confused. 'What do you mean?'

'You don't bundle Mr Day into your car and make off quietly while I'm turning into your exasperating cousin again. If you don't promise me to wait, I come as I am.'

'George, you've been involved quite enough in this. Probably we're now going to show those people a clean pair of heels. But we can't be sure. And it just isn't right that you should be –'

'But you've got to get me out of this, Richard. Think of that woman. She'd recognize me again in a flash – ghastly stockings or no ghastly stockings. And where should I be, supposing she and her friends came upon me defencelessly tramping through these wilds? I've earned your protection, Richard Cranston, and I claim it.'

George, it seemed, could manage drama after all. In a way, she was just being too clever for him. At the same time, there was a positive truth in the proposition with which she had trapped him. He ought to have thought of it. It was a sober fact that he had involved this girl not only in an episode of danger but in a continuing danger – whether they parted or kept together.

'All right,' he said. 'I promise.'

'Then out you get, both of you. And I think I'll get into my walking things again, rather than that frock. If you don't mind, that is to say.'

'I don't care tuppence.' Aware that this was rather a boorish reply, Cranston made the more haste to throw open the door of the ambulance. The action revealed Sandy Morrison, scratching his tousled head and gazing round the deserted quarry in slow consternation. 'Sandy,' he called out, 'what's taken you?'

'It's no' onything that's tak'n me, ye great gaup. It's some loon that's tak'n your auld rattletrap.'

Cranston leapt to the ground. A single glance told him that Sandy spoke the truth. His car was gone.

Chapter 10

'You're sure it's the same place?' Day spoke from the interior of the ambulance. He had not been prevented by Sandy Morrison's inelegant vocabulary from tumbling instantly to what had happened.

'Of course it's the same place – damn you!' Hearing himself swear, Cranston knew that he was rattled. His plan had been clever – but it looked as if somebody else had been cleverer still. And there was this girl. She was a tiresome irruption, certainly, from her uncouth wilderness. But she had played up very decently. And now he had allowed himself to land her in a trap. A single quick look round this lonely quarry had left him with no illusions. It was not the sort of spot in which professional car-thieves find it profitable to lurk. His car had vanished as a move – probably a final and decisive move – in the melodrama in which this accursed John Day had involved him.

'In that case we know where we are.' Day's tone had all its irritating calm.

'And what the hell does it matter to you?' Cranston rounded on him stupidly. 'You're going to die – aren't you? But we don't all share your blasted simple plan. Do you think I want to see this girl riddled with bullets – or Sandy here, or myself?'

'I'm sure you don't. And that being so, perhaps we should attempt to drive on in this ambulance. It's what they call a forlorn hope.'

'We can try.' Recovering himself, Cranston swung round quickly. 'Sandy, climb in – and drive for all you're worth. I'll explain later. But it's life or death, I promise you.'

'But, man, I've got to be back in the forenoon!' Sandy raised a protesting wail. 'Gin I jine in your daft ploy ony mair, d'ye think I'll ever hae that hearse?'

'You'll have a hearse, all right – if we don't get out of this.' It was Day who spoke, and again impassively. 'But first, they'll have to collect what's left of you with a shovel.'

'And what sort of a daft speak is that, ye plook-faced –'

A sharp report from the edge of the quarry made Sandy break off. It was followed by a quick hiss of escaping air. Cranston turned round in time to see one of the rear wheels settle flat on its rim. By a single neat shot the ambulance had been virtually immobilized.

*

So that was that. Cranston took a quick survey of the terrain and acknowl-edged – what he already knew – that it could not be worse. Behind them, in an unbroken semicircle, was the face of the quarry. In front was the unfrequented road leading to the glen and to the moors beyond. On the other side of the road a bare brae rose gently to a sky-line perhaps a couple of hundred yards away. The enemy was presumably looking down from somewhere at the top of the quarry. Even if no more than a single person lurked there, it was a position admirably chosen. There was no conceivable line of flight that offered the slightest hope of a successful get-away . . . He found that George was standing beside him. 'Get back,' he said. 'Get back at once.'

'Nonsense. I was brought up on this.' Very deliberately, she took a dozen paces into the open. And he saw suddenly that she was an extraordinary sight. His joke about Apollo's big sister had been only too near the mark; she was a divinity disguised as divinities must be disguised in opera – with grotesque inadequacy. In Elspeth's clothes she had the appearance of some resplendent symbol of earth – say a great sheaf of corn – unconvincingly masquerading as a scare-crow. That whole business at the castle had been too clever by half. Or rather it had been too light-hearted – the sort of thing one contrives in a rag, and not in a desperate battle for survival. He watched her with compunction as she strolled back to him.

'I mean, of course, in my reading. Bush-rangers. Here's a coach or a waggon, and there' – she pointed upwards to the lip of the quarry – 'is Ned Kelly . . . Sandy Morrison, did you ever hear of Ned Kelly?'

Cranston realized that the incredible girl was acting with deliberation and in the interest of Sandy's morale. Something of the sort was needed, for this was plainly his baptism of fire and he had been a little taken aback by it. Now he grinned slowly, although his eye was apprehensively on the quarry. 'I've seen something like,' he said, 'at the picture-hoose in Dindervie. Ye mind the way they end episodes in the serials? A fine skirry-whirry we're landit in.'

'Will they do . . . absolutely anything?' She had turned to Cranston. 'Is this it?'

He nodded. 'Yes,' he said quietly. 'I'm terribly sorry – and it seems incredible. But they're – well, entirely serious.'

'Then I propose to get into other clothes.' George swung herself back into the ambulance. 'And you needn't turn out our purblind friend. I don't mind him. But I do mind going to my last account dressed like something in Sir James Barrie.'

'Day – come out!' Cranston had realized what he must do. 'We're beaten.'

'So soon?' Day came to the rear of the ambulance but made no move to emerge. George was wasting no time; Cranston could see her scrambling out of her dress in the semi-darkness beyond. 'Right at the start, in fact?' Day was almost mocking. 'Is that what you call resource?'

'Don't be a fool, man. They've caught us, and the circumstances leave only one thing to do. Will you do it?'

'I think I know what you mean.' Day paused and appeared to be listening carefully. 'Doesn't it strike you as odd that they seem in no hurry with their next move? My guess is that it's just as it was last night. There's only one man. He's taken your car, and he's got us, I suppose, neatly immobilized. There's no cover to get away behind?'

'Not a scrap.'

'On the other hand, he may be immobilized too.'

Cranston shook his head. 'I don't see it. Again, it's just like last night. All he need do is come over and blow our brains out.'

'He can't be certain that by this time we haven't got a gun – or several guns – ourselves.' Day was patiently expository, like a teacher before a dull class. 'He may be reckoning that he can do no more than just pin us here until some of his associates turn up. Actually, something else may turn up instead – and entirely to our advantage. It's unlikely, but one never knows. So I don't at all see that we need throw up the sponge. Courage, my dear young man, courage.'

'My guess is that they've mustered quite a force by now.' Cranston kept his temper with difficulty. 'And if they simply open up on us here there'll be a massacre – including this girl. I think you'd better consider whether it isn't up to you –'

'To go quietly?' Day asked the question reasonably. 'To walk straight towards the cliff or quarry or whatever it is and let them finish me? You think they'd then let the rest of the party off?'

'I want you to come with me – you need a guiding hand, after all – and talk to them, whoever they are.'

'You're a fool. You don't know them.' Day was sharply impatient. 'They'd shoot us down, I tell you, and then turn on the others. They're going to leave no witness of this. Our only –'

'Mr John Day!'

Cranston swung round. The voice had come from somewhere high up in the quarry – and even as he searched the rock the figure of a man stood boldly up on the sky-line and then dropped out of sight again.

'Mr John Day!' It was a second voice – and simultaneously a second figure rose momentarily into view. The first had been English; this was markedly foreign.

'Mr John Day – please!' A third voice, also foreign, quickly followed, and again the owner briefly showed himself. But this time the same voice continued to speak from cover. 'Will Mr John Day please join us? Nobody else need come. Will Mr John Day kindly join us?'

The summons was utterly bizarre – like the call of a pageboy in a nightmarish hotel. But Day appeared unperturbed by it. 'You see? They're not really anxious to present themselves in person. But they'd be quite willing to get on with the job from a distance. I'd advise the young man and yourself to come inside.'

Cranston thought for a moment. 'Sandy – can we make a dash for it? We can drive on as we are?'

'Aye, Dick – we can that, at a kin' o' crawl. But ye maun mind they've got your rattletrap – and mebbe a car o' their ain foreby roon the next bend. It's an unco awkward thing.' Sandy scratched his head again. 'I dinna ken what for's a' this stour. Thae voices are fair scunnererfu' and I canna' thole them. But I'm thinking I hear an engine. Might it be the polis, do you think, in their bit car from Dindervie?'

Cranston listened. There was certainly an odd throb or rumble in the air. But it didn't sound like a car. 'Farm machinery somewhere,' he said . . . 'Listen.'

Again one of the voices was speaking from the quarry. This time it was nearer, and from lower down on the left. 'We're coming,' it said. 'I think you have a lady? There need be no violence – nothing distressing. Simply an appointment with Mr Day. We advise him to join us.'

'Awa' and bile your heids!' Suddenly moved to wrath, Sandy Morrison made the quarry ring with this rude injunction. Then he made a dash for the cabin of his ambulance, and reappeared brandishing a spanner. 'I'll learn ye!' he bawled. 'Come awa' doon here, ye lurking loupers, and I'll learn ye.'

It was a challenge that was immediately accepted. There was a whistle from somewhere in the quarry, and two men appeared simultaneously at each end of it. A fifth rose up from behind a heap of stone straight in front of them. Cranston caught a glint on his face that he recognized. He had doffed his trilby, but there could be no doubt about his identity. All the men began to advance with deliberation in a contracting half-circle. They were all much like the man in the middle. They all wore the same sort of townee clothes. If anything could be more sinister than the simple fact of their threatening advance it was this displeasing incongruity with their surroundings. They should have been lurking under lamp-posts in disreputable streets or keeping furtive observation on others of their own kind in undesirable pubs.

The advance continued. The men made no display of weapons, but each kept one hand in a pocket of his jacket. George dropped to the ground again beside Cranston. She was once more in her khaki walking kit. 'It's not quite real – is it?' Her voice was steady. 'It ought to be flickering faintly – and in glorious Technicolor.' She was watching the man with the glinting glasses. 'And they ought to keep on coming at us until they're enormously larger than life.'

'Life-size will do.' From behind them in the ambulance Day's voice for the first time was savage. 'There's no sign of traffic in this damned solitude you've trapped us in? Don't I hear something?'

Even as Day spoke the line of men came to a halt. The throb and rumble in the air had rapidly increased – and now there was added to it a sort of clattering tramp, as of an army of booted giants pounding up the road to the glen. Cranston swung round. What was in fact advancing upon them was a line of tanks.

The uproar grew. A second line of the monsters had appeared over the brae straight ahead. They had enormous guns that gave them the appearance of a herd of trumpeting elephants. And they came lumbering and lurching down the hill, apparently intent upon a rendezvous with their fellows at this point where the quarry made a great scar on the answering slope. For a second Cranston stared unbelievingly. He could think of the irruption only in terms of a planned spectacular act of rescue, and the forces being hurled into the battle seemed fantastically disproportioned to their task. Then he realized that the appearance was of course fortuitous. The tanks had no interest in the ambulance standing in the quarry. And presently they would be gone.

He turned round again. The five men had vanished. Very understandably, this abrupt appearance of the armed forces of the Crown had a little thrown them out of their stride.

'It's thae Tank Corps chiels frae the camps ahint Drumtoul. They've been scurryvaiging ouer the moors these ten days syne. It's tairrible bad for the birrds.' Sandy was wholly disapproving. 'And they'll no' even gae lounlie on the sabbath. The meenister at Auchinputtock has preached a sairmon on it.'

When not more than twenty yards away, the first of the monsters drew to a halt. One by one, lurching, coughing, and spluttering, the others did the same. There was a long line of them on the road. Those on the brae had spread out as they descended, and they were now immobile on its slopes as if they had been frozen while they grazed. Trapdoors opened and beret-clad heads looked out. A group of officers appeared from nowhere and applied themselves to conversing importantly over a map. Some of the beret-clad heads, becoming aware of George, emitted significant whistles and cautiously improper cries. Cranston glanced at the girl. 'Well,' he said, 'Day was right. Something *has* turned up. And I'd better go and nobble that Major.'

'No!' She put an urgent hand on his arm. 'You wouldn't think of throwing up the sponge if you didn't feel you had me on your hands. Sandy and you must change the wheel, and get clean away from under their noses. If you like, I'll stop behind.'

'With the licentious soldiery?'

'I expect they'll be frightfully decent. The Major looks most fatherly.'

'Sandy, man – come on.' Cranston made a dive for the tool-kit. 'We'll get away yet.'

'And that we will.' Sandy Morrison dropped the spanner with which he had armed himself and went to work furiously. The ambulance was jacked up before he spoke again. 'Dick,' he said in a low voice, 'ye'll no really leave the quean-bairn wi' the sodjers?'

'We ought to, Sandy. You see now what sort of a business this is. It's not for a girl.'

'I dinna' ken that she's ony less apt to it than ye are yersel', Dickie Cranston. See her getting oot the spare whiles you dae na' mair than stand by like a gumphie.' Sandy was withering. Then he paused to draw from a pocket an enormous watch. 'I can get ye a' to Drumtoul halt, man, in time for the wee diesel-car tae the junction. And there ye can tak' the express. Hae ye siller?'

'Quite a lot. And Day claims to have a fortune.'

'Does he that?' Sandy spoke with respect. 'Haud the thing fast, man, whiles I gets the nuts off. The tanks are no' for moving yet?'

'No, thank goodness. Some of the men are out on the heather and smoking. My guess is that the Major has got lost and won't admit it.'

'Praise the Lord!' Sandy ejaculated this with genuine piety. 'And the preen-heidit foo's in the quarry?'

'They're not so witless, if you ask me. But they're giving no sign.'

'We'll jink them yet . . . Right, lassie – pass it ou'er.' Sandy took the spare-wheel from George with an approving nod. 'Ye're warth twa o' this feckless loon Dickie. Ye'll hae the hearse, mebbe, afore mysel'. There's a lum-hat gaes wi' it. You'd look braw in that.' Sandy laughed extravagantly at this fantasy. 'Praise-be-thankit, it's on.' Sandy looked up, and paused indignantly. Several of the more enterprising youths from the tank-crews had slipped across the road and formed an admiring group round the ambulance. Ostensibly they were appraising the technique of its driver. But their real interest was, of course, in George. The classically educated among them might have likened her to an Amazon, dropped in, appropriately girt, to do a turn of work in Vulcan's smithy. The bolder could be heard comparing her points, audibly and favourably, with those of such young ladies as had recently figured on the front page of *Blighty*. Sandy tightened a final nut with energy. 'It's no daecent,' he said. 'A loon has but tae put on a bit uniform and syne he sheds a' the godliness that was skelpit into him as a wean. Awa' wi' ye!' He looked up and waved an oily hand at the young men. 'First scaring the birrds that ought to be reservit for the gentry in the lodges and the half-gentry in the hotels. And then making profane talk aboot the fore and aft o' a maiden that's worth the pack o' ye. Awa', I say.'

Much as if endorsing the injunction, the Major at this point gave a shout, and somebody farther back blew a whistle. The soldiers went off at the double. Tanks here and there began to snort and shake themselves. George finished strapping the punctured wheel into its place and turned to Sandy. 'Where will they be going?'

'Back to Drumtoul for their brose. Eating by day, and sprunting after the village lasses by nicht, is a' they're fit for.'

'Then we can go too.' George gave a single glance at Cranston – too swift to be an appeal – and swung herself up into the seat beside the driver's. In a moment Sandy had followed her.

Cranston picked up the jack and pitched it into the ambulance. He took a careful look at the quarry. There was no sign of the enemy, but he had no doubt that they were still lurking there. The first of the tanks were already moving. It was clear that the exercise was in fact over, and that they were minded to trundle decorously home. He glanced into the ambulance. Day was sitting quietly on a stretcher. In Sir Alex Blair's expensive tweeds and the dark glasses he was unrecognizable. Cranston could almost persuade himself that here was somebody with whom he had nothing to do. But that, unfortunately, would be an illusion. 'You were right,' he said abruptly. 'And we're getting away. For the moment.'

'It's from moment to moment, my dear fellow, that I've lately learned to live.' Day stretched himself. 'We've picked up some sort of miraculous convoy to a place called Drumtoul?'

'Just that. As my friend here would say, the deil looks after his ain.'

'How long until we get there?'

'At the pace we're likely to make with this circus, I'd say over an hour.'

'Then I think – do you know? – I'll sleep. There's nothing like swimming for making you drowsy.' Day yawned, and then placidly lay down.

For a second Cranston stared at him. Day, he was sure, was not posing. Lying there, he was perfectly relaxed. Relaxation was for the moment the rational thing, and the man was able to command it. He himself, on the other hand, felt his heart thumping and his limbs trembling. He was no longer frightened of being afraid, but he couldn't remotely pretend that he wasn't in a state of tension. 'In that case,' he said shortly, 'I'll get in with them in front.'

Day made no reply. He was taking off the dark glasses and settling himself on the stretcher. The ambulance had a faint antiseptic smell that made Cranston think of his father's surgery. George's rucksack and Elspeth's abandoned clothes were lying in one corner. For some reason he had a sudden sharp vision of Sally – of Sally at a summer dance, very exquisite and rather beautiful . . . He shut the door with a snap, ran round to the front of the ambulance, and scrambled up. 'There's room?' he asked.

George nodded without speaking. She was watching the line of tanks. 'There!' she said suddenly to Sandy. He slipped into gear and the ambulance jolted over the floor of the quarry and inserted itself neatly between one tank and another. 'Will they mind, do you think?'

'They'll only mind that they're shut down in their daft contraptions and no' able to be casting their immodest regard upon your person.' Sandy gave her a sidelong glance that was entirely austere. 'And they canna' bid us pass and go ahead, sin frae here through tae Drumtoul the road's scarce wide enough for the muckle-douped things theirsel's.'

'Is it a long climb?'

'Aye – we climb right tae the top o' the moor. You and Mr Cranston here will be able to look awa' doon tae the sea and tak' a last glink at Dinwiddie Castle. If it's ony satisfaction tae either of you.'

Chapter 11

For some time they were silent as the long line of monsters laboured towards the summit of the moor. They were out of the glen and the heather rolled away monotonously on either side of them, unrelieved except by a line of shooting-butts a mile on their left and here and there a deserted sheep-fold piled up out of weathered grey stone. A burn ran by the side of the road, its murmur entirely drowned by the clatter before and behind them. It was hard not to believe that the whole moor was exhaling exhaust gases. Presently Cranston pointed ahead. 'You see that cairn?' he said to George. 'The road goes off on a long curve there. If we look back, we should be able to see the whole line behind us – and tell if they've joined in.'

'Whether they have or not, I suppose they're unlikely just to give up? They really feel Day to be terrifically important?'

Cranston nodded. 'I'm sure they do. There was a big effort – and a lightning effort – getting five chaps on top of us like that. What more they can mobilize, I've no idea. But everything they've got. Within twelve hours, I'd say, everything they've got in these islands.'

'Sandy – do you hear that?' George appeared to be in remarkably good spirits. 'You are at grips with the entire forces of atheistic communism.'

'Maybe I am, Miss. But I maun be back at the Infirmary the forenoon, all the same. I canna' see the Superintendent, coarse chiel that he is, making much o' a tale o' Sandy Morrison at grips wi' the Kremlin . . . If you want to spy back adoon the road, there's a pair o' glasses in the bag at your fut.'

Cranston stooped and rummaged. Presently he produced a pair of excellent binoculars. 'And what, Sandy,' he asked, 'is the use you find for these?'

'Bird watching.' Sandy was dour. 'It's an improving ploy, Dick Cranston, that you must mind them urging us to in the school.' He gave a swift wicked grin. 'I'm a great one for keeping an eye on the birds.'

'You're a great one for keeping an eye on Lord Urquhart's or Sir Alex's keepers, if you ask me.' Cranston leant far out of the window and scanned the curve of road behind them. 'There's nothing. Only tanks, and more tanks. If they're after us, it's not at the tail-end of this queer procession . . . George, have you got your maps?'

'They're in the rucksack in the back – unless Day's eaten them. Why?'

'Just that it strikes me –' Cranston broke off. 'There's the sea,' he said. 'And there's the castle.'

'Dinwiddie?'

'Dinwiddie.' For a moment he continued to stare. The place was bumping up and down in his field of vision, but he had it perfectly in focus. It seemed very near – and there was a queer shock in its suddenly being so. Part ruin and part mansion, it stood out boldly on its cliff against a sea still silvery in the morning light. And somehow it was ominous and evil. He tried to recall the sharp vision of Sally that he had experienced only half an hour before. But all he saw was Caryl's flesh in moonlight – that and her husband Alex Blair, spruce and polished and facetious. He handed the glasses silently to George, and sat back so that she could focus them across his chest. For some horrible seconds he was gripped by what he thought of as his dream-feeling – the sense of a sudden recollection, seizing the mind as it swam up out of oblivion, of an irrevocable thing done . . . 'Clear – isn't it?' He had forced himself to speak.

'There's something I don't like about it.'

'Something *you* don't like?' He was vastly struck by this.

'I don't like medieval things.' George was puzzled, yet decided. 'I thought I'd find them marvellous. But the Tower cured me.'

'The Tower of London – you've been there?' He was amused.

'Of course I've been there. It's horrifying. Do you realize that London was once a Roman city – a civilized place that you and I would recognize? And that centuries and centuries later, all that people could manage was a ghastly mixture of slum and prison – like the Tower, or like Castle This and Castle That? It's terrifying. It shows how civilization can just seep away.'

'I suppose it does. But the medieval people built the cathedrals. Have you seen them?'

'You can build cathedrals without knowing about drains – or even baths.' George lowered the binoculars for a moment and looked at him with what appeared to be perfect seriousness. 'And when did they put baths into Dinwiddie? Probably not more than fifty years ago.'

Cranston laughed. Five minutes before, it was something he would have believed himself become permanently incapable of. 'Do all Australians believe that godliness is next to cleanliness?'

'There's something coming out.' George had the glasses focused once more on the castle. 'It must be a tradesman's van. It's a brilliant yellow. But it's going very fast.'

'Yellow?' Suddenly he remembered. 'But that's Blair's car – Sir Alex Blair's Cadillac.' He laughed again. 'Would you expect a Scottish baronet – and an intellectual one at that – to paint a Cadillac bright yellow?'

'I'm afraid I don't know at all.'

'Well, you wouldn't. But there's something odd in him.'

'Blair? What is he, anyway?'

'What I've just told you – a baronet, and our local bigwig Number Two. He comes after old Lord Urquhart, who's his deadly enemy. And he's a physicist – a *ci-devant* physicist, I should say. He was on the way to eminence when the baronetcy – and something soft inside him, I expect – stepped in and sank him.'

'He might have been what John Day is?'

Cranston stared at her. 'Well, yes – but there's something decidedly *ci-devant* about Day too now, I'd say.'

'In rather a different sense.' George had swept the binoculars round in a curve. 'I suppose Cadillacs are pretty hot? It's travelling very fast indeed.'

'It's a pleasure to hear o' something that's no behaving like a funeral.' Sandy Morrison was peevish. 'I'll no mind crawling like this when I'm set up wi' my hearse. 'Twill be but reverent-like. But an ambulance is anither matter. I've got a wee bit bell here – doon there at my fut – that's for clearing the traffic awa' frae in front o' me in the toon. D'ye think, Dick, I might gie a bit ding wi' it noo?'

'It wouldn't do the slightest good. The pace of this whole column is set by someone in an armoured car at the front.'

'Yin o' the high heed-yins, nae doot.' Sandy was disgusted. 'The great dunderclunk might hae a thought tae my Superintendent.' He pulled out his watch again. 'Frae Drumtoul tae the Infirmary's nae sma' loup. And I mun mak' it in the forenoon.'

'We're not likely to forget it.' Cranston turned to George. 'What would you say they know about us?'

'That here we are. And perhaps that's about enough. I suppose there are other roads to this Drumtoul.'

'There certainly are. But what would they know about us once we definitely broke the trail?'

'One of them has seen me close-up – in that queer rig. Five of them have seen the two of us – and Sandy – at a middle distance. As for Day, I suppose at least one of them knows him very well. But do they know about his eyes?'

Cranston shook his head. 'I don't see that they can. At least, it would be something worth taking a risk on. But what isn't worth taking a risk on is driving into Drumtoul in this ambulance. And that's why I asked you about your maps . . . Sandy, would you have the nerve to stop?'

'And what for no'?' Sandy was indignant. 'Hae I no' a right to halt upon the guid Queen's highway for my lawful occasions – whether or no' all the Queen's tanks are a wee bit impeded the while?' Sandy paused. 'Are ye thinking, man, o' taking to the heather?'

'Yes, I am.'

'Wi' Miss Cranston here and the blinter?'

'Day's eyes are the trouble, all right – and have been from the start. But I've got a plan.'

'Ye aye had plans as a wean, Dickie Cranston, and fair daft some o' them were.'

'That's true enough. My plan at the castle this morning was daft. But I think I've thought of a better one.'

'Which is?'

'I'm not going to tell you.'

'Ye'll no' let on tae your auld schoolfellow?' Sandy was deeply offended. 'And would it be owerweening, Mr Cranston, to spier what for no'?'

'If you don't know you can't tell. Not even if the Kremlin catches you in a corner and asks you not too gently.'

'Lordsake!' Not unnaturally, Sandy received this with some dismay. 'Are you telling me they'd accord me waur than death?'

Cranston nodded. 'Undoubtedly. But fortunately their interest in you won't last very long. Within twenty-four hours, if I have my way in the matter, you won't be worth twopence to them. Nor will George here, thank goodness . . . Sandy, you must get yourself jailed. The constable in Drumtoul – isn't his name Carfrae? – was telling me only the other day that they've built him a grand new lock-up at the bottom of his garden.'

George, who had been listening to all this attentively, interrupted. 'And what put it into a policeman's head to tell you that?'

'He was having a little joke.' Cranston grinned at her. 'About salmon . . . And, Sandy – that will do for you. You must get Carfrae to clap you in his grand new lock-up for poaching salmon. You'll be safe enough there.'

'Me jailed?' Sandy was indignant. 'And with sic a record wad they ever promote me tae that –'

'Unjust suspicion, Sandy. Carfrae must let you out tomorrow evening, without troubling a magistrate. He can give you a note to your Superintendent. Or you can get your mother to write in that you were poorish.'

Sandy took a hand from the wheel to scratch his head. This fertility in expedients was plainly something he remembered from of old. 'It maun be as ye will,' he said resignedly. 'But will the tank laddies no' think it strange tae see three folk get oot o' an ambulance and gae louping ower the heather?'

'Not a bit. We'll look just like walkers you've given a lift to . . . And you can stop any time now.'

'Verra weel.' Sandy hesitated and gave a sly glance at his former schoolfellow. 'Might it no' be better', he asked, 'if Miss Cranston here came tae Carfrae's new jile too?'

'It would wreck your chances at once.' Cranston was decisive. 'Carfrae's a decent shameful loon, Sandy, that would panic at the thought of it.'

'He's got his auld auntie.' Sandy held out this prospect of chaperonage without conviction.

'Stop havering, man – and signal them you're going to stop. I'll nip round behind and get out Day and the rucksack in no time.'

Sandy Morrison did as he was bid. 'D'ye ken what I think?' he asked. 'That Day, whatever he hauds himsel' oot for, is but a coarse creature and no' worth a' this stour.'

Chapter 12

Cranston had been prepared for difficulty, but their progress across the moor was even slower than he had feared. Day's eyes, although horribly inflamed, were beginning to be of some use to him – but they were no help with the heather at his feet. It looked as if the ten miles – and it was certainly a good ten miles to Urquhart – might take them four hours to cover.

For some time they had moved silently. The road had dropped out of sight behind them and the rumble of the tank column had died away. The only sound was the cry of peewits high in air, and sometimes a faint tinkle of water dropping in tiny invisible runlets down the slope they were painfully climbing. Helping Day was laborious, and after no more than half an hour they were glad to pause for breath. George had brought Sandy's binoculars, and she turned to sweep with them the ground over which they had come. The road, although below them, was still invisible behind some swell of the moor, and beyond it the heather stretched in reaches of dull purple to the sea. Nothing moved. In the whole prospect there was no hint of habitation. There was nowhere – whether in hut or tree or post – a single perpendicular line. Cranston, although he loved it, was prompted to apologize for the scene. 'It's pretty bleak, isn't it? Vast and empty and useless.'

'Vast?' George was amused. 'If you came from Australia, you'd feel that this was no more than elbow-room.'

Day had sat down, his head sunk between his hands. Now he raised it. 'Australia – is that where you come from? I nearly went there once.'

'Really?' George looked at him coldly, and Cranston realized that she was unable to see in this queer fugitive anything remotely resembling a figure of sympathy. 'A great deal of it is very like this, you know. Almost nothing to destroy.'

'To destroy?' For a moment he seemed not to understand. 'You think of me as a destroyer?'

'I don't know that I do. Perhaps it wouldn't be fair. Say just chief technical adviser to the Death Wish.'

Day shook his head. Cranston noticed – as he had noticed when the man first came out of the sea – what a fine head it was. 'It's a matter, of course, of what we're urged to – and given funds to go after. But it might have been called creative, not destructive – the Australian idea. Getting at artesian water – enormously far down. Transforming a continent.'

George was silent for a moment. 'But you didn't go.'

'There were difficulties.' Day looked up sombrely. Dimly, it appeared, he could now distinguish them as figures. 'Had we better be getting along?'

They moved forward. It was still heavy going – the more so because, as George had foretold, the day was indeed a cow. A light breeze that had been whispering in the dried bells of the old heather had now died away, and the warm dry scent came up to them in waves. They had made another mile before George spoke. 'Is it like this all the way?'

'We finish on a road – if we think it safe.' Cranston stopped and fished out the map. 'Let's get it clear. The high-road runs parallel to the road to Drumtoul we were travelling on. The distance between the two roads is about eight miles across this moor. But after about six miles we begin to have Urquhart Forest on our right. We could take to it, if the worst came to the worst.'

'As it very conceivably may.' Day, unable to see the map, was looking up at the sky. 'I don't deny that this is a good move of yours, Cranston. But it's one they may well take a guess at. *They* would see that *we* must see the danger of simply driving into Drumtoul.'

'That's clear enough.' George was impatient. 'But would they reckon on our moving almost due north?'

'They'd consider it. But they certainly couldn't risk throwing all their force into quartering this moor.' Day spoke slowly, as one carefully weighing chances. 'They haven't got companies at their command – or even platoons – after all. Their best chance is with the roads. What are they like round here?' He tapped the map irritably. 'I wish I could see that damned thing.'

'Imagine two adjacent squares,' Cranston said. 'Imagine them lying almost north and south. The southernmost line is the sea – the Firth. The line which they have in common is the Drumtoul road. And the line to the north is the high-road.'

'Which we have to cross?'

'We have to cross the high-road to get to Urquhart, which is two miles beyond. We're going to make the high-road, I hope, at a pub, the Canty Quean. And there we can leave the heather. Imagine an inverted T. The arms are the high-road. We go straight down the stem, which is a by-road leading to Urquhart.'

'I see. Would it be right to say that, until we get over the arms of the T, we are on a rectangle of bare moor, bounded by straight and virtually unfrequented roads?'

'Yes – and we are on a line that pretty well bisects that rectangle now. And it's bare enough – except for the forest, which lies north-east of us.'

Day nodded. 'Their plan will be to contain us, won't it? It's not too difficult to keep an eye on long stretches of straight moorland road.'

'Quite so.' Cranston folded up the map and prepared to walk on. 'That's why I want to cross the high-road by the Canty Quean. The woods come right up to it there, both on this and the Urquhart side. We can reconnoitre without being seen . . . George, it's my turn with the rucksack.'

She handed it over. 'What about people at this pub?'

'There may be nobody more than the man and his wife. And after that I don't think there's a habitation until we drop into the clachan of Urquhart itself.'

'The what?' George was at a loss.

'The village. It lies just south of the house.'

Again they moved forward. It seemed to Cranston that Day was tiring. Perhaps it was the man's terrific swim beginning to tell. 'If we just make the Canty Quean', he said, '– or the forest close by it – you can shelter, if you like, and I can go on. Lord Urquhart would send down a car.'

Day shook his head. 'I don't think I shall be beaten by a remaining six or seven miles. But aren't you rather confidently banking on the benevolent interest of this nobleman?'

Cranston laughed. 'It's going to involve telling some lies. Do you mind?'

'Not if they are convincing lies, my dear young man.'

'Well – I rather do mind, as a matter of fact.' Cranston felt a now familiar irritation rising in him. 'I rather like old Lord Urquhart.'

'But I understood you to say that he was the deadly enemy of your good friends at the castle. Perhaps that's irrelevant?'

'It's not, I'm afraid.' Cranston frowned. 'It's what I'll have to exploit. And I'll have to exploit your eyes, damn them.' He flushed. 'I'm sorry.'

'Not at all, not at all.' Day was bland. 'You interest me. Did the castle folk blind me in an access of hideous barbarity?'

'Something of the sort. You'll have to back up the story that –'

Cranston broke off. George had stopped dead. 'Listen!' she said.

'I wondered when you'd hear it.' Day was at his most detached. 'An aeroplane, without a doubt.'

The sound hung, minute after minute, in air. In volume it rose, dropped, rose again, and then once more dropped. The suggestion was unmistakable; it was of a machine lazily circling somewhere far to the south. George searched the horizon with the binoculars. 'Nothing to be seen. And I hardly suppose –' She was silent for a moment. 'But one does come to feel that anything's possible.'

Cranston nodded, but without much appearance of worry. 'That's true enough. And it may be worth while, as we get along, keeping an eye open for cover.'

'Are we likely', Day asked, 'to find any – short of that forest?'

'I don't know that we are. But my guess is that the thing's harmless. If it comes in sight, we'll think again.'

'Wait.' George had turned a little to the west. 'There it is – just coming over the horizon. It must be flying quite low. And it's only a little one.'

'The job scarcely requires a B.47.' Day had one of his flashes of savagery. 'A ditch would help.'

'Unfortunately we've hardly time to dig one.' George got her own back with some energy. 'There's just heather. Given a little time, you could do something quite effective with that. But it's not exactly stuff you can climb under. What about sitting down on it for a start? They say it's movement that's first spotted from the air.'

'Then we'll sit down.' Cranston was still easy. 'It should pass straight over us.'

They sat down. The plane was revealing itself as a small flimsy thing. But for the increasingly audible throb of the engine one might have taken it for a glider. 'A sort of run-about,' George said.

Cranston followed it with his eye. 'It's going straight home.'

'Home?' She was puzzled.

'Lunch-time.' Cranston spoke confidently. 'And I'm hungry myself. Let's get on.'

'Wait.' George pointed. 'You're wrong – whatever you mean by home. It's started fooling around again.'

This was true. The little plane had banked and begun its lazy circling. It dropped in a wide spiral and rose again. Its movement was entirely the movement of a mechanical thing. Nevertheless, the suggestion it conveyed was that of a hawk.

Cranston spoke abruptly. 'We'll take no extra risks. Down on our tummies is the thing. Heads under heather – and feet too, if it can be managed. Then don't move. And don't look up.'

They got down as he directed, and lay quite still. 'What's odd', George said, 'is that we can talk – or even sing. Do you still think it isn't the enemy?'

Cranston laughed. 'I think it's somebody quite different – our prospective host.'

'Whatever are you talking about?'

'Old Lord Urquhart. He's air crazy, and has a little fleet of aircraft of his own. He's one of the Scottish Representative Peers –'

'What does that mean?'

'That he's in the House of Lords. And he's constantly making speeches there about opening up the Highlands by means of air transport. Most enterprising, too.' Cranston raised his voice, for the sound of the engine was now rapidly increasing. 'Last summer he sold a herd of Highland cattle to the Duke of Horton – and dropped them by parachute into the park at Scamnum Court. And he does a lot of flying himself. It's my guess that here he is, having a little morning spin.'

'I hope you're right. And I hope it's cooler up there than it is grovelling like this . . . Listen!'

What there was to listen to was sudden silence. It was a good deal more unnerving than the mounting roar of the engine had been. Then suddenly the heather was whipping and tossing around them, and for a fraction of a second they lay not in bright sunshine but in shadow. It passed over them like a blade and in the same instant the engine broke into life again. Cranston looked up. The little plane seemed to skim the heather straight in front of his nose. Then it climbed and vanished from his field of vision. He had caught a glimpse of the pilot, a white-helmeted figure in an open cockpit. He had a confused impression that the man had waved an arm.

For minutes they continued to lie still. But the sound of the engine now steadily receded, and as it died away they sat up. It was only a speck in the sky in front of them. It glinted momentarily in the sun and then vanished.

'I hope you were right.' Day spoke rather grimly as they trudged on.

'It's in the direction of Urquhart, more or less, that it has vanished.' Cranston was still cheerful. 'So I still think it's our eccentric peer. And I hope I'm right about his going home to lunch. If we don't find him about the place, we shall be badly help up.'

George, who had retrieved the rucksack, hitched it higher on her shoulders. 'Richard, what sort of a place is this Urquhart anyway? Is it grander than Dinwiddie Castle?'

'Good lord, yes. It's one of Scotland's best attempts at a great house.'

Day had taken off the dark glasses and was cautiously dabbing at his eyes with a handkerchief. 'And you really have the entrée, my dear young man, to its splendours? We shall try not to be visibly over-awed.'

'I know Lord Urquhart quite well.' Cranston was curt. 'How are your eyes?'

'Call them five per cent – which is a good deal better than they were. But they get more deucedly painful as they insist on seeing a little. Your father with his bandages might have been not a bad idea . . . Isn't there a breeze again?'

George stopped. She was excited. 'There is. And it's because we're at the top. Richard, what a tremendous view!'

'I hope I may be told about it.' Day was ironic. 'But if this means that we're posturing happily on a sky-line, I suggest that we move down a little.'

'Quite right.' Cranston moved on, pointing ahead as he did so. 'There's Urquhart Forest, George, in the distance on the right. You can just see the high-road running from the left and plunging into it.'

'And just there I see smoke – blue smoke.'

'Peat smoke. That's the Canty Quean. It's all a good deal farther than it looks. Nearly a couple of hours, I'd say. Now look a little to the left – at about ten o'clock from the edge of the forest and on the very horizon. Can you just see a pale streak? That's Urquhart. A tremendous Doric façade.'

'We'll make it yet.' George spoke with sober confidence. 'And I think I can now take a guess at why it's so desirable. You're reckoning that Lord Urquhart, if properly approached, will –'

George paused, and Cranston nodded. 'Yes . . . fly us out.'

Chapter 13

Day was suddenly in a fever. It was as if energy had poured back into him so abundantly that he was unable to use it with economy. Cranston realized that until this moment he had been accompanying a man without hope.

When in the quarry he had told Day that they were beaten, it had been something which Day already believed. He had been carrying on not out of any substantial hope but as the consequence of a sheer effort of will. Now he had seen a real chance. Only a few miles away there was waiting something that could transform his situation. He was moving forward with complete concentration on the physical task of covering with all possible speed this uneven and impeded ground. He was treating the moor as he had treated the ocean not many hours before.

But it was still a slow progress. Sandy Morrison – if he had been sufficiently impressed to do as he was told – was by this time in Constable Carfrae's lock-up in Drumtoul. Lord Urquhart had landed and was addressing himself to his luncheon – with a copy of *The Aeroplane*, Cranston seemed to remember, propped up against a large kebbuck of cheese. Caryl Blair was very probably consulting his father about her sprained ankle – and perhaps asking more questions than she ought to about the movements of the doctor's son. Sally –

Cranston checked himself and carefully scanned the country ahead. 'I think', he said presently, 'that we had better bear to the right now and skirt the forest. When we come to the last stretch – I mean before the high-road and the Canty Quean – we ought to do it through the trees. It's bound to slow us down a lot, but we can afford to be prudent before the last lap.'

'And on the other side of the high-road?' Sweat was trickling down Day's forehead. It was clear that he still found it difficult and almost useless to open his eyes. His face looked as if it had been brutally scrubbed with some abrasive substance.

'We can either chance it and walk straight along the road. Or we can do a sort of Red Indian approach through the trees.'

'Pine trees, I suppose?'

'Almost entirely.' Cranston turned to George. 'Did you ever play hide-and-seek in a pine wood? It's rather fun. You don't make a sound, because the ground is thick with the fallen needles. But you can't just hide behind a tree. It doesn't often have sufficient girth. And there's hardly any undergrowth. You have to keep far enough away from the chap that's after you to be screened by a whole band of trunks. It's like a game in some enormous colonnade . . . Do you notice how the smell of the forest is getting on top of the smell of the heather as we approach? Do you like it?'

George sniffed. 'It's all right. But it's not my idea of what trees should smell like. Did you ever smell eucalypts?'

'Gum trees?' He smiled. 'Only in a botanic garden. Is it something hard to do without?'

She nodded. 'Impossible.'

Cranston glanced at her curiously. It hadn't occurred to him that a sun-goddess could be home-sick. 'We'll get into the trees just there,' he said – and pointed ahead. 'But have a go at the high-road with the glasses first.'

George sat down and carefully focused the binoculars, balancing bare elbows on bare knees. 'There's no sign of life about the pub. What did you say it's called?'

'The Canty Quean. It means the cheerful girl.'

'It doesn't look cheerful – only rather lonely and forlorn. I can't think where it gets its customers.' George swept the binoculars to the left. 'But wait a minute. Perhaps there are some approaching now? Can you see? A car – a large closed car – coming slowly along the high-road from the west.'

'I can see. It probably hasn't any idea of stopping. But we'll approach with a good deal of caution if it does. And now we take to the woods.'

And presently they were moving silently through the trees. It made, quite suddenly, another world. Day would no longer be guided. The going had ceased to be treacherous underfoot, and out of the sunlight he seemed to find himself among massively distinguishable shapes. He went forward groping and peering. The effect was of something curiously savage. It was possible to feel that he would have been more congruously dressed in skins than in Sir Alex Blair's eminently civilized clothes. And if his sight was virtually useless still, his other senses appeared to have gained an almost primitive acuteness. 'Listen.' He had stopped – and the word was uttered only in a whisper. 'There's a noise – a queer whistle.' He relaxed. 'Are there telephone wires?'

Cranston thought for a moment. 'I think so.'

George nodded. 'I know there are – along the high-road. I noticed the posts.'

'Then it's only the wind in them.' Day had a strained smile that showed ghastly on his injured face. 'But there's another thing. Somebody's cooking.'

Cranston sniffed, but was aware of nothing. 'Picnickers? It's more likely to be the old wife in the pub. It's not fifty yards away. But I don't think we'll linger to see what she has in the pot. Let's trust Lord Urquhart to put on a magnificent cold collation round about three o'clock.'

'Do I get in on that?' George presented this question with some urgency. 'Your mother's was a dinkum breakfast. But I'm beginning to feel –'

Cranston nodded. The sun in some mysterious way manufactures its own fuel. But it would be only reasonable to suppose that George required substantial stoking. 'You're a problem,' he said. 'But my idea is to treat you as Lord Urquhart's problem, and not mine. I hope that *noblesse oblige* will do the rest . . . And now, if you ask me, the critical moment comes. Once across the high-road, and I think we've beaten them. Come along.'

They advanced until they were once more looking out into bright sunlight. They were here among larches, and these, running right up to the yard of the Canty Quean, cast perpendicular lines of shadow across its white-washed walls. The outlines of the building were uncertain, and from their vantage-point it had the appearance of some shapeless fleecy creature slumbering behind enormous bars. The only sounds at first were that of a turkey gobbling and a few poultry scratching in dust. It was possible that to the high-road the Canty Quean presented an aspect more in keeping with its name. The back was dismal.

Cranston put his mouth to Day's ear. 'Stay where you are. I'll move round a bit and see what's doing.'

Day nodded. 'Very well. But be careful. I thought I heard voices. And hadn't we better go east for a little way and cross the high-road where it's running through the forest?'

'Perhaps so – but I'll spy out the land.' There was a low tumbledown wall round the yard, and Cranston began to skirt it. The turkey still gobbled and there was the smell of a pig. He found that George was by his side. 'Hadn't you better stop with him?' he murmured.

She shook her head. 'Let's leave him for a minute. With any luck he may vanish.'

'Vanish?' he was alarmed.

'Magically, I mean. Perhaps he isn't true. I'm sure I hope so.'

Cranston glanced at her oddly, but had no time to speak. For suddenly there were voices from the front of the building. They stood quite still, straining their ears.

'Gentry,' George whispered. 'Or is it what Sandy calls half-gentry? I wouldn't know. But I think they must be from that car.' Without waiting for a reply she tiptoed away, and he saw that she was determined to have first peep. He let her go. For he knew by now that George, although physically overwhelming, had a very adequate command over her slightest movements. And within a minute she was back. 'It is. An enormous vintage Daimler, I think. And it's stopped with its bonnet turned down the road to Urquhart. It looks as if it might belong to your old Lord Urquhart's grandmother.'

'It may at least belong to one of his venerable friends. I wonder –' Cranston hesitated. 'Could you see who'd got out?'

'No – but it sounds like an elderly man. And I think he's talking to the woman of the place – the pub-keeper's wife.'

'Mrs Brash, I think she's called. If this is somebody going to Urquhart, do you think we might bag a lift? Could there be any risk – after we've taken a better look? It would mean we had it in the bag. Let's go round.'

She looked at him in surprise – perhaps guessing that he had somehow become infected with Day's new impatience. Then she put her hand on his arm. 'I'll go. A lone girl's more appealing at a first shot. If he's nice I can spin a yarn and fetch you both out. But I won't break cover until I get a better look.'

'George, no –'

She slipped away before he could say more. He had been on the verge of going forward himself, and her action was taken on the strength of some sharp instinct. She rounded the corner of the yard and looked up the high-road as it ran through the forest. For as far as she could see, it was deserted. She looked across to the road that led, as she knew, to Urquhart. The big car was still stationary – but in shadow, so that she could not distinguish its occupants. She took a few steps farther and peeped cautiously round the corner of the building. The main door was there, sheltered by a small porch. The elderly man appeared just about to turn away from it, and his voice now came to her clearly. It was a Scottish voice – dry, cultivated, and full of authority.

'Then good day to you, Mrs Brash. If your son still seeks the tenancy, send him to see my factor. And I'll speak to Lord Urquhart this afternoon.'

The elderly man turned away from the door with a nod. George made up her mind, and stepped into the road. The elderly man saw her at once, and took off his hat politely as he turned away to his car. His glance had been appraising, courteously brief, and carefully unsurprised and unamused. She made up her mind that he was a judge. 'Excuse me,' she said, 'but can you tell me the road to Urquhart?'

He raised a silver-topped walking-stick and pointed. 'Two miles ahead – and well worth seeing. You can't miss it.' He appeared about to walk on, when a further thought struck him. 'Would you by any chance care for a lift? And have you friends with you? I think there is room for two or three.'

'Thank you very much. I –' George stopped. Her eye had gone past the elderly man to the front of the Canty Quean. It was as forlorn as the back. But for the noise of domestic animals, one would have taken it to be deserted. She glanced at the little porch and the door within it – and suddenly her heart pounded. A shaft of sunlight, creeping round from the south-west, was playing full upon a large cobweb that draped alike the handle and the jamb of the door. The thing was as good as a seal. The elderly man had been conversing with nothing but a surface of blank wood.

He was looking at her with a changed expression. But it was only for a split second that she distinguished it, for a sound behind her made her turn in a flash. The doors of the big car were open, and she had a glimpse of a figure disappearing behind a dyke. She shouted with all her might. 'It's a trap!' Then she ran.

The elderly man attempted no pursuit of her. She had the impression that he had instantly turned away, shouting orders. She ran to retrace her steps to the point at which she had left Cranston. Then it came to her that this was to give too much away. She wheeled and ran for the other side of the building. The move was a bad one. Another man was coming head on at her, and she had a confused impression of being caught between high walls. The man held something in a raised arm. It was as if he was going to strike her down as he ran and then hurry on to other quarry. There was a door on her left. She had no time to turn a handle, but she lunged at it and it gave. She was inside and she banged it to. There was a bolt and she shot it. The door rattled briefly, furiously, and then she heard the man hurry on. Despite the uproar outside, there was no sound inside the building. She appeared to be alone in the Canty Quean.

She saw in a swift glance that it was a miserable place; she was even conscious that it smelled dismally of stale beer and stale tobacco. She was in a low back passage, and she ran forward into a kitchen. There was somebody in the place after all. A bent old woman was standing by a stove, stirring at something in a frying-pan. George called out and the old woman turned round. She stared at George vacantly and without surprise. Then she turned back, muttering, to her cookery. There could be no help there, and George ran on. She found herself in some sort of tap-room or bar. It was deserted except for a black cat, asleep on top of a barrel. She looked quickly round. It was her idea to find a weapon. She had a dim notion, picked up from stories, that such places often, for some reason, kept a loaded shot-gun over a fire-place. But what her eye fell upon was a telephone.

For a moment she stared at it, stupid and incredulous. The notion that she could have any link with an outer world seemed quite unreal. Then she ran to it. The instrument was fixed to the wall. There was a handle to turn – rather as if one were going to crank up an ancient car . . . But almost at once a soft Scottish voice spoke. 'Number please?'

She found that her mind was a blank. And then she remembered. 'I want the police-station, please. The police-station at Drumtoul.'

Chapter 14

George's shout had brought Cranston out on the high-road at the double. For the first time since that fatal moment on the beach beneath Dinwiddie, when John Day had risen from the waters to fasten mysteriously upon him like an incubus, his mind was free of any thought of the man from the sea. There was nothing in his head but the girl – whom he had unforgivably let push forward as she had done. He had no hope that her shout was a false alarm – George was too reliable for that – and not much that he could in any way redeem the situation. But he made his dash all the same. He was in time to see her disappear round the other side of the Canty Quean. Simultaneously he was aware of several figures moving on the road, and he heard a call which told him he had been spotted.

He turned and doubled round the building, expecting to meet George that way. But she had vanished. There was a wall in front of him, and she might have got on the farther side of that – in which case its shelter would take her right to the fringe of the trees. His best course was to bank on this, and himself beat a retreat. If they could all three reunite, then they might contrive to withdraw into the forest and find another plan. He heard more shouts as he ran – not random shouts, but the sharp calling out of one and another command. It seemed to him that they were in English. The impression – quite irrationally – angered him more than anything had done yet.

He supposed that in addition to their own secret agents – who must at least be brave men – they hired anybody they could get. He hoped that it wouldn't be before one of the hirelings that he would go down – if go down he must. And things looked bleak. A trap like this would take some escaping from. Once more he had been far too confident. He remembered his conviction that the little aeroplane had carried Lord Urquhart, and the recollection made him grin wryly as he ran.

Day was before him. Day was standing with his back to a slender larch and in an attitude that suggested desperate defiance. His face beneath its injuries was pale and blotched and his nostrils were quivering. The man did, at least, intensely care. And whether it was for his queer scheme of atonement, or for some cunningly concealed design, or again for mere life – the little of life that remained to him anyway seemed at the moment unimportant. He would fight. Blinded and with bare hands he would yet fight. And Cranston felt once more the tug of whatever it had been that had first drawn him to the man. It was something very primitive and probably entirely worthless. It shocked him now, even as he felt it. For he ought still to have no other thought than for George. 'Where is she?' he called. 'Where's the girl?'

'Ssh!' Day had gone rigid. Now he turned on him his furious purblind face. 'You fool – don't shout! What have you done? Another bungle?'

'Just that.' Cranston lowered his voice. He felt no animosity. 'But haven't you seen her?'

'Have I seen anything – except men ás trees walking?' Day's hiss was again savage. 'Get me out of this! Haven't you landed me in it?'

It seemed to Cranston that the man was cracking. His fighting would be that of a cornered animal. His swift brain would no longer be behind it. Cranston put out a hand to him. 'Take hold,' he said. 'I'll get you a couple of hundred yards back into the forest, and then I must have another look for George. I don't believe she made the trees at all. Perhaps she got into the pub.'

He led Day back as he had promised. The enemy, he guessed, were doing nothing precipitate. They would be stringing out along the high-road, and across the last stretch of the moor, preparatory to making a drive through this corner of the forest. They still couldn't be legion – it strained credulity that there could be more than, say, a dozen of them all told – and they would have to spread themselves out thin, while carefully maintaining contact all the while.

Once more the Canty Quean appeared through the last fringe of trees. This time he decided to skirt it on the west, for it was on that side that George had vanished. He rounded the building – and there she was. But it was only for a second. She had darted out of some side door and bolted straight for the high-road before he could give a call. He ran after her. He supposed that she had got her directions wrong, and he risked a shout. 'George – it's this way!'

He was too late. George had vanished round the front of the building. He followed – so precipitately that he tripped on a loose cobble and lost ground. When he reached the high-road she was over it. Suddenly he saw that she knew where she was going, and he stopped. The nearest man was twenty yards up the road where it plunged into the forest. And straight in front was the big car, apparently empty. George was making a brilliant bid to capture the enemy's transport. The man up the road had seen her and was pounding back towards the pub. It was just possible that she would bring it off, all the same. But even as her hand was on the door-handle she was beaten. Dead in front of her a second man sprang up as if from nowhere. George saw her danger, dashed across the narrow side-road, and vanished into the trees. Both men were after her. Cranston saw what he must do. 'Day,' he shouted, 'this way – quick!'

The trick worked. Even as Cranston bolted he saw both men turn and make for the pub. He had a good start, and was securely invisible among the trees before they could catch a glimpse of him.

George was over the high-road. Provided she tried no more tricks, she was tolerably safe in the northern part of the forest, for the enemy was unlikely to spare it much immediate attention while they knew that their true quarry was close at hand in the south. And now he had better find Day again, if that was possible. It would be rash to shout, or even to give a low call. He must simply find his bearings, and then push cautiously about. Day could not be more than a couple of hundred yards away now.

He came upon him quite suddenly, sitting with his back against a tree, but alert and listening. 'It's me – Cranston.' He dropped down beside Day. The man was evidently tiring, but he knew how to conserve his strength. 'Listen. It's not too bad.'

'And what about your colonial giant?' Day had recovered his poise, and his question sounded decently concerned. 'Have we lost her?'

'Yes. But I think she's got away. And we can get away too. We have this whole forest, after all. And these people can't run their hue and cry indefinitely.'

'They have pertinacity.'

'No doubt. And these are lonely parts. But it's not Siberia, and there are limits to what they can get away with. All this land is Lord Urquhart's – and he's pretty strict and enormously wealthy. He has no end of keepers. They'll be on top of this invasion in no time.' Cranston realized that he had taken up the role of encouraging an exhausted man. 'Even if there are a dozen of these chaps – two dozen – we can extend them hopelessly. We needn't turn back. We can move eastwards through the forest, parallel to the high-road. And after a couple of miles we can reconnoitre it again. With luck we can be across it after all – and within an hour. After that, Urquhart's no distance, and we'll put our first plan through. You'll be air-borne, man, by tea-time. So come along.'

Day had listened in silence to the whispered words. Now he was on his feet. 'That damned swim,' he murmured. 'Astonishing that I could race you straight after it, and feel like death now. But I can do another couple of hours. Or six at a pinch.' His laugh was low but harsh. 'Lead the way. I can make you out.'

Cranston turned silently and moved off through the trees. It came to him that whether he in his turn could make Day out was an open question still.

Within five minutes he knew that he had been wildly optimistic in speaking of reaching Urquhart by tea-time. If they could have brought themselves to walk straight forward, with no more deviation than was required in order to thread their way among the trees, the estimate would no doubt have been reasonable. But that was impossible – because foolishly rash. Anywhere on their left the enemy might be infiltrating into the forest. Indeed, they were bound to do so, since they could scarcely afford merely to command the high-road and play a waiting game. Some sort of driving or encircling movement was essential if they were to succeed. At any moment one of them might appear, working forward from the road. Against this threat there was considerable advantage to be gained by studying the configuration of the trees so as to find a route affording a maximum of concealment. This made progress very slow – and also distance hard to calculate. Cranston aimed at getting at least two miles east of the Canty Quean before any attempt to break through to the north.

They made perhaps a little more than half that distance in an hour. He was beginning to think of risking a turn to the left when something pulled him up. Only a short distance ahead, and directly across their path if they went on, there lay what it first occurred to him to think of as a great bar of light. For a moment the effect was of an enormous searchlight trained upon the forest. And then he realized that the occasion of it was very simple. What lay ahead was clear sunshine. But it could not, he knew, be the eastern boundary of Urquhart Forest. That, at this point, could not be less than five miles away. 'Wait,' he said to Day, and went cautiously forward.

A great straight ride was here cut through the forest – whether as a fire-break or for the convenience of sportsmen, Cranston didn't know. But for one set of hunters its utility was obvious. He stood still, listening. The only sound was the cooing of pigeons, invisible in the tree-tops overhead. It was a peaceful sleepy sound that made him only more aware of his own strained nerves. He moved forward to the edge of the ride – once more it was a matter of nerve-racking, time-consuming caution – and found a couple of tree-trunks from between which he could make a survey with reasonable safety. The high-road was a quarter of a mile away, beyond a long straight fall of ground. He could distinguish a figure on it – immobile and looking down the ride. Still with steady precaution, he looked the other way. At about an equal distance up the ride there was another figure.

Cranston turned and walked back to Day. 'About turn,' he said briefly. 'We can't go on?'

'There's a straight swathe cut through the forest. They command it.'

Day nodded. He seemed again to be the calm Day of the earlier stages of the adventure. 'Which leaves?'

'A damned sight less room for manoeuvre, one has to admit. A triangle, in fact, bounded by this ride, the open moor, and the high-road.'

'Listen.'

It was the sound of a motor-horn – particularly sepulchral in tone – that had caught Day's attention. 'Something on the road,' Cranston said. 'Another proof that this isn't Siberia. If we risk getting right up to the edge we might be able to dash out and intercept something. There's military traffic, for one thing.'

'We could do quite a lot with just one of those tanks.' Day turned round on this note of grim pleasantry, prepared to follow Cranston's retreat. Then he swayed on his feet and abruptly sat down. 'Damn,' he said. 'Give me just a couple of minutes. Damn, damn.'

'Take a rest – and spare your breath.' Cranston stood beside the exhausted man, frowning. The conviction was coming to him that it was the end of their tether. If the enemy really had a dozen men, seven or eight of them could effectively seal this corner of the forest. And the rest could beat through it at their leisure. He strained his ears, but heard nothing except the same motor-horn, grown fainter. Within the forest twenty men could be moving in perfect silence over the deep carpeting fallen from the pines. 'We'll try.' He spoke quietly but sharply in Day's ear. 'Get up. You can do it. You said you could. We'll make for the high-road – and either lurk for a passing car or try a straight dash. Lean on me, if it's any help.'

Day rose. His swollen eyelids had closed and he appeared drowsy. But he staggered on. 'This Lord Urquhart,' he murmured presently. 'Might he know me?'

For a moment Cranston thought that Day's mind was wandering. 'Know you?'

'I know he's not another titled dabbler in physics, like our friend Blair. But my notoriety – and the photographs?'

'Time enough to worry about that if we ever make Urquhart. And your face is a bit of a mess, you know. I doubt if anybody would recognize you who wasn't on the look-out for you.'

'It's really nasty?'

'It certainly looks uncommonly painful.'

'Rather a shock for my poor wife?'

Cranston made no reply. There was something false in the question which queerly jarred on him. And he wanted absolute silence. They must now be very near the road. Once he thought he heard voices – quite far away. Round about – and apart from the laboured breathing of the man beside him – it was almost ominously soundless. It was a relief when, some minutes later, there were unquestionably voices. They were not near, but they were nearer. They were the voices of men calling to one another as they moved systematically through the trees. The outer guards were all posted. The drive had begun.

'Come on.' Cranston quickened his pace, and tightened his grip on Day's arm. 'It's now or never, if you ask me.'

They hurried on. The voices had ceased and there was the silence again. But there was something wrong with it. Something that was wrong with it hammered at Cranston's brain. Of course there were the peaceful sleepy pigeons – but their sound was so constant that it counted with the silence itself . . . He stopped dead in his tracks. Hundreds of pigeons. Perhaps thousands of them. But among them – a pigeon that was no pigeon at all . . .

He wondered if he could recall the knack of it. He pursed his lips. '*Coo-too!*'

'Coo-too!'

'*Coo-too!*'

'In heaven's name!' Day had swung round on him, bewildered and furious.

'Quiet.' Cranston breathed the word. He was intently listening. 'I can't be wrong,' he whispered. 'I can't be.'

'Coo-too!'

'This way.' He dragged Day forward. The voices made themselves heard again – very briefly, this time, but again from nearer at hand.

'*Coo-too!*'

'Coo-too!' The sound came from close to them. They advanced a few more paces. Cranston caught a glimpse of the road, and of a dark vehicle which had apparently been run a few yards off it into a small clearing. Then, immediately before them, a figure stepped from behind a tree – an extraordinary figure enveloped in black garments and wearing an ancient silk-hat.

'Quick, man – for mercy's sake!' The freckled and perspiring face of Sandy Morrison was in violent agitation beneath the hat. 'They're a' roon' us in thae lairicks.' He gestured at the larch trees. 'An' patrolling the road as thick as polis on a Saturday night on Edinburgh's Royal Mile. I'm jist hoping they'll tak' it I've steppit amang the trees for the sake o' daecency . . . Noo, come awa'.'

Sandy made a dash towards the road and they followed. The vehicle was a hearse. Beside the driver's empty seat was another sombrely clothed and hatted figure, oddly immobile. Sandy flung open a door and seized this appearance unceremoniously by the neck. Within a second he had it in the shelter of the trees, and Cranston found himself staring in stupor at a tailor's dummy. Sandy was tearing off its coat. 'Frae auld Munroe's shop,' he said. 'I thievit it, the Lord help me, frae the window and dressed it as ye see. Lord sakes, Dickie, ye muckle looster – get yoursel' into the thing. They'll be doon the road ony minute.'

Cranston did as he was told. 'But Day?'

'The coffin, ye puir croot!' Sandy was in a frenzy. 'I've backit the hearse so it canna well be seen. Ye maun thrust in the coarse creature and doon wi' the lid. I've bored yin-twa holes – God forgi' me for an irreligious man – that he can breathe through in the bottom. Quick man! Then I'll come oot, looking as I should, and awa' we gae.'

Within a minute this extraordinary programme had accomplished itself. As Cranston jumped in beside Sandy he had a glimpse of a man sweeping up on a bicycle. Sandy slipped into gear and the hearse moved decorously forward. 'Ye needna' look ower reverent,' Sandy whispered. 'In the profession, ye keep that until ye see the mourners. But let the big lum hat come well down ower your e'en. Did the chiel Day mind the coffin?'

'I think he was a bit taken aback.'

'He'd be mair taken aback by a lang way if thae gomerils got at him with their guns. What kind of a daft gallivanting is this, I ask ye, to be rampaging in the ancient an' godly kingdom o' Scotland?' Sandy accelerated. 'Where are ye for?'

'Urquhart. It's the first road on the right.'

'Is it indeed?' Sandy was contemptuous. 'If I didna' ken these pairts weel, d'ye think ye'd be riding in your carriage at this moment, Dickie Cranston?'

'No, indeed, Sandy. But how –?'

'Get your heid doon, man. Here's more o' them.'

Cranston glanced ahead. It was the big Daimler – drawn up at the side of the road as if for a picnic. A cloth had been laid, and there was a hamper apparently ready to be unpacked. The only person visible was an elderly man of distinguished appearance, in dark clothes and a black hat. He might, Cranston thought, have been an eminent Q.C. Somewhat surprisingly, he seemed to be occupying himself with a portable radio. But as the hearse approached he rose and strolled to the edge of the road. At the same moment another man, dressed like a chauffeur, appeared on the other side of the road, one hand deep in a pocket. Both men scrutinized the hearse. And then the eminent Q.C. respectfully took off his hat. The chauffeur, accepting the cue, saluted. The hearse was past them. The Canty Quean was in sight.

'But, Sandy – how did you do it?'

The hearse was trundling down the side-road to Urquhart. The surface was bad, for Lord Urquhart disapproved of useless expenditure on facilitating surface travel. The trip could not be very comfortable for Day, but they had agreed that it would be imprudent to resurrect him yet.

'Man – it wasna' me. It was the lassie.'

'The lassie?' For a moment Cranston's mind was blank.

'The lassie frae Australia, ye gaup. She rang up the polis at Drumtoul – rang them up frae the Canty Quean – and persuaded that great sloupe Carfrae to let me oot. And me jiled na' mair than twenty meenits. The puir traicle came for me tae the lock-up tae mak' sense o' it. So awa' I went to find the ambulance. And then I saw there was little sense in that, for they'd mind it at yince after a' that cookuddy in the quarry. So I got oot the hearse instead.' Sandy Morrison paused mournfully. 'It seems no' likely, Dick Cranston, that I'll ever hae the chaunce o' driving it again.'

Cranston laughed. 'That you will, Sandy. I'll speak to Lord Urquhart. Isn't his word law from here to Inverness?'

'Even wi' the Superintendent?'

'He appoints the Superintendent – and the folk that superintend the Superintendent as well.'

'Would that be so, now?' This was a new vista to Sandy, and he received it with gravity. 'But here's the lodge. Had we no' better have oot the creature Day?'

Cranston thought for a moment. 'No,' he said. 'Decidedly not. We'll drive up exactly as we are.'

Chapter 15

'I wouldn't have believed it.' Lord Urquhart flourished the knife with which he was dissecting a cold ham. 'Not, that is to say, if I hadn't seen it with my own eyes.' He turned to Lady Urquhart. 'Might be something in a shocker – eh?'

Lady Urquhart, who was combing a Dandie Dinmont, shook her head. 'No, Ian – not a Cocker. I never cared for their ears. But we might consider a Golden Retriever.' Lady Urquhart was very deaf. She was also a woman of somewhat circumscribed interests.

'But deuced like Alex Blair. Mark you, I never speak ill of a neighbour.' With great rapidity Lord Urquhart cut half a dozen slices from the ham. 'And much less of a neighbour's wife. It's something I never knew good come of yet. The servants pick it up, you know, and pass it on to the tenantry. And that's not good for any of us. So I never do it. What was I saying? Ah, yes. Damned foolish of Blair to marry that bitch.'

'A bitch?' Lady Urquhart was doubtful. 'But don't you think Alice would prefer a dog? One has to be so careful, in a town.'

'An eminent ichthyologist.' He turned to Cranston. 'I think that's what you say the fellow is?'

'Yes, sir.'

'And name of Knight?'

'John Knight.'

'Quite so. I've heard of him, of course. Positively an outrage. I'm uncommonly shocked.'

'No, dear – certainly not docked.' This time Lady Urquhart was decided. 'I never approved of it. Of course it may be different with sheep. There, I would never interfere.' She turned to Cranston. 'Is your friend Mr Knight interested in dogs?'

'I think he may know about Russian setters.'

'How very interesting! But such troublesome dogs to groom. A woolly and matted coat.'

'Now, why doesn't the fellow join us?' Lord Urquhart looked about him hospitably. 'Why doesn't he come and get something to eat?'

Lady Urquhart nodded. 'Yes, Ian – that's just what I was saying. In town, *not* a bitch.'

'Knight's making a long-distance call, sir. I believe he's trying to make certain of the whereabouts of his wife.'

'To be sure. The poor lady will be very much distressed. Sheer barbarity. To be quite frank, I never regarded Alex Blair as one of us. Not even before that shocking low marriage.' Lord Urquhart looked at Cranston. 'Know Lady Blair, my boy?'

'I've got to know her a little better, just lately.' Cranston wondered if he looked a fool. It was positively – odd, he found, to be speaking a fragment of the truth.

'Take my advice and keep clear. If you ask me, the whole household's a bit strange.'

'All spaniels do.' Lady Urquhart appeared to admit this with regret. 'But it always means that something has been wrong with the diet. And much can be done by treating the skin at once.'

'Lady Blair's girl, now – can you remember her name?'

Habituated to deceit, Cranston gave the impression of exercising his memory. 'Sally Dalrymple.'

'That's right . . . Have some salad, my boy.' For a few moments Lord Urquhart busied himself about the table. 'Although who Dalrymple was, heaven alone knows. Certainly not one of the Dalrymples. Queer girl, too.'

'Sally's quite sound.' Cranston found that, most indiscreetly, he had spoken with sudden fierce conviction.

'A hound?' Lady Urquhart took up politely what she plainly regarded as an inept suggestion. 'An otter-hound would be a possibility. But they are undeniably quarrelsome, you know. And there's that oily underfur to consider. Definitely not a dog that is *ever* at home in a drawing-room. And poor Alice, I fear, is scarcely at home anywhere else. I always advised against a political marriage.'

'Quite right – quite right.' For the first time, Lord Urquhart arrived at some sort of cloudy contact with his wife. 'The political people have gone to the devil. No enterprise. Won't look forward. Travel in stage-coaches, if they had a chance. Now, take my grandfather. He wouldn't let the old Caledonian Railway, you know, put a line across his estate. Suffered a lot of abuse as a result. Called a backwoodsman and a Stone Age Pict and things of that sort. But not a bit of it. What he had was prospectiveness, my boy. Knew that all that railroad stuff would be obsolete within his own son's lifetime. Dipt into the future, as Tennyson said. Saw the heavens filled with commerce . . . Have I told you my scheme for flying fresh herring from

Cromarty to Chicago?' Lord Urquhart broke off reluctantly. 'Ah – here's Knight.'

An ancient manservant had appeared at the door. His words were unexpected. 'Miss Cranston, your ladyship.'

'My cousin, Georgiana Cranston.' As George made her necessarily somewhat surprising appearance, Cranston offered what explanation he could. She was safe and sound, and his relief was enormous. But he did a little wonder what the Urquharts would make of her, and how much it would be necessary to fit her into the extravagant yarn he had delivered himself of. 'Georgiana lives in Australia.'

'Australia? How very interesting!' Lady Urquhart received her new guest with cordiality. 'You must tell me about the dingoes.'

'Dingoes?' Lord Urquhart was puzzled. 'Never heard of such a family in my life. You can't mean the Stillgoes, Anne – the people poor Kinross's daughter married into?'

'Of course not, Ian. Dingoes are dogs. But are they pariah dogs? Nobody appears to know.'

'Oh – dogs.' Lord Urquhart's interest evaporated. 'Can I give you some ham? Did you come with the hearse?'

George accepted ham. 'I walked – through the forest.'

'Perfectly proper, perfectly proper. I've no doubt you took reasonable care. You don't carry matches?'

'Never.' George shook her head as she munched. Being introduced into the presence of the ancient nobility of Scotland did not appear to induce in her any access of self-consciousness. 'Just a map and a compass and some lollies.'

'Some –?' Lord Urquhart was at a loss.

'Sweets – usually barley-sugar. That sees you through twenty-four hours easily, if you get lost in a mist.'

'Perfectly true, perfectly true.' Lord Urquhart was delighted. He turned to his wife. 'You see how well informed and well conducted the younger people are, Anne? And then a fellow like Blair goes and behaves in this disgraceful way. Has a gun fired under the nose of an eminent scientist – more eminent by a long way than Blair himself is, I don't doubt – and virtually blinds him and then hounds him over a moor. Supposes that everyone interested in fish must be a poacher.'

'Certainly not. A lurcher would be quite impossible, Ian. We might as well send a greyhound while we were about it.'

'Keeps keepers that are no better than thugs. Young Cranston here actually has to smuggle the fellow away in a hearse. Think of it – an ichthyologist in a hearse! But I must remember to commend this young Sandy Morrison. Most resourceful. I'm minded to give him a job on my ground staff.' Lord Urquhart looked at Cranston. 'How would that be?'

'Capital, sir – although Sandy has rather looked forward to doing funerals all the time.'

'Then why shouldn't he?' Lord Urquhart was suddenly inspired. 'Why not get that line of business into the air? Tiresome things, funerals, among surface traffic. Do it by helicopter, eh? I must consult my nephew. My nephew Porp, you know. He's the great helicopter-wallah.' Lord Urquhart turned to George. 'What about Australia? Any room for air-funerals there?'

'Well, there's plenty of *room*.'

'We must think of it. What does your father do – make paper-bags?' Lord Urquhart paused and then appeared to recognize this as a somewhat random question. 'Just that I get some money, from time to time, from people who do that out there. Make them out of gum-trees, I'm told. Deuced odd trade.'

'My father raises sheep.'

'Does he, indeed?' Lord Urquhart was interested. 'Graze many acres?'

'I'm afraid I can't say how many. It's rather a hard sum.' George considered. 'But it works out at just under eight hundred square miles.'

'God bless my soul!' Lord Urquhart was impressed.

'What breed does he go in for?'

'Merinos, mostly.'

'Capital, capital.' Suddenly Lord Urquhart put down his carving-knife and looked at George with something like awe. 'Not the Cranston Merino?'

'You're telling me. And aren't they beaut?' George was enthusiastic. She caught Cranston's eye, and seemed to be moved by it to a further exercise of her vernacular. 'Dinkum,' she said.

Lord Urquhart accepted it gravely. 'Precisely, my dear. The only word for that astonishing sheep. But – let me see – how did we get to sheep from fish? Cranston, what about your fish man? Isn't he going to join us?'

'I think he will in a minute, sir. But he's in a good deal of pain. You saw his eyes. They're in a shocking mess.'

'Bless my soul – why didn't I think of a doctor?' Lord Urquhart was contrite. 'Could we get your father over?'

'I doubt whether he could come, sir, just at the moment. He's standing by for rather a difficult confinement.'

'I see, I see.' Lord Urquhart considered. 'What about old Anderson, then? He's said to be not bad. Some of the tenants swear by him.'

'Then perhaps we'd better have him, sir, although he mayn't know a great deal about eyes. But one can't pick and choose at the back of beyond.'

'Eh – what's that?' Lord Urquhart was instantly indignant.

'Sorry, sir – but you know what I mean. The Highlands are shockingly out of reach of the great medical centres. Sir Mungo Lockhart of Edinburgh would be the man. My father says he's one of the best oculists in the country. But there's no hope of making Edinburgh under seven or eight hours.'

'Indeed?' Lord Urquhart had risen and was eyeing his young guest with unusual severity. 'And just where is this Lockhart to be found in Edinburgh?'

'Moray Place.'

'Very well. Do you know Turnhouse?'

'Is that some sort of little airfield?'

'It is an airfield.' Lord Urquhart contrived to utter this through a sort of snort. 'And how long, do you think, would it take some wretched taxi-cab to get from Turnhouse to Moray Place?'

'I'm afraid I've no idea. But my guess would be half an hour.'

'Very well. Add an hour and a half to that – or two hours with the devil of a head-wind – and you've got the time in which I can deliver this Lockhart his patient.'

Cranston looked at his host with every appearance of astonishment. 'You mean, sir, that you'll fly him there?'

'I'll fly the lot of you.' Lord Urquhart had taken to pacing up and down in high excitement. 'Go and find him. Go and tell him about it. And then send a telegram to Lockhart . . . Sir Mungo, did you say? He must be one of the Lockharts of Lee. Perfectly sound people . . . Ah, here your fellow is.'

Day was led in by Lord Urquhart's butler. He wore the dark glasses Sally had provided in the summer-house, and Cranston wondered whether he was really still as blind as he made out. His appearance in this fashion, guiding himself on the arm of a venerable family retainer, had for Cranston a displeasing effect of masquerade. But then the whole thing was that, and he himself was up to the neck in it. And he was suddenly abominably ashamed.

He was both ashamed and bewildered – bewildered that the quality of his shame over this merely graceless aspect of his situation was indistinguishable from that which he had been experiencing at what he thought of as his betrayal of Sally in the horror of his affair with her mother. Only some hours ago he had been feeling that to be utter dishonour – and the feeling had landed him, as a species of penance, with this queer mission. He still felt it as that now. But he found that he was quite as ashamed of this present charade – which was a mere harmless vulgar deception – as he had been of fornication and adultery. And the unexpectedness of this worried him. He could have enjoyed playing all sorts of outrageous jokes on old Lord Urquhart, just as a year or two ago he could have enjoyed stealing his trout. But this was the wrong sort of joke. And he found that he greatly cared about being committed to it.

But the feeling only made him plunge the more resolutely now. In for a penny, in for a pound. 'Lady Urquhart,' he said, 'this is my friend John Knight.' He had to put some emphasis on the name. He was afraid that Day might have forgotten it. And, even as he spoke, he had a sudden absurd panic about something else. Again and again since this adventure began, it seemed to him, he had blundered through over-confidence. And perhaps he had done it once more. It was wildly unlikely that either of the Urquharts had ever set eyes on John Day, the eminent nuclear physicist. Even if they had, it was most improbable that they would recognize him now. But it was not merely John Day who had just come into the room. It was also a complete outfit of Sir Alex Blair's. What if Lord Urquhart was accustomed to cast a noticing and satirical eye at his detested neighbour's sartorial tastes? What if he now gave a cry of astonishment and indignation? Cranston had managed a harrowing account of his friend's brutal treatment at the hands of hirelings of the Laird of of Dinwiddie. It would take some explaining if it appeared that his friend was dressed in the Laird's clothing now.

The fear was, of course, baseless. Day – or Knight – was civilly received and accommodated with whisky and cold ham. He was convincing enough in his role – remarkably so, considering that he had to pick up much of it as he went along – but at the same time he was to Cranston's eye discernibly ill at ease. And Cranston conjectured with astonishment that it was a species of social embarrassment that was at work. The man who had been so confident with Caryl Blair was uncertain with harmless old doggy Lady Urquhart. He must have had dealings, in his final years of importance in England, with all sorts of eminent and exalted persons. Yet he couldn't quite get the Urquharts right. Not that it mattered. They were accustomed to it. But it was queer that this inwardly driven and outwardly hunted man, with his *idée fixe* and his passions and his small span of years or months to live, should retain the slightest responsiveness to the notion of comparative social elevations. Surely Day –

Abruptly Cranston realized that he had got it all wrong. Day's trouble was not embarrassment but some sort of distraction. The man was failing to keep his attention civilly on what was being said – whether by Lady Urquhart on the subject of Skye Terriers or by her husband on the insufficiencies of the Ministry of Civil Aviation. Perhaps it was sheer fatigue. Perhaps it was pain. Or perhaps – Cranston suddenly found himself thinking – it was a trick. Perhaps it was some sort of trick within his own trick – a matter of Day going one better.

'Cranston tells me that the man we had better get you to is Lockhart in Edinburgh.' Lord Urquhart had come back to his plan. 'I have told him to send the fellow a wire, to make sure you don't miss him. Eyes, you know, are not things to take risks with. It would be a thousand pities, my dear Dr Knight, if this deplorable incident were to cripple a career like yours. Dash it all, we can't – um – know too much about fish. All very well for old savages like myself to catch them and eat them and order plaster casts of the big ones. But science is another matter.' Having delivered himself of this amiable generality, Lord Urquhart returned to business. 'So I propose, as I was saying, to fly you to Edinburgh . . . By the way, I hope you got through on the telephone to your wife?'

'Not actually to my wife, Lord Urquhart.' Day passed a hand across his forehead. 'I had, as a matter of fact, rather worrying news. It bothers me much more than this business of my eyes.'

'My dear sir, I am sorry to hear it.' Lord Urquhart was concerned and benevolent. 'Not, I hope, sudden serious illness?'

'A street-accident. You must forgive me if I am rather upset, and inattentive to your great kindness. My wife is in one of the metropolitan hospitals. And it seems that she is on the danger list.' Day paused. 'If you will really have the extreme goodness to fly me to Edinburgh, I can possibly get a commercial plane from there, or at least catch the night train.'

'There is not a moment to lose.' Lord Urquhart strode to the side of the room and rang a bell. 'I shall fly you straight in to Northolt myself.'

'My dear Lord Urquhart!' Day appeared painfully agitated. 'I really could not think of it.'

'Nonsense, my dear sir. It is my pleasure.' Lord Urquhart was courteously concerned to minimize the sense of obligation his offer must impose. 'Cranston will tell you that this is my great interest. There ought to be nobody in a position like mine in this country who is not equipped, and willing, to do precisely this. We must come down at Turnhouse to refuel, but after that it will be only one hop. And at Northolt my town car will be waiting to take you straight to your wife, and to such treatment as you require yourself.'

Lord Urquhart, flushed and triumphant, turned aside to give orders to a servant who had entered the room. Cranston looked cautiously at George. It was evident that she shared his discomfort before this mounting duplicity. But decidedly they were in for it now. And with luck this amiable peer would never know that his confidence had been abused. Not, that was to say, unless the enemy won out after all, and riddled the anxious husband with a burst of bullets. Or unless . . . Cranston knew – indefinably but with increasing certainty – that there were other possibilities. For John Day continued to be an enigma. His story was plausible – even convincing. But it remained true that to stick to him was to make oneself a fellow-traveller into the unknown. It was possible –

Cranston's speculations got no further. Lord Urquhart had turned to his wife. 'My dear,' he said, 'I find that I must fly our guests south. Expect me home tomorrow. And don't blame our friends if their leave-taking seems a little abrupt. I am hurrying them along. We must leave now.'

Lady Urquhart had listened carefully – and now her face lit up. 'Precisely!' she said. 'It has been in my own mind all the time. Alice shall have a Chow.'

Chapter 16

They skimmed over Scotland. Lord Urquhart – Cranston had found with relief – admitted the company of some sort of technical assistant in aeronautics. These two sat in front, and the three passengers in a small compartment behind. But Day had once more dropped off to sleep, and Cranston and George talked. He told her now all that he knew about the man from the sea. He tried to make clearer – he scarcely knew whether it was to her or to himself – the impulse prompting him to see Day through. But George appeared not much disposed to any large analysis. She was looking ahead. 'Let's accept this business of seeing his wife. Even if it's genuine I'm not clear that it's admirable. But we can't possibly pretend to judge it, so we must take it as read. The question is: what then?'

'Yes – I know.'

'I suppose, by the way, that the business about a street-accident *was* a pure lie – something cooked up to prompt Lord Urquhart to take him all the way south?'

Cranston shook his head. 'I haven't had a chance to ask him – and I'm not inclined to wake him up now. But I suppose it's almost certainly untrue.'

'Did he really make a long-distance call from Urquhart?'

'I can't even tell you that. But I suppose so. It would be a pointless deception, surely, simply to say he had. He wasn't going to ring up his wife herself. That would spoil the surprise.'

'I think it's horrible.' George was suddenly emphatic. 'His eye must be entirely on himself.'

'You said we couldn't judge.'

'All right. But what about this telephone call?'

'It was to be a cautious inquiry, I gathered, made somewhere else, to find out if his wife was still where he left her.'

George looked puzzled. 'Isn't that precisely where he might expect *not* to find her? Didn't you say there were children – sons? Surely when a thing like that happens one makes what break one can?'

'I suppose one might be determined to face it out. The address is somewhere in Kensington, and it seems she has remained there. I suppose it's an anonymous sort of place. And it's where Day asks to be taken to for this horrible reunion.'

George was silent. She had turned away to look down at the country beneath. Its character was changing. There was a town. The sight of it prompted George to another topic. 'Richard, what happened to my rucksack?'

He stared. 'I'm frightfully sorry. It simply got left behind during the chase. I can't even remember where. Is it a disaster?'

She laughed. 'We'll do well if we get away with no worse disaster than that – although I did like that frock. Is Turnhouse any sort of fashionable resort?'

'I'd hardly suppose so.'

'Or Northolt? I do cut a frightful figure.'

Cranston was taken by surprise. He even felt some sort of sudden shyness. His respect for George was now very wholesome, but he had started by regarding her as a figure of fun. This sudden unselfconscious emergence in her of matters of purely feminine concern for a moment disconcerted him.

'You'll be all right if it doesn't turn cold,' he said – and glanced at her cautiously to see how she would take this determined masculine impercipience. 'And I have an aunt in London. She could –'

'That's all right.' George was clearly not enchanted with the prospect of being rescued by Cranston's aunt. 'My own base is in London for the time being, you know. I'm sharing a flat with another girl. And I do possess a spare frock there.'

'Then that's fine.' He hesitated. 'Are you thinking of stopping in this country long?'

'Oh, no.' She was briskly decided. 'I'll make that visit to your mother, if I'm still wanted. But soon after that I'll be off. I've a job at home, you know.'

'With the Merinos?'

Instead of replying, George pointed. 'Are we there? Is that Edinburgh Castle?'

'Stirling. But we shall be at Turnhouse in no time now. The old boy wasn't boasting about the turn of speed he can manage.'

'Must he really take us all the way? Isn't it a bit steep? There must be ordinary passenger flights from this Turnhouse place?'

Cranston nodded. 'There are. In fact, there's bound to be one out just about the time we get there. But I suppose Day is going to feel safer tucked up cosily in private.'

'It seems to me that John Day has it all his own way. If you ask me, this doomed-to-die business has got us both down.'

'Perhaps. But it's only fair to remember that it has got him down too. I think we can trust Day to die.'

'Do we leave him to it?'

For a moment Cranston was silent, staring in sombre perplexity at the sleeping man. 'I'm sure it's true – that part of his story. But I'm not clear about just when the thing is – well, scheduled. It would be irresponsible, wouldn't it, just to say good-bye to him at the moment of tipping him into the bosom of his family?'

'Decidedly.'

'In fact, one must whistle up a policeman at just that point? I've absolutely not given any undertaking not to. But it seems pretty squalid, all the same.' He looked at her anxiously – caught himself, indeed, so looking, and suddenly realized that he was in a sense handing over to her. 'Or doesn't it?'

George seemed not immediately disposed to tackle the question head-on. 'Perhaps he means to do away with himself. That must have occurred to you.'

'Yes, it has. I can't imagine that the sort of disease one gets from a slip-up with his kind of stuff can be other than unspeakably horrible. Suicide must almost certainly be in his mind. But it seems a bit mean to hope that the poor devil will hang himself just in order to get me out of a hole. I should never be quite sure afterwards that I hadn't actually bought him the rope.'

'You've certainly given him a lot already.' George shot this at him. 'I'm a crude self-confident colonial, as you've noticed. But *your* self-confidence – your awful cheek, Richard Cranston, positively takes my breath away.'

'My cheek?' He was startled and disturbed.

'Taking on a thing like this by way of getting straight with yourself over some small hole-and-corner immorality. It's outrageous. My younger brother once nearly started a bush fire.'

'I don't see –'

'He had been shockingly careless. And it was about the very worst thing that he could have done. *He* saw it, poor kid, as a crime, a sin. He came back to the homestead feeling like death. But do you know what I found him doing half an hour later? Juggling with Dad's billiard balls before a mirror and showing off to himself no end.'

'And I'm like that?' Cranston was looking at her round-eyed.

'Exactly. Except that your billiard balls are fissionable.'

Cranston was silent for some minutes. The Firth of Forth had begun to broaden out on their left. The first part of their flight was almost over. 'I wasn't regardless,' he said. 'I did think of bringing in Sir Alex Blair. But I found I just couldn't.'

'Because of something about Blair himself? Or because he stood for society, the law – that sort of thing?'

Cranston found himself bewildered. 'I don't know,' he said. 'Although obviously I ought to.' He seized on a clarifying idea. 'If Blair stands for society, then there's something rotten in the state of Denmark.'

'So instead of Sir Alex Blair you brought in his step-daughter, who is unquestionably sound? At least I think you described her to Lord Urquhart that way?'

'It wasn't like that, George. I've told you how Sally was dragged in. It was absolutely rotten for her, and she was frightfully decent.'

'You don't think she –' George checked herself. 'Do you think the enemy can have another shot?'

He nodded seriously. 'I think they can. The business of the hearse wouldn't baffle them for long, and they would see that the trail led to Urquhart. When they saw Lord Urquhart's plane take off they would feel decidedly interested. I don't suggest we're going to be shot down in the air – but it's not at all certain what may be waiting for us, whether here at Turnhouse or in London. Then again, there's Day's wife. It wouldn't be beyond their imagination to fancy that he might make for her. And he *is* making for her. They may be waiting on her doorstep for him. In other words, despite bringing off this rapid move south, we have quite a bit of thinking to do.'

'And surely with Day in on it? Mightn't it be suggested to him that he could find a healthier place for his bit of theatre than the known home of his wife?' She pointed. 'Isn't that the Forth Bridge?'

'Yes – and we're coming down.'

The plane banked and turned. An airfield appeared and disappeared, to be replaced alarmingly by hurtling roofs and haystacks. There was the slightest of quivers beneath them. 'Nicely done,' George said.

'There's the plane for London – that Admiral.' Cranston nodded at a farther corner of the airfield. He glanced at his watch. 'Due out, I think, in about half an hour.'

'It will beat us, won't it?'

'I've no idea. Presumably we'll be off again within ten minutes ourselves. But there'll be time to stretch our legs. This plane isn't really built for you and me.'

'I'd say we'd stretched them quite substantially today already.'

For a moment they found themselves contemplating each other's sprawled limbs with frank amusement and satisfaction. Then Lord Urquhart turned round and gave them a triumphant wave. 'First stage,' he said.

They got a cup of tea, and afterwards George wandered off by herself. The whole business of air-travel fascinated her almost as much as it did Lord Urquhart. The great Constellations were to her generation what the mail-steamers had been to her parents' – the magically punctual carpets that carried one home – always, in a sense, 'home' whether one were travelling in the one direction or the other. And the small fry – the D. H. Drovers and the Doves – represented the means of fetching the doctor or dropping in on the neighbours. But on this occasion she had only an absent eye for the traffic of the place. It had become clear to her that there was a sense in which her cousin Richard Cranston had been hypnotized by his man from the sea. Cunningly – she was sure it was that – John Day had touched off in him something that was not so much simply romantic as positively atavistic – a touchy quirky sense of personal honour that she knew in Cranstons on the other side of the world as well. Her own father called it the pride of folk who fetch long pedigrees from small places. And she wondered if the day's events didn't show her as a little tarred with the same brush – as indeed it was only natural that she should be.

So far, they had been rescuing Day from the people to whom he had formerly, for one reason or another, sold himself. What if the situation suddenly and sharply changed, and they had to shelter him – positively and immediately, in some concrete situation – from the law of his own country? How far was her cousin prepared to carry this hazardous business of a private judgement on the thing? And how far was she?

George stopped to look at the Admiral that would presently be taking off for London. Was it possible that the law had already been invoked, and that interest in John Day had spread beyond the small band of secret agents

565

who had made all the running so far? Was Richard perhaps too confident that –

She turned away, seeing that it was time to go back to Lord Urquhart's plane. She was walking rapidly when she happened to turn her glance on the main entrance to the airfield. It was like the crisis when she had first spied the tell-tale cobweb on the door of the Canty Quean. But it was, for the moment, a good deal more bewildering. There was no sense in it. There was no sense in it unless – George found that she had stopped dead in her tracks. She heard a faint hail and turned her head to see her cousin standing by their plane and waving to her. She hurried forward. By the time she reached him her mind was made up. 'Richard,' she said, 'I'm not coming further.'

'Not coming?' He spoke above the roar of the engine. The plane was ready to take off. He was astonished and dismayed. 'Why ever not?'

'I can't tell you.'

'George!' He made a movement towards her.

'I can't tell you – yet.'

'You're not –?' He paused, confused.

'Do you think I would?' She flashed it at him. 'Where can I contact you?'

He saw that she meant it. 'At my aunt's. Malvern Court. It's a big block of flats off –'

'I know. And now – get in.'

Cranston gave her a single long look and obeyed.

'I'll be seeing you,' she said – and turned away.

He didn't see it, she said to herself. For a wonder he didn't see it. And it sticks out a mile. It would be quite noticeable if it were black or a sober grey. But as it is –

There was only a chauffeur left in the great yellow car. It was drawing away from the low building marked *Departures*. George remembered thankfully that she had a belt – like Day she had a belt – and that there was quite a lot of money in it. Until she knew what was happening she couldn't afford to let go. She wished she was less absurdly dressed. Probably she was as noticeable as the yellow Cadillac itself.

She glanced quickly at the nearest group of people, with a notion that she would find them staring, and instead found to her astonishment that they were dressed exactly like herself. She drew nearer. They were young men and women of about her own age, talking a foreign language. For a brief moment – such is the power of recent associations – she was suspicious and alarmed. Then she slipped into the middle of them. They were blonde, and most of them were enormous. She guessed that they were Norwegians or Swedes. Certainly they were perfect cover. She stood in the middle of them, amiably smiling, and knew that for the moment she had found a sort of cloak of invisibility.

Not that there was any reason to suppose that Sir Alex Blair would know her from Adam – or Eve. Whatever he was up to – and to discover that was decidedly the point – he was presumably without the advantage of any information derived from the late enemy. From his own lodge-keeper, Patullo, he might vaguely have heard of the incident of the mysterious housemaid – supposing Patullo had in fact noticed anything. But that was the nearest, surely, that he could be to any knowledge of her existence.

And correspondingly she didn't know him. Her mind worked largely in pictures, and she had indeed invented an Alex Blair. She had invented, for that matter – and with rather more particularity – an image that she called Sally Dalrymple. But neither of these inventions would much serve for the purpose of positive identification . . . She glanced about the species of assembly hall in which she was standing. There was no great crowd – only, she guessed, the passengers going to London on the Admiral, and an answering group going the other way to Aberdeen. And in a moment this conjecture confirmed itself. With the usual ritual of disembodied voices and lines of coloured lights the Aberdeen contingent was shepherded away. But her Scandinavians were going south – which was so far, so good. And so was she – or ten to one she was. The odds were sufficient to justify her buying a ticket at once. Without much trepidation now, she broke cover to do so. Fortunately the plane wasn't booked out. She returned to her adopted companions. They received her without surprise, and one or two even appeared to murmur casual words. Presumably their travels were young and they were some of them unknown to one another.

She scanned the remaining people in the hall. None of them answered to anything she could conceive of as a retired scientist turned Scottish country gentleman. She abandoned the men and studied the women. And almost at once she knew she was looking at Sally Dalrymple. Richard's Sally, she said to herself. Richard's sound Sally.

She was easy on the eyes. George framed this vulgar description to herself with deliberate relish. A sweetly pretty girl. No – that wouldn't do. It wasn't at all fair. Sally Dalrymple was beautiful. She was beautiful and knew how to get herself up to match. But she had told tales.

George took a grip on herself. One wanted a clear head. And to say – or think – a thing like that was less fair still. If the girl had gone straight to her step-father with the story of John Day one couldn't honestly and faithfully say that she had done wrong. And the consequence wasn't any sort of hue and cry. Turnhouse wasn't swarming with officers from whatever was the Scottish equivalent of Scotland Yard. Sir Alex Blair had acted swiftly – but unobtrusively. If the term didn't quite fit his Cadillac, George couldn't blame him for that. Had it not attracted her attention when she was scanning Dinwiddie Castle that morning, its sweeping on to the airfield would have meant nothing to her now.

Again she hunted around – for she couldn't believe that Sally Dalrymple was here alone. Sir Alex must be somewhere about. Unless indeed – it struck her suddenly as a possibility – the girl's travelling south to catch a plane was sheer coincidence. But something about the girl herself indefinably insisted that it wasn't so. She was not only what is called perfectly groomed; she was also perfectly self-possessed. But if you watched her face you saw that it was set and strained. She was here because of John Day.

And she was here because she could identify John Day. Even if only in an imperfect early morning light, she had seen him as he now was. The moment must come at which the girl would have to point and say *There*! It couldn't be something she was looking forward to, poor kid – and it explained the tension discernible in her now.

The disembodied voice was telling the London passengers to get ready. And still there was no sign of Sir Alex. How, George wondered, did the girl feel about Richard? There was no doubt how Richard felt towards the girl. Or about the whole story. George looked at the story steadily – much as she had been looking at Sally. There was nothing easy on the eyes about it. Still, her mind didn't exactly reel before it. Apparently poor Richard's did. He felt –

She caught herself up. All that wasn't, at the moment, the point. It was the point that this man Blair had been told of young Richard Cranston's rash involvement with the returned John Day. And what he was now doing – surely the facts could bear no other interpretation – was acting quickly and quietly to relieve the youth of at least some part of the burden of his folly. Presumably Sir Alex didn't know about the behaviour – about what newspapers or lawyers called the misconduct – of his wife. He thought of Richard as his step-daughter's friend and the family doctor's son. He would do what he could to get the matter briskly settled and effectively hushed up.

The voice was speaking again. They were being exhorted to follow the blue light. George's Scandinavians shouldered their rucksacks and bundles. The other passengers picked up their hand-baggage. There was a general shuffle across the hall. And then she saw him.

Sir Alex Blair was as unmistakable as Sally Dalrymple had been. He was the only person in the place, George thought, who had Ruling Class written all over him. If there was anything unexpected about him it was perhaps that the writing was a shade too large. He certainly wasn't showy or obtrusive or arrogant. There was nothing about him that corresponded, so to speak, directly to the colour of his car. Still, what the car spoke in one language the man himself contrived somehow to speak in another. Perhaps, George told herself, it was all to the good. He looked the sort of man who would prize powerful friends and cherish influential contacts. If Richard were threatened with serious trouble – and he might well be – this was the man who would know just where to go and what to say. Like his step-daughter he was beautifully turned out – in admirable clothes that were just not quite new. He was extremely well preserved, but not offensively so. He would smell – very very faintly – of some superb shaving-soap.

George had not much time to remark that these observations and responses fell some way short of enthusiasm. For now they were in the open air and had been taken over by a young lady in uniform. George managed to get right at the tail of her large blonde companions and thus to have Sally Dalrymple immediately behind her. Sir Alex, she realized, had been in a little office, and as he advanced she saw out of the corner of her eye that he was carrying a telegram.

'Just in time.' His voice – pleasant, confident, and not exactly subdued – came to her clearly. 'It ought to have been waiting for us, but it came in only thirty seconds ago. A near thing. I asked –'

A sudden roar of engines drowned what followed. The Aberdeen plane was off down its runway. When the noise faded the two people behind George had fallen silent. The little ragged procession was nearing its aircraft. Two or three rude persons, having a mind to some favourite seat, began a sort of modified jostling designed to get them to the front. The Scandinavians stood politely aside. George decided to do the same. Without assertiveness – one couldn't indeed quite see how it was done – Sir Alex was first aboard after all, with his step-daughter beside him. George, glimpsing them together as they went past, had an odd sensation of hearing with her inner ear the voice of old Lord Urquhart, repeating something he had already said that afternoon. Then she was on board herself. She didn't want to sit down beside a conversable Swede, and she moved forward. When she found a seat it was directly in front of the pair from Dinwiddie.

They were still, as far as she could judge, silent. But the engines were now roaring, and in a minute they were moving forward. It was only when they had been airborne for some time that she felt at all confident of being able to catch even fragments of anything that was said. It was years since she had eavesdropped in a serious way. She settled down to it now.

'There are a great many difficulties, you know, still.' It was Sir Alex's voice. But its quality had changed. The tone matched the words. It was worried and almost sombre. 'The biggest is the mere uncertainty.'

'Are you so uncertain?'

'We have this one specific indication. Day is making for his wife. But it may be all lies. Do you think young Cranston realizes that?'

'I don't know. I suppose he would. Wouldn't he?' Sally Dalrymple's voice, although distinguishable only with difficulty, came to George as oddly uncomfortable and constrained. It was as if she found talking about Richard difficult. And that, George thought, might well be.

'I know precious little about him.' Sir Alex sounded impatient. 'I suppose he's a fool. Most young people are.'

'Thank you!' Now Sally's voice seemed to tremble. It might almost have been with anger. George frowned. Probably the impression was no more than a trick of the queer acoustics of the hurtling cylinder in which they were seated.

'Now, don't go off into idiocy, Sally. And stick to the point. We have this one positive line. Marlow.'

'Marlow?'

'Weren't you listening? That's what Mason's telegram said. For the last twelve months the wretched woman has been living in a cottage at Marlow. So if it's *not* lies –'

'Yes – I see.' Sally's voice sank, and George could only just catch the words. They sounded desperate. 'I don't think I can take it. Dick –'

Sir Alex said something that George didn't catch. Nor did she hear Sally Dalrymple's reply. She had an impression indeed that it was less an articulate response than a quickly drawn breath or a gasp. And then neither said anything at all. The young lady in uniform had put on a different jacket and was handing out cups of coffee and sandwiches. The sandwiches were so sharply triangular that they might have been the product of precision instruments normally concerned with turning out components for the aircraft itself. Perhaps the people behind were munching them. For their silence continued.

England, slightly tilting from time to time as if it floated on a gently heaving sea, drifted beneath them on a leisurely trip to the North Pole. The Scandinavians, tired of cricking their necks in order to contemplate its dull mottle, buried themselves in guide-books to Cambridge, Oxford, Stoke-upon-Trent, and other serious places. George began to think that her eavesdropping was over. At least she already had plenty to think about.

But perhaps half an hour later something more was said. Indeed, the two must have been murmuring inaudibly together for some time, since what she now heard plainly hitched on to other words just spoken.

'And if it is?' Sally's question seemed to be at once sharp and weary. 'If it's an utterly false cast, is there anything else you can try?'

'Certainly there is. I can think of a good many possibilities. Perhaps Day had deserted his recent friends simply because he has secured a promise of more advantageous employment elsewhere. And he'll have brought with him on paper everything he can't carry in his head.'

'But, Alex, where else –'

'My dear girl, plenty of countries are anxious to start up on all that. For instance, some in South America.'

'South America? I don't see how –'

'You have no idea what I'm talking about.' He was impatient again. 'You seldom have. It's one of the points in which I find you rather like your mother. But you may think comparisons are –'

George heard no more. Two Scandinavians across the gangway on her left hand had started a noisy argument. It was earnest and good-humoured and went on interminably. For a long time she sat very still. She found herself wondering why she felt chilly. These things were air-conditioned, surely. And the late-afternoon sunshine was beating in on her right cheek as she sat. She had a queer impulse to look at the people behind her. If she could see them again it might help her to make sense of what she had heard. But she could do nothing by just turning round. The seats were more than head-high. She would have to stand up and deliberately stare.

That would never do. For a time the impulse left her and she felt sleepy. It had been a tearing-around sort of day. She must really – at least for minutes or seconds – have dropped off, because presently she had the sensation of starting suddenly awake. And again she wanted to have a look.

She remembered – it was absurd to have forgotten it – that there was some sort of wash-place at the tail of the plane. She had only to stand up and make for that. But now, oddly, she was reluctant. She tried to interest herself in the argumentative Swedes. They had got out some coins and banknotes. The whole dispute appeared to be about the mysteries of British currency. She wondered whether she should lean across and explain it to them. She could do it in French. But that was stupid. They mightn't know French, and almost certainly they had a lot of English . . .

Abruptly George stood up, turned, and began to walk down the gangway. She looked straight at Sally Dalrymple – Richard's Sally – and Sir Alex Blair. It was only a fleeting glance, and now she was moving steadily on.

But she felt very cold indeed.

Chapter 17

Lord Urquhart's town car turned into the quiet Kensington square, glided smoothly and silently half-way round, and stopped. Lord Urquhart's chauffeur got out and impassively opened the door. Lord Urquhart had said good-bye at the airport and left them to give their own directions. Rather like a man who is careful of the stabling of his horse, he had explained that he had immediate instructions to give about his machine. But his quick withdrawal had been a matter of delicate feeling. Cranston wondered whether the chauffeur, when orders had been telephoned to him from Scotland, had been told that his destination was one of the big London hospitals. If he had, he had shown no surprise at this different destination.

Still sitting in the car, John Day peered intently round the square. Cranston knew that his sight had been clearing steadily all through the afternoon. The effect he gave was myopic, but he was in no difficulty. 'It seems all clear,' he said.

Cranston agreed. He was experiencing a sense of mingled relief and anticlimax. The more he thought about this moment, the more he had been inclined to see it in terms of melodrama. The enemy agents had lost their quarry in Urquhart Forest. Their next move – unless they simply decided to give up – would be to man any point where he was likely to reappear. And they would be bound to think of his wife. That they did not know her whereabouts was most improbable. And if they could raise, within a matter of hours, a force of a dozen agents in a remote part of Scotland, it was very clear that they would have no difficulty in finding whatever they required in London.

'But it *would* seem all clear.' Day's former ironical manner had returned. 'They wouldn't, when you come to think of it, have a couple of machine-guns waiting on the pavement. What one likes about these London squares is the gardens in the middle. Trees and shrubs galore. You could hide a small army in them.' For a moment he sat back in the big limousine. 'And, of course, a lot can be done from windows, too.'

'No doubt.' Cranston spoke shortly. Day's were certainly pertinent observations, but there seemed nothing to be gained by not getting the thing over. The chauffeur, moreover, was listening to these remarks with a wooden expression which Cranston found embarrassing. Cranston had been remembering the bullets spraying about the beach at Dinwiddie. But although it was a recollection which he found thoroughly uncomfortable, it did not exclude from his consciousness the absurdly incongruous discomfort of talking and behaving incomprehensibly before this waiting man. 'We must chance it,' he said. 'We'll get out.'

'Are *you* getting out?' Day appeared surprised.

'Of course I am.' Cranston stepped on the pavement. 'Thank you very much,' he said to the chauffeur. 'We don't want you to wait.'

'Very good, sir.' The man was looking not at Cranston but at Day, who was now descending from the car. 'Good afternoon, sir.' He was about to close the door when he glanced inside and stopped. 'Excuse me.' He reached forward to a seat. 'I think these are yours, sir?' What he had picked up was Sally Dalrymple's dark glasses. He was still looking at Day as he handed them over. Perhaps, Cranston thought, he was quartered from time to time at Urquhart, and had on some occasion been more noticing than his employer of the neighbouring Sir Alex Blair's clothes. But this was unlikely. And now the man had climbed back into his seat. In a moment the car had drawn away from the kerb and was gone.

'Well – thank you very much.' Day, standing on the pavement, had turned to Cranston as a man might do to a friend by whom he has been given a casual lift.

It was the moment, Cranston knew, for which he ought to have been better prepared. He glanced round the square, almost wishing for the missing melodrama. But there was no hint of it. Behind its high iron railings the garden in the centre appeared deserted. The score or so of cars parked round about were all empty. The dusty London summer light was draining away, and sucking the dusk down into the great grey tank of a square. A boy was delivering evening papers, and down a side street a woman with high heels returned from shopping – the superior sort of shopping that declares itself in cartons and band-boxes of modish design. There was no help in this commonplace scene. Cranston turned and looked at the doorway by which they stood. 'It's here?' he asked. 'Your . . . home?'

Day nodded. 'The top flat.'

'You're going to stay?'

'In a sense – yes.'

The man was inscrutable. One could be certain of nothing except that some inflexible purpose drove him. 'You want me to go?' Cranston asked.

'To go?' For a moment Day looked at him as at somebody he had forgotten about. 'Well – yes. Don't think me ungrateful. But for the moment – decidedly yes. It's scarcely an occasion, is it, for outsiders?'

'I suppose not. Shall you be here if I come back tomorrow?'

'That's difficult to say.' Day fell silent. It might have been because a policeman was going past with a heavy and unhurried tread. Or it might have been in calculation – only by this time, surely, all his calculating had been done. 'That's difficult,' he repeated. 'But I think not.'

'Why?' Cranston made the question a challenge.

Day slightly shook his head. It was like a gesture of embarrassment. 'Look,' he said, 'need we end on any sort of dismal note? We've had rather a good show.'

'I want you to tell me, please.'

'It's the top flat – five storeys up. Don't ask how I propose to leave it. Say . . . just rather suddenly.'

'You can't. It's abominable!' Cranston suddenly knew that he was revolted. 'I can't criticize the act. I've no right to. But you should have done it at once – long before you got yourself on that ship and within hail of this country. Let alone within hail of this house! Go away. Go away, man, and drown yourself. Only, if your wife's here, spare her this vicious stunt. You once said you wondered if what you'd got in your head was crazy. Well, it is. I see it now as utterly that. I ought never to have brought you.'

Day's reply to this was to walk up the short flight of steps to the door of the house. There was a row of bells, but the door was open upon a staircase leading to the flats above. He turned. '*If* my wife is here? You don't believe me? I think you never did.'

'If your story's true, and if you mean to do as you say, I can't see that there's anything I can do.' Looking up at Day from the pavement, Cranston was seeing him rather as he had done during their first exchange of words among the rocks at Dinwiddie. 'I urge you to give up this plan. But I can't do more . . . *Is* it true?'

'It is true.' Day's inflamed eyes held his squarely. 'I give you my word of honour as a gentleman.'

'Very well.' Cranston turned and walked away.

It seemed to him that he had walked for hours. It was dark by the time he went into a café and ate something – something tasteless and lumpish, washed down with what was perhaps coffee. He went out and again walked about London. He hadn't solved his problem; he had simply dropped it. He saw that he must begin with what he really knew – with what he really knew about the man from the sea. But his mind, as it tried to face this, went off elsewhere. Sally looking down at him as he descended the cliff – looking at him as if she never expected to see him again, as if it was all hopeless, as if this was the end . . . It meant something, he now knew, that he didn't understand. This enigma worried at his mind. But so did another – and perhaps more keenly. George hadn't walked out on him. He was certain of that. Almost the only thing he had to hold to was that she was stopping in. But then why –?

He drove his mind back to Day. He tried to imagine George walking beside him – here in the London dark – and giving him a line on Day. He tried this for a long time. The spectral colloquy seemed fruitless – but presently he noticed the direction he was now walking in. He was going back to Kensington.

He must begin with what he really knew about the man from the sea. And the area of certainty was quite small. When one's head was clear it could be surveyed at a glance. The man from the sea was John Day – a scientist deeply compromised and immensely dangerous. Cranston found that his pace had quickened. When he reached the square he walked to the house with certainty and mounted the steps. There was a little frame for a card beside each bell, and a light good enough for reading. He looked at the one on top. It was something that he might have done before, he thought. If it said *Day* then his mind could be a little at rest, surely, about the man from the sea. If it didn't, he was little farther forward. The poor woman might well be prompted to live behind somebody else's name . . . There was a printed card in the frame. *DAY*.

For a moment he stared at it fixedly. He heard his own breath going out in a gasp of relief. The business was over – or over so far as he was concerned. Up there the abominable *dénouement* had by this time accomplished itself. Day had made his submission, penance, apology – whatever he conceived it. By this time, perhaps, he was dead. It was to be supposed that he would have the decency to choose a window at the back . . . Cranston turned, descended the steps, and walked away. It wasn't for him, he supposed, to do anything about the poor devil's wife – or not now. He didn't even know how she would feel about it. Perhaps she was not altogether hating that it had happened that way. Perhaps she was proud, happy, exalted. Day in his action might have been absolutely right. Cranston quickened his pace. It was beyond his experience. He just couldn't know.

He had walked a hundred yards when he suddenly pulled up dead. They wouldn't, Day had said, have a couple of machine-guns waiting on the pavement. But didn't that mean that he had left Day – been obliged to leave him – just at the very most dangerous point of all? Would Day's late employers much consider the feeling, or for that matter the life, of his wife? Had the affair had – or was it even now still having – a *dénouement* quite other than he had lately been imagining?

Cranston turned and walked quickly back. He must know. Even if it was

574

the end of him – and it might be – he must know. He stopped and stared again at the card. *DAY*. It looked, he now saw, oddly new. Perhaps the poor lady lived here no longer, and it was by some trick that Day had been persuaded she did. Perhaps the top flat had been empty – until hastily invaded and transformed into a trap this very afternoon. With his imagination racing and his heart pounding, Cranston walked into the house and hurried upstairs, taking the treads two at a time. There would be another bell at the top. He had only to ring it and he could hardly escape finding out the truth either way.

He reached the top landing without consciousness of physical effort. There was another bell – and another little frame also. But this frame was empty. He could only barely distinguish the fact, because the landing was poorly lit. He paused to let his eyes grow accustomed to the gloom. He thought he heard voices.

Cranston strained his ears. One got odd effects in flats, and these voices might really be coming up from somewhere down below. If not, he thought, he knew where he was. Because they were the voices of men – several men – and they all appeared to be talking together. He put his ear to the door, and at once he was certain that the sound came not from downstairs but from inside. Suddenly the voices were louder, as if some inner door had been opened. And now he could distinguish something of their quality. They were foreign voices.

Some instinct made him draw back. Almost in the same moment the door by which he had been crouching opened. It opened precipitately and a man hurried out. He was thrusting a soft dark hat on his head, and the movement took him past Cranston unheeding. He ran downstairs. The door began to close, as if somebody was shoving it to with a foot from inside. The voices were still talking, and in some sort of mounting excitement. Cranston couldn't be said to have made up his mind. His body acted for him. He moved up to the door, shoved against it hard, and walked into the flat.

Chapter 18

He was confronting a small dark man with frightened eyes. The man began stuttering and stammering in an unknown tongue. As a door-keeper he was distinctly not formidable, but Cranston didn't delude himself he would find only the same sort inside. He put a hand on the small man's neck, swept him without much gentleness against the wall, and walked on.

He was making, he supposed, a demonstration – showing his private little Cranston flag. Well, that was how he had begun, and it did seem up to him to carry it through. Once more he recalled the bullets spraying on the beach. And this time he remembered also the voices calling from the quarry. They had been particularly detestable. And presumably it was the same voices –

or the same sort of voices – that now came to him from some farther room. Decidedly, Day's pursuers had won. Day must have known about just this risk. But he had gone ahead. Dead or alive, he was worth some sort of salute . . . Cranston pushed open another door. 'Good evening,' he said.

There was sudden dead silence, and then a small startling crash as somebody knocked over what must have been a bottle or a glass. Day was in a corner, and four men appeared to have been sitting round him in a close circle. Now they had sprung up and turned upon Cranston, staring. Only Day made no move. Even his bloodshot eyes were motionless in a face that had gone like chalk.

One of the men threw a swift question at Cranston – but not in English. Then he turned and talked volubly to one of his companions. A third joined in. But the fourth was silent, and this drew Cranston's eyes to him. Like the other three he was dark, and in dress he was not much distinguished from them. But he was very different, all the same. It was difficult to tell why. Perhaps it was simply because he assumed he was. And now he spoke a single sharp word. There was immediate silence.

Cranston took advantage of it. 'It's all right, Day. I've got things in hand.' He spoke slowly and distinctly. Then he turned to the others. 'I suppose', he said, 'that your trade makes it necessary for you to understand English. So listen. You are in the heart of London, and your chances are even smaller than those of your friends in the Highlands. I think you'd better give over. These antics are fit only for a comic strip – a decadent, bourgeois comic strip. I don't know whether this is still Mrs Day's flat. But I'm pretty sure it's not yours. Clear out.'

At least they were startled. The fourth man glanced at Cranston for a moment and then looked at Day. It almost had the appearance of being interrogatively. 'This is altogether unforeseen,' he said in English. 'And most awkward. I appear to have been badly served.' He turned and spoke rapidly to his companions in his own language. Cranston didn't understand a word. And yet suddenly the language told him a great deal. It was, in a fashion, speaking to him. It couldn't be the language it ought to have been. It wasn't nearly remote enough. In fact, it was Latin, not Slavonic, and distinguishably first or second cousin to languages he knew.

He took another look about the room – and then turned to the corner in which, according to his first impression, Day had been surrounded by a threatening group. Beside Day he now saw a low table. It held a decanter, a syphon, glasses, and an open box of cigars. Cranston, who had been without consciousness of fear, suddenly felt rather sick. He walked up to Day and just managed to speak to him steadily. 'Your wife – does she live here?'

They looked at each other directly. A muscle quivered at the corner of Day's mouth, and then with an effort he seemed to turn his face to stone. 'My wife? Certainly not.' He spoke with his old irony. 'You must have been misled by the little card downstairs. But that was provided by these gentlemen, you know – just in case you happened to take a look.'

'Have you a wife?'

'Dear me, yes. She is said to be living at Marlow.' He shook his head. 'But I doubt whether she would care to see me again. I would certainly not be so inconsiderate as to intrude upon her.'

'I see.'

There was a long silence. Cranston found that he was hoping to feel in himself some flare of anger. But it didn't come. Only the sense – the acute physical sensation – of sickness increased. He was learning that betrayal is the worst thing of all.

The fourth man took a step forward. 'There is a distressing side to this,' he said. 'But, sir, you must take a balanced view. Thanks to you – for I am sure it is largely your doing – our friend here has got safely through. And from this point we know how to look after him. He is enlisted once more under the banner of the free peoples.'

With an enormous effort, Cranston gave some attention to the man thus orotundly addressing him. 'Are you Spanish?' he asked.

'My culture is Spanish. Let that for the moment suffice.'

'In fact you come from South America somewhere? And you're proposing to smuggle Day away in your own interest? He's been plotting this with you – for a long time, and under the noses of the people he's been working for? If he managed to get clear of them and make this rendezvous you'd pick him up and get him away?'

'I must dispute the terms in which you express the matter.' The fourth man suddenly smiled charmingly. 'May I offer you a whisky-and-soda? No? Then let me put it rather differently. Let me ask you to consider this matter from the point of view of a civilized man, unfettered by narrow nationalistic notions. Our friend here is in great difficulty. He has abjured the errors into which he had lately fallen. You agree?' The fourth man paused. He was clearly pleased with his own excellent English. 'But his own country can scarcely welcome him, or at once reinstate him in his labours – labours, mark you, invaluable for the cause of the free world. There would be vulgar outcry at once. You follow me, Mr –?'

'Cranston.' It was Day who composedly supplied the name.

'Thank you. We see, then, that Mr Day is obliged to seek asylum – would you agree that asylum is the word? – elsewhere. And my country is honoured to provide it.'

'I see.' Cranston felt horribly tired. The whole business appeared weary, stale, flat, and unprofitable. He couldn't look at Day now. It would be like looking on the very face of treachery . . . Yet underneath the numbness and shock his brain was working. 'Oughtn't you', he said to the fourth man, 'to have a little talk about this with our Foreign Secretary? And haven't you, in joining in personally like this, rather overreached yourself?' He pointed to the fourth man's silent companions. 'It's all very well sending people of that sort along to play a hand like this. But weighing in yourself is another matter. As you said a few minutes ago, it's most awkward.'

The fourth man took a second to turn this over. 'May I ask,' he said, 'what you take me for?'

'I don't know your country. Perhaps it's a big one or perhaps it's a little one. In either case it may well stand high in the world's regard.' Cranston paused. 'But I should take you to be its Minister at the Court of St James's – or its Ambassador, if it runs to one. As I say, you've been indiscreet.'

'It is arguable, Mr Cranston, that you have been guilty of some little indiscretion yourself.' The voice of the fourth man had taken on a new edge. 'Let it be granted that publicity in the present matter would not be welcome to me. But no more, surely, would it be to you. There is again the factor of vulgar outcry. For nearly twenty-four hours you have been sheltering Mr Day from the law. An inhuman law, no doubt, which enlightened persons like ourselves must be anxious to mitigate. But there it is. Technically, Mr Day is chargeable with some very serious offence – and you have known it ever since you identified him.' Abruptly the voice of the fourth man changed once more. 'My dear young man – had you and I not better come to an understanding?'

'Look at Day.' Cranston now spoke with energy. '*I* don't want to – but do *you* look at him. You'll see he knows that that's no good.' Cranston tilted his chin. 'At least he knows *that* – that I won't just say thank you and walk out quietly, promising to keep mum. Do you know what he is wondering? He's wondering if you're up to the standard of his former friends – those that he's been plotting to swop for you. Are you tough enough? That's his question. He knows that his only hope is in screwing you to murder.'

'There is something in that.' As Day spoke he reached for the decanter. 'Our young friend, who began so decidedly as a romantic, is developing a realistic temper very fast. Unfortunately he clings to certain ideals of conduct. He won't, in fact, let go.' Day turned to the fourth man. 'In other words, my dear Sagasta, the decision lies with you.'

The man called Sagasta drummed with his fingers on the back of a chair. He didn't like it. He walked slowly across the room and back, frowning. Then he gave a sudden nod. One of his assistants stepped instantly to the door.

Day laughed softly. 'That's a little better. It looks as if we may reach your friends at Porthkennack – is it? – after all. But you'll have to keep your nerve.'

Sagasta liked this still less. He had turned very pale. Cranston decided that the game wasn't quite lost. 'It will never do,' he said. 'Even if you brought it off, your Government would never support you in it. They may want a big man in his line, like Day here, very much. They may be prepared to put him right at the top of a whole big show – which is what it's now clear to me he's prepared to sell and re-sell himself for, poor devil. But your Government won't stand for a big risk. They have no stomach, you know, for that sort of thing. Why should they have? The blood of the hidalgos doesn't exactly run in them – does it? Merchants and shop-keepers. They'd let you down.'

This was a bow drawn decidedly at a venture. Yet it discernibly went home. Sagasta produced a handkerchief and delicately mopped his forehead. 'I will take my chance, Mr Cranston. There needn't, I think, be much risk of unpleasant publicity. If we can smuggle Mr Day out of England alive, we can smuggle you out – how should I put it? – in another state of being. And we needn't take you so far. Say, just a little beyond the Lizard.'

Sagasta gave a nod at another of his assistants. The man's hand went to a pocket. And at that moment an electric bell rang sharply somewhere in the flat.

Cranston sat down. He was uncertain whether he did so as a gesture or because he was doubtful about the state of his knees. He still didn't believe that he was frightened, but he felt physically fagged out. It was how the truth about John Day had taken him. His voice, however, was perfectly steady. 'I imagine', he said, 'that we are now to be joined by the police. Tiresome for you all . . . Yes, there they are.'

The ringing of the bell had been immediately succeeded by a formidable knocking on an outer door. Sagasta snapped out an order to one of the men, who made a dash from the room. It was as if they had recalled the unreliable character of their janitor. But it was too late. There was a sound of brief expostulation in the hall, and then a new figure walked into the room. It was not, however, a policeman. It was Sir Alex Blair.

'Sorry to make such a row.' He advanced, genial and confident, and swept the company with a rapid glance. 'Good evening, Dick, my boy. No – don't get up. A pretty pickle you've contrived, I must say. And we must sort it out, I suppose – we must sort it out.' Sir Alex drew off a pair of gloves, tossed them on a table, and briskly rubbed one against the other the palms of two perfectly manicured hands. 'And John Day? Well, well – what a lot you must have to tell us. And what a change good Scotch whisky must be.' He turned to Sagasta. 'Your Excellency has a reputation as a man of enterprise – but I hardly expected to find you here in person. These gentlemen – yes.' He waved a contemptuous hand at Sagasta's assistants. 'I happened to know they operate here. And I decided to drop in.'

'I don't understand you. There is, I think, some misapprehension.' Sagasta was plainly discomposed, and for the moment could only fall back on conventional phrases.

'A misapprehension? I'd say there have been a good many. We believed, my dear Day, that you were interested in your wife. And your late friends – shall we call them the Hyperboreans? – appear to have been banking on that too. Marlow is swarming with them. But I had a shrewd idea you were really minded to other company. And here you are.'

Sagasta had taken his little turn up and down the room. 'You have brought your police with you?' he asked.

'The police will appear when it is appropriate that they should do so.' Sir

Alex's manner had changed. He had become grave and weighty. 'I admit that the matter has its complications, Sagasta. This young man has got himself most undesirably involved in an affair he has had no proper understanding of. You follow me?'

Sagasta slightly inclined his head. 'Possibilities open out,' he said smoothly.

'And *you* follow me?' Sir Alex looked hard at Cranston.

'I suppose so.' Cranston was confused. He was aware that he had to get new bearings.

'Then I think you had better go.' Sir Alex was kindly but curt. 'No purpose will be served by your remaining.'

'But, Sir Alex – are you here alone? These people are –' Cranston paused, doubtful whether he was talking sense. 'It's decent of you to try to get me out. But I'd like to know –'

'You must know already.' Sir Alex appeared to misinterpret the unfinished question. 'Sally told me – almost at once. She's a good girl, and you mustn't blame her. It was the only reasonable thing to do.'

Cranston was silent. Of course the man was right. He himself ought to say something at once – something to the effect that he indeed didn't blame Sally. But he found it impossible. The silence became strained.

'It's true, you know, that you *haven't* properly understood what you were about.' Sir Alex was still kindly. 'It was no affair, believe me, for romantic scurrying over the heather. Your first duty was to the security of your country, my dear boy. Well, that aspect of the matter is all right now. You can leave it to me. Go straight home and forget it. Forget it *entirely*. Do you understand me?'

Cranston nodded. Confusedly, he thought he did understand. Sir Alex was stretching a point – was stretching a point pretty far – in order to disentangle him from his follies. It was, as he had said, decent of Sir Alex. And over the face of this benevolent intention there lay a hideous and humiliating irony. The man who was thus taking risks with his own reputation – for it must amount to that – was Caryl's husband. Treachery all round. That was what it came to. Himself treacherous to Sir Alex. Day treacherous to him . . . Yes, he had better clear out. Sir Alex's standing by him in this way was the only decent spot in the affair. He had better do what he was told.

And Cranston stood up and moved towards the door. Nobody else stirred or said a word. There was some sort of doubt in his mind, but he couldn't place it. Something rather unexpected was happening. Or rather the unexpectedness was in the fact that something wasn't happening. The South Americans, who had been preparing a few minutes before to cut his throat, were doing nothing. They were simply letting him go. They were letting Sir Alex have it all his own way. But the puzzle, if there was a puzzle, was no longer any business of his. He had been charitably dismissed from the horrible involvement, and he had better go.

He had reached the door when behind him he heard a queer sound. It was a short high hysterical laugh.

Cranston swung round and looked at Day. The face of the man from the sea was as it had been – frozen into stone. But it was from Day, he knew, that the sound had come. Day had cracked. He was in a state of tension that had suddenly become intolerable. And for a second he had lost control of himself and given that meaningless laugh. But it was meaningless only because Cranston couldn't understand it. And he *must* understand. He walked back to the centre of the room. 'It won't do,' he said.

They were almost random words – for his mind was merely groping. But they had the effect of bringing Sagasta into action again. Once more he motioned one of his assistants to the door. 'No, indeed,' he said. 'It won't do. Blair, can't you see –?'

'Leave us!' Sir Alex had swung round upon Cranston with a new uncontrolled vehemence. 'Do as I say. If you remain –'

'But he must remain.' Sagasta was suddenly vehement too. 'Don't you see that the risk's too great?'

'Be quiet, you fool!' Sir Alex had turned upon him in a fury.

But it was too late. Cranston felt that he was now probably as pale as Day. But at least knowledge had come to him. He turned to Sagasta. 'The idea', he asked quietly, 'is that you're all going to talk business? Sir Alex, having tumbled to your game, is going to get in on some neat three-cornered deal?'

Sagasta's reply, if he proposed to give one, was forestalled by Day. Once more he gave his crazy laugh. But this time there was triumph in it. 'You see?' he asked. 'The boy has some sort of brain. He knows. It's the end of him, I'm afraid. But at least he knows.' He stood up and tapped his waist. 'Do you know, Cranston, what I have here? Enough –'

'You'll regret this.' Sir Alex had turned on him savagely.

'Blair knows, my dear young man, that I must be carrying the records of enough new physics to give him what he has always wanted: a reputation. With this' – and again he tapped the hidden belt – 'he could enter the field again and be no end of a swell. And he's prepared to do a deal. I leave him the stuff, and am free to take myself off with my new friends here – to another hemisphere. Would you say the proposal was reasonable? Do you advise me to accept?'

Cranston took one look at Sir Alex. A second wasn't necessary. The thing was true. Here again was betrayal, treachery. Without even knowing that he was doing so, Sir Alex had paid him back.

'But can I trust him?' With his inflamed eyes Day gave Sir Alex a glance that was ironically appraising. 'Or can *you* trust him?' He had turned to Sagasta. 'You see, now, where we stand? It's not just a question of the young man. It's a question of our venturesome friend Blair as well. A little time ago you mentioned the police. Well, as you see, you can put them out of your head. Blair is here on his own. It is really very rash of him.'

'Do you think I'd be fool enough to come here without taking precautions?' Sir Alex's tone was contemptuous. 'You may as well know –' He broke off. 'What's that?'

It was the electric bell once more. It rang once and then for seconds there was absolute silence. The small man with the frightened eyes hurried into the room and whispered to Sagasta. And Sagasta turned to Sir Alex. 'At least it's true that somebody knows you're here. You're being asked for now. Will it much advance matters to deny your presence? I think not.' He gave a brief order to the small man, who left the room.

A moment later, Sally Dalrymple entered it.

Cranston sprang towards her. The place was a trap. It had closed on him. It had closed on the treacherous Sir Alex. And now it was closing on Sally. Her step-father had committed some horrible outrage in thus exposing her. For she could know nothing of the true state of affairs. She could have no other notion of it than he himself had had only a few minutes before: that Sir Alex's concern was to bring the adventure to an honourable close and extricate the young man who had so rashly got involved in it.

But it was Sally who must be extricated now. The only chance was to use his fists, a bottle, a chair – anything that came to hand – and fight a way out for her at once. As he took his spring to her side their eyes met. And in the same moment she cried out.

'*Alex, quick! He's getting away!*'

She had queerly misinterpreted his movement. And he felt himself go numb. His eyes continued to hold hers, and in a blinding moment her features interpreted themselves. Mysteriously and utterly, she was committed – and all-knowingly committed – to the other side. She was this against some smothered longing, some broken hope within herself. And this was why now, as before, she looked despair.

'Pull yourself together.' Sir Alex had turned on her. 'Why did you come up?'

'Because they're here.' Now she seemed almost dazed. 'Because it's all found out.'

Sagasta gave a sharp exclamation. 'Found out? It's the police?'

'Yes . . . I think so.' She was almost incoherent now. 'A chauffeur – Lord Urquhart's chauffeur –'

'*Quick!*' Day had sprung to his feet, and his ghastly eyes were blazing. 'I wondered – but I couldn't remember. It was the way he looked at me when he handed me the glasses . . . He recognized me. He used to drive for the Ministry.' He whirled on Sagasta. 'Is there a back way? If not, I'm trapped. And so are you.'

One of Sagasta's assistants was flinging open a door at the back of the room. There was a moment of complete confusion. Cranston's mind seemed to swim in it and then rise clear. He knew what he must do. He must get

Day. He took a step forward, and in the same moment was hit on the head from behind.

He was down on the floor – in darkness, but aware of running feet, banging doors. The blow had been a glancing one, and he was up again. There was blood in his eyes. But he saw that only Sir Alex and Sally were left in the room. He threw himself at the door which he had seen flung open. It was firmly closed – bolted, it seemed, on the other side. He guessed that at the back of the building there would be either another staircase or a fire-escape. The South Americans would have got Day away down that. But now there was no way through. His only chance was to leave as he had come.

Cranston ran from the room. He didn't give a glance at the two people left there. He dashed from the flat and pounded down the staircase. If the police had really arrived – and Sally had seemed uncertain – he must contact them instantly. If not –

Hurtling round a turn on the stairs, he pulled up just in time to avoid violent collision with somebody coming up nearly as fast.

'Richard!'

It was George.

Chapter 19

The great moon had passed its zenith. Far below them on their right the soft contours of Dorset rose and fell beneath its pale diffused light like a sleeper breathing beneath an eiderdown. On their left the still Channel was all silvered. It might, Cranston thought, have been last night's sea. But it was a different sea. And a different man was looking at it.

'Won't there be an awful row?' George had turned curiously to Lord Urquhart. 'I mean, has he any business to have it out?'

'Porp?' Lord Urquhart chuckled happily. 'No business at all. And I've no doubt that a missing naval helicopter is a serious matter. Almost as serious as a missing nuclear physicist . . . Isn't that what you said the fellow was?'

'Yes. John Day.'

'To be sure – John Day.' Lord Urquhart was not particularly impressed. It was the aeronautical aspect of the expedition that interested him. 'But I wouldn't worry about my nephew. Believe me, Porp Urquhart has taken on odder jobs than this. He did work with submarine-borne aircraft, you know. That's how he came to be called Porp. Short for Porpoise, you see – short for Porpoise. And as for a row – well, I telephoned the First Lord. We were at school together. He'll see Porp through, if necessary, with the salt-water chaps.'

'And Porp can really find it?'

'I'm sure he can. A wonderful navigator is Porp. I thought of him at once, as soon as you explained the job to me. We'll be there, believe me, in under an hour.' Lord Urquhart yawned contentedly. 'You young people mind if I take a nap? No doubt you've things to talk about.'

Like the sea and land below, Lord Urquhart slumbered.

'I hope you didn't get that name wrong.' George looked anxiously at Cranston. 'I can't see that the circumstances can have been favourable for accurate reception.'

'Porthkennack? I got it correctly, all right. And I don't believe that Day noticed he gave it away – or that the other folk did either. They were all a bit strained, I'd say.'

'And you know it?'

'I've been there. I don't say I'd recognize it. But that's this Porp's job. It's an out-of-the-way sort of cove, but I know that sea-going craft sometimes put in there.' Cranston paused. 'I still don't know how you did it. Or how you began to tumble to the sort of affair it was.'

George made no immediate reply. A helicopter is noisy. One wants to talk only in bursts. But presently she said: 'Shall I take the hard question first?'

'The hard one?'

'How I came to guess the sort of affair it was. Their talk – when I sat in front of them on the flight to London, I mean – was queer. It would have been hard to tell just why. But it wasn't, somehow, the talk of two people who were acting quite simply in the interest of their country and of a rash young friend. But there was something else.' George stopped and looked out on the quiet land and the quiet sea. 'We seem a long way from it all, here,' she said.

'Go on.' Cranston too was looking far out over the dim landscape.

'It wasn't quite the talk of a man and his step-daughter either. And then I got up and took a look at them. They weren't aware of it. And I saw.'

There was a long silence. 'I don't know how it could have happened,' Cranston said. His voice was husky.

'Things do happen.'

'Yes.'

'There is something powerful about Sir Alex. And he must have exploited some horrible underground current of feeling. You get that in families, sometimes.'

'Yes.' Suddenly Cranston remembered. 'She said that she knew how I felt . . . that at least she knew how I felt.' He shivered. 'Lord Urquhart understood what he was talking about, I suppose, when he said something about Dinwiddie being all wrong. He told me to keep clear.'

'So I felt I had a better idea how things stood.' George pushed on more briskly. 'Sir Alex Blair just couldn't be more – well, corrupt. And it might take him just as much one way as another. And then I began thinking about

Day too. He had told you his wife lived in Kensington. But Sir Alex had got that telegram, saying she had lived for a year at Marlow. I was sure there was more to the discrepancy than just a mistake. Day was trying to reach some address in Kensington, but not to see his wife. He had told you a lie.'

'Quite a lot of lies.' Cranston looked at her wryly. 'Lies and lies and lies.'

'I wondered what I ought to do. I could either try to hang on to – to those people, or I could go to the police. I had that address of your aunt's, but I knew that – well, that all sorts of things might have happened before I contacted you that way. I decided I'd stick to the trail. It was an idiotic notion.'

'Idiotic?'

'Try it, and you'll see. In books people jump into a taxi, yelling *Follow that car*. Well, there was a car – and it was another yellow car, which might have helped. It was waiting for them at Northolt, and of course they simply got in and drove off. They had vanished from the landscape before I found anything. All I could do was to have myself driven to Marlow, and hope for the best.'

'And it was a wild-goose chase?'

'Completely. I just didn't see those people and their yellow car again. And no end of people called Day live in Marlow, as I discovered from the telephone book. I could hardly go round the lot, inquiring whether they were related to a disgraced scientist. There seemed nothing for it but the police.' George paused. 'But then I felt that going to the police would be giving in.'

'You felt that?' He was astonished.

George smiled. 'Isn't it something that runs in our family? Anyway, I thought I'd make one more push in the name of private enterprise. And I thought of Lord Urquhart. He had a town house. Probably he had gone there.'

'I think it was a wonderful idea.'

'It was frightful cheek. I was very nervous about how he'd take it. And when I found him, he was interviewing his chauffeur. You know what the man was telling him – that he had driven yourself and the man called Knight to an address in Kensington, not to a hospital; and that he was sure Knight wasn't Knight at all, but Day. He had driven Day about a lot during the war, and he was certain of him.'

'And the old boy wasn't furious?'

'At first he wasn't too pleased.' George glanced cautiously at Lord Urquhart, who continued in slumber. 'But I talked to him. I said I didn't want to let you down – because it isn't a good thing to do in families. He agreed. And in the end he consented to my coming to explore the address to which his chauffeur had driven you. He insisted only on two things. One was that he should come too. And the other was that he should bring along some important old crony of his who could, if necessary, call out the whole

British Army in thirty seconds. You know the rest. The real crisis was just after I'd found you – persuading him to make this one final bid of our own. The crony didn't much approve. But then luckily Lord Urquhart thought of his nephew Porp, and the idea went to his head. So here we are.'

'And I think we must be nearly there.' Cranston was scanning the coast below. 'We mustn't muck it. We just mustn't let these South Americans get Day away on whatever ship they have waiting.'

'What happens if we do?'

'An emergency meeting of the Cabinet, I expect, and a decision whether to stop on the high seas a ship belonging to a friendly power . . . It's a pity you dislike the Tower of London, George.'

'The Tower?'

He grinned at her. 'It's where you and I will be incarcerated before being shot.'

'Oh, dear! And Lord Urquhart?'

'He and Sandy Morrison will both be put in Constable Carfrae's new lock-up. Fortunately they'll get along together very well.'

'We'd better not muck it, all the same. You really think our chances are good?'

'They're certainly not bad.'

'And we'll be first on the scene?'

'We're bound to be – unless they have some means of flying down too. And I doubt that. Their resources are probably not on the scale of our earlier enemy's. They will just have some craft waiting off Porthkennack – probably a regular cargo vessel which has been instructed to take on the job. And they're motoring Day down to it now.'

George nodded. 'Will the chief man – Sagasta – be with them?'

'Not on your life. He's back in his Legation or Embassy by this time, resolved to leave this sort of thing to underlings in future. He didn't really have what it takes. And I don't think his assistants will have it, either. They want Day, but it's my guess that they'll ditch him as soon as they're thoroughly scared. And that's what we're out to have a shot at.'

'Yes.' George was silent for a moment. 'Are you sorry for him?'

'For Day? I think I am. He seems to have guessed so damned badly.'

'He began doing that a long time ago. Shall we ever understand him?'

Cranston considered. 'He's not a venal man in the common sense. He hasn't been after money or the other obvious bribes. But he's no sort of political animal either, I'd say. Essentially, he's a misfit – a pathological egoist and individualist caught up in an activity requiring vast co-operative effort. His *idée fixe* is to be all alone at the top. And if he made South America he might, I suppose, end his days as a little dictator in his own virgin field there.'

'He'd be top of his form – but still no more than one of the back-room boys.'

'Just that. With all his near-genius, he's not exactly a far-sighted man.'

Chapter 20

There was a small beach set in a deep rocky cove. The sea was empty, the night still, and the moon sinking towards the west. It was uncannily like – and unlike – the night before.

The helicopter had taken off again. It was invisible but they could faintly hear its engine in the distance. After dropping them it had moved inland. If it could locate a likely car on the road to Porthkennack there would be an opportunity for a first stroke in the war of nerves.

In the warm night they sat side by side with their backs against a rock. Sometimes they talked. But for the most part they were straining their ears, waiting to catch a first low throb from the sea. Cranston wished it was over. He didn't think there was going to be any violence or danger this time. But perhaps he ought not to have let George come, all the same. Perhaps he ought to have insisted on her staying in the machine with Lord Urquhart and his nephew. But he didn't at all know, for that matter, whether George would accept a word of command from him. And there was much more about her that he didn't know . . . He realized that here was another reason why he was wishing it was over. It was all part of something that was dead to him. But there was a lot he wanted to ask George. And tell George. He turned to her now and was about to speak. But she had raised a hand. 'Listen!' she said.

There could be no doubt about it. For a moment it was no more than a tremor; then it was as if the sea had somewhere begun to throb to a deep slow pulse; then the sound became louder and more commonplace. 'Something quite large,' Cranston said.

The engines stopped as he spoke. They waited in a breathless silence, gazing out beyond the line of rock that formed the western arm of the cove. For a fraction of a second the dark rock appeared to change shape against the glimmer of the sea. Then they were seeing the bows of a steamer. It glided forward without a sound. Small waves began to break among the rocks, and the whole surface of the cove shimmered. The steamer was almost stationary. There was a splash and a brief rattle. George stood up. 'Anchored,' she said. 'We can't – thank goodness – have made any mistake. But what about finding some cover?'

He nodded, and scrambled to his feet. George in moonlight was like a statue cut in some dark golden stone. 'The rocks,' he said. They moved into shelter. 'I think I hear the helicopter – and something else as well.'

'Yes – it's a car. And travelling fast. Can a helicopter drop down to pass the time of day – or night – with a car going at seventy?'

'I'm sure it can, with the redoubtable Porp in charge . . . And there he is.'

The helicopter had appeared low on their right. Like a vast lazy insect it drifted across the face of the moon, and for a moment they could see the tail-rotor spinning. Then it moved out across the cove.

'They've lowered a launch from the steamer.' George pointed. 'And I can hear the car on the road down to the beach.'

Cranston nodded. 'It's a well-synchronized rendezvous, isn't it? But they're just going to become aware of the unexpected factor.'

The launch was in the water. They watched it begin to cut across the cove on a straight course for the beach. Suddenly it swerved and its engine faltered. 'It's happened.' George's voice – and it was for the first time, Cranston reflected, in their acquaintance – trembled with excitement. 'They've seen it. Porp's dipping on them. It's a nasty shock.'

The launch recovered and drove for the beach. The helicopter continued across the cove. It was hovering, mast-high, above the steamer. The launch beached, and almost at the same moment the car appeared. It was a big saloon. It drove to the edge of the beach and stopped. A door was flung open and four men tumbled out. They could be seen at once looking up at the sky. There could be no doubt that they too had been made aware of the menacing presence moving in it. The open door was shut violently from within. The car backed, turned, and tore off through the night. The driver, at least, had had enough.

The four men were running for the launch. Cranston could see that Day was in front. From the launch itself a couple of men had landed and were standing knee-deep in the sea, holding on to the gunwales. They could hear voices now – voluble Latin voices – raised in fierce dispute. One of the men from the launch was pointing back at the steamer. The helicopter had circled it and was now rising. And as it rose a light began to flash from it. It appeared to be sending a signal far out to sea.

The voices at the edge of the cove rose higher. Anger and panic could be heard in them. And suddenly there was a shouted command, a scuffle, a cry of pain. The men clustered round the launch were clambering into it, and in a moment it was streaking back across the cove. But one figure remained – prone on the beach. It was all over. John Day had been betrayed.

The launch disappeared within the shadow of the steamer. They could hear the engines starting and the anchor being raised. Within what seemed less than a minute the steamer was gliding from the cove, desperately seeking the immunity of the high seas. The helicopter accompanied it – grimly speeding the departing guest. The noises of both craft faded on the night. The ripples subsided. The cove and the spreading moonlit waters beyond it were void and still.

Day had got on his feet. He was standing quite immobile with his back to them. He might have been a holiday-maker with a taste for nocturnal seascapes. He was still in Sir Alex Blair's expensive clothes. 'Wait,' Cranston said. He rose from the rocks and walked slowly across the beach.

He was within arm's length of Day before the man turned. Cranston looked at him. 'It's me,' he said. The words were as flat as he could make them. He didn't want to import an ounce of drama into this last scene.

'It's you.' Day eyed him wearily for a moment, and then turned and walked away. He was making for the nearest rocks. Cranston followed him. Day chose a flat ledge with apparent care and sat down. 'Well?' he said.

'The helicopter will land presently. We go back to London in that.' Cranston spoke quietly, finally. 'Lord Urquhart has a friend who will see that the right things are done.'

'The right things? But of course.' Day had his old ironical smile. 'And I nearly brought it off.'

'You nearly brought it off.' Handsomely, Cranston acknowledged it. Compunction faintly stirred in him. 'I suppose it mayn't be so bad. After all, you *have* . . . come back.'

'So I have.' Day was amused. 'By the way, one thing was true.'

'That you haven't long to live?' Cranston accepted it gravely. 'I never doubted it. And I don't doubt it now.' He hesitated. 'I'd suppose there is more than one way that you might feel about it.'

'So wise so young, they say . . .' Again Day smiled. 'You remember?'

'I remember.'

'And our race?'

'Yes.'

Day stood up slowly. He seemed prepared for indefinite talk. 'It wasn't quite on fair terms, you know – last night. I'd just done that swim. I can do better now.'

Even as he spoke, he flashed into motion. It was totally unexpected, and he was fifteen yards ahead before Cranston started. On the beach he gained another ten yards. He had certainly been a sprinter. He was in the water and swimming.

'Day – come back!' Cranston paused for the one shout, and then flung himself into the sea. But Day was too far ahead. Cranston swam for a long time, but he glimpsed him only once. Or he thought he glimpsed him. But what he saw might have been only a clot of seaweed floating out with the tide.

He was very tired when he reached shore – but at once he scaled the highest rock he could find. The surface of the cove, and of the sea beyond it, was a great still empty sheet under the moon. Even as he had come, the man from the sea had departed again. The waters from which he had risen had closed over his head for ever.

'Richard!'

It was George calling anxiously from the farther rocks. Cranston was very tired indeed. But he turned towards the voice and ran.

MORE ABOUT PENGUINS
AND PELICANS

For further information about books available from Penguins please write to Dept EP, Penguin Books Ltd, Harmondsworth, Middlesex UB7 ODA.

In the U.S.A.: For a complete list of books available from Penguins in the United States write to Dept CS, Penguin Books, 625 Madison Avenue, New York, New York 10022.

In Canada: For a complete list of books available from Penguins in Canada write to Penguin Books Canada Ltd, 2801 John Street, Markham, Ontario L3R 1B4.

In Australia: For a complete list of books available from Penguins in Australia write to the Marketing Department, Penguin Books Australia Ltd, P.O. Box 275, Ringwood, Victoria 3134.

In New Zealand: For a complete list of books available from Penguins in New Zealand write to the Marketing Department, Penguin Books (N.Z.) Ltd, P.O. Box 4019, Auckland 10.